Isaac's Story

A novel by

Roy Goodman

This is a work of historical fiction. Except as noted in Notes and Acknowledgements *at the end of the book, names and characters are the product of either the author's imagination or are used fictitiously. Any resemblance to real people, living or dead, is entirely coincidental.*

ISAAC'S STORY

First Edition

Published by Roy Goodman

ISBN: 979-8-600-81070-9

Cover design by Angela Stewart
Photographs by Roy Goodman and Laurie Goodman

To

Uncle Max

and

Uncle Frank

Chapter 1

My body is almost not here. There are times when I feel like a ghost, like I can't weigh more than a couple of ounces. I feel myself riding on the breeze. I know my end is near and, frankly, I have had more than enough of this place. I am ready to lie eternally in a hole in the ground. If I knew who my maker was, I'd be happy to meet him or her. I might even have a word or two to say.

My name is Isaac Simon and I am one hundred and two years old. I was born in the year 1900. That's the truth. In fact, I only lied about my age one time. Big mistake. I'll tell you all about it later.

Of course, I'm telling this story in my head. I can't move. I certainly couldn't sit upright and hold a pen. Sometimes I feel someone touch my hand or stroke my cheek. It's nice. Reminds me of when I was first married. Reminds me of my beloved Virginia. She was a marvel - strong, bold, with a passion for life that was explosive, and a warmth that was all-embracing. We used to hold hands a lot and other things there is no need to get into details about.

My mind and my memory, unlike my body, seem to be working just fine. I remember everything almost from the day I was born. Well, not quite, but I do remember the shtetl in Lithuania where we lived until I was ten years old. Linkeve.

I remember our two-room house with the steep roof that leaked when it rained. I remember mud in the spring, and snow and cold in the winter. My brother Chaim and I had to get up early to bring in snow so Mama could melt it to make tea for my father. From the age of six, I had to feed the chickens, clean out their coop and bring in the eggs. Chaim, who was four years older than me, milked our cow. I envied him until my father lost the cow in a game of chance, and Chaim had to milk a goat my mother bought with money from vegetables and eggs she sold at the market.

That goat was an unpleasant animal. It was always trying to escape and it hated being milked. Maybe that's why its milk tasted a little bitter.

Mara - that's the name Chaim gave her - kicked poor Chaim several times. He threatened to take her to the butcher, but he never did. I would hear him cursing her while I picked my way through the hen house.

Over the years I have met many folks from the old country; they all talk of their parents like they were saints. Their fathers were very learned and wise. It seems like everyone had a father or grandfather who was a rabbi, and their mothers were the best cooks and bakers in the world. Mine were not like that. My father was an ignorant peasant who worked as a builder's helper from time to time and spent most of the money he earned gambling and getting drunk.

He would quote a selected few passages from the Book, but could not read a word. His favorite teaching was the story of Noah who got drunk and, in his drunken state, was embarrassed by one of his sons. Noah then cursed that son for not respecting his father. I think my father really believed the Bible gave him permission to drink and mistreat us.

Like many drunks I've run into in my life, he was mean and loud. He often shouted at my mother and Chaim and me. When we were little, my mother would wrap us in her dress and we all hid from him. It was warm there. When we got too big, Chaim and I would go outside to escape him, unless it was too cold; then we would crawl under the bed we shared.

My mother was a wonderful, strong, warm person, but a terrible cook. It seemed to me that her cooking was the cause of many of the arguments between my parents. But not all.

My mother had a baby girl who was born a year after Chaim. The baby died when she was only a week old. Mama never talked about her. I did not even learn about my lost sister until Uncle Kalner, my mother's older brother, told me the story during the journey to America. I had often wondered why my parents had only two children; so many of the families in Linkeve had at least five. I remember in one household up the road from us, there were twelve children. Uncle Kalner told me my mother almost died when I was born, and she was not able to have any children after that. I think it was a blessing.

Chaim was the scholar. At least, that's what my mother used to say. I hated school and preferred to spend time wandering in the woods near the shtetl, watching the birds, and catching frogs in the stream. I loved to draw the things I saw. My father called me a dreamer, which, I think, was meant as an admonition to be more practical. I took it as a compliment.

Often, before dark, Chaim sat with me and reviewed the drawings I had made. He would ask me to tell him about the creatures that populated my pictures and he encouraged me to be more observant about how they moved and interacted with their surroundings. In looking back, he was prodding me in the direction of science, art, and critical thinking. He wanted me to try to understand how things worked. He was my first and most important teacher. And my protector.

My father would shout about my "useless meandering in the woods." He went on and on about me not getting my chores done, not helping my mother, not doing well in school, not learning the Book. I think I spent more time trying to avoid him than anything else.

Then one evening in February 1910, two months before my birthday, everything changed.

My father took one drink too many and slipped on the ice in a snowstorm as he was making his way home from the tavern. He rolled into a ditch and was not found until the sun came out three days later. Uncle Kalner told us about my father's death.

My mother breathed in deeply, but said nothing. How could she say out loud that a burden had been lifted from her?

We sat Shiva for the full seven days, as was the rule. My mother, dressed in black, sat on a low stool in the front room when family members and neighbors were in the house. We talked little, and ate the food they brought us. After everyone left, my mother would take off her mourning clothes and put on her most colorful blouse and go about her daily routine. I almost said she went about her daily routine "as if nothing had happened," but that is not true. She was noticeably more at ease, happier, more in control of her life. She even sang softly to herself. The people of the shtetl would have been appalled if they had known this, but since the ritual and rules of mourning were so well established and ordered it was easy for her to change her behavior and her clothes before anyone came to the house to sit with us.

My Uncle Kalner was always the first to arrive in the morning during that week of Shiva. He would stop by on his way to work at the shtetl's only general store. He would kiss my mother on the forehead, then sit down opposite her and hold her hands in his for a few minutes. Uncle

Kalner was not a very warm person and this moment of affection towards his little sister was unusual. Mama used to say that his spark was snuffed out when his wife died in childbirth the year after I was born. The baby was stillborn. It would have been his first child. He lived with us for a while after his wife's death, then moved into a small shack which he slowly filled with books.

I was a little afraid to visit him; his home was always so orderly, so clean. My fear, however, was counterbalanced by the presence of all those books, and the understanding that I could look at any of them so long as I handled them with care. No one else in the shtetl owned books except the rabbi - and all of his books were about the religion.

But Uncle Kalner had all kinds of books, written in languages I did not know. "One day, you will learn Russian and English," he said. "In the meantime, you can look at the pictures."

I loved to page through the books on art and science and biology. They transported me to a world completely outside what I knew.

I remember one time when I was no more than six or seven, Mama brought me to stay with him because she was going to the market, and my father was drunk in bed. Uncle Kalner sat me down on a chair by the big table and placed his newest acquisition in front of me. He carefully opened the book to reveal a picture of a strange-looking animal with a huge set of antlers. He told me it was an American moose. The animal was knee-deep in the water of a rushing river. The forested mountains behind it glowed with the golds and reds of fall.

A few weeks after my father's funeral, Uncle Kalner announced that he was selling everything and moving the family to America, to a place called Lowell, Massachusetts, where my Uncle Ben was living. He said my mother could work in the textile mills there and that Chaim and I could get a better education.

For reasons he never explained to me, Chaim said he did not want to go to America; his dreams were set on South Africa. Uncle Kalner became angry with him, but my mother said he should go to Africa if that was what he wanted.

"A person can be poor anywhere in the world," she said.

So, that spring we planted nothing. My mother and Uncle Kalner worked in all kinds of jobs to raise money. They sold the chickens and the goat and the gardening things. They even sold many of Uncle Kalner's books. They sold my father's carpentry tools and his clothes and his few other possessions, including his silver Shabbes cup: it had his name engraved on it and he would let no one touch it. It was the one thing in the house he took care of.

We packed our clothes and whatever else we could into suitcases and boxes, and a neighbor brought us to the train station in his wagon. Chaim came to see us off. His journey was not to begin for another few months. He hugged and kissed us before we got onto the train and he waved to us as we chugged away.

That was the last time I saw my brother - a boy of fourteen, on his own. I cried. I think I cried for days.

I remember little of the train ride, except that it was very cramped and crowded and seemed to go on forever. We arrived at the port city of Hamburg on the River Elbe in the evening. There were thousands of Jews waiting on the dock with their bundles and boxes. Fortunately it was summer, so being outside was not too bad, except that the smell was terrible. There were so few facilities for people to use. A lot of people were sick.

I found a place on a low wall, not too far from where Mama and Uncle Kalner had settled on the dock. I sat there for hours during daytime making drawings of this mass of people who had left their homes and were waiting to sail across the ocean to an unknown world. I think I still have some of those drawings in a folder somewhere in my home.

I remember one drawing, in particular. I was watching a little girl who was sitting next to her mother on a bundle of gray blankets. She was thin with unevenly cropped short brown hair. She was holding a chunk of hard bread with both hands and, every so often, would struggle to take a bite out of it. As she sat there chewing laboriously, a seagull swooped down and snatched the bread from her. After her initial fright and fear, a smile of delight and wonder lit up her face, as though she were enthralled that such a creature would visit her.

When I finished the drawing, I tried to give it to her, but her mother shooed me away. I never understood why. I told my mother about the incident and she told me to forget it.

"Some people do not know how to receive a gift," she said, "just like others have never learned how to give one. It is her misfortune."

***

I can hear voices as I lie here: my grandson, Allen, and his daughter, Ginnie, named after my beloved. I was so grateful for that. They visit often. I can understand what they are saying. Eavesdropping. I am the fly on the wall.

Mostly, they talk to one another as if I am not here at all. But, every now and then, they will say something to me, especially when they arrive or leave. Ginnie always gives me a little peck on the face when she arrives. She has been very sad lately. I wish I could help.

I hear their clothes rustle; I think they are hugging.

"How're you doing today, sweetie?" Allen says. "I'm so glad you come to see Grandpa Isaac. Somehow I think he knows you're here."

She kisses me on the forehead. "I'm OK, I guess... Actually, I'm not really OK. Not OK yet. I mean, I still wake up in the middle of the night and reach for him."

I hear her pace back and forth. "They look so fragile," she says.

"What do you mean?" Allen asks.

"The Prudential Center and the John Hancock tower. They looked so fragile, so exposed." She stops pacing. "I still can't believe what has happened."

"I know," Allen responds.

"I never told you that Jake proposed to me the night before he left for that job interview in New York. He asked me to marry him." Ginnie hesitates, sniffs. "I told him I was too young. I told him to ask me again in a year - after graduation. He said we didn't need to get married right away, but that we should get engaged."

She sniffs again. "I wish I hadn't been so stubborn. I told him I wanted to wait before making such a big commitment. I loved him, Dad. I love him. I can't believe that the last thought he had of me was anything other than that I love him."

In their silence, I visualize them: her head on his shoulder, his arm wrapped around her, patting her gently.

She comes to sit on the bed next to me. "Remember when we used to visit Grandpa Isaac and I would cuddle up on his lap and he would tell me those wild stories about his childhood?"

"He always was a great storyteller," Allen says. "I wonder how much truth there was in them."

"Doesn't matter how true they were, Dad. What matters is that he told them. I felt like he made them up just for me. He made me feel a part of things. Important." She leans forward and touches my cheek. "It's what I love about Jake. He always had time for me. He always had a way of making me feel good."

I am not exactly sure where I am. I don't think it's actually a hospital, although there are people around all the time, and the ever-present sound of machines purring as they monitor me and keep me going. Every so often, I hear various beeps, and sometimes one of the machines issues a faint "puff-puff" sound as if it is blowing off a little steam.

I often hear the sound of an elevator - that whooshing noise as it goes up or down, the annoying bell when the doors open. So I guess I'm in a tall building somewhere. I know I'm in Boston, in sight of the Hancock tower and the Prudential. Also, Allen lives near Boston and Ginnie goes to university in Boston. What a lovely young woman she is.

I like Boston. I spent most of my life working and living around here. Virginia and I used to come into the city often to visit the Museum of Fine Arts, the Gardner and the galleries on Newbury Street. We liked to eat in the North End and then walk down to the waterfront and watch the big ships slowly move through the water.

I've always had an ambivalent feeling about big ships, starting with that first crossing from Hamburg to New York.

***

Somehow Uncle Kalner managed to get us onto our ship after a few days. The ship was called the President Lincoln. It was a huge vessel that I soon discovered was separated into two different worlds. Above were the first and second class cabins, with all the lovely décor and the fancy dining halls. Below were the immigrants. Fortunately we were in a third class cabin. This meant that we shared our little space with a family of five from Latvia, but it was a lot better than steerage, which was further below deck and seemed to be one huge stinking space packed with hundreds and

7

hundreds of people. I only went down there one time. It was enough. I learned later that there were almost two thousand people in that place. Four died before we reached America.

As third class passengers, we were allowed in some areas of the main deck. I tried to venture to the upper decks: not a good idea. A sailor caught me before I was halfway up the stairway and he made it very clear to me that if I took one more step he would throw me overboard.

I thought it would be good to make friends with the oldest of the three Latvian children. He was a couple of years younger than me and seemed scared of everything and everyone. He stayed close to his mother and father and avoided my attempts to engage him. I showed him some of my drawings, but he turned away and shrank further into his mother's arms. My offer to show him around on the main deck was refused. For most of the journey there was no communication between our families. I found that strange.

My mother was seasick almost from the moment we left Hamburg. She kept throwing up. Even when she had nothing left to throw she heaved and groaned. She looked terrible; pale with sunken dark eyes. She could not eat or drink anything. I thought she was going to die, and I told Uncle Kalner of my fear.

He told me that some people have a hard time being on a ship, but Mama was strong and she would be OK. He tried to reassure me nothing bad would happen to Mama. And then he told me about the sister I never knew. Her name was Tzipora, which means little bird. I always thought it was such a nice name for her. She flew away so young. I could never understand why he chose that particular time to tell me about her.

On the third day the ocean calmed down and my mother began to feel better. She even ate some hard bread she had brought, and some dried apples. I loved being on the ocean, with nothing to do except walk around, watch for seabirds, and make sketches in my notebook.

One day we saw a pair of whales less than a hundred yards from the ship. They swam alongside for several minutes. Another day, a school of dolphins crisscrossed in front of the ship - leaping out of the water then diving under the hull and turning to cross again. Mama laughed so hard. They played like this long enough for me to make a few sketches. Even Uncle Kalner broke a smile.

But the next day a storm came up and we huddled together in the pounding rain as the boat rocked and swayed. Even in this weather, it was better to be on deck in the fresh air than in the sweltering little cabin with the five Latvians. Mama, I think, was too scared to be sea-sick again, but she ate nothing and looked awful. She sang to me, softly, as I clung to her. I can hear her voice, strong but gentle.

And then one morning the Statue of Liberty rose out of the ocean. All the passengers cheered and hugged one another. Everyone stood near the front of the ship, watching the statue and the city come closer and closer. Someone started chanting the "Birkat HaGomel" - the prayer for deliverance from peril.

Chapter 2

I was wondering today how I survive. I can't eat or drink. I think the doctors stuck a bunch of tubes into my stomach and they feed me directly - no need to chew or swallow. I didn't ask for this.

And then I started thinking about what the word 'today' means. I can't tell the difference between light and dark. My guess is that when there is less activity around me, and no visitors, it is nighttime. Also, one of the nurses always greets me with a cheerful, "Good morning, Isaac. How are you doing today?" So, I assume when she comes, it's morning. She feels for my pulse, listens to my breathing and my heartbeat with her stethoscope. She is always kind enough to warm it before she touches it to my skin. But I don't know if she comes in every day - I hope not, for her sake. She has to have time away from here for family and friends.

I love it when she talks to me; sometimes she sings softly when she is nearby. She told me her name is Wanda.

***

I don't want to remember Ellis Island, but I can't really help it. It was a terrifying experience.

When the President Lincoln docked in New York, the first and second class passengers disembarked. Then the steerage and third class passengers - the immigrants - were loaded onto barges each carrying about seven hundred people, and were ferried across to Ellis Island.

We were inspected by customs officials and doctors and nurses, all seemingly looking for some reason to not let us into America. I have this image of a cavernous gray room; people's voices, in dozens of different languages, echoing through the huge space. We were made to move forward one at a time as the inspections proceeded. About six or seven people ahead of me was a young woman carrying her infant daughter against her shoulder. I could see that the child's eyes were swollen shut. A man in a white coat looked the woman and child up and down, then made a white chalk mark on the child's coat. The mother and child were taken away.

Mama, as I said earlier, had been terribly seasick and had eaten little. She was pale and not very strong. She was in line behind me, followed by Uncle Kalner. Fearfully, I passed that man in the white coat, then turned just in time to see him lean towards Mama and mark her coat. Uncle Kalner and I called out helplessly as she was led off to a side room.

Uncle Kalner and I were directed into another large room to face the questions of the immigration officer. Where were we from? Where were we going? Do we have family to vouch for us in America? How much money do we have? Do we have money for train tickets to our destination? What work do we do? What languages do we speak? The questions were repeated in different ways as if to try to confuse us. Sometimes he would have Uncle Kalner answer the questions, sometimes I would have to.

There was one question that made my heart almost stop beating; "Where is your mother?"

"They took her away," I mumbled, and then started to cry. Uncle Kalner explained about the chalk mark.

The officer paused, checking our papers again. "Welcome to America," he said, as he stamped the papers. "You can wait for her in the waiting room." He waved in the direction of a doorway off to the side.

Uncle and I had made it through all the inspections and testing and bureaucracy and were officially granted immigration status, but here we sat in that hot, crowded, airless room on the doorstep to America, waiting for Mama to be given permission to join us.

The windows were open, but the thick summer air did not move. In Linkeve we were on a hill; there was always a slight breeze and the fresh scent of the nearby forest. Here, in New York harbor, we were surrounded by the stink of the ocean that was the sewer and refuse bucket of the city. I stood by a window staring out at the brown water, looking for any sign of life. The gulls circled above, but few dared to splash down.

An ocean liner enter the harbor. The deck was crowded with hundreds of immigrants like us - hopeful, fearful, expectant, and completely unaware of the ordeal they were about to go through. I watched as they were loaded onto the barges and brought over to the island. I could not see where they disembarked, but I could hear them talking nervously, comforting the wailing children, trying to reassure family members that all would soon be well.

A few hours later, some of them began to trickle into the waiting room.

Uncle Kalner was asleep when I rejoined him on the hard bench he had secured for us. I pulled my sketchpad and pencils from my bag and looked around the room. There were many people who seemed to be alone as they waited for their loved ones. I remember thinking how few large groups there were, how so many of the people in this room, and people passing through this building, had left the security and support of their extended families to come to this country.

We had left Chaim behind, not knowing if we would ever see him again. He was my brother, my protector, and he was not with us. I tried to remember everything about him - how he looked, talked, sang, smelled, laughed, moved, walked; how he shielded and comforted me when my father shouted at me. I began to cry, the tears dripping from my chin onto my sketchbook.

I felt Uncle Kalner's arm circle my shoulders. "Don't worry, Itzik," he said, "I am sure your Mama will come back to us soon." I pressed myself against him and we remained like that in silence for a long time.

I looked down at my sketchbook. The tears had dried, but had left faint traces of their presence. I began to follow their shapes with my pencil, then fill them in. It was a strangely personal and intimate process - drawing my tears. To someone who did not know, the drawing looked totally abstract, but to me it was as real as the ocean we had just crossed.

**

I feel the weight of someone sitting down next to me on the bed. I feel a hand on my forehead and I catch a whiff of Chanel Number 5 - Danielle. "You're looking pretty good for an old man," she says, and chuckles.

I smile, or at least, I think I am smiling. I get the impression from all those who come to this room that they are unable to detect any movement I make. I find that unfortunate and frustrating.

"Sorry to drop in so late," she says, as if I know the difference. "I saw Allen on his way out. He's looking good."

I have known Danielle her whole life. Her father and I were close friends, buddies - he saved my life. She was always the caretaker, even as a little girl. She is about seventy years old now. I think of her as my daughter, sometimes even as the sister I never got to meet.

She takes my hand in hers. "Your hands are cold," she says, and she gently rubs each of my fingers and my wrists. I try to respond. Strange how I can feel her touch, but cannot move a muscle. Quite amazing this human body - as it breaks down, its various functions seem to separate, to differentiate one from the other. I wonder if neurobiologists have studied this. Let me be a guinea pig - at least I could do something useful as I lie here.

"Allen said that he and Martha and Ginnie are going away for the long weekend. They'll be in a cabin in way-northern Vermont. He calls it a 'graduation getaway'."

I wonder what long weekend she is talking about; I have no sense of seasons in here. The place is always the same. The temperature is constant. I used to curse the cold snowy winters and grumble about the steamy summer days. Now I live in a bland unchanging comfort zone.

"Ginnie is still grieving for Jake. The whole country is still in shock over nine-eleven, but for poor Ginnie it is so much more painful." She sighed. "He was such a gentle young man."

I remember Jake well. He and Ginnie visited me often in my home. They were good together. Ginnie thought I would be shocked to learn that she was living with her boyfriend. I surprised them both with a big hug and a bottle of champagne when they finally told me. I had guessed they were together months before they plucked up the nerve to actually say something.

Separation is hard. Loss is worse.

***

"Why did that man make a chalk mark on Mama?" I asked Uncle Kalner. "What does it mean?"

He explained that it meant they thought she might be sick and they wanted to examine her more carefully to be sure she was well enough to travel further.

"But, what if she is not well enough?"

"Don't worry, Itzik. She'll be fine."

And so I sat in that stifling room next to Uncle and we waited for the door to open and for Mama to rejoin us. Through the windows I could see that the sun was setting and the sky was slowly turning from pale blue to gray and black. We would have to spend the night in this awful room, now lit by a few electric lights pressed against the ceiling.

I watched as the dozens of people made adjustments for the night, pulling blankets or coats up over their bodies, children nuzzling in close to their parents. In the gloom, against the far wall, a boy about my age was already asleep, resting his head on the shoulder of a man who was probably his father. The pair looked much like us. I tried to draw them but it was too dark.

It was one of the longest nights of my life. The sharpness of the hard bench, the noises of people snoring, whispering, and coughing, overlaid with the sounds of babies crying and the horns from ships passing outside in the harbor, all kept me awake. I could not stop worrying about Mama. What were they doing to her? Where was she? Was she really too sick? What would I do without her?

At last, I saw the sky growing lighter and after some time people began to stir. I am sure I was not the only one who had not slept. There was a tangible sense of anxiety and fear in that room. It was too quiet, too unreal. We all knew that this coming day could bring good news or terrible news or nothing at all except more waiting.

The day started well for some. The door opened and four people entered. Immediately shouts burst from four different parts of the room, as families rushed to be reunited. I looked on enviously as people hugged, then gathered up their belongings and made their way to the exit. A sad silence settled on those who remained. I heard a child whimper. It might have been me.

Some time later an officer entered and called out a name. A man stood, whispered something to his child, then walked over to the officer. They talked briefly. The man let out a loud cry of pain and disbelief, then returned to his child. He wearily picked up his suitcase and bundles, and father and daughter moved uneasily toward the exit. "She is being sent back," I heard him say to no one in particular.

"What does he mean?" I asked Uncle Kalner.

"I don't know," he said. This was the first time my uncle had no answer. I realized that he, too, was scared and tired. He squeezed my shoulders and when I looked into his face, his eyes were full.

Hours passed. The spaces vacated by the families who had departed to continue their journeys were soon filled by other families - different but the same. Uncle Kalner bought some bread and cheese from the canteen. I know he hated to spend the money, but we had to eat. I chewed my food as slowly as I could, trying to make the time go by, trying not to think about what could be.

By mid-afternoon five other families had been reunited and left the building, but Uncle and I remained, waiting. As the sky slowly darkened I realized we would have to go through another night in that horrible place. Uncle Kalner sat motionless, his face like stone. I leaned my head on his shoulder. He was too weary to even wrap his arm around me.

The second night was even worse than the first. It started off not too badly. I think I even fell asleep for a little while. Suddenly there was a huge commotion in the room. Someone was yelling, "Gonif - thief!" I saw two men fighting. One wielded a long knife while the other was waving a heavy club. People were shouting, children were screaming. Everyone pressed back as far as they could. Uncle Kalner turned my face into his chest and covered my ears with his hands so that I would not see or hear.

I did hear the sharp whistles of the officers who rushed into the room. Uncle Kalner released his grip on my head and I turned just in time to see the officers holding the two men face-down on the floor and putting them in handcuffs. They then marched the two men out of the room, but before they left, one of the officers announced, "These two are undesirables. They will be on the next ship back to where they came from!" A boy of about six or seven cried helplessly as his father was led away. He appeared to be alone.

Uncle Kalner went over to the boy, knelt down beside him and talked softly to him. Then he picked up all of their belongings and brought them to where we were. The boy followed and sat down next to me. Uncle told me to look after him, while he went to look for an officer. Uncle was gone for a long time.

The boy's name was Shlomo and he was coming to America with his father and oldest brother, Reuven, who was fifteen. His mother and three sisters were still in Zagere. A man had made a chalk mark on Reuven's coat, so now they had to wait for him. He told me that his brother was big and brave. I thought of my brother, Chaim. I hoped that he too would be brave in his new life.

When Uncle finally returned he said there was nothing to be done until morning when the higher ups came to work. He tried to reassure Shlomo that everything would be alright, but I could tell he was not sure. Shlomo and I sat on either side of him. He spread his coat around us, encircling us in his arms, and we tried to sleep. After a while I could hear Shlomo's steady breathing, but my mind kept turning over and over. My fears about Mama now mixing with concern for Shlomo and his father and brother, and with the sadness of leaving Chaim behind.

A light rain was falling as night slowly turned to day. Shlomo woke up and looked confused. "Where's my Papa?" he asked, "Who are you?" There were tears in his eyes. Uncle Kalner tried to comfort him, but the more Uncle talked, the more Shlomo cried.

Suddenly I heard a man call Uncle Kalner's name. My blood froze. Was the officer going to tell him that Mama was being sent home? Uncle Kalner took my face between his hands and said, "This is about Shlomo. Look after the boy. Don't worry." I watched as he strode to the officer and left the room with him. Shlomo grabbed my arm and we both sat in fear, our eyes not moving from that door.

It was only a few minutes before the door opened and in walked Shlomo's father and brother. Right behind them were Uncle Kalner and Mama. The joy of that moment is still with me.

Uncle Kalner introduced me to Mr. Novitz and Reuven, Shlomo's father and brother, then we said our goodbyes, gathered up our belongings and made our way to the railway station.

On the train from New York to Massachusetts, Mama would not let go of my hand. She talked about the two long days and nights she had been away from us in the hospital, being inspected and poked and tested. When she had tried to explain that her weakness was simply because of seasickness and lack of food and water, they would not listen. "It took them forty-eight hours to figure out I was tired, hungry and thirsty!" she said.

I asked Uncle Kalner what had happened with Shlomo's father and where the family was going. He said the officers came to the conclusion that Shlomo's father was not a bad man; he was only trying to defend himself and his son from a thief who had a big knife. The thief was arrested, and Shlomo's father was allowed to stay. It was pure coincidence that both Reuven and Mama were discharged from the hospital together and right when Shlomo's father and Uncle Kalner were returning to the waiting room.

"Shlomo's family is going to meet up with a cousin in New York City," Uncle Kalner told me. "I gave them the address of Uncle Ben. I hope they will write."

Many weeks later I did receive a letter, but it was not from Shlomo - it was from Reuven, who I had met for only a few minutes, but who was to become a very important person in my life.

***

Dear, sweet Danielle, who sits beside me on this bed, is my good friend Reuven's daughter. There is much more to tell about him and her.

Chapter 3

I can no longer detect Danielle's perfume. I don't remember her leaving, but she is definitely not here. The room is quiet except for the purring and gurgling sounds of the machines, and the ringing of that damned elevator.

I hear faint footsteps, as if someone is walking in felt shoes. I remember reading an article about the "Silent Prison" in Port Arthur, Tasmania. The English would send prisoners there who were troublemakers in the main prison. This was the end of the line. Prisoners lived in complete silence and isolation. No one was allowed to speak or make sounds - not even the guards, who were required to wrap their boots in soft cloth to dull their footsteps. When prisoners were moved to the exercise area or to the chapel for Sunday services, their heads were completely covered with bags that had tiny openings for them to see through - but they saw no other human face. A few months of this and prisoners lost their minds. The prison, reportedly, had an excellent mental hospital right next door. There is something diabolical about the English.

"Sorry I woke you, Mr. Simon." His voice is deep, gentle. How did he know he woke me? "I'm simply going to do a quick check of your vitals. Routine stuff." I feel him lift my wrist. A few minutes later the blood pressure strap is clamped around my upper arm and I hear him pumping it up, then releasing the air. "Looking good," he says. "I'll leave you now. Goodnight."

How does he know he woke me? He did wake me, I'm pretty sure of that. But how did he know? I have been under the impression that I have no way to communicate anything, that my appearance and behavior were constant, unchanging. If *he* knows, why do others not know?

He never told me his name. Who is he?

***

Our first home was with Uncle Ben, Mama's youngest brother. He had left the shtetl a year after I was born and made his way to Lowell, Massachusetts. He worked as a mechanic in one of the big textile mills in the city, and he rented a small apartment only a few blocks from his job. Mama started working in the same place as Uncle Ben three days after we arrived. Uncle Ben wanted me to work there, too - but Mama insisted I go to school. I hated the school and wanted to work. Uncle Ben was not married and liked to go out with the factory girls. Mama thought he was a bad influence on me and urged Uncle Kalner to find us another place to live.

There was a lot of shouting in that apartment.

After a few months Uncle Kalner found a place for us to live in Lawrence, a nearby city with even more textile factories. We moved to our new apartment in September 1910. It had one bedroom, a parlor and a small kitchen and indoor plumbing, which was new for us, and a wonderful thing, especially in the winter.

The bedroom was Mama's. Uncle Kalner slept on a sofa in the parlor. If one of them was working at night, I slept in their bed – otherwise I slept in a cot in Mama's room. It was very close.

From the day we arrived in Lawrence Uncle Kalner refused to speak to me in Yiddish. I don't know where he had learned English; probably from the few English books he bought in Linkeve, but whatever words he had, those were the only ones he used. For the first year or so in America, he always kept a Yiddish-English dictionary nearby. If I asked for something in Yiddish, he ignored me and pretended I wasn't there, or he would push that tattered dictionary towards me. "Look it up," he would say, "You have got to learn this confounding language." It took me a long time to understand what he meant. He was not as strict with my mother, so I would sometimes ask her questions to ask him.

Mama soon found work on the looms in one of the factories in Lawrence. She was a lot older than most of the workers there - many of them were farm girls on their own, away from their families; I think they liked to pretend she was their mother. My uncle also worked there for about a year, but he was not well suited to factory work.

The day he got fired was the day he became a labor organizer. "I am not part of a machine, and neither are you, Rivka," he said to my mother. "The one thing I now know about this place called America is that working people will get nothing if we don't fight to get something." He banged his fist on the kitchen table. "Wait and see. We will shut this city down."

My Uncle Kalner became an organizer for the IWW, the International Workers of the World, the Wobblies. Such a funny name for such bold people. In that one year he spent working in the textile mill Uncle Kalner not only taught himself English, but became quite fluent in Italian, as well. And, of course, he could speak Russian and Yiddish from the old country. So Uncle Kalner was able to talk with many of the workers in their own language, which made him important to the Wobblies.

Before the big strike in the winter early in 1912, and during that strike, many of the Wobblie leaders would come to our apartment to talk about how the union organizing was going. I had to stay in the bedroom much of the time, but I could hear most of what was being said. As their conversations became more and more intense, less and less attention was paid to me, and I would sneak out of the bedroom and sit in the corner of the parlor, watching and listening.

Mama became a strike leader, too. This came about, not because she was Uncle Kalner's sister, but because the younger women respected and loved her, and she was very brave in standing up to the bosses and the goons and strikebreakers. She was on the picket lines every day, face to face with the police and the company thugs.

One evening Uncle Kalner came home and sat me down at the table. He told me there had been a fight between the police and the workers on the picket line and Mama had been hurt and taken away by the police. He promised he would find Mama and bring her home. He said I was not to leave the apartment, not even to go to school. He said I must keep the door locked and not let anyone in unless I knew who they were. I was left alone, not knowing how long he and Mama would be gone. There was very little food. That night I ate a bit of bread and some raw cabbage. There was no wood for the fire and I was cold. I crept to Mama's bed and took all her blankets and brought them into the parlor. I piled them on top of Uncle Kalner's blankets on the sofa and burrowed underneath them, like a little fox in a hole.

Next morning I sat at the table not knowing what to do, except worry. If someone had offered to take me back to Linkeve that day, I think I would have gone. I started to draw pictures of the people I had seen coming and going from the apartment; the strike organizers. They were all such interesting people; loud, strong, passionate.

There was a young woman from Ireland. She had short curly dark hair and freckled white skin. Her eyes were grayish green, and sparkled fiercely when she spoke. I could barely understand her, but I was burned by the fire in her voice. A thin older man always sat at the head of the table. He talked little, but when he did everyone in the room became quiet.

There was a man from Italy with a long droopy moustache, who slapped his hand on the table when he spoke. His had a deep baritone voice and would often burst into song in the middle of a meeting. Sometimes the others would join in, sometimes they would tell him to be quiet and get back to the discussion. I liked him.

I spent a lot of time working on those drawings, trying to portray the features of each person. I did one drawing of the group around the table in the cramped parlor with the man from Italy standing and singing while the others clapped their hands and sang along with him.

The apartment was freezing; frost spread across the inside of the windows and blocked out the rest of the world. I never left. I just waited for Mama and Uncle Kalner to come home. I was so hungry. I knew that everything was scarce during the strike. I had heard the Wobblies talk about how the police and the companies were trying not to let food and other supplies into the city. The strike leaders had even talked about sending the children to other towns so they would not starve in Lawrence.

On the third day after Uncle Kalner had left to find Mama I heard someone approaching our apartment and then knocking on the door. I sat as quietly as I could. The man cleared his throat. "It's me, Ben," he said. "Is anyone home?"

I had not seen Uncle Ben in almost a year. I ran to the door, unlocked it and let him in. It was so good to see him. We hugged and then I told him about Mama and the police. He said he had read about the strike, and he wanted to be sure we were taking care of ourselves. "From what you tell me, Itzik, my worries were not made up. But," he said, reaching into his jacket pocket, "the main reason I came is to deliver this letter from Chaim. It arrived yesterday, and I wanted to bring it personally."

He put the letter on the table in front of me, then looked around the kitchen and asked if there was any food or firewood. I said, "No." He asked me when I had last eaten anything, and I said I had a raw potato in the morning. He told me to wait, and he rushed out to see if he could find food and wood to buy. Before he left, he told me not to open the letter from Chaim. "It's addressed to your Mama."

I stared at that white envelope with the blue stamp in the corner, and Chaim's writing. How could I not open it? I held it up to the gray light of the frosty window, but could not read anything inside. It wasn't fair - I had not heard a word from my brother in a year and a half, and Uncle Ben said I could not open the letter.

It was dark outside when I heard people coming up the stairs and stopping outside our apartment door. I blew out the one candle I had lit. I was so scared. Then I heard a key go into the lock and in a moment Mama and Uncle Kalner came into the apartment. I rushed toward Mama, but Uncle Kalner stepped between us and held me. "Your mother has a lot of pain," he said, "hug her gently."

He released me and it was then that I noticed her right arm was in a sling and she had a bandage on her head. "Come here, my boy," she said and wrapped her good arm around me and held me close. We sat down on the old sofa, not talking, enjoying the feeling of being together again.

A short while later there was a tap on the door and Uncle Ben announced himself. Uncle Kalner opened the door for him and he entered carrying a large bag filled with food in one hand, and a bundle of wood for the stove in the other. Mama embraced him, and he told everyone to sit while he started to cook.

It was a banquet - pumpkin soup, followed by scrambled eggs with onions and cheese. I ate until I was ready to pop.

"So what did you do while your Mama and uncle were gone?" Uncle Ben asked me after I had pushed my very full self away from the table.

"Not much," I said. "I made a few drawings."

"No school work?" Uncle Kalner asked.

I did not answer.

"Can I see your drawings?" Mama said. I went to the bedroom to fetch them, proud and excited to show off my work. I knew that I had created very realistic portraits of Uncle Kalner's Wobblie friends.

When I handed the papers to Mama I saw immediately that something was wrong - her initial smile quickly left her face and I could see she was not happy with the pictures.

"You don't like them, Mama?"

She set the drawings on the table then slid them toward Uncle Kalner. She placed her elbows on the table and pressed her fingertips together. This was not a good sign. Uncle picked up the drawings and examined each one carefully. His face went hard. He stood up from the table and walked around behind my chair. I felt his strong hands grip my shoulders.

Mama said, "These are wonderful drawings, Itzik. They are too good."

"I don't understand," I said.

"They are too good. They look exactly like the people they are supposed to look like - and that is the problem."

"That doesn't make any sense, Mama."

"You have to understand, Itzik, that the police and the company only know some of the strike leaders and organizers. They would like to be able to identify everyone, and these drawings would help them do that. We can't take a chance that the drawings would fall into their hands."

Uncle Kalner cut in, "We could get a visit from them at any time. I'm afraid, Isaac, that as wonderful as these drawings are, we have to burn them. And if any stranger ever asks you if there have been strike meetings here, you have to say no."

And with that, he picked up my drawings and dropped them into the fire.

"I'm really sorry, Itzik," Mama said, "they are very good drawings."

I watched the flames race across the papers, devour them, then curl and shrink them until they were nothing more than black flakes. The room was so quiet and I could hear my drawings crinkle as they shriveled. I listened until the sound was gone, then I went to Mama's bedroom and cried. My mother came in and sat down next to me on the bed. She sang softly to me, and stroked my face and dried my tears with the sleeve of her blouse.

***

I feel my great-granddaughter Ginnie's hand on my cheek. She sits next to me on the bed. I think she is crying. "I miss you. I miss your stories, Grandpa," she says. She pauses for what seems to be a long time, then says, "I even miss your advice. I could use it now." She hugs me. If my arms weren't lumps of lead I would wrap her in them. I would love to be able to say even two or three words to her.

Chapter 4

I did not ask for my mother's advice. I knew what she would have said and I didn't want to hear it.

But, I am racing ahead. I must go back to that letter from Chaim. In my joy at having Mama home and my sadness and anger over Uncle Kalner burning my drawings, I had forgotten all about the letter.

It was not until the next morning, after my two uncles had left the apartment, when Mama was putting away all the dishes and other things from supper that she found the letter in the middle of the table. She let out a loud shriek. I jumped out of bed and ran to her. She held the envelope out to me with her good hand. "Open it," she said, "carefully."

I took a sharp knife from the drawer, sliced open the envelope, and handed the two page letter to her. She unfolded the pages with her good hand and began to read. Tears formed in the corners of her eyes; she did not try to stop them.

She read the letter again then handed it to me. It was dated December 1911. Chaim wrote that his journey from the shtetl to South Africa was fine. He was well and he had seen our cousin Shmuel who had been in South Africa for five or more years. He said he was in a large town called Pretoria and had started a job as a builder's helper – "like our father, except without the schnapps," he joked.

"Why are you crying, Mama? He says he is fine and he has a job."

"It is what he does not say, Itzik. He does not say why it took him so long to write. He does not say even when he left Linkeve, nor does he give any details of the journey. He does not say how he lived all this time without a job. He does not say that he is continuing with his studies. He does not say where he is living, what kind of place. He does not say that Shmuel, that greedy good-for-nothing, offered him no help or hospitality."

She took the letter from my hands, folded it carefully and returned it to its envelope. "Your brother has been through such difficulty in his short life, and without his Mama to hold him and sing to him." She stood up and went into her bedroom, closing the door behind her. I heard the bed creak as she sat down. I heard her sobbing for a while, then silence.

About ten minutes later she came out of her room. "I have to go to the picket line," she said.

"Can I come with you?"

"Yes," she answered without a moment of hesitation and to my great surprise, "I think that would be good."

The chanting of the strikers grew louder as we walked down the street toward the textile mill. When we turned the last corner I saw hundreds of people in front of the gates before the huge building. As we got closer I could see the signs they carried. They were in Yiddish and English and Italian and French and other languages I did not recognize.

I saw many children on the picket line – some younger than me. "Why didn't you bring me here before?" I asked Mama. "Other people have brought their children."

"These children work here, Itzik," she said.

I stared at them in awe.

Someone in the crowd saw my mother approaching and began to wave and cheer. Soon the whole picket line was chanting, "Riv-ka! Riv-ka! Riv-ka!"

I saw a group of militiamen move toward us. The crowd saw it, too, and their chanting grew louder. A determined smile flashed across my mother's face, and she raised her good fist and shouted, "We will never be broken!"

The crowd roared in response and about ten big strong men stepped out of line and rushed to protect us before the militiamen could cut us off from the strikers. Inexplicably, the militiamen turned back; I wondered whether they actually realized they were fighting against their own people.

I have mentioned a few times that my Mama would sing to me when I was sad. She always sang soft, gentle songs with images of family, of friendship and peace. That day on the picket line the workers lifted her up onto a big box – something they had obviously done many times over the past few weeks – and called on her to sing.

And she did. I saw my mother as I had never seen her before. She was defiant, full of energy, with a strength in her voice that could conjure up a whirlwind. She sang working people's songs in English and Yiddish and even one in French. The crowd joined in and spurred her on. She sang until her voice was gone.

She raised her fist. "We will not be broken," she rasped as they helped her down. She hugged me and we both withdrew into the crowd to continue singing and chanting as the Italian baritone who I had seen many times in our apartment was pushed up onto the box.

***

Someone is singing near me. It is a man's voice. I do not recognize it. "Good evening, Mr. Simon. I am Damon, your new night nurse." His speaking voice is deep, earthy. I like him, even though I am still getting used to the idea of male nurses. "I need to adjust a few things," he says, and I feel him pulling on the sheets and touching where the tubes and wires are connected to me.

His hands move quickly, but gently. He is singing again, a song about lost love.

He stops. I feel him close to my ear, "Mr. Simon, blink your eyes if you hear me," he says.

I am stunned, panicked. No one has asked me to communicate in ages. I can't remember when last anyone has actually directed a question at me that they expected me to respond to. What does this nurse Damon want? Why?

Why not? It's not like the inquisition. He's trying something no one else has done in a very long time. What's the harm? I blink.

He sighs. "Nothing," he says. "Well, we can try again some other time."

Now I am truly depressed. I thought I had moved my eyelids - but he did not see it. Can I really not even do that! I will have to practice. Maybe tomorrow I'll show him. For now I will call him Damon the Unobservant.

***

The strike lasted until the middle of March: two months of picketing and fighting and arrests. One striker was killed and the police tried to blame the Wobblies. Two Wobblie leaders were arrested, including my baritone friend. But they could not get the charges to stick because everyone knew that the killers were really militiamen.

With the strike over, things began to return to normal. I went back to school, as much as I hated it. My Uncle Kalner went off to organize in Chicago and New York, working for the International Ladies' Garment Workers Union. We did not see him often, but when he did come to visit, he always had remarkable stories to tell about the people he met and the battles they fought.

My mother was earning a little more money. She worked in that textile mill until the day she died. One time during those first few years I asked her whether she missed Linkeve. It was early in the morning on a raw and rainy day and she was getting ready to leave for work. "We were a wonderful community. I miss that. I miss the big family – my cousins and aunts and uncles. But we were going nowhere. It was like we were walking around in circles with one foot nailed to the ground." She sighed as she pulled on her boots. "The mud is about the same." And with that she left, reminding me not to be late for school, again.

My brother Chaim was not a frequent letter writer. I wrote him several times about our life here, and begged him to write to Mama, but his letters came only every three or four months. The arrival of each letter became a ritual in our home. I would find the letter in our mailbox when I returned from school, bring it up to the apartment and position it on the kitchen table facing the door so Mama would see it the moment she entered. She would pick it up carefully, examine the envelope as if she were a detective looking for clues, then pass it to me and instruct me to open it, carefully.

She would read, and sigh. I would wait for her to give the pages to me. Chaim's first letters were written in Yiddish, but by the fourth or fifth letter he was writing mostly in English. The content was almost always the same: he was fine, working hard, seeing a few family members.

I had started collecting stamps, so I was eager to get to the letters, but Mama would not let me tear off the stamp. I was allowed to keep the whole envelope. In February 1915 a letter arrived from Chaim. I remember it well, partly because there was no stamp on the envelope, but mostly because he had written to say that he was in the South African Army in German South West Africa. He was a private in something called the Witwatersrand Rifles! Mama was stunned. She could not believe that her son had signed up to be a soldier. She wondered what hardships had driven him to this unfortunate decision.

"Why did he have to get involved in this war between greedy colonial powers?" she said after his second letter from the army arrived only three weeks after the first. This time she did not cry. She was angry. "Stupid boy," she muttered, "and we all thought he was such a scholar, such a wise young man!" She tossed the letter at me. "He says nothing because he has nothing to say!"

I read the letter and had to agree with her. All he said was that he was fine, and he complained about not getting enough sleep. I suspected the rubber stamp of the army censor might have had something to do with the lack of any actual news or information about his life as a soldier. I put the letter away with my small collection and then went out to sit on the front steps of our apartment building until Mama called me for supper.

***

It is quiet in here right now. No visitors. No nurses. I need to practice my blinking. I am determined to surprise Damon the Unsuspecting. I try to focus all of my attention on my eyes. I realize that I do not even know whether my eyes are closed or open. All I see – if "see" is the right word – is gray. I squeeze the muscles around my eyes. Then I relax. I do it again, and again. After several attempts I seem to sense a slight shift in the level of gray. Is it possible?

Chapter 5

Allen, my grandson, is talking to someone. His voice is low but intense as if he thinks I might overhear him. Little does he know! He is having an argument. The other person says, "I can't stay. I have to get back to New York."

"But, you haven't seen Grandpa Isaac in months. Surely you can spend a little more time."

"I have to go. I can't take any more time away from the office."

"Then what did you come here for? To sniff the air in Boston?"

Good one, Allen, I say to myself. I realize he is talking to his hot-shot Wall Street trader son: the one who has more money than sense.

"What's the big deal? Grandpa Isaac doesn't even know anyone's here!"

"You don't know that!"

"C'mon, Dad! Be realistic. Isaac has no idea. He's not aware of anything!"

"He's probably more in touch than you are!"

"This is bullshit! I'm gone. Tell Ginnie I said hi."

I hear his expensive shoes striding out the door. Allen sits down near me and touches my hand. "I hope you didn't hear that," he says, "David can be such an ass."

I figure now is not a good time to practice my blinking.

***

Stubbornness does run in the family. Or maybe it is a universal response to that feeling of not being entirely sure of oneself.

Which brings me back to my brother, the soldier. The next letter from Chaim came from an army hospital somewhere in the desert of South West Africa. He had not been wounded, but he was exhausted. A few days later, a short letter from the hospital administration said that Chaim had no signs of injury and his mental capacities had returned to normal and he was returning to active duty.

Back in those days people called it 'shell shock.' The officers said it showed weakness, and the best way to treat it was to get back into action. I've seen it close up. It is not that simple.

Poor Chaim. He was so lost as a soldier. I could not understand Mama's reaction to the letters, which came more frequently now that he was a soldier. Sometimes she would cry, but mostly she would read them, hand them to me and then stare blankly at nothing. His letters never talked about what he was doing or what he wanted to be doing. They were like small signals, just to let us know he was still there. I felt like I no longer knew him, as if he was disappearing.

Then, in July 1915 the newspapers announced the German defeat in South West Africa. Chaim had survived. His next letter talked of returning to Pretoria to his old job and finding a room with a widow from the old country. He seemed happy and the tone of his letter suggested it was more than a lodging arrangement. Mama did not offer a comment on this detail. She was too filled with relief to care.

But the happiness did not last. In December we received a letter from him from a hospital in England. My brother Chaim had signed up again. He had joined the South African Third Infantry Regiment and had shipped out to England in September, where his unit trained for a few weeks before being sent to Egypt to fight the Ottomans. He had managed to get sick and missed the trip to North Africa. He wrote that he had become friendly with the only other Jewish fellow in his unit. His name was Moish Zweig, who was originally from the town of Zeimelis, which was not far from Linkeve.

Mama was furious he had returned to being a soldier, but thankful he was safe in an army hospital, and afraid that his illness was serious. He gave no details, although I will say that I saw his military records many years later. Turns out he had gonorrhea. The poor lost soul. My sweet big brother!

Mama never found out.

***

All I am aware of in my room is the sound of the machines that keep me alive. They purr like kittens. Every now and then they give a little "puff-puff," followed by a few moments of silence, then the kittens return.

I have named them the "cat-machine."

So frustrating to be here, connected to these things, but unable to connect to the people who come and go.

I seem to be alone in this room. I must practice my blinking for Damon the Demanding. I need to find something to do that isn't all inside my head and memories.

I have outlived my three children. How does a person understand something like that? Albert, Allen's father, was the oldest, yet he died long after the other two – Mark and Emma. They were both too young. At least my dear Virginia did not see her eldest go. But she, too, is long gone – more than twenty years I have lived without her.

Am I practicing my blinking, or am I trying not to cry? I hope Damon the Determined is not around. I don't want to confuse him.

***

At the time we received Chaim's first letter from England, I was fifteen years old. I was still going to school, but had started working at the Lawrence Eagle Tribune on Essex Street, about six blocks from the mill where Mama worked. I wanted to learn the printing trade, and to help Mama with the bills. The job they gave me was on the loading dock – taking materials off the delivery wagons and moving them into the warehouse, and loading the wagons with the evening editions of the newspaper.

It was hard work. For the first few weeks my muscles ached and Mama would rub smelly ointments into my arms and back every evening to ease the pain. Part of me hated the work, but over time, another part of me enjoyed seeing my body get stronger and feeling the sense of accomplishment when I reached a point where I could lift a sixty pound crate of printing ink without even thinking about it.

I was, however, learning nothing about printing. One evening, after my shift was over, I snuck into the main part of the plant and squeezed myself into a dark corner where I could see the presses and watch the men set up the printing plates, fill the ink cylinders and ready the huge machines for the next print run. I had brought my sketchbook and pencils and was soon completely absorbed in drawing everything I saw around me.

Suddenly, I heard the blast of the steam whistle; it was ten minutes before the midnight shift change. I was panicked. I knew Mama would be worried. I was supposed to have been home by nine o'clock. And, as circumstances would have it, I couldn't sneak out then because there were even more people around with the midnight crew arriving.

I closed my sketchbook and pressed it to my chest; and as I did this a pencil dropped and rolled out onto the floor, right in front of one of the men. He picked it up and turned his head in my direction. His eyes rested on my frightened face. Then he straightened up. He was a big man; well over six feet and thick around the shoulders and neck.

"Come out of your hole, fella," he commanded.

I moved forward nervously, clutching my drawings tightly.

"What have we here?" and he reached out for my sketchpad. Reluctantly, I handed it to him. He turned the pages slowly, looking at each drawing long enough for me to hope he might like them. Then my whole body tensed up as I remembered that awful night when Uncle Kalner burned my drawings of the union people.

"Please, give them back," I mumbled. "I won't come in here again."

He ignored my plea. By now several other men had gathered around. "I seen you on the loading dock, right?"

I nodded.

"You should stay there, fella!" he said, and was about to push the sketchbook back into my hands when another man came up.

"Let me have that," he said, and grabbed the book. "And get to bloody work, you lot."

I recognized him as one of the foremen. He glanced at my drawings. "You come see Mr. Hardwicke before you start your shift tomorrow. Maybe he'll give this back to you. Maybe he won't." He tucked my pad under his arm, turned and shouted over his shoulder as he strode away, "Now get outta here!"

I was in trouble. Mr. Hardwicke was a high level manager. I'd heard his name uttered a few times on the loading dock, and not very nice things had been said about him. I had no idea what his position actually was, but I knew he had a big office, far above the noise of the printing presses.

It was almost one in the morning when I arrived home. Mama had reached a point where she was more scared than angry. I told her what had happened. All she said was that I had better put on a clean shirt if I was going to see Mr. Hardwicke.

***

Fear is something I have not encountered in a long time. I know, as I lie here, I am looking in the face of Death, but it is not fear that I feel. I have seen Death too many times to be afraid of him now. How can I fear what I am waiting for? But, when you are young, Death is a whole other matter. And so is fear.

I hear Damon singing. I wonder whether he is singing to me or simply singing to pass the time. No matter. I can enjoy it all the same. His hands are warm as he touches me, checks my pulse and all the wires and tubes going in and out of me. I hate to think how scary I must look.

"Everything looking fine tonight, Mr. Simon," he says, as he gently wipes my face with a warm cloth. "Your beard's getting pretty wild, though. White as snow. Let's see if I can comb it."

He sits on the bed beside me. I feel the comb moving slowly down my cheeks and chin. Several times.

"Now, that looks a whole lot better," Damon says. He stands, "See you tomorrow." he says, and I hear him walking from the room, the squeak of his shoes fading quickly.

I did not get to show him my blinking. I was enjoying his touch so much, I forgot all about it. Well, I will practice some more, and be ready for tomorrow.

Chapter 6

I hear someone's steady breathing. Every now and then there is a rustle of papers, as if the person is examining a stack of documents. I wish I could let this person know I am awake and listening. It's so upsetting. I know I'm here, awake and aware, but no one around me can see it. I try to say something; to make a sound, any sound, but nothing happens. I try blinking, but realize that even if I was actually succeeding in clenching my eyelids, if the person sitting there with the pile of papers is not looking at my face, he – or she – will not notice. And even if he or she did see, would they know that it was actually me, Isaac Simon, who was communicating?

It's getting to be too much.

"Grandpa Isaac's looking pretty good this morning. Someone combed out his beard – very Walt Whitman." It's Ginnie. I didn't hear her come in. Guess I was too busy feeling sorry for myself.

"What're you reading, Dad?"

"This is amazing stuff," Allen replies. "I was going through some of those boxes in Grandpa Isaac's closet and found this envelope containing his brother Chaim's service records. It's fascinating and heartbreaking. It seems like many of those stories Isaac used to tell us about his brother were mostly true. Isaac did leave out the worst parts, though, and some of the potentially scandalous episodes as well."

"Scandalous?"

"Well, he was hospitalized twice for treatment of venereal disease. Not the kind of diagnosis one would write home about."

"Uncle Chaim and those wild French girls!" Ginnie giggled.

"And English young ladies," Allen said. "But, more seriously," he continued, "he saw some terrible combat. Do you remember the stories Grandpa Isaac told you about Charlie, the lost little mouse?

"Of course I remember Charlie."

"They were all about his brother Chaim, except Isaac usually found a happy ending. He actually wrote some of them down and kept them in the envelope with Chaim's service records."

I remember. Ginnie would sit on my knee and plead with me to tell her about the adventures of Charlie. How could she have known how much it hurt?

Charlie was alone in the world. He had become disconnected from his family because of a big rain storm that flooded their home and washed away all the roads and bridges. He was trying to cross a small stream to return to where he thought they all were, but the current was too strong for him. He managed to cling to a fallen twig from an oak tree as it sailed by, and he was carried far, far away.

When the storm finally ended, Charlie found himself in a foreign land. He sniffed around looking for something, anything, that was familiar, but the only scent he recognized was the smell of the earth itself. He was very hungry, so he tasted a berry he found. It was so bitter that he spat it out. Then he tried to nibble on the bark of a tree, but that was too hard. Finally, he dug a hole in the ground and went to sleep, exhausted and still hungry.

Charlie woke up the next morning to find the sun shining and the sounds of life all around. Carefully he crept to the edge of his hole and sniffed the air. He listened to the birds and the bugs as they sang and chatted. He strained his ears and poked his head a little further out of his hole when he thought he heard the squeak of a mouse. He squeaked in response and was happy to hear the other mouse answer him. A new friend, he thought.

Suddenly everything went quiet for a moment. Charlie poked his head out even further to see why everyone was so silent. "Get back," he heard his new friend shout, and seconds later all the birds, chipmunks and other creatures began to scream, panicked. Charlie pulled back into his hole just in time to allow his new friend to squeeze in beside him.

"Hawk," said the new arrival.

"Pleased to meet you, Hawk," Charlie said. "What a funny name for a mouse." (Ginnie always giggled loudly at this part of the story.)

"My name isn't Hawk; it's Ruby," the newcomer replied indignantly. "There's a hawk circling the field out there, ready to swoop down to grab someone for her dinner. What's your name?"

But there was no time for chit-chat. The two mice needed to dig a deeper hole to be sure the hawk could not find them. They worked steadily for a long time. Poor Charlie's stomach growled and growled, but Ruby convinced him it was too dangerous to go out in search of food while the hawk was still flying around.

Finally, when the birds sounded the "All clear," Charlie and Ruby ventured out to find food and to play. They came to a field thick with ripening corn. What a feast they had!

"Look out for snakes," Ruby said, as they made their way cautiously through the corn in the direction of the bubbling sounds of a nearby stream.

Charlie did not know what a snake was, or how it looked, or what he should do if he saw one. But he said nothing. All he wanted was to get to the stream, and to find his way across it and return home.

When they finally emerged from the corn field they were confronted not by a small stream, but by a wide river with strong swirling currents. Charlie knew he could not cross it. He flopped down on the muddy river bank and cried. Ruby nuzzled up beside him. "I will be your family," she said. "We will look after each other."

Suddenly they heard a screech. "Hawk!" Ruby shouted. "Quick, run behind that rock and start digging!"

And the hole they dug together behind the rock became their home.

Allen continues to recite the facts of Chaim's last years on earth. I am glad that he found those papers. They are like a skeleton – stark and scary, but there is no blood or skin or muscle. No heart. I know what Chaim went through. I was there. I walked where he had walked. And I could not talk about it with anyone. Even my dear Virginia only knew a small part of what I knew. She did know about my nightmares. She would hold me tight, and sing to me, rescue me from those terrors.

"Chaim clearly suffered mentally from his experiences," Allen went on. "He went AWOL several times and was punished by loss of pay and reduced rations for weeks. He was hospitalized more than once for treatment of 'shell shock' – what we call PTSD today. The treatment was not much more than a short rest, then get back on the horse, soldier!"

"Shit," my so elegant great-granddaughter said.

"He was killed in at the Battle of Arras in April 1917 – days after the United States declared war on Germany."

They were silent a long time. Finally Ginnie said, "You're right – he did keep the worst of it from us."

"I can't believe Grandpa Isaac never shared these papers with anyone in the family. I never thought of him as a secretive person. It must have been too hard to talk about what really happened."

Tears are rolling from my eyes into my beard.

Ginnie is pacing. "I have to go," she says. "I have a huge paper due on Thursday and I'm not even halfway through all the reading. I'll come by the house Friday night." She sits on the bed next to me and I feel her lean over me and kiss my cheek.

"He's crying!" she says. "Look Dad, Grandpa Isaac is crying." Her voice gets softer, almost as if she is afraid I will hear what she is saying. "Do you think he heard us talking about his brother?"

"Maybe. Who knows?"

"I think he did. Maybe he is more aware than we think!"

She cups my face gently in her hands like she used to do when she was a little girl sitting on my knee, listening to my stories.

I feel as though my whole body is smiling. I try to blink, but she does not acknowledge my effort. But she will one day, soon.

She stands up and says goodbye.

After some time, Allen pats my hand. "I found Chaim's letters. And yours. What a life you have lived," he says.

The room is silent except for the purring of my machines.

I am alone again. For the first time in years I am afraid to sleep for fear of those nightmares. Yes, a short while ago I said I did not fear Death – but I do fear pain and loss. I fear the explosions and the chaos. I fear the process. I remember the horror of it all.

My chest is tightening, like someone is strapping me down. I can feel my heart racing. The blood is pounding in my ears – like rhythmic rounds of cannon fire.

I hear one of the nurses calling, "Isaac's in trouble," and I hear people rushing into my room. They stand there, silently. I remember that I had signed a DNR order. So they wait, and in knowing they are watching over me, I feel my panic recede.

I can hear my machines purring and pausing. I feel the strap across my chest relax. The pounding of my heart subsides. The explosions in my ears fade away.

"False alarm," a man says.

"I'll keep an eye on him." It is Wanda. I feel her take my hand.

People shuffle out. "You gave us a little scare, there, Mr. Simon," she says. She inspects all my tubes and wires then sits down beside me on the bed. "I won't have you checking out on my shift."

I wish she would sing to me, but she says she has to look in on another patient.

She leaves. I try not to think about anything.

Chapter 7

Wanda is singing softly to herself. I recognize her voice. It has a lovely throatiness to it. She wipes my face with a warm cloth. I'm not sure how I feel about her taking my tears away – they were a form of communication. Of course, they are dry by now and no one could see them anyway. But *I* could feel them, somehow, and I liked that feeling. I know that keeping me clean is part of her job, so I guess I have to get over it.

At least I have her singing.

***

Allen's description of Chaim's time in the army has set me off course. I am not ready to talk about it yet.

I need to go back to Mr. Hardwicke and my drawings. I went straight from school to the newspaper. Usually, I would have time to go home for a little lunch and to do some homework, but I was told to be at Mr. Hardwicke's office before my shift, so I hurried down Essex Street and into the front door of the newspaper building. The young lady at the reception desk told me that Mr. Hardwicke was on the fourth floor, room 401. She directed me to the elevator. I was panicked. I had never been on an elevator before.

"Just press the button," she said. "Tell the operator you want to get off at the fourth floor."

I heard her giggle.

I was dressed in my best clothes. Mama had washed and pressed my white shirt and gray slacks. My shoes were in need of new soles, but the tops were well polished and looked pretty good to me. The elevator opened and I stepped in, cautiously. I asked for the fourth floor and up we went.

When the elevator stopped and the door opened, I stepped out into a world I had never imagined before; a large well-lit landing area with wide hallways stretching to the left and right. The floor was a rich dark wood that had been waxed and buffed till it glowed. The walls were paneled in the same wood to a height of about three feet and the surface above the paneling was painted a light beige. Large gilt-framed paintings of landscapes and portraits adorned the walls.

Room 401 was directly opposite the elevator. A wooden plaque with gold letters was placed at eye-level on the door. "Reginald Hardwicke - Editor."

I tapped nervously on the door and waited. Nothing. I knocked a little louder. The door was opened by a thin gray-haired lady in a dark blue dress. Her spectacles were perched on the edge of her nose, and she seemed to be annoyed by my presence. "What is it you want, lad?" she said.

"I was told to see Mr. Hardwicke before my shift," I stammered.

"Your name?"

"Isaac Simon."

"Ah, the boy with the sketchpad," she said, "Mr. Hardwicke is expecting you." She motioned me into the office, pointed to a chair, and then returned to her desk. "Mr. Hardwicke has a gentleman with him at this moment. He will see you shortly."

I sat down in the comfortable chair and surveyed my surroundings. The office had the same floor and paneling as the hallways, but the un-paneled portion of the walls was painted a muted deep purplish color, like the skin of an eggplant. There was only one painting in the room: a portrait of a well-dressed older man reading a newspaper: it hung on the wall beside the door to the inner office. In the center of the floor was a Persian rug with vines and stylized animals and plants on a deep red ground. It was mesmerizing, even though it clashed horribly with the color of the walls. I was amazed that something so beautiful was lying on the floor for people to walk on.

The one window in the office was open and a ceiling fan turned slowly, moving the air without moving the papers on Miss Westin's desk. I knew her name was Miss Westin, because she had a sign on her desk with her name painted on it. It struck me that Mr. Hardwicke's name on the door was in gold; Miss Westin's name was in black. I understood the power relationship – and if *she* could be in those nice clothes in this rich office, where did I stand in relation to Mr. Hardwicke and his world?

I thought of the strike that had ended only a couple of years before and the long discussions in our kitchen about the bosses and their greed and evil intentions. I knew the workers had stood up to them and won. Power was not infinite.

I was no longer nervous about having to see Mr. Hardwicke. I wanted my sketchbook back, but if he refused to give it to me, I would be fine. He could not take away my ability to draw. I knew I could even recreate those sketches from memory if I wanted to.

And so, I waited. I heard the distant whistle signaling the start of my shift, but I had been told to see Mr. Hardwicke before reporting to work, so here I sat in this cool, comfortable, clean and colorful place.

***

It seems like I am very good at waiting. Lying here in my bed, listening to the machines and the nurses. I wait and I listen. I can now distinguish between the people who take care of me. I know some of their names, while others I have given names that match the sound and quality of their voice or other characteristics.

There is Wanda, of course, who is here most often in the daytime (I think), and Damon the Instigator who is here at the most still time – late night, I assume. I don't know why, but the nurse who comes in after Wanda is always so quiet and business-like. She rarely says anything to me; she just checks things and leaves. Every now and then she'll mutter something like, "Still chugging," or, "Still on track." I've named her Trainwreck because of the railway references and also because I heard her cursing one day after she dropped a tray of pills or something.

A doctor comes to see me every now and then. He's about as warm and friendly as a raw herring. His hands are always cold and he treats the nurses like servants. I don't like him. I named him Doctor Fish. If my grandson Allen happens to be here when Doctor Fish is around, the doctor always takes Allen outside my room to talk to him. I'm not sure if this is because Doctor Fish has an instinctual fear of saying something inappropriate in front of his patients no matter what their state of consciousness, or whether he actually thinks I might overhear his conversation.

***

Mama used to call me by my Yiddish name – Itzik. It is a biblical name which means, "He made me laugh." It's what Abraham's wife, Sarah, said when she found out she was pregnant at a very old age. And she gave the name to her first-born son. The King James Bible called him Isaac. I guess it would not have sounded too theologically austere or poetic to call the kid, "Laughter-boy," or something like that. I like my name. It always makes me smile.

And I found myself smiling as I waited for Mr. Hardwicke. Finally the door to the inner office opened and a tall man dressed in a smart dark gray suit emerged. He strode towards the exit door without even acknowledging Miss Westin or me, then turned and took a few steps back in the direction of Mr. Hardwicke's office. "You will not get away with this, Hardwicke," he shouted. "You'll be hearing from my lawyers!" He stormed out, slamming the door behind him.

Miss Westin smiled uncomfortably at me. She opened the door to Mr. Hardwicke's office. I heard her mention my name.

"Mr. Hardwicke is ready to see you. Go on in, young man." She closed the door behind me.

"Sit."

I lowered myself into a soft leather chair. He had my sketchbook open on the desk in front of him. He flipped slowly through the pages, stopping from time to time, but saying nothing. The book contained several drawings in addition to the ones I had done in the press room: sketches of animals, several portraits of my mother, and some of the houses in our neighborhood.

I recognized Mr. Hardwicke from the painting that hung outside his office, except that in real life he had a much stronger presence. It was not that he was bigger or more powerful physically, but there was an energy to the way he moved and carried himself. The artist had failed to capture the dynamism of the man, his bearing, the intensity in his eyes. I watched him carefully as I waited for him to review the entire book.

"How old are you, son?" His voice was strangely high-pitched and thin.

"Fifteen," I replied. "I'll be sixteen next month."

"Still in school?"

"Yes, sir."

"Working on the loading dock after school?"

"Yes, sir. I've been there about six months."

He spread his hands out on top of my sketchbook. "You are a talented young man," he said. "These drawings are very good."

I smiled and shifted nervously in my chair. "Thank you."

"If I gave you a much better and more interesting job where you could use this talent, would you promise to continue your education in the evening?"

"Y-yes," He completely surprised me. I had come to his office expecting a reprimand and the real possibility he would not return my drawings, and here he was offering me a job where I could continue to draw.

"Good." He stood up and leaned across his desk, extending his right hand to me. I, too, stood and we shook hands. Then he went to the door and asked Miss Westin to bring in some tea and cookies.

"What do you know about advertising?" he asked.

I knew nothing, other than that I'd seen advertisements in the newspapers. I mostly ignored them because they were always trying to sell things I could never afford. Why make myself feel bad about things I couldn't have?

"Not much," I replied.

"No matter. You'll soon get the hang of how it works. Businesses try to promote their products, to make them look so good that people will want to buy them. That is where you come in, Isaac. I want you to be one of the advertising artists on the Tribune. You need to make their products look irresistible."

Even if they aren't? I said to myself. To Mr. Hardwicke I said: "That sounds very interesting and challenging, sir. I am sure I can do it."

"Good. I will introduce you to Mr. Clemente. He's in charge of the art department, and he will be your supervisor."

He stood up and handed me my sketchpad. "Come," he said, not waiting for Miss Westin to return with the tea and cookies. I was a little disappointed and hungry, too; I had eaten nothing since leaving for school early in the morning.

I followed him out of the office to the elevator. We rode down to the second floor in silence. I really did not know what to say. I was entering an unfamiliar world. It was exciting and a little scary.

***

It is so quiet in here. I strain to hear any sound besides the purring of my cat-machine, but I hear nothing. I wonder what time it is, although the numbers on a clock are meaningless to me – I don't even know if it is winter or summer, let alone day or night. I don't remember if Damon the Dynamo has checked on me recently. I don't think he has. I should practice my blinking.

I squeeze my eyelids tight, then relax. I do it again and again. I am sure that I notice a difference in the depth of the gray fog before my eyes. What would it be like to see again? A little blob of color would be nice. How about green instead of all that gray?

I can actually imagine the colors. They used to be essential to my life. My paintings were all about the colors – seemingly amorphous regions of color that played with one another; advancing, drawing back, surrounding, exploring, concealing, revealing. There was never a speck of paint I put on the canvas that was not intended. I was conscious of every hue, every tone, every location, every shape.

Many people think that artists use "abstraction" because we don't know how to depict the "real" world, whatever that is. That's nonsense. In the Museum of Fine Arts in Boston two paintings by Picasso hang side by side. One, painted in 1906, is a beautiful, delicate, realistic portrait of a young woman. The second, painted less than two years later is a bold cubist abstraction. Some people find it hard to believe that the same artist was responsible for both of these works - but, for me, the transition and the connection is obvious.

Sure, there are some hacks in the art world who couldn't draw a straight line with a ruler. Once, a critic accused me of being one of those hacks. But, I knew exactly what I was doing. I had complete control. In my next show I included a realistic portrait of him with his head up his ass. He laughed out loud, apologized, bought that painting and hung it in his office.

We became good friends. I went to his memorial service years ago. We had quite a party – he should have been there. Well, he kind of was there – twice: his partner had my painting hanging above the pedestal that

45

held the urn with his ashes. He died of AIDS.

Damon the Dutiful is humming around me. He holds my hand as he wipes my forehead with a warm cloth. I hear him move to the cat-machine side of the bed. Then he checks my plumbing. I am anxious to show him that I know he is there. I know I have to wait till he talks to me directly, asks me to respond, to blink. I am anxious, holding my breath.

"Isaac," he says, "I love your beard. Your family loves it, too. I am going to brush it a little for you."

I hear him opening the drawer in the nightstand, then he sits down next to me and gently brushes my beard.

"Pure golden white," he says, then laughs. "Yeh, I know gold is not white, but that's what I see when I see your face."

I feel like I am smiling. He has his own unique perception of color.

I feel him suddenly stand up. My body tenses. He can't go away without asking!

"Gotta run, Isaac. Red light flashing down the hall. I'll be back as soon as I can. We still have things to do." And he is gone.

I've seen my share of flashing lights. I know what they mean. I know he must run towards them.

***

Mr. Hardwicke introduced me to Mr. Clemente, who looked me up and down, grunted then pointed me to a tilted drawing board and tall stool. "You'll be here," he said. "My office is in the back. Pencils and paper are in the cabinet over there." He did a lot of pointing. I had no idea where to look.

"See those shoes on the table?" he said, and nodded in the direction of a pair of stylish black leather men's shoes. "Your first assignment. Make them look like they're really worth ten bucks."

Ten dollars, I thought, *that's more than my Mama brings home in a week.* To Mr. Clemente, I said: "Yes sir, but I have a couple of questions."

"What?"

"What are my hours of work? How much will you pay me?"

"This is not full-time work, boy. Be here at eight Tuesday through Friday. You will work till four. Your pay is twenty-five cents an hour.

Now get to work on those shoes - you only have one hour before the end of your day. See me when you have something to show me."

He rushed off to his office before I could respond. Twenty-five cents! That was almost double what I was making loading and unloading trucks. It was more than Mama made. It would really help.

As I stood by my drafting board trying to take in my sudden turn of fortune, I heard a voice from the other side of the room. "Welcome to picture-town," he said. "My name is Roland Ramsay and I am to show you the ropes around here. You can call me Mr. Ramsay." He advanced towards me, right hand extended and a huge grin on his face as if he was enjoying a private joke.

I shook his hand. "Call me Mr. Simon," I said.

He laughed out loud. "You're Isaac the little Jew kid from the loading dock. You're no 'mister,' boy!" His voice had a sinister edge to it. My defenses went up. He was not the first anti-Semite I'd encountered in my life. He had power over me in my new job. I knew I had to be careful.

"What do I need to know before I start work on the shoes?" I asked, very matter-of-fact.

"It's for a five inch, two column ad. You'll need to leave about half the height for the ad writers to fill in the text. Make the shoes no more than four inches wide. Strong, but modulated lines. Not a lot of shading. Nothing fancy. Crisp and clean is how Clemente likes it. Do several sketches to show him so he can approve one, before you spend too much time on something he might reject." Roland Ramsay liked giving directions.

I began to focus my attention on the expensive shoes.

***

Damon the Dasher is back. "False alarm, fortunately," he says. He sits down next to me and resumes gently brushing my beard as if there had been no interruption. "Lovely lady down the hall had a little panic 'cause she couldn't find the light-switch. She pressed the 'help-me-come-quick' button. She gets so anxious. I think she needs a nice quiet guy like you to calm her down." He chuckles.

Quiet? Me?

He stops brushing and I feel him lean a little closer to me. "Isaac, blink if you hear me."

I squeeze my eyes tight, then relax. I do it again. I hear him catch his breath. "Let's try that one more time, Mr. Simon."

I squeeze my eyes as hard as I can, then relax. I feel my eyelids flutter. I feel a laugh rising in my throat but hear no sound.

"I don't fucking believe it," Damon the Delightful exclaims. "I want you to do that again, Isaac. Just wait, I'm going to get someone." He rushes off and returns a minute or two later with the nurse I call Trainwreck.

"Can you do that one more time, Isaac? Nurse Melinda doesn't believe me."

I am getting tired, but I squeeze my eyes as hard as I can.

"Holy shit!" she says.

"Easy, Melinda, the man can hear you!" They laugh, and Trainwreck gives me a peck on the cheek.

"I'll write this up before I leave," he says. "Be sure to tell the doctor."

I feel like I've just played Carnegie Hall – the performance of my life!

Chapter 8

There is a lot of activity and excitement in my room. Wanda it flitting about, humming quietly. She wipes my forehead with a cool cloth. "How are things this morning, Mr. Blink?" she says. I sense the smile on her face.

My grandson Allen is talking to Doctor Fish, who has not talked to me since he came in, prodded my chest, lifted my eyelids with his cold fingers and grunted.

"Very unlikely, Mr. Simon," I hear him say. "I don't see that he has the functionality. If necessary, we can continue this discussion in the hallway, Mr. Simon?"

"Hey, doc! You're talking about me," I yell in my head. "Take a look! Bring your fishy ass over here and ask me to blink!"

But I hear him walk out in his creaky ten dollar shoes – well, probably four hundred bucks by now.

Allen sits in the chair beside me. "Is it true, Grandpa Isaac? Did you really blink for the nurse?" His voice is unsteady, nervous, as if he's not sure whether he wants to know the answer. I can almost hear his mind turning. Finally, he takes my hand in his. "Can you do it again?"

I feel him leaning close to me. I squeeze my eyelids, then relax, suddenly expecting to actually see something as I do so. But all is still gray.

"You did it! You did it!"

These excited words conjure up a lovely old memory - when Allen was three or four years old. I was in my studio, painting, and he arrived unexpectedly with his dad, my son, Albert. Albert had told him I could make a picture of anything, so little Allen asked me to draw a fire truck. I remember feeling a bit pissed off by the intrusion into my time, but I took up my sketchpad and a couple of colored pencils and whipped off a picture of a fire truck racing to a fire. He was delighted! "You did it, Grandpa Isaac," he yelled and gave me a big hug. I got over being pissed off.

Allen is pacing back and forth in my room. He is muttering to himself, but I can't make out the words. After some time he sits again and takes my hand. "I have to be sure," he says. "The doctor says it's impossible, so we have to try again." He pauses, then says, "If you can hear me, blink two times."

I squeeze, then relax. I wait a long moment. He has suspended his breathing. I feel the tension in his grip on my hand. I squeeze my eyelids tight again.

"Wow!" he says. "Wow!"

He gently strokes my beard. "I wonder how long you've been able to hear." His voice is shaking, he is almost crying. "I wonder how aware you are of what's going on around you. How long you've been conscious of your isolation."

I wish I could answer all his questions. I'd tell him that I have no real awareness of the passage of time, but I have been aware of everything going on for what seems like forever. I would so like to tell him and all my family exactly what is going on in my head. I am not sure whether telling my story is a joy or a curse. Many of the memories are so painful, but many are not.

***

Of course, my first drawings for Mr. Clemente were pretty important, and I had so little time to do the basic concept. I sketched the shoes as they sat side by side on the table. It was a good likeness, but boring. I turned one of the shoes on its side to show a more interesting perspective. Then I turned them away from me, and drew them from above – kind of what they would look like to the person about to put them on.

I brought the three sketches into Mr. Clemente's office. He barely glanced at them, and then held out the boring one to me and told me it had promise. "Work this one up in the morning," he said, and waved me out of his office.

And so ended my first day of work as a professional artist. It was Tuesday, August twenty-fourth, 1915.

I hurried home, arriving some time before Mama's shift was over. I could not wait to tell her my exciting change of fortune.

***

Allen is pacing again; back and forth he goes at the foot of my bed. He stops. The room is quiet except for the cat-machine, which issues a little "puff-puff" into the silence.

"Martha! Hello, dear. I've got some news about Grandpa Isaac. He can hear us! I know it seems impossible, but he's just responded directly to me. It's amazing. Yeah, I know. Well, he's been here for almost six weeks, but he stopped talking long before that. Yeah. Come as soon as you can. Will you call Ginnie? OK, Martha – see you soon."

Martha is his wife of twenty-eight years. I liked her from the moment he introduced us, although there are certain subjects we cannot talk about. Martha and Allen met when they were both students at the Hebrew University in Jerusalem. Long story that I'm too tired to tell right now. This blinking on request can suck all the energy out of a person.

Despite Doctor Fish's skepticism I have become the talk of the place, particularly amongst the nursing staff. I have heard them buzzing about, whispering to one another - I guess they believe I can hear them, so they're careful about what they say. Not that I could repeat anything, but you never know. I hear the name "Doctor Watson" and the words "arrogant asshole" used in the same sentence. They are most likely not talking about Sherlock Holmes stories. I feel like I am smiling.

***

When I arrived home after that first day as an illustrator at the Eagle, I found two letters in our mailbox. One was from Chaim, who was somewhere in France with the South African Army; I would have to wait for Mama before opening it. The other was addressed to me from Reuven Novitz. There had been no contact between us in years. There was his brief letter about two months after our short meeting at Ellis Island. I had responded right away and we exchanged a few letters over the next year or so; and then nothing until now, almost four years later.

Reuven apologized for the long silence, but offered no excuse. He wrote that his mother and sister had finally arrived from the old country and they were now living in Providence, Rhode Island. But Reuven's main reason for writing was that he was moving to Boston at the end of the month to go to Suffolk Law School. He hoped we would be able to find time to get together.

Even though Boston was a short train ride from Lawrence - less than an hour - I had never ventured into the city. It seemed so big and unwelcoming, but having an old friend there to explore the city with did sound exciting.

I began my reply immediately, telling him I looked forward to seeing him in Boston. I was still writing to Reuven when Mama arrived home from work. She was surprised to find me there so early. "Did you get fired?" she said, "I can't believe your drawings could get you into so much trouble."

"I did not get fired, Mama. I got a new job. In the office, drawing things for advertisements."

She hugged me and wanted to know all about my meeting with Mr. Hardwicke, and my first day in the art department. I recounted every detail of the place and the interview - from the splendor of Mr. Hardwicke's office to the arrogance of Mr. Clemente. I avoided mention of the undercurrent of anti-Semitism from Roland Ramsay. I ended my account of the day with the news of my wages - twenty-five cents an hour.

She clapped her hands. "We are not rich," she said, "but for the first time since we arrived here, I feel like we will be all right." She jumped up from the kitchen table, put on her sweater and said, "We deserve a special meal. A celebration. I need to go to the store." And with that she went out, leaving me alone in the apartment.

Chaim's letter from the trenches lay unopened on the table.

***

Chanel Number 5 floats into my room. Danielle is back.

"Allen told me your news," she says, as she takes my hand. "He says there've been a lot of people coming in and out of here. You must be exhausted. I am not going to ask you to perform for me. I just want to be here to hold your hand."

Did I mention that she is Reuven's daughter? She is also Allen's stepmother, and one of my best friends, like her father was. There was a time when he held my hand, too. I will get to that in good time. It is not an easy story.

Someone with squeaky rubber-soled shoes approaches. "Mr. Simon, I am Doctor Jerzak," he says. His voice is high, almost as squeaky as his shoes. "I am a neurologist. I am told that you have responded to direct questions by blinking your eyes. I would like to examine you."

I feel Danielle release my hand and stand up. "I'll be back later," she says. "Let the doctor do his thing." I wish she had stayed.

Doctor Squeak places his soft, cool hand on my forehead and lifts each eyelid. I think he shines a bright light into each eye as he examines them - I can detect a slight change in the intensity of the gray I see. He then uncovers my right arm and runs a cold smooth object slowly from my shoulder to my wrist, and then squeezes each fingertip. Then he goes through the same things to my left arm. He uncovers my feet and seems to be trying to tickle them, but I don't really feel much that far away from my brain.

"Let's try the blinking, Mr. Simon. Blink two times if you can hear me, please."

I try my best. I am not sure if it is good enough. He says nothing.

"How about blinking one time if you are tired, or two times if you are able to continue this examination."

There's a dilemma. I want him to continue, but I'm wiped out from all the goings on. I hesitate. I sense a major opportunity. I go for two.

"Very good," Doctor Squeak says.

He uncovers my right arm again. "I noticed when I tested this arm that you appear to have some small nerve and muscle function in your fingers. I am not sure whether it is reflex, or whether you can actually exercise some control." He places my hand gently on top of his. "Try to squeeze my hand," he says.

I can visualize the energy moving from my brain down to my fingertips, telling them to tighten, but I don't think the message gets through.

"Okay," he says, "How about trying to lift a finger."

Again, I visualize that flow of energy. I think I actually feel movement.

"Good," he says. "I think that's enough for today. I am going to have a physical therapist work with you on your hands and arms. There is potential. I'll be back tomorrow." And with that he squeaks his way out of the room.

Mama came in with a big bag of fresh vegetables, bread and a chicken.

"There is a letter from Chaim," I said.

She placed the bag on top of the stove. "Read it to me, Itzik."

I carefully sliced the envelope and took out the single page, written in pencil. He was in hospital, again. He said it was not a war wound but some kind of infection that he "picked up" and it was being taken care of. He expected to be in hospital for about a month. He told us not to worry - he was enjoying the down time.

He also wrote that the army had reduced his pay because his time in the hospital was not related to war wounds. I asked Mama what she thought that meant. "Who knows?" she answered, "All I know is that the life of a soldier is hard. There are dangers in the most unexpected places." Then she stood up and set to preparing one of the best meals she was capable of creating.

While we were eating I told her about my letter from Reuven.

"So, he's going to be a lawyer," she said. "When is he moving to Boston?"

"Soon. The school year starts in a few weeks."

"You should visit him," she said. "He is a good boy, and I'm sure Boston is a very interesting city. I hear there are wonderful art museums there. You will enjoy them."

I waited anxiously for Reuven's next letter to arrive.

***

I cannot think of Reuven without thinking of Danielle. How happy I am that she is here beside me, holding my hand. "You've had quite a day," she says, and, like her father, she offers no explanation and requires no response. "They tell me you can hear us. How about I read some of your favorite poems?" I appreciate not having to do anything for her.

I hear her opening her pocket book and rummaging around. Usually she lugs around something the size of a steamer trunk so it always takes a while for her to locate whatever she is searching for in it.

I expect her to read Mary Oliver or T.S. Eliot, but she starts off in a different mood - Ogden Nash. "The Lord in his wisdom made the fly," she reads, "and then forgot to tell us why." Her laughter explodes, and she slaps my hand. "Gotcha," she says. "We need a little levity in this place."

She giggles her way through a few more of Nash's silly poems, then I feel her put that book down on the bed. "OK," she pauses, "Wild Geese."

It is one of my favorite Oliver poems, but I had not thought of it in ages. As Danielle reads, I can almost feel myself forming the words. "Tell me about despair, yours, and I will tell you mine. Meanwhile the world goes on."

I think I am crying.

***

My first visit to Reuven in Boston was on a Sunday in early December 1915. It was a cold cloudy day. The wind cut through my thin coat as I stepped down from the train at North Station and looked around for him. I hadn't seen him in over five years, and I was not sure who exactly I was searching for. Finally, a tall slender young man, dressed in a dark suit and darker overcoat approached me. He was definitely no longer the immigrant boy; he appeared to be so much a part of this big city.

"Isaac?"

I nodded. "Reuven?"

We hugged and he led me out of the station into the noisy crowded street. As we walked to the Boston Common he told me about his family, and then he asked me how my job as an illustrator was going and how I was getting along at night school. It was as though we had known each other all our lives. We chatted easily. We stopped briefly to watch people skating on the frozen pond. I immediately thought of my old home, Linkeve, where we used to skate on the river in the middle of winter. That was where I first encountered anti-Semitism; a gang of older kids chased us away with taunts and snowballs. It did not deter me from skating. I wished I had a pair of skates right then in Boston.

Reuven loved the city - its mix of people, the nightlife, the law school and most particularly, the Museum of Fine Arts, which was our destination for the day.

How do I describe the experience of my first visit to the MFA? I was a boy from the shtetl who liked to draw, who had not seen anything of the art of the world except for some poor quality reproductions I remembered from Uncle Kalner's books. Here I was in another world - another universe. I walked through that building with my mouth open. I could not believe the beauty, the amazing collections from all over the world, and across the centuries. From ancient Rome and Greece, to the works of contemporary artists in Paris and New York. Even architectural features from China and Egypt. I was mesmerized by the Renaissance works from northern Europe; some so dramatic and moody, others so peaceful and domestic.

I could have spent a week there. I barely talked to Reuven as we wandered from gallery to gallery. Occasionally I would hear him say something like, "This is beautiful," or, "This sculpture is one of my favorites." What could I respond? What more was there to say?

We stayed until the museum closed, and then took a trolley downtown, and he walked with me back to the train station. As we approached the station, he asked, "What do you hear from Chaim? How is he faring in South Africa?"

"He's in the war," I said. "In Europe. We hear from him infrequently. It's a scary and terrible thing. My mother is anxious when a letter arrives, and is more anxious when there is no letter. I am too."

"I didn't know," he replied, and we continued in silence the rest of the way.

It was strange to think that across the ocean hundreds of thousands of men, including my brother, were fighting in a horrible war, and here we were in Boston, having thoroughly enjoyed a wonderful day in the museum. Our time would come.

Chapter 9

There is someone new in my room. I do not recognize the footsteps or the movements. The person pauses at the end of my bed, presumably reading my chart. Then I feel my left forearm being lifted and replaced on the bed. The person moves to the other side of the bed and raises and lowers my right forearm. I wish they'd talk or whistle, or something.

I don't like not knowing what's going on.

"Is he awake?" It is a woman's voice; kind of low and hoarse but definitely a woman.

I hear Wanda respond, "Hard to tell, but assume that he is."

"I'm Chris, your physical therapist, Mr. Simon. I'm here to help you with your arms and hands. OK?"

This is going to take some work. I've been through physical therapy - long ago. It was no fun.

"So here's the thing, Isaac," Chris says. "You haven't used these muscles in a long time. They're weak, but still there. My job is to try to slowly build them up." She begins to massage and manipulate the fingers on my right hand. I try to disconnect myself from what she is doing.

***

On the train ride home from Boston I could think only of Chaim. The wonder of the museum was overshadowed by a feeling of dread. What was happening to him? How could my kind, gentle brother survive being a soldier? Why did he sign up? What was his life like alone in South Africa?

Up until this time I had not paid a lot of attention to the war in Europe. Chaim's involvement was personal, almost unrelated to the greater goings on. But somehow that question from Reuven about Chaim was like a flare, lighting up the whole world. All we had to do was look and we would see what was there.

I became obsessed with the war and how it progressed. I put up a map of Europe on the parlor wall, and I followed the news in the Eagle every day. Of course, the reports in our newspaper had little detail about specific British army units, so trying to find out about the activities of the South African Third Infantry Regiment was almost impossible.

I do remember the reports in late July 1916 of the involvement of the South African Third Infantry in the battle of Delville Wood, which was part of what was later called the Battle of the Somme. The hill was thick with beech trees and hazel bushes. It was gloomy during the day and darker at night. Because it was a forest, the web of roots prevented the soldiers from digging proper trenches. At one point the Germans were launching hundred of artillery shells a minute into the woods. Not to mention the gas. By the end of that battle, hardly a tree was left standing. The South African casualties were almost eighty percent of their forces - over two and a half thousand men.

And I knew Chaim was there. I circled the area on my map, and we waited for a letter.

His next letter did not arrive until the last week of August. Mama had not waited for me to return from work before opening it. I found her sitting at the kitchen table gripping the one page letter tightly in her hands. She did not look up when I entered; she simply nodded for me to sit, then handed the letter to me. It was stained with her tears. I remembered the drawing I had made while we waited on Ellis Island for Mama; the drawing of my teardrops that had fallen on the page of my sketchpad.

Chaim's letter was written in pencil, and I could barely decipher his handwriting. He wrote that he was alright and back in a rest area after being at the front for several weeks. He did not, or could not, mention Deville Wood by name. One sentence he had written was cut out with a blade by the censor. I still wonder what it was he had said that made the censor so aggressive - it was like a piece of my brother had been removed.

"He says he's OK, Mama," I said, without much conviction.

"But he isn't," she replied, "I read it, but I didn't have to read the words to know he is not right. His body might not have been damaged, but he was hurt, hurt very deeply. He can't even hold a pencil, or finish a thought."

I gave Mama a hug, then put the letter away with all the others from Chaim, and went out to sit on the front step. It was a dark moonless evening. A rainstorm was approaching; you could see the broken clouds filling in, and you could feel and smell it in the wind. For America, the war in Europe was not much more than an article or two in the newspapers, but for many recent immigrants it presented a daily cycle of fear for a loved one who was there, in the trenches or living under occupation. Chaim was one of those millions of lost souls.

I looked up hoping to find a break in the clouds, to see the stars, to see the night sky he might have seen a few hours earlier. How awfully different the world was under that same sky. How unreal.

***

"Are you with me, Isaac?" Chris's voice breaks through my memories. "Where'd you go?"

Where did I go? If I could tell her, I'm not so sure she could bear it.

"It's your turn now, Isaac. I need you to try a few things."

My hands are tingling; she must have worked them pretty hard. It is a strange sensation. I wonder what she did to make them feel like this.

"I'm going to place a spongy ball in your right hand. When I give the word, I want you to squeeze it as hard as you can."

I feel her place something in my hand and close my fingers over it. "Before we start," she says, "I want you to blink two times if you understand what I'm asking you to do. OK?"

The blinky-blink again! I do it.

"Great! Now squeeze the ball."

I try as hard as I can to make my fingers contract around that ball, but I don't feel it happening. I relax my grip - if that is the opposite of unnoticeable squeeze - and I feel the ball slip from my hand. I hear Chris bending down to pick it up.

"Hmm," she says, "you cannot close your fingers, but you can open them a little. Hmm. I need to talk with Doctor Jerzak about that."

She walks around to the other side of the bed. "Let's try the same thing with your left hand." I can do nothing. I can feel that ball in my hand, but it stays there, unchanged, no matter what I try to do.

I hear her writing in her notepad. "That's enough for one day, Mr. Simon. I'll be back Wednesday - day after tomorrow."

So it's Monday. Fancy that. A brand new week. My hands are still tingling from the physical therapy. I try several times to clench and unclench them. Then I do my blinking exercises. I have become unused to physical work. I am tired.

Doctor Squeak is speaking to Allen. I can't hear the whole conversation, but the phrase that comes up several times is "Locked-in Syndrome." I wonder what that is. It seems to describe how I feel when people are saying and doing things around me and to me, when I know what's going on, but I just cannot do anything about it.

It's kind of how I feel right now. Locked in. I would really like to be a part of the conversation.

The squeaky shoes approach the bed. "The physical therapist says she was able to generate some slight movements in your fingers, Mr. Simon. We are not yet sure what that means, so I would like to run an EEG to see what brain activity is present, and then, perhaps, some electrical stimulation of your hand and finger muscles."

Doctor Squeak actually addresses all of this to me and seems to be waiting for my response.

I blink twice.

He says, "Very good," as if I do this kind of thing all the time. "I'll schedule the EEG for tomorrow morning." He pats my shoulder. "In the meantime, keep on blinking."

I hear him leave and Allen sits down in the chair beside the bed. "What an amazing few days this has been, Grandpa Isaac. Absolutely amazing!"

You should see it from my side!

"Doctor Jerzak, the neurologist, thinks you might have a rare condition called Locked-in Syndrome. Nobody is quite sure how it works, and it seems to have several causes ranging from some snake bites, to diseases of the circulatory system, to certain types of strokes. Since we are pretty sure you weren't around any poisonous snakes in recent years, and there was no evidence of a stroke or circulatory disease when you first lost your ability to communicate, the doctor is not sure what might have caused this - if, in fact, it is Locked-in Syndrome. So the first step is the EEG to see whether you do have more brain activity than would be expected from someone in a non-communicative state."

When was it that I lost it? I never had a time when my mind stopped working. There were always stories, images, even conversations going on in there. And I never stopped being able to hear things or smell things or even feel things. But, at some point nothing was going out, nothing came out of my mouth, nothing moved. I no longer felt like I was being heard. I don't remember the process, the progression of things. I'm not even sure if it was something I actually wanted. I know my body was shot to hell; I was in pain from head to toe. It hurt to stand, it hurt to move, and lying down killed. Maybe I just wanted to shut it all down, or, at least not think or talk about it.

And I had been alone for so long - Virginia was long gone, the kids were all gone. Sure, I had visitors who I love and I felt their love for me. But I was still too much alone. Maybe I just flipped the switch.

I can hear Reuven saying; "You only have two choices - you deal with the shit, Itzik, or you fall off the planet. I have no intention of falling off the planet." That was his life's philosophy, and it served him well. What am *I* doing? Am I dealing with it, or am I falling off the planet?

Chapter 10

Damon the Instigator is singing. I recognize the words; Allen used to play that song in the car all the time. Something about feeling fine. He wipes my forehead with a warm cloth, then goes through his usual routine of adjusting the plumbing and fiddling with the cat-machine.

"Let's brush your golden white beard, Mr. Simon," he says, and sits down next to me on the bed. "I love to see it glow." He is so gentle, so calm. "So, I hear we've caused quite a commotion, Mr. Simon. Nurse Melinda tells me there's been a parade of all kinds of doctors and specialists and therapists and the like, causing a traffic jam in the hall-way." He laughs softly.

There are more of them than I know about?

"Yup, you certainly have gotten this place in a tizzy!" He touches my beard. "That looks pretty good, 'though it's getting a little scruffy. I'll give it a trim tomorrow."

I blink a couple of times; my way of saying, "Thank you."

He laughs, then stands up. "See you later," he says, and is gone. All I can hear is that machine purring.

***

The next letter from Chaim was bad. It was not mailed free at his usual Army Post Office, but arrived with ten cents postage due and a postmark from the French town of Corbie. I searched my map, and found the town in the Somme valley, not far from Delville Wood. Even though it was not mailed at the Army Post Office, it had found its way to the base censor's office.

The censor had two main functions, I found out many years after the war. The obvious one was to ensure that no information in the letter could jeopardize an operation or anyone in the service. The other important reason for the omnipresent censor was to gauge the morale of the troops.

Chaim's letter was almost completely obliterated by the censor's black pen. There was almost nothing in the letter we could read. Not a single complete sentence. The only words we could read were his name, the date: "July 25, 1916" and, "I love you both." That was all that the censor had left us. Chaim was more lost than I could have imagined. How could he possibly live, remain sane, having witnessed four out of every five people around him being killed or wounded in the course of a few days?

How can you not feel utterly destroyed when you realize you are using the dead body of your comrade as a shield against the onslaught of bullets and flying shrapnel? How do you cleanse yourself of that guilt? No rabbi or priest can bless away that chasm of despair. No punishment any authority could impose would make you feel you have atoned for what you did.

"Tell me about despair, yours, and I will tell you mine." Oh, Mary Oliver, I don't think even you know how deep this cuts.

Poor Chaim had run away from his unit only a few days after being withdrawn from Delville Wood and had tried to drown himself in drink and the whorehouses of this nearby French town. When he sobered up enough, he wrote home, pouring out his grief and guilt and sorrow, only for the censor to wipe out his words and to notify the Military Police where to look for him.

They found him sleeping off the absinthe under a bridge. He was dragged back to his unit where he was sentenced to three days of hard labor without pay. A few weeks later he was back at the front, assigned to a tunneling unit. A week underground, hearing and feeling the explosions of heavy artillery shells above him, and he broke down.

They sent him to a hospital to rest and recover from his "shell shock" - and to deal with his second bout of gonorrhea. In a little over a month they sent him back out into the battlefield.

How do I know all this? I made it my mission to find out everything I could about what happened to him. There is more, too much more, but I can't tell it now.

***

"It looks like Grandpa Isaac has been crying again." Ginnie's the one who always seems to pick up on my tears. Unfortunately, I think it is because she has so many of her own. Of all the people who come to see me, she is the one I would most want to talk to. I hear her pain and sorrow. I know it, and I fear for her. She kisses me on the forehead. I am thankful that she does not wipe my tears away.

"My mom's here, too." she says.

"How are you, Isaac? It's Martha." She pats my hand. "Allen told me all about the exciting recent developments." I try to remember the last time Allen's wife came to see me. It could not have been all that long ago. She had apologized for being so busy; meetings all the time to organize some big event to raise more money for the Hadassah Hospital in Israel, as if they need it. Want to get Martha going? Suggest they give the money to a Palestinian hospital in Ramallah instead. Then stand back.

Don't get me wrong; I like Martha. She has been a wonderful partner to Allen, and is a great mother to Ginnie and David. She has also always been kind to me and was especially warm towards my son Albert, Allen's dad, before he died. She is a good person. But we do have our differences. She seems to see a particular corner of the world in simple black and white. Good guys and bad guys. I try to stay away from talking about that corner of the world with her, but it's not easy, since it dominates most of her thoughts and efforts.

On her last visit, I now remember, she talked about a new psychiatric wing they were helping finance. Not a bad thing to do, but after a while I began to wish I could not hear. Talk about feeling locked in!

"So, the gala went off spectacularly. We had this very funny comedian from Tel Aviv acting as master of ceremonies. He was hysterical. Then we had a local Klezmer band - the Dynamic Dreidels - you might remember them, Isaac; they performed at the fundraiser you were at five years ago, and after that we had the speeches and a 'thank you' message from the Chair of the Hadassah Hospital Board of Directors in Israel, which I read to the crowd…"

"Mom." My dear Ginnie has come to the rescue. I was getting that locked in feeling again.

But Martha is relentless. "They - the Hadassah Hospital Board - were so gracious in their comments about the work our committee has done over the years. Anyhow, so after the speeches we had more music - dance music by a swing band, and then we closed the silent auction. The food was wonderful - grilled salmon with asparagus and this marvelous smoked

Gouda mashed potato…"

"Mom, I think Grandpa Isaac is getting a little tired."

Tired is not the word I would have used.

"One last thing. Allen and I donated one of your paintings to the fundraiser. It went for ten thousand dollars; the all-around highest bid of the night."

Ten thousand for one of my paintings! The most I ever got was half that! Do they think I'm dead already? Rich jack-asses. I'd rather the money had gone to that hospital in Ramallah!

Both women are quiet for a minute, then Martha says, "See you for dinner Friday, Ginnie?"

"Yes. I'll be there around seven."

"See you soon, Isaac. I have to run." Martha pats my hand one more time and rushes off.

Ginnie kisses me on the forehead again. "I need to leave, too. I have a major assignment due in a couple of days. I wish Mom hadn't taken over; I had hoped to have some quiet time with you. I have a lot on my mind, and I wanted to talk."

A different kind of locked in feeling. Stay. Talk. I wish I could hug her, hold her close.

***

Uncle Kalner came to visit a few days after we received that bad letter from Chaim. I think Mama must have sent word to him. He tried to reassure her, but it didn't help. For the two weeks he stayed with us Mama walked around like a robot doing whatever she had to do; working, cooking, cleaning, but she had no life in her. At night I heard her crying softly.

On the evening before he was due to go back to his job in Chicago, Uncle Kalner sat with me on the front step. Mama would not come out, even though it was a beautiful warm evening with a full moon and a light breeze. I asked him what he thought would happen in Europe.

He shrugged. "They're a bunch of gangsters fighting over who will get to own everything. And they're using millions of people, like Chaim, to achieve their objectives."

"How will it end? Who will win?"

"In many ways, it doesn't really matter who wins. Germany, France, England, Russia - all they care about is expanding their own empires. They have no concern for the people." He paused, leaned back and looked up at the brilliant moon. "America will be dragged into this mess sooner or later." He stood up and went back to the apartment, leaving me on the step wondering if what he said was true.

It was more than six weeks before Chaim's next letter arrived. It was short; not even a full page. He said nothing about what had transpired since his last letter. He was doing better, he wrote, and was being discharged from the hospital. He asked Mama to send him socks and gloves. We knew that meant he was going back to the front.

***

"It's a beautiful morning, Mr. Simon. The sky is as blue as can be, the sun is warm and there is a gentle breeze. A perfect spring day." Wanda is cheerful today. The cat-machine issues a few soft purrs in her honor, although I guess she probably doesn't even hear it anymore after working in this environment for so long.

"We have to get you ready for that EEG today," she says. "They'll be here pretty soon." I hear her moving things about, making room for the equipment. I feel her wipe my face with a warm cloth. She combs my beard. "I'll see you when they get here. It's a big day."

Everyone is calling today a big day. I don't even know what that means. How can a day be big? Important or crazy, maybe - but a day doesn't really have a size. It's a riddle. What is always the same size but is infinitely variable with respect to what you can put in it? I smile to myself. Wish I could communicate that thought.

I hear something being wheeled into the room.

"Good morning Mr. Simon. We're here to do the EEG. OK?" I feel his hand on my head. "Please blink twice if you understand me."

I squeeze my eyes two times.

Doctor Squeak says, "Good. Nurse, can we elevate his head a little more?" and I feel the bed behind my back pushing me up.

"There are three steps to this test, Mr. Simon. First, we will attach a number of electrodes to your head. This should take about fifteen minutes. Then we fire up the machine and it will pick up and record whatever is going on in there," and he taps the top of my head. "It is best if you stay awake during this step. And then when we're done buzzing your brain, we remove the electrodes and I go away and I analyze what the machine tells us."

I blink twice, again.

"Good. This might feel a little funny, but it's non-invasive and will not hurt." Then to his technician, who I have detected by the smell of cigarette smoke on his or her clothes, he says, "OK, let's wire him up."

I'm not sure I like his metaphors.

I try to think of the process of placing the electrodes as a head massage. I relax, remembering a faraway place and time when Virginia and I were in the Northeast Kingdom of Vermont, near the Canadian border, camping on the shore of Lake Willoughby. It was late June in our first year of marriage and Virginia was pregnant. It had been a wonderful day; I saw my first real moose at the water's edge - so much like the picture I'd seen in Uncle Kalner's book. And a bald eagle soaring high above the lake. We played in the water for hours, then built a fire as night fell and cooked steak and corn. The night sky was carpeted with stars. I remember us lying side by side, looking up, and I marveled at how lucky I was to be here, with this strong, beautiful woman, who was my wife.

When I had asked her to marry me, she had smiled, and then responded playfully, "Well, it depends. Do you snore?"

I laughed, and then said seriously, "No, but I do have nightmares."

"Those I can deal with," she replied, and she cupped my face in her hands. "Yes, I would love to be married to you."

And that first night on the lakeside I had one of my terrifying nightmares. I woke up to find her sitting cross-legged with my head in her lap and her hands gently massaging my head and face. "It will be OK," she kept repeating, "It will be OK."

I miss her. I miss her every day.

"You still with us, Isaac?" Doctor Squeak says, "We're almost done with the electrodes."

I blink.

"All set, Johnny?"

"Last one," Smokey John says and locates the last electrode on my forehead between my eyes. "OK" he says.

"Here we go, Mr. Simon. This will take about forty minutes. Try to stay awake."

I blink twice.

The room is strangely quiet. I know there are a few people standing around, but no one says a word. The EEG machine is silent except for a low hum. The cat-machine continues to purr, continues to emit its sporadic "puff-puff." I can hear intermittent scratching sounds; I figure it is someone writing notes every so often.

I would love to hear someone sing.

My Virginia had a lovely voice. Her favorite song in our first years together was, "By the Light of the Silvery Moon." She sang it to me that first night by the lake, and she would sing it to Albert and Mark and Emma when they were little. Have I mentioned Mark or Emma before? I don't remember. There is too much sadness there, but I will get to their stories soon enough. I promised to tell it all. It is hard when you out-live your children.

***

Mama worked. I worked and went to school at night. We did little else except wait for Chaim's letters. Even a card from Reuven inviting me to spend a day with him in Boston, exploring the Isabella Stewart Gardner Museum did not crack the dark mood that overwhelmed our home. I replied, "Sorry – some other time. I need to be with my mother."

We would go for weeks without word from Chaim, and then when a letter finally arrived it did nothing to cheer us up. Chaim's letters were short and without news. I am fine. Weather is rainy/cold/hot/sunny... Thanks for the socks. Food is not bad. Sometimes he would mention having run into an old friend. Don't worry about me. The only real news about where he was or how he was actually coping was wiped out by the censor.

One day in late January, after a month with no letters, three letters came together. Mama had waited for me to return from school so I could read them with her. Despite the fact that Chaim had written them over the course of three weeks, they were almost identical. In one of the letters he wrote that he and Moish, the fellow from the old country, were given a weekend pass, and they enjoyed a visit to a nearby town which he could not name. Mama suppressed her fears, but said nothing.

Three weeks later a Field Service Card arrived. In its starkness, it was one of the most foreboding pieces of paper I have ever seen. It was a multiple choice; the soldier sending the card simply crossed out the sentences that did not apply. Chaim had left only two lines; "I am quite well," and, "I have received no letter from you for a long time." It was dated February tenth, 1917. The signature was shaky, barely legible.

I learned later from Moish that this card was sent towards the end of Chaim serving fourteen days of Field Punishment for punching his sergeant. His mail was withheld until the end of the fourteen days.

I never told Mama what I had learned.

***

There is a definite change in the sounds of my room: the EEG machine has stopped. "All done with the test, Mr. Simon." It's Smokey John. "Here comes the worst part, I'm afraid. We have to remove the electrodes. It might pinch a bit."

My skin is pretty thin and brittle these days. Getting those damned electrodes off my bald head hurts like hell. I feel the tears welling up in my eyes.

"Sorry about that, Mr. Simon. Three more."

It's finally over. Doctor Squeak says, "I'll see you tomorrow with the results, Isaac."

I hear him leave the room. I wonder if he wears those squeaky shoes to let people know when he's coming and going, or whether he's simply oblivious.

Wanda is back. She is soothing my poor old head with ointment, and she is singing just loud enough for me to hear. "There is a balm in Gilead..."

Chapter 11

After all the activity with people and testing, and machines buzzing and humming, everything is so quiet now. I am floating in silence. My body is weightless. I can see myself lying on the bed. I look peaceful, young, smiling. Then I drift off through the window and out high above the city. The river reflects the blue of the sky as it curves and twists down to the ocean. I am not sure whether I am guiding myself or if I am drifting on the wind.

I am racing across the tips of the waves. I feel the spray on my face and can smell the salt water. Suddenly the land; hills, trees, and fields spread out below me.

Linkeve. The town I was born in. My father is slumping by the side of the road, his back propped up against a boulder, his feet dangling in a ditch. He is singing but I cannot make out the words. Perhaps I am floating too far above him; more likely he is drunk and incoherent.

I move on to our cottage. Mama is kneeling, weeding her garden. She, too, is singing; "Gonna lay down my sword and shield, down by the riverside." It does not seem odd that she knows this song. Her voice is sad. She sings the tune as a drawn out lament.

"Ain't gonna study war no more!"

She screams that last line and I am suddenly choking on the smoke and smell above the battlefield on the banks of the Marne River. I see the network of trenches of both armies. I see the gun emplacements. I see thousands of men, scared and miserable, hungry and horrified. "Over the top! Go! Go! Go!" I hear the shouts and watch them scrambling over the trench wall and the barbed wire and charging into no-man's-land. I hear machine guns and the explosion of artillery shells.

My heart is racing. The blood is pounding in my ears. I feel the pain in my left shoulder. I am falling.

"Isaac. You're OK. I got you." Damon's voice is breaking through.

"Are you with me, Isaac?" I can feel his hand on mine. "This is not the time to cash in your chips, Isaac. We're not ready for that."

He wipes my forehead with a cool cloth. I feel my breathing getting more steady, my fear receding. True, now is not the moment to leave. I have to know whether Doctor Squeak has found me inside my bag of bones.

I hear Damon moving about. I feel his stethoscope on my chest, feel him clamp the oxygen monitor on my middle finger. My cat-machine purrs on. "Looking good, now," Damon the Diligent says. "I'll be back before the end of my shift to comb that beautiful beard so you're shining for Doctor Jerzak in the morning."

He leaves me in the quiet again.

***

The newspaper announced that the United States had severed relations with Germany. This was February third, 1917 - three days after Germany had announced that all ships, including American ships, were subject to submarine attack. Uncle Kalner's prediction was coming true; America was getting involved in the war. Two months later, April sixth, war was declared.

On April ninth, on the first day of the Battle of Arras, my brother was killed. I will never forget the day when we received the letter from a captain in the British Army telling us of Chaim's death in battle. I had worked late that evening at the newspaper and did not get home until almost eight o'clock. Mama was sitting at the table. She did not say a word: she just lifted the letter to me as if it weighed a hundred pounds. It was short, to the point.

"Chaim Simon served bravely and gave his life in service to a greater cause." The captain had obviously written letters like this too many times. I wonder whether he even believed the words on the page, but at the time they cut into me, deeply. Service!

Mama and I sat Shiva for the week, but in truth, she mourned for him until the day she died. I still mourn for him.

Uncle Kalner and Uncle Ben came to sit with us. Some of the Wobblie leaders came, too, as well as many people from Mama's work. It was a strange thing having all these different people in our little apartment, sharing the ageless tradition and ritual of mourning. A rabbi did visit, but since we were not regulars in his congregation, he did not stay too long.

There was no body to bury, so there was no real service. The few people in the room who had known Chaim in Linkeve talked about him, remembering his kindness and his humor, and his sharp mind. Also his stubbornness. Others talked about the waste of war and the tragedy of so many young lives destroyed. Most of the time Mama wept silently, and I sat with her.

Chaim's last letter to us actually arrived while we were still sitting Shiva. Uncle Kalner found it in the mailbox on his return from a meeting with the Wobblie leaders in a restaurant downtown. He handed it to Mama, and she gave it to me to open. "Read it aloud, Itzik," she said.

Our little parlor was filled with people, and they all fell silent and looked at me as I opened the letter. I wish I could say there was something profound or prophetic in that letter, but it was much like so many of his others. He thanked Mama for the socks and cigarettes she had sent. He shared the cigarettes with Moish. He said he was fine and the food was still as awful as ever. He said his unit was on the move, but could not say where he had been or where they were going. He said he missed us all. And that was it. Love, Chaim.

Chaim's death hurt me, changed me. I had lost my big brother to the Germans, the Hun, the barbarians, a few days before my seventeenth birthday. More than anything else, I wanted vengeance. I stewed in this anger for a month, then decided I needed to do something.

I said at the beginning of this story that I had only lied about my age one time. Well, this was it. I went down to the army recruiting office and stood in line with hundreds of other young men. I filled out all the forms to join the Massachusetts National Guard. I told them I was eighteen, but that I never had a birth certificate because none were issued in the town in which I was born. They were happy to sign me up. My medical examination was set for the next week. I wrote to Reuven telling him I had enlisted. He replied that he had done the same.

I passed the physical and was told I would receive my call-up notice within a month. But it wasn't until the end of July that the notice arrived, telling me to report on August fifth to the embarkation point at North Station in Boston. I wrote a letter to Moish Zweig, Chaim's friend in the

South African army, and told him I would soon be in Europe and would try to find him. How naïve was I?

Those months between signing up and leaving home were so hard. I avoided telling Mama; I knew she would be devastated no matter when I told her. So I delayed and delayed, and I worried. I tried to work longer hours and to spend more time on my school work. I was afraid I would let something slip, so seeing her less seemed to be the solution. She did not appear to be aware of the changes in my behavior; she was still preoccupied with Chaim.

As the days passed my desire for vengeance acquired an added dimension; I wanted to know exactly what had happened to Chaim - what he had experienced, what he had faced. I needed to know the pain, "to walk where he had walked," as they say. And so, when I finally told Mama four days before I was due to report, I talked about my need to find out about Chaim, so that I could understand it, and help her to come to terms with all that had happened to him.

In retrospect, it was all bullshit. Yes, I did want to know - and, in fact, I was able to find out a lot - but, I knew as I was telling all this to Mama that I would never be able to tell her anything that could help her, that could lessen her grief. I could not admit it to myself back then, but I was only adding to her sorrow.

***

"Are you ready for the big reveal, Isaac?" Damon is back. What the hell is he talking about? "I'm going to comb that luxurious mane," he says. "Doctor Jerzak should be here in about an hour with the results of your EEG."

Does Doctor Squeak know that I'm here? Did he find me? What absurd questions. *I* know I am here, but does the good Doctor Squeak know that?

"See you later, Isaac. My shift's over. Got things to do, places to go." Damon laughs. "Good luck, Isaac." He has such a reassuring voice. "Wanda will be in to see you in a few minutes."

He leaves me with my thoughts and memories. I don't really want to be with them right now, so I try to focus my attention on the purring of my cat-machine.

Mama packed a box with bread and cheese and fruit for me to take to Boston. She did not come with me to the train station in Lawrence; she was too upset and angry. When I had told her I had signed up for the war, she slapped my face and stormed into her bedroom, slamming the door behind her. She refused to talk to me about my decision. In fact, she barely talked to me at all, or even looked at me.

As I got ready to leave the apartment that August morning, she finally took my hands and stared deeply into my eyes. "You do what you feel you must do, Itzik," she said, "but there is one thing you must do for me. You must come back!" She kissed me on both cheeks. "Go." She dropped my hands and sat down at the kitchen table.

***

I feel someone sitting down next to me on the bed. A soft kiss on the forehead. My dear Ginnie. "I had a little time before my class this morning," she says. She strokes my beard. "Someone is really looking after you here, Grandpa Isaac. Your beard is magnificent." She laughs, but I sense her sadness has not eased.

"Come here, Ginnie. Let me give you a big hug," I say inside my head. I never feel more 'locked-in' than when I am with her.

"Actually, I made a point of coming early because I want to talk to you. I know you will listen, without judgment." She laughs uncomfortable, "Well, I don't really know if there will be judgment or not. I know I never felt it in the past, so I'm assuming you are still the same old supportive guy."

I wish I could smile.

"I'm almost done with school. I graduate in a couple of weeks and I'll have my B.A. in American Literature, with minors in American History and Creative Writing." She sighs. "It's been a ton of work, and I've loved it. But what the hell can I do with it? I mean, there aren't too many companies looking for Lit majors."

I hear her stand up and begin pacing back and forth at the foot of my bed. "I always thought I would go to grad school and then find a job teaching at a college somewhere. But, it all seems so futile now. The world has changed so much in the last year. I mean, after Jake was killed on nine-eleven, everything seems so pointless. American Literature! Huh! It's ludicrous!"

She sits down in a chair - I hear it scrape on the floor. "What do I do? It's like there's nothing worthwhile to do." She is quiet and then, over the purring of my cat-machine, I hear her sobbing.

There is so much for you to do, my dear girl. Literature, art - they embody who we are. They reflect the souls of each of us as individuals, but more importantly, they elevate the soul of the entire community. Now, in these terrible times, is exactly the moment when these are called for.

"I'm sorry I dumped this on you, Grandpa Isaac. I wish you could let me know you are there."

She is pacing at the foot of the bed again. I hear someone else enter the room - undoubtedly Doctor Squeak.

"I guess I need to go now," Ginnie says, and she leans over to kiss my forehead.

I blink, twice.

"Did you see that? He blinked when I kissed him!"

"Yes, he can do that," says Doctor Squeak, with no inflection in his voice.

"Do it again, please, Grandpa Isaac," and I feel her hand gently on my shoulder.

I blink three times. Ginnie hugs me, and it seems like she doesn't want to let go.

Another person enters the room. "Good morning, Doctor Jerzak. I'm sorry I'm a little late. Traffic." Allen is here to listen to the EEG report.

"I have to go, Grandpa. Thank you. Hi, Dad. Bye."

I wish she'd stay.

***

North Station in Boston was chaos. Hundreds of young men were milling about trying to figure out what we were supposed to be doing, where we were supposed to be going. Many were surrounded by swarms of family members and friends. As I wandered through the crowd jostling with men and women and children from all walks of life (except the upper classes, as I would find out later) hugging and kissing their "soldier-boys," the enormity of what I had done to Mama hit me.

I found a bench on the platform and sat down, holding the box of food Mama had given me on my lap. It was like a lifeline - my only tangible connection to her. I opened it and found a note pinned to the inside cover; "Promise me you will come back, Love, Your Mama." I removed it, folded it carefully and put it in my shirt pocket, alongside that letter from Chaim which had been almost completely wiped out by the censor. I carried that note and that letter with me till the day I walked through the apartment door almost two years later.

As I sat waiting for someone to tell us what to do, I heard my name being called. I turned and saw Reuven pushing his way through the mob towards me.

"It's so good to see a familiar face" he said as he finally broke through.

I could not resist hugging him. "Reuven! What a joy it is to see you."

"Are you here alone?"

I nodded. "What about you?"

He told me he had visited with his family in Rhode Island. They saw him off at the station in Providence.

We chatted about family and art museums and law school, avoiding any talk of the war. I did not even mention Chaim's death. He did not ask why I had lied about my age.

***

"I am so often astonished by the workings of the human brain," Doctor Squeak says. "I have been studying it for over twenty years, and I am still in awe." He pauses. "Do you hear me, Mr. Simon?"

I blink.

"Good. Good." He hesitates, clears his throat. "So, as I say, the brain is an amazing machine, and it is composed of a number of different parts - for want of a better word - each with its own function. With the EEG we are able to look at how those different parts of that machine are working."

I can feel the tension in the room. Danielle had arrived at some point; I can smell her Chanel Number 5. Wanda is here, too.

"I spent a good deal of time reviewing the results of the test, and met with a few colleagues to discuss my observations. This is what I can tell you." He clears his throat again.

Why is he so nervous?

"What we have with Mr. Simon is this: the parts of the brain that control motor skills and movement show almost no activity. He cannot tell his hand to close, or his foot to move. His eye movements are related to a particular section of the brain, and as we have seen, he has some control there: the ability to blink. There might be some chance he could move his eyes from side to side. We will have to experiment and try some further tests and exercises."

Allen says, "OK."

Doctor Squeak pauses for what seems a very long time. "There are some other findings that are surprising."

Allen says, "Oh."

"The areas of the brain that show sensory perception - touch, pain, smell and taste - are quite active, as well as hearing." He pauses to emphasize what he is saying. "Isaac knows we are here. He can feel it when you touch his face or sit down next to him on the bed, and he can hear much of what is going on around him. Even more interesting is his ability to identify and organize what he hears and feels. Add to that, he is actively and continuously accessing his memory, and we believe that Isaac is not only engaged in what is happening in his environment, but he is able to reference it to things that he has experienced in the past."

Allen says, "Wow!"

What's up with the guy today? Cat got his tongue?

"I don't like the term 'Locked-in Syndrome', but Isaac's situation does match the literature. I'd prefer a term that captures the fact that there is significant inner life." He sits down on the bed and takes my hand. "We know you are there, Isaac. We will do all we can to help you communicate whatever it is you want to tell us."

I like Doctor Squeak. He seems to get it. I blink three times. He laughs and touches my shoulder. "See you later, Isaac." I do like this man.

He stands, "Allen, Danielle, do you have any questions?"

"Hundreds," Allen replies, "But it's going to take me a while to sort them all out."

"I understand. This is a highly unusual situation."

"What's next? What can we do?" Danielle asks. Always the practical one. The helper. She has approached the bed and I feel her lean over and kiss me on both cheeks. "Hi there, Isaac old friend." She sits on the chair beside me and places her hand gently on my shoulder.

I blink. She chuckles.

"As I said," Doctor Squeak continues, "We do have more tests to run, but in the meantime all you need to do is be here and engage him. Talk, touch."

"Thanks, Doctor," Allen says after a long pause.

I hear the doc leaving the room.

"Wow," says my very articulate grandson, the high school English teacher, the novelist. He sits on the bed and takes my hand.

"Grandpa, I have to ask you some basic questions before I can even begin to wrap my head around all of this." He pats my hand several times, then says; "Blink once if the answer is no, twice if the answer is yes." He pats my hand again. I can sense the nervousness in his actions and voice.

"Is your name Isaac?"

I blink twice.

"Is my name Allen?"

Twice.

"Is my name Mary?" Danielle says.

I blink once.

"Danielle?"

Twice. I am beginning to tire.

"Amazing! He can recognize us." she says to Allen.

"Wow," the grandson with a Master's Degree in English says, again. Did I mention that Allen is a published novelist? He has two books out there and is working on the third.

"He must be getting tired," Danielle says, then continues, "I'm sorry, Isaac; I should have asked you. Do you want to take a break?"

I sure do. It has been quite a day. The beginning of a whole new phase in my life - right when I'm on my way out. I blink twice.

Chapter 12

I was lucky to be assigned to the same company as Reuven - Company D of the one hundred and first engineers. I have no idea why I was put in an engineering company - maybe it had something to do with my drawing skills. Reuven was selected because he was a college man, even though his college training had nothing to do with engineering and was not exactly required for the kind of work we did. I never did learn to understand army logic.

Reuven and I were both late recruits to this unit, and we got in at the tail end of the engineering training at Wentworth. Most of the men had been there for months. We missed a majority of the class-room training, the theoretical side of being in an engineering unit. What we experienced, mainly, were the military drills - rifles, bayonets, hand-to-hand combat, how to survive gas or mortar attacks and so on. And, a lot of hard physical work on how to dig and reinforce trenches, place barbed wire, and build roads, bridges and fortifications of various types.

I was not as fit and strong as I had been when I was loading and unloading trucks at the Eagle, but I soon got back into top condition. Reuven, on the other hand had spent the past few years in lecture halls and libraries. By the end of each day he was aching all over and wondering why he had volunteered to put himself through this agony. We knew this was nothing compared to what lay ahead for us on the far side of the Atlantic.

I received my first letter about three weeks after arriving at the camp. It was not from my mother; it was from Uncle Kalner and he was furious at me for getting "sucked into this imperialist war," and more furious for what I had done to my mother. I did not need him to make me feel even more guilty about Mama, and I was not interested in his political views. I was here for revenge and to find out what happened to Chaim. That was how I justified it to myself. I did not reply to him.

Mama's letter arrived two days later. She was calm and concerned.

Was I getting enough to eat? Was I making friends? Was I coping with the training? She did not mention how she felt and I was grateful for that. I responded that I was fine and that Reuven was in the same unit as me. Before I sealed it, I re-read my letter; it sounded familiar, like the news-less ones we had received from Chaim. I almost threw it away, but sent it off anyway.

Our training was shorter than I thought it would be, shorter than it needed to be, and by the end of September we were on the British ship Andania sailing from New York to Liverpool.

Seeing the Statue of Liberty recede and slowly slip behind the horizon was a strange feeling. I remembered the elation when we had first seen it seven years earlier followed by the horrible experience of Ellis Island.

Being on the Andania was like being in a floating, rolling sardine can. Our entire regiment was crammed into that tub. There were rows and rows of bunks so closely arranged you could barely move. The only good part of the trip was when I was put on sub watch. I was high up in the summer breeze, scanning the ocean and away from the stink of the lower deck. I could watch the sea-birds and also our escort of destroyers. I wish I could have had my sketchpad with me.

On our eighth day out one of our spotters saw the periscope of a German U-boat about seven hundred yards off to our right. He raised the alarm and everyone scrambled to the main deck, life jackets on. I was on sub watch at the left of the ship, but I could see the two destroyers on the right veer toward the U-boat just as the traces of a pair of torpedoes made their way towards us. They missed by a few dozen feet.

The destroyers raced towards the U-boat, firing everything they had at it. When they were close enough to where they figured the U-boat had dived, they each rolled several depth charges into the ocean and steamed away as fast as they could. Less than a minute later huge plumes of water roared upward.

We watched and waited. I focused my binoculars on the area where the depth charges had exploded. I saw nothing. The ocean grew strangely calm, then suddenly the U-boat began to surface directly ahead of our convoy. I thought I saw the hatch lifting. The destroyers opened fire again and within moments the conning tower of the U-boat was blown apart and the ocean rushed into the gaping holes. As the vessel sank, a bizarre collection of things started to bob to the surface - random objects, ripped from wherever they had been, floated upward. I did not see a single sailor, alive or dead. I put my hand over the shirt pocket that held Mama's note and Chaim's letter.

We steamed on to Liverpool without further incident. The Andania was not so lucky. The old tub was sunk by a U-boat about four months later as it was heading back to America to pick up a fresh supply of cannon fodder.

***

Someone is fidgeting with my bedding. "Time for a sponge bath, Mr. Simon. OK?" I feel the covers being lifted off my body. "My name is Tracey," she says. "I'm one of the aides on this floor."

"And I'm Megan. Also an aide."

They sound like the same person. Maybe they're twins. Who knows?

"We're going to wash your front, then Megan and I will need to roll you onto your side so that we can sponge your back. OK?"

Not so OK. Last time someone did this my shoulder hurt for days.

The water is warm, and as they gently wash me down I become aware of all parts of my body that I haven't noticed or thought about in ages. And I mean ALL parts. How weird it is! I guess a good clean-up isn't such a bad idea. Megan and Tracey are chatting with one another about one of the nurses who is "so-o-o-o cute!" with a beautiful smile and a voice that "just wants you to say yes." They giggle.

No one gave them the message that I can hear pretty much everything. I wonder if they are talking about Damon the Divine, perhaps. He does have a warm and reassuring voice.

"Time to move you onto your side, Mr. S," one says.

I feel my old bones creak as they roll me onto my right side. They must have read in my notes somewhere that I have no cartilage in my left shoulder socket and any pressure on that shoulder hurts like hell. Or maybe they just guessed right; it's a fifty-fifty shot. They prop me up with pillows so I don't roll back before they are done.

"OK, Meg, I can take it from here."

"OK. See ya later." I hear Tracey leaving the room.

"A couple more minutes, Mr. S."

The water has cooled. It is no longer soothing. I want this to be over. Tracey works methodically, washing me from neck to heel. It is not a fun job, I'm sure. I don't know how she manages to keep my sheet dry.

"All set, Mr. S. Let me roll you back and I'll be off." She moves me carefully. "There! See you later, Mr. S." She pats my shoulder and is gone.

***

Army logic landed us in Liverpool, then decided we needed to be in Southampton, about two hundred and fifty miles away, in order to catch the transport ship to France. That's a long way to go on foot, loaded down with all our gear. They said the march was part of our training, designed to make us more physically prepared. It seemed endless, and as lovely as the green English countryside was, we were too miserable to appreciate it. It rained often; no heavy downpours, just a light drizzle that soaked everything.

A couple of days before the end of the march we arrived in Salisbury in the early afternoon. It was one of the rare bright days and we were given a few hours to rest or to venture into that beautiful old city. Most of our unit simply collapsed on the ground and slept the afternoon away. I convinced Reuven to join me on a visit to the cathedral. Long ago I had seen pictures of it in one of Uncle Kalner's books.

Despite the fact that I hadn't been into a synagogue since I was a boy and I am probably more of an atheist than anything else, my Jewish origins have left deep feelings about my history and culture. So, stepping into a Christian cathedral was a very unfamiliar experience: all those religious paintings and stained glass, the sculptures of saints and the tombs of rich and important people, and the crosses. But most memorable was the soaring space - the otherworldly, spiritual feeling created by the architecture.

"How old is this place?" Reuven asked.

"Parts of it have been here since the twelve hundreds."

We climbed the spire and were able to walk out onto a platform high above the ground. I retrieved my sketchpad and pencils from my pack and began to draw. I focused on the structural elements of the building, ignoring the rich embellishments and decorations. Then I turned my attention to the view; the day was so clear I swore I could see the ocean.

"We have to go, Itzik," Reuven said.

Back at our camp I continued to draw as much as I could remember; from the cavernous interior to close-ups of the garish gargoyles I had seen. I was so absorbed in my drawing that I didn't notice Captain Swan touring the camp. Swan was the officer in charge of our company. He was a "straight arrow" - everything by the book. He was strict but fair and most of us grew to appreciate his leadership. He would not make us do what he was unwilling to do himself, and when people are shooting at you and firing mortars and gas and grenades, having a leader like that is pretty important.

After the war ended he wrote a book about Company D. He called it *My Company*, and he sent a copy to everyone in the unit. A nice gesture. Frankly, I found the book a little too long on how great the adventure was, and very short on the realities of war. You know; the death, killing, pain, disease, fear, horror…

Anyhow, as I say, I didn't notice him walking around until I saw a shadow cross my sketchpad. I looked up, and there was Swan. I began to scramble to my feet.

"No need, soldier. This is down time," he said. "Very good drawings - you must have gone into town this afternoon."

"Yessir. Novitz and I went to the cathedral."

"Interesting destination for a pair of good Jewish boys," he chuckled. "We might find some use for your artistic skills. Let me think on it."

***

"Puff-puff." Nurse Trainwreck is imitating my cat-machine. I wonder if she'll purr. She's not much of a talker. There is something soothing about her quiet, methodical manner, though. She's wearing a muted lilac fragrance. I haven't noticed this before today. It's very nice, it reminds me of our garden - well, it really was Virginia's garden because she did all the work. We loved to sit out on the deck during the spring, sipping red wine, and watching the birds at the feeders. Every so often the breeze would carry the smell of the lilacs in our direction, envelop us. It was so perfect.

Chapter 13

The place is quiet. Damon the Instigator is here. "I heard what Doctor Jerzak had to say. Pretty amazing. There are so many things I would love to ask you. I hope we can figure out a way for you to communicate more than just yes and no."

Me too. I should think about how to do that.

Damon is more chatty than usual, and that's fine with me. He has a beautiful voice and I enjoy his company. "It's peaceful up here tonight. No drama so far. I like it that way; it means I get to spend a little more time with my favorite people, and you, Isaac, are definitely one of them."

I hear him move the chair closer to the bed and sit down.

He pats my hand. "I can't imagine what it must be like for you," he says. "I mean, to be aware of what is going on all this time, but not being able to let anyone know."

Actually, most of the time I am OK being inside my head. I'm able to tell my stories, to create my own reality. Would I like to communicate? Of course. But I have gotten to know myself quite well, and I'm comfortable with that. Which is not to say there haven't been times when I've wanted to interject my thoughts, and more importantly, to reach out and hug someone, to offer comfort. Those are the difficult times. I wonder if one can blink a hug.

"I see a light flashing. Gotta go, Isaac. So much for the no drama."

Yes, run to the flashing light.

***

We disembarked at the port of Le Havre on October nineteenth. I remember the date because it is my mother's birthday. I wrote a letter to her while we sat on the dock waiting for instructions on where to go next. A British hospital train was parked on the wharf. Hundreds of wounded soldiers were slowly and painfully moved from the train and helped onto the transport ship we had recently left. Many were on stretchers, others leaned on crutches or were pushed in wheelchairs. I could hear their cries and groans.

Reuven squeezed my arms. "What have we gotten ourselves into, Itzik, my friend?"

What could I say? I thought of Chaim, patted the pieces of paper secured in my shirt pocket, and shook my head.

"We'll make it," he said. "You and I will look out for each other!"

"No turning back," I said, and put my arm around his shoulder.

We boarded the train having no idea where we were heading. The officers said nothing and the rumors flew. Some of the men were sure we were being sent straight to the front to take the place of those poor bastards we had just seen being loaded onto the transport ship. Reuven, in his direct and logical way pointed out that we were a newly arrived American unit and the Army brass would not break us up and send us off to who knows how many different British regiments. "Furthermore," his lawyerliness showing, "we have a lot more training to do before they send us into battle."

He was correct, of course. The next morning the train stopped at the station of a small village on the Marne River about a hundred and twenty miles south-east of Paris. We were initially billeted with people in the village. I was going to say families, but the families were all fragmented - the young men were gone to the war. One mother had lost three of her eight sons on the front, and a fourth was brought home in a pine box during the two months we spent in this beautiful place.

We built barracks and bath-houses, mess-halls and stables and laid out firing ranges and other training facilities. And we learned how to kill and how to defend ourselves and each other.

In a strange way, the war seemed unreal, distant. We played football on Thanksgiving and were given a great feast with turkey, potatoes and gravy, even apple pie. We had a gramophone which played music all through the meal and after. We sang along. But when one walked through that village, with its fields turned to barracks and its missing young men, you could not shut out the underlying sense of dread and loss.

Reuven and I were billeted in a tiny three-roomed cottage. Our hosts were a man in his fifties, Monsieur Chaisson, and his daughter, Yvette. Reuven had learned some French in high school and college, and was able to hold up his end of a conversation with them. Monsieur Chaisson told us his wife died before the war, and his two sons were at the front. Yvette's husband was also on the battlefield. Their one child had died of influenza at the age of two, while his father was in the trenches.

They were warm and generous and did not seem to mind our intrusion into their lives. They even thanked us for coming to the defense of France. Every night I could hear them praying for the end of the war and the return of the young men. We were able to sneak food out of our mess hall and bring it to them. They were a little saddened when our barracks were completed and we moved out of their home.

We did not have much down time, and when we did all we wanted to do was sleep. But Reuven and I made a point of visiting our former hosts a few times. A couple of days before Christmas we were walking to their cottage. It was cold and felt like snow was on its way. From a distance we could see Monsieur Chaisson sitting on the front step, his head buried in his hands, and we heard the sound of someone wailing uncontrollably.

Monsieur Chaisson lifted his head as we approached and then pointed over his shoulder to the open door. Yvette was on her knees, weeping and pounding the floor with her clenched fists. It seemed like a very long time before she realized we were there. "Philippe death," she said, and continued her wailing. An official looking letter lay on the floor in front of her.

We sat on either side of her, and each of us put an arm around her shoulders. I found myself thinking of my mother and I'm sure Reuven was thinking of his. I felt tears trickling down my face, and that old feeling of uncertainty and fear from the time on Ellis Island came pouring down on me. I will never forget that afternoon with Yvette; three young people crying our eyes out.

***

"Are you crying, Grandpa Isaac? It's OK. Cry if you need to." My dear Ginnie is sitting beside me and stroking my beard. She always seems to catch me crying. She is tuned in because of her own story.

"Dad told me about the EEG findings. I am stunned and a little confused," she sighs deeply. "So I guess you heard my last rant about graduating with a worthless degree."

She pauses and I blink two times.

"Sorry I unloaded all that on you," she continues, as if I am now fully a participant in the conversation. "Well, I'm not really sorry I expressed my feelings, because I am confused and you've so often been the one person who would give me a straight answer."

I blink twice, again. I wonder if she remembers the conversation we had before she made the decision to major in English Literature.

I was visiting Allen and his family one Sunday and, over lunch, Ginnie started fretting about what to study in college. She said she really wanted to be in the liberal arts. Her older brother, David, the future Wall Street whiz, was pressing her to study something "useful" like business or engineering. He called her naïve and without direction.

"But I don't give a damn about business and I am not good at math and science. I freaking hated the biology course I had to take, and chemistry made me want to hurl." She was rather emphatic and dramatic as a teenager. She has mellowed a little since - life has caught up with her in a big way.

There was a lull in the argument and for some reason everyone looked at me. "What do you love?" I asked.

Without hesitation, Ginnie responded, "I love to read. I love literature."

"Then do it!" I said. "You'll figure out a career along the way. Hell, it took me a damned war and more to point me in the direction of what I wanted to do for a living. Study what makes you happy."

I believe I gave her the best advice back then. I am sure she'll work it out now.

"So, Grandpa Isaac, what do you think? Should I go to grad school or should I do something else?"

I cannot answer this question with a blink or two. I have not yet learned to say what I said to her five years ago. I try hard not to blink at all.

"You're leaving it up to me? Smart man." She cups my face in her hands. "I know what Jake would say. He's like you in many ways. He'd tell me to follow my heart. But now that he's gone, my heart is broken. I'm not sure…"

Her voice falters. She stops in mid-sentence and lays her head gently on my chest. I feel the weight of her on me. I try to will my arms to move, to encircle her.

***

We were woken up before daylight on Christmas day. "We're moving out." The word spread through the camp. Men groaned and grumbled as we packed our equipment and prepared to march on. A fine snow was coming down steadily and settling on everything. By the time we were assembled three or four inches had shrouded the landscape. One could not tell the road from the fields that bordered it. The sumptuous holiday dinner of the evening before seemed like a fantasy.

Why they moved us to Betancourt, a pretty village a few miles west of Chartres, is beyond me. Again we were billeted with local families while we built barracks, mess-halls and so on for ourselves and for the troops who would come after us.

We were given one free afternoon, so Reuven and I hopped a ride to Chartres. Its cathedral has been there since the eleven hundreds and most of the stained glass is original. It is breathtaking. I set out determined to explore it and draw as much of the building as I could.

We arrived around one o'clock and entered through the huge main door. There is a soft, embracing light that permeates the interior, reducing one's vision, encouraging one to look inward, to be calm. We sat in one of the first pews and I distinctly remember bowing my head and closing my eyes. Immediately, I could hear the old rabbi in Linkeve almost having a fit, but I was able to push him out of my mind and allow myself to gradually relax, steady my breathing, and let go of all my guilt and fears. It is an amazing place. I felt no need to move.

After some time - I have no idea how long - I lifted my head and looked around me. Reuven had wandered off and I sat by myself totally in awe of this remarkable space. I could see a few other people in the building; women sitting alone in the pews, deep in prayer or thought. About twenty feet in front of me two young men in French Army uniforms were standing side by side, and as my eyes became more accustomed to the light I could see they were both leaning on crutches and that each of them had lost a leg.

"What the hell am I doing here?" I whispered to myself, but apparently louder than I had intended, since one of the young men turned to me and nodded his head slowly several times.

I did not make a single sketch that afternoon in the cathedral. I sat in the pew, overwhelmed, until Reuven came and led me back to our unit. In the evening I drew a one-legged French soldier looking at me over his shoulder and framed by the soaring Gothic interior. I could not get him out of my mind. I can still see him there, right in front of me, nodding his head, jaw clenched, and his eyes burning with loss.

Six weeks later we were on the move again, this time for final training before being sent to the front. We did not have to construct anything - another Engineering regiment had built the place for us.

We practiced hand-to-hand combat with bayonets and knives. We had drills to rapidly put on our gas masks, and continue fighting. We rehearsed going 'over-the-top' - it was getting all too real. On the Sunday before we were to be sent off to the front, our whole regiment came together for the first time since arriving in France. It was a bright early February morning. The sunlight brilliant as it reflected off the thin coating of snow that had fallen during the night. Flags flew, bugles sounded and officers strutted down the rows, inspecting the troops.

Then the regimental chaplain strode to the podium to bless us and to send us into battle. He talked about God and country and the joy of heading to war to protect our great democracy and liberty. I could not help but think of Uncle Kalner's first letter to me. Were we all no more than pawns in a fight between soulless empires?

Chapter 14

I think Ginnie has fallen asleep next to me. She doesn't move and her breathing is steady. I hear someone enter the room. "Good morning, Isaac," she whispers. It is Wanda. "Looks like your great-granddaughter is taking a nap. I can come back in a little while; no need to disturb her."

When Ginnie was about five years old, Allen brought her to visit me. They showed up unexpectedly and found me in my studio in front of an easel, painting. She plopped herself down on the floor next to me. "Daddy said you can draw anything," she announced. I recalled a similar interaction with Allen. "Can you make me a picture of a garden with trees and flowers and a bench where I can sit and read?"

I was in the middle of work on a series of large abstracts in acrylics. I had a show scheduled less than two months away and, as usual, I was far behind. I looked down at her in her Rolling Stones T-shirt, blue jeans and flashy pink sneakers, and her bright green eyes staring directly at me. How could I refuse?

I went over to my drawing board, taped a sheet of paper to it and began to sketch out the garden scene. She stood beside me, holding her breath as the flowers, trees, birds and bench emerged on the paper. I saved the most important for last; a portrait of her, dressed as she was that morning, sitting on the bench reading a book. As an afterthought I placed a squirrel looking admiringly at her from his perch on a branch above her.

"That little squirrel is me," I said to her as I handed her the drawing, "I love to see you happy!" She was in awe. It surely was one of my most appreciated works.

"We need to let Grandpa Isaac get back to his big painting," Allen said. "Thanks so much. Remember the fire truck?"

"Of course I do."

"I still have it, you know."

"I know."

I feel Ginnie stirring, then sitting up. "Wow! I fell asleep." She stands. "I really needed that! I was up all night and came over to see you as soon as the doors opened. Hope I didn't get in the way."

You are never in the way, my dear. It is wonderful having you close by. It got me thinking of you when you were a little girl. Such lovely memories. If there was only one word I could express, other than 'yes' and 'no', it would be 'hug'. I need to work on it.

***

The march to the front was grueling. We carried our full packs, trudging through the slick, semi-frozen mud. At times the ice crust would give way and you found yourself ankle deep in freezing muck. Our hands and feet were burning with cold. We could not light fires at night because we did not want to give away our position.

On our third day of the march traces of gray smoke began to appear on the horizon, and we soon became aware of a dull undulating roar, punctuated with louder staccato bursts, and the unmistakable sound of men shouting and screaming. We were a few hours away from the battle lines. We were told to take a break in a nearby cratered and barren field while our officers conferred with a small group of French officers who had been sent to meet us and coordinate our entry into the line with their forces.

Reuven and I sat back to back, surveying the scene. He was facing the front, I was looking into the desolation of a forest that once bordered this field and was now barely more than a crazed arrangement of burnt and twisted shapes. The ruins of a stone farmhouse stood between me and the forest. I carried a small sketchpad with me and a couple of pencils. I made two quick sketches - one of what I saw before me, the other of what I envisioned the place looked like before the war. I handed them to Reuven.

"This is insane," he said after a long pause. "Bloody insane." And then, after another long silence, "Can I keep these?"

"Sure, I drew them for you."

We sat listening to the sounds of the battle raging not too far away. A bright yellow bird flew from the dead forest into the burned out farmhouse. It carried a few dry sticks in its mouth. Moments later it flew back into the desolate forest and then returned with more dead grass. I wanted to go over to watch her building her nest, but dared not take the risk of scaring her away. I marveled at how this small creature was able to make the best of things, was able to press on in the face of all this chaos and devastation. I patted my pocket, and thought of Chaim and Mama.

"Captain Swan and the rest of them are coming back," Reuven said. Our corporal shouted to us to get into formation. "This is it." We struggled to our feet with our heavy packs on our backs and our Enfield rifles in our hands. "God help us, now."

"Amen!" The response came from half a dozen men who were in earshot. We got into formation then marched ahead.

As we came to the top of a long slope we saw four or five observation balloons hovering above the battle line. A network of trenches crisscrossed the valley below us, and beyond them rows of barbed wire stretched from as far as we could see on our left to as far as we could see on our right. About two hundred yards past our wire was a canal and beyond that was more barbed wire - the German side. And, like on our side, balloons shimmered in the afternoon light above their trenches and fortifications.

The space between the opposing barbed wire installations - no-man's land - was empty. And when I say empty, I mean there was nothing there except mounds of bare dirt that had been churned over and over again by exploding shells. The canal looked like a gash in the land, like an exposed vein. The smoke and the smell of cannon fire were unworldly. The sounds of the men and the gunfire were ungodly.

"Holy shit!" Reuven said, in his not so college boy manner.

"Amen," I replied, along with several others.

***

Doctor Squeak is talking to Allen. They are keeping their voices low, but not low enough so that I can't hear. "His case is quite rare. I have been doing some research. There is not a lot of scientific data and even less information on how to manage his condition."

"I've been reading up on it, too," Allen says. "It seems like there have been some breakthroughs in coming up with a language based on eye movements."

"There is anecdotal evidence for that and I am willing to give it a try. It will take a lot of experimentation, a lot of hard work on his part."

"I know."

"Do you think Mr. Simon is up for that?"

"One thing I do know about my grandfather is that he has never run away from a challenge. If there's a way, he will want to find it."

Within reason, dear boy. I'm a hundred and two years old, for crying out loud; there's only so much running I can do! Yes, I do want to be able to communicate, but learning a whole new language now is going a little too far. I can tell the stories in my head - and I'm OK with that. All I really want is to be able to embrace all of you.

I hear Doctor Squeak move to the side of my bed. "Mr. Simon, are you awake?"

I blink twice.

"Good. I'm going to do a few more tests. OK?"

I blink twice, again.

"I would like to test your sense of touch, Mr. Simon?"

He does not wait for me to blink. He takes my right hand. "I am going to squeeze one of your fingers. Blink once if I squeeze your thumb, twice for your index finger, three times for your middle finger, four..."

I got it, Doc! Squeeze away.

"Ready? OK which finger am I squeezing?"

It feels like my index finger. I squeeze twice.

"OK," he says. "Let's try another."

Bastard; he would pick my pinkie! I blink five times. He goes through the same procedure with my left hand. He doesn't say whether I got the squeeze test right or not.

"I think we've done enough for one day, Mr. Simon. We have a baseline to work from." He pauses and I hear him squeak towards the door, then stop. "There is something I'd like you to try some time, Mr. Simon." He returns to the bedside. "I have noticed that your eyes are always fixed in one position; straight ahead. I would like you to see if you can move them from side to side and up and down."

Never thought about that before. When you can't see anything, what's the point of looking around?

"Will you give it try, Isaac?" he says.

I will try. I blink twice.

"Thanks, Doctor Jerzak," Allen says. I had forgotten that he was in the room; he had been so quiet. He sits down in the chair next to the bed and covers my hand with his. "This is pretty exciting, Grandpa Isaac. I mean, who'd have thought you would be starting a whole new journey at this time of your life?"

A new journey! An adventure! I've been sold that bill of goods before, but at least this time no one's shooting at me. I'm tired. Thank you for being here, Allen. You are so much like your father.

***

We marched in formation towards the line and entered a wide gully we had not been able to see from the ridge of the hill. Soon we found ourselves in a warren of trenches, dugouts, caves, mess-halls - everything an army needed - all underground or dug deep. Our barracks was an enormous cave crammed with tightly packed bunks filled with straw. We were to share it with a French company of engineers that had been there since October. The Germans had previously held this land and we were, in fact, staying in structures they had dug and built.

Since that battle in October which pushed the Germans back across the canal, thousands of men had been killed or wounded by the unending rounds of artillery shells fired from both sides, and in the several futile attempts to mount ground assaults across no-man's-land and the canal. The line had not moved an inch. Each side built more and more fortifications, gun emplacements, traps and roads in anticipation of the next big push.

The Germans kept us awake most of the night with barrage after barrage of artillery shells that exploded around our cave. The French soldiers assured us the cave was strong enough to withstand anything the Germans might send our way, and they seemed to sleep like babies. The French guns were not exactly silent either.

During one of the lulls in the shelling, one of our guys muttered, "They sure know how to welcome us poor travelers from a far-off land."

Reuven, who was in the bunk above me, replied, "A cup of tea would have been nice."

"Amen," and a few chuckles came from all around. Reuven had apparently become our spiritual advisor.

The next morning we received our first assignments. Our platoon was to work with a French unit to rebuild a bridge for a narrow gauge railway line that the Germans had partially destroyed in their October retreat. Our side needed the bridge to bring ammunition and supplies up to the front row of trenches and fortifications.

We set out at first light in small groups so as not to attract the attention of the German spotters in their balloons, but it didn't take long before a shell exploded about a hundred yards in front of us. Then another landed about fifty yards to our left. The French officer in charge of our expedition guided us into a deep crater to wait for the shelling to stop.

There were sixteen of us in that shell hole - six Frenchmen and ten Americans. Reuven was the only one in the group who could converse in both languages and he tried to translate everything that was said. It was comical, in a way, because most of the words that came out of our mouths were variations on swear-words. He developed quite a repertoire. The explosions were happening all around us, and they were getting closer and closer.

One showered us with wet dirt. When it hit, one of the Frenchmen flattened himself against the floor of the crater and began shaking uncontrollably. His comrades pressed up against him and held him. "Shell shock," the French officer said. We needed no translation.

Finally there was a pause in the shelling. The French officer said something which Reuven translated; "They've stopped to grease their guns. Let's move!" We scampered out of the hole, dashed across the broken field in the direction of the bridge we were supposed to repair, and dived into another, larger crater. One advantage to being in a place that has been bombed a million times is that there is always a hole to jump into.

***

Allen is still here. I think he is sleeping. It is quiet; all I can hear is my cat-machine purring steadily. I try to move my eyes to the left, then the right. I do it several times, having no idea if my efforts are noticeable to anyone who might be watching. I try moving them up and down.

When you are fully able to do everything that the body needs or wants to do, you don't think about little things like which way your eyes move, or whether your eyelids are open or closed. These things just happen. But when moving them takes conscious, controlled effort it is a whole other story, especially when you don't even know whether what you are trying to do is recognizable to the outside world. And so much depends on what you do; I am so dependent on others. I am unable to initiate any interaction.

***

I am sure the generals and other high ranking officers plan things; they spend hours poring over maps, reading intelligence reports, discussing questions of troop strength, availability of supplies and ammunition, weather conditions, and who knows what else. But to the poor souls on the ground doing the dirty work and dodging the flying pieces of metal, it all seems pretty random. For no rational reason, the Germans stopped firing at us that day once we started working on the bridge. We could hear the chaos not too far away, but we kept working furiously as if nothing was happening.

As evening approached, the sounds of the shelling from both side intensified. "Musique de nuit," one of our French comrades said.

Reuven translated; "Not exactly a lullaby."

We waited for the night music to recede, then made our way back to the cave. Before being dismissed for the night, our lieutenant called my name before the entire platoon. "Simon, do you know what day it is tomorrow?"

I had no idea what he was talking about. "Tuesday," I stammered.

"Novitz, do you know?

Reuven was equally perplexed.

Then he called on the only other Jewish person in the unit, Benny Samuels, who by now had figured out that the question had something to do with our Jewishness. "I think it is Passover, sir," he responded.

"At least one of you knows. Yes, tomorrow is Wednesday, March twenty-seventh, the first night of Passover. You three will work on cleaning this rat-hole of a cave tomorrow, then leave at fifteen-thirty to arrive at the regimental mess hall for the Passover service and meal at eighteen hundred hours. You will stay there overnight and attend morning services after which you will return to the cave by seventeen hundred. Got it?"

That came out of nowhere. Who would have thought the army would make a consideration like that, especially in the battle zone. None of us - Reuven, Benny, or I - was particularly religious. We ate non-kosher food and worked on the Sabbath along with our comrades. Even at home I had not attended a synagogue in years. Mama did make some attempt to prepare a special meal for the two of us on Passover, but she ignored most of the other holidays. I think she missed the big family affairs she had grown up with in Linkeve, with lots of aunts and uncles and cousins and an abundance of food.

But, what the hell, we had time off and that was great. Suddenly, a whole lot more of the guys professed to being Jewish.

There were close to fifty men at the Passover Seder, about a third were from French units. The army had done a remarkable job with the set-up; they provided white table-cloths, real silverware and porcelain dishes, and candles. The rabbi who led the Seder was French, but spoke passable English. The Seder, for the most part, was according to the ancient text and in Hebrew. I was surprised how much of it I remembered from my childhood.

As we approached the 'Four Questions,' I wondered how the rabbi was going to handle them. According to tradition, they were supposed to be read by the four youngest children in attendance. Reuven leaned over to me and whispered loud enough for many to hear; "I think you're going to have the honor, my young friend."

"I've done it more than once," I whispered back.

But, in typical army style, the rabbi called for volunteers. When no one raised their hand and everyone laughed over the lack of response - we had all become conditioned to keeping our hands in our pockets when the word 'volunteer' was heard - he selected two Frenchmen and two Americans to read.

It was, in so many ways, one of the most surreal evenings of my life. The food was wonderful. It was as if there was a group of Jewish grandmothers in the kitchen; they served us matzo ball soup, followed by roast chicken with potatoes and peas and a dessert of fruit compote. You could hear the sounds of the war behind the crunching of matzo, the clinking of wine glasses and the voices of men who were away from family and loved ones, away from the children who had always been such an essential part of the holidays.

During the meal, the rabbi circulated through the room chatting with us, asking about our families and our hopes. There were photographs and stories and tears. I showed him the note from Mama. He read it slowly and said, "You need to do what she says, Itzik. You need to make it home." He patted my arm, and then moved on to the next table.

Chapter 15

"I've been thinking about you a lot," Danielle says, "trying to figure out what is going on inside your head and wondering what you need to help maintain a sense of reality." She is sitting on the bed next to me. Her perfume as lovely as ever. Her thoughtfulness is even lovelier. "I have been trying to think of those basic things I take for granted, that you could not know unless someone actually told you."

Her voice is becoming more animated. She takes my hand. "It hit me this morning, the moment I woke up: I knew the second I opened my eyes that it was morning, it was sunny, and when I looked at the clock next to my bed that it was six-forty-five on Friday, May seventeenth, 2002. And I said to myself; 'This is information *I* need to anchor my day. I bet Isaac would like to know this kind of stuff, too!' So here I am!"

She kissed my cheek. As I said, her thoughtfulness was lovely. She has found a way for me to start to build a framework. I love it!

"So, Isaac, I am going to ask you a bunch of questions. Answer yes or no. OK?"

I blink twice.

"Would you like to know what day of the week it is, every day?"

I blink twice.

"The date?"

Twice.

"Weather, time of day."

Yes. Yes.

"OK," she says, "I will make sure that you get all this information every day. Oh, by the way, it is now ten-fifteen in the morning."

I blink twice, pause, then blink twice again. That is my way of saying, "Thank you."

***

The morning Passover service was rather dismal; the French soldiers were not there and only a dozen or so Americans showed up. The room in which we had feasted the night before had reverted to its primary use - an officers' mess-hall - so the service was conducted outdoors, behind the building. The rabbi kept it short, wished us all courage and safety and sent us on our way before eleven.

Benny, Reuven and I looked at each other not knowing quite what to do. It was about a three hour walk back to the cave, so we had about three extra hours to kill. "Let's take our time getting back. Rest a lot along the way," Benny said.

"Not a bad idea," Reuven responded.

As we walked we could see and hear the artillery fire from both sides, and the showers of smoke and mud wherever the shells landed. It was all still far from us; we had no need to be concerned or vigilant, but its presence was constant.

The road went through an abandoned village sacked and ravaged over and over again during the years of war in this area. Not a single home appeared to remain intact. The stones from the destroyed buildings were piled along the sides of the main road to allow men and vehicles to pass. No one lived here. No one could possibly still live here.

About halfway through the village we decided to detour off the main road up a short side street that led to an open square which had, perhaps, once been a park or a village garden. The stones and rubble had not been cleared so it was slow going. At the far end of the square stood the charred ruins of the church - its roof, windows and doors gone.

We entered through the vacant arched doorway to find that the interior had been cleared of all stones which might have fallen, all glass, all burned wood. The ceramic tiled floor, laid out in a pattern of red and yellow diamonds, was swept and clean and an empty ammunition crate had been placed where the altar would have been. A cross, the remnant of two partially burned roof beams, leaned in the window opening behind the makeshift altar.

We sat down in the middle of the floor, spontaneously silent. This was a sacred place. I found myself thinking about my future. I felt certain that I would fulfill my mother's demand that I return. And then what? I looked around me at this structure, this timeless space, and my mind drifted to our visits to Salisbury Cathedral and Chartres. I had been fascinated by the relationship between the physical elements and the atmosphere they created. How the materials are used to evoke the non-material emotions and yearnings. It was in this destroyed, yet alive, little church that I decided I wanted to be an architect.

Through a lull in the noises of the war I heard the erratic tinkling of bells. I got up and walked towards the sound. Behind the church, a set of chimes had been constructed using empty shell casings cut to different lengths to create different tones, and each one fitted with a clapper. They were mounted on a frame high on the wall. A rope hung down. I was tempted to pull on it, but held back, happy to hear the random music as the wind rocked these makeshift bells from side to side.

I felt Reuven's hand on my shoulder. "Lovely sound," he said, "but we'd better get moving."

The road from the village sloped down into the valley and ever closer to the front. In the distance, the canal cut across the landscape. We walked in silence for some time, not wanting to break the spell of that wonderful little church. We still had plenty of time before we had to report at the cave, so we walked slowly. Shells were exploding about a thousand yards to our right. We watched them as we went.

We descended further and as we rounded a sharp bend we had to jump out of the way of two speeding trucks as they came roaring up the road kicking up dust and stones. Reuven cursed at the drivers. A shell exploded sixty or seventy feet in front of us. Benny shouted, "Hell! That one was close!"

A moment later a second shell exploded. I felt my legs blow out from underneath me as I was lifted off the ground. Then I landed hard. My right thigh was screaming and I remember reaching for it and feeling the sticky wet ooze of my own blood. I felt like throwing up.

Reuven was shouting and dragging me into a crater near the road. Another shell explodes. Reuven is tying a tourniquet around my upper leg. "Where's Benny?" I hear myself say.

Reuven shakes his head slowly. "You need to be still, Itzik. Don't worry, I'll get you to a medic."

I have a fleeting memory of Reuven carrying me over his shoulder. Then the aid station. Reuven holding my hand tightly, telling me, "You're going to be fine. The doc is patching you up. You're gonna be OK, Itzik."

He kept talking and squeezing my hand as I faded in and out of consciousness.

Chapter 16

"You awake, Isaac?" Damon's voice is soft and deep.

I blink twice.

"It's Saturday morning, just before two o'clock, May eighteenth, 2002. It's a dark cloudy night. It was pretty chilly when I came in at midnight."

I blink twice, twice. *Thank you.* I am not sure he notices, but I am thankful to Danielle for spreading the word, and thankful to Damon the Decent for following through.

He checks my wiring and plumbing. "Looking fine," he says. "All quiet up here for now." He pats my shoulder gently, and I hear him sit in the chair next to the bed.

"I did notice your double-double. Does that have meaning?"

I blink twice.

He pauses. "Let's see if I can figure it out?"

He is quiet for a few more moments, then says; "Alright. I will say words that I think match what your double-double means. When I hit the right one, give me a double-double; if I am wrong, do nothing. Make sense?"

I blink twice. I am excited and a little nervous about this experiment. What if he is able to connect? What if he is not?

"Here goes. You did it right after I told you the date and time, so the first one is 'good morning.'"

I do not respond.

"How about 'hello?'"

He waits and I remain unmoving. I hope I haven't gotten into something too open-ended. How many words are there in the English language? I mean, you weren't just plucking a random word out of the air. I blink one time. *No.*

"I gave you information you never had before and really wanted. How about 'thank you?'"

Smart man, Damon. I could hug you. I give him a strong double-

double, as he calls it. He laughs and squeezes my hand. "You are awesome, Mr. Simon."

***

Stretcher, ambulance, train. I have sporadic memories of these. I remember the stabbing pain in my thigh as I was moved from one mode of transportation to the next. I remember the crushing headaches. I remember lots of flashing lights.

When I finally emerged from my fog, I was in a bed in a large tent, along with about twenty other wounded soldiers. My right leg was secured at several places in a contraption that kept it straight, and elevated my foot about eighteen inches above the bed. My thigh was wrapped in bandages. I also had a large cotton swab taped over my ribcage on my left side. It hurt to breathe. I could see a couple of nurses moving from bed to bed, talking softly with the men, bringing food, medications, and checking bandages and waste basins. I lifted my right arm and wiggled my fingers.

One of the nurses came to my bedside. "You're awake, then, Private Simon," she said. "I will tell the doctor."

It looked like she was about to walk away. "Wait. Where am I? How bad am I?"

She smiled. "I'm Nurse Kathleen. You're in Base Hospital Number Nine in Rouen. It's good to see your open eyes. You've been unconscious for several days." She patted my hand. "I'll have the doctor talk with you about your injuries. He won't be long."

"I'm thirsty," I said.

"I'll bring you some water." She walked off. I watched her leave the tent. About ten minutes later she returned with a tray of food; mashed potatoes, ground meat, canned carrots and peas. And a large glass of water.

I was in the middle of my meal when the doctor arrived. "Good to see you awake and eating, Private. I am Captain Bell. I'm in charge of this ward."

He struck me as kind of arrogant. Seems to be a thing with doctors, no matter where they are. "I see my leg hanging in the air and I feel bandages on my side. What's going on?" I say.

"The good news is that nothing that happened to you should cause long-term problems. You were hit by shell fragments that tore a hole in your thigh and broke your thigh-bone. You are lucky the fracture itself was clean and did not require surgery to realign the bone or remove bone chips. We need to keep it immobilized while the bone knits itself back together and the wound heals. Fortunately, too, the shrapnel missed the major artery in your leg by about half an inch. You also cracked two ribs and you had quite a serious concussion. Our main concern now is to avoid infection. Whoever treated you in the field did an excellent job of cleaning that wound."

Reuven, my friend, I have so much to thank you for.

"Any other questions, Private?"

"Will I walk again?"

"I expect you will be back with your unit in five or six months, fully able to carry out all your duties."

"Thank you," I said, not too happy about going back to the front. Well, maybe it will all be over by then.

He walked over to another bed. Nurse Kathleen hovered nearby. "Where's all my stuff?" I asked her.

"You didn't arrive with much, Private Simon; just the uniform you were in, and I'm afraid most of it was ruined."

"There were things in my pockets. Letters, pictures, my wallet."

"Whatever is able to be saved is locked away for safe-keeping until the soldier can take care of them himself. I'll see what we have for you. Give me a few minutes."

My whole body seemed to tense up as she left. My head was pounding. I was not sure whether it was the concussion or my anxiety over Mama's note and Chaim's letter. I finished my now-cold meal without tasting it.

Another nurse came to take the tray away. "It's nice to have you awake and aware, Isaac. We'll take good care of you here. I'm Nurse Elizabeth; you can call me Liz. The doctors are excellent. The best - from Lakeside Hospital in Chicago."

I thanked her and closed my eyes and waited.

"I have your things, Private Simon." I must have dozed off. When I opened my eyes Nurse Kathleen was standing nearby holding out a large envelope to me. It was sealed, and had my name and number on it.

I thanked her and carefully tore it open. There were only two things in it; Mama's note and Chaim's letter, which now had a small smear of dried blood near one edge. I shuddered. I reread them both, several times, then put them in the pocket of the pajamas I was wearing and closed my eyes. I could feel the tears rolling down my face.

"Isaac, would you like some writing paper?" I opened my eyes to find a woman about my mother's age standing next to me. "I am Agnes, a volunteer with the Red Cross. Would you like to write a letter home?"

"Thank you, Agnes. There are few letters I would like to write."

She gave me a pencil and several sheets of paper and a few envelopes. They had the Red Cross logo on them. She also gave me a small tray to press on. "When you're done, put the letters on that table next to you. I'll be back in a couple of hours to pick them up."

The first letter I wrote was to Mama, telling her I had been injured and was being taken care of in the hospital and expected to be out in a few of months. I told her not to worry, and that I still carried her note in my pocket. My letter was so much like Chaim's, so much like almost every other letter I had sent her. Vague. Completely lacking any detail of what I was going through.

I was about to sign off when I realized I had not written to her since before the Passover Seder, so I added a few paragraphs describing the evening, the meal, the service, the friendliness of the rabbi and the camaraderie of the group of Jewish American and French soldiers. I also described the wonderful church we had discovered in the ruins of the village - how peaceful it was and how someone had cleaned it up and created a set of bells. On the last page of the letter I created a drawing showing Reuven, Benny and me sitting on the floor of the ruined roofless church. I did not mention that Benny was dead.

My next letter was to Reuven, thanking him for saving my life and letting him know I was going to be fine and back with the Company in a matter of months. I also asked him if he had any idea where my pack was, with all my equipment, warm socks and gloves, as well as all the letters from home, the many sketches I had done and a few mementos I'd picked up along the way.

I was getting tired, but I wrote a third letter, a brief one, to Moish Zweig, the South African fellow who served with Chaim and knew more than anyone what Chaim had experienced. I asked him to get in touch with me, and I told him I was determined to meet with him before we went home. I used the same address Mama and I had used when we wrote to Chaim, hoping that it would find him.

And then I fell asleep.

***

"Would you like me to read to you?" Danielle asks, as she touches my hand and sits down. "I brought Mary Oliver again and Winnie the Pooh.

I need to find a way to say 'smile.'

"But first; it's early Saturday morning - seven thirty. Blue sky with thin high clouds. Looks like it will be a perfect day: dry, sunny, but not too warm. Spring in New England. I love it!"

I do too. I blink twice, and then again.

"Oh. The double-double. I talked with Damon a few minutes ago. He waved me down when I got off the elevator and told me about your latest move. Well, thank you for saying 'thank you!' Damon is such a caring young man."

I have been giving him all kinds of appellations, but I think from now on I will stick with Damon the Good. I like that.

"So, Mary or Pooh?"

I do love her poetry, but I'm more in the mood for the bear. I used to read the A.A. Milne books to my children. They loved them, as did I.

"One blink for Pooh, two for Mary O."

I blink once.

"Good choice, Isaac. I had hoped you'd go for the wise and funny little bear."

***

Agnes returned to pick up my letters. She had a cart with a few dozen books, and she asked whether I would like one. "Do you have any on architecture?" I asked. "I'm going to study to be an architect when I get back home."

"I'm sorry, son, I only have novels," she replied, "but I'll see what I can come up with."

"What would you recommend?"

"You should try Zane Grey. I have a few books by him." She placed a book on the table. "I'm sure you'll enjoy it; most of the men do."

"Is there any chance I could have more paper?"

"More letters?"

"Not today - but I like to draw. I was a commercial artist before I signed up." She reached into a large envelope on her cart and produced a small stack of paper and two pencils. "I'll try to find some better drawing paper for you; in the meantime I hope these Red Cross letter sheets will be OK."

"Thank you, Agnes."

She moved on to the next bed and I started on a sketch of her and her cart. I gave the drawing to her when she was doing her rounds the next week. She was "quite astonished" and gave me a peck on the cheek.

***

Danielle is still reading Winnie the Pooh. I must have drifted off.

"Sorry to interrupt your story, Isaac." It is Wanda. She is not her usual self; her voice is dull and she sounds tired, but more troubling is the absence of the joy that I usually sense in her. Something very difficult is going on in her life.

"I'm afraid it's time for me to leave, Isaac," Danielle says. "It's almost nine and I'm meeting Ginnie downtown for a cup of coffee. Yesterday was her last day of school and she asked me to get together for a long chat. I so love that girl!"

Me, too.

"I'll leave the books in your cabinet so someone else can pick up where we left off. I marked the page. Allen will be here after lunch." She gives me a kiss on the cheek and is gone.

Lunch - now there's an interesting concept. It is so weird to me that I do not eat. Food was always such an important part of our lives. Virginia and I loved to cook, and having the family together for a meal was one of our greatest joys. We even planted vegetable and herb gardens. To be honest, I was not much of a gardener, but Virginia kept it going until the end.

I remember when 'a liquid lunch' used to mean a couple of beers; now it's some concocted goo that's dribbled into me on a regular schedule. Not what I envisioned.

Wanda is still here, fiddling with my tubes. I am losing all patience for this. How do I blink 'enough'?

***

At around seven-thirty every morning in the hospital tent, an orderly made the rounds distributing mail. That is one way you could tell who was new in the ward and who had been here a long time. New patients got nothing. It was four weeks before my mail caught up with me; I received three letters from my mother and one from Uncle Kalner. All four letters were written before they had received word of my injury. The letters had been sent to my Company Army Post Office Number 709 first, then forwarded to some Divisional office and finally redirected to Base Hospital Number 9.

The big news was that Uncle Kalner had remarried. He had not told anyone he was even seeing someone, then, "out of the blues," as my mother wrote, "he announced that he was married, and that he and his new bride were coming to Lawrence to visit."

My mother, despite her tenuous adherence to Judaism, was "taken aback" when she was introduced to Kalner's new wife, Mary, "a Catholic woman at least ten years older than your uncle," she wrote.

The wedding had been a civil ceremony in a courthouse in New York. Mary was divorced from her first husband and could not remarry in the church even if she had wanted to. She was, as Uncle Kalner wrote, "A smart, warm, caring, fiery woman of Irish descent, who has no need for the oppressive dogma of any church." Sounded like my uncle's type of person!

The first meeting between his new wife and his younger sister, according to Uncle Kalner's letter, was "a little frosty." I could imagine. Uncle Kalner paved the way for me - but, I will get to that later.

I never learned whether Mama's initial reaction to Mary was primarily because of her age or because of her religion. In a short time, however, the distance between them dissipated and they became good friends and comrades in the fight for women's voting rights and against child labor. They saw each other infrequently but corresponded regularly for years.

My ribs were healing well. I was able to sit up straighter and breathe without pain. Even though it was over a month since I was admitted, my leg was still hanging in space. This made any movement in the bed nearly impossible. Every few days the doctor would lower my leg and remove the splint and bandages on my thigh to look at how the leg wound was healing. Then they would wrap me up and strap me in again, and I would have to just lie there, immobilized, with my foot in the air.

The first time they unwrapped my leg I did not know what to expect. I still felt a constant dull pain in my thigh, with an occasional sharp stabbing sensation. I looked at my bare skin as if I were studying a painting in the Museum of Fine Arts. About five inches above the knee was a perfect arc cut into my flesh, sewn closed with stitches of black thread evenly positioned every quarter of an inch. There were at least twenty-five stitches; I could not see the end of the scar since it curved behind my leg. The skin was pale pink, with an under-wash of mixed blues, purples and reds.

I tried to roll my body so that I could see where the scar ended, but the doctor pushed me back. "Please don't move, private, unless I ask you to." He slowly lifted my knee, bending my leg slightly. Pain shot through my thigh and I let out a cry. "Your leg muscles were significantly injured. They are healing well but are stiff and weak." He stretched out my leg so that it was now lying flat on the bed. He repeated the leg movements several times, and each time it hurt a little less.

After about a month of this routine, I asked, "When can the stitches come out, doc? They look awful. And this damned splint."

"Actually, Private, the stitches are looking good. There are no signs of leakage or infection. I would say we can take them out in about two weeks. In the meantime, we're going to make some changes to your life so that you can get some sunshine." They reinstalled the splint but did not hook me up to the device that elevated the leg. When they were done, I was moved to a wheelchair and, with my leg sticking out straight in front of me, one of the nurses rolled me out of the tent into the sunlight.

"The doctor said you can be out here for one hour today, and then back to bed," she said.

As I felt the warmth of the sun soak into my body, I suddenly realized I had not been out-doors since the day I was wounded. My eyes took some time to adjust to the light and when they did I found myself sitting with four other men, each one with combinations of bandages, casts or missing limbs. Agnes was chatting animatedly with the group and when I arrived she introduced me all around, saying what a "wonderful artist" I was and even showing everyone the drawing I had done of her.

"This is pretty good," one of the men said, looking at the drawing and then tapping lightly on my splint. "Good thing you don't draw with your leg." Everyone laughed.

I looked around me at the rows of large tents laid out in a grid pattern in the middle of a huge flat tree-less field. Most of them housed injured or sick men. In the far distance I could make out the tops of buildings and, of course, the steeples and bell-towers of several churches. Save for the voices of our little group, it was strangely quiet.

"My first time outside since this happened," I said, waving at my outstretched leg. "I could get used to it." I lifted my face and closed my eyes enjoying the warmth.

"Don't get too comfortable. Today is unusually warm - tomorrow it could be in the fifties."

"What is this place?" I asked, "I mean, what was it before we all showed up?"

"The place used to be a racetrack," one of my companions said. "Back in the day when France was fun."

We sat silently. Agnes trundled off with her cart of books and paper and envelopes. It was hard to imagine horses racing around here.

"I need to write a letter," I said, and picked up the paper and pencil Agnes had given me.

Chapter 17

"How are you doing this afternoon, Grandpa Isaac?" Allen is sitting in the chair near my bed. "I talked with Danielle before I came here. She said she spent some time with you earlier this morning, reading Winnie the Pooh," he laughed. "I remember when you read it to me, and to Ginnie and David." He paused, then added, "Would you like me to continue reading?"

How do I say, 'yes, but not yet?' I am thinking, then blink one time.

"No," Allen says. "Actually, I'm glad you are not into it right now - there is something else on my mind, something else I wanted to let you know. OK?"

I have no idea what he wants to talk about, but I'm curious enough so I blink twice.

"Thank you," he says. "Oh, almost forgot - Danielle told be about the double-double, the 'thank you.' That's great!" He pauses a long while. I begin to think he has forgotten what he wanted to tell me. Finally, he says, "Do you remember I said the other day that I was going through some boxes of old papers in your apartment?"

I certainly do and despite my mixed feelings about him digging into my life I am intrigued. I blink twice. What did he find?

"I came across all the letters you wrote home from France to your mother, from the day you got on the train in Boston to the day, almost two years later, when you wrote that you had been discharged and were on your way home. To be honest, the letters don't say much about what you experienced, although there are some beautiful descriptive pieces about places you saw. There are also several wonderful drawings - including one of you, Reuven and a third soldier in what looks like a bombed-out church. Do you remember it?"

Of course I do. Like it was yesterday. I blink twice, not entirely sure if I was indicating "yes" or trying to hold back tears.

"There are also some letters and drawings on Red Cross paper from when you were in the hospital. One drawing shows you seated in a wheelchair with your leg in a cast or splint sticking straight out in front of you. I didn't even know you'd been injured. The letters give little detail. I wish you could tell me about it all."

I wish I could. I wish I had told you, but there is never a right time to talk about horror. I guess now you'll just have to read my mind. It's all there.

***

The day following my first day in the sun it rained without interruption. It was also the day I received a letter from Reuven. He told me they were working hard, building fortifications and repairing roads. Not much had changed and everyone seemed to be in fine spirits. He also apologized for leaving my pack in a ditch on the side of the road. "I had other priorities, and anyway it was pretty torn up," he wrote. "I don't know how you carried all that junk around, but it probably saved your life! I found a chunk of shrapnel the size of a meat cleaver in there. It sliced through your pile of drawings and letters and lodged itself in the handle of your shovel."

That's probably what broke my ribs. He did not mention Benny or how the guys reacted to his death. I thought of the letter Mama and I had received from Chaim's commanding officer who, through three years of war, found himself having to write so many similar letters. I wondered what Captain Swan had written to Benny's family concerning the first combat death in his company.

The rain was drumming on the tent. I was sitting in my wheelchair next to my bed struggling to read Zane Grey's *Riders of the Purple Sage*. I had never heard of Mormons and the story seemed almost Old Testament in its rigidity. I think I read the first chapter twice, and was still having a hard time with it.

"Listen up!"

I looked up and saw a tall, thin man in full dress uniform standing at the entrance to the tent, his silver lieutenant bars, well-polished and shining even in the dull light. "Major General Clarence R. Edwards will be arriving shortly to present the Purple Heart to members of the Twenty-sixth Division. Return to your beds and make yourselves presentable, gentlemen!" He turned sharply and marched out.

I put my book on my table, moved my chair so that I was stationed with my outstretched leg parallel to the bed and waited. Moments later in walked the General, all pressed and shiny, except for the muddy boots. He saluted the room, but since none of us was in uniform, no one returned the salute. It seemed a little odd. The lieutenant who had announced the general's impending arrival was at his side carrying a tray with several dark boxes on it.

The lieutenant called my name.

"Sir!" I responded.

General Edwards came over to me carrying one of the boxes. He opened it, removed the medal and pinned it to my pajama shirt. "Thank you for your service, son," he said. "I hope we shall see you back in the line soon." He shook my hand, then placed the empty box on the table next to Zane Grey.

The general and his lieutenant repeated this procedure with three other men in the ward, saying the exact same words to each one. And then they were gone. I could hear a similar scene re-enacted in the nearby tents.

I looked at my medal, then flipped it over and saw my name and rank inscribed on the back. Returning to the line was the last thing I wanted to do.

I decided to give Zane Grey one more try, but must have fallen asleep. I woke to find Nurse Liz crouching next to me, patting my hand and whispering, "It's OK, Isaac. It's just a dream. There is no need to worry. It'll be OK."

I had no idea what she was talking about. My whole body was tense, but I had no recollection of a dream or anything else. Apparently in my sleep, I had been twisting and turning violently in the wheelchair, and shouting and cursing.

"Who is Benny?" she asked, "You called out his name several times. And Reuven? Do you want to tell me about them?"

"Benny is dead," I said, and I could not stop myself. "We were walking together, the three of us, when the shell exploded close behind us. There had been no shelling anywhere near us, and then... Benny took most of it. What missed him, hit me. I remember being blown off my feet and landing hard. I remember Benny's scream, and then silence. Reuven was untouched; he patched me up and carried me to a medic. At least, that is what I think happened. Reuven saved my life. I have known him since I was ten years old. We met at Ellis Island. He saved my life."

I felt my body shaking. The nurse stayed with me until I calmed down, then she stood up and said, "This will pass in time, Isaac. We can talk some more, later, if you want."

I did not know Benny well at all, but after the war I went to visit his parents in Providence, Rhode Island. There was an aura of emptiness in their small apartment. Benny's picture was everywhere. There were several photographs showing him in a tuxedo playing a clarinet in front of a six piece band, with people dancing. I had not even known he could play an instrument. I felt terrible that I could tell them so little about their only son. Mostly we talked about what a good time we had at the Seder. I lied and told them that after the Seder someone produced a clarinet and a guitar, and Benny and another soldier entertained us for over an hour. They wished me well. I remember the guilt I felt that I was glad that if someone had to be killed it was Benny and not Reuven.

I lay awake listening to the sounds of the men around me: the writhing and screaming of sleeping men. In the dark, I could make out a nurse moving quietly from bed to bed, trying to soothe them. Why I had not been aware of this before, I don't know. Maybe I had been able to sleep very deeply, or, perhaps I had heard these anguished sounds and not connected them to my own reality. But, whatever the reason, that innocence was now gone. I came to know the sound of profound pain.

The next morning was bright and warm. I was exhausted from not being able to sleep. I needed to get outside, to escape the agony that seemed to hang in the air inside that tent. Before breakfast I talked Nurse Liz into helping me into my wheelchair, and I wheeled myself out of the tent. It was early and I was the first one out. A huge cloud of starlings suddenly broke over the tops of the tents and moved and tumbled like waves crashing in on themselves. The noise was deafening. The performance lasted less than a minute, and then they were gone.

"Did you see that?" It was the mailman. "Absolutely amazing! Do you know what kind of birds they were?"

"Starlings," I said.

"You're Private Simon, right? I have two letters for you." He handed the letters to me. "Have a good day."

"You too. Thanks."

The first letter was from Mama; it was addressed to me at the hospital. She had finally received my letter telling her I had been wounded. She was upset, and angry. She begged me to tell her everything that had happened and what the doctors were saying about my wounds. "Are you really not seriously wounded? Being laid up for a few months is a long time. Tell me straight, Itzik. I need to know."

The second letter was from Moish Zweig. The return address was Base Hospital Number 3, BEF, Rouen. I tore open the letter. War is crazy and random, and sometimes the strangest coincidences occur. Moish had been shot in the shoulder and had been sent to a British hospital in the same town where I was recuperating. He wrote that he was doing well and expected to be sent home in a few weeks.

I wheeled myself back into the tent as fast as I could and rolled directly towards the nearest nurse, almost knocking her over. "I need help finding someone."

"I'm not sure what you're asking me to do for you," Nurse Liz said.

I told her about my brother Chaim, and about needing to meet Moish to find out what had happened to my brother, and then Moish's letter from in a British hospital right here in Rouen. "He says he's being sent home soon. I have to talk with him."

"I'll see what we can do, Isaac. I happen to know some of the British nurses at Number three - we worked with them when we first arrived here. Give me a little time."

"There isn't much time!"

"I understand. I'll do the best I can."

***

I am awake listening to my cat-machine. I don't remember Allen leaving, but I am pretty sure he is no longer here. I could really use a little *Winnie the Pooh* right now; I need a little cheering up. The place is too quiet. Maybe I should practice my eye movements.

I am aware of the slight change in light when I open my eyes. Everything is still all gray, but the intensity is definitely different. But it is still colorless! I move my eyes to the left, then over to the right. Left again. What the hell am I doing? Where will this eye gymnastics ever get me? I am too old to learn a new language and, anyway, what do I have to say that could possibly be conveyed by moving my eyes around! These eyes have seen too much!

"His pulse has been fluctuating wildly for the last few hours." Trainwreck is saying. "I got concerned when it hit one-seventy-five then dropped suddenly to sixty and then elevated to one-thirty and stayed there for some time. His breathing was also shallow and rapid. As you can see, his pulse rate is still a little erratic."

"Hmmm." It is Doctor Fish. He plops his clammy cold hand on my forehead. "Thermometer."

I feel him move my head slightly to the left and insert something in my right ear. I hear a tiny chime.

"Ninety-nine." He moves the blankets and fiddles with my pajama top. Then his cold stethoscope is on my chest and ribcage. "Hmmm." Pause. "We are going to sit you up for a minute, Mr. Simon." I feel the bed fold up behind my back. "Hold him up, nurse." I feel Trainwreck's arm brace my shoulders and I hear the bed being returned to its previous position. The cold stethoscope again. "Lungs are clear. Hmmm." They lay me down. "Check on him every half hour and let me know if he does not stabilize."

"Yes, Doctor."

I hear him stride out of the room. "You gave us a scare, Isaac. But you seem to be returning to normal." She makes sure all my plumbing is still in order and then she walks off, leaving me back in the quiet again.

***

Three days later I was sitting in my wheelchair fully absorbed in the drawing I was working on and enjoying the sun, when a shadow fell across my sketchpad. I looked up to find Nurse Liz with a broad smile on her face. "There is someone to see you, Isaac." She stepped aside and I saw a soldier, with South African Expeditionary Forces insignia on his uniform, and the empty right sleeve of his shirt pinned up.

"I'm Moish," he said, extending his left hand. I wanted to hug him.

"I'll get you a chair," Nurse Liz said.

"I'm leaving for home this coming Thursday," he said. "One of the nurses tracked me down yesterday and told me you were here. She was able to arrange for someone to drive me over."

Liz brought the chair and Moish sat down. "They're picking me up at noon." He looked at his watch. "Two-and-a half hours."

"You're going home," I said. I had so many questions I did not know where to begin. I just looked at him.

"Yes, quite a price to pay for a ticket home," he slapped the empty sleeve. "Good thing I'm left-handed." He laughed awkwardly, and we were both silent.

"How well did you know Chaim?" I asked, at last.

He took a deep breath, held it, then exhaled slowly. "Since we have so little time I'll tell you all I can. And I will be blunt. OK?"

I nodded.

"We met in August 1915, soon after I arrived at training camp. Chaim and I were the only Jewish boys in our company and we somehow found each other. He took me under his wing, since he was a veteran because of his experience in German South West. He was a corporal during training, but lost the stripe days before we boarded ship because he got drunk at a farewell party."

"My father's curse," I muttered.

"Yes, he told me about Linkeve and your father's drunkenness." He continued; "Chaim confided in me that he didn't care about losing the stripe. He said he didn't want to be responsible for anyone or to be the lackey for the officers. He had that chip on his shoulder all the time. He wasn't big, but he was strong. He didn't take crap from anyone. One time one of the boys in our unit called him 'a bloody Kike' and Chaim was on him in a flash, leaving him with a bloody nose and a couple of missing teeth. The incident earned him three days of punishment."

I had always thought of my older brother as strong-willed, but also gentle and easy-going. I could barely recognize the man Moish was describing.

"But that didn't stop him," Moish continued. "On our first leave in France, he went straight to the local bar and brothel where he spent time with at least two women and got falling-down drunk. Fortunately I was able to get him back to camp without anyone seeing him in this state, but the next morning he couldn't make it out of his bunk. The sergeant smelled the drink on him and he was given another three days of punishment. And then he spent a couple of weeks in the infirmary being treated for something he picked up from those women.

"But, despite all the stuff Chaim got up to, our lieutenant liked him because Chaim was unafraid. If the lieutenant needed a volunteer, he could count on Chaim to step forward. And most of the time he did what he was told to do, and he did it well." He paused a long while, then added, "That was until Delville Wood."

I knew about the battle in Delville Wood in July 1916, and I knew from Chaim's letters that this battle was a turning point for him, a place from which he was unable to return.

"I won't - no I can't - go into detail about Delville Wood." Moish paused and I saw his face clench. His voice was hoarse, almost a whisper. "It was worse than I ever imagined hell could be. It wasn't just the unceasing fire and noise and screams, but it was what we all did to protect ourselves. We did things that are unimaginable. I do not believe any one of us who came out of there alive sleeps well at night. It changed us all. I think we all doubt our very humanity."

There were tears in his eyes and I reached out to touch his shoulder. He pulled back and wiped his eyes.

"Soon after we were withdrawn from the line, we were given a two day pass and we descended on the bars in the nearest town. I was not much of a drinker, but even I had a few too many. When I got back to our unit, Chaim was nowhere to be found. It was another three or four days before the military police found him semi-conscious in a ditch near a whorehouse in the town. His uniform was gone and he was wearing a lady's red bathrobe. The only thing that identified him as a South African soldier was the tags around his neck. They charged him with going absent without permission. His hearing was brief and he was sentenced to ten days of hard labor. He also forfeited all pay until his new uniform was paid for. He was broken, Itzik. Broken."

I showed Moish the letter that Chaim had written at this time; the letter where more was censored than left. He shook his head and swallowed hard. The tears were now running freely down his face, and he made no effort to wipe them away.

"After he had done his time he barely spoke, not even to me. He did what he was told, without questioning, but was consumed by a simmering ferocity. He suffered a minor battlefield injury in August when he led a charge, and he actually spent three or four weeks recuperating here, in Rouen, before being sent back to the front. Sometime late in 1916 he was assigned, with no explanation, to a Scots tunneling unit. When he returned to our company after a month or so, he told me nothing about the experience, other than to comment that he had survived it. Later he got into a fist-fight with our sergeant, which earned him two weeks of Field Punishment Number One. It was horrible. He was tied to the wheel of a cannon for an hour a day. It was January and freezing cold and his fingers were cracked from frostbite. He just stood there screaming angrily as the shells fell and exploded not too far away, and our cannons returned fire."

Moish suddenly stood up and began pacing back and forth on the short path that led between us and the entrance to the tent. I looked at my watch, it was almost noon. Moish returned to his chair.

"And then came Arras in early April. We were entrenched to the east of the town. Our engineers had spent months establishing the trench network, gun emplacements and other structures. The tunneling units, maybe even the one Chaim had been assigned to, had dug deep and far toward the German line. We sat in our bunkers for four days while our artillery pounded the other side. I watched him seething with anger and impatience, barely able to wait for the order to go. Then on April ninth we poured out and began the advance across no-man's-land. A freak spring snow-storm blew in from behind us, but on we charged. Chaim was just ahead of me on my right as we scrambled across that snow-covered plain. I could hear him shouting and cursing at the Boche as he ran, and I followed his voice. Through the whirling snow we could barely see each other, but we could see the flashes of rifle and machine-gun fire in front of us. It was ghostly. And then Chaim's shouting suddenly stopped and I thought I saw him stumble. I ran to where I thought he was and found him face down in the snow. 'Keep moving, soldier,' our sergeant shouted, and so I charged on, leaving him behind. I was told later by the medic who found him that he had died instantly - he had been hit by a large caliber machine gun bullet right in the middle of his chest."

He sighed deeply, then was silent. His tears stopped and he sat looking down at his one hand gripping his knee. After a long while he said, "Chaim was a tormented man, Itzik. Broken. I am not sure he could have survived in the world."

My poor brother. I had signed up to avenge his death, and to find out what had happened to him. I wanted to experience what he had experienced. I did not want that anymore. I wanted to get the hell out of there and go home. I had not seen anything close to what Chaim had seen, but I had seen and felt enough to be able to imagine it. Moish's ticket home was the empty right sleeve of his uniform. Was the price really all that high?

Chapter 18

Damon the Good is wiping my face with a warm cloth. "You've been crying again, Isaac. Memories?"

I blink twice. I'm not sure I could tell them to you even if I could talk out loud.

"Sometimes sad memories can also be good memories."

I do not respond. To me Chaim had always been a boy, the big brother who understood me and took care of me and protected me. But there was another side to him I never knew, the disruptive part of him that pushed him away from his family and directed him to South Africa and then into the war.

"And sometimes sad can just be sad," Damon says. "I know." He is silent for some time, then says, "I think your beard could use a little sprucing up. Do you mind if I give it a bit of a trim?"

I blink one time, and wonder if he will interpret this as "no I don't mind" or "no, don't trim." It doesn't matter either way.

"I'll get a pair of scissors."

I hear the snip-snip and feel the slight tugs on my beard as he works. "It's Sunday, May nineteenth, four o'clock in the morning. Remember, I am the night-shift nurse. I will not be here tomorrow night or the next; it's my weekend."

I do the double-double.

"Looking good! I love that beard." He rises to leave. "I'll come by a little later to check on you."

I hear him move towards the door, then stop and turn. He sits down again and takes my hand. "Were you remembering the war, Isaac? Is that what made you cry?"

Yes.

"I've been there, Isaac. Desert Storm in 1991. I was a medic with the infantry - First Division. Signed up a few years after high school. While our casualties were fairly low, I saw some horrible things that still have me waking up shaking. It was mostly injured Iraqi soldiers and civilians that I found myself trying to keep alive. But, people are people - flesh is flesh, no matter where the hell you live or what you believe. My war lasted a few months, and to be honest, our enemy was not that well-armed or organized, but it was still an experience I would not wish on anyone. I can't imagine what you went through being in trench warfare and hand-to-hand combat, with poison gas and everything else."

He stopped talking for some time, and then blew his nose.

"It's the reason I work night shift - my nightmares. They scared the hell out of my wife, so I started working at night and she worked during the day so that we would sleep at different times. But, it all got to be too much for her and she left eight months ago."

I wish I could put my arms around him.

"As much as I wanted children, it's probably a good thing that we never had any. I think my issues would have scared the hell out of them."

I know that fear, young man. How I thank my dear Virginia for living through it with me. We had three kids. It wasn't easy in so many ways.

"And there's other stuff, too," he added, his voice trailing off. He offered no explanation.

Well, it's his business.

"Gotta go!" he announces abruptly, "Red light flashing. You know what that means. See you later, Isaac. Thanks for listening." He hurries out.

How could I know whether there really is a flashing red light? Perhaps he felt he had said more than he intended and needed to get away.

***

Nurse Liz found me slumped down in my wheelchair after Moish had left. My sketchpad and pencils had fallen to the ground at some point during our meeting and I could not muster the energy or will to reach for them. She sat down in the chair that Moish had vacated a few minutes earlier.

"I can see it was a difficult talk with your South African soldier. I am sorry." She stood up and placed her hand on my shoulder. "You missed lunch, but I can find something for you if you're hungry."

I shook my head

"OK, then," she said. Before she left she retrieved my sketchpad and pencils and handed them to me.

What a waste! We, the Americans, had been in this mess for not even a year and anyone could see it was all insane. The British, French, Germans and others had been at it for three-and-a-half years! It had nothing to do with freedom or honor. It was about blood and death. It was all about millions of people dying so that people who cared nothing for us poor bastards in the trenches could exert their will and power over other similarly despotic megalomaniacs.

I remember saying to myself; "From this moment, Itzik Simon, your one and only mission is to survive this insanity and get back home."

This war had taken my brother and turned him into our father - and worse. After it had drowned him in booze, it undermined his very humanity and then threw him into a meat-grinder. Moish's parting statement were seared into my brain, and I wrote them in heavy letters on my sketchpad: "He was a tormented man, Itzik. Broken. I am not sure he could have survived in the world." And then, below this text, I began to draw Chaim's last moments - the cratered no-man's-land, the swirling snow, the flash of weapons, the exploding shells, and the thin shadowy line of soldiers with fixed bayonets raging across this field. Chaim was at the far right, his whole body lifted off the ground, almost horizontal, his rifle falling from his hand and a gaping wound in his chest. He had an otherworldly look on his face, more of relief than of fear or pain.

Below the drawing I wrote; "This is insanity!" I slipped the drawing into the middle of the pad. I knew I could not mail it home. It portrayed too much, and the censor would destroy it. Even showing it to someone might present a problem, so it remained hidden. I did not have the heart to show it to Mama after I got home, nor did Virginia ever see it, but I kept it my whole life.

***

"Sorry I dumped all my stuff on you, Isaac. It was out of line."

No need to apologize, Damon. I wish I could say it. Mental telepathy. The ability of two people to communicate with one another using only the power of their thoughts. I wonder if that would work. I remember when it was the craze in the first part of the nineteen hundreds. Famous people from Sir Arthur Conan Doyle to Albert Einstein and author Upton Sinclair were taken up with it. You couldn't pick up a newspaper without some article about these amazing mental feats. Unfortunately, they were all shown to be frauds. It would be nice, though.

"My shift is over, Isaac. It's almost eight in the morning. I'll see you in a few days."

I give him a double-double.

"Thank you! What's that for?"

I wish I could smile. In fact, I try to smile.

I might as well try the eye movements. Left, right, up, down - I go through this exercise ten times, trying to picture myself sitting on the deck of our house and looking at the bird-feeders and nearby bushes on the left, the tomatoes and vegetables on the right, the roses directly ahead of me, and the table with my bottle of stout and bowl of peanuts in front of me. And Virginia by my side. Birds, veggies, roses, beer! A whole lot more interesting than the points on a compass.

Chapter 19

"Good morning, Grandpa Isaac. It's just after ten on a gloomy, drizzly Sunday. I think it is May nineteenth. Sorry."

Nothing to be sorry about dear Ginnie.

She sits on the bed next to me. "Someone trimmed your beard. It looks really good." She holds my face gently between both hands and kisses my forehead. "So, the big news is that I am finished with school. Graduation was yesterday! I'm not sure what comes next. In the meantime I will continue to be one of the many well-educated baristas at Starbucks. It pays for my car and even covers the wonderfully low rent I'm giving my folks for the apartment above the garage. Oh, I probably forgot to tell you I gave up the place Jake and I had in Boston, and moved back with them. I think I really need to be near them right now."

It is so nice to see her so chatty, so animated. For months the sorrow of Jake's death seemed to overwhelm her. She was able to focus on her school work, but whenever she did not have a specific task that needed her full attention, the wave of sadness swelled and enveloped her.

I hate the expression, "Time heals all wounds." It doesn't. What time does is dilute the pain in everything else that happens, but the pain is never altogether gone. Time gives you the option to let go without forgetting. Time teaches you that you can endure. But the scar remains.

***

"Well, Private," the doctor said, "it is time to remove those stitches. The wound is healing nicely." And with that he deftly began to snip each stitch with a scissors and yank each thread with a pointed tweezer and then drop them into a basin Nurse Kathleen was holding. My skin had kind of grown into the threads and it stung each time he yanked one out. When he was done, the nurse rubbed some ointment into the skin and then wrapped my thigh in a loose bandage.

It was two months since my injury. Finally the stitches were out.

I was now allowed to spend most of the day out of bed. I was still in the splint, but only needed to have the leg elevated at night. There was a YMCA hut about a quarter mile away; I was able to wheel myself down there, have a cup of coffee and doughnuts, and play cards and socialize with other patients. No one talked about what had happened to them; how they had come to be in this place with their missing limbs, scarred faces, and damaged bodies. It was a dark humor that bound us together - descriptive and ironic nicknames were created. I became known as Isaac the Terrible, both for my near-Russian ancestry and for the nasty wound on my thigh. I remember Sam the Stump (no legs), Tom Thumb (no thumbs), and Gorgeous George (terribly disfigured face). It was sick, but somehow it provided an understanding of what we had each experienced without us having to utter a single word about it.

I made sketches of many of the men and we put them up on the walls. Gorgeous George was the first of our group to be sent home, and when he said his farewells to us, he asked if he could take his picture with him. We replaced it with a little sign inscribed with his real name, his nickname and the words, "Gone Home." It became a way of keeping track of the comings and goings.

It was now mid-June, and the summer heat was building. The hospital tent was hot, with little ventilation. Outside, the nearest shade trees were a few hundred yards away, across a pathless uneven field. There were wooden benches under the trees and I looked enviously at the men who had made their way out there. One particularly hot and muggy afternoon I tried to wheel myself over to join them but soon managed to get my wheelchair stuck in a ditch. As I struggled to move on, the chair flipped on its side and I landed in the muddy grass, and smacked my outstretched leg on the ground. I screamed from the pain, which got the attention of the men under the trees. Two of them navigated their way to me on their crutches, realized immediately that they could not lift me up, so they went to the tent and returned minutes later with two nurses and a doctor who dragged me and my wheelchair back to the path and got me back to my bed.

"This fall could have set back the bone healing process," the doctor scowled. "I need to remove the splint and take a look."

After about ten minutes of poking and prodding, he announced that he did not see any obvious problem. He reapplied the splint, and hooked it up to the contraption that kept my leg elevated. "We'll keep it in traction for two weeks, before we ease back on it."

I wasn't sure whether it was a punishment for doing something so stupid as to try to cross an uneven field in the chair, or whether it was really a medical necessity. Either way, I had no control over the situation, and the prospect of not being able to get out of bed for two weeks was depressing. On the bright side, it might delay my return to the front by a few weeks, and I was certainly OK with that.

The next morning I received two items in the mail - a letter from Reuven and a picture card of Southampton from Moish saying he was about to board the ship that would bring him home. I was happy for him, but can't deny I was also envious. I wished him a safe journey home.

Reuven's letter was upsetting. He was now the only Jewish man in the company, and he was feeling isolated. He made a comment about an incident that occurred while they were enjoying some down-time after several days of hard work. The censor had obliterated part of Reuven's description, but he did leave Reuven's statement that the incident involved "Billy B and his crew."

I knew exactly what he meant. Billy Baldwin had never been subtle in his attitude towards Reuven, Benny and me. We made a point of avoiding him as much as possible, but Reuven now alone, had become the target for his anti-Semitism. As I read the letter, I hoped our lieutenant, who censored it, was able to read between the lines and figure out what Reuven was saying and, more importantly, take action to get Baldwin in line.

I remembered Moish's account of Chaim punching out a fellow soldier who had called him a "Kike." I could see this happening in Company D if the lieutenant didn't do something to put Baldwin in his place. I wondered about Lieutenant McAdoo's views and sensitivities around these issues. I certainly didn't feel that he was overtly anti-Semitic, but was he aware enough of what was going on? Reuven was well-liked and respected by most of the men - for his smarts, as well as his sense of humor and, of course, his ability to do the work. I knew that the most important thing to McAdoo was to keep his boys focused and to avoid strife within the ranks. I hoped he would deal with this situation before it got out of hand.

In his next letter Reuven wrote, "The Billy B problem has been resolved. You might even be seeing him in your part of the world." I learned later from Reuven that three days after he had sent the letter talking about Baldwin and his crew, the unit had come under fire while walking to their work-site (another bridge that needed repair). While they hunkered down as best they could, McAdoo had sent Baldwin and two others to scout the area for better shelter. Baldwin had been badly injured by an exploding shell. Reuven was inclined to think that McAdoo wanted Baldwin out of the way.

***

Ginnie is combing my beard and humming to herself. She stops. "I know you're there, Grandpa Isaac, but I have a sense that you kind of come and go. I'm not sure what it is, 'cause I can't tell whether you're awake or asleep, but I feel that sometimes you *are* listening and other times you're far away in your thoughts and memories."

I blink twice.

She giggles like a little girl. "So you're back from your mind-wanderings now?"

Yes.

"I was thinking this morning while I was on the subway coming to visit you about one of your Charlie the mouse stories - the one where the other mice pick on him and call him names. You didn't tell it to me very often. Do you remember it?"

I remember it well. It was the last one I thought up.

"I don't think I fully realized it when I was little but, unlike all the other Charlie stories, this one did not end on a positive note. The ending was ambiguous and actually quite sad. Charlie was teased so much that he couldn't be comforted, even when his best friend tried so hard to help." She hesitated.

Yes, and I didn't tell it more than a couple of times because it was so hard to tell. I couldn't find any up-side to the story of Chaim's last months on earth. I could not find a way to sugar-coat the fact that if you put a person through hell, they live in hell and it is hard, sometimes impossible, for them to climb out of hell.

"I loved those Charlie stories."

I did too. They helped me to think about Chaim and to introduce him to my children and grandchildren and great-grandchildren.

***

July Fourth was the first day after my roll-over in the field that my leg was taken out of traction and I was allowed to leave the tent. All of the men who were able to be out of bed were wheeled or walked to a parade ground in the center of the hospital complex. There had to be over five hundred men there. We were parked in rows under the blazing sun opposite a temporary stage on which were seated about a dozen officers in spiffy uniforms with multiple ribbons and shiny bars and leaves. The stage was under a canopy and flanked by flagpoles flying the American flag and flags of the different branches of the military. A brass band, also under a canopy, was off to the side playing patriotic songs.

The band stopped and an army chaplain prayed for us all, then launched into a fiery speech about service, sacrifice and love of God and country. Then a general gave the exact same speech, and even the colonel in charge of the hospital seemed to repeat it. The one person not in uniform on the stage was introduced as "the Senator from the great state of Illinois." His speech was indistinguishable from the others. The only thing that kept me awake was the smell of chicken and steak being cooked on open fires at the far end of the parade ground.

Finally, the speeches ended, the band got going again and those of us that could, hobbled, rolled or limped over to the food. It was a good meal - by far the best I ate since arriving at the hospital. I looked around for anyone I knew - I somehow expected to find Baldwin, but fortunately did not see him.

A few of the dignitaries who had been up on the stage circulated through the crowd of wounded men, shaking hands that were still there and slapping people on the back. The senator worked the crowd like he was courting our votes. He approached the soldier sitting right next to me. The young man was strapped into a wheelchair having lost both his legs, and the left side of his face was severely scarred from burns. The Senator reached out to shake his hand, but the soldier did not move. "I'm from Chicago, Illinois," he said. "I voted for you, Senator Lewis, because you said you would keep us out of this bloody war. I believed you, but your promise has gone the same way as my legs - except that you, Senator, can get up and walk away. I can't."

The senator's jaw dropped. He stammered, patted the soldier on his back and mumbled, "Thank you for your service, son," and he turned and skulked away, but not before the soldier's response.

"Thanks for nothing, Senator!"

He ruined my first opportunity to shake hands with a senator! Big deal. "I'm Isaac Simon, from Massachusetts," I said.

"Winston Evans," he replied. "Chicago."

We shook hands. "Yes, I did hear you were from that part of the world."

He laughed. "I can't tell you the shock when I saw that bastard up on the stage. I actually helped out on his campaign. I even got to shake his hand two years ago at the July Fourth parade. How's that for irony! I tell you, when I saw him up there I was ready to blow a gasket. And then when he came up to me," his voice was angry, bitter, "I could not hold back."

"There was no need for you to hold back."

"At least I didn't curse at him."

"Not that he didn't deserve it."

"I guess," he said, and then after a long pause he continued, "I'm going home in a month or two. They're sending me home like this! What the hell am I going to do? I was a high school science teacher before I got into this mess. I have a hard time seeing myself back in the classroom. I try to picture myself up there in front of them, and I can't. Hell, I can't even see how I can get myself up the stairs and through the front door of the school."

There was nothing I could say.

"Time to get you back to the ward, Isaac." It was Nurse Liz. "Can you manage by yourself, or do you need a push?"

"I can do it." I shook Winston's hand again, and wished him good luck.

I have said before that war is random. I learned many years after my conversation with Winston Evans that he was one of thirty five men killed on the USS Mont Vernon in early September when it was hit by a torpedo during the journey back to America. Senator Lewis was on that same ship, and he survived.

"My dad said he found the Charlie the mouse stories amongst your papers. They were all there except the last one; he didn't find a copy of that last story, the one about Charlie being teased."

No, I could not bring myself to write it down. I'm not sure why. Perhaps it was too close, too raw. I think about my brother every day of my life. He is still in my thoughts as I lie here today.

"How about a little *Winnie the Pooh*?" Ginnie asks, after a prolonged silence. "Danielle said she left it here."

I blink twice. I hear her opening and closing the drawer in the table next to the bed.

"OK, it looks like Danielle stopped at the beginning of this chapter, 'Tiggers don't climb trees.'"

I listen to her reading about the exploits of the inquisitive and adventurous little bear and his friends. She has created different voices and speech patterns for each character. I am enchanted. Wonderful! I feel my body relax as if I am smiling from head to toe.

"They're funny things, Accidents," she reads in her slow, deep Eeyore voice. "You never have them till you're having them."

She stops. "How true that is," she says. "I think I need to think about what you just said - wise and sad old Eeyore."

Eeyore's insight into the randomness of life. I wonder what Ginnie will think about this. Will it help to dilute the pain, or will it make it all that much more meaningless? She is young, not quite twenty-three, but she is older than I was when I lost my brother. When I hear people say things like, "Oh! He's young - it will take time, but he'll get over it. He has his whole life ahead of him," I want to scream. Pain does not discriminate - it doesn't matter how old or young you are, pain is pain and loss is loss. It becomes a part of you. I think of it like an ice cube in a glass of water. The cube is cold and hard and obvious; as it melts, it becomes part of the water, but it never goes away. It changes form, but its essential character is still there - completely fused into the water.

Ginnie is silent. I can barely even hear her breathing, but I know she is still there because she is holding my hand, drumming her fingers lightly on mine. It is a habit from her childhood; something she would do when she was deep in thought. I can see her sitting on the couch next to Danielle, her step-grandmother. It's a week before her ninth birthday and she is trying to find a way to tell Danielle that she wants a CD player for her birthday - a desire that Danielle is well aware of. In fact, the CD player is already purchased and wrapped and is sitting on a high shelf in the closet in her bedroom.

Ginnie is dressed in blue jeans and a Michael Jackson T-shirt. Her bare feet are tucked under her as she leans over and takes Danielle's hand in hers. I am watching them from across the room. I see a subtle smile flash across Danielle's face as she looks down at Ginnie's fingers drumming away. "What's on your mind, Ginnie?"

"Oh, nothing."

"OK."

"Well, there *is* something," Ginnie says after a while, "but I don't know how to say it."

"Try."

Another long pause. "You see this shirt, Grammy, with Michael Jackson?"

"Uh-huh. It's beautiful."

"Well, I really like his music and the best way to listen to music is on a CD player."

"So I've been told," Danielle says, and I see that smile again.

"CD's are much better than old-fashioned records. The sound is better and they don't get scratched." Her fingers are almost making music on Danielle's wrist.

"I've heard that too."

"Well, Grammy, I was thinking how nice it would be for us to have a CD player."

"It would be very nice, Ginnie. Is that what you want for your birthday?"

I can see Ginnie's body relax and the drumming stops. She grabs Danielle's hands in hers, and kisses her on the cheek. "Thanks, Grammy," she says, and runs off. Moments later I hear Michael Jackson's "The Way You Make Me Feel" coming from her room.

I feel the rhythm on my hand. I wish I could read her thoughts.

Chapter 20

Mama wrote several letters telling me how hard they were working to make the fabric for uniforms, blankets, and other clothing for the soldiers. After four months in the hospital, all I had to wear were some donated pajamas, socks and underwear. I didn't even have a uniform and didn't expect to get one till I was ready to be sent back to the front.

I was now on a routine that allowed me to be outside most of the day and even permitted me to wheel on down to the YMCA hut in the afternoons. Some of the old crowd was there, but there were many newcomers. "Isaac the Terrible is back," I heard someone shout on my first day back. "Where've you been?" It was Sam the Stump.

I explained about my tumble and reinjuring my leg. "It bought me a few extra weeks in this lovely place."

"A few more weeks away from the front," Sam said.

"You still here, Sam? I thought you'd be long gone by now."

"They're putting me on a train to Brest day after tomorrow. Then home." He raised his voice above the drone of the place. "So this, boys, is my farewell. I will think of you all." The place fell silent. He rolled over to the wall, removed his picture and tucked it into his pocket. "How could I ever forget?"

One morning Agnes was making her rounds. She had not been in to see us for quite a while, so I asked her where she had been. "Influenza. I was in the hospital, but I'm OK now. How have you been?"

"Same as ever, Agnes."

"Are you able to draw much?"

"I don't do a hell of a lot else," I said, then apologized for my rough language.

"I've heard worse." Before she moved on to the next patient, she said, "I'll be back tomorrow with care packages collected by the Red Cross. A whole crate of them arrived and they're being sorted for distribution. And I'm still looking for an architecture book for you. I haven't forgotten."

Care packages? I had heard about them but never received one. Mama had sent some parcels over the months containing dried fruit, cookies, socks and gum, but I had never received one from a stranger.

True to her word, Agnes was back late the next afternoon with a small mountain of boxes on her cart. I was already back on my bed enduring, for the millionth time it seemed, the process of hooking up my leg to the traction contraption. Agnes handed one box to each of us in the ward.

I carefully opened my box. On top was a short note; "Dear Soldier, I hope this package finds you in good health and that it brings a small measure of comfort to you. Best wishes, Miss Virginia Appleton." There was a return address on Beacon Street in Boston.

I liked the note. I liked the fact that she did not thank me for my service - I was getting sick of that tired and empty old platitude. I liked that she realized what she could offer was small and that she had used the word "comfort." I especially liked that she was a "Miss," although it did not necessarily mean she was not a seventy year old spinster with nothing to do except knit woolen socks and mittens for soldiers.

I unpacked the box methodically. There were three undershirts, three pairs of woolen socks, a pair of gloves, a toothbrush and toothpaste, shaving soap, a razor and blades, tinned peaches and pears, three packs of cigarettes, gum, a packet of homemade shortbread cookies and, to my amazement, a box of twelve colored pencils and a pencil sharpener. I put everything except the cookies and the colored pencils into the drawer next to my bed and immediately began to draw a picture of what I could see from where I lay.

I had drawn similar pictures dozens of times, but never in color. It was an entirely different experience and I had to do it several times before I was satisfied with the result. My leg, suspended in space, was in the forefront. Behind it were the men either in their beds or sitting beside them. Some were reading, but most were in small groups enjoying the contents of the packages they had received; sharing dried fruit, nuts and cookies, trading magazines, gum and cigarettes.

By the time I was done with the drawing it was almost dark in the tent and I had nibbled my way through half the cookies.

Early the next morning I wrote a letter; *Dear Miss Appleton, Thank you so much for the package which I received yesterday. It is hard to explain how important all these things are to me. Let me simply say that everything I once had was abandoned in a ditch somewhere on the Front. The cookies are delicious. And, how could you have known to send the colored pencils! I enclose a drawing I did using them. Yours sincerely, Isaac Simon, Private, from Lawrence, Mass.*

I agonized over every word of my letter. I wanted to convey to her not only my thanks, but the strange feeling I had that she somehow knew me and I knew her. At the same time, I did not want to be too forward or inappropriate. I knew Beacon Street was a very upper class and selective part of Boston - near the Common and the State House - and the names Virginia and Appleton were not exactly names I had encountered in the working class Jewish neighborhood I had grown up in. But somehow I felt a connection to Miss Virginia.

Or maybe it was just a lonely soldier's yearning for a kind word from a woman, and the softness of her touch.

I gave the letter to the mail man, then ate my breakfast and nibbled another cookie, and waited for the nurse to come around and detach me from my traction contraption.

***

I do not recognize the movements or the touch of the nurse who is flitting around me. She (or he) makes no sound, not even breathing. My guess is this person is replacing Damon the Good while he has a couple of days off, but I can't know for sure unless someone tells me. Apparently this person did not get the memo to fill me in on the date, time, etcetera.

The person leaves without a word and I am left to fume about the communication that didn't happen. I have so little - don't they understand how important those simple bits of information are to me! I feel my pulse begin to climb, and the blood is pounding in my ears. I force myself to calm down, but not before someone is back checking on me, no doubt examining the display on my cat-machine.

It must be the same nurse who was here earlier, because not a word is spoken, no attempt made to explain why she (or he) returned to my room. "Don't get all riled up again," I tell myself. I breathe in as deeply as I can and exhale. And one more time. And then I am alone in my room again.

I mailed the letter to Virginia on July twenty-fourth. My experience with letters to and from Mama was that it took at least six weeks from the time I wrote to the time I received a reply. So I could not realistically expect anything from Virginia, if she were to write at all, until early September.

In the meantime, my medical situation was improving. I was issued a pair of crutches and soon learned to get about with great speed and efficiency. Even more importantly, the traction contraption was taken away and I could actually now sleep on my side or roll over when I wanted to. Also, I started doing exercises to flex my knee and strengthen the muscles in my leg. The doctor anticipated sending me back to my Company and the front around September fifteenth.

On August twenty-eighth, exactly five weeks after posting my letter to Virginia, the mailman handed me a letter from her. She, apparently, was even able to bend time. I sailed on my crutches to one of the benches in the shade and opened the envelope. She had written four pages! She started by saying she loved the drawing and had put it under the glass of her dressing table, and then she wrote several pages about a recent visit she and her mother had made to the Elizabeth Stewart Gardner Museum on the Fenway in Boston. She commented on the paintings and furniture, many of which I remembered from my visit there with Reuven. She told me she had baked the shortbread cookies herself - her "one and only domestic accomplishment" - and was happy that I enjoyed them.

She wished me a safe return home, soon. Her last words had me shaking. "I don't know why this is," she wrote, "but I have a feeling we shall meet someday. Best Wishes, Virginia."

***

Time moves slowly in this place. It seems like eons since I had a visitor, or even since the anonymous nurse was here. I picture our garden and do my eye movement exercises. Birds, veggies, roses, beer! I think Monday is approaching and Doctor Squeak, the neurologist, said he would return on Monday. His visit will let me know whether my eye gymnastics are real or not.

In the meantime, I have been thinking of variations to the blinking.

There is not only the number of blinks, but their duration. And once I have short and long blinks, there is the sequence in which they are used. Like Morse code, if I knew Morse code. But then, would I want to, or even have the energy to spell out every word, letter by letter? I need to find a shortcut, at least to express the important words.

***

I was sitting in the shade working on a self-portrait to enclose in the letter I planned to write to Virginia when I became aware of someone standing in front of me. His boots shone, his uniform was impeccable and his lieutenant's bars flashed in the sunlight. "On your feet, Private Simon!"

I stood hastily, gave a half-hearted salute, and waited for him to speak.

He handed me a package and an envelope. "Your orders to return to your Company, and a uniform. Good luck." He turned and walked away.

I ripped open the envelope. It contained an official-looking document that told me to report to my company commander no later than sixteen hundred hours on Friday, September thirteenth. There was also some money and a train ticket to Reims where I would be met at the train station by someone from my unit. Further instructions would follow. Of course, I had no idea where Company D was. What I did know, judging from the steady flow of new arrivals at the hospital, was that the war was not winding down.

I packed up my drawing things and made my way slowly back to the ward. Nurse Liz met me at the entrance. "We heard the news that you are to be discharged. Congratulations."

"I have to be back in about two weeks, and I'm still on crutches."

"You're getting stronger every day."

I grunted and moved to my bed, put away everything except the half-finished self-portrait and the colored pencils, and made my way outside again, deliberately leaving my crutches on the bed. If they're sending me back, I have to be able to walk! Nurse Liz watched me, but did not say a word.

I walked carefully to the YMCA hut, feeling the muscles in my leg ease and then contract. I felt I still had a long way to go before I would be fit enough for the front again, but apparently the doctors and the brass felt otherwise. There were a few men in the hut, none of whom I knew. I got a cup of coffee and a doughnut and sat alone at a table in the corner. I took out my drawing and pencils and continued to work.

No one approached me, and I was glad for that. It was a courtesy in that place - you did not interfere with someone who had withdrawn himself. I completed the self-portrait and was more than satisfied with it. I remember feeling surprised by how well I remembered the contours of my own face.

There was always writing paper available at the Y hut so I began the letter to Virginia. My letter was quite short - only a single page. I thanked her for her long descriptive letter, and told her of my visit to the Gardner Museum with a childhood friend who was now a comrade in the field. And I told her I was being discharged from the hospital to rejoin my unit in about two weeks. "I do not know what the immediate future will bring," I wrote, "but I, too, believe that when all of this is over, you and I will meet. I enclose a self-portrait. I hope you will keep it close, as I will keep your letter with me always."

I have heard of 'love at first sight.' I can honestly say that with Virginia it was 'love at first reading.' When I read that first letter, I knew we were going to spend the rest of our lives together. I just knew - and I had to convey that to her, especially as I was preparing to go back into war.

***

"Good morning, Isaac." It's Wanda. "It's about eight-thirty Monday morning, May twentieth. The weatherman says it's going to be a beautiful sunny day."

I blink twice. I am happy to hear that the joy has returned to her voice.

"Doctor Jerzak is scheduled to be here in an hour, but he's never on time."

I hear her humming as she goes through her routine. Lovely.

"Everything's looking fine, Isaac. I'll see you later."

An hour or more till Doctor Squeak gets here. I wonder what he'll have to say. I hope Allen or Danielle is here when he comes. Maybe I should do a little more of my eye gymnastics.

I hear Martha before she enters the room. She is having a conversation with someone whose voice I don't recognize and which is too soft, anyway, for me to figure out what he or she is saying. I hear two people enter the room.

"Good morning, Isaac. It's Martha. I just popped in for a minute. My friend, Sharon, and I are on our way to a meeting, but she begged me to bring her to meet you. Sharon and her husband purchased your painting at the auction."

"Pleased to meet you, Mr. Simon. I absolutely love your work."

Is it just me, or is this extremely odd? I'll try to be polite! I'd love to shake your hand! I blink a double-double, but Martha doesn't notice.

"Someone's been reading Winnie the Pooh to you. How charming. The book is beside your bed. When David and Ginnie were little they both had Pooh-bear sheets and pajamas."

"My kids did, too," Sharon responds.

An awkward silence follows. I hope they are not expecting me to jump in.

"Well, I'm afraid we have to rush off."

"Good-bye, Mr. Simon."

Don't get me wrong, I do like Martha, but she's sometimes not quite aware of what's happening around her. She seems to have missed that little lesson about walking in the shoes of another.

***

I plucked my Isaac the Terrible picture from the wall in the YMCA hut and said farewell to the men who had gathered. I was never one inclined to making speeches, but I did manage to stand up in front of the group and wish them a safe return home. I was wearing my new uniform for the first time - it felt strange but fit surprisingly well.

Before sunrise the next morning, September eleventh, I dressed and made sure that the note from Mama, Chaim's heavily censored letter and Virginia's four-page letter were all safely buttoned in my shirt pocket. I packed my few things into a back pack and walked to the parade area where I was met by the truck that would bring me to the railway station in Rouen. There were six of us in the back of the truck - none from my unit. Very little was said. Each of us had a sense of what lay ahead. I had received a letter from Captain Swan instructing me to take the Rouen to Reims train that would arrive before noon on September eleventh. I was to wait in the tea-room in the Reims station until my escort from the Company arrived.

I found my train and took a seat in the third class compartment. Besides a handful of elderly men and women, and a few soldiers, the carriage was empty. I had to change trains in Paris. The station there was busy and enormous. It took me some time to find the right platform for the train to Reims, and when I did I discovered that the train was delayed and would not be leaving for another hour. I looked at the huge clock that hung above the platform - it was nine-fifteen. If things went according to plan, I'd be arriving at Reims minutes before noon.

I entered a station coffee-shop and found a table near the door. The place was filled with men in uniform from all different parts of the world - French colonial soldiers from Africa, British, Belgians, Dutch, and Americans - but despite the crowd, there was an eerie quiet about the place. I made a few quick pencil sketches.

The train pulled into Reims at five minutes before noon. I stood by the doorway to the tea-room, scanning the room looking for a familiar face. Suddenly I was seized from behind; "Itzik! Itzik! You're back! How are you, old friend?"

"Reuven!" We hugged, then found a table and ordered a large lunch.

"How are you feeling, Itzik?"

"My body is doing OK. Still a little pain, but not too bad. I have a long way to go before my strength is back to where it was before, but I'll be OK. How are you?"

"You get used to it."

I was not sure what he meant, but it didn't sound good. I decided not to press him further. He had lost weight and his eyes were sunken and ringed with dark circles. There was a dullness to them that was unnerving. "You saved my life, Reuven."

He did not reply. Our meal arrived and we ate in silence.

"You still drawing?" he asked, as we ate our dessert.

"Of course. It's what keeps me sane, I think."

"How about the nurses in the hospital? Anything interesting in that regard?"

"They were all friendly and competent - but not the kind of friendly you're suggesting."

There was so much I wanted to talk with him about - what I had learned about Chaim, the news from home about Uncle Kalner's new wife, and, of course, Miss Virginia Appleton. But I felt uneasy. It was almost like I had recently enjoyed a six month vacation, while Reuven was being drawn more deeply and horrifyingly into the uncompromising realities of the war. I felt guilt for being wounded.

"We'll spend the night in Reims," he said. "I've found us a place. Then tomorrow we set off to find the company. We've been on the move a lot recently, gaining a lot of ground, although one place looks pretty much like the next - scarred land, barbed wire and bodies." He paused and touched my hand. "You do get used to it." He fell silent.

"I see you earned yourself a stripe - corporal."

"Somebody's got to do it."

"Did you imply that we have the rest of this day off?" I asked.

"I did. Is there anything you'd like to do? See a big, beautiful old Catholic cathedral, perhaps, my good little Yiddisher boy?"

"You know me well. Lead on!"

"Our lodging is between here and the cathedral. We'll drop your things there along the way."

As we walked to our small hotel we passed an art supply and framing store. I went in to buy a couple of sketchbooks and more colored pencils. The store-keeper asked what I could possibly want with these items in the middle of a war. I pulled my old sketchpad from my pack and gave him one of the drawings I had done in the coffee shop in Paris. He asked me to sign it, and took twenty percent off the price of the sale. That was the first artwork I ever sold.

The cathedral had been badly damaged by German shells during the first years of the war. The roof was mostly gone and the stone walls and pointed arches were charred. There were gaping holes where the windows had been - the stained glass had fortunately been taken down and hidden in a safe place when the war started. Most of the rubble had been removed and a cleanup process was underway. I sat on the floor, as we had done in that little village church the day after the Seder, and marveled at the awesome beauty and peacefulness of the stark skeletal remains of the seven-hundred year old cathedral: the soaring interior, the window opening, the sculptures, the structure. A brilliant late summer light poured in, making every detail stand out in sharp relief. It was awfully quiet, except for the noises of crows that had made their nests on the exposed tops of the walls.

"One thing I've never understood about Christianity," Reuven said while we were having a late dinner in a rather fancy restaurant that I could not afford, "is why they have an implement of torture as the main symbol of the religion."

"I really don't know," I replied, "but they sure know how to surround it with beauty."

***

Danielle is here. "Good morning, Isaac. It's ten-thirty on a warm, sunny Monday. Doctor Jerzak, the neurologist, is here to see how you're doing."

"Do you hear me, Mr. Simon?"

I blink twice.

"Good. If you remember last time I saw you I asked you to try to work on moving your eyes from side to side and up and down. Do you remember?"

Yes.

"Did you try to do it?"

I've been doing the eye gymnastics all weekend! *Yes.*

"Well, then let's see how you're doing. I'm going to shine my light into your eyes. Keep them both open and when I give the word, let's see how your eyes have responded. OK?"

OK.

"Look to your right. Now left. Right again. Front. Left…"

How long is this going to go on, doc? I'm waving my eyes around like a surrender flag!

"Good. Now let's try up. Down. Up. Down. Right…"

I surrender, doc! Tell me if you see me!

I hear him writing his notes. "There is a small amount of directional movement from left to right. Up and down is not detectable, but the fact that I can discern some side to side movement does mean there is a chance there could be more, with work."

And I thought I was performing like a star gymnast! A small amount of directional movement - what the hell does that mean! This is depressing.

"What kind of work are you talking about, Doctor?" Danielle asks.

"We need an exercise regime, like an athlete. Start out with ten reps three times a day. Each rep is up, down, left, right, front. We'll see how things look in a week, maybe ramp up to fifteen reps. We don't want to overdo it."

"Did you hear what the doctor recommends, Isaac?"

I did. Sounds like torture, but I'll give it a try. I blink twice, and Doctor Squeak departs.

Danielle sits. "Let's continue with the little bear, OK?" She kisses me lightly on the cheek.

Chapter 21

The next morning we wondered around the ancient Roman Mars Gate, and also spent more time at the cathedral. After lunch we picked up our things at the hotel and walked to the train station. As we sat next to each other on the train, I realized that Reuven and I had barely spoken all day. Not that there was any tension between us, it was more a sense of detachment, the feeling that you don't want to get too close for fear of potential loss. He had seen too much.

When he had said earlier that you get used to it, I knew what he meant - you get used to death, to seeing people around you being killed and maimed. And you get used to killing. Although, of course, what he really meant was that you never get used to these things. Ever.

We arrived in Verdun in just under two hours and we were immediately aware that something big was happening. Trains with wounded soldiers trundled slowly through the station without stopping, heading towards Reims. The city was bursting with military vehicles moving in the opposite direction - towards the front. Reuven approached a French Military Police officer and asked him what was going on. "Big push. Americans and French. Big push, move fast."

By the time we found a place to stay it was night and a light but steady rain had begun to fall. It would continue for days. Next morning we hitched a ride on an American ambulance that was going in our direction - the town of Les Eparges, where the Company had been when Reuven left it two days before. They were gone. We found a medical station and asked if anyone had any idea where our unit was. The only advice we received was to walk south-east, and listen for the guns. "They're all on the move," one of the wounded men said.

Reuven opened his compass, glanced at the dial, then at the surrounding landscape. "That pile of rubble about a mile down the valley," he said, and we began our arduous trudge through the mud and rain. We crossed our abandoned trenches and barbed wire and picked our way between the craters and gray stumps of trees. The smell of the aftermath of battle was overpowering - clearly not all the dead had been collected.

We came across the body of a soldier lying face down in the mud. "You'd better take his rifle and his ammunition, Itzik. You might be needing them. His bayonet, too." Reuven helped me remove the things I needed.

"Shouldn't we bury him?"

"No time," he said, and we moved on. We found a bombed out farmhouse that provided enough shelter from the rain for me to disassemble and clean and oil the rifle and put it back together. I fired off a couple of shots into the air to make sure it was working. Reuven consulted his compass again and pointed into the vast oozing lifeless terrain. "Let's go."

***

"Nurse Melinda told me about Doctor Jerzak's visit. I guess we have some work to do." Damon the Good is back from his weekend. I hope he had a relaxing time. I hope he was able to keep his demons at bay. "I know it's one o'clock in the morning, but are you up for your eye exercises, Isaac?"

I blink once. *No.*

"That's OK. I can't make you, nor would I. I guess you're old enough to make your own decisions." He laughs.

I laugh in my own way, then give him a double-double.

"You're welcome. Anything else I can do for you?"

Yes, I'm pretty sure there are a couple of things you could do for me, but how do I tell you.

He does not wait for my answer. I'm sure he wasn't expecting one. "See you later, Isaac." He touches my shoulder and leaves.

How could I convey my Morse code-like idea to him? If I go down that path, will I end up lost in some endless space without a map? How do I get him to pick up on what I'm trying to do? Or maybe I should wait for Danielle; she's the one person who can sense my needs. The problem with any puzzle is where to begin, and how to know when you're not making progress and need to begin again somewhere else. But I am at an even more difficult stage - how do I convey that I have the beginnings of a good solution when everyone is looking in a totally different direction.

Reuven and I spoke very little as we moved across the battlefield. We approached the rows of barbed wire that the Germans had set up, and crossed them where our tanks had plowed through as if they weren't there. We continued toward the network of trenches. The smell hit us first. It was ungodly. Dozens of abandoned bodies lay half-buried in the mud.

I had come to war seeking revenge for the death of my brother. This was my first close-up encounter with the enemy, the first time I had crossed no-man's-land into the German side, and all I saw was rotting corpses and marauding rats.

"We've gotta get past this, Reuven."

He didn't answer, but kept moving. We could see the tracks made by our tanks as they had plunged across the trenches, so we followed them.

At some point we both became aware of the sound of cannon-fire, and we could see smoke lifting in the distance. We were at the top of a small rise. Far off to our right we noticed a line of vehicles moving slowly towards the front. "The highway to hell," Reuven muttered. "Let's go there."

As we were nearing the road we heard an unusual roar from above us and, looking up, we saw six German bi-planes streaking towards the jam-packed row of vehicles.

"I've heard of these flying machines, but this is the first time I've ever seen them," I said.

"Yes. They add a whole other dimension to this chaos. You can't only look across the field anymore, you've got to keep one eye always searching the heavens."

We were close enough by now to see the American insignia on the vehicles. The planes flew low over the column and dropped dozens of bombs hitting several trucks. Moments later, a group of French planes arrived and went after the Germans. Reuven and I took shelter in a crater and watched the dogfight, which lasted only about ten minutes before the Germans flew off, leaving two of their number in fiery ruins on the field. Reuven cheered as the German planes hit the ground.

When we reached the road we discovered the one-hundred-and first Infantry, which was part of our Division, making its way to the front. One of the military policemen who was trying to sort out the traffic jam told us our Company was about five hundred yards further down the road working on repairing a bridge which had been partially blown up by the retreating Germans.

Twenty minutes later we reported to Lieutenant McAdoo and five minutes after that I was given a pick-axe and shovel and we joined the work on the bridge. It was after dark before we had the bridge stable enough to allow one vehicle at a time to pass slowly over it. I hadn't eaten all day, nor had I worked this hard in six months. I fell exhausted on my bunk and slept until I was woken by Reuven before dawn. He gave me something resembling dry bread and an apple and then pulled me out of the bunker and back to the bridge to begin shoring it up.

By around noon traffic was flowing steadily and we were given a break. Captain Swan found me half asleep under the bridge. He tapped me on the shoulder. "Good to have you back, Simon, Don't get up. I trust you are fully recovered."

My whole body ached from the exertion of the past twenty-four hours, and my stomach growled, but my injured leg, surprisingly, seemed to be fine. "My leg and ribs are OK, sir, but I'm not used to all the work," I replied. "I'm sure I'll be fine in a couple of days."

"Carry on," he said, and walked off.

"We go through periods like this - working like crazy for weeks, trying to keep up with the line of advance," Reuven said. "Then we have a little down-time when we do maintenance sorts of things, and wait. Then we move again, and things go nuts. And, of course, there are times when we actually are thrown into the fighting."

"So, what phase are we in right now?"

He held up his hand as if to silence me. The noise of the battle a few hundred yards away was unceasing. "The guns are moving. We'll be moving before too long. Get some rest. Eat something."

And so it went on for endless days.

***

"I thought I'd stop by for a quick visit on my way to work," Allen says. "Danielle told me about Doctor Jerzak's eye movement test. She says there is hope."

Hope. What the hell is that! I've been through enough battles to know that survival has little to do with hope. It's eighty percent dumb luck, ten percent effort, and ten percent keeping your big head down. I'm not going to do Doctor Squeak's eye gymnastics! It's too much work and I'm too old. Maybe I'll see if I can get through to Danielle with my sort-of Morse-code idea, but I'm not even sure I want to attempt that. Just leave me to my memories and my...

"I almost forgot. It's a little before seven on Tuesday morning, May twenty-first, 2002. Traffic into Boston was surprisingly light. The weather is gloomy, although it is supposed to clear up this afternoon."

He pauses. I thank him.

"Ginnie is back living at home. It is nice to have her, even though she and Martha have their moments."

Martha is not easy to take in large doses. I like the fact that I can think these things without ever fearing I would accidently say something not very nice.

"More importantly, she knows we are near if she wants to talk. She's lonely. I wish I could make her world better."

It is still too soon, but I wonder if Ginnie will take the risk to love again. I've lived through a lot, but I've never had to deal with the kind of loss she has experienced. Yes, when my Virginia died I was heartbroken. But she was ill for so long, I had time to adjust to the inevitability of her death. We talked about it - she and I, and we made plans. But Jake's death was so sudden, so unreal, impossible to comprehend.

I can only hope that dear Ginnie is able to find the courage to take the risk. What did I just say about hope? Oh, Itzik, you are too cynical! Hope is the starting point for every new thing. Without it we would do nothing more than sit on our fat asses and eat.

***

Miraculously a letter from Miss Virginia Appleton found me at the front on the last day of October. We were having a brief period of down time after working for twenty hours straight setting up machine gun emplacements and dodging German shells in what once was a beautiful forest west of the Meuse River.

I opened her letter carefully. Nestling between the two folded sheets of writing paper was a photograph of the most wonderful person I had ever seen. She was looking directly at the camera (at me); a broad smile lit up her face. She appeared to be about my age. Her hair, parted at the side, hung in gentle curls down to her shoulders. The picture showed someone who was care-free and independent, and the fact that she had sent it to me, also suggested a person who had her own mind and lived by her own rules.

She knew we came from different worlds, but that clearly did not bother her. In fact, it intrigued her. Her brief letter thanked me for my self-portrait, which was now also under the glass on her dressing table. There were a few lines about spending time at the Red Cross building putting together care packages, but she also said she was sending me more cookies, colored pencils and other things. In signing off she wrote, "I hope you like this photograph - I had it taken just for you. Maybe, hopefully, one day soon you will see the real person."

Virginia was always very bold, even in those old days when women were supposed to be quiet and demure and do whatever their husbands or fathers told them to do. In that sense she reminded me of my mother who refused to be bossed around by anyone. It was Virginia, in fact, who introduced my mother to the Right to Vote movement. There are several legendary stories of my working class Jewish mother meeting with the fancy high-brow Beacon Street ladies. Shall we say that she impressed them with her blunt manner of speaking. Remember, she was a union organizer - she did not waste time with the niceties.

When I think about those first letters Virginia and I exchanged, I am astounded by how direct we were with one another. Perhaps it was the war, or maybe it was simply our youth, but those letters had a seething undercurrent of passion. We had never met, we knew almost nothing about each other, but there I was in the middle of the battlefield with shells exploding, and the mud, the stench, the chaos, and I was making plans with this lovely woman to meet after the insanity was over.

Chapter 22

Trainwreck is wiping my face with a warm cloth. It feels so good. I give her a double-double and she laughs a little. "Thank you, too, Isaac." She pats my hand and squeezes it. "It's almost the end of my shift. Damon will be in soon."

She's more talkative than usual. There is an easy, relaxed quality to her voice today. "It's been a quiet evening," she continues. "You were very tired, I guess, because you slept through your visits. Your grandson Allen was here for a while, and so was your friend, Danielle. They both said they'd be back tomorrow."

I do have a vague recollection of them being here, but time seems to merge and collapse. There are times, too, when I simply cannot generate the energy to wake up. I hover in that in-between place where I feel like I am dreaming but have some degree of control over where the dream is going. I often find myself flying over large distances and back and forth in time - from Linkeve to Boston, to France, to our home, to Virginia's grave. I love these journeys, despite the unhappy memories they sometimes bring.

***

November eleventh was another soggy, muddy, cold day - and glorious. We had been told that the armistice would go into effect at eleven in the morning. Somehow, some politicians or military brass, or both, saw poetry in the idea of the eleventh hour, of the eleventh day, of the eleventh month. For those of us on the front, the idea that we should keep fighting and killing until a randomly appointed time was crazy. We kept our heads down and prayed that we would not be the last casualty before the clock ticked to that fateful moment.

And then it happened. The guns went quiet and for a few beautiful seconds all you heard was the sound of the rain drops in the mud. After that, a giant exhale followed by shouts of joy. Reuven climbed up onto the top of the bunker wall, then called down to me. I scrambled up. Through the mist we could see our men running and dancing and jumping and, while we could not see them, we could hear the Germans cavorting as wildly as we were.

"We made it Itzik! We made it!" Reuven hugged me and lifted me off my feet.

"I never doubted it for a moment." We laughed and lost our balance and landed in the mud. And we could not stop laughing.

Our officers let us go wild. I don't think they had a choice. Bottles of wine and whiskey materialized, along with candy and cookies and all kinds of tinned food. Fires were lit and we sat around them eating and drinking, ignoring the light rain. By nightfall the clouds had moved on and the stars came out. I couldn't remember when last I had seen them, because even if there were no clouds, there was always a pall of smoke from the cannon-fire and the burning woods. We slept under the stars that night. It was cold, but I didn't care.

The next morning was bright and clear; you could see for miles, and what we saw was mind-boggling. The harsh light of day shone dispassionately on the devastation all around us - the charred trees, the empty fields, the churned land and the knowledge that there were hundreds, thousands, of dead men out there.

Our job for the next number of days was to scour the battlefield looking for bodies. When we found one, we were to cover it with a blanket and place a marker at the head so that the graves people - many of them Black soldiers in the Pioneer units - could find them more easily and remove them for proper burial. I remembered Reuven's words to me when he met me at the train station on my return from the hospital. "You get used to it." You never do. You get numb, perhaps, but you never feel like it is normal.

***

"It's seven a.m. Wednesday morning, May twenty-second. The sun is up, the sky is blue and all is well." Damon the Good is cheerful today; I hope things are on the mend for him. "Have you been doing your eye movements, Isaac?"

No. I have not been in the right frame of mind; too many memories. And it's too much work.

"It's up to you, Isaac. No one, not even me, can force you to do it if you don't want to."

Thank you. I appreciate the fact that you recognize it is my choice, my decision.

"Your beard could use a little care." He sits beside me and begins to comb.

I hear footsteps. "So, *you're* the groomer. I'm Ginnie, Isaac's great-granddaughter. I've noticed your stylings before." Her voice has a little giggle under it.

"Pleased to meet you, Ginnie. I'm Damon - groomer and nurse. Isaac has such a rich beard; I just love to comb it."

"You should have seen his hair. Not that I saw it in real life, but there are pictures of him in his sixties with pure white flowing locks, parted in the middle and reaching below his shoulders. He was a real hippie! Bell-bottomed jeans and all!"

"I'd love to see that!"

"I'll bring in the evidence," she laughs. "Unfortunately, by the time I was old enough to notice, most of his hair was gone, and what was left he kept pretty short."

What the hell, so I was born forty-five years too soon! I loved that period - the music, the freedom, the political activism, the sense of being together. I never did get into the marijuana although I must confess I did try it once; it brought out a flood of bad memories which I did not want to encounter again. It scared me straight.

"Well, I have to move on," Damon says. "Nice meeting you."

"Yes. Nice meeting you, too."

Don't read too much into the tone of voice, their intonation, Itzik. But wouldn't it be a wonderful thing if they could soothe each other's wounds.

***

The shooting had ceased, but we remained in France. We spent a lot of time helping the French fix roads and bridges, rebuild town halls and other government buildings. We had a fair amount of free time to travel, visit old friends, or do whatever we wanted. I went alone or with Reuven to explore nearby villages and towns and I made dozens of sketches. I went back to the art store in Reims where the store-keeper remembered me and welcomed me with a warm hug followed by strong coffee and delicious flaky French pastries. I was able to trade six sketches of the Reims cathedral for a fifty percent discount on a set of watercolors, brushes and some paper-board. Over the following weeks I found the time to teach myself how to work in this medium.

Reuven and I made a special trip in early March to visit the family we had been billeted with when we first arrived in France. We found Monsieur Chaisson working in his field with both of his sons. He was thrilled to see us, introduced us to Daniel and Jean, and brought us into the cottage where they served us coffee and sweet butter cookies. We asked about Yvette, and were told she had recently married a young man from the village and had moved to Brest with her new husband. He worked on the docks, loading American soldiers and their equipment onto the transport ships. She worked in a restaurant that served the departing troops.

The drawings I had made of Yvette and her father when we lived with them were lost when I had been injured, so I asked him if I could draw him and his sons. We went outside and I had them sit on a bench beside the cottage. I drew quickly in pencil, finishing two drawings one of which I gave to him, and the other I kept.

Signs of normal life were gradually returning to France. As Reuven and I traveled we found people hard at work rebuilding, repairing and planting. There were also so many men with missing limbs and scarred bodies. Many more with scarred minds that no one was able to talk about - least of all the men themselves.

I received almost a letter a week from Virginia. We corresponded as if we had known each other since childhood, although I have to confess some of the things she wrote about, like the high society parties she felt obligated to attend, were beyond me. I had glimpsed this world in Mr. Hardwicke's office with its opulent paintings, carpets, and furniture, but it was only a glimpse; I had no idea how people actually lived in that world. I worried how she would react if she were to visit Mama and me in our small apartment in Lawrence, and I raised my concern to her.

"I really don't care where you come from, Isaac," she responded. "I care about what you do and who you are; and I'm perfectly happy with what I've learned thus far."

We were writing to each other so frequently that I was sure her parents must have been aware of my existence, but Virginia wrote nothing about their reaction to me, so I asked her. Her response was simply that her parents were aware of me, but, "the matter has not been discussed." She added that they were forward-thinking people, Unitarians, and she did not foresee any problem with me calling on her when I returned. I had never heard of Unitarians and I was sure there had to be a reason Virginia had not discussed "the matter" with them.

Of course, I had not discussed "the matter" with my mother either. Virginia did not question me on this.

In mid-March, 1919, our division made its way by train to Brest. Reuven and I visited several restaurants near the docks hoping to find Yvette, but without success. A week later we were sailing to Boston.

On the march from the dock to the railway station in Boston the route was lined with cheering people who brought us candy and cigarettes and flowers. Then we went on to Camp Devens. I sent cards to everyone I knew letting them know that I was back in Massachusetts.

It was almost a month before we were demobilized. On May first Reuven and I, and many others, were on a train back to Boston. We parted company there - he to Providence to see his family, and I to Lawrence.

I returned to a city that was in chaos. Police and militiamen were everywhere and as I got closer to our apartment, which was not far from the mills, I could hear the familiar sounds of picket line chants and songs. I redirected myself toward the mills. I approached cautiously and watched from a safe distance; thousands of men, women and children confronted the police. I scanned the crowd looking for my mother but could not see her. In a far corner of the open space in front of the building I saw a group of about twenty militiamen with rifles and fixed bayonets. My stomach turned and I almost vomited.

I ran to our apartment and threw myself on the couch, burying my face in the pillows. My hands trembled and I felt the sweat on the back of my neck. It took some time for my body to relax and my breathing to return to normal. I got up, put the kettle on for tea and began to pace back and forth. The apartment was virtually unchanged - the old couch where I had slept after Uncle Kalner had left, the table and chairs, the wood stove. The wall above the sofa was now decorated with half a dozen drawings I had sent home from England and France.

Suddenly the door swung open and my mother ran towards me. I hugged her and lifted her off her feet. "I kept my promise, Mama. I have come home in one piece."

She sat me down at the table while she fussed about. She moved back and forth between me and the stove as she finished preparing tea and a feast. I could not count how many times she touched my face, my arms, my hair, how many times she cupped my face in her hands and looked into my eyes, kissed me. "You are really back, Itzik," she said, over and over.

I went to bed early, exhausted, and slept late, waking to find that Mama had stayed home from the picket line. We drank countless cups of tea and ate bread she baked fresh that morning and talked about how she had coped with me being gone all that time.

"What's the strike all about?" I asked.

"We've been out since February. Why we do this in the winter, I don't know! Anyway, the reason is when we managed to negotiate a reduction in the work week from fifty-four to forty-eight hours, we saw our weekly pay go down by more than ten percent. That hurt a lot of people, so we tried to get a pay raise. Owners said 'No' - so we went on strike."

"Are you one of the leaders, again?"

"No. I was happy to give that role up to the younger women."

"How have you managed? Money, food?"

"We've had a lot of support from local stores, churches and even some rich folks in Boston have sent money to the strike fund. I've been getting along OK. Kalner has sent money, and Ben has brought baskets of food and firewood."

"Like 1912 all over again."

She held my hands. "And you, my boy, how are you doing?"

"Too soon to tell, Mama," I shrugged. "It's so good to be home, to be away from all of that."

She commented on my news-less letters, all of which she had kept.

I tried to explain to her that I did not write about my experiences because of the censor; but in truth, I simply could not have written about them. She asked me about my wound and I showed her the garish semicircular scar on my thigh. She gasped and gently touched the skin. "Does it still hurt?"

"No, Mama. That wound is healed."

Tears filled her eyes, but she asked no more questions, not even about what I had learned about Chaim. I was glad of that.

Chapter 23

Chanel Number 5. Danielle is sitting beside the bed. I wonder how long she's been here. I blink three times to let her know I am awake. The idea just came to me.

"A new trick, Isaac?" She laughs.

Yes.

"Three blinks means you're awake?"

Yes.

"And a very good thing." She laughs, again. "I've been sitting here for ten minutes not wanting to disturb you; you looked so peaceful."

I thought I had only one look. How can I look peaceful now? And how is that any different from how I looked an hour ago or a month ago? I wonder if I look a little agitated right now. Because I think I am!

She puts her hand on mine, perhaps actually sensing my little tantrum. "It's almost three in the afternoon on Wednesday, May twenty-second. You're looking good - someone has been taking care of that lovely flowing beard." She pauses. "The nurse told me you have not being doing the eye movement exercises that Doctor Jerzak suggested. Is that true?"

Yes.

"Too much effort?"

Mostly I don't see the point of it. I respond with an unambiguous blink-blink.

"I wish you would try, Isaac, but it's OK if you don't feel up to it."

Thank you. With an exclamation point!

"Did the physical therapist come today?"

I don't think she did. I don't remember, but I do feel a new pain in my right hand that I don't think was there a while ago. Who knows? I blink once. *No.*

***

Our apartment, as I have said, was small and provided me little privacy. I wanted to write to Virginia, but didn't want Mama to know. In the early afternoon I told her I needed to go to the newspaper to see Mr. Hardwicke to let them know I was back and hoped to return to work soon.

"What's the urgency, Itzik? You haven't even been home twenty-four hours and you want to go back to work? You deserve a long vacation. Mr. Hardwicke can wait. I didn't hear anything about *his* sons going off to France!"

I ignored her dig at the upper class. "I can't just sit around, Mama. And, anyhow, you'll be going to the picket line tomorrow."

She threw up her hands, shrugged. "Go, then. I'll put together something for a nice supper."

I stopped at the general store on the way to the Tribune, bought some writing paper and envelopes, and found a place to sit at a small café nearby. I began to write my first letter to Virginia as a civilian; no more "Miss Appleton," no more "Private Isaac Simon."

I told her as unambiguously as I could that I wanted to see her as soon as possible. It was a short letter - not even a full page. I looked at the empty space below and could not leave it that way. I drew a picture of two birds sitting close together on the branch of a tree, singing. As I was about to fold the letter to place it in the envelope, I glanced up and saw my mother looking at me through the café window. She hurriedly turned away and walked on.

I would have to tell her about Virginia.

It was after four when I arrived at the newspaper building. I had this sudden impulse to go back to the loading dock to see whether any of my old co-workers were there. More than half of the people unloading the delivery truck were young women; most of the men had not yet returned from the war.

I went around to the front and took the elevator up to the fourth floor. Miss Westin welcomed me with a stiff handshake, invited me to sit while she went into Mr. Hardwicke's office. A few moments later, he emerged and extended his hand to me.

"Come in. Come in young man. Tea, Miss Westin, please."

He led me into his office. "Sit, Isaac. It's good to see you. I heard you had been injured."

"I was hit in the leg and spent a few months in the hospital, but I'm fine now."

"Good. Good. We need you back. The art department is a little thin. I don't know whether you heard that Mr. Ramsay was badly burned during the war and cannot work. Old Clemente has had to get his hands dirty, poor man. He'll be happy to see you."

"Sorry to hear about Roland Ramsay," I stammered, "that must be very difficult for his wife and daughter. What will he do?"

"When can you return to us, Isaac? How about Monday next?" he asked, ignoring my question. I could not believe Hardwicke's callous detachment. All he seemed concerned about was his paper. I was tempted to tell him to go to hell, but I needed to work, so I gave him a date two weeks away. He pushed me to come back sooner but I stood firm and he reluctantly acquiesced.

On my way out I asked Miss Westin for Roland Ramsay's address. She consulted her files, then wrote it on a piece of company stationary. Not surprisingly, he lived quite close to our apartment. His wife answered the door and I introduced myself, adding that I had just returned from France.

"Rolly is not often up for visitors. I'll ask."

She closed the door most of the way and I could hear them whispering. She returned and invited me in to the kitchen.

Ramsay was seated at the table, an army blanket wrapped around his shoulders. He waved a terribly red and disfigured hand limply at me, indicating a chair across from him. Both his arms and hands were covered in bright pink scar tissue that extended up his neck. His face, miraculously, was untouched. "Can't shake your hand," he said.

I shook my head. "I'm really sorry about this, Mr. Ramsay."

"Why'd you come?"

"I just met with Hardwicke. He told me about your injuries. His main concern, frankly, was that you are not able to come back to the paper which is under-staffed."

"Ah. Mr. Hardwicke is all business!" he snorted. "He doesn't give a damn about anyone."

"I came away with a similar impression. He asked if I could start on Monday. Hell, I only got home yesterday."

"What did you tell him?"

"I told him I could come back in two weeks. He wasn't happy but he finally agreed."

"Did you see Clemente?"

"No."

"You know, neither one of those bastards has had the decency to visit, or even send me a note. Hell, Elsa, my wife, went down to the building a week after I got home to let them know my situation. You know what she got for her troubles? Nothing. Not even a handshake."

What could I say?

Elsa sat quietly next to him. She adjusted the blanket which had fallen from his shoulders revealing the scars across his chest. "Don't get upset, Rolly. They're not worth the effort."

"Rumor has it that you caught one, too," he said, after a long silence. "Doesn't show."

"I took a chunk of shrapnel in the leg. I also broke a few ribs. I was lucky - I healed up pretty well. I spent six months in the hospital which was fine 'cause it was six months away from the front."

"Amen to that."

I left their apartment after promising to return in a week or two. Mama was sitting at the table peeling vegetables when I arrived home. "I'm making a nice beef stew for supper. It will be a while."

I took a sharp knife from the drawer and sat opposite her and began to slice the vegetables. "I saw you looking at me in the café."

"You were writing a letter?"

"I was." I put down the knife and waited for her to stop peeling, to look at me. "I need to tell you about a young woman I met. Well, I didn't really meet her face to face, but we corresponded from the time I was in the hospital." I talked about receiving the care package with the cookies and the colored pencils and what that meant to me. I pointed out that a couple of the drawings Mama had pinned to the wall were drawn using those pencils. I showed her the photograph Virginia had sent.

"Very pretty," Mama said.

"Yes, Virginia is very pretty." I watched her expression as I spoke, trying to gauge her reaction to that not-Jewish name, but her face said nothing.

"Where does this Virginia live, Itzik?"

"She lives in Boston. When I wrote her that I was being sent home from France she asked me to contact her as soon as I got home so we could arrange for me to visit her. I was writing that letter in the café."

My mother stood up from the table, gathered all the vegetables and put them in a pot. Then she placed a large heavy pan on the stove, added some oil and while it was heating she unwrapped the meat and cut it into smaller chunks which she added to the oil. She turned the meat several times until the pieces were browned on all side, then she threw the vegetables into the pan, added some water and salt and pepper, and then she covered the pan.

Finally, she turned to me and said, "Your Uncle Kalner's new wife, Mary, is a good person."

***

"Are you up for a little more Winnie the Pooh?" Danielle asks.

I am beginning to tire of the little bear and his friends, but I love to hear Danielle's voice and, besides, I'm in no hurry to get anywhere.

I remember a Christmas a couple of years before Virginia died. She was in a lot of pain but insisted on having the whole family and some friends over for coffee and dessert after their individual holiday dinners. Christmas morning found us in the kitchen early, baking three pies - apple, pumpkin and pecan - as well as a large batch of her famous apple, ginger, walnut and cranberry cookie bars, which were a family favorite. Our house smelled of spice and warmth.

We had a light lunch - she ate so little - then laid out the mugs and plates and forks, as well as the cookie bars and pies, and set up the coffee. As we moved about she started humming.

"What song is that?" I asked

"It's the theme song to Sesame Street, a wonderful kid's show on Public Television. You need to watch it sometime, Isaac. We are in that cycle of life again; there's a new baby in the family, a new generation. Allen and Martha are bringing our first great-grandson."

I can see Virginia in her big dark blue chair holding David for the first time. The Christmas tree is beside them and the baby is looking up at the sparkling lights while Virginia is smiling and cooing. The room is crowded with people but she seems unaware of them. She hums the Sesame Street song softly to him. I hear her voice through all the laughter and the chatter around us. I can't take my eyes off her.

***

The days passed painfully slowly as I waited for Virginia's letter of invitation. I spent much of my time walking along the river, sketching and experimenting with watercolors, and worrying about whether Virginia had come to her senses and had decided this foolish infatuation with the poor Jewish boy had gone too far. I almost wrote her another letter to suggest we slow down, but fortunately did not follow through.

On the Tuesday morning I stayed in the apartment and reread all of her letters; I became even more convinced the feelings we shared in our relationship-by-mail were real. My biggest concern now was that we had created expectations we could not possibly live up to. I imagined her in heated arguments with her parents about me, and I feared our relationship would cause terrible harm within her family.

I wrote a letter to Uncle Kalner to ask his advice about dealing with Virginia's family, should the occasion arise. I wished I'd written the letter before the one I'd sent to Virginia - I felt I needed his wise words right away.

Virginia, true to her habit, replied to my letter the day she received it. She was overjoyed I was home safely and said she was anxious to meet me in person, as were her mother and father. "Isaac, is it possible for you to visit this coming Saturday (May tenth) at two o'clock?"

It was already Thursday. There was not enough time to respond to her by mail, so I raced to the Western Union office and sent a telegram accepting her invitation. And then I panicked. What do I wear? Do I bring a gift - for Virginia? For her mother? Both? What kind of gift? I started walking up and down the main shopping streets of Lawrence, peering into shop windows trying to see something that looked appropriate. I didn't want, nor could I afford, to buy expensive ostentatious gifts - I did not want to present myself as something I was not. At the same time I wanted them to see me as a thoughtful, creative person who had a lot of potential to do well, whatever that meant.

I returned to the apartment with nothing, except a churning in my gut. Mama was sipping her tea, so I poured myself a cup and sat down opposite her at the table. "I need your advice, Mama."

"The girl?"

"Yes. She invited me to her parents' home this Saturday."

"Hoo! And now you are all worked up."

"Well, I don't know what to bring, what to wear. We are so different."

"That was your choice, Itzik. You knew that." She placed her cup in its saucer and reached out to pat my hand. "Different is fine, Isaac. Look at the mill; there are people from all over the world there with different languages, religions, traditions, young, old and in-between. We do OK; we look out for one another."

"I know, Mama, but the difference between us and Virginia's family is more than religion or language - it is class, money - and that's a very big difference."

She sighed. "Yes, it is. But if you love this girl, and if Virginia loves you, the two of you will find a way."

I walked around behind her and kissed her on the cheek. "Thank you, Mama."

"Now, about what you should bring. I never met a woman who did not love flowers and chocolate. Bring both and give them to Virginia. If her mother is a reasonable person she does not need to be flattered - she will judge you based on how you treat her daughter."

I kissed her again.

"The father is a different matter. I'm not good with men, and the couple of upper crust ones I have had to deal with were like another species altogether. All I can say is be polite, and try not to talk politics unless by a miracle you somehow agree with him." She paused and stood up to place her empty tea-cup in the sink. "You'd better get yourself a new suit, and a white shirt."

***

Danielle kisses me on the cheek. "I'm on my way, Isaac. I'll be back tomorrow afternoon. In the meantime I'm going to think about communication, and I will tell the nurse about your awake signal."

I now have four words - yes, no, thank-you and awake. Not bad for a one-hundred-and-two year-old guy!

Chapter 24

.

I arrived in Boston before noon that Saturday. I sat on a bench in the shade of an old maple tree in the Public Garden and studied the facade of the Appleton house which stood across Beacon Street opposite the Garden. It was a three-storied brick building with a basement and attic rooms, probably for live-in servants. A large bay window on the ground floor projected toward the sidewalk. The front double-door was heavy dark-stained oak with thick beveled blue tinted glass panels and shiny brass hardware.

Then I moved on toward the Swan Boats. I took a small pad and pencil from my jacket pocket and made a few sketches. Around one-fifteen I strolled through the park to the downtown shopping district. I found a fancy candy store on Tremont Street and bought a pound of chocolate covered caramels. Then I bought a dozen deep red roses from a vendor near the entrance to the Park Street subway station. "The first roses of the season," the seller told me, and I took that as a good omen.

"Well, here goes!" I said out loud as I started walking quickly down Beacon Street. It wasn't anything like going over the top, but I sure had a tight knot in my stomach.

As a distant bell chimed two o'clock I lifted the large brass lion's-head knocker on the front door and knocked twice. A few moments later Virginia opened the door.

***

Damon the Good is here; I recognize his movements. I blink three times. He laughs, "You're awake, Isaac! I heard about your new word. As you probably know because I'm here, it's very late at night - actually almost four o'clock in the morning on Thursday the twenty-third of May."

Thank you.

"Got any other new tricks?"

Is this the time to try out my phony Morse-code idea? It is really only an idea, I have not figured out how to actually implement it. Am I opening a door to better communication or to the entrance of an endless maze? What the hell! Let's go! I blink twice. *Yes.*

"You do?" Damon is clearly surprised. He sits beside the bed. "OK, Isaac. Try me."

I give two short and one long blink. Then one long, followed by two short.

"Duration! And sequence! Looks like Morse code to me. Am I right?"

I figured he'd jump to this. And I had also thought of how I would respond. I blinked once, paused, then twice. *No, yes* - which in my new blinky language means "sort of" or "maybe," and because I put "no" first, I mean that it is mostly not Morse Code, but that duration and sequence can be used to mean different words.

"Hmm. Now I am confused. No. Yes."

Well, Damon, it can't be both so it must be something in between. Makes sense to me.

"Shoot. Red light. I'll be back!"

I think he is inventing this one. I guess he needs time to think. That's OK. I never expected it would be easy.

***

"It is so wonderful to actually meet you, Isaac. Please come in." She was beautiful, so much more beautiful than she appeared in the photograph I had carried with me through the last months of the war, and which I still carried. I can see her now in that sky blue dress with a square neckline and accented with a sheer layer of darker lacy blue. Her dark hair in soft curls resting on her shoulders. The dress reflecting the color of her eyes.

I stood there speechless, then extended the flowers and the box of chocolates to her. She took them, thanked me and turned, and I followed her through the front hall into the parlor - the room with the big bay window.

Her mother was seated in a heavy red velvet covered armchair beside the window. "Good afternoon, Mr. Simon," she said.

I bowed slightly. "Pleased to meet you Mrs. Appleton. Thank you for inviting me to your home. It is lovely." I had not had much time to look at the house, but it seemed like the polite thing to say.

Virginia directed me to sit at the end of the couch close to her mother. "These are gorgeous roses, Isaac, and very bold," Virginia said. "I need to find a vase." And she left me alone in the parlor with her mother.

"First roses of the season," Mrs. Appleton observed. "They are special."

I smiled. "Yes, they are. That's why I chose them. I thought Virginia would like them."

"You are a talented artist, Mr. Simon. Virginia showed me your drawings. I believe we saw you across the street in the Garden earlier today. We recognized you from the self-portrait you sent."

"Yes, I arrived early. I enjoyed my time in the Garden."

"You were drawing?"

"The Swan Boats. They are a lot of fun for the children."

Virginia finally returned with the roses in a crystal vase which she placed on a low table beside her mother. She sat down on the couch leaving a respectable distance between us. "What have you two been talking about?"

I wanted to sit sideways on the couch so that I could simply look at her. I wanted to take her in my arms and hold her. "Your mother mentioned you had observed me earlier today across the street with my sketchpad."

"Yes, we did. Can I see what you drew?"

I withdrew the pad from my pocket and flipped to the Swan Boats. She moved a little closer so she could see. "I love the way you capture the children. They appear to be having a wonderful time." She took the pad and handed it to her mother who spent some time looking at the sketch, then randomly turned to another page in the pad - which happened to be a drawing of milk bottles on the front steps to our apartment building in Lawrence. I had been intrigued by the smooth shiny surface of the bottles against the texture and grain of the weathered wood.

"I draw what I see," I said.

"Quite dramatic," said Mrs. Appleton.

"Lovely," Virginia said.

An ornate banjo clock on the wall behind Mrs. Appleton chimed two-fifteen. "Mr. Appleton will be down in a minute. Virginia, please tell Bea to bring the tea."

I was left alone again with Mrs. Appleton.

"Virginia admires your artwork, Mr. Simon, and she says that you have a charming sense of humor."

"She is too kind."

"Yes, she is. But she has a mind of her own - a bit of a stubborn streak."

"I have seen that in her letters. She is also very open-minded." What the hell, I might as well stir up the waters a bit. It was bound to happen sooner or later.

"Yes, she is. It is something my husband and I are most proud of."

Virginia returned and moments later her father entered the room and advanced toward me. He was a tall, slim, imposing man. I stood immediately. "I am pleased to meet you, Mr. Appleton." We shook hands, firmly.

"The young artist my daughter has been going on about. Well, sit down, young man." He lowered himself into a chair on the far side of the bay window.

"Tea will be here shortly," Virginia announced.

"So, Mr. Simon, Virginia has told us a little about you, but I am sure there is more to tell. Where are your people from?"

Nothing like getting straight to the point. I glanced at the large oil painting - an idealized agricultural landscape - on the wall behind him, and then at the rich oriental carpet on the floor. I wished Virginia would give me a clue on how to begin, but she sat silently looking at her clasped hands resting on her lap. In my letters I told her of my background and my decision to be an architect after the war. She said that she had shared some of it with her parents before inviting me here.

I knew the questions would be coming. I had even rehearsed my responses. "To be honest, sir, I come from a different world than what I see here. I was brought to Massachusetts when I was ten years old by my mother and uncle. We come from a village in Lithuania called Linkeve. Our family is Jewish, although we are not particularly observant."

His face displayed no clue as to what he was thinking. "My mother works in a textile mill in Lawrence. Before the war I worked on the loading dock and then as an illustrator for advertisements at the Lawrence Eagle Tribune. I will be returning to that position in a week, although my intention is to find an apprenticeship with an architect and to enter architecture school."

"Where is your father?"

"He died in Linkeve about a year before we came to America." No need to give any more details.

"That must have been difficult for your mother. Do you have brothers or sisters?"

"My only brother decided to go to South Africa instead of coming here with us. I never learned why; we had been very close even though he was four years older. He served with the South African forces in German South West Africa and then in France. He was killed at Arras in April 1917."

"I'm sorry to hear that. Losing a brother is very painful."

"It is."

While we were talking, Bea had arrived with tea and cakes and she set them on the table in front of the couch. Virginia poured and passed a cup to each of us. She waited for her father to finish before asking me if I wanted lemon or vanilla cake. I chose the vanilla - it looked less elaborate and therefore less messy. I was not exactly used to dealing with all the fine china and silverware.

I took the opportunity to look around the room, particularly at the paintings. I was astonished to see a large abstract oil on the wall above the couch. It was a composition of irregular shapes that seemed to suggest an image of a female acrobat: the colors were muted browns and greens and grays. It seemed so out of place in this otherwise formal room, with its Persian carpets, classic landscapes and silver and crystal ornaments placed all around.

"It is by Jean Metzinger," Mrs. Appleton said. "We were in Paris in the April before the war and we saw this at an exhibit. I was transfixed by its audacity. Mr. Appleton is not yet convinced."

"I'm not sure I ever will be, my dear."

"It does make one think about the nature of art," I said. "I saw an exhibit of the modernists while on furlough in Paris a month before I was sent home. I still have not made up my mind about them, but seeing this in your home is amazing. I think I do like it."

"I think it is fascinating," Virginia offered. "There are some days when I actually find myself looking at it for hours. It draws me in and I get lost."

I remembered the picture of the teardrops I had drawn at Ellis Island. It was my first 'abstract' although I did not go in that direction until many years later. But, here I was in the parlor of Virginia's family's home staring at this remarkable work. "I can see how one could almost disappear in it, Virginia. It is simultaneously almost two-dimensional and infinitely deep. I can't figure out how he does that, but it is fascinating. It presents a challenge."

"Do you think you might try something like this, Isaac?" Virginia asked.

"I don't know. I would have to see things the way this artist sees them in order to do something like this. But the painting does challenge one to try to look at the world differently."

"Mr. Metzinger wrote a book about the Cubist theory of art. It is quite fascinating. We picked it up when we bought the painting. Do you read French, Mr. Simon? I would be happy to lend it to you."

"Thank you, Mrs. Appleton. I'm afraid the only French I learned was in the trenches. It does not exactly extend to the philosophy of art."

She laughed, as did her husband and daughter.

"Well, perhaps Virginia could translate it for you."

"I'd be delighted," Virginia said, "but my French is not that good."

Teacups had been emptied, cake eaten. Bea had cleared away everything. I felt the afternoon was progressing well, but I was anxious to get even a few moments alone with Virginia. But how?

"Have you worked in oils at all, Mr. Simon?" It was Mr. Appleton.

"No, sir. Before the war I was happy to use an ordinary pencil. It was Virginia who introduced me to colored pencils. I was able to buy some watercolors in Reims after the armistice, but oils are too cumbersome and time-consuming for the life of a soldier. Hopefully, now that I am home, I will be able to give them a try."

"Yes, of course."

I was not sure what he meant by that, and neither, it seems, was anyone else. The four of us sat in silence until Mrs. Appleton finally said; "Why don't you two young people take a walk in the Garden? It's a splendid afternoon."

I could have kissed her. I think Virginia and I were out of the house and across the street before her mother could finish her sentence.

***

"It's seven on Thursday morning." My Ginnie is sitting on the bed beside me. "Did I wake you?"

No.

"I spent most of yesterday researching grad schools and scholarships. I've pretty much decided to do a Masters in American Literature. I know there's no money in it, but so what! I'll just have to marry some rich old guy!" she laughs. "But, seriously, I can't see myself going through grad school studying something that doesn't get me excited. So long as I can get enough scholarship money to help pay for school and keep me out of eternal heaps of debt, I'll be OK."

There's an expression I've heard on TV that seems to apply here. "You go girl!" How could I possibly blink that? Instead, I give her a double-double - *thank you.* Thank you for following your heart.

"Hello, Ginnie. You're here early again." Damon the Good is here.

"Yes. I've always been an early bird."

As he fiddles with my plumbing, he says: "So, Isaac presented me with a puzzle a couple of hours ago." He pauses then asks, "Isaac, can I share this with Ginnie?"

Of course.

"I think Isaac is working on a form of communication that involves blinking his eyes. We know he has a few signals - yes, no, thank you. Yesterday he came up with 'I'm awake,' which is three blinks. But, he has now introduced a new feature - the duration of the blink, and related to that, the sequence of short and long blinks."

"Like Morse Code?"

"Well, that's what I immediately thought of, so I asked him and he responded with 'No,' followed by 'Yes.' I have no idea what he means by that."

Ginnie the English Literature major sighs. "Putting 'no' and 'yes' together could suggest ambivalence; it is neither one nor the other, but something in between. Grandpa, does 'no-yes' mean 'maybe?'"

Smart girl! *Yes.*

"So your new idea is maybe like Morse Code, but not exactly?"

Yes.

"Hmm. I'm not sure where that takes us. Kind of like Morse - but how? I'm going to have to think about this, Grandpa Isaac. I'll talk with everyone and see if we can figure this out. Danielle is an amazing puzzle-solver."

They are both silent. "I'll work on it, too," Damon says. "It's another step along the road."

"It's a puzzle, a true-life word game."

Yes. A game! Think CHARADES! I think that's the key! I want to shout it. I'm thinking of a word. Three letters...

"He said 'yes,'" Ginnie says. "Grandpa Isaac, did you say yes when I said 'word game?'"

Yes. We are getting somewhere.

"I do have to rush off - but I will think about this. We'll figure it out!" She kisses me hurriedly on the cheek, and says goodbye to Damon.

"You're a pretty smart old guy," Damon chuckles.

And a wise guy, too. *Yes. No.*

* * *

"Would you like to take a ride on a Swan Boat?"

Virginia giggled, "You know, I see them every day from the window of my room, but have not taken a ride since I was ten years old. It sounds like a fine idea." She took my arm as we walked along the path towards the lagoon to wait in line.

After the stiffness and tension of the past couple of hours, it was so good to be able to begin to relax. "Well, that wasn't too bad. I was prepared for much more of a grilling from your parents."

"I told you there was nothing to worry about. They like you, Isaac. I know them, and they really do like you."

I had not feared open hostility or bigotry from them. Far from it. But my concern was simply that our worlds were so alien to one another that we barely breathed the same air. And yet, here I was with their daughter waiting in line with a dozen or so other folks out enjoying the beautiful spring afternoon.

"How do you know they like me?"

"Do you think my mother would have suggested this walk if she didn't like you?"

"Probably not," I replied, "but I'm pretty sure they're standing in that big bay window right now and watching our every move."

"Well, they are my parents. I would not expect anything less!" She laughed and bumped her upper arm against mine. I wanted to hug her, to hold her close to me.

We bought our tickets and sat on a nearby bench.

"That painting by Metzinger is fascinating," I said after a long silence. "I can't stop thinking about what it means."

"It doesn't mean anything. It just is."

"I'm not looking for the meaning of the painting itself; I'm wondering what it says that your parents own it and like it."

She thought a while, then turned to me and said, "It means what I have told you before, Isaac; they are open-minded people. They are not bound to the conventional, the traditional. They are not fearful of new ideas, of new ways of understanding the world. They have brought me up the same way."

"It's a remarkable painting. I would like to copy it some time."

"I'm sure my parents would allow you to." She squeezed my arm and smiled.

"It's our turn," she said, as we watched the Swan Boat unload its passengers. "Let's sit in the back. We can watch the children."

We took our seats. As the boat pushed off, she put her hand in mine and squeezed a little. "This will not be easy," she said, "but somehow I know it is right."

"Yes." I felt my heart doing summersaults in my chest and I put my second hand on top of hers. "This is good." I half-closed my eyes and listened to the shouts and laughter of the children, the yells of delight when we passed a family of mallards and a turtle sunning herself on a rock, and the groans of protest when we came to a stop back at the loading point.

Virginia and I went to the same bench I had occupied earlier in the day. She was still holding my hand. "That ride brought back so many memories," she said. "The last time I was on a Swan Boat was with my grandfather - my father's father. He had come to live with us about six months earlier, after my grandmother passed on. Grandfather was not well, either."

She hesitated, and when she continued speaking her grip tightened on my hand. "He had been a major in the Union Army. During the war he suffered wounds which damaged his lungs and made it difficult for him breathe. He used to have terrible nightmares and he would shout and writhe violently in his bed. Sometimes he would even get up in his sleep and beat on the walls. It got so bad that my father had all the mirrors and paintings removed from his room, and a bureau was placed in front of the window so that he could not break the glass. The walls were draped with heavy fabrics to prevent him from damaging his fists. And the door to his bedroom was locked at night so he would not wander about the house. I was terrified and my parents tried repeatedly to explain his night-time illness to me.

"Yet, by day he was the sweetest, kindest man. He would wait for me to come home from school, then we would have lunch together and he would bring me to the park to play. Every day I'd beg him to take me on the Swan Boats, and he would give in to me about once every couple of weeks - just infrequently and irregularly enough to make each ride special. After the ride which became our last together, we went back to the house and I heard him say to my mother that he was going up to his room because he was not feeling well and she should lock him in because he thought he would sleep.

"He had a bell on the night-table beside his bed which he rang in the morning when he was awake. I remember thinking how unusual it was that I had not heard his bell before I went to school. He was not there to greet me on my return; he had passed sometime during the night. I learned only a year ago that he had taken a bottle-full of pills prescribed for his lung condition and his unrelenting pain. My father said his father had never talked about his experiences in the war; he carried those demons to his grave."

Tears welled up in her eyes and began to roll down her cheeks. I offered her my brand new, starched white handkerchief which she accepted. I put my arm around her shoulders and she pressed closer. "I know about those night terrors," I said.

There were many times I almost talked to Mama about my experiences in the war, but I never did - not in any detail. I told her a sanitized version of Chaim's life and death, painting a picture of him fighting and dying like so many hundreds of thousands of others. I never mentioned the drinking, the women, the battlefield punishments or the brokenness his friend Moish had described to me.

The only good thing I can say about the war is that it brought me to this wonderful woman who has filled my life. "Will you ever tell me what you endured?" Virginia asked, her head still pressed against my shoulder, "I think it would help to talk about it."

"In time. Many of my drawings portray the reality of it. I will show them to you some day." I was going to add, "When I get to know you better," but I felt like I had known her forever.

A distant bell struck six o'clock. "That's our church on Arlington Street telling me it's time to go home." She took my arm as we walked back to the house. We saw the curtains in the bay window move. "I wonder if they really have been standing there for hours," she laughed, then answered her own question, "Probably. I am their only child and they are very protective."

We climbed the steps. Virginia took my hands and looked into my eyes. "I am so glad to meet you, Mr. Simon," she said and kissed me momentarily on the cheek. "Will I see you the same time next Saturday?"

"Of course!" I said, and she pecked me on the other cheek.

***

Danielle is here; I am aware of her perfume before she says a word. I signal I am awake and she sits in the chair next to me. "It is mid-afternoon on Thursday," she says. "The weather has become gloomy and chilly. If it weren't late in May I would say that it feels like snow. It has that kind of grayness and stillness."

Thank you. I wonder if she has talked with Ginnie.

"So how are you doing, Isaac? Are you up for some more adventures of the little bear?"

Apparently Ginnie and Danielle have not talked yet, so I might as well listen to a story.

I hear her opening and closing the drawer beside the bed. She begins to read and I begin to drift off on one of my mind-flights. I am hovering above the Boston Public Garden looking at people strolling happily along the pathways or sitting on blankets in the sun enjoying picnics. I see a young couple sitting cross-legged under one of the huge willow trees near the lagoon. They are deep in conversation. They touch each other's hands, knees, faces - lovingly, but almost unknowingly - instinctual, perhaps. I am transfixed by them, drawn in. The moment I realize it is Virginia and me that I am watching, the image recedes and I find myself flying over the ocean. I am in control enough to stop the flight - I have no desire to go back to France.

I try to focus on Danielle's voice. The painful truth is that as much as I love her, she reminds me of Reuven, her father, and he reminds me of the war. Yet I would do anything to have him by my side, to hear his voice again. When Reuven was dying Danielle brought me to visit him at his home in Falmouth on Cape Cod. He lived alone in a small house, not much more than a bedroom, living room, kitchen and bathroom, with a deck that ran the full length of the house in the back, which is where we found him. He was sitting in a wheelchair under an umbrella and sipping iced tea through a straw. He looked terrible; he had lost a lot of weight, his face was so thin and his eyes so sunken that he looked almost skeletal.

Before I leaned in to hug him, Danielle said softly to me, "Careful. His bones are very brittle." Then she left us alone to talk.

"How are you, my old friend?" I said, as I pulled up a wicker chair next to him.

"Holding on," he replied, weakly, then added. "Who'm I kidding, Itzik. I feel like shit."

What could I say? I suddenly thought of the YMCA tent in Rouen and the bizarre nicknames we gave one another. "Yeah, old friend, and you don't look a whole lot better either."

He laughed and reached for my hand. "This is one battle I'm not going to win, Itzik. There's no bullet, bayonet or bomb that will take down this cancer. I've tried them all." Then he squeezed my hand harder than I would have thought he could, and said. "Listen, I don't want any military stuff when I go. I told this to Danielle and I want you to be sure she does what I asked. She thinks I'm some kind of war hero, but my life was not defined by that war. Yes, I did some things that won me a couple of trinkets, but they are mostly bad memories. No fine orations, no bugles, no flags, and definitely no rifle shots. Just make sure they put me in a hole in the ground like any other non-observant dead Jewish guy! That's all!"

The speech had exhausted him and he relaxed his grip on my hand

and leaned back into his wheelchair. "I'll talk with Danielle, Reuven. Don't worry."

"And you, Itzik, if you decide to say a few words - see if you can do it without mentioning the war."

I looked into his pale watery eyes that were now barely able to see. "That would not be easy, Reuven. You saved my life."

"I just happened to be there."

"I know, my friend, but it was *you* who was there."

He sighed, then drew in a deep breath and winced. "It even hurts to breathe."

We sat silently in the late summer sunlight, listening to the birds and watching squirrels chasing around the old maple tree in the neighbor's yard. Danielle came out of the house with a fresh tray of iced tea, but Reuven said he was tired and needed to go in for a nap. He refused Danielle's help to wheel him into the house, and I watched him struggle to propel himself up the slight incline from the deck into the kitchen. Finally we were in the living room. Danielle covered him with a light blanket, kissed him on both cheeks and went out to her car.

"Anything else I can do for you, Reuven?"

He shook his head. "Don't get sick," he said, and smiled weakly.

"I'll do my best."

That was the last time I saw him. My good friend Reuven died less than a week later. The funeral was short and simple. The rabbi who presided had obviously never met him and so had nothing but platitudes to say. I talked for less than a minute, saying Reuven and I had known each other from the day we stepped foot into America, that he had lived an amazingly full and courageous life, and he had always looked out for me. It was as though the war had never happened. It's what he wanted.

Chapter 25

Mama was waiting for me at the kitchen table; she wanted to know everything about my afternoon with Virginia and her family. She was impressed with the first roses and astonished that her mother had suggested the walk in the park. "They watched us the whole time from the big window," I said, and Mama nodded approval.

"So, you have told me what you did, Itzik," she said, "but what were they like? How did the Appletons make you feel?"

I had to think about how to answer. "I had expected to feel uncomfortable and out of place in their big, opulent, non-Jewish house and for the most part, that is exactly how I felt. 'Like a penny waiting for change,' as Reuven is fond of saying. On the other hand, Mr. and Mrs. Appleton were actually quite friendly in a formal kind of way. And I was pretty open with them. He asked where 'my people' were from and I told him. He had no reaction other than to nod thoughtfully and then ask about my father and any brothers and sisters. I told him the big picture - no details, and he responded kindly to the loss of Chaim."

"And what about Virginia - is she as you thought she would be?"

"Yes - and more! She invited me back same time next Saturday."

"You're young, Itzik. Don't rush into anything."

"It was our first in-person meeting, Mama. No one is sending out wedding invitations."

"You need to get established first," she said, not convinced by my response.

"I know. We will take our time, Mama. I promise."

On the Monday after my first visit with Virginia I found myself almost wishing I had not been so obstinate about needing two weeks before returning to work. The week ahead seemed endless. I moped about the apartment, drinking cups of tea and trying, unsuccessfully, to produce a watercolor portrait of Virginia. Finally, I pushed myself out the door. I was determined not to go near the picket lines so I started walking towards the heart of the city. I stopped at one of my favorite cafes for lunch. As always, I had a sketchbook with me and I began to draw the interior of the place.

When I was getting ready to leave, the owner approached me. "I've been watching you for a while," he said. "Will you trade that drawing for your lunch?"

"Sure," I said, and tore the sheet from the pad and handed it to him. "I should have had the steak."

He laughed, "Come back tomorrow, and the steak will be on me."

I walked down Essex Street without any particular destination in mind. On a painted glass panel in the entryway to one of the tall office buildings, I saw a sign for A.L. Wilkins, Architect. In the next block, I saw another architect's office, and further down, across the street, yet another.

I hurried home and spent the rest of the afternoon and evening combing through all my drawings and watercolors, selecting the ones that best showed my ability to capture architectural detail. By the time I was done, I had a portfolio of thirty pieces depicting both ruined and intact buildings in France (the ones from England were in a ditch somewhere), as well as a few that I had done of the factory buildings, bridges and other structures around Lawrence.

The next morning I put on my new suit and set out with my portfolio. By lunch time I had knocked on the doors of five architecture firms, showed my portfolio to two of them and had set up an appointment with one other for the afternoon. Three interviews in one day - not bad. I went back to the café I had lunched at the day before and enjoyed my free steak.

The interviews all followed much the same format. I introduced myself as someone whose interest in architecture was sparked by my visits to the architectural masterpieces I had explored in France and England, as well as my more recent discovery of modern styles. I presented my portfolio, which was well received, but which did not show, according to all the men I talked with, the skills of a working draftsman. I conceded the lack of experience but assured them I could learn, and that I intended to go to architecture school. I also pointed out that many architectural drawings presented to the clients were, in fact, artistic renderings of proposed buildings, and my skills in that regard could be beneficial.

Two of the three said they would contact me by the end of the week.

As I walked home I had the sense - for the second time in the matter of a few days - that my life was about to change. On Thursday I received a telegram from Mr. A.L. Wilkins asking me to come to his office at nine o'clock Friday morning, which I did, and by ten on Friday morning I was an apprenticed draftsman earning forty-three cents an hour. My first day of work was the following Monday, May nineteenth.

Mama was on the picket line and I wanted to tell her my good news. I had not been close to that part of the city since the day I'd returned home. As I looked across the line of police officers standing between me and the thousands of workers, I could not see a way to get through, even if I could locate my mother. I started walking along the sidewalk parallel to the mill trying to decide what to do, when I noticed a gap of about fifteen feet in the ranks of the police. Placed prominently in that gap was a machine gun pointing at the picketers! No one was actually manning the thing and I saw no bullet belt - but there it was in full view to the strikers and onlookers.

I had put my life on the line for this! I had seen comrades blown apart. I had killed other poor fools like me so that I could come home to see a machine gun aimed at my mother!

I crossed the street and marched toward the group of policemen standing near the machine gun. I had no idea what I was going to do or say. One of them turned to me and held up his hand. "Sir, you can't be here." His voice was firm, but respectful.

I was a little taken aback by his tone, until I realized I was dressed for my job interview in a suit and tie and looked more professional than working class. "What's that machine gun doing here?" I demanded. "I arrived home from the war ten days ago - the last thing I expected was to find a damned machine gun positioned in the streets of my home town!"

"To be honest, it's purely for show, sir. It isn't loaded."

"Who do I have to speak to to get it out of here?"

"I believe that would be the mayor, sir. Mr. John Hurley. It was his big idea."

"It's outrageous!"

"The strikers know there are no bullets. If you ask me, sir, the whole thing is crazy."

I turned and walked back to the downtown, not quite knowing what, if anything, I could do about the machine gun. I also still needed to let Mr.

Hardwicke at the newspaper know of my change in plans. I found a place to get a cup of coffee and a sandwich, and to figure out what I would say to Mr. Hardwicke.

My meeting with him was brief and to the point. He was not happy with my announcement. He did not wish me 'good luck' nor did he acknowledge that my new position was a great opportunity to advance in my career; he simply said, "Well then, Mr. Simon, I'll have to find someone else." And that was it.

I decided to pay a visit to Roland Ramsay; I thought he would appreciate hearing about my encounter with his old boss. I found him sitting on the front step of his apartment building sipping a glass of lemonade. He offered me a drink, which I declined. I tried to remember whether he had been able to hold something in his hand during my previous visit. I couldn't be sure.

He told me his wife was starting a job in a store on Monday. "Don't get me wrong - that's a good thing because we really need the money, but I think I'm going to lose my mind sitting around alone for hours brooding about my injuries."

"You'll have your daughter to take care of, to distract you," I said.

"Aye, that's the one little blessing."

I described my conversation with Mr. Hardwicke and he burst into a raucous laugh. "Well done, Isaac. I'd have loved to have seen that old dragon's face! Heartless bastard - you gave him a little taste of his own medicine!"

"Are you able to draw, at all?" I asked.

"I haven't tried. I'm just not up for it." He held out his red mangled hands in front of him. "My daughter calls me the lobster-man. She means no harm. She is, in fact, very sweet and gentle, and will often ask if I want her to rub my hands and arms with the ointment."

"How old is she?"

"She'll be four next month." A smile broke across his face, and he lifted his right arm to point down the block. "There she is now, coming home from shopping with her Mum."

The small girl ran to her father and hugged him carefully, then crept behind him so that his body shielded her from me.

I smiled. "Hello. My name is Isaac. Your father and I have known each other for a long time - from when you were a little baby. And now you are almost four!"

She held up four fingers, then turned and ran into the building, followed by her mother.

"I need to go in. Thanks for stopping by, Isaac." He paused, then continued, "I was not very decent to you when you started at the paper, and I'm sorry for that. Good luck in the new job."

"Thank you, Roland." I wanted to shake his hand.

***

Damon the Good is here, humming a song I don't recognize. He seems a little distracted as he fiddles with my plumbing. I blink three times. He does not respond. That's the problem with this system - if the person is not looking at me, they don't 'hear' me. Not much I can do about that. Or maybe they don't respond because they just don't want to deal with me. Not much I can do about that, either.

I said a while back that if there was one thing I would like to be able to do it is to hug people - Ginnie, Danielle, Allen, and all the nurses who look after me. I've been thinking about this evolving language I call 'blinky-blink' and I have tried to visualize a hug. I see it as a big heart with two strong arms. In blinky-blink, that translates to a long blink on either side of a very long blink. I will try this on Danielle as soon as she gets here - hopefully she has talked with Ginnie.

***

There was a letter from Reuven in our mailbox. He wrote that he was returning to Boston at the end of July to pick up where he had left off his studies at law school. He suggested I share an apartment with him and he talked about the museums we could visit and the music and night-life we could enjoy. It was tempting to be in the city, close not only to the museums, and the Boston Architectural Club, but most importantly, to Virginia. But I had committed to Mr. Wilkins and I knew the opportunity he was giving me was one I could not walk away from.

I responded to Reuven explaining about my new job. I also wrote in some detail about my afternoon with Virginia and meeting her mother and father; the questions asked, the Metzinger painting, the Swan Boat ride, and the invitation to return. I asked him whether the news of the mill strike in Lawrence had reached Rhode Island, and I told him about the machine gun and my conversation with the policeman.

It was long after dark when Mama arrived home. She had a bandage on her left forearm and scrapes on both hands. "Nothing to worry about, Itzik." She put a kettle of water on the stove, fixed herself a cheese and tomato sandwich then sat opposite me at the table. "So, what did you do today?" she asked, "Anything exciting?"

"I came to see you this morning at the picket line. I couldn't find you. I did see all the police, and the machine gun."

"That toothless thing!"

"I've seen what those things can do, Mama."

"They have no bullets. It scared us the first time they brought it out, but now it's like a piece of the scenery in a vaudeville show. So why were you coming to see me?"

"Good news, Mama. I have a job with an architect. I start on Monday."

"Wonderful!" She grabbed my face and kissed me on both cheeks. "Where is this architect?"

"Essex Street."

She kissed me again, then got up to start preparing dinner. "So, you're going to Boston tomorrow to see Virginia?"

"I am. Any advice?"

"Chocolates for Virginia, and perhaps something small for Mrs. Appleton."

"I can't imagine she could need that I can afford."

"Itzik, I doubt she *needs* anything - other than a little thoughtfulness. You can't go wrong with flowers. Perhaps pink carnations. I read somewhere they symbolize gratitude. And you are surely grateful that she is allowing you to see her daughter!"

Chapter 26

"We need to talk, Isaac." It's Danielle.

She must have had a conversation with Ginnie. *Yes.*

She hugs me and kisses both cheeks. "But first, the date-time report. It is around ten o'clock Friday morning, May twenty-fourth. The weather is miserable - a fine steady rain that seems to soak into everything."

Thank you.

"I had a terrible night. I couldn't sleep. My arthritis always flares up in this kind of weather and no amount of Advil helps. On the plus side, it gave me the time to think about you and your blinking language." She laughed. "The pun is intended."

I blink three times - my usual sign for "I'm awake," but I figured it could also mean, "I'm paying attention." I think I hear the sound of raindrops on a window.

***

It rained for all it was worth the Saturday of my second visit to Virginia. I emerged from the Park Street subway station around twelve-thirty into a downpour coupled with gusty winds; within seconds my umbrella was turned inside out. I took shelter in the doorway of a store on Tremont Street hoping the rain would slacken.

I had plenty of time before I needed to be at Virginia's. I was standing in the doorway of a men's haberdashery. In the display window on the left was a selection of silk neckties and I thought it would be a good idea to spend some of my remaining soldier's pay on a second tie; the one I was wearing - the only one I owned - had been abandoned by Uncle Kalner when he left Lawrence. I entered the store and approached a rack of neckties. I found one I liked; it was dark blue, with small regularly spaced light blue dots. Elegant, not too brash and it matched Virginia's eyes.

"Can I be of assistance, sir?" The salesman was impeccably dressed, almost intimidating.

I indicated the tie I was interested in. He removed it from the rack and held it up close to my suit. "It will look very good, sir. Excellent choice. Will that be all?"

I nodded.

"That is a dollar and seventy-five cents, sir."

I gulped. That was a few days' pay in the trenches. It took my mother several hours to earn that much. I opened my wallet and handed the salesman my last five dollar bill. Good thing I'd bought a round trip train ticket when I came to the city.

"I'm visiting a young lady," I explained, as I pocketed my change.

He offered me the use of a mirror. I thanked him and quickly removed my old tie and replaced it with the new. The salesman smiled knowingly.

The rain continued, but a little less heavily. I darted from sheltered doorway to sheltered doorway making my way to the chocolatier I had visited the previous week. I lingered as long as I could in the store, enjoying the wonderful smells, before buying a small box of fresh strawberries dipped in dark chocolate.

By the time I left the store, the rain had turned to drizzle and the wind had died down. I turned up my collar, walked back to Park Street station and bought a bunch of pink carnations and then headed down Beacon Street toward the Appleton home. The clock on a nearby church showed five minutes before two. I quickened my pace, not wanting to be late. I was not more than a hundred yards from the house, when the skies opened and a new deluge began.

I arrived on their doorstep drenched. The box of chocolates was soaked and the carnations were in disarray. Virginia opened the door before I knocked. "Oh my!" she exclaimed. "Give me your coat."

I handed her the soaking gifts, followed by my soaking overcoat and hat and stepped into the front hall. She looked down at my shoes. "I think those need to come off, too."

I obeyed.

"I'll get a towel." She disappeared and returned moments later with a large crimson towel which she draped across my shoulders.

"The wind flipped my umbrella inside out," I muttered, then added, "The carnations are for your mother."

"She'll love them. Come into the parlor."

"Virginia, have Bea get a fire going. We need to warm this young man," Mrs. Appleton said as we entered the room. She was sitting in her red velvet chair, and waved me in the direction of the fireplace on the far wall. "We don't want you catching the influenza that is going around."

Virginia sat me down on a chair in front of the hearth, then hurried off to find Bea. I looked down at my shoe-less feet, thankful I was wearing a relatively new pair of socks. Bea entered and a few minutes later she had a roaring fire going. I could see the steam rising from the cuffs of my trousers.

"Bea is making the tea a little early. It will warm you up."

I was feeling miserable, defeated by a burst of rain. I think if I had still been wearing my shoes I would have made some excuse and left.

Virginia pulled up a chair next to me. "I'm glad you came, Isaac. I was worried that the weather might have deterred you."

"It would take more than a few raindrops to keep me away," I said, with a flourish of false bravado. "How has your week been?"

"It has been a remarkable week. Mother and I have been campaigning for women's voting rights. The United States House of Representatives is to vote on the Nineteenth Amendment next week, so we have attended several meetings and rallies. Yesterday afternoon we marched to the State House - there were over a thousand women and quite a few men who supported us."

"If I'd known, I would have been there," I said.

"Really?"

"No question."

She squeezed my hand briefly. "Did you hear that, Mother? Isaac said he would have marched with us yesterday."

Mrs. Appleton was still in her chair at the other end of the large room, but she must have heard what Virginia said, because she came over and sat in her husband's chair nearby. "I'm pleased to hear that, Mr. Simon. Do you think your mother would have joined us?"

Bea entered with the tea before I could reply.

I thought of my mother's scraped and bandaged hands, the machine gun facing the picket line, the thousands of strikers, the police and militiamen - and I looked around me at the rich carpets, the paintings, the silver and crystal, the fine porcelain tea cups, the roaring fire. I wondered if the Appletons could have any idea of what my background was really like, of the daily struggle for survival and dignity my mother endured, and how ferociously she fought.

"I cannot speak for my mother," I said, "but I believe she would have been in the front of the line. She has been a fighter for as long as I can remember."

Clearly, neither Virginia nor her mother had expected my answer, and it showed in the expressions on their faces.

"However," I continued, "she could not have been here yesterday because she was on the picket line in front of the mill building where she works. They have been on strike since early February. We have not talked about voting rights, but I don't doubt that she would be in support."

"What is the strike about?" It was Mr. Appleton, who had entered the parlor as the tea was being poured.

I stood and shook his hand. He looked down at my shoeless feet, and I involuntarily glanced at his polished leather shoes. "Sit, sit, young man. What is this strike all about?" he repeated.

"Money and working conditions - what they are all about." I was not anxious to get into the details.

"Yes, but there are always particular issues."

Did he really want an answer? Did I want to give it? I tried to be as matter-of-fact as possible. "As I understand it, sir, with the end of the war the mill owners and the unions agreed to reduce the work week from fifty-four to forty-eight hours. What they did not agree on was the union demand that workers get an increase in hourly pay to compensate for the loss of hours."

"So the workers are demanding more money for less work?"

"No. They are demanding the same money."

"But they will be working fewer hours."

"True - but they still have to eat and pay for rent and fuel. Those prices have not gone down."

"Why is that the owners' problem? Should they have to pay for labor that doesn't happen?"

"It is the mill owners' problem because they need the workers to produce their fortunes, and if the workers won't work, their fortunes are impacted."

"That's coercion."

"The workers know that the owners can easily afford it. It is not right that so many work so hard for so little, while so few do so little and earn so much."

"Sounds like socialist propaganda to me!"

I paused and looked at Virginia. She was holding her breath as if she were trying to stop time, to prevent what she saw was rapidly unfolding in front of her. She reached out and touched my hand briefly.

"Father, perhaps you can continue this some other time."

"No, my dear, if this young man is to court my daughter, I need to know who he is."

Well, if my family background, life experience and understanding of the world were going to be a problem, I figured it was better to get everything on the table sooner rather than later. "I belong to no organization - political, labor, or otherwise - nor do I find value in placing labels on people, sir," I responded, paused a moment, then continued, "You might recall that when I visited last week, sir, I observed that my background was very different from what I see here. I do not believe, sir, that you could understand what it is like to live on a worker's wages…"

"I don't see how that is relevant, Mr. Simon!"

I took a deep breath. "I noticed your shoes when you greeted me earlier. They are very elegant and similar to ones I was assigned to draw for my very first advertisement at the Tribune. I was astonished at the price - ten dollars. That was the equivalent of almost a week's pay for my mother. And how many pairs of shoes do you have, sir? She has one. I have one. Almost everyone I know has only one. The economy is not only inherently unfair to the vast majority of people, it is also unsustainable - if we cannot buy the products, the factory owners cannot sell them."

Virginia was looking down at her clasped hands. Her mother looked anxiously at her husband then stood and said. "I think this has gone far enough." She turned to me and said, "Another cup of tea, Isaac?"

"Yes, thank you, Mrs. Appleton."

I heard Virginia exhale. "And how was your week, Isaac?"

I felt my body start to relax, a little. I was not sure whether Mr. Appleton would continue this confrontation or back off. "Actually, Virginia, I have had a remarkable week, a life-changing week. I am starting work on Monday - but not at the newspaper. I am taking my first step towards becoming an architect; I will be an apprentice draftsman at a small architectural firm in Lawrence."

Even Mr. Appleton congratulated me. But he remained silent while Virginia, her mother and I chatted about how I came to get the position and then went on to talk about my drawings. Bea came in to remove the tea, and Mr. Appleton soon followed her out of the room.

"It is too wet for a walk," Mrs. Appleton said. "I'll leave you two to continue the discussion."

"Did I go too far?" I said, as her mother walked away.

"It was a little close - but he provoked you."

"Thank you for trying to intervene. I really did not want to get into an argument with your father."

"I know."

"But I couldn't walk away without saying my piece."

"I understand."

How much could she understand? How much should I say?

***

"Are you with me, Isaac? You seem to have drifted off." Danielle touches my shoulder.

I blink three times. I'm back.

"Sometimes I wonder where you travel to in that head of yours." She taps me lightly on my forehead and laughs. "Anyway, we've been thinking about this word game of yours, this puzzle. Ginnie and I spent a couple of hours trying to come up with a method. Like most things in life, they start out complicated, but as you work through them, they simplify. When you arrive at the end, you look at the result and wonder why the hell it took so long!"

Less is more. Mies van der Rohe; one of my architecture icons.

"The method we came up with puts *you* in control. I'll run through it, then we'll try it. OK?"

Yes.

"Step one is for you to have a signal that means you have a word in mind you want to create a blink pattern for. When we acknowledge the signal, you create that blink pattern for the word you have in mind. We confirm. You with me, so far?"

Yes.

"Good. Then we ask, 'how many letters?' and you blink that number of times, and we confirm. Next is the spelling part, taking one letter at a time; we will slowly go through the alphabet and when we come to the correct letter, you blink twice. We confirm, then move on to the next letter, and so on till we know the word. The final step will be us saying that blink pattern such-and-such means the word just spelled out."

A little cumbersome, but it actually sounds do-able. I like it.

"Shall we give it a try?"

Yes. I can't wait!

"Have you thought of that initial signal that means 'I have as word?'"

I think for a few moments. *Yes.* Then I give three long blinks.

"Three long blinks means 'new word?'"

Yes.

"This is exciting. Do you have a blink pattern for a word?"

Yes. I've been holding on to this for a long time. I give one long blink, then a longer one, then another long blink.

"Huh? I'm not sure I see the difference between that and the new word signal. Can you do it again?"

Long, longer, long.

"Was the middle blink longer than the other two"

Yes.

"So your code has short, long and longer blinks?"

Yes. This is amazing. I feel like Shakespeare holding a quill for the first time. Well, I'm allowed a little exaggeration!

"Great! Next step - how many letters in the word?"

I blink three times, and Danielle acknowledges.

She begins to recite the alphabet. I blink twice when she comes to the letter 'H'. She confirms, and starts the alphabet again. It is a long wait for the letter 'U'.

"Three letter word starting with 'HU' - is your word 'hug?'"

Yes!

She hugs me. "So, long, longer, long means hug? Blink it for me!"

I do as told and she hugs me again.

"I will tell the world!" She kisses my cheeks. "This is fuckin' amazing!"

Yeah, it is.

***

"Will your father let me back into your home?"

"He was upset, but he didn't tell you to leave."

"I was pretty direct with him."

"Yes," she said, and placed her hand on mine. "It is one of your attractive features."

"Not if it gets me thrown out of your house."

"It won't. Mother will talk with him." She turned in her chair and faced me. "You challenged him. You put a human face on his progressive philosophy; you bring it down to flesh and bone, to shoes, not just words and ideas. He - we - have little experience of that. It will take time, but he will come around. We all will."

"Virginia, what I struggle to make clear is how immediate, how visceral, this all is."

She looked confused, but said nothing.

"When I came home from the war in Europe, I arrived home to the continuation of the class war here. On my first day back in Lawrence I saw the strike - the workers on one side, the police and the militia with their rifles with fixed bayonets on the other. A few days later I returned to the picket line; there was a machine gun facing the strikers. It has, fortunately, not been used yet."

"Unbelievable!"

"I saw these things with my own eyes. I have seen up close what bayonets and machine guns can do. And there they were confronting my mother and her co-workers. It is very real. My mother feared for my life every moment I was in Europe; and now I have to fear for hers in our own hometown."

She sat silently, squeezing my hands. "My father is a lawyer," she said, "he deals mostly with business contracts and the laws of commerce. He doesn't see the human dimension - for him it is all laws, regulations and numbers."

Bea came into the room and approached us. "Your shoes, sir. I dried and polished them for you." She placed them on the floor next to my feet.

191

"Thank you, Bea. That was very thoughtful."

"It's my job, sir," she replied, then turned and left.

I watched Bea walking out of the room, limping slightly, but head and shoulders held high. "Virginia - your father doesn't see the human dimension not because it is not there, but because he has never had to see it. But, that reality is right here. In this house every day. In the person of that Negro lady who cooks your food, cleans up after you, does the laundry. Did you see her worn-out shoes? Probably her only pair. How well do you all know her? Do you ever wonder how often she gets to see her children and grandchildren? Do you even know whether she has children or grandchildren?"

"Bea has been with us since before I was born. We are her family."

"Do you honestly think she sees it that way?"

Virginia squeezed my hands and leaned forward and kissed me quickly in the cheek, but did not answer my question for some time. Finally, she said, "I need to think about that."

The banjo clock on the wall chimed six o'clock. Virginia stood and started pacing slowly in front of the dying fire. "It's strange; when I first started thinking about meeting you and getting to know you, my fear was that our different religions might present the biggest obstacle, but I never thought about class. I saw our different economic circumstances as simply a matter of a disparity in things, not as a way of experiencing and understanding the world." She knelt down in front of me and clasped my hands. "Are we that far apart, Isaac?"

I wanted to say the old cliché, "Love conquers all," but it was too soon to express what was held so deep inside me. Instead, I said, "I don't think so." I kissed her hands. "I learned how to build bridges in the army. I was pretty good at it despite being shot at. This is just another kind of bridge - and we can build it together."

"And no one will be shooting at us."

"I certainly hope not."

We stood, still holding hands. "Mother and I will keep an eye on my father."

I nodded and smiled. "I do need to go now."

I looked around the room. Oh - the Metzinger! One of the things I had hoped to do during that visit was to copy the Metzinger.

We walked to the door, and as she handed me my coat and hat, she said, "Same time next Saturday?"

Yes.

***

I've been lying here trying to think of my next word or two. It's so odd - to be in a position where you can communicate only six of the hundreds of thousands of words in the English language and have to make a decision about which word will be number seven. Do I go with something very utilitarian like "tired" or something that expresses feelings like, "like" or "dislike". What if I went with something totally random - "salamander" or "crucible"?

I hear someone shuffling papers in the chair next to my bed. I guess it's Allen, going through a new trove of my letters, no doubt. *I'm awake.*

"Good evening, Grandpa Isaac. I've been very anxious to see you today." It is Allen.

I give him the long, longer, long signal and I feel him lean over me and give me a gentle hug.

He laughs. "It is true! Not that I didn't believe what Danielle told me - but still, it's wonderful to see."

Yes.

"First - it's four o'clock on Friday afternoon, May twenty-fourth. It was a rainy, gloomy day, but the clouds have finally begun to clear and we expect good weather for the holiday weekend. It's Memorial Day on Monday."

Thank you, Allen.

"I'm afraid I can't stay long. Martha, Ginnie and I are leaving soon for a mini-vacation in northern Vermont, so we won't see you until Tuesday. Danielle will be here often, and hopefully a few other folks who you haven't seen in a while. It'll be a surprise."

I'm not quite up for surprises. I'd rather know who to expect. Perhaps he isn't telling me because he's not certain they're coming. Now I'm going to lie here trying to guess who might show up. Pain in the ass!

"Danielle says she hopes to build up your word list over the next few days. I can't wait to see what you come up with by the time I get back. She's going to put a big chart up on the wall so anyone who comes to visit will understand you."

I am thinking of Memorial Day and of the many young men I've known who died in wars. Chaim and Benny were the first. There were too many others - from boys in my unit, to boys who died in the hospital at Rouen, to those who were killed in World War Two and Korea and Vietnam. I knew so many; the list goes on and on. Many were close to me.

And then there are those who came back scarred for life in body and in spirit. Broken boys. And I call them 'boys' because they were all so young.

I feel the tears rolling down my cheeks into my beard. The room is quiet except for my cat-machine.

Suddenly I am back in France with shells exploding all around me. I keep myself down in the trench dreading the command to attack. I look down the line at my comrades - tired, dirty, vacant-faced. Reuven is to my right. My eyes focus on the white of his knuckles as he grips his rifle. Yesterday we had tried to cross no-man's-land but had been thrown back by torrents of machine gun fire and unending shells. We had gone out during a lull after dark and dug shallow graves for our dead and buried them right where they lay.

The order to advance sounds and we scramble over the trench wall. As I run forward I see that the shells have churned the ground yet again and many of those we buried are now exposed. We keep on running, screaming wildly.

"It's OK, Isaac. I think you've been having another nightmare." I hear my cat-machine beeping rapidly. Nurse Trainwreck is wiping my forehead with a cool cloth. Her voice is gentle, calm., and as I feel my body start to relax, the beeping slows and finally stops.

I blink three times.

"You're awake. Good. I wish we had a way to keep those nightmares away."

Me too. Eighty-four years after the war, and I'm still having these dreams! How did Virginia put up with it?

"They send your blood pressure through the roof." She checks my plumbing. "Happily, your vitals are almost back to normal now. I hope you have a restful sleep, Mr. Simon. I'll check on you later."

I lie awake thinking of words, doing what I can to not fall asleep.

***

A letter arrived from Virginia on the Tuesday after that rather tense visit. When I first saw it I feared she was writing to tell me I could not see her again. I sat at the table and slit the envelope open, preparing for the worst.

"My Dear Isaac," she wrote, "It is only a few hours since you left, and I have not been able to stop thinking about the question you posed; the one about Bea. Does she see herself as part of our family? I have watched her closely all evening, trying to see her from a different viewpoint, and trying to remember her in various situations over the years. I recall a Christmas gathering two years ago. Father and Mother had invited several members of our church for cocktails. Bea spent all day cooking and preparing canapes, finger sandwiches, savory puffs and a host of other wonderful light snacks for the event. When the guests started arriving around seven-thirty, she hung their coats, hats and scarves in the hall closet and by eight-thirty she was circulating through the parlor and dining room serving the appetizers.

"At some point my mother was chatting with one of the church women and Bea approached with her tray of food. The lady helped herself to a canape, took a small bite and exclaimed how exquisite it was. Mother gushed, praising Bea for her cooking prowess. Then Mother said; 'Bea is wonderful. She has been with us for so long - she is practically one of the family.' I remember seeing a strange look cross Bea's face, then she turned away and headed straight to the kitchen. I did not think much of that incident at the time, but I did not forget it. I think, Isaac, your question has forced me to confront a reality I have never been aware of despite the fact that it has been right there in front of me my whole life."

She ended her letter with the following: "You are a remarkable and interesting man, Isaac Simon. I look forward to building bridges with you! Fondly, Virginia."

How could I wait till Saturday to see her again?

That week, of course, was also my first week at the architecture firm of Mr. A.L. Wilkins, who assigned me to work and learn under the strict eye of Mr. John Jackson, the chief (and only) draftsman in the firm. I spent my entire first three days practicing writing the alphabet and numbers in block letters. "Every drawing has notes and dimension," Mr. Jackson explained, "and the draftsman has to learn how to apply these with precision, style, consistency and clarity."

Surprisingly, it was not a boring task. I actually delighted in seeing my abilities improve, and comparing what I had done on the first day, to the product by the end of the third; the difference was subtle and quite amazing. At first glance, the examples looked similar, but it was as though I was looking through a lens which I rotated and suddenly brought everything into sharper focus. By Thursday I graduated to drawing lines; the art of maintaining a pencil line with a constant thickness and weight.

I was also given several books to read that covered a variety of architectural subjects; the physical properties of different construction materials, electrical wiring, lighting, and plumbing as well as landscape design. My experience in the engineering regiment gave me more practical knowledge of construction principles and techniques than I had realized, and I was able to make some connections between what I read in the books and what I had actually done in the mud of France. Mr. Jackson was impressed, as was Mr. Wilkins. And, from the books, I began to more deeply appreciate the engineering genius of the builders of those medieval cathedrals and abbeys I had visited and sketched.

On the Friday of that week I came home from work to find Mama and about a dozen of her co-workers crammed into our small apartment. The vodka and beer were flowing freely and my mother was leading the singing of picket line songs. "The strike is over, Itzik. We won!" Everyone cheered and someone pressed a glass of vodka into my hand. I set it on the table and went over to my mother and hugged her.

"You are a tiger," I whispered in her ear.

She let out a loud roar, then laughed and slapped me on the back. "Eat, Itzik. There's plenty of bread and cheese." She fixed me a sandwich while the joy and loud conversation rose and fell around us. It wasn't until after ten o'clock that the last of the people left; many were not so steady on their feet.

"It's a good day, Itzik. A really good day." We were sitting across from each other at the kitchen table, which was covered in dirty dishes and glasses and sprinkled with bread crumbs.

"I'm glad it's over, Mama. I was worried about you."

"On the picket line they call me the tough old lady." She chuckled, then was silent for a long while and I noticed tears welling up in her eyes. "It was your father that made me so tough. I had to be." She leaned forward and reached for my hands. "Soon after I moved into his house after our wedding I learned that I could not trust him. I was still a girl, seventeen! He was ten years older. There was no love. He treated me like a servant; worse than a servant! I had begged my father not to make me marry him, but I was told to be patient, to give it time."

Her speech was slightly slurred - the vodka had allowed her to drop her guard, to let old memories and pains return. "I ran away a month after our wedding, to a friend who lived in the neighboring shtetl, but her parents told my father where I was and he came and fetched me and brought me back to my husband's house. When my father left me there, weeping on the floor, my husband threw himself at me and..." She could not continue. The tears were cascading down her face and she made no attempt to stop them or wipe them away.

"It's OK, Mama." I had never seen her this sad. I did not know what to say. In all the years since my father's death she had never told me anything about her relationship with him. She rarely mentioned him at all.

She gripped my hands tightly. "When he was done, he dressed and went to the tavern. I lay on the sofa and curled up as tightly as I could. Two of his friends carried him home very late and very drunk. I told them to leave him on the floor and I went to bed. I slept with one eye open that night and many other nights. The only good thing from that night was your brother, Chaim. He saved me. He gave me something to live for." She leaned forward 'til her forehead touched the table. "And now Chaim is gone."

Chapter 27

Damon the Good is singing, "If I had the wings of an angel," his soft, deep voice sounding like Louis Armstrong without the gravel goes right to my heart. Such memories of the music and dancing with Virginia in those first years. I have said before that she had a beautiful voice.

I wait for him to finish the song. *I'm here.* Then I give him the double-double. *Thank you.*

"Hello, Isaac." I can hear the smile in his voice. "Thank you for what?"

I suddenly know what my next word has to be! Sing.

"Never mind. It's six-thirty-five on Saturday morning, May twenty-fifth. It's still 2002." He touches my forehead. "Word on the floor is that you have a new word."

Yes.

"Do you want to show me?"

I like Damon, but he's not family. He's a nurse; he works here. Is asking him for a hug overstepping some line? What the hell - all he can say is no. *Hug.*

He laughs out loud, says, "OK," then leans in and gives me a long, gentle hug. "You're all right, Isaac."

Yes, but I mean: "you are all right, too, young man." My blinky-blink language is so inadequate.

He checks my plumbing and vital signs. "I'm off for three days, Isaac. You have a good weekend." He hugs me briefly.

***

Virginia's father approached me as I was walking through the Public Garden towards their house on the Saturday following our rather pointed interaction the week before. "I was hoping to talk with you before you came to our door," he said, stiffly. We shook hands. "Shall we sit a moment?" I had no idea what to expect, but it couldn't be good. I wondered if Virginia knew he had come out to find me; was she watching from behind the curtains of that big bay window, or maybe from her bedroom on the second floor?

I sat and waited for him to speak. He remained standing a few feet in front of me. I observed that the shoes he was wearing were not the same pair he had worn the week before - was that intentional, or simply a matter of fashion or comfort? Were these his walk-in-the-park shoes? I tried not to smile.

"Let me be direct with you, Mr. Simon." He was looking down at me, somewhat intimidating. "I have come to appreciate that you are a bright, thoughtful and forward-looking young man and in other circumstances I would be quite satisfied with my daughter's choice. But, in this circumstance, I am not so certain."

He was a lawyer, accustomed to speaking and being listened to, expecting respect, and comfortable in his ability to control the situation. I felt my best approach was to let him finish his words, which he had probably written and rehearsed, without any interruption or comment from me. Let him put his whole case on the table.

"My concern is that we are so far apart. You yourself have spoken more than once about the different backgrounds of our two families. To be blunt; I am concerned that your Jewish heritage is incompatible with our Unitarian Christianity. I even spoke with our minister, the Reverend Frothingham, and while he did not rule out such a relationship, he certainly had some reservations."

Mr. Appleton finally sat down, but continued speaking; "Even more troubling for me is, to be direct, our difference in social standing. For better or for worse, our family has certain standards to uphold, and Virginia is our only child. If I were to announce to my peers that our daughter was being courted by the son of a widowed Jewish factory worker, the reaction would be one of universal astonishment, and could negatively impact my position."

He stood again, and looking down at me, he said; "You are a fine young man, Mr. Simon, but I have serious misgivings about your relationship with my daughter, and I have informed her of my feelings." He began to walk away.

"Mr. Appleton, sir. I would hope you would allow me to respond, because, to be blunt, I *do* want your approval to court Virginia." He stopped and turned to me. "Please, sir, won't you sit."

Reluctantly he sat down beside me. "You're not going to make this easy, are you, Isaac?"

He used my first name; I knew that somewhere in all his bluster there existed a small soft spot for me. I also knew it was important to talk about me, and to avoid attacking him and his views directly. "It is true, Mr. Appleton, that there is a large gap between your family and mine. The obvious truth is that a person has no say in where their road begins, but one does have a great deal of say in where the road goes. My family has already come a long way - from where we began as barely literate peasant farmers in rural Lithuania, to urbanized workers in Massachusetts. And now I am on a path to becoming a professional architect.

"As for my Jewish-ness. Again, I cannot change the religion I was born into, but the truth is that I find little comfort or value in religion or God, even. Whatever belief I might have had in the almighty was blown away in the trenches of France."

"You are an atheist?" The look on his face was almost one of horror.

"In truth, sir, I don't know how to answer that."

"Well, Isaac, what *do* you believe in?"

I looked around us at the park, with the flowers in bloom and the dozens of people strolling or sitting alone or in small groups under a vibrant blue sky scattered with white bubbly clouds. I saw the sculptures in the gardens and the surrounding graceful buildings. I saw the golden dome of the State House and the large bay window of the Appleton residence. "I believe in this," I said, gesturing to our surroundings, "I believe in people, in nature, in art, in science, in love. That's more than enough for me."

"You are an interesting young man, Isaac," he said, after a long silence, "and eloquent, too." He rose. "Let's get back to the house. The ladies must be getting impatient."

"Does this mean, sir, that you've had a change of heart?"

"You always make me think - and I like that about you, despite my misgivings. Let's just say I am reserving judgement."

"A stay of execution?"

"I suppose you could put it that way. Perhaps you should give up architecture and become a lawyer."

I smiled. "I'll leave the lawyering to my good friend Reuven," I said.

***

Danielle is here, but her Chanel Number 5 does not cover the stale smell of cigarette smoke on the person who is with her. I hear a man cough. One of Allen's surprise guests?

"Remember, Isaac can hear everything," Danielle whispers.

"I'll try not to use bad language." He chuckles, and coughs again. His voice is not entirely unfamiliar, but I can't place it. At least he seems to have a bit of a sense of humor - and that's a good thing. I don't like the cigarettes. "How do we know if he's awake?" the man asks.

"He'll blink three times."

"So we keep an eye on his eyes?"

Danielle laughs. "That's what we do."

He breathes deeply then exhales loudly. "Dad talked about Isaac so often. The last time I saw him was at Dad's funeral, over twenty years ago, and he was old then."

It's Reuven's son, Sam! He's right - I haven't seen him since we buried my good friend.

"He's a hundred and two now."

"Tough old guy."

"And as sweet as there ever was."

I think I'm ready to be here. I blink three times.

"Hi there, Isaac. I'm here with my brother, Sam. Do you remember him?"

Yes. Of course I remember him. I was at his bris, his bar mitzvah, his wedding and a whole bunch of lesser gatherings.

"Sam, we always start each visit with what I call the date-stamp." She touches my hand. "It's about half an hour after noon on Saturday, May twenty-fifth. A beautiful spring day with warm skies and a few puffy clouds. The flowers are in bloom and folks with allergies are complaining."

"Hello, Isaac. It's been way too long since I saw you last. It's good to see you."

Yes.

"He blinked twice - that means 'yes.'"

"My dad told us so many stories about you - from the day you met at

Ellis Island, through the Great War and beyond. He loved you."

There's another word I need. Love. I wonder if I could steer the conversation towards building my list of words, or would it be rude to interrupt the flow of things.

"Sam is visiting me for the long weekend. He flew in early this morning from San Diego."

"A long red-eye flight with a stop at some ridiculous hour in Chicago. I got in to Logan about four hours ago."

I wonder where his wife, Sarah, is. Sam was too young to serve in the Second World War, but he went to Palestine in June 1948 to fight in the Israeli war of Independence. He spent almost three years there living on a kibbutz in the Negev desert, where he met Sarah. She was a Belsen survivor, the only one of her immediate family. She had grown up wealthy in Budapest, and her family had been active collectors of contemporary art. She learned piano and sang in her middle school opera group before the Nazis invaded. When she arrived on the kibbutz she had little more than the clothes on her back, and her beautiful voice. They were married in Providence, Rhode Island, in 1952. As a gift to Sam, and to all their guests, she sang a lovely aria from Bellini's La Sonnambula.

"I told Sam that you and I had some work to do today. I showed him the big chart of your words I am making. I'm going to tape it to the wall above your bed so people can learn your language." There is a school teacher tone to Danielle's voice, but she actually followed in her father's footsteps and became a lawyer.

"It's an impressive chart," Sam says. "It's clear and easy to read."

"OK, Isaac, are you ready to begin?"

Yes.

New word. The trickiest part is coming up with what Danielle called the "blink pattern" for the new word. I can't just make it a random arrangement of short, long and longer blinks; it has to mean something to me, to convey the feeling of the word.

I give four longer blinks. Danielle says, "Four longer," and I respond in the affirmative. I had decided on four longer blinks because they take time, they require me and the observer to pay attention, to listen to the heartbeats.

Four letters.

She goes through the alphabet. L then O. "Is the word "love?"
Yes.

"Four longer blinks means love?"
Yes.

"I will add it to the chart!" Danielle says, then adds, "I four-longer-blinks you, Isaac."
Hug.

She hugs me and kisses both my cheeks.

"Are you up for another word, Isaac?"
Yes.

We create "sing" - short, long, long.

"You really don't want me to sing for you. Not with my voice." Danielle exclaims.

No. I'm keeping that for some other folks - Damon and Wanda and Ginnie.

"Do you have another word in that head?"

No. I'm thinking my next word needs to be "tired" but I don't have the energy to work on it right now.

"Are you up for more adventures of the little bear and his friends?"

Yes. Danielle has a lovely, soothing voice.

***

Virginia had been watching her father and me from her bedroom window, and when she saw us walking together towards the house she came running out of the building, crossed the street and into the park. She wrapped her arms around her father's shoulders and gave him a quick kiss on the cheek. "Thank you."

He returned the embrace, smiled, but said nothing.

She took my arm. "Father, could Isaac and I spend a few minutes in the garden before tea?"

"Don't be too long. You know how Bea gets when things don't go according to schedule." I watched him walk back to his house. There was lightness in his gait that I had never noticed before.

"Was he awful to you?"

"He's concerned. He wants to be sure that no one, particularly you, is hurt by our relationship."

We were walking towards the Swan Boats. She stopped and she turned to face me. "And just what is our relationship, Isaac?"

"Let's sit somewhere." The park was crowded and all the benches in sight seemed to be occupied, so we leaned up against the trunk of a huge willow tree. "We have known each other for about a year, although this is only our third meeting. I have felt a deep bond with you from the moment I read your first note written to a soldier you had never heard of." I took her hands in mine and moved closer to her. "My dear Virginia, if I could wave a magic wand I would marry you this afternoon! And I know we would be happy together for the rest of our lives."

She pressed her body against mine and we kissed. "I would accept your magic, but we need to be a little more practical."

"I know."

"Shall we consider ourselves engaged?"

"Yes!" We kissed again.

A nearby church bell chimed. "We need to go in for tea," she said.

"Should we say anything to your parents?"

"I think we need to give them a little more time to get used to seeing us together."

I assumed that Mr. and Mrs. Appleton had seen us kissing in the park. I didn't care, and nor did Virginia.

We walked back to the house. Virginia stopped at the foot of the steps and took my hands. "This is a big thing for them - this thing between you and me. We need to tread lightly. It is unnerving for both of them, and, to be honest, for me too. It is easy to be open-minded here," she turned and gestured to our affluent surroundings, "but it is when reality begins to touch one's life that one's high-sounding ideas are put to the test. Your very presence here forces us to reexamine what we believe, and more importantly, how we put our beliefs into practice."

"I understand, Virginia, but it is even more complicated; there are two sides to this coin."

"I'm not sure what you mean."

"What I mean is that I grew up with certain perceptions of the upper class, the rich. I have seen the class warfare first hand and have always felt anger, distrust, even hatred toward the owning class. While your father fears his loss of standing because of our relationship, I fear that I might be seen as selling out by my family and our friends and comrades in the struggle for workers' rights."

"I see." I could not read her face.

***

Wanda is moving around, humming as she checks everything. I let her know I'm awake.

"Good morning, Isaac. You've had a nice quiet night; it's half past eight on Sunday morning, May twenty-sixth."

Huh? The last thing I remember it was yesterday afternoon and Danielle and Sam were here. I must have slept well - it was an exhausting visit, creating two new words. How crazy is that? I remember when I could run ten miles and barely break a sweat - but that came with the promise of blood and bullets so I'd rather be here, thank you.

"I see you have a word chart on the wall. Impressive."

I do. Let's see if it works. Short, long, long.

"Sorry, Isaac, I missed that. Could you do it again, please?"

I repeat the word.

"Sing? You want me to sing?"

Yes.

"OK, but I'm a little rusty so early in the day." She clears her throat then breathes in deeply. "Let it be a dance we do, may I have this dance with you? In the good times and the bad times too - let it be a dance!" Her rich voice moves and sways with the tune.

How does Wanda know this song? It is a Unitarian Universalist modern classic by the Reverend Ric Masten. Our son, Albert, brought us to a service Ric led at the Arlington Street Church in 1979. It was a few months before my Virginia died and she was very weak. When Ric started singing "Let it be a dance," a broad smile lit up Virginia's face; she sang along, rocking her body from side to side. On the ride home she sang the refrain several times. She asked that we sing the song at her memorial service, and we did.

I feel the tears on my cheeks. Wanda stops singing. "I love that song," she says. "We had a guest chorus at our church the Sunday before Thanksgiving and they sang it for us. Our choir director was able to get the music and we sang it in church last week. It brought people to tears."

Thank you. The world is even more intertwined than we imagine. Dear Wanda, I cannot tell you how much I thank you.

Chapter 28

Virginia and I sat on the sofa sipping our tea. We sensed that we had been seen kissing in the Gardens, but neither Mr. Appleton nor his wife said anything. It was awkward. Finally, Mrs. Appleton, seated in her usual chair by the bay window, asked; "How is your mother faring, Isaac?"

"I'm pleased to say the strike ended yesterday and she is happy it is over. And so am I. The workers won most of what they were seeking. We had quite a party in our home last evening!"

"That's very good." She offered me a second slice of Bea's famous ginger cake, and handed it to me before I could answer.

"Mother, Isaac would like to make some drawings of the Metzinger."

"Of course. I'll ring for Bea to take the tea things away."

A minute or two later, Bea gathered up the cups, saucers, plates, forks and pots and brought them back to the kitchen. Mr. and Mrs. Appleton followed her out, leaving Virginia and me alone in the parlor.

"That was uncomfortable," I said.

"It certainly was. I have never seen my father at a loss for words. If nothing else, he is always the most perfect host."

I took her hand. "Well, at least they didn't invite me to leave; in fact, they left us here by ourselves."

She sat silently, looking down at her hand in mine. Then she said; "I know what is bothering him, Isaac. It really is quite simple. My father wants not to like you, but he can't. Every time you talk, he is more impressed by you. He just does not want to admit to himself that he likes you."

"I hope he comes around."

"He will. Father is a good man, an honest man."

"Sometimes being honest with oneself is the most difficult."

"He is struggling with this, but he will come around." She stood. "Why don't you start your drawing? I'll go into the music room and practice my Chopin." She pecked me on the cheek then strode across the room, opened the double doors at the far end and disappeared into the adjoining room. Moments later she started playing the piano.

I moved one of the chairs so that I could sit facing the Metzinger and began to draw as the music spilled into the space. In my mind's eye I reconstructed the painting; it was as if Metzinger had seen the subject through multiple prisms and then flattened what he saw onto the canvas. The shapes were sharp, geometric, but not quite two-dimensional. He created the sense of movement by the angles and rhythms of the intersecting and overlapping shapes, and their subtle changes in color. And then he used solid simple blocks of strong colors to accent certain features and to force the eye to keep moving across the surface of the painting. With Virginia playing Chopin in the background and this mesmerizing painting before my eyes I felt I was in a dream.

***

It occurs to me that I haven't seen a doctor in a long time. More precisely, I have not been aware of a doctor's visit in a long time. Is it because no doctor has been, or have I simply not been aware? Or have I been aware at the time, but blocked them out or forgotten? The same goes for the physical therapist. I'm sure she is supposed to be here every day, but I have no memory of her for days. I don't like this. Is my mind playing tricks on me, developing holes? Or, maybe I'm actually sleeping more than I think I am.

My cat-machine has started beeping. That means my pulse has risen too high. Anxiety. I breathe in as slowly and deeply as I can. Exhale slowly. Repeat several times. The beeping stops moments after a nurse enters the room. She takes my wrist to check my pulse. I guess she doesn't fully trust the machine. "False alarm," she says as she places my wrist back on the bed. I do not recognize her voice.

***

Virginia invited me to return again the following Saturday, but on Wednesday when I arrived home from work I found a letter from her with a package containing two publications. In her letter she asked if I could change my visit to Sunday afternoon at two-thirty because her father wanted Reverend Frothingham to meet me and he was not free on

Saturday. "I hope you do not see this as an attempted ambush, Isaac," she wrote, "but to prepare you for the meeting I thought these two pamphlets might be helpful. One is a sermon given by the Reverend on Britain's Day last December. The other is a small collection of Unitarian hymns that expresses the Unitarian view of the world. I know you will read them with an open mind."

She went on to suggest I read the hymnal first, and she asked me to return the books to her on Sunday, if I was able to come that day. I wondered if her father knew she had sent these items to me.

I wrote a hasty note saying I looked forward to meeting the Reverend and I thanked her for the reading material. I ran down to the mailbox three blocks away, then returned to the apartment and settled down to read.

I began with the introduction to *The Unitarian Faith as set forth in Fifty Unitarian Hymns,* trying to figure out how to approach the subject. It was so alien to me. I knew little about Christianity, and I certainly knew nothing about the nuances of belief that distinguished a Catholic from a Methodist, a Lutheran, a Baptist, a Unitarian or any other denomination.

But Virginia had implied that I prepare for an ambush! She also asked me to read with an open mind - a term she had used more than once to describe her parents. She had talked, also, about the difficulty they confronted in seeing their beliefs and ideas reflected in the real world, in real people. So, as I read through the book, I searched for passages that talked about breaking with tradition, expanding the mind, the relationship of people to one another, being open to change - and I found several, which I copied into a note book. I also found a number of other ideas that were hard to accept; I copied those, too.

Mama came home as I was reading. She set the kettle on the stove for tea, then sat opposite me at the table. "More books from mister architect?"

"No, Mama, books from Virginia. Her father has invited their minister to meet me next Sunday. Virginia sent me some material to study so that I don't make a fool of myself."

"Is it interesting?"

"In a way. If you're worried that I am suddenly going to become a Christian, don't be. It's interesting in the same way that watching a fire is interesting. I have no desire to jump in."

She laughed, then stood and leaned across the table to ruffle my hair.

"You love this young woman, don't you Itzik?"

"I do, Mama. She is wonderful to be with, wonderful to know."

"And when do you think you will introduce her to your mother? When will I meet her family?"

I had expected this would come up at some point, but I was still not prepared for it. I hesitated, then replied; "I'll bring up the question with Virginia and her parents when I see them on Sunday."

"Good. A mother needs to know who her son is spending time with."

She poured the tea and we drank in silence. I returned to the hymn book and my notes, while Mama warmed up some soup and fried some eggs for supper.

It was almost midnight by the time I was done reading the book of hymns. If I was to be engaged in a conversation with Mr. Appleton and the Reverend I wanted to know how they saw the world. But, as I lay in bed thinking about the upcoming meeting, an equally important issue arose: where did they place me - the working class, non-observant Jewish young man - in their perception of the world. I was very tired, but the question kept rolling over and over in my mind.

The next day seemed to last forever. I spent the morning working on my first set of elevation drawings for a small wood-framed house that Mr. Wilkins was designing. In the afternoon Mr. Jackson introduced me to the techniques and frustrations of drawing in India ink. By the end of the day I was irritated and exhausted. I arrived back at the apartment and picked up *Our Debt to Great Britain* by the Reverend Paul Revere Frothingham. Seriously - that's the man's name! I decided I was in no mood for it. Instead I spread out the drawings I had made of the Metzinger painting and began to study them.

When Mama came home I asked her if I could draw her while she prepared supper. I tried to create her in the style of Metzinger, breaking down her form, as well as the table and stove, into contoured, interwoven geometric shapes. I added pieces of other elements of the room - the window, the sofa, the pictures on the walls. It was like learning a new language, one that was filled with words and phrases which could be both precise and ambiguous at the same time. It allowed for multiple levels of meaning and appreciation. I understood, too, that this was not an easy language to learn, but it was definitely worth the effort.

Mama thought the picture was "pretty, but nuts," and I felt good about that.

The next evening, Friday, I settled down after supper with the Reverend's Britain's Day speech. The intent of the speech was to honor the sacrifices of the British people in the war - and it certainly did. It was luxuriant in its praise and overflowed with grand statements of their heroism and courage and "dogged perseverance." From the first paragraphs it reminded me of the blustering self-righteousness of that senator from Illinois who spoke at the July Fourth commemoration at the hospital in Rouen.

The Reverend did give credit to Britain's attempts before the war to avert the conflict through diplomacy, but, basically he saw the war as a struggle between good and evil. Towards the end of the speech, the Reverend returned to the theme of Britain's sacrifice and he asserted that compared to the losses that the British people suffered, America lost "but a scattered few."

I threw the pamphlet onto the floor. He had no idea! To him it was all bugles, flags and ceremonies, including the burials. My impulse was to cancel the visit; I did not think I could meet with this man without getting into an argument. How could I respond to this pompous "man of God" without alienating Mr. Appleton and in so doing, losing Virginia?

"What's got you so upset, Itzik?" my mother asked. She had been sitting at the table while I was reading and heard my frequent bursts of anger and contempt.

I picked the pamphlet off the floor and said, "You read it! You'll see why I'm angry at this Reverend Paul Revere Frothingham!"

"Whew! Quite the name!"

"It goes well with his little book!"

"You really want me to read it?"

"Actually, Mama, I do," I replied after I had thought about it. "Maybe I'm over-reacting. Maybe it's because the war is too close to me. Perhaps you will have a more neutral view of it."

"I'm too tired tonight. I'll read it first thing in the morning." She stood and went into her room. "By the way, Itzik," she said before closing the bedroom door, "I had another look at your nutty drawings - I like them!"

I woke up late the next morning to find my mother at the kitchen table sipping her tea. She poured a cup for me then said, "Well, Itzik, I read Mr. Frothing's booklet. I also read most of the other one. The one about Britain is just a lot of hot air trapped in very fancy language. I would ignore it - he was being a politician and you know how they are." She lifted the book of hymns and continued, "This one, if you could get rid of all the Jesus and Almighty stuff, has some interesting things to say."

"Mama, I think the God and Jesus stuff is what holds them all together. You can't simply throw them out."

"Itzik. This is about beliefs and thoughts and ideas. Philosophy. And in philosophy you certainly can push aside the things that don't make sense."

"Really?"

"Yes, and as I was about to say, there are interesting observations here about science and learning and peace. I even found a reference to the importance of working people."

"I found a few words or phrases, but..."

She cut me off. "This is not only philosophy, it is poetry, and in poetry you can't expect long paragraphs about important subjects. In poetry all you get is a word or two, a hint. If you're lucky you might get one full sentence. So, when you see the word 'labor' set in a positive context, you see it as respecting labor."

"But, does it really have any idea what labor is? Or peace, or justice?"

"That's what you have to find out tomorrow, my boy. But be polite."

"You are a wise woman, Mama."

"Between your Uncle Kalner's books and work in the union I've learned a thing or two." She laughed, then added seriously. "I've also lived through more than my share of life's troubles."

***

I hear Sam's coughing. I wish he would stop smoking, but that's not very likely. I catch a trace of Danielle's perfume. I blink three times.

"He's awake!" Sam has a flash of childlike wonder in his voice - as if he has just seen, for the first time, a fish jump out of a pond.

"We're back, Isaac. Sam wanted to see you before he left; I'm bringing him to the airport in a couple of hours."

Thank you.

"It's Sunday evening, May twenty-sixth. We had a spectacular sunset - you would have loved it. There were two types of clouds - high streaky ones in bands across the horizon and random small low puffy ones. The colors lit them all up - reds, yellows, orange, purple. We stopped the car for about twenty minutes to look."

"I took dozens of photographs."

I am long past feeling jealous or sorry for myself for not being able to see things like this. I try to visualize them as they are described to me - the more detail the better. I wish I could smile. I blink "Thank you," again, and Danielle takes my hand.

When my children were young, during the Depression, we used to have a game we called the "Colors and Shapes Game." We would go to some open space and I would bring my paints and a canvas. I'd mix a color and put it on the canvas in a particular shape and the kids would have to find something in the area that matched what I had painted. Once they called it out, I would add another area of color. They got to be pretty good at it, and they learned to actually see things. It was also a great way for me to work while looking after the children. Of course, they got bored with the whole thing after a while, so I let them play whatever they wanted while I continued to paint, and keep an eye on them.

Chapter 29

I knocked on the door at a few minutes before two-thirty. I was dressed in my best clothes with my new blue necktie, and my shoes well shined. Bea opened the door, took my hat, and showed me into the parlor. "The family will be here shortly," she said.

"Thank you, Bea. You don't attend the same church?"

"No. My church has services on Sunday evenings, Mr. Isaac."

I waited, standing in front of the Metzinger and wondering where the Appleton's and the Reverend were. After some time, I turned and looked out the big bay window into the Boston Garden and saw Virginia, her parents and a man, who I assumed to be the Reverend Paul Revere Frothingham, walking through the gardens towards the house. I had hoped Virginia and I would have a few minutes together before the Reverend arrived but that was not to be.

I watched them as they crossed the street. The two men were deep in conversation while Virginia and her mother seemed to be enjoying the warmth and color of the spring afternoon. They were all dressed formally in their church clothes. I felt out of place, but that was the reality of the situation.

Virginia entered the parlor first. "I'm sorry I was not here to greet you, Isaac. We decided to go to the parish house to meet the Reverend and walk with him. He's a busy man and was a little behind schedule."

"It's quite all right," I smiled, "You are always worth waiting for."

"Reverend Frothingham, this is Mr. Simon, the young man I have been telling you about." It was Mr. Appleton.

"I am pleased to meet you, Mr. Simon." We shook hands. "Mr. Appleton has told me a great deal about you. As has Virginia." He seemed almost as uncomfortable as me.

"Pleased to meet you, too, sir."

"Well, why don't we all sit down?" Mr. Appleton motioned to the Reverend to sit in a chair between the couch and his chair. Then he directed Virginia and me to sit on the couch, with me closer to the Reverend and himself. Mrs. Appleton sat in her usual chair next to the bay window.

I felt everyone looking at me, as if I was expected to initiate the conversation. But I thought it wiser to defer to the Reverend or to Mr. Appleton, so I remained silent, staring at Virginia's tightly clasped hands resting on her lap. Finally, Mrs. Appleton said, "Virginia, dear, could you please ask Bea to bring in the tea as soon as it is ready."

As Virginia left the room, the Reverend said, "Mr. Simon, Mr. Appleton tells me that you were with the Yankee Division."

I had no desire to talk about the war, especially with someone I did not know. "Yes, sir. I was with the one hundred and first engineers." I needed to redirect the conversation. "Now I am working as an architectural draftsman and planning to be an architect. Some of the skills I learned in the engineers are applicable to my current endeavors."

But the Reverend plowed on. "I visited several of the training camps around Boston during the war. I was always so impressed with the spirit and enthusiasm of the men."

Please don't go down that road. "Yes." I looked around for Virginia, for Bea and the tea things - anything to stop this.

"I remember talking with a colonel at one of the training centers - his family were long-time members of our church - and he talked so glowingly of the Army's ability to unify men from so many different backgrounds."

"Very true, sir. When the men on the other side are shooting and firing cannons at you there are more pressing needs than worrying about where the fellows next to you were born, or what languages they grew up speaking. Although, even in a war, there is enough down time for the bigots to crawl out from under their rocks." I immediately wished I had not said that last sentence.

He didn't miss a beat. "Did you experience much anti-Semitism?"

I recalled Reuven's letters to me while I was in the hospital. "There were a few unpleasant incidents. Fortunately, our lieutenant was able to take care of the situation before it got out of control."

"Very good. And how did he accomplish that?"

He asked for it. "Well, sir, he sent the three perpetrators on what amounted to a suicide mission. Only one of them came back, and he was seriously wounded."

Mrs. Appleton gasped. The Reverend lowered his head.

"With all due respect, Reverend Frothingham, I would prefer not to talk about the war. I would just ask this; I assume, as a minister, you also visited the hospitals that wounded men came home to. Can you honestly say that you found the same spirit and enthusiasm there as you found in the training camps?" I wanted to stop, but could not. "Terrible things happen to people in war, sir. I was wounded. I almost lost my leg. But it is not the memory or occasional recurring pain from that incident that give me nightmares; it is what I saw and what I did over there that haunt me."

Virginia had returned and was sitting next to me. She put her hand on mine.

"You did what you had to, Mr. Simon," the Reverend responded, trying to sound supportive. "And you did it for an honorable and noble cause."

"There is nothing honorable or noble about killing. This was a war about big powers trying to re-divide the world, and it was millions of poor fools like me on both sides of no-man's-land who paid the price."

Thankfully, Mrs. Appleton announced that the tea had arrived before the Reverend could respond. Tea was poured and distributed. Then the cakes. Somehow Mrs. Appleton managed to keep the conversation light or, at least, non-controversial. We talked about the upcoming votes in the states to ratify the nineteenth amendment allowing women to vote and the Reverend said that he would be delivering a sermon in support of that issue within the coming weeks.

After the tea things were taken away by Bea, Virginia and her mother left the parlor as if by pre-arranged signal, leaving me alone with Mr. Appleton and Reverend Frothingham, who began to speak the moment the women had exited. "Mr. Simon, I appreciate your reluctance to talk about the war, but I do want to close the discussion on the matter by saying that before the war I was deeply involved in organizations for peace, meeting with government officials here and abroad and attending many conferences, including the International Church Peace Congress in August 1914 in Germany and England, a few days before the declaration of war. But soon after, I became convinced of Germany's aggressions and malice and threw my support behind the British and their allies, and later behind

President Wilson. I believe it was the war to end all wars. I still hold that dream of world peace and am an ardent advocate for the League of Nations."

"I certainly like the idea of the League of Nations," I said, hoping that we were now about to move to a different subject. And I was not to be disappointed!

"On a more immediate matter, Mr. Simon; Mr. Appleton has discussed with me his concerns about you courting Virginia. I will not beat around the bush; if you are considering marriage, would you be willing to renounce your Jewish faith and marry within the Unitarian church?"

Both men were leaning back in their chairs. Both had their arms folded and their eyes were fixed on me. "Reverend Frothingham, I appreciate your directness so I will try to answer as directly as I can, but this is not a simple matter," I began, hesitating, searching for words. "Virginia and I have not seriously discussed marriage, but I certainly have thought about it, and I suspect she has, too. We have talked on several occasions about the differences between us - differences of religion as well as class. Virginia and I both believe these differences are not un-bridgeable. We can learn to build bridges of the heart. It is a matter of will and love, both of which we have in abundance."

I took a deep breath. "To the specifics of your question. I have mentioned to you, Mr. Appleton, that I do not consider myself a religious person. I grew up Jewish and am very much imbued with that tradition and history, but the idea of an almighty God who looks over me and cares for me or guides me or listens to my prayers, is an idea that has little meaning for me. I believe in science, in reason, in art, in nature, in people - and I think you and I have some common ground there - and that is enough for me. I regret mentioning the war again right after I asked not to discuss it any further, but any lingering beliefs in God I might have had have been sucked into the blood-drenched mud of France.

"Having said that, I could no less dismiss my Jewish heritage than a zebra could lose its stripes; it is part of who I am although I am not defined or constrained by it. To the second part of your question, if Virginia and I were to marry, would I be willing to marry within the church? I have to answer that I really don't know enough about Unitarianism to make a decision. Virginia did send me some reading material, parts of which I found quite interesting and forward-looking and other parts, frankly, I found to be outside my experience of reality. "

"What did she send you?" Mr. Appleton asked.

I described the book of hymns and the Reverend's sermon.

"That collection of hymns represents some aspects of our faith," the Reverend responded, "but we are a cantankerous group and each church has a significant degree of independence. Some churches tend to be more spiritually and biblically based, others are more directed towards what we do on earth rather than continually looking towards the heavens. It is a matter of emphasis and is manifested in the person of the minister, who has the freedom to preach his mind from the pulpit. Our church here on Arlington Street leans more toward the human person of Jesus than the divine; we see in His life an example for how we should live ours. We worry less about the Kingdom of God and more about our deeds on earth." He leaned forward. "Everything starts and ends with love, Isaac. That is what is important."

"If everything starts and ends with love, Reverend and Mr. Appleton, then why would you need us to marry in your church?"

"Because God is love and the church is His house."

I could not win an argument on theology with a minister, but I was young and pig-headed, so I pushed on. "There are probably thousands of different religions in the world, each with its own description of god. It stands to reason from this situation, that god is a creation of man, not the other way around. Who is to say that the gods revered by the Zulu people of South Africa are less great or powerful or loving than your Christian God? And when you do start comparing gods, and claiming that one god is better than another, then you soon find yourself at war - and that benefits no one, except those who seek more power."

"It is true, Mr. Simon, that religions were created as a means of organizing and ordering society. But God has always existed and always will, throughout eternity. Perhaps the different religions of the world each describe a small fraction of the different facets of the one God." Reverend Frothingham sighed, then stood up and began to pace back and forth on the Persian carpet in front of the couch. "I fear we have gone off in a direction that is not very fruitful, Isaac. The theory and the theology are less important to me, and to my church, than the deeds, the way we conduct our lives. That is what counts: that we act with love and caring to each other and to the world. I try to live this way with the love and guidance of God - the God I have come to see. Others, I am sure, experience this love in other ways. Who am I to say that their experience is any less valid, any less important?"

"Sir, I..."

He held up his hand. "Please Isaac, allow me to finish." He stopped pacing a few feet in front of me. "I am sure that I am the first Christian minister you have had a lengthy discussion with, and you undoubtedly have some preconceived ideas about me. That is understandable, but what I want you to know about my faith - Unitarianism - is that it is not static; it is ever evolving. So while we recognize the supremacy of God, we are always questioning and investigating our relationship to Him, and our relationships to one another. We do not believe in eternal truths - that laws and rules which were written thousands of years ago are all directly applicable to today. The Bible, and particularly the stories of the life of Jesus, is a guide to us on how we should live. Further, we are not so narrow as to seek wisdom and guidance only in that one holy book. For example, before I came to the Arlington Street Church I preached a sermon at Easter, which traditionally is the holiday commemorating the resurrection of Christ, and I used readings from Buddhist texts instead of the Bible."

Reverend Frothingham sat down on the couch beside me. "What I am saying, Isaac, is that we - Mr. Appleton and I - came to this meeting preparing to judge you. That was wrong. I can clearly see that you are a thoughtful, caring young man. I hope and trust that you will not judge us. I hope you will take the time and make the effort to get to know this church."

I should have thanked him, promised to consider his words, and left it there. But there were still questions gnawing it me. "Reverend, you have asked me whether I would be willing to accept your church. If I were to agree, I wonder how willing your congregation would be to accept me, Isaac Simon, the poor working class person whose widowed mother works in a textile mill and is a union activist. My people, for the most part, were ignorant peasants and tradesmen. How welcoming would the intellectual and financial elite of Boston be of all of that? As I see it, sir, the major area of concern is not about religion, but about class, and we have not talked about that at all this afternoon."

We were all silent. I heard the soft chime of the banjo clock; five o'clock. The Reverend looked at his pocket watch and confirmed the hour. "Goodness. I need to rush back to the parish house and prepare for vespers." He rose from the couch and I followed. "You raise a valid question, Isaac; one which needs more time to discuss than I, unfortunately, can devote right now. Mr. Appleton, Virginia and I talked about this very question. Perhaps they can fill you in."

I thanked him for his time and for the interesting discussion, as did Mr. Appleton who accompanied him to the door. I heard the Reverend say; "He is a fine young man, George, and remarkably articulate for one with his level of education. Give him time."

The front door closed and Mr. Appleton returned to the parlor. "Would you like a sherry, Isaac?"

"No thank you, sir."

"You don't drink?"

"I drink very little, sir." Should I tell him more? Today's the day to put it all out on the table. "My father was a heavy drinker. He actually died when he fell down drunk in a winter storm and froze to death before he could be found. My brother also drank excessively, using it during the war to dull his senses. It got him into trouble several times. As a result, I am wary of its effects."

He poured his sherry and we both sat down. Mrs. Appleton and Virginia returned. "Did you gentlemen have a fruitful discussion?" Mrs. Appleton asked.

"We did. Yes, I'd say it was. Would you agree, Isaac?"

"I would."

"Although it ran longer than expected and the Reverend had to hurry off for vespers, leaving some still unexplored questions."

Virginia commented; "The Reverend is fond of saying that the process is as important as the outcome - which translated into English means that he enjoys talking." We all laughed.

"To be fair, I found myself going on a bit, too," I said.

"Complex questions cannot be explored with simple answers. I appreciated the depth of your responses, Isaac, even as I am still trying to weigh their impact."

I was not sure what her father meant. I looked at Virginia; she had the same quizzical expression on her face as I suspected I had on mine.

Mr. Appleton stood and started walking to the door, then he stopped and looked back at both of us. "We'll work it out," he said, and left the room. Mrs. Appleton followed without saying a word.

***

I am aware of my cat-machine. Besides its purrs and occasional puffs, there is complete silence. I must have drifted off while Danielle and Sam were here. I wish I hadn't done that; I was not polite, and more importantly, I love her like my own daughter.

My daughter! Oh Emma! Dear child. I have said nothing about you, though I think about you all the time. You are like a never-ending glow inside me - an ember that brings both warmth and pain. There was a song, I think by Bob Dylan. "Forever Young" it was called. It came along years after you died, but in my mind it holds you. I wept when I first heard the words. I still weep. "May you always be courageous, Stand upright and be strong, And may you stay Forever young." And you are. And Mark, my son, is right beside you - another burning fire. What can I say?

"Are you saying something, Isaac?" It's Wanda.

My eyes are blinking as the tears roll down my face. I am not saying a word, but I cannot control my eyelids.

"Oh, you're crying. That's OK, Isaac. Crying is good medicine."

It is. I focus all of my attention to feel the tears, to watch them flow over my wrinkled old skin, and be diverted by the grooves in my face, and finally meander between the hairs of my beard. I can almost paint it like a vast shimmering river-scape inside my head.

Wanda gives me time, quietly going about doing what she needs to do. I am thankful that she does not wipe away my tears. I can feel them slowly drying on my skin.

Finally she says, "I'm working Damon's usual shift tonight, then I'm off for a couple of days. I'm going to spend some time with my Mama in upstate New York. I haven't seen her since Christmas. See you in a few days, Isaac."

Bye. I blink "Thank you," but I do not know whether she sees it. She forgot to give me the date-stamp. The room is quiet again except for the cat-machine.

Chapter 30

"So, how was it really?" Virginia was next to me on the couch, holding my hand.

"I like Reverend Frothingham. I do. He's an honest man and sincere."

"But?"

"But, we are worlds apart."

After a long pause, she said; "I've been thinking about you, Isaac. You've never explained how someone who ten years ago was, as you say, an ignorant Lithuanian peasant, has become so articulate, so at ease in conversation with high-ranking men with generations of Harvard education, and in a language that is foreign to you."

"I would not say I'm 'at ease' in these conversations, but I'm not afraid of them. I don't want to sound like some wizened old seer, but I have seen enough of the world and met enough people of different rank to regard everyone as equal and so I'm not intimidated by them. I suppose it begins with my Uncle Kalner. He's my mother's older brother and he took care of us both before and after my father died. He was the one who brought us to America. My Uncle Kalner is a remarkable man, the opposite of my father who truly was an ignorant, drunken bully.

"Back in Linkeve, Uncle Kalner worked in one of the few stores in town. It was something like an American general store, selling everything from seeds, lumber and tools, to fabrics and thread. It also sold books; not many, because not many people in the village could read. Uncle Kalner taught himself to read - Hebrew and Yiddish, and also Russian and a bit of English. That's not only four different languages, but three completely different alphabets! I have no idea how he did it."

"An amazing man," Virginia interjected.

"Yes, he is," I continued. "He collected books on whatever subjects interested him and he spent most of his wages on those books and most of his free time reading them. He built a wide and varied library which he delighted in showing me and my brother. We would talk about history and art and architecture, animals and the stars. He encouraged me to draw even when my own father thought I was a foolish dreamer wasting my time."

Virginia took my hand but said nothing. She seemed entranced by my story.

"My Uncle Kalner would read poetry to me in these foreign languages that I did not understand: Keats and Shakespeare, and some obscure Russian name Fofanov, whose name tickled me and I never forgot, although his poetry is long gone. But my uncle's favorite was a poet named Yehudah Leib Gordon who promoted the ideas of a liberal enlightened Jewish identity and involvement in the wider world.

"Uncle Kalner also showed me pictures of moose and tigers, the cathedrals and palaces of Moscow and Saint Petersburg and Paris, and we talked about ideas. I did not know the word 'philosophy' then but when I think back to those visits to his small house, philosophy is mostly what we talked about.

"And he forced me to learn English," I continued. "Almost from the moment we set foot on American soil he refused to speak to me in Yiddish and he would not respond to anything I said that wasn't in English. Once I learned to read in English, I couldn't stop. Uncle Kalner was not as hard with my mother, but hard enough so that she became fluent in this 'confounding language', as he called it, within a couple of years. Meanwhile, he was working in the mill and learned French and Italian as well."

"Astonishing. I would love to meet him. Where is he now?"

"He lives in New York City. He is a union organizer, a Socialist. He recently remarried - to a divorced Catholic woman who I have yet to meet, but I am thankful to them for breaking that barrier."

"You certainly do have a rather interesting family," she said.

"It's all pretty normal to me," I replied. "But, speaking of family, my mother wants to meet you. She says that a mother needs to know who her son is spending time with."

Virginia hesitated. "I would like to meet her, too. Perhaps she can accompany you on a future visit. I will speak with my mother."

"She read the publications you sent me and offered very insightful and positive advice on how to understand and discuss them."

"Does she hold similar views to you?"

"It's the other way around - I learned from her." I took both her hands in mine. "Does it bother you that I do not believe in God?"

"One of the things about Unitarians is that we are almost never one hundred percent certain about anything. Questioning, re-examining, is in our nature. However, the existence of God is the one unshakeable thing."

"And those of us who do not believe are damned?"

She laughed. "No. We don't believe in eternal punishment. No, Isaac, you are not damned, but I believe you do miss something wonderful - that sense of wholeness and all-embracing, unconditional love."

I wanted to say, "You and I have that together," but felt that was too forward. Instead I said, "It must be a reassuring feeling, but I just can't flip a switch and turn it on."

***

Chanel Number 5. Danielle. *I am here.*

"Good morning, Isaac."

I signal for a hug. She laughs and lays her head gently on my chest.

"It's almost eleven in the morning of May twenty-seventh, Memorial Day. I've been at the cemetery for a while, visiting Albert and Emma and a few others."

Thank you.

"Lots of people out there this morning. Too many flags; it always saddens me how many of our people were soldiers - generation after generation. We don't seem to have learned much from our past!"

Danielle never knew Emma, or Mark - and Mark has no headstone; there is no place for one to visit except the ocean. Mark's B-24 Liberator went down in the English Channel in June 1944.

I was in my studio in the back of the house when the knock on the door came. Virginia was volunteering at the Red Cross, as she had seventeen years before in that war to end all wars. When she came home she found me at the kitchen table with the telegram in my hand and tears streaming from my eyes. I just said, "Mark," and she fell on her knees beside me, threw her arms around me and we wept together.

He was our second son; a little guy with a broad smile and a heart of gold. He was kind and creative; he wrote plays for his high school drama club, and wanted to be a screen-writer for the movies. He wrote in one of his first letters after being posted to England that he saw the war as a way to "gain experience of life so that I can write with authenticity." There's nothing more real than death.

About ten or twelve years ago Allen asked me if I wanted to see some World War Two planes. "What kind of planes?" I asked.

"I'm not sure, Grandpa Isaac. I think there are some bombers and a couple of fighters. They're at a small airfield in Nashua. It's less than an hour from here."

It was a beautiful late summer day, almost fall - a few leaves had already begun to change color; the sky was cloudless, brilliant blue and the air was fresh and vibrant. We drove with the windows down. I remember the feel of the wind in my beard. We parked outside the fence and I could see the four aircraft lined up side by side on the apron.

There was one fighter, a P-51 Mustang, and three bombers, a B-17 Flying Fortress, a B-25 Mitchell, and a B-24 Liberator. People were walking around the planes, taking pictures, checking out the guns and the paintings on the noses. The bomb bay doors were open on all three of the big planes and people were climbing underneath and looking up.

As we walked toward the planes I began to feel a little uneasy. "I'm not sure about this," I said to Allen.

"It will be OK," he replied, and took my arm.

I breathed deeply, trying to focus my energy. It was one of those situations that you did not want to be in, but you also knew that if you walked away you would never forgive yourself.

"Let's take a look at the Liberator," I said, and we walked slowly toward it.

The four huge engines hung from the wings that were mounted high on the fuselage. I had read about this plane, how the set and size of the wings made it faster and able to travel longer distances than the B-17, but it was also less maneuverable, less agile and so more vulnerable to attack.

This Liberator had the word "Witchcraft" painted on the side of its nose, accompanied by a painting of a witch on a broomstick. I wondered how they had come up with that name. Mark had written that his craft was called "Old Bettie."

Allen guided me under the wing. I wished I could have gotten down low enough to look up into the bomb bay, but my old bones would not allow it. Behind the bomb bay was the bubble for the underside gunner. It was tiny - I couldn't imagine anyone getting in there, let alone flying in that thing. We went around to the rear, and I looked up at the tail gunner's position. I remember standing there a long time, my hands clasped behind my back, tears rolling down my face.

"Do you want to see inside?" Allen asked.

I nodded.

He helped me up the short ladder into the fuselage. As I found my footing inside the plane, the Liberator suddenly seemed so small. I stretched out my arms and could almost touch both sides of the interior. Looking back toward the tail gunner's position, the whole thing was unimaginable to me. There was a crawlway the gunner had to navigate before he got to the bubble. There was almost no room for him to move once he was settled in. It must have been unbelievably cold and noisy when they were airborne. Not to mention that feeling of being dangled out into nothingness. Being a little guy is probably what got Mark the job.

Mark's last letter home was dated June eighth 1944. He wrote about flying in the tail gunner's bubble suspended above the broken clouds and looking down, being able to see the spreading wakes of countless vessels as they headed from England to France. He wrote that he knew his brother Albert was on one of those landing craft, and he felt like he was looking out for him.

Less than a week later, Mark was killed during a mission over central France. Their Liberator was attacked from the rear by three German fighters. He was only able to hit one of them before his little bubble was ripped apart. Other crew members managed to deal with the two remaining fighters, but the craft was badly damaged and was leaking fuel. The captain turned the plane back towards England but they never made it. The details of what happened to Mark's craft and the location where they went down were reported by others in his squadron. Several air and sea searches were unable to find the wreckage or anyone.

Allen touched my arm. "Someone is trying to get past you, Grandpa Isaac."

"Can we go?'

"You don't want to see the other planes?"

"I've seen all I need to see," I replied, and for sure, I had seen enough.

I had been able to get a sense of how my son had spent the last moments of his life - sitting on fire at the edge of the world.

We drove home in silence. Allen walked me to my apartment. "I wish you could have known him," I said. "Your Uncle Mark was a unique person."

He hugged me.

"Thank you for today, Allen. I really needed to be there. It was important, cathartic."

I realize that I have drifted off from Danielle again, but fortunately her perfume is still here and I can hear her steady breathing. I wonder if she is asleep, but soon I hear her turn the page of a book. I blink that I am back.

"You there, Isaac?"

Yes. I'm thinking that the next word for me to say is "sorry," because I find myself ignoring people who come to see me and that is very impolite. I need to be able to apologize.

"Are you ready for another word or two?"

Yes.

"Actually, I have a word in mind. We need to know if you like something or not - so, can you come up with a signal for 'like' and we can use its reverse order for 'don't like.'"

Good words to know. *Yes.*

"Give me the new word signal when you are ready."

I think of a check mark - short stroke down, then longer stroke up. So, short-long can be "like" and long-short can be "don't like." Pretty soon the signals are created and Danielle has added them to the chart. We also create the signal for 'sorry' which I visualized as an upside-down smile and translated to long-short-short-long.

"You have nothing to be sorry for, Isaac," she said, after she added the word to the chart.

Thank you.

"But, I do. I'm afraid I have to leave now. Hug?"

Hug.

***

I had to cancel plans to visit Virginia the following Saturday because

Mr. Wilkins asked me to work; he had an appointment with a client on the Monday and we were behind schedule with the drawings. He also wanted me to work on a watercolor rendering of the design. I worked all day Saturday and came in for a few hours on Sunday to finish. Mr. Wilkins thanked me for my extra effort, and even praised my work to the clients - a young couple who were building their first home together.

My next visit to Virginia was on Saturday, June fourteenth. We had exchanged letters during the intervening weeks and she had agreed to accompany me to lunch, followed by a visit to the Museum of Fine Arts. This was to be our first time together away from the watchful eyes of her parents. I was a little nervous.

I arrived at the Appleton home at noon, and was greeted at the door by Mrs. Appleton. "Come in, Isaac. Virginia will be down in a minute or two." I followed her into the parlor and she motioned me to sit. She sat in her usual chair. "Virginia mentioned that your mother was interested in meeting us."

"Yes, she is."

"Well, Virginia and I have an idea. The Massachusetts House is preparing to vote on the ratification of the women's suffrage amendment within the next couple of weeks. There will be a large rally in support of the amendment in the Common near the State House steps next Saturday morning at ten o'clock. I would like to invite you and your mother to join Virginia and me at the rally, and then come back to the house afterwards for an informal luncheon."

"That sounds like something my mother would want to do. Of course, I cannot make a commitment for her, but I will extend the invitation and write immediately to let you know her answer."

Virginia entered and I stood. She was dressed for summer in a calf-length light blue dress, square cut at the neck and with short sleeves. I think she selected it to match my necktie. Her hair had been cut quite short, framing her face. She was beautiful. I could not resist kissing her briefly on the cheek right in front of her mother!

"Did you tell Isaac of our idea for next Saturday, mother?"

"I did - and he thinks his mother would love to join us."

"Wonderful. I am so looking forward to meeting her. Will you be participating in the rally, Isaac?"

"Of course."

She gave me a quick hug. "Then, let's be off."

"You'll be home by five-thirty?"

"Yes, Mother. We won't be late."

She took my arm and we walked up Beacon Street towards the business heart of the city. "Where shall we eat?" I asked.

"Wherever you wish. I am not particular."

The only restaurant I had heard of in Boston was Locke-Ober on Winter Street. Reuven had mentioned it while he was a student before the war, so I suggested we go there.

When we arrived at the restaurant, we looked at the menu posted beside the door. What Reuven had failed to mention was that Locke-Ober was also very expensive. Lunch for two would cost me half a week's pay! "French cuisine," Virginia said, sensing my alarm at the prices. "You probably had your share of that in France. Let's find someplace else."

Part of me was relieved, and part was embarrassed and a little angry. "All right," I said.

We walked in silence until we found a small restaurant that looked more in my financial range. We both ordered vegetable soup with a large salad, followed by apple pie and coffee. "I'm sorry about Locke-Ober," I said. "It might have been nice."

"Actually, Mother and I had luncheon there last month; the food was nothing special. Bea does a better job with salmon."

"My friend Reuven worked there as a waiter before the war. He recommended it. Perhaps the quality has gone down over the past few years."

"I'm not particularly impressed with fancy food with fancy names." She laughed. "This vegetable soup is excellent."

I agreed.

"When last were you at the museum of art, Isaac?"

"The spring before the war; it seems like forever ago. Reuven and I spent several hours there. How about you?"

"I went with a friend to see the new acquisitions exhibit about a year ago. They have added a whole gallery of works of the so-called 'Impressionists.' I found them so refreshing. I am sure those are my favorite paintings in the museum."

"Does the museum have any of the recent artists, like Metzinger, Picasso or Braque?"

"I do not believe they have ventured there yet."

We spent a lovely afternoon at the museum which had recently added a small collection of works by the French artist Millet. What we both enjoyed about them was their depiction of everyday people - farmers and tradesmen shown at work and relaxing. In fact, as we meandered through the rest of the galleries we found ourselves being drawn to the works that showed working people rather than the rich and powerful. Whether we were looking at artifacts brought back from ancient Egypt, or paintings from the Renaissance in the Netherlands, these were the items we sought out. Virginia, I think, began to get a new perspective on class relations through these items from different places and ranging across the millennia.

Chapter 31

I feel a cold hand on my face, lifting my eyelids. Must be Doctor Fish - no one else would touch me without at least announcing their presence. He moves my blankets, opens my shirt and places his cold stethoscope on my chest near my heart, then lower to listen to my lungs and who knows what else. I blink three times; *I am here.* Nothing. I hear him entering something on my chart. He departs without saying a word.

A nurse or aide buttons my pajama shirt and pulls the blankets up.

I am here.

"Good morning."

I don't recognize her voice, and she leaves without introducing herself. I wonder if it's still Memorial Day. I hope not - Memorial Day requires that we remember and there are too many heartbreaking things to remember.

***

It was the Sunday before Memorial Day, 1970. The family and friends were coming together at Albert's home to observe the first anniversary of Colin's death in Vietnam. Colin was Albert and Charlotte's eldest, Allen's older brother.

Allen arrived home from his first year at college in Amherst. I watched him park his car on the street behind Beth's VW minibus. Beth had been Colin's girlfriend since they were juniors in high school. Charlotte and Albert were like parents to her. Beth was at the house that terrible Thursday afternoon when the messenger of death came knocking on the door.

Allen stood for a moment on the walkway of the house he had grown up in. The maple trees along the property line were taller than the two-story building. When he was six and Colin was nine, the two boys helped their father plant those trees – three on either side of the house. Allen had asked Albert why they planted the trees so far apart from one another.

They looked so puny, so inconsequential; to imagine them as full grown, brushing their leaves together, was impossible.

The next year they planted a row of spruces along the back edge of their property – it took the three of them most of the day to dig the holes, add the rich dirt, set the trees and fill in the holes. Their neighborhood was new. All of the families there were new, pioneers of urban sprawl. By the time the trees were strong and big enough to be climbed Allen and Colin were interested in other things.

Charlotte had draped the flag the army had sent home over the railing of the front porch. The Purple Heart and a few other items that arrived with the flag were on display on the table in the hallway. A framed picture of Colin taken at his senior prom was mounted on the wall above the table. It was so like his mother to want to remember him as a kid.

Virginia and I watched Allen standing and contemplating the small shrine. You never get over the death of a brother. I know. "From a high school dance to a soldier's grave in about a year," I muttered, and tugged on Allen's shoulder-length hair. "Give your grandfather a kiss, and your Granny, too."

We embraced, then entered the large living room.

Charlotte was kneeling at the coffee table in front of the sofa, slowly turning the pages of a photograph album. "How're you doing, Mom?" Allen stooped to hug her, and her grasp on him would not let him straighten. He fell back on the sofa behind her and she leaned against his knees. Her hair had gone from black to gray in the year since Colin's death. She kept it cut short exposing the wrinkles in the pale skin of her neck. Virginia sat on the floor next to her, and kissed her on the cheek.

In the dining room, through the arched opening in the far wall, I could see that Charlotte had set out cold cuts and salads, as well as cakes, cookies and coffee. Albert was sitting alone near the table. His head was bowed and his eyes closed. He had seen more than his share of horror in World War Two; North Africa, Sicily, Normandy, Battle of the Bulge, Germany and the concentration camps. He, too, had lost a brother - Mark. And a sister - Emma. And now a son.

I went to him and put my hands on his shoulders. He looked up at me. "How do you get through it, Dad? Every day?"

"I don't know, son. Somehow you just do."

"Charlotte is falling apart. She is inconsolable. I don't know if she ever sleeps," Albert said, "and I can't get her to talk about it, either."

Charlotte had moved herself up onto the sofa next to Allen. "Do you remember the trip we took to the Bridge at Concord? Look at this picture, Allen; you and Colin pretending you were fighting the redcoats." The expression on her face was grim, joyless.

"I do, Mom." He put his arm around her and rested his cheek on the top of her head.

So long ago. Always fighting. This world has been insane since our earliest ancestors.

***

Damon is back, humming softly. I'm awake, but I like to listen. When he stops I blink to let him know I'm here.

"Good to see you, Isaac. I see we have a few new words on the chart. That's great!"

Yes. He had said that he was going to be away for three days. It seems much longer.

"I'm still on the overnight shift. It's six-fifteen on Tuesday morning, May twenty-eighth. A drizzly morning. It was cold last night - strange for this time of year."

He moved around me, checking my plumbing.

"Don't mind me saying so, Isaac, but your beard's a mess. For someone who can't move, you do manage to create your own bit of disorder!" He laughed. "Let me get a warm cloth and I'll wipe your face, then I'll comb that splendid golden mane."

I wanted to laugh, too. That will be my next word.

He sits in the chair beside the bed. I feel the warm damp cloth on my face. He is so gentle. Then the comb moving slowly through my beard. *Like.*

"I'm glad to be back at work. These long weekends can really drag." Damon hesitates. "I went to my dad's grave yesterday - Memorial Day. He died when I was fourteen. He suffered for years from the effects of Agent Orange, but, of course he was never able to get anything from the VA. The only thing he ever told me about his experience in Vietnam was about the day a couple of helicopters swooped over the jungle spraying that stuff all over the place, not knowing his platoon was there. Not one of the guys in his platoon showed up at his funeral; I remember thinking they must all be dead."

Too much pain. For some, Memorial Day is just another big shopping day wrapped around burgers and beer. For others…He touches my hand.

Hug.

I feel his hands on my shoulders and his head resting gently on my chest. He stays this way a long time. "Thank you, Isaac. You know just what to say."

***

Mama liked the idea of going to the women's voting rights rally, and meeting Virginia and her mother in such a setting struck her as auspicious and also fairly neutral. She was not so sure about the luncheon at the Appleton house.

"So, Itzik, tell me about the mansion."

"It's big, in a part of Boston occupied by old families with old money. It overlooks the Public Garden - an enormous garden that's in full bloom right now. As for the inside; I have not seen more than the entry hall and the front parlor. They have beautiful carpets, paintings, silver, crystal and porcelain. The furniture is comfortable. They have one servant; a Negro woman named Bea who appears to be about fifty years old and is an excellent cook and baker, and does all of the housework."

"What do they all do for work?"

"Mr. Appleton is a lawyer. I don't think Mrs. Appleton works, nor does Virginia."

"That must be nice."

I looked at her as she sat across from me in our small kitchen. She had worked her whole life - first in her father's hen-house, then in his fields, and after marriage at anything she could to buy food and escape her husband. In America, she had worked in the mill almost since the day she arrived. She had not taken a vacation ever. "It's a different world, Mama. Some things that seem so obvious to us simply do not register with them."

"So how will you and Virginia find a place where you are both at ease?"

"We will. Somehow I feel we already have. Simply being with her breaks down those walls."

"You're in love, Itzik, and that is more than wonderful. But keep your eyes open, my boy."

"Don't worry."

I wrote to Virginia telling her we would be at the rally and suggesting we meet near the entrance to the subway station.

We took an early train to Boston. Mama wanted to get there before the crowds and to walk through the Commons and the Garden. She woke up before sunrise and spent an hour or more getting ready. She wore her best dress and a jacket I had only seen her wear once - at my Uncle Ben's wedding. I sensed she was nervous and she remained quiet for most of the train ride. When we arrived at Park Station she rushed towards the exit, climbing the stairs two at a time. Once out in the open air she slowed down, took my arm and asked me to walk her to the Swan Boats.

I looked at the clock on a nearby church; it was almost eight-thirty. "They're not operating yet, Mama."

"No matter, I want to walk there anyway."

The morning sun lit up the willows and flooded the flower beds. There were not too many people about. We walked slowly until we got to the pond, then found a bench and sat. We watched the ducks paddling about and a family of turtles sunning themselves on a log.

"Which one is their house?" Mama turned and scanned the row of buildings across from the park.

"That one with the big bay window, three or four houses from the corner."

"Very nice!" She slapped my knee and stood up. "Come, Itzik. Let's go and make some noise."

She strode back across the park with me struggling to keep up. At some point she stopped. "Your leg's still not right. I forgot. I'm sorry, Itzik."

"Don't worry. I'm fine." We walked on at a slightly slower pace.

People had started to gather below a stage which had been set up at the foot of the steps near the State House. It was unoccupied, except for six folding chairs and a podium. A very big "Votes for Women" banner fluttered between two poles above the stage. Behind the stage, on the sidewalk opposite the State House we saw a row of policemen standing ready. Mother snickered.

"We should go back to the station to meet Virginia and her mother," I said. It was a short walk down the path, but we were going against the stream of hundreds of people converging on the rally and it took some time to reach our destination. Virginia and her mother had not arrived yet. My mother and I waited, watching the excited throng pouring out of the subway station and marching up towards the State House.

Finally I saw Mrs. Appleton and Virginia pushing their way through the crowd. I waved and Virginia waved back. "There they are, Mama. Let's go."

After brief introductions, we joined the tide and moved closer to the stage. By now, five of the six chairs were occupied and a fashionably dressed woman of about Mrs. Appleton's age was standing at the podium trying to quiet the crowd that had begun chanting, "Votes for women! Vote now!" over and over again with a steady increase in volume as more and more people joined in.

A young woman circulated through the gathering handing out posters declaring "Votes for Women." Virginia and her mother each took one. She approached my mother. "Thank you, I brought my own," my mother said. With that, she reached into her pocket and unfolded a rectangle of white fabric on which she had boldly written; "Freedom for Women!"

Virginia smiled broadly at my mother. "Yes, Mrs. Simon. I like it!" Mrs. Appleton nodded.

The crowd started singing, "Come vote, ladies," (to the tune of "Good night, ladies") and Mama joined in with passion, spurring on the people around us. Even Mrs. Appleton joined in, despite her discomfort at the growing disorganization.

After about ten minutes of this, all the women who had been seated on the stage stood and held up their hands, begging for quiet from the crowd. Slowly order was restored.

There followed six speeches, some inspiring, some rather boring. They were, fortunately, interspersed with bursts of singing and chanting. I looked around at the crowd that was about three-quarters women, and I was pleased to see they were not all upper-crust ladies of Anglo-Saxon origins. One could distinguish the working class and recent immigrants by their clothes and demeanor. Some had brought signs and banners in languages other than English. I even noticed a few Black women standing off to the side. Yet, despite the diversity of the crowd, there was uniformity among the speakers.

My mother was fired up by the time the rally ended almost two hours later. "I feel so alive!" she said as the crowd began to disperse. "It is so good to stand together with all these people, these women! I wish there had been less talking and more singing, though. Singing raises people up."

We started walking arm-in-arm through the Common; my mother was on the right, then Virginia, me and Mrs. Appleton. "Tell me about your banner, Mrs. Simon," Virginia asked.

"Freedom for Women. Yes. I've been thinking about the rally since Itzik - Isaac - mentioned it to me. At work, I looked around me at all the women working there on those machines, young women and older women. Some with children, some not. Some with husbands, others not married. I looked at the children in that mill, working until their fingers bled. I realized that voting was just the beginning; a small step at the start of so much that needs to be done."

By now we were approaching the Appleton home and we stopped at the edge of the park. Mother continued; "Women need education, better pay, more job opportunities. We need our children in school, not in the factories. We need a full say in our lives. We need respect and we need freedom!"

Virginia and her mother were staring at her in awe, speechless.

Mother smiled, and looked down. "It seems like I've been rehearsing that speech my whole life. Thank you for listening."

"No, Mrs. Simon, it is we who should thank you." Virginia said, then took her arm. "I'm starving. Let's go in."

The dining room was through a pair of double doors and down a short passage to the right of the staircase. The large table was set for four. "I'm afraid my husband has an unanticipated business appointment. Hopefully, he will be home before you need to leave, Mrs. Simon."

My mother did not respond. She sat staring at the gleaming porcelain plates and array of knives, forks and spoons laid out in front of her. I was equally at a loss; on my previous visits I had managed to deal with tea cups and saucers, cake plates and forks, but this was a whole lot more than I had expected for an informal luncheon.

Bea entered and placed a bowl in front of each of us. Then she circulated with a tureen of soup which she ladled into the bowls. My mother and I watched our hosts to see which spoon they picked up, then followed suit.

"How is your job going, Isaac?" Mrs. Appleton asked.

"I'm enjoying it. My immediate supervisor is strict but, most importantly, he is a good teacher. Mr. Wilkins, the architect, is encouraging and seems to appreciate the work I do, not only the working drawings, but also the watercolor presentations."

"Will you enter architecture school soon?"

"I think in about a year. Getting the direct experience in the field will serve as a good foundation for formal study. And, of course, I need to put some money aside for school."

Bea removed the soup bowls and returned with a tray of sliced turkey breast, accompanied by mashed potatoes and a soggy green vegetable which I learned later was called broccoli. She placed a silver basket filled with warm bread rolls on the table.

"Virginia, dear, pass the rolls to Mrs. Simon."

"Thank you," my mother answered, carefully moving a roll from the basket to her side plate. The meal was painful for her. She had barely spoken since we sat down. She was not good at small talk - I doubt she even knew what the phrase meant. I could see her struggling to find something to say, hesitating. Finally, she set her knife and fork down on her plate and asked, "Mrs. Appleton, when do you think the vote will take place in the State House?"

"I believe it is scheduled for this coming Wednesday afternoon."

"Will you be there to make sure they vote for us?"

Mrs. Appleton looked at my mother with determination. "I think I will, Mrs. Simon. The visitor galleries are open to the public and I will be there."

"I will, too," Virginia said. "Those men need to get used to seeing women in the halls of power."

"Good!" my mother said. "I wish I could join you, but ..."

Silence dropped over the table, again. After a few minutes I said, "Virginia, Mrs. Appleton, do you know any of the women who spoke at the rally?"

"Yes. Mrs. Langley, who spoke second, and Miss Bernard, who followed her, are members of our church. We know them quite well," Mrs. Appleton replied.

"And I was in the children's program at the church with Mrs. Langley's daughter. We were good friends. I saw her briefly this morning."

I wondered why they were no longer friends, but decided not to ask. The awkward silence returned. Finally, Mrs. Appleton suggested we move to the more comfortable seating of the parlor where we could have our tea and cake. As we left the dining room Mrs. Appleton asked Virginia to play her Chopin.

Virginia crossed the parlor and opened the doors to the music room. "Isaac, would you like to join me?"

I glanced at my mother who had a panicked expression on her face. "I'd love to," I said, "I'll be there in a few minutes."

Mrs. Appleton sat in her usual chair and my mother and I sat on the couch. My mother was sitting stiffly, leaning forward, and gripping her handbag in front of her. Virginia started playing. "I love this piece," Mrs. Appleton said, "And Virginia plays it so well."

"She does," I replied.

My mother was trying to survey the room and all its fine furniture and artworks without being too obvious. She stopped at the Metzinger. "Ah, Itzik, now I see where your inspiration came from for those nutty sketches you made of me. I do like it, though."

"Yes, there are times I sit here and can stare at it for hours," Mrs. Appleton said.

My mother held back her response. I knew she wanted to say something like, "It must be wonderful to have so much free time," but she stopped herself. Then she turned to Mrs. Appleton and said, "Our next fight, Mrs. Appleton, must be for the children."

"I'm not sure I know what you mean, Mrs. Simon."

"Children should be in school, not in the factories, mines and mills."

"Aren't there laws protecting children?"

"Very few, and they are not enforced."

It looked like the two mothers were about to delve into a subject important to both of them. They didn't need me around. "I think I'll join Virginia."

"Go," my mother said, and turned to Mrs. Appleton to continue their discussion.

The music room was almost as large as the parlor. Its side walls were draped with heavy burgundy-colored velvet curtains and the floor was carpeted in a matching color. Virginia was sitting at the Steinway grand piano with her back to the parlor doors. On the far side of the piano, a number of comfortable chairs were arranged in a semicircle facing the piano, and behind them was a table with six chairs. Across the entire back wall, a dark floor to ceiling wooden bookcase displayed a collection of books, many bound in leather.

I stood behind Virginia, watching her play, listening to the music spilling almost effortlessly into the room. She was so comfortable here, so very much a part of this environment that was so alien to me. I went closer to her and placed my hands lightly on her shoulders. She missed a note, shook her head, and continued playing. Then she leaned back against me.

Chapter 32

I feel someone take my hand. "Hi, Grandpa Isaac. Are you awake?" Ginnie says, softly. They are back from their mini-vacation in Vermont. I lie a while enjoying the sensation of Ginnie gently rubbing my fingers, then I signal that I am here.

She chuckles and gives me a hug. "We got home late last night. We should have been home before dark, but we blew a tire minutes after we left the bed-and-breakfast so Dad took back roads and drove slowly on that stupid donut. He's paranoid about things like that; I don't think he went above forty all the way home. Anyway, we did have a nice relaxing few days."

She continues to rub my fingers. I sense that she has more to say. I wonder if she's noticed all the words on the chart. I signal for a hug. No response, so I blink again.

"Did you say something, Grandpa Isaac? I saw you blinking, but it didn't quite register."

Hug.

I feel her head touch on my chest and her hands gently pressing my shoulders. She remains like this for a while. I'm happy that I can comfort her.

She sits up. "I'm glad that I went to the lake. I needed the time. But I also felt like I should be somewhere else, especially on Memorial Day."

That day, again!

"Of course, Jake's ashes were sent to his family in Seattle and are buried there." She sniffed loudly. "I borrowed the car on Monday and took off early, driving without a destination in mind. After about an hour I found myself on the Canadian border in a town called Derby Line. I came to a church with a cemetery and parked the car. I wandered back and forth between the gravestones, reading the inscriptions and the dates and calculating the age of each person. I found one man who was twenty-three, Jake's age. By the year of his death, I imagined he died in the Civil War. I knelt by his grave and cried. I wished I had brought flowers for him. When I drove back to meet my folks for lunch, I could not remember that young man's name."

I feel the tears rolling down my cheeks into my beard. Ginnie dabs them gently with a soft cloth. "I didn't mean to make you cry, Grandpa Isaac. I'm sorry." She hugs me again.

When she sits up I give her the signal for "love" - four extra-long blinks.

"I love you, too," she says and sighs deeply. "I forgot the date-stamp. Sorry. It's Tuesday, May twenty-eighth, around four-thirty in the afternoon."

Thank you.

"I expect my dad will be arriving soon. I hope he gets here before I have to leave for work - I'm on evenings for a few days. I have to be there by six."

***

"I like that woman, Mrs. Appleton. She has a spark in her," my mother said as we walked toward the subway station. "Although I can't imagine what these people do with all their time! Me, I hate working, but I'd go crazy if I had nothing to do except sit around all day and look beautiful."

"And Virginia - what did you think of her?"

"Smart. Too smart to do nothing. She needs to go to college or work in some fancy office."

"But, Mama, do you like her?"

She stopped and took both of my hands in hers. "I do like her, Itzik. She's a kind, clever young woman. But, to be honest, Itzik, how you two are going to make this relationship work is a mystery to me." She kissed me on the cheek, then turned back to survey the Appleton home and the surrounding opulence.

By late summer the Appletons had become accustomed to seeing me almost every Saturday. A second meeting with the Reverend Frothingham went remarkably well, although we did not come to any agreement on his big question concerning marriage in the church. For me the question of marriage was premature. Virginia and I were both still nineteen years old, I was only back a few months from the war and beginning what I hoped would be my new profession. While the possibility of our marriage seemed to be at the forefront of our parent's minds, Virginia and I were much more interested in getting to know each other better and having fun together. There was, in both of us, a sense that we would spend our lives together, but it was too soon to talk seriously about marriage.

Reuven moved to Boston in mid-August to continue his studies in law. His first weekend back I visited him after my afternoon with Virginia. He had a small apartment in the north end of the city, a community of immigrants of mostly Italian origins, although a few Jewish and Irish families remained. He was anxious to know all about Virginia and her family, especially her father, the lawyer.

"Don't get any ideas, Reuven. Mr. Appleton deals with big business and commercial contracts. We actually get along quite well, now, but he sees the world very differently than you and me."

"It's all about the money?"

"You get to the point quickly, my friend."

He laughed. "I wouldn't mind a little extra every so often." He gestured broadly to his barely furnished bland apartment.

"We're not talking 'a little.'"

I glanced out the window - it was still light. "Do you want to go on a short expedition? I'll show you the house."

We walked through the narrow streets of the heart of Boston and arrived at the Common at the corner of Park and Tremont Streets, then crossed the park towards the lagoon and the Swan Boats. I pointed out the Appleton house to him. He whistled, then said; "And you think you can make this work with Virginia?"

"I do, Reuven. There is something so honest and open about her. The more I get to know her, the more I get to know myself. And I think the same is true for her. So, I do believe we can overcome the differences."

"Truth is, my friend, I don't know any wealthy people, but from what I can see we live on different planets with different rules. She was born with a silver spoon in her mouth - you and I arrived with a muddy boot on our backs."

"I know, Reuven, but you'll meet her and you'll see."

We crossed the park back towards the State House and then ascended the steps to the top of Beacon Street. "The first time my mother met Virginia and Mrs. Appleton was near these steps, at a Votes for Women rally. It was a good setting for their first meeting; my mother is no stranger to that type of gathering. She was able to form a bond with the Appleton women on her own turf, so to speak, before we went for luncheon at the house."

"And all went well with your mother once you were inside the house?"

"It wasn't easy, but my mother came away saying how she really liked Virginia and her mother. The two mothers have actually corresponded several times since that meeting."

"Amazing."

"Yes. Maybe the world is changing."

"I wouldn't hold my breath."

With Reuven back in Boston, I now had a place to stay overnight in the city, which made it easier for Virginia and me to be together in the evening and go to the movies or dancing. In early September we went to a jazz club where she introduced me to some of her friends. We were having a wonderful evening, dancing our shoes off and drinking a little more than we should have, when the clarinet player launched into a slow haunting solo. I found myself thinking of Benny who was killed when I had been injured and the lie I told his parents about him playing his clarinet after the Passover Seder.

Virginia noticed my sudden change in mood. "Are you all right, Isaac?"

"Just a little light-headed. I never told you this is my first time ever in a jazz club."

"That explains your dancing." She laughed and kissed my cheek. "Let's sit." We returned to our table and watched the people on the dance floor. The club we were in was one of the fashionable establishments that catered to the moneyed young adults of Boston. It was chic, glamorous and beyond my budget. I would have to work as much overtime as Mr. Wilkins would give me for the next two or three weeks just to cover this one evening.

Virginia's friends, Phillip and Dot, joined us at the table after a short while. Phillip offered to buy another round of drinks. I declined, as did

Virginia. "You two are no fun," Dot said, laughing. She continued to talk about parties and vacations and the plans for their upcoming wedding while he went on and on about his automobile which he had purchased that week. I was growing increasingly uncomfortable. I enjoyed the music and the dancing but I knew I did not belong in this place, with these people. How had Phillip avoided the war? He was my age, maybe a year or two older. He should have been in the mud with me.

As it approached midnight Virginia asked me if I was ready to leave.

"I'm sorry I've been such a lead balloon," I said as we stepped out onto the sidewalk. Phillip had offered to drive her home, but she said she'd prefer to walk.

She took my arm and we started toward her home. "No need to be sorry, Isaac." We walked for some time in silence, then she said; "I haven't seen Dot and Phillip since their engagement party about six months ago. So much has happened in my life since then - mainly you - and I have become more restless, more questioning of my life. Being with them was actually a little strange."

We were approaching the Appleton house. "You are a wise and wonderful woman, Virginia," I said. We climbed the steps and then she turned to me, wrapped her arms around me and we kissed, long and warm.

***

I have a sudden pain in my right leg. My old wound. It hasn't bothered me in a long time, but now, out of nowhere it is screaming at me. It doesn't make sense; the wound has been healed for over eighty years. The muscle and bone and nerves have all meshed together the way they were supposed to, but every now and then the pain explodes again as if those pieces of flying metal were cutting into me for the first time. Except, this time I cannot call out and Reuven is not here to help, nor is Virginia here to soothe the pain.

I hear my cat-machine emit a few loud electronic beeps. Moments later Damon is talking. "I know you have a DNR, Isaac, but I'm not gonna let you go." I feel a cool cloth on my forehead.

I blink "new word."

Immediately, Damon responds, "What's the signal for the new word?"

I hadn't really thought about it, then give one very long blink.

"One very long?"

Yes.

"How many letters?"

Four.

He starts going through the alphabet. I blink "yes" at P, then at A...

"Is the word 'pain?'"

Yes.

"Where's the pain, Isaac?" he says, then obviously realizes that I can't tell him, because he follows his question with, "Oh shit! Let me think a minute."

The sharpness of the pain is being replaced by a deep, dull ache.

"OK, Isaac, I am going to touch different places. Give me a 'Yes' when I'm close. OK?"

Yes.

I feel his finger on my forehead, then my chest, and then he moves to my stomach. "I know," he mutters, and he sets his finger lightly on my right thigh exactly on the scar.

Yes.

"The old wound. Dammit, man, they never go away! I'll be right back."

He returns in less than a minute. "I'm going to apply a cream that has a topical pain-killer, like Novocain." Damon begins to gently massage the area around the wound, rubbing the cream into my skin. Slowly the ache recedes.

Thank you.

"You're welcome, Isaac. I'll put your new word on the chart."

***

The Saturday afternoon following our outing with Phillip and Dot, Virginia and I were walking hand-in-hand in the Gardens near the Swan Boats. "Last Saturday night - what was it that upset you? Was it the place, the music, Dot and Phillip, me?"

"It definitely was not you. I would be happy to be with you anywhere." I put my arm around her shoulders and she leaned into me as we slowed our pace. "I enjoyed the music, but there was a moment when a clarinet solo ignited a memory from the war and from then on I couldn't get back into the mood. Also, to be blunt, I can't afford places like that."

"I didn't realize…"

"No matter. I will recover."

"What about Dot and Phillip?"

"I'm sure you know how I felt about them," I replied, "but, there is a broader, related question my mother raised a while ago that has been gnawing at me. It was when she and I were walking back to the subway after her first meeting with you."

"What is it, Isaac?"

"Well, she asked what you do with all your time."

It was a while before she answered. We had found a bench away from the trees and we sat soaking in the warm late September sun. "In truth, I do very little," she said. "And when that realization hit me not too long after the rally, it began to really bother me. During the war I was busy raising money and putting together care packages. The church had several members in the war, so my mother and I would visit their families and so on. But, even that did not fill my time. Of course, I play piano and read constantly, but it is not enough, not nearly."

She sighed and took my hands. "It's all your fault, you know. If I had never met you, Isaac, I would probably have been happy to shop for lovely clothes and go to parties and sit around waiting to get married and have babies. But now, I'm not content with that prospect. I don't mean I don't want to get married and have children. But, I want more than that. As much as I love you, Isaac, I never want my life to be defined only in relation to you."

"Freedom for women," I said.

"Yes!"

"So, where do you go from here?"

"I'm not certain, but the first step is education. I'm going to see if I can get accepted to Radcliffe College. I'm not sure what courses I'll take, but I'm leaning towards teaching."

I could not resist hugging her. "Wonderful!"

"Thank you."

"What do your parents say about this?" I asked.

"I have not mentioned it yet, but I expect Mother will be enthusiastic and Father will be accepting."

I looked in the direction of their church which stood across from the bottom corner of the Garden. "And Reverend Frothingham, would he have an opinion?"

"The Reverend has an opinion on just about everything. I think he would wholeheartedly support me and I intend to ask him for a letter of recommendation."

"He probably has a few connections, too."

"I'm sure he does." She tilted her head and a mischievous smile flashed across her face. "Would you like to take a look inside the church? It's beautiful, with wonderful windows by Tiffany."

"It's open on a Saturday afternoon?"

"It's always open. Come on." She stood and grabbed my hand. "I promise, no bolt of lightning will descend from the heavens to smite you."

As we neared the church we heard the sounds of the organ. "Oh dear, I forgot there's a wedding. We'll have to sneak in."

"Are you sure?"

"Just follow me."

Virginia led me through the open doors and up a stairway to the gallery. The interior walls of the church were all white, accenting the dark wood box pews on the main level below us and in the gallery. I did not have a direct view of the stained glass windows since they were all on the main level, but their soft purplish light touched the hundred or more people who were gathered below for the wedding.

I took my small sketchpad and a few colored pencils from my coat pocket and began to draw the scene.

"You can't resist, can you?" Virginia said.

"I can't. It's lovely in here; so tranquil."

We sat quietly, me making my drawings, Virginia listening to the ceremony and watching me draw. We stayed in the gallery until everyone had left except the sexton who was going through the pews, picking up trash and organizing the hymnals. Then we went down into the main level and spent time looking at the Tiffany windows. The colors and craftsmanship were astonishing, but I found the style too romantic and dramatic for my taste. The light pouring through those windows, however, was magical.

"Did you really forget there was a wedding here?"

"I really did. I promise. But I must say I'm glad we came."

"I am, too."

***

Wanda is singing one of her church songs in that soft rich voice of hers. I listen. *I'm awake.*

"Morning, Isaac. It's wonderful to see you today. I see you added the word for 'pain' to your chart. Are you still hurting?

No.

"Good. Damon told me about it before he left. I'm glad to know he was able to help." She checks my plumbing. "It is Wednesday, May twenty-ninth at ten minutes before nine in the morning. Your physical therapist, Chris, should be here at nine. Are you OK with that?"

Yes.

"Good. I'll check in on you later."

Chris arrives. "We're going to try something a little different today, Mr. Simon."

She takes my right hand and lifts it, bending my arm at the elbow. She moves it all the way until I feel my fingertips touch my shoulder. I kind of like that feeling. Then she lifts my elbow rotating my arm at the shoulder. She returns my hand to its original position, then repeats the exercise about a dozen times. I hear her move to the other side of my bed.

Does she remember that the cartilage is gone in my left shoulder? Do not try to move my arm!

I feel her lift my hand to my shoulder. Then she pushes her fingers under my elbow and begins to lift. Pain shoots through my arm, shoulder and chest. I feel tears burst from my eyes. After the third or fourth repetition my cat-machine starts going crazy. I can feel my pulse racing and the blood pounding in my ears.

Wanda rushes in at a moment when Chris has my elbow high off the bed. "Don't move!" Wanda commands. I feel her take my hand from Chris and slowly lower my arm back to the bed. She starts to gently rub my shoulder. "Tell me if this eases the pain."

No. It is like fire in my shoulder, my whole body.

"I'm going to see about getting you some pain killer, Isaac. I won't be a minute." She curses under her breath. "You! Don't come back until you've read his chart!" She says to Chris.

"I'm sorry, Mr. Simon," Chris whimpers and runs from my room.

Chapter 33

"So, when am I going to meet Virginia, Itzik? You talk about her all the time, you use my apartment as your city residence when you come to visit her, but you have yet to introduce me."

I had just arrived at Reuven's apartment after spending the afternoon and evening with Virginia. I still had my coat on. Virginia and I had eaten dinner in the little restaurant we went to after what we had dubbed 'the Locke-Ober deflection.' It had become our favorite dining spot.

"You're right, Reuven, it's about time. I want you to meet her and I'm sure she'll be happy to meet you; I've talked about you often enough! I'll suggest the three of us go for a walk in the Garden next Saturday."

"Maybe she can invite a friend for me?"

"I can ask."

He paused. "Actually, don't. If I'm to meet her, I don't need any distractions. I want to know who this woman is that has so enchanted you."

The following Saturday Reuven met me at the exit from Park Station. He was dressed in his best suit and coat. "You're hoping to meet her father, aren't you?" I said.

"There is that possibility. I didn't want to look like a bum if I were to be introduced. Anyway, I'd get dressed up to meet Virginia."

It was a chilly mid-October afternoon. The leaves had changed color and were beginning to fall. A sharp wind cut through the trees as we walked across the park. "We should go on the Swan Boats before they close for the season."

"Sure, Itzik. Very romantic."

Virginia opened the door. She gave me a peck on the cheek and I introduced her to Reuven. "The famous Reuven," she said. "I have been looking forward to meeting you. As has my father." I noticed Reuven give me a sly smile as Virginia led us into the parlor. Mr. and Mrs. Appleton were each in their usual chairs. They both rose when we entered and the introductions were made. Reuven and I sat on the couch, with Virginia between us. He was at the end closer to her father.

"How is your work going, Isaac?"

"Very well, sir. Our senior draftsman was out sick most of last week and I have had to pick up some of his assignments."

"And your artwork, Isaac?"

"Unfortunately, Mrs. Appleton, I don't have as much time for it as I would like. I was able to do some watercolors after work during the summer, but the days have gotten shorter and I'm usually not out of the office before dark. I do have weekends - when I'm not here." I touched Virginia's hand.

"And you, Reuven, Virginia tells me you are studying the law."

"Yes, sir. I've finally returned to it after the interruption of the war."

"I find it to be a noble profession. Where are you studying?"

"I'm in in my second year at Suffolk Law School."

Mr. Appleton replied with a rather haughty, "I see," then suggested the young folks take a walk in the gardens before the weather turned.

"Will you be back in time for tea?" Mrs. Appleton asked.

Virginia, Reuven and I looked at one another for an instant, then Virginia said. "Of course, Mother, Bea has made some rather lovely cakes for us."

We crossed the street together and into the park. Reuven had a scowl on his face. "We all can't go to Harvard!" He exclaimed, then quickly turned to Virginia. "I apologize for that little outburst."

"No need, Reuven. My father can be rather clannish at times. I think he was quite rude, and I noticed the look my mother gave him."

"How about a ride on the Swan Boats?" I suggested.

"I'm not sure we have enough time. Let's take a look at the schedule."

By the time we reached the ticket office we had just missed the three o'clock ride, and the next one wasn't until three-thirty. "That will be cutting it a little too close. Mother likes her tea no later than four. We should not disappoint her."

"Let's walk, then," I said.

"Virginia, Isaac says you're entering Radcliffe College?"

"Yes, I'll be taking a couple of courses right after the Christmas break. I start full time next fall. The first few terms will be general studies in the liberal arts. After that I'll focus on teaching."

"Congratulations. Education is the key to life, and you are acquiring it so that you can distribute it."

"Thank you, Reuven. That's a nice way to look at it."

We were walking down the gentle slope of the Boston Garden. Reuven pointed to the Unitarian church on the corner. "So, Virginia, that's your church?"

"It is."

"Did Isaac tell you about our visits to some of the great cathedrals of France and England?"

"And some of the small churches and chapels, too. He showed me his drawings, as well."

"I can't believe he carried those around with him wherever he went."

"He did?"

Reuven glanced at me, then continued, "Did Isaac tell you that his drawings saved his life?"

"Well, I'm sure they helped to keep his mind off the war, to keep him sane."

"Much more than that; in a very real and practical way Isaac's drawings saved him from more serious injury."

"My drawings and a shovel," I said. I had no idea why Reuven had pushed the conversation in this direction. We almost never spoke about the war, and when we did it was usually about silly things that happened. We avoided the painful and horrifying things. Virginia rarely asked me about the war, either. I had told her some of the basics about how I was wounded and how Reuven had carried me to an aid station, but I spared her the details.

Virginia took my hand. "I'm sure Isaac will tell me all about it when the time is right."

We stopped near the corner of the park and looked across Arlington Street at the church. "This façade is suddenly familiar," I said. "It reminds me of a church I saw in one of my Uncle Kalner's books on world architecture."

"It is, in fact, designed after St. Martin in the Fields in London. You have a remarkable memory, Isaac."

"Have you been to London?" Reuven asked.

"No, but my parents were there before the war. They brought back post cards of St. Martin's." We remained looking at the church for a while. "We should probably start back for tea," Virginia said.

We arrived at the house and entered the parlor to find Mr. and Mrs. Appleton in their chairs and the tea things on the table. "Sorry we're late, mother."

"You are not late, dear. Your father and I were just a little thirsty. Virginia, why don't you pour for the boys?"

We sat, sipped our tea and ate Bea's wonderful almond cake and pumpkin pie. Mr. Appleton requested a second cup of tea. He shifted in his chair, crossing then uncrossing his legs. Mrs. Appleton kept her eyes on him, saying nothing. Finally, Mr. Appleton said, "Reuven, what area of the law are you most interested in?"

I could see Reuven struggling to formulate his answer in a way that would not drive a wedge between himself and Mr. Appleton. Reuven and I had talked endlessly about his interests in the law, and they seemed quite different from our host's. "Well, sir, I think it comes down to Constitutional law."

"Could you elaborate a little?"

"Of course. As I see it, the Constitution, and in particular the amendments contained in the Bill of Rights, are designed to protect the rights of all the people. That is where I hope to focus my practice of the law."

"Have you been able to find a firm to intern with?"

"Not yet, sir. I might have to move to New York after I finish my formal studies."

Mr. Appleton breathed in deeply, took a final sip of tea and set his cup down on the table next to him. "There might be other opportunities, Reuven. I'll make some inquiries."

"Thank you sir. Thank you so much," Reuven stammered in appreciation and disbelief.

"You do understand, Reuven, this choice of yours is not the most remunerative, and in some circles it is even seen as bordering on subversive."

"I am well aware of both of those observations, sir. What a sad sign of the times that a defense of the Constitution would be viewed as insurrectionary."

"Indeed." Mr. Appleton stood, and Reuven and I did, too. We shook hands. "Reuven, put together a little information about yourself and your studies and experience. Isaac can pass it along."

"Yes, Mr. Appleton. Thank you."

He strode from the room. Mrs. Appleton smiled broadly. "He's not the old grizzly bear he sometimes likes to portray," she said.

"He's really more like a Teddy bear when you get to know him," Virginia added and giggled.

"I really can't fully express my appreciation," Reuven said.

"No need, young man. He is happy to do it," Mrs. Appleton said, then continued, "I have a feeling that if he were at the start of his career he might have followed a similar path."

***

Allen is here. I can hear him talking with Dr. Fish, although I can't make out what they're saying. Fish is so secretive; it drives me nuts. Finally, I feel Fish move my blankets and pajama top aside and place his cold stethoscope on my chest. He says, "Hmm." Very helpful! He moves the stethoscope. "Hmm," again.

The ache in my shoulder has mostly subsided. I feel something taped on the top of my left hand. It hurts a little. I seem to recall Wanda saying something about having to install an IV port before she could give me the pain-killer. Doctor Fish touches around where the needle rests in the back of my hand. He says, "Hmm," one more time, and I hear him say, "Stable." I assume he is talking about me and not a horse. Then I hear him say, "I'll be back tomorrow," and moments later Allen sits on the chair beside me. He lets out a soft groan, as if this whole business of watching out for me and visiting me is becoming too much.

It was never my intention to drag this out so long. If I could flip the switch, I probably would. I'm not sure if I should let Allen know I'm awake. I wonder if it's easier for him if he thinks I'm asleep. Probably. If he knows I'm awake, he feels obligated to communicate with me, and we know how expansive that can be!

He must be reading; I hear the pages turning every so often. He chuckles. Must be a humorous book. After some time he closes the book and sighs. I blink to let him know I'm here, but he does not respond. His breathing slows and I listen. I think he is falling asleep. I remember him as a baby - he loved to be held tight as he drifted into sleep. When he spent the night with Virginia and me she would wrap him in his soft yellow blanket at bed-time and then hold him in her arms and rock him and sing to him. She had a lovely voice, surprisingly deep and mellow. She would sing songs from the old women's suffrage campaigns and even a few union songs that she had learned from my mother - the same songs she had sung to our children and to me at times.

I hear Allen stir, stand and begin to walk slowly back and forth at the foot of my bed. "I need a cup of coffee," he says. I hear him leave. My cat-machine is purring softly. The pain in my shoulder has returned to its usual level. I begin to wonder what Doctor Fish meant when he said I was stable. Is there something new they are monitoring in me? Is there yet another function of my body that is no longer doing what it is expected to do?

Allen is back and sitting next to me. I signal that I am awake.

"Hi, Grandpa Isaac. How are you this evening? I'm afraid I dozed off. I don't know why I'm so tired today. I think my body still wants to be on vacation."

Yes.

"We did have a good time away from everything. The lake was beautiful although still too cold to swim much, the sunsets were spectacular. It was a nice, lazy time. We all needed it." He paused. "I think it was good for Ginnie. She spent the morning of Memorial Day on her own; she took the car and drove off somewhere. She never told us much about what she did. When she returned she was pensive, but in a better frame of mind, as if she had arrived at a different place in her grieving. It's hard to explain, but she seemed more accepting. She is still grieving, but it's like the 'why' question is no longer weighing as heavily on her."

What do I say? Even if I could talk, I would not know what to say. She is no longer looking for an explanation, realizing, at last, that there isn't one, there can't be one. It'd hard to accept the randomness of life and death, and the worst part is that it's not at all liberating when you do. It's more a sense of resignation.

Allen is quiet. I'm waiting for him to say something, anything.

Nurse Trainwreck breaks the spell. She is huffing around me, checking on things. "New IV port," she says, "a direct line. Good."

"The doctor said that he was having some pain," Allen says. "Do you know any more about it?"

"Only what's in his chart. As I remember, it says something about severe left shoulder pain earlier today. There was also an episode during the night with pain in his right leg."

"Are you still having pain, Grandpa Isaac?"

No. Well, nothing more than the usual.

"Gotta move along," Trainwreck says.

Silence. Then Allen says, "Oops, I forgot the date-stamp. It's Wednesday evening, around nine o'clock. May twenty-ninth."

Thank you. I'm glad people are remembering to give me the date-stamp. Somehow, it keeps me in the present, prevents me from whirling off into timelessness.

***

"Do you really think Mr. Appleton will help me find a position in Boston?" Reuven asked as we walked toward the subway station.

"Why would he offer if he didn't mean it?"

"True, he owes me absolutely nothing. However, it's pretty obvious that Virginia's mother put him up to it."

"She certainly prodded him in that direction. I'd have loved to have been a fly on the wall during that conversation."

Reuven laughed. We were almost at the station. "You've found a wonderful girl there, Itzik my friend."

"I have. Thank you."

"Will I see you next weekend?"

"I don't think so, but I have some thoughts about the following weekend. I'll let you know when I've figured out exactly what I want to do."

On the train ride back to Lawrence I began to plan for the weekend two weeks away. It would be the Sunday before the first anniversary of the Armistice and I felt certain there would be events in Boston to mark that date. But those did not interest me; what I really wanted to hear was what the Reverend Paul Revere Frothingham had to say about it. I was planning to put the Reverend to the test.

I wondered whether I should tell Virginia I was thinking of attending the service. I wanted to surprise her, but if I showed up without preparing her and her parents, would they be upset, embarrassed, pleased? Would Mr. and Mrs. Appleton feel uncomfortable acknowledging me in front of their friends? What if I snuck into the back of the gallery where they couldn't see me and waited till everyone had left the church after the service? Could I even get into the church undetected by her and her family or the Reverend?

As it turned out, any further scheming and fretting were pre-empted by a letter I received from the Reverend Frothingham himself, inviting me to attend the service on November ninth as his guest, although, he said, he would understand if I "chose to sit with the Appleton family, who encouraged me to offer this invitation." The service was to be "dedicated to those who served in the Great War and to the cause of World Peace." He also encouraged me to wear my uniform and service medals.

The next day, Virginia's letter arrived urging me to come to the service. "This will not be our usual kind of service," she wrote, "and, knowing Reverend Frothingham I am sure he will make it a worthy and uplifting observance." She went on to write that her parents would "be happy to share their pew with me," and I should come to their house at nine in the morning so that we could all walk together to church.

How could I refuse? I wrote to Virginia, and then to the Reverend accepting his invitation and telling him I would be sitting with the Appleton family. I also said that I preferred not wear my uniform because, "I am no longer a soldier."

***

"Are you awake, Mr. Simon?" Doctor Squeak, the neurologist, is back. He lifts my eyelids and I think he is shining a bright light into my eyes. Now what?

I try to ignore him. Do I want to know what new ideas he has for me, or do I just want him to go away?

"Mr. Simon. It's Doctor Jerzak."

OK doc. I signal that I am awake.

"Good morning, Isaac. It is Thursday, May thirtieth at a few minutes past ten."

Thank you.

"I see you have a large chart on the wall with all your words. I would like to verify them. OK?"

Yes.

He reads off the words one at I time and I blink for him.

"Excellent!" he says, and I think he actually claps his hands.

I feel like a second-grader at a spelling bee.

"I read about your incident with the physical therapist. I am truly sorry about what happened, and so is she. So, there is another word I think it would be useful for you to have, and that word is 'stop.' Do you agree?"

Yes.

Chapter 34

When I told my mother about the invitation to attend the church service and my response to the Reverend, she looked me straight in the eyes and said, "Itzik, you should wear your uniform; you deserve to be recognized for what you went through. Do not dismiss being honored; it doesn't happen too often in life."

"There's no honor in killing people, Mama. I am going, but no uniform."

"They wish to honor you for your sacrifice, Itzik."

"It is hard to separate my sacrifice from that of the boys I killed. I go to honor them, too."

We were sitting at the table eating supper. She put down her knife and fork and pushed her plate away. "I hear your fearful dreams sometimes, my boy. I wish I could help those memories to go away." She stood to clear the plates. I could see the tears forming in her eyes.

"I wish that, too."

The next evening I returned home from work to find that she had bought me a new necktie, shoes and a coat. "You're going to a church - you need to look respectful," is all she said. When I pressed her about the money, she said she had been saving for something special. She insisted I try everything on. "You do look good," she said, and I had to agree.

"There is more news. I received a letter from your Uncle Kalner; he and his new wife, Mary, are coming to visit at the beginning of December. He has a big union meeting in Boston, so they are taking a little vacation together."

I hadn't seen my uncle since before the war; there was so much for us to talk about. He had taken the role of my father even before my father had died. He shaped me in so many ways, and he encouraged me to explore whatever interested me. "I can't wait to see him," I said, and I gave my mother a big hug.

I feel someone's head on my chest and hands gently on my shoulders. "Hope I didn't disturb you. I just had to do that." It's my Ginnie.

I am here.

She hugs me again. "This is a quick visit. I'm on my way to work."

Smile.

"Did Dad make it here yesterday?"

Yes.

"Good. What about Mom?"

No. Truth is, I haven't seen Martha in ages. She's too busy raising money for the wrong causes. Well, that's a little harsh, but I'm old, I have a right to think what I want!

"She's the busiest non-employed person I know."

Smile. Martha gave up her accounting job when David was born and never returned to full time work. It always amazed me that she had been in college at the height of the Women's Lib movement, yet it didn't seem to have rubbed off on her. Equally amazing was how Allen, who was always politically involved, found himself in love with this totally a-political person.

I remember the anti-war march in Boston in October, 1969. Allen arrived at our house early in the morning and found me, dressed in blue jeans and a bright painted shirt, sitting on the front step with a bowl of granola and a mug of coffee for each of us. He sat for a few moments in the car, smiling at me - all ready to go, to join battle again.

"Like the shirt?" I asked, "I worked on it all week just for this occasion."

It was a spectacular shirt, covered in a pattern depicting red banners with anti-war slogans and raised fists. The background was a texture of earth tones – pale ochre, sepia and greens. The shirt was long and loose, hanging almost to my knees. The long sleeves were wide at the wrists, the neck was open and without a collar.

"You made the shirt?" asked Allen, as he got out of the car. He accepted a coffee and a bowl and sat down next to me. "That's a fantastic shirt. They'll sure be able to pick you out of the crowd!"

I chuckled.

"The last time I marched I wore a uniform, with a couple of medals and..." My voice trailed off and I looked up at the clear pale pink morning sky.

"World War One?"

"No..."

Allen waited for me to say something about my last march, but I couldn't. "Some other time, perhaps," I said, more to myself than to him.

We finished our breakfast in silence. Then I went back into the house to take care of the dishes and to pick up my backpack. Virginia was still asleep. I wanted to wake her, to show off the shirt, to get a farewell hug. I sat down next to her on the bed. She moved but did not open her eyes, so I kissed her softly on the forehead and pressed her hand.

"Don't worry about me," she said, "I'll be fine."

"I know. So will I. See you later." I kissed her again.

"Beautiful shirt," I heard her say as I left the room.

I emerged from the house carrying my rucksack and two six-foot long poles. "I made a banner," I said in response to Allen's puzzled look. "It's in the rucksack. We'll need the poles to support it." He threw the pack onto the back seat and maneuvered the poles so that they were suspended between the dashboard and the rear seat, down the center of the car.

"You really have done a lot of work for this," Allen said, as he backed the car out of the driveway. I looked up at the bedroom window. Virginia stood there with her hand over her heart, clasping her nightgown. I blew her a kiss

"I have," I said. "It's not often that one goes marching. I want to be part of the crowd, but, somehow, I also want to stand out." I leaned forward a little and turned to look directly at Allen. "This is not the first war I've suffered through, and I want the bastards to know that!"

I could see the surprise in Allen's face at the sudden anger and bitterness in my voice. "Love that shirt!" he said.

The march went from the Prudential Center straight down Boylston Street to the Common, then up towards the State House. There were thousands and thousands of people. The speakers' stage was set up in the exact same location as the one for the Votes for Women rally fifty years before.

"You still there, Grandpa Isaac? You seem to have drifted off."

I'm here. Sorry.

"I was saying that it's time for me to go to work. I talked with Danielle earlier; she's had a little cold for a couple of days and didn't want to bring it here, which is why you haven't seen her. She's over the worst of it now so she'll probably be here in the morning."

Thank you. Hug.

Ginnie giggles and gives me a hug and a kiss on the cheek.

***

"You know, Itzik, you should think about moving to Boston. You could share this place with me." It was the evening before the Armistice Day service and I had come into the city late on Saturday afternoon so that I could stay with Reuven over-night and be at the Appleton home before nine the next morning. Reuven and I were having dinner at his apartment. He had cooked one of his scrambled egg concoctions with onions, mushrooms, sausage, garlic and cheese. It was delicious.

"I've been thinking about it. I could start taking some architecture classes."

"And you'd be closer to Virginia."

"Of course. But I would need to find a job before I could consider moving. And I'd need to make sure my mother would be OK on her own."

"She'll be fine. She's tougher than most people."

"That's true, but I still need to discuss it with her."

We finished eating and I cleared up and washed the dishes, while Reuven put a record on his new gramophone, "After You're Gone," sung by Marion Harris. "Sad, but beautiful," he said. He poured us each a glass of wine and we sat listening to his small, but growing collection of jazz music.

"Things are falling apart in this country, Itzik," Reuven said, after his second glass of wine. "Something is going to happen that will make your head spin."

"What the hell are you talking about?"

"This big 'Red Scare' campaign. The government is targeting foreigners, particularly union organizers, and branding them as anarchists, communists and socialists. Pretty soon the hammer is going to fall."

"What makes you think this?" I asked, and I wondered if my Uncle

Kalner had a similar view of things. I wondered if he was in danger.

"Have you heard about all the strikes, the violence on the picket lines, the police beatings, the race riots? The whole country is in upheaval. And then yesterday they raided the offices of the Union of Russian Workers in New York and detained a couple of hundred people. I tell you, that's just the beginning!" He stood and started pacing unsteadily across the small room. "So many men came back from Europe to unemployment and rising prices. It's barely a year since the end of the war and already those 'heroic men' - people like you and me - are now being called treasonous bums. People are angry and the government has no real answers, so they're going after the unions and foreigners. Have you read what the attorney general has been saying lately? We're heading for bad times, Itzik, mark my words."

"What makes you so sure?"

"Mark my words, my friend; the storm is just over the horizon."

He began to pour a third glass for us, but I declined. "I have a big day tomorrow."

I went to bed, leaving Reuven slouching in a chair.

In the morning I found an envelope on the table addressed to Mr. Appleton, and a note asking me to deliver it. I put it in my coat pocket and left the apartment before eight-thirty. Reuven was still asleep. I walked quickly through the back streets of the city and through the market, which was buzzing with activity. I thought about getting something for breakfast, but was afraid I might spill on my new coat and tie. I made my way up to the Common. It was a cold, cloudy morning and it felt like it might rain.

I arrived at the Appleton house and knocked on the door. Bea let me in and led me into the dining room where Mr. Appleton sat alone at the table finishing his breakfast. "Sit, Isaac, have something to eat," he said. Bea offered me a cup of coffee and a bowl of stewed fruit.

"The ladies will be down in a few minutes. They're making the finishing touches to their attire." He paused, then continued, "How have you been, Isaac? We haven't seen you in a couple of weeks."

"I've been well, sir. Nothing new to report."

"And what of your friend, Reuven?"

"Reuven is studying hard. I spent last evening with him. He asked me to give this to you." I handed him the envelope.

"Thank you." He slipped it into his coat pocket.

Virginia and her mother entered. "Are we all ready to go, then?" Mrs. Appleton said, and moved to the door without waiting for a reply. Mr. Appleton, Virginia and I followed. As we descended the front steps, Virginia took my arm, "Good morning, Isaac. How are you feeling?"

"A little apprehensive, but I've been looking forward to this. I'm trying to keep an open mind."

"If nothing else, you will find the service interesting, I'm certain of that."

We walked a few steps behind her parents. I surveyed the Garden and could see several dozen small groups of people making their way toward the church. The men were all dressed in dark suits and coats, the majority of the women wore muted colors. Virginia had taken a bolder approach; she was wearing a vibrant emerald green dress under an off-white coat. She wore no jewelry except for a simple short pearl necklace. She was beautiful.

"You look lovely this morning," I said.

She squeezed my arm. "So do you. Splendid new coat and tie."

I did not say that my mother had bought them for me.

We exited the park and crossed Arlington Street with a throng of people. I noticed several young men in uniform. Reverend Frothingham was standing at the open door of the church, chatting with people and welcoming them as they entered. "I'm so pleased you decided to be with us today, Mr. Simon." He shook my hand, leaned closer to me and added in a low voice, "And I do understand about the uniform. There were a few others who shared your feelings."

The Appleton family pew was in the center section on the left, a little more than half way toward the pulpit. The organ was playing a non-descript piece that seemed more to fill the silence than to inspire. Unfortunately, the gloomy day did little to light up the Tiffany windows; they remained flat and lifeless, setting a fitting tone.

The organ stopped and Reverend Frothingham walked down the aisle toward the pulpit. I looked around me at the sparse and lofty interior. The pews on the main level were filled, as were the galleries. "Is it always this full?" I whispered to Virginia.

"No. This is a special day. Shh."

The Reverend ascended the pulpit which towered high above the congregation. He scanned the gathering. "Today we honor, we remember, and we pray for peace." His voice was full, but weary. Over the past few months I had learned a little more about him and most particularly about his ardent fight for the League of Nations. He was active and outspoken and traveled broadly, promoting the organization and its ideals. His chief adversary was another Massachusetts Unitarian, the powerful Senator Henry Cabot Lodge who was chair of the Senate Foreign Relations Committee.

There followed a long prayer, asking God to bestow peace upon the world, to guide our political leaders down the path of peace and to ensure that the sacrifices made in the War to End All Wars would not have been in vain.

Then we all stood and sang a hymn for peace. I watched Virginia throw herself into the song, her warm voice blending with those all around us. As the hymn ended and we sat, I noticed tears in her eyes. I took her hand and she turned to me and smiled. Mr. Appleton leaned forward a little and shot a quick glance at Virginia's hand resting in mine, but he said nothing.

"In our usual service, now would be the time for a reading from the scriptures or some other inspirational work," the Reverend said, "but this is not a normal service, nor are we living in normal times. Instead of an inspirational reading, let us be inspired by the men who served and sacrificed for our freedom. Forty-three young men from this congregation answered the call, and many of them are here this morning. One of those forty-three men, David Weld did not return home. In addition, over the past year or so, we have met several men who served and many of them are with us this morning." He paused and organized his papers. "I am going to read the names of all those men, and I ask them to rise when their names are called."

I had not expected this. When the first name was read, a young man in uniform rose unsteadily to his feet a few pews in front of us. I did not count how many names were read, but the sight of this growing number standing silently with the eyes of the congregation upon them was difficult to witness. Obviously, I did not know what each individual had endured, but I knew what I had, and that sense of collective horror was unbearable.

When my name was inevitably called, I struggled to stand. The pain in my leg had suddenly returned and I winced. And, once standing, I could not raise my head to look around me. I heard Virginia gasp and I saw that I was holding her hand so tightly that her fingertips were white. I had to force myself to loosen my grip.

Finally the last name was read and after a long pause the Reverend asked the congregation to remain in silent contemplation of us and of those who did not come home. I thought of my brother, Chaim, and Benny and many others, even the trio of anti-Semites that had been sent out on a suicide mission. And I thought of the unnamed hundreds on both sides that I had seen fall.

And then I started thinking about the word "fall," and how words are used to hide the truth. Those boys did not fall. They were not leaves that dropped from trees when the season turned. They were killed, torn apart by weapons used by other boys at the command of rich and powerful rulers far away from the carnage, rulers using sanitized language and waving their flags to obscure the reality of their crimes. I remembered Senator Lewis from Illinois who spoke so artlessly and ignorantly about sacrifice on the battlefield at the July Fourth parade at the hospital in Rouen and the severely wounded soldier from Chicago who confronted him.

Finally, the Reverend asked us to sit. It took all my strength not to run from that church. I wondered how my fellow soldiers felt. As the service continued I stood when everyone stood, and I sat when they all sat, but I paid little attention to what was being said. I kept telling myself that I must get through this - for Virginia. She was the future, the war was the past.

Virginia squeezed my hand. "Are you all right?" she whispered. "You look ashen." Reverend Frothingham had finished his sermon, and introduced the final hymn.

"I'll be fine."

"It's almost over."

I did not respond, but felt the tension in my body begin to ease. I focused all my energy on Virginia's singing.

And then it was over and the crowd began to inch toward the doors. "Can we sit a few minutes?" I said to Virginia.

"Of course," and we turned sideways to allow her parents to pass us into the aisle.

A few people shook my hand as they passed, saying something like, "Thank you for your service." I acknowledged them politely.

Finally the crowd had thinned. Virginia took both my hands and looked into my eyes. "I never realized how difficult this might be for you, Isaac. I'm so sorry."

"No need to apologize. I was looking forward to coming." I felt a sadness descend on me. "I did not know what to expect, Virginia, nor could I have known how I might react. I was overcome with the horrible waste of it all, and the stupidity and ignorance that comes out of the mouths of those powerful leaders who send young men to war."

We sat a while longer. The sanctuary was virtually empty. Through the gallery windows one could see that the clouds had broken up and the sun was shining. The Tiffany windows glowed, spreading their soft light. I breathed deeply several times. "This is a lovely tranquil place."

"It is, but we should go," Virginia said. "Mother and Father will be waiting for us in the Garden. We like to walk home together."

The Reverend was still lingering by the door, chatting with groups of his congregants who were milling about. When he saw Virginia and me approaching he moved towards us. "I am so thankful you came, Isaac." He put both hands on my shoulders. "I could tell it was a difficult experience for you. I believe time and love will help you overcome this pain."

"Thank you."

Mr. and Mrs. Appleton were across the street in the Garden talking with a couple and their three grown children, one of whom was in uniform. I was introduced to the Winslows as Virginia's friend. We shook hands. Andrew, the young man in uniform displaying lieutenant's bars, said he had seen me standing when the names were called. He asked what unit I was with and I told him. He said he was with a supply unit that, fortunately, had spent most of the war in Le Havre unloading and organizing equipment and sending it off to the front.

"You were very lucky," I said.

"I was."

Virginia took my arm. "It's time for lunch. The service went longer than usual and Mother and Father are anxious to get home."

Mr. Appleton walked beside us. "Mr. Winslow is a colleague who works with a new organization representing Negroes on issues of voting rights and other civil liberties matters, the National Association for the Advancement of Colored People," he said. "They opened a small office in Boston a few years before the war. Have you heard of it, Isaac?"

"No, sir."

"They're an interesting organization. Winslow's a fine man and an excellent attorney. He told me he was looking for legal assistants and I mentioned your friend Reuven to him. Tell Reuven, if he is interested, to pay him a visit next week. His office is on Bromfield Street."

"Thank you, sir. I'm sure he will be interested."

"He seems like a dedicated young man, your friend."

Sunday dinner was a sumptuous event. It started with creamed corn soup, then a course of small pieces of fried fish with a tangy lemon and parsley sauce, followed by a salad of greens. The main course was roasted turkey with potatoes, peas and carrots and a buttery walnut bread. Finally, caramel custard with dried fruit. I don't think I had ever seen so much food or that many knives, forks, spoons and plates in front of four people in my life. The Appletons were clearly emerging rapidly from the conservation efforts of the war years.

Discussion over dinner was sparse. It was as though the Appletons viewed this as a time to contemplate the Sunday service, to let the message sink in. I watched Virginia for clues on how to conduct myself. We remained at the dining room table even after the meal and after Bea had removed all the dishes and cutlery.

"Bea will bring in the coffee shortly," Mrs. Appleton said.

That seemed to be the cue Mr. Appleton was waiting for. "So, Isaac, how did you find the service this morning?"

I wasn't sure what to say. It wasn't as if I didn't anticipate the question, but I felt at a loss for words, especially since I heard so little of the service. What would Mr. Appleton think if I said I did not listen to the sermon and had no idea even what the main theme was? "I like Reverend Frothingham," I said after a long silence. "I find him to be a passionate and compassionate person."

"He certainly is," Virginia said.

"How did you feel about standing and being recognized by the congregation?" Mrs. Appleton asked.

"To be honest, Mrs. Appleton, I found it difficult. I had thought I would feel some solidarity, some sense of common accomplishment with the other men who stood, but I'm afraid the war is still too recent for me to see it in any positive light." I took a sip of my coffee, trying to give myself time to find the words to continue, but I could not.

Virginia offered me another slice of apple pie. I declined.

"How did you find the sermon?" Mr. Appleton asked.

I looked helplessly at Virginia. I had not told her that most of the service was a complete blank to me, but I hoped she had realized that, or, at least, she would see my discomfort and find a way to divert the question. She tilted her head and looked back at me, and smiled. "I think the Reverend sailed rather close to the edge today," she said, "virtually calling the Senator a war-monger."

"I did not hear that at all, Virginia," Mrs. Appleton interjected, "In fact, I think he was more than generous to Mr. Cabot Lodge, who, after all, seems to think that war is the answer to every international conflict."

"My dear, I think Virginia is correct, except that I think Frothingham has every good reason to call the Senator what he is."

"So, we all seem to agree that Cabot Lodge is on the wrong side of this matter, it's a question of whether we think the Reverend was too direct in calling him out." Virginia always had a remarkable way of getting to the heart of things. "What do you think, Isaac?"

I could take any position on this question, since her parents obviously heard different things from the Reverend. "Thank you Virginia!" I said to myself, "you are so incredible!"

"Well," I said, hesitating a moment, "since I have not been aware of this dispute between Reverend Frothingham and the Senator I can only say my impression was that the Reverend appeared somewhat angry and frustrated by the opposition to what he sees as the most important reason for us going to war - the chance for world peace embodied in the League of Nations."

"Indeed. I think he finds it incomprehensible that a fellow Unitarian would take such a position," Virginia said.

"Well, he should know we are not always the most united people," Mr. Appleton responded, "We have taken diametrically opposite positions on many important issues in our history. In your part of the state, Isaac, where the economy is built on textiles, many Unitarians who were textile mill owners were in favor of slavery because they benefitted from the low cost of slave-produced cotton."

"It doesn't make them right," Virginia said.

"No, dear, but people tend to act out of self-interest no matter what the Bible says."

"I thought we were better than that!"

"We try to be."

I stayed out of the discussion as best I could, but at some point Mrs. Appleton asked why I had not worn my uniform as most of the others had. "I am no longer a soldier," I said, then added; "I will say that what impressed me most about Reverend Frothingham was when he read the names of those who had served, he read only the names - without rank or unit or awards. He placed us as equals in the context of civilian life, of society."

"I never thought of that," Mr. Appleton said.

Chapter 35

Damon is humming, as he often does.

I'm here.

"Hello, Isaac. I hope I didn't wake you."

No.

"Are you doing OK?"

Yes.

"Any more pain?"

No. Nothing more than the usual, that is.

"Good. That lovely mane of yours could use some help. How about I comb your beard?"

Yes.

He sits beside me and I hear him rummaging in the drawer next to the bed. "Before I begin: the time-stamp. It's quarter after five in the morning on Friday, May thirty-first. The sky is growing light already and the sun is beginning to appear. Not a cloud in sight."

Thank you.

I feel the comb moving gently through my beard.

Sing.

"Sorry, Isaac, I missed your word.

Sing.

"You want me to sing?"

Yes. I need to have a blinky-blink signal for "please."

"OK. Give me a minute to think of something." He is quiet, continuing to comb. Finally he asks, "Do you like James Taylor?"

Yes.

"Well, a lot of people think this song was written by James Taylor, but it was actually written by Carol King and sung by James Taylor."

Smile. I know it the moment I hear the first couple of words. It is one of my favorite songs.

"When you're down and troubled and you need a helping hand ..."

Damon, are you sure you didn't know me years ago! Allen used to play this record all the time, and in her last days Virginia would often ask to listen to it. At her memorial service, a friend sang it for her, for me. Tears spill from my eyes. I hope Damon doesn't see them because I don't want him to stop singing. I feel him squeeze my hand as he completes the song.

Thank you.

"You're very welcome, Isaac."

I want to ask for a hug, but perhaps that is going too far.

"I need to visit a few other patients. I'll try to see you before I leave." He squeezes my hand again and is gone.

***

Virginia died on October twenty-second, 1979, a week after Ginnie was born. She hung on just long enough to hold her great-granddaughter. She died smiling, despite all the pain she endured. She was like that. She never made a fuss, never expected the world to adapt to her situation. When she set her mind to doing something, nothing, not even cancer, could hold her back.

In Jewish tradition, children are named after a person who has died. Several years after Virginia's death, Allen told me that Martha had not wanted to name her new daughter after Virginia because Virginia was still living when the baby was born. Allen tried to persuade her that it would be honoring Virginia to give the baby her name. They finally compromised on Virginia as a middle name, but no one has ever called Ginnie "Hannah," which is her given first name after Martha's favorite great aunt.

I am drifting off somewhere; one of my flying half-dreams. Skimming over the ocean, over a ship weighed down with emigrants from the old country. I see my ten-year-old self on the deck, my sketchpad in my hands. I am drawing a picture of my sea-sick mother. Then onward, over the French coast line. I feel the spray on my face billowing up from the waves pounding the rocks. I listen for the sounds of war and watch for the snaking lines of trenches. I am holding my breath trying to direct my mind away from the inevitable. But in vain, and I am hovering over no-man's-land seeing the bodies, damp with morning dew and glistening as the sun climbs in the heavens.

And suddenly I am standing in the cemetery at Athies near Arras in France crying over a white gravestone with a Star of David and my brother's name carved into it. His stone is one of thousands, arranged in perfect lines, so orderly and pristine; the antithesis of the chaos that brought these people here. I bend and pick up a small flat stone and I set it on the corner of Chaim's marker. Ginnie is standing next to me, and so are Virginia and Mama. We all are here at Chaim's final place of rest, the place where they put his torn body, freed from his tormented soul.

Everything seems to collapse inward simultaneously. Time has collided with itself. A slow rhythmic drumbeat begins softly and then starts to increases in tempo and volume until it is a barrier of unbroken sound. I am tumbling in complete darkness. I feel my arms flailing. My breath burns in my nose and throat.

It is the stabbing pain in my chest that breaks me out of my fall. I focus all my attention on the pain and I force the drumming to recede. Almost imperceptibly the darkness begins to transition from impenetrable black to translucent gray.

I hear Wanda's voice and Doctor Fish. I cannot make out what they are saying over the crazy beeps of my cat-machine. I hear Wanda approach.

I'm here.

"Good to see you, Isaac. I'm going to draw a little blood," she says, "So that we can run some tests."

I feel her poke a needle into my arm. I also feel some unusual pulling at different spots on my chest.

"We have you hooked up to an EKG," she says, as if she were reading my mind.

"You appear to have had a heart attack, Mr. Simon." It is Dr. Fish. "We're trying to ascertain the extent of it."

Don't like.

"Did you blink something, Isaac?" Wanda says. "Can you do it again, please? I missed it the first time."

I blink long, short.

"Got it. Let me check your word chart." She pauses, then continues, "Did you say 'don't like?'"

Yes.

"Well, no one likes a heart attack, but the fact that you can still remember your words is a good sign."

The cat-machine stops beeping. "We can stop the EKG, nurse. I'll be back in about half an hour to check in on him." Dr. Fish is still pretending that I can't hear him or communicate. What's blinky-blink for 'shithead'?

"Are you still having pain, Isaac?"

No.

"That's good." Wanda begins to remove the electrodes from my chest. "You gotta stop scaring us like this, Mr. Simon. We like you hanging around up here."

***

Ten days after the Sunday service honoring the soldiers, the United States Senate voted not to join the League of Nations. My next visit to Virginia was on the Saturday afternoon after that vote. She was waiting for me on the front steps of her home and she ran to me the moment she saw me walking down Beacon Street. She hugged me briefly.

"I'm so sorry, Isaac. So deeply sad and sorry." Her eyes were full, shimmering.

"What are you sorry about?"

"The vote. Everything you did in the war, everything you suffered through was for nothing."

I took her hands. "I knew that long before the vote. I think I knew it the first day I saw battle."

"But, there was the hope that something good would come of it. And now that's gone!" She leaned forward and pressed her cheek against my chest. I pulled her closer to me.

After some time she leaned back. "We'd better move on; neighbors will talk." She said. "Mother is expecting us for tea."

"Your father isn't home?"

"No, he's meeting with Reverend Frothingham and some other members of the church. They are concerned the vote in the Senate will cause a schism in the congregation because there are ardent supporters of both sides. They have to figure out how to keep the church together."

"Without Reverend Frothingham compromising his own rather strong convictions on the issue."

"Exactly."

"I never thought a religious leader also needed to be a diplomat."

Virginia laughed. "The Reverend can be rather stubborn. This will be a challenge for him. But I have faith." We walked in silence to the house.

Mrs. Appleton was in the parlor seated in the chair usually occupied by her husband. It had been turned to face the glowing fire in the fireplace. She closed her book and stood as we entered. "Good afternoon, Isaac, it's good to see you again. Sit, you two." She indicated the chairs on either side of her.

"Good afternoon, Mrs. Appleton."

"Mr. Appleton will not be joining us for tea, I'm afraid. He asked me to apologize for him."

"Virginia told me the circumstances. There is no need for an apology."

"The Reverend is in a froth over this whole business."

I had to admire her use of the pun. "I understand he is passionate about the League," I responded.

"He's more than passionate. And he feels betrayed by his own churchmen. I think if Cabot Lodge were to step over the threshold of the church, the Reverend would personally escort him from the building."

I had nothing to add. I looked at Virginia who had not spoken since we entered the room. "Did I tell you that my Uncle Kalner and his new wife are coming to visit in a couple of weeks?" I said.

"I had a letter from your mother yesterday," Mrs. Appleton said. "She mentioned that her brother and his wife would be visiting. She seemed a little concerned."

"My mother has met Mary, my uncle's wife, only once or twice. Mary did not grow up Jewish and there might be a little tension."

"No, your mother is over that. It has more to do with the campaign to end child labor. She said something about Mary trying to persuade her to speak at a hearing in Washington, which she doesn't want to do. I, frankly, think she would be an excellent speaker, and I told her so."

Mrs. Appleton knew more about what was going on in my mother's life than I did.

"Freedom for Women," Virginia said. "I often find myself thinking about her sign."

"I do, too. And I told her that as well."

Bea arrived with the tea and a still-steaming apple pie and set them on the table.

"So, how have you been since that service, Isaac? Virginia said you were deeply affected by it."

"The war is with me constantly. Most of the time I can press it into the background, but the service brought it back. I don't think anyone can fully grasp the cost of that war. Whatever might have come out of it, even a League of Nations, for those of us who were there I think the price would have been much too high."

I accepted a cup of tea and a large slice of pie from Virginia. I looked around the room and it struck me that I had become used to this environment; it no longer seemed out of the ordinary to me. Certainly, the Metzinger still danced and intrigued every time I saw it, but the rest of the place looked neutral. I even noticed all was not perfect; the large Persian rug was frayed along one edge, the wallpaper on the wall behind the fireplace showed signs of lifting along the ceiling, and the fine porcelain plate which held my pie had a small chip.

"Reverend Frothingham asked after you last week," Virginia said. "He sought me out before the service. I told him you had written in a letter shortly after the service that you were not always able to predict or control your emotional responses to the war, but that time was working for you."

I had written that, but I was not so sure about the healing powers of time. Time is more like a filter - less gets through, but what does make it is the essence of the past, in its finest, most vivid detail with all the feelings exposed and sharpened.

"Please tell him I appreciate his concern," I responded, "and that I'll be fine."

We finished our tea. I walked over to the bay window. It had started to rain heavily. Virginia stood beside me and placed her hand on my back. "Are you really fine, Isaac?"

I hesitated. "I am," I said, "There will probably always will be some bad days, but I won't allow my life to be defined or controlled by those years."

"Will you come back to our church again?"

"I don't know. Maybe. Probably, but don't ask me when."

"OK. I can accept that." She grabbed my hand and pulled. "Let's walk in the rain! We can use Father's large umbrella."

Before I could respond we were on the top step outside the house. She unfolded the umbrella and handed it to me. "Let's go to the library. It's a beautiful building and they have astonishing exhibits from their rare books collection. A while ago I saw some Shakespeare first folios."

There were few people on the street. We splashed our way past the church then up Boylston Street, the rain unrelenting. Virginia was laughing like a schoolgirl. "I love to be out in the rain!" she shouted and dashed out from under the umbrella twirling several times with arms outstretched before returning to my side and hugging me. About a block before the library she pulled me into a men's clothing store. We stood just inside the door, dripping.

"What are we doing here?" I asked.

"I want to get you a new necktie."

I started to object, but she placed her fingertips on my lips. "Isaac, almost every time you visit you bring me something - chocolates, flowers, books. I'd like to get something for you."

"You've been planning this. The library was a ruse."

"Of course."

"I never took you to be a devious person."

"Only when I want to do something nice." She kissed me quickly and we advanced further into the store.

By the time we left the store with my new deep green necktie the rain had almost stopped. Virginia took my arm. "I asked Mother to invite you and your mother to Thanksgiving, but she said it was too soon. We always have a big family dinner with hordes of aunts, uncles and cousins, many of whom we only see on holidays."

"I agree with your mother completely. I don't think my mother and I are ready to take on such an Appleton gathering."

"They're pretty harmless, for the most part."

"I'm sure they are, but I'm not particularly comfortable in crowds of strangers, especially ones filled with people who are trying to figure out who I am and why I'm there. I'll see you on the Saturday after."

"Come for luncheon," she laughed, "We'll still have tons of leftovers."

Chapter 36

We had been in America nine years, but Mama and I had not yet quite understood the meaning of Thanksgiving, other than that it was a day off work and a day when extended families got together. She invited my uncle Ben and his wife for dinner, but they couldn't make it. Uncle Kalner was in New York and was coming to Boston in a couple of weeks, anyway. So, we spent a quiet day together with our usual kind of meal. Mama made an attempt at a pumpkin pie for dessert, because she heard that was a traditional thing to do, but it failed terribly with a burnt crust and a filling that would not set.

After the meal I decided to take a walk and do a few drawings. It was a cold gray day, threatening snow. I made my way towards downtown and found a low wall to sit on. The streets of the city were deserted; the tall, dark buildings seemed to lean in under the weight of the gloomy sky.

I had started to experiment more and more with abstracted views and was completely immersed in my drawing when I heard someone call my name. I turned and saw Roland Ramsay crossing the street toward me. "Isaac! What brings you out here on this Thanksgiving day?"

"Hello Roland. I came out to make a few sketches. It's nice and quiet." I almost stretched out my hand to shake his when I remembered his terribly deformed hands. "I could ask you the same question."

"About the same - except the drawing. I like to walk around the city when it's almost empty."

"How's your family? Your little girl?"

"We're all fine, I suppose. My wife is working and I am finally getting a small benefit from the government for my wounds. We're getting by. I'm starting a training program in the new year that will hopefully help me get back to work."

"Good."

"And how about you? How is the architecture world going?"

"Well, very well. I'm learning a lot and the pay is much better than at the newspaper."

"I wouldn't doubt that. Hardwicke is a cheap old bastard!" The resentment flared then died down. "I'm trying to force my fingers to move, to be strong enough to grip a pencil or a brush. I think if I could just do that, I'd be able to draw and paint again." He extended his mangled right hand to demonstrate and I could see slight movement in the fingers and wrists.

"That would be wonderful!"

"I'm working at it, millimeter by millimeter. Exercises, creams, warm towels."

"Keep it up. How long have you been doing this?"

"About a month. It all began when my little girl and I were playing hide-and-seek and she hid in my closet. While I was looking for her, she found the old portfolio of drawings I had put together when I was looking for a job several years before the war. She couldn't believe that her Daddy had done them and asked why I stopped making pictures. I didn't know how to explain. I decided right then I was going to find a way to draw again."

"I wish you all the best, Roland."

"I'll let you get back to your drawing. Nice seeing you, Isaac." He started to walk away, but stopped. "Will you be here Christmas Day?"

"I really haven't given it any thought."

"I'll be here in the afternoon, about this time. I plan to be sitting right where you are now, with pencil and sketchpad."

"I'll try to be here, too."

***

Chanel Number 5. Danielle. I hear her sipping a cup of tea and slowly turning the pages of a book. I worry that my recent possible heart attack has robbed me of some part of me. I feel like I need to take stock. I know I can still hear and smell things. My brain seems to be working; otherwise I wouldn't be going through this exercise.

I am awake.

No response. Is she not paying attention, or am I really not opening and closing my eyelids? I wait till I hear her sip her tea, and try again.

I feel her touch my hand. Good, I can still feel things and the blinky-blink is working. "Hi there, Isaac. You've been dozing for some time. You actually snored a little. Really surprised me; it's been so long since any sound has come from you that even a snore is music."

Smile. Hug.

Danielle leans in and gently squeezes my upper arms. "Sorry I haven't been around for a few days. I was fighting off a cold. Anyway... it's Friday afternoon on May thirty-first."

Thank you.

"I saw Nurse Wanda when I came in; she said you had another episode. I'm not sure what the hell that means, but she also said that you're OK now. Are you OK?"

Yes. Whatever the hell that means.

"Sure?"

Yes.

"I asked the nurse to tell the doctor I'd like to talk with him. I'll keep you posted. Are you up for a bit of Winnie the Pooh?"

No. Then I signal that I want to create a new word.

"New word?"

Yes. And we create the signal for "please." Short, short, long, long.

"I'll add it to your chart. It will be number fourteen."

I wonder if I can remember them all.

"Now are you ready for some tales of the bear and his friends?"

Yes. Please.

She chuckles and begins to read.

***

Uncle Kalner and Mary arrived at our apartment around two o'clock in the afternoon on the first Saturday in December. He hugged me warmly and introduced me to Mary, "The woman who has saved me from myself." We shook hands.

"How long can you stay, Kalner?" my mother asked.

"We have to get the five-thirty train back to Boston. There's a dinner meeting I need to attend."

"So short?" She was disappointed.

"These are busy times, Rivka. The labor movement is growing fast, exploding, and the government doesn't like it."

I remembered Reuven's dire prediction; "Uncle, what do you think will happen?"

"I think the government, especially attorney general Palmer, is going to try to put his foot on our necks."

"Reuven is saying the same things."

"Enough of that talk, Itzik. How are you? I have not seen you for years."

"I'm OK, Uncle."

"Your mother wrote to say you have a young woman in your life."

"I do. Her name in Virginia Appleton, from Boston."

"Nice Jewish girl, just like mine!" He winks, and puts his arm around Mary. "I'm happy for you, Itzik. Love is the most important thing in the world."

Having Mary in his life had changed him in some ways; he seemed less angry, less stern. Mary was the perfect complement to my uncle; where he was assertive, she was laid back, and where he was loud and challenging, she was quietly persuasive. This is not to say she did not have strong opinions, and she launched into the issues surrounding child labor as soon as there was a lull in the conversation. She urged my mother to come to Washington the following week to meet with representatives and speak at a congressional hearing.

"What more can I say than children should not work?"

"You can talk about your own life experience and about the children you see day in, day out in the mill."

My mother sighed, "Don't you see, Mary, one of the big problems with the way this democracy works is that even though we legally have a right to say our piece and be heard, working people can't afford to risk their jobs to take the time to go to Washington to plead our case. Not to mention the loss of pay, the travel expenses and so on."

"But, you know how important this is."

"I know. But I can't go."

There was a prolonged silence. Finally, Uncle Kalner said, "Well, we can't make you do something you have made up your mind about." He turned to me, "Your mother wrote that you are working for an architect. How is it going?"

"Very well. It's a small firm - the owner, a senior draftsman and me -

so I'm exposed to a wide range of different details that go into designing and constructing a building. I'm thinking of entering architecture school in Boston in the fall."

"Little Itzik is growing up, Rivka. Soon he will be off on his own."

I paused, waiting to catch my mother's eye. "Reuven has suggested I share his apartment."

"Really," my mother said and she sat up a little straighter and pressed the tips of her fingers together - a sign of concern. "And when were you going to tell your mother about this?"

"I haven't made a decision about moving, yet. I thought I would talk it over with you first."

"Good."

I took a deep breath. "I'd like to change the subject. I have a question I'm hoping Mary can help me with."

Mary looked at me apprehensively, "I'll try."

Ever since the non-invitation for Thanksgiving dinner at the Appletons, I had been worrying about Christmas. If Thanksgiving was difficult for me to understand, Christmas was terrifying. While the whole idea of a virgin giving birth to the son of God seemed bizarre, and all the dogma and ritual built up around that belief only made it less comprehensible, it was the simple requirement of exchanging gifts that kept me up at night. What could I possibly get for Virginia that she didn't have and that I could afford?

"This will be the first Christmas Virginia and I will be together. I know people give gifts at this time of year, but I have no idea what is appropriate. Do you have any suggestions?"

She looked at me as though I was asking her to solve some deeply profound problem. "I really can't help you, Isaac. I don't know Virginia. I have not given or received a Christmas gift since I was twelve years old. In my family, it was only the children who received things - usually clothes or boots, and the occasional toy. You're dipping your toes in a world I know little about. I'm afraid I have no idea what to suggest."

"A gift doesn't always have to be a surprise, Itzik," my mother said. "Virginia knows your background and lack of experience in this holiday. Talk to her. Let her know your confusion."

"Hmm. This is one of the many bridges Virginia and I will need to build together. You're a wise woman, Mama." I leaned across the table and kissed her on the cheek.

***

I have been lying here thinking I have no idea what is going on in the world. The last events I can recall all had to do with the aftermath of that terrible attack in New York on September eleventh last year. I know the President and others are beating the drums for war. I wonder if anyone is challenging him. I wonder what else is going on.

I always used to spend time reading the newspapers and Newsweek, and watching the news on the television. I tried to keep myself informed. Now, I'm just a lump. I could be anywhere, anytime, and it wouldn't matter because I have no connection to what is going on.

Danielle is reading. I'm pretty sick of the cute little bear for today. I want news. I wait for her to pause, then signal for a new word.

"Something on your mind, Isaac?" she says.

Yes. New word.

I signal a five letter word and it takes until I have indicated GLOB for Danielle to catch on to the word "Globe."

"Globe?" she asks.

Yes.

"Do you want me to read the *Boston Globe*?" There is a note of apprehension in her voice.

Yes.

"Now?"

Yes. If at all possible.

"OK. I'll go down to the lobby. They probably have them on sale in the gift store."

Thank you. I am feeling energized, like I am about to get some nourishment I didn't even realize I'd been missing. She seems to be gone a long time. I try to maintain my focus.

Nurse Trainwreck is buzzing about, checking on my pipes. I pretend I am sleeping because I don't really want to interact with her right now.

"Still chugging," she says as she leaves the room.

Danielle is back, sitting next to the bed. I hear the newspaper rustling. Love that sound! "How about I read the headlines, and you blink 'yes' if

285

you want me to read that article."

Yes. Thank you.

"OK, first one: 'Somber rite as World Trade Center site closes a Chapter.'"

Yes.

She starts to read: "NEW YORK - A nationally televised ceremony yesterday marked the end of the massive cleanup of the World Trade Center site, the start of the rebuilding of the nation's financial center, and a new phase in the recovery from the Sept. 11 attacks." She pauses. "Do you want me to read on?"

Yes.

"Music from drums and bagpipes wafted through this wounded city as work crews rose from the empty canyon now cleared of tons of twisted metal, carrying the last beam of the World Trade Center. The solemn ceremony began with the ringing of a fire bell 40 times to honor 343 fallen firefighters at 10:29 a.m., the exact time the north tower collapsed into blinding dust and screeching concrete. The haunting sound of Taps echoed, as dignitaries, emergency crews, and relatives of the 2,823 people who were killed gathered at the 60-foot-deep pit."

Stop.

"Enough of that one? Do you want something else?"

No. I had heard enough. Watching those towers fall was one of the last visual images I have. It was soon after that terrible morning when I began to notice my already blurry vision diminishing dramatically. And the mention of the "haunting sound of Taps" brings on too much for me.

"Next time I'll start with baseball," Danielle says.

Yes. Although I had no great expectations for the Red Sox.

***

The following Saturday afternoon I worked until almost three. I had no way of letting Virginia know I was running late and I did not get to her home until after five o'clock. A light snow was falling as I stood outside the door and rang the bell. Mr. Appleton opened it. "You're late, Isaac," he said, bluntly.

"I know, sir. Mr. Wilkins kept me later than usual."

"Deadline?"

"Yes, sir. He is meeting with the client on Monday. I will need to go into the office tomorrow to finish the watercolor rendering."

"Virginia is in her bedroom. Take a seat in the parlor; I'll let her know you're here."

I sat on one of the chairs near the fire. On the small table next to me was the latest issue of Arts and Decoration magazine. I began to flip through the pages. At top center of a page with an article on current art shows was a photograph of a sculptural mask from the Ivory Coast. This was the first time I had ever seen work from Africa and it astonished me in its boldness, and clarity of line and form. Everything I had read and seen (and there wasn't much, I have to admit) about the modern movement seemed to find a point of recognition in this one work. It was simple and complex at the same time. It was expressionless and simultaneously seething with emotional power.

"Mother recently started subscribing to that magazine." I had not heard Virginia enter the room. I stood and kissed her lightly on the cheek. "Frankly, I found much of it too staid for my taste."

"Did you see this?" I held out the photograph of the African mask to her.

"No. I missed it. Remarkable."

"I am entranced. Sorry I'm so late, by the way."

"I've been trying to convince Father to get a telephone. It would make things so much easier."

"Well, I'd have to have one, too, although I think they have installed a pay phone at the railway station in Lawrence. I've never given it much thought."

"Well, no matter. Father said you had to work later than usual."

"Yes, and tomorrow, too. I'll have to get an early train."

"Staying at Reuven's tonight? How is he?"

"I haven't seen him since he was here. I did have a letter to say that he had been able to set up an interview with the lawyer your father recommended him to. He asked me to convey his gratitude to your father."

"I'll let him know."

"So, what shall we do this evening? Fancy a light dinner somewhere and a movie?"

"I think I'd prefer to stay home, if that's all right with you. It's miserably cold out there, and this fire is so nice and warm. Bea has left for the evening, but I'm sure we can raid the kitchen and find something to eat when we get hungry."

We sat side by side holding hands and staring into the fire. "Christmas is less than two weeks away," Virginia said. "Do you have any plans?"

"No," I answered, cautiously. That was my second Christmas fear - that I, or both my mother and I, would be invited to the Appletons for some Christmas party or other observance. I had at some time found myself visualizing the Appleton family showing up for a Passover Seder in Linkeve. It was an impossibly bizarre scene.

"We are going out tomorrow after church to find a Christmas tree. It will be fun. I wish you could join us."

"Afraid..."

"I know. You have to work."

"Virginia, I have to tell you that I am confused by Christmas, and a little scared. It's so outside my culture."

"Don't get caught up in all the magical stuff, Isaac. We see it as a holiday to celebrate the message of Peace and goodness and generosity. It is more about the message than the messenger. It's a fun, warm family and friends time in the darkest period of winter. But, don't worry, I'm not going to ask you to come to Christmas dinner, or the Christmas Eve party that my mother always gives."

I sighed in relief.

"But, I am going to ask you and Reuven to come to a party I'm giving for my friends on the Saturday night after Christmas. There'll be about twenty people, with lots of good food and drink, and the latest music. Father is getting me a gramophone and some records for Christmas, and people will bring their records, too."

There's that gift issue. "Reuven has a good collection of jazz records."

"He should bring them, definitely!"

"It sounds like fun!" I think she detected a note of apprehension in my voice, so I added, quickly, "I'll invite Reuven."

"My friends are anxious to meet you. Ever since our evening with Dot and Phillip the word is out about my mysterious Jewish soldier-boy companion."

"I'm not sure whether I should be intrigued or terrified."

"You can handle them. And remember, I have chosen to be with you, and if they have a problem with that, they can walk. By the way, Dot and Phillip declined the invitation, but I have had positive responses from about a dozen people so far. My friends are, if nothing else, a curious bunch. You should also tell Reuven there are several unattached women who will be coming."

"You are an instigator!"

"I am." She stood. "Getting hungry? Let's see what we can scrape up in the kitchen." She took my hand and led me out the parlor and down the hall past the door to the dining room and into the kitchen, which was almost the size of our entire apartment! It was dominated by an elaborate new pale yellow porcelain gas stove and oven along-side an old wood-stove against the far wall. A large table occupied the center of the room, and two of the four walls held rows of shelves and cabinets. A large icebox stood next to the rear door.

"I don't cook," Virginia admitted. "We'll have to make do with what we find." She opened the doors to the icebox and pulled out a block of cheese and a plate with slices of meat which she placed on the table. She went into the pantry and returned with a loaf of bread and the remains of an apple pie. "I think we'll have enough with all this," she said, "I'll make some sandwiches."

"Looks fine to me." And yet, here was such a simple, everyday activity where our class differences were starkly exposed. How could she not know anything about cooking? "Should we put water on for tea?"

"I don't know how to use the fancy new gas stove, and the fire is out in the wood-stove."

We sat at the kitchen table and ate our sandwiches. "One thing we should resolve is to be a lot more self-sufficient. We both need to learn to cook!"

"Or, at least, boil a pot of water!" she said. "It is pretty pathetic. I have everything I need, but I'd die of starvation if I was left alone in this house for more than a few days."

Here was my cue to talk about the question that had been gnawing at me for days. "So, something has been worrying me for some time, and I'm just going to say it." I set my half-eaten sandwich on my plate and took her hands. "I know that Christmas is a time when people exchange gifts, but I have no idea what is considered appropriate."

"This shouldn't be a problem."

"I know, but it is. From my perspective, the question that forms in my mind is: what do I get for someone who has, as you said, everything she needs?"

"I might have everything I need, but I do not have everything I want." She smiled. "I don't mean to be flip, but life is more than being able to meet only one's basic needs. Or, maybe the line between needs and wants is not a line at all, but a large fuzzy area. You're an artist, Isaac. Is art a need or a want? Or is it both? Perhaps it is a need for some, a want for others, and yet for many others it is neither."

"You're not helping me."

She kissed me quickly on the cheek. "I want something of you, Isaac."

And that was all she was willing to offer. When I arrived at Reuven's apartment later that evening he was deep into his studies, preparing for two major tests coming up the following week, and had no time to talk. I made myself a cup of tea then sat on the couch and contemplated the gift question.

It seemed obvious that the something of me that Virginia wanted was a painting, but a painting of what? The problem was that I was going through a period of indecision with my art. Most of what I drew was realistic, but I had begun to experiment more and more with abstraction and I had not yet built up a confidence in my work. I liked the freshness and experimental nature of the new work, but I found myself throwing away more pieces than I kept. I was also running into the limitations of pencils and watercolors. I needed a medium that gave me bolder colors and more nuanced transitions. Working in oils seemed a realistic and natural new direction, but for that I would need more space and there was none in our small apartment in Lawrence, nor in Reuven's place in Boston. And, of course, oils and canvases were expensive, not to mention I knew nothing about the medium and I would need to find someone to teach me the basics.

Reuven stood and stretched. "I'm done studying for tonight. How's Virginia?'

I told him my Christmas gift dilemma and he laughed. "I wish I had your problem."

"You're no damned help! By the way, you're invited to Virginia's party on the Saturday after Christmas. She told me to be sure to inform you there will be several unattached women there."

"How could I say no?"

"She'd also like you to bring some of your jazz records. She's getting a gramophone from her parents as a Christmas gift."

"Very nice."

"So, seriously Reuven, what do I give her?"

"How much can you afford?"

"About nothing - I'm trying to save for architecture school next year."

"She wants an artwork from you, Itzik. Create something romantic."

I paused. "Actually, Reuven my friend, you've given me an idea."

"Glad I could help. Wine?"

"Thanks."

"You know this is going away soon," He said as he handed a glass to me.

"What's going away?"

"This. Wine, alcoholic drinks. Prohibition goes into effect on the twentieth of next month. Crazy people - they see nothing immoral in sending hundreds of thousands of men to die in their wars, but they get all upset about us enjoying a glass or two at the end of the day."

I was aware of Prohibition, but hadn't given it much thought. Somehow, I had felt it was such a ridiculous idea that it would never happen.

"The magician and the confidence man call it misdirection. You get people to focus on the shiny nickel while you're pulling the dollar bills out of their pockets."

"Are you beginning to hoard your favorite vintage?"

"I'd love to, but prices have climbed spectacularly. There already is a black market. This is the last bottle I'll be able to afford for a long time."

"Thank you for sharing it with me, my friend."

"You do know what's going to happen? Criminal syndicates will smuggle booze into the country, or they'll find ways to produce it here, and it will become a whole new industry - along with the street wars to carve out territory. And of course, the money will flow to buy off cops, police chiefs, prosecutors and politicians. If the fools were worried about the negative effects of alcohol, they're in for a big surprise when they see the effects of taking alcohol away!"

"To optimism," I said, as I raised my glass then downed the last of my wine.

Chapter 37

On Christmas day I was up before sunrise; I had set this day aside to work on Virginia's gift and I was anxious to get going. I had made several preliminary sketches of different ideas over the last week or so until I had finally came to a decision on what it would be. Actually, I decided to do two renditions of the same romantic scene - the Swan Boats. One painting would be a realistic depiction using watercolors; the other would be the same scene, abstracted, and using various media. I came to the conclusion that since I did not have the vibrancy and texture of oils, the second painting would incorporate pieces of colored paper and other found objects to provide the effects I was trying to evoke. It was a bold departure for me, but I felt it would work.

I started with two eleven by seventeen sheets of watercolor paper and did quick almost identical pencil sketches of the Boston Garden lagoon with a Swan Boat in the center and surrounded by willows and flower beds, and a young couple embracing under one of the trees. Then I began adding the colors to both. At some point I set one sheet aside so I could complete the realistic version.

My mother tried not to disturb me, but after several hours she coaxed me into joining her for a lunch of beef stew. I sensed there was something she wanted to talk about, but I told her I needed to take a walk to clear my head. As I made my way towards the downtown, I remembered Roland Ramsay saying that he planned to be there with sketchpad and pencils in hand.

And so he was, sitting on the same low wall I had occupied a month before. I came up beside him and looked over his shoulder at his drawing. It consisted of no more than a few dozen lines, but he had captured the elegance of the towering buildings leaning in above the deserted street. "You're doing it, Roland!"

"I told you I'd be here."

"That you did. It must feel good."

"I feel better than I've felt in years. I managed to draw a picture of a baby doll for my little girl for Christmas. The way she reacted you would have thought I'd given her a pony with a pot of gold."

"Wonderful."

"And how are you doing, Isaac? Still seeing that girl in Boston?"

"I am. I'm struggling over a painting I'm doing for her. A Christmas gift. I needed a walk to think about it."

We were quiet for a while, enjoying the silence. The sun was centered between the buildings, shining brilliantly. Roland added a few more lines to his drawing to emphasize the sun and its shadows, then he turned to me. "I apologize again for how I treated you when you came to work at the paper, Isaac. If there's one thing the war has taught me, it's where the real lines are in this world."

"Thank you, Roland. I appreciate it."

"You should stop by the house some time. My little girl remembers you."

"I will."

He returned to his drawing and I walked home quickly, re-energized.

I started right away on the second work. In thinking about it while walking home, I realized that the most important element was the couple embracing, so I redrew them in briefest outline, at what was to be the focal point of the work - slightly right of center. The swan - the symbol of purity and love - I drew larger and directly behind the couple. Then I tore my colored papers into various geometric shapes of different sizes and pasted them, overlapping, onto the sheet to form a background of shimmering abstracted flowers. I used several layers of watercolor to fill in the couple, and black ink to enhance their merging outlines. The original sketch, a duplicate of the first stages of the development of the realistic scene, was glimpsed just enough in the abstract collage to suggest that the two works were designed to complement one another.

It was almost dark by the time I was done. I taped the two works side by side on the wall. Our low power electric lamps did not really give enough light to see, but I really liked the way they both came out, and how they looked together. The next morning I signed and dated them, and inscribed each one, "To Virginia, with Love." I stopped at a picture framer's store on the way to work and selected simple varnished wood frames for both pieces.

I arrived in Boston late on the Saturday afternoon and made my way slowly to Reuven's apartment. A light snow had fallen in the morning leaving the city covered in a clean, white, fluffy, and dangerously slippery sheet. I was carrying an old suitcase with the clothes I was to wear to the party in one hand, and in the other, the package containing the two framed paintings I had picked up when I got out of work at noon.

The cold seemed to focus its attention on my wound, and a dull ache gripped my thigh. By the time I reached Reuven's I was grimacing with pain and not in the mood for a party. He saw the expression on my face and guided me to the one comfortable chair he owned. "Tea with lots of sugar," he said, prescribing a cure my grandmother might have suggested.

"What time is it?" I asked.

"Almost four-thirty. What time are we supposed to arrive?"

"Virginia said most of the guests would start arriving after eight, but she asked me to be there a little earlier to help move furniture to make space for dancing in the music room. We should leave here no later than seven."

"Unless we take a cab." He rose, poured the tea and handed me a cup.

"That's not in my budget, Reuven. I spent half a week's pay just to get these pictures framed."

"It is in my budget," he replied. "Yesterday I met with Mr. Winslow for the second time. He offered me a position as a legal assistant. I start the day after New Year. It is exactly the kind of law firm I want to be with."

"Congratulations, my friend!"

"Not only does he work with the NAACP, but his firm also represents several labor unions and organizations involved in a variety of civil rights issues. I would work for this man for nothing to get that experience, but he is, in fact, paying me very well."

"Does he share the same concern that you - and, by the way, also my Uncle Kalner - have about the so-called Red Scare?"

"He does. He told me to be prepared to be extremely busy."

The pain in my leg was subsiding. I drank a second cup of sweet tea while Reuven talked about the growing anti-foreigner sentiment being stoked by the attorney general and other political leaders. And also the growing power of the Ku Klux Klan which was spreading throughout the whole country, fueled by the anti-immigrant, anti-labor, and anti-socialist hysteria.

"Do you know there were more raids late last month? And last week over two hundred people were deported for their political views."

"I saw it in the papers. Emma Goldman and Alexander Berkman were in that number."

"Yes. There were no trials." He slapped his hand on his knee, then stood up. "And we are still only at the beginning of this. Winslow has contacts; he says there's a lot more to come!"

It had grown dark outside. "I think we need to get ready for a party. Let's try to put the politics aside and have fun."

"I can always get myself into the mood for fun, Itzik."

Shortly after seven o'clock we were riding in the back seat of a cab. I carried my paintings, Reuven held his records.

Virginia met us at the door. She was wearing a calf-length sapphire blue silk dress, with a scooped neckline and tight-fitting sleeves. Her matching gold necklace and ear-rings were reminiscent of ancient Egypt. She hugged me warmly and kissed me on the cheek. "Thank you so much for coming early. I see you brought records, Reuven. Thank you." We followed her through the parlor to the music room.

"I brought you something, too."

"I had noticed that rather large rectangular package under your arm. Shall I open it now?"

"Please do," said Reuven. "He would not say a word about it, let alone show it to me."

I handed her the package and stood nervously beside her. She placed it on the table and proceeded to unwrap it. "There are two framed pictures," she said, surprised.

"Wait," I said. "Close your eyes and I'll set them up so you can see them simultaneously."

She did as asked and I arranged them with the realistic one on the left. I glanced at Reuven; his face betrayed no reaction. "All right, Virginia, you may look."

I held my breath as she looked at one painting then the other, moving her head slightly as she studied the two works side by side, and leaning in a little to get a closer look at the abstract. Finally, she turned and hugged me.

"I love them, Isaac! And they go so well together. You and me and the Swan Boat. You could not have chosen a better subject. And so bold and fresh!" She pulled my face to hers and kissed me on the lips. "Thank you!"

I sighed loudly. "I am so happy, and relieved, that you like them," I said. "I was worried I had undertaken something so new and different for me."

"They are both so alive, vibrant. I must show them to Mother. And I have something to fetch for you." She hurried from the room.

"Are you sure you want to waste your time on architecture, Itzik? Maybe you should devote yourself one hundred percent to art."

"I'd love to, Reuven, but how many artists do you know that make a living? I can do both."

Virginia returned carrying a large colorfully wrapped box. "For you, merry Christmas, Isaac." I took the box from her and placed it on the table beside the paintings. "Open it."

The box contained half a dozen pre-stretched canvasses, a variety of brushes, a wooden palette, a palette knife and twenty-four tubes of oil paint. I was overwhelmed. I hugged her and thanked her. "Now you have no choice, Isaac. You have to learn how to use them."

Mrs. Appleton entered while we were still embracing. "Good evening, Isaac, Reuven. Virginia insisted I come down to see your paintings." She strode to the table. "Wonderful! I see Mr. Metzinger had an influence on you."

"He forced the gears of my brain to turn."

"I do like them. Where are you going to hang them, Virginia?"

"In my bedroom, of course, where I can see them every day."

A clock chimed eight. "Oh dear, we're late. I'll put the paintings and the paints in a safe place. Will you and Reuven move all these chairs and the table up against the walls so that there is room to dance in here? The gramophone is there in the corner," she pointed. "Reuven, would you like to put on some music?"

The first guests arrived about twenty minutes later. I recognized Andrew Winslow accompanied by a young woman I did not know. Reuven and I were standing near the gramophone and I asked him if he would like to meet his boss's son.

"I was introduced to him at the office," he said. "Andrew's working for his father while attending Harvard law school. Small world."

"He has two sisters. I suspect they'll be here too, although I don't know whether they are attached or not."

"I'll stay clear of them. The last thing I need is to get mixed up with the boss's daughter!" He laughed.

I went in search of Virginia and found her standing near the entrance to the parlor chatting with some new arrivals. She noticed me and waved to me to join her. The room was already quite full; the twenty or so guests that Virginia had said she expected soon blossomed to over thirty. Fine suits and dresses and jewelry were on display. I vaguely remembered some of the people from my morning in the church.

Two waiters circulated with glasses of white and red wine. A third carried a tray of hot appetizers. I wondered whether Bea had been corralled into working in the kitchen that evening. I tasted one of the appetizers and concluded they were good, but below her standard.

Virginia introduced me to her friends as her "beau," which raised a few eyebrows and questions about how we met and had we made plans for the future. We avoided long conversations. Virginia always had the excuse that she needed to circulate, and I followed. Mr. and Mrs. Appleton came down only once during the evening to greet their daughter's friends, before retiring to the upper floors.

The music from the adjacent room was getting louder, as was the noise of the people who had begun dancing. I saw Reuven standing near the gramophone readying the next record; he had apparently become the de facto person in charge of the music, and he appeared to be enjoying it. After he put on a record he would be out on the floor, dancing with someone.

The music was intoxicating, as was the never-ending supply of wine. By midnight a few people had collapsed onto the parlor chairs and fallen asleep. Virginia went over to Reuven and asked him to hold off playing the next record. In the sudden silence, the crowd all turned to her. "First," she said, "let me assure you that the party is not over." The crowd cheered. "But, before anyone else nods off on my mother's parlor couch, I want to thank everyone for coming this evening, and I want to wish you all a happy New Year!" More cheers. "Reuven - more music please!"

The sound of Jelly Roll Morton and his band filled the room, and the dancing continued. I did notice that the waiters with wine did not return - there was only so much of his hoard that Mr. Appleton was willing to part with, less than four weeks ahead of the spigot being shut. The party was winding down slowly. The last guests departed around two o'clock, leaving Reuven, Virginia and me alone in the parlor, which was littered with wine glasses, small plates and napkins.

"A wonderful party, Virginia! I had a really good time."

"Thank you for taking control of the music, Reuven. I can't imagine how it would have been without you."

"It was great. I got to play all the music I like, and hear a lot I hadn't heard before."

I looked around at the chaos of the room. "We need to straighten up a bit in here."

"Don't worry about it. Bea can take care of it in the morning."

"That's not quite fair. She has enough to do getting you all ready for church. Let's at least bring all the glasses and plates into the kitchen."

It took less than twenty minutes for the three of us to clear all the dirty dishes and reposition the furniture. When we were done, Virginia said, "You know, this was the first time I've ever done anything like that. Thank you, Isaac." She kissed me.

"We should be going," I said. "It's very late."

"Thank you for the paintings. I love them." We embraced again. "Let me get your paints."

There were no cabs about at that time of night, so we had to walk to Reuven's apartment in the cold. But it did not bother me; I was elated. This gift exchange I had feared, the party with all of her friends that had terrified me, were done and had all gone so well. Reuven and I stayed up listening to music and talking till dawn. I wished I could have done that with Virginia.

***

I am listening to the purr of my cat-machine. I have no idea how long I have been listening, but there is a steady reassuring rhythm to it, as if I am connected to a greater flowing world. We never had any pets when I was growing up - I certainly would not put the chickens or that mean goat in a category of pets. They were our sustenance and they supplemented our livelihood. There was no space or time in our tiny apartment in Lawrence. My mother did get a canary, but that was a few years after I left home.

When our children were small a big short-haired gray cat adopted us. He showed up at the back door one Sunday morning and darted into the kitchen when I opened the door to take the trash out. Emma was no more than four years old and she claimed ownership of the cat and named him "Bunny." Albert and Mark thought it was a dumb name for a cat, but Emma insisted, so we lived with a cat named Bunny. He was a warm, cuddly, playful cat who slept every night on Emma's bed till the day she died. About a week after her accident, Bunny escaped from the house and never returned.

"You're crying again, Grandpa Isaac." It was my dear Ginnie. "You have too many sad memories."

I do. But many are mixed happy and sad. They seem to go together. I blink that I am awake.

She hugs me gently. "It's June first, around nine in the morning. Summer is here a little early. It's going to get into the nineties today and stay that way for several days. You're lucky you have air conditioning. I might just move in with you!"

How do I say, "I'd love to have you spend time with me?" Instead, I blink "Yes."

"So, I've spent much of the past week frantically filling out and submitting applications for grad school. The deadline is today. I'm only applying to three schools - UMass, University of Vermont in Burlington, and Brandeis. Now I wait. I really want to go to Vermont; I've been to the campus a few times over the last year or two and it's really nice. And Burlington is an exciting city with a lot of cool things happening despite its relatively small size. But if I don't get in there, I'll be happy with either of the others. It also depends a lot on financial aid. I am researching all kinds of scholarships."

Smile.

"I can see it, Grandpa Isaac, that little smile of yours!"

I have to invent a blinky-blink word for "laugh."

"Danielle said you have decided you'd like to read the Globe. I brought today's with me. Would you like me to read it?"

Yes.

"She said to start with baseball. OK?"

Yes.

She reads the article describing the Red Sox victory in Yankee Stadium after a delay of over an hour. Good to hear that our team is doing so well and beating those overpaid blustering Yankees. But by the time she reaches the end of the article, I'm anxious for a bit of real news. I signal "Globe."

"You want more?"

Yes.

"Sports?"

No.

"All right. Page one." I hear the paper rustling. "How about this headline: 'Cold feet at the Pentagon?'"

Sounds interesting. *Yes.*

The article deals with President Bush's visit to Paris where he was met with numerous protests against his foreign policy and his denial of climate change, as well as the ominous possibility of invading Iraq. I did not want to think about another generation going to war. I signal to Ginnie to stop, which she does. She sets the newspaper on the floor and takes my hand in both of hers.

"I hope I don't have to wait too long for an answer from the schools and the scholarship folks. Working at Starbucks is beginning to wear me down. There are far too many people with college degrees serving fancy coffees and being forced to be friendly to total assholes! Oops - sorry about that, Grandpa Isaac, but there are days when I feel like I don't exist. If it weren't for the arrogant insults from certain customers there'd be nothing. It scares me."

Very expressive and colorful. I hope Ginnie goes home and writes all this down. Writing runs in the family. Her father is a writer and so were her grand-mother and her great-aunt Emma, who she never met.

Emma was much like Virginia - strong-willed, daring, unconventional. As a girl she would spend a lot of her time in my studio watching me paint and writing in a notebook she carried with her all the time. If you asked her what she was writing about, she would answer vaguely, something like, "Whatever's in my head." She was very private, but seemed happy most of the time. As a young teenager she was typically

301

moody and occasionally angry. She liked to be alone in her room, but also enjoyed hanging out with friends. She showed little interest in boys, once proclaiming that every boy she had ever met was "barely human." She was quick to feel hurt, and quick to forgive.

But after her brother Mark was killed in the war she became noticeably more withdrawn. The blow our family took with his loss hit her deeply. On New Year's Day, 1945, she announced that she had quit school and taken a job at the Fore River Shipyard in Quincy. She was to become a welder. Virginia and I were furious, but nothing would change her mind. She reminded me of myself when I had made that fateful decision to join the army.

"Winnie the Welder" and "Rosie the Riveter" were the names given to the almost two thousand women who worked in the shipyards during the war. All of them lost their jobs as the men returned, but my Emma lost her life. The platform she was standing on as she welded the steel plates of a destroyer collapsed, and she fell thirty feet to the concrete floor, amidst an avalanche of tumbling wood and metal. She was seventeen years old. It was only days before Germany surrendered.

When we went through her room we found three wooden boxes of notebooks she had filled and kept, going back to when she was nine years old. Those boxes are somewhere in my apartment; I'm sure Allen will find them. It was months after we buried Emma, and after Albert had returned home safely, that Virginia and I were able to read Emma's notebooks. She wrote whatever was in her head, and heart; her thoughts about what she had seen and heard, and how she felt about those things. There were also detailed descriptions of what she saw, from sunlight on a dusty floor, to snow storms and birds in flight.

In her last journals, she wrote about the loss of her brother and the pain of never seeing him again. And she wrote about building gigantic ships and the strength and power she felt in doing the task well. Her last few entries were about finding love and the experience of intimacy. She never mentioned a name, just the letter "L," but she wrote openly about "L" as a woman, and their fear that they would be discovered, and not caring if they were.

Virginia read these entries before I did, and as she handed the journal to me she said, "Do you remember that young woman who came to the funeral and sat on her own, weeping uncontrollably near the back. I wish I had known who she was, how important she was to Emma. I wish I had talked with her. I wish I could hug her."

Chapter 38

On Friday, January second 1920, federal agents rounded up thousands of people across the country. Thousands more were taken into custody in the following days. They were accused of being foreign agitators - anarchists, socialists, communists. Many were labor activists and organizers. Attorney General A. Mitchell Palmer put into action what Reuven and others had predicted. A week later Mama received a telegram from Mary saying Uncle Kalner had been detained late Thursday night along with many others. Mary did not know where he was or what would happen to him. Mama was frantic and helpless.

"I'm going to Boston tomorrow afternoon to see Virginia," I said. "I'll go to Reuven first and ask if he can find out anything; he's working for a lawyer who helps people in this kind of situation."

"Good. Good."

I took an early morning train to Boston. I walked to Reuven's apartment as fast as the snow-covered sidewalks would allow, but he was not home. I remembered Mr. Appleton had said that Mr. Winslow's law office was on Bromfield Street, so I hurried there. Fortunately, it is a short street - only two blocks - and I managed to find the building fairly easily. I took the stairs to the third floor. The door to the office of Joseph J. Winslow Esquire was not locked so I let myself in. The receptionist was on the telephone and looked like she needed some sleep. She motioned to me to take a seat and continued talking and taking notes. The moment she hung up, the telephone rang again and she picked it up.

Finally, she was able to talk with me. "Sorry, sir, but we are extremely busy today. How can we help?"

"I'm looking for my friend, Reuven Novitz. He started working here a few days ago."

"Is Mr. Novitz expecting you?"

"No, but my uncle, who he knows, was detained on Thursday."

"One moment." She came out from behind her desk and walked down a long hallway, returning a minute later. "He'll be out shortly."

Reuven, too, looked like he hadn't slept in some time. He had a few days' beard and his shirt was wrinkled and stained. "Well, you look like hell," I said as we hugged.

"I sure picked the perfect time to start my new job. Baptism by fire, they call it. The back offices are crazy, as is the conference room. We'll have to talk here."

We sat. "I've learned more in the last week than in the three years at law school. It's been intense."

"When last were you home? I stopped by your apartment before I came here - it looked like something exploded."

"And smells like something died. I know. I've probably spent a total of ten hours there since Monday. I just pop back when I can to wash and change my clothes. Mr. Winslow has Wendy go out and bring in food for us. There are some cots set up in one of the empty offices so we can nap. Anyhow, enough about my life. I can only take a couple of minutes, so what's going on with your Uncle Kalner?"

I told him all I knew from Mary's telegram, and filled him in on my uncle's involvement with the Wobblies, and later with the Ladies' Garment Workers Union in New York. I really knew few details. I did not even know whether he was a citizen.

"He was detained in another state. I'll have to talk with Mr. Winslow to see whether I can help on this. I'm sure he'll at least let me make a phone call or two. I assume you're off to see Virginia this afternoon; come back here before you head home. Hopefully we'll have some information."

I thanked him and watched him hurry back into the depths of the office.

Snow was falling when I left the building. It was too early to go to Virginia's so I walked to our favorite restaurant and ordered my usual soup and green salad. While I waited for my lunch, I started to draw a portrait of my uncle. My first inclination was towards the realistic, but I forced myself to try to see him more objectively, more in the spirit of that African mask I had seen in the magazine.

I allowed my soup to get cold and never touched my salad, but I left the restaurant with a drawing that astonished even me. The portrait was composed of simple interwoven shapes and, in its simplicity, it showed my uncle with his stoic expression blended with his smiling eyes. It was abstracted, cubist, but still conveyed the real character and look of the man.

"You have to meet him," I said to Virginia when I showed her the drawing and told her about his detention.

"Is he really a socialist?" she asked.

"Does it matter? He's a union organizer. He's been detained without a warrant, held in an undisclosed location and has had no communication with anyone since he was picked up. I think those are all violations of the law."

"People are afraid of socialists."

"People are afraid of what they don't understand, and the owning class is afraid of any challenge to their economic and political power." We were seated alone in the music room. This was the first time we had seen each other since the party and I knew Virginia would have preferred to talk about that, but I was worried about my uncle and my mother. It had struck me while I was on the train to Boston that if they were carting off union activists of foreign origins, then they could go after my mother, too, even though she had pulled back from her leadership role in favor of younger workers. Fortunately, she and I had both become naturalized citizens in 1916, so I felt she had some protection.

"Will Reuven be able to do anything?"

"I don't know. I'm going back to see him before I go home. My Uncle Kalner is one of the most wonderful people I have ever known. He can also be quite stubborn. I'm really worried about him."

"I know," she said, and we sat quietly for some time.

Bea came in with a tray of tea and cookies. She was smiling. I watched her leave, then said, "So, tell me what people have said about the party."

"I received notes from several of my guests; they were all very complimentary of you. Gillian even wrote that I had made a 'lovely and intriguing' choice. I have to agree."

"It was a wonderful party. I have to admit I was apprehensive, but I enjoyed it, and I enjoyed being with you."

"You definitely have Bea's approval. She was quite stunned to find that we had brought all the dirty glasses and plates into the kitchen. She was not surprised it was you who suggested we clean up. She's been humming that Marion Harris song, 'A good man is hard to find,' all week."

I laughed.

"I must confess that I've been playing it on the gramophone all week, too. I went out and bought it on Monday morning." She walked over to the gramophone and put the record on. When it ended, she opened the piano and played the same song. I loved to listen to her sing.

Mr. and Mrs. Appleton came into the room. "We're going to see Aunt Ethel at the hospital. We'll be home for supper. Will you be joining us, Isaac?"

"Thank you, but no. I have some errands to attend to in the city before I return home."

"Influenza," Virginia said. "Everyone was saying that the epidemic was over, but it isn't. Aunt Ethel was admitted two days ago. She's my mother's baby sister and very Presbyterian - which is to say that she disapproves of us Unitarians. She's convinced we are all on our way to hell because of our free-thinking ways."

"And are you?"

"I don't believe in hell. But it is rather scandalous that my parents should leave their daughter alone in the house with her young man." She walked over to me and sat on my knees and embraced and kissed me. Then she stood up, as did I. "I am so happy we found each other, Isaac! Our story is quite amazing."

"Improbable. Yet, here we are." We heard Bea approaching to pick up the tea things.

"We are not quite so alone," I said, and we exchanged a quick kiss. "I need to get back to see Reuven."

She walked with me to the door, and embraced me on the front steps.

"I don't care who sees us," she said.

"Nor do I. But then, I know no one in this part of town except you."

It was almost dark when I opened the door to the law office. Wendy, the receptionist was not at her post. I waited a few minutes but she did not return, so I made my way slowly down the long hallway. I could hear Reuven's voice. He seemed to be talking with someone on the telephone. I found him alone in a small office with three desks, three chairs, and rows of filing cabinets. He waved to me to sit. Finally he hung up the telephone, leaned back in his chair and sighed deeply.

"I'm exhausted, Itzik. The detentions are continuing. We heard of another twenty people here in Massachusetts today."

I shook my head. "Have you been able to find out anything about my uncle?"

He sat forward and reached for a pad of paper. "I was, in fact, able to track him down. He is being held in a Federal facility near Albany, New York. According to the authorities the men in that facility are still being processed - whatever that means."

"Has he been charged with anything?"

"Not yet. We do know from our contacts in the area, that some men have been released within the last couple of days. They were American citizens wrongfully detained. We also know that conditions are bad. The facility they are in was designed for twenty prisoners; we believe there are over sixty men being kept there."

"Does he have a lawyer? Can he receive visitors?"

"No visitors, yet. As for legal representation, there are civil liberties groups working on all the detentions, nationwide. It is hard to know what is going on with specific cases."

"So what can we do?"

"First is to find out if he is a citizen and if he is, to get his naturalization number to me so that I can forward it to the people in Albany. This would be the best case and the quickest way to get him out."

"And if he is not a citizen?"

"Then we have to wait for charges to be filed and take it from there."

"That's it?"

"Itzik, your Uncle Reuven is one of several thousand. The dust hasn't cleared yet and we really don't know which way this whole business is going. It's frustrating, and frightening."

There was a clock on the wall behind him; it was after six. "You leaving anytime soon?"

"I still have a couple of hours of work to do."

"I need to go. My mother is waiting on the edge of her chair for news. Thanks for everything, Reuven. I'll see what I can find out about his citizenship. Write down your telephone number for me and I'll call as soon as I hear anything."

"Mary could call me. It would be quicker. If I'm not here for some reason, Wendy will take a message."

The Western Union office at the North Station was still open, so I sent a telegram to Mary with the necessary information, questions, and instructions to call Reuven. It cost me almost all the money I had on me. It was after eight o'clock when I got home. Mama was sitting at the table, drinking tea and worrying. "What did Reuven tell you? Did he find out anything?"

I hugged her then told her what he had told me, and also about the telegram I had sent to Mary. She listened while she warmed a bowl of beef stew for me. "So. Mama, the big question is whether Uncle Kalner is a citizen or not."

"I don't know," she replied. "He never said anything to me about it."

***

People don't send telegrams anymore. They have their cell phones and email for instant communication. In the past, the telegram was the way people conveyed urgent news. You never wanted to receive a telegram unexpectedly - they were always bad news, especially during war-time. I know, but I don't want to think about it now. Later, maybe.

Danielle is here. I remember I wanted to create the word "laugh," so I signal that I am awake.

"Hi Isaac. You've been sleeping for some time. I was about to leave, but I'm glad you've noticed me here."

Smile.

"I'm smiling, too. It is a beautiful day - nice and warm. I spent the day on the beach, enjoying the early summer. The water is still cold, but the day was beautiful. Not many people out, so there were lots of shore birds and a few ducks. Lovely. So, now it is evening - Sunday, June second."

Thank you. New word.

"You have a new word to build?

Yes.

We create the signal for "Laugh," and she adds it to the chart. Short, long, short, long.

Danielle chuckles. "Trust you to want that word! I love it." She laughs again. "I suppose you want me to tell you a funny story now."

Yes.

"OK. Let me think a minute." There is a long silence. Finally, she says, "Did I ever tell you the story about when my father took me to the Catholic church when I was a little girl?"

No. I couldn't imagine why Reuven would ever do such a thing. He was a confirmed non-believer and the idea of him bringing his daughter to church seemed impossible.

"I was about seven years old and I had a friend named Sally who was a Catholic. One day my dad overheard Sally and me playing with our dolls and making up a story about our dolls going to church together. Since I had never been in a church, I had no idea what Sally was talking about when she used words like pews, pulpit, incense, altar, communion, and so on. He could tell I was thoroughly confused, so after Sally left, he asked me if I wanted him to bring me to Sally's church to see what it looks like. Of course, I said yes."

She touches my hand and continues, "Can you imagine my dad dressing up on a Sunday morning to go to the Catholic church? My mother thought he had lost his mind. I overheard him whispering to her, 'I have no idea what I'm doing. I've never been to a service inside one of those places. Do I need a yarmulke, a tallis?'"

Laugh. I could hear Reuven saying that.

"My mother laughed, shook her head, and sent us on our way. The Catholic church was only about four blocks from our house so we walked, hand in hand. I had told Sally we were coming to church that day, and she and her family were waiting for us at the foot of the steps that led up to the enormous gray building. We went in together. It was beautiful, with high ceilings, stained glass windows and a gentle, sweet smell. I was immediately captivated by the atmosphere of the place. My father and I sat in the pew behind Sally's large family. I remember being transported by the grandeur of the space and being completely unaware of my father. But, when the organ started playing he let out a soft, but very audible, 'Oy!' People three rows ahead of us turned around and stared, and he started to giggle. 'Danni, my girl,' he said, straining to suppress his giggles, 'I have something in my throat. I need to get some water.' And he ran from the sanctuary."

Laugh. Reuven, you old heretic!

"When he finally returned, the service was well under way and it went from boring to alarming. I was afraid to speak at all, so I saved my big, scary observation until we were out of the church and on our way home. I looked around to be sure no one was near, then blurted out, 'I think they are cannibals.' My father, without skipping a beat, replied, 'No Danni, they're not cannibals; they're just not too sophisticated. How could they possibly have wine and crackers without the cheese?'"

Laugh. Brie or cheddar?

"After we arrived home, he did follow up with an explanation of what the wine and crackers symbolized to Catholics, and he assured me they were not actually drinking the blood and eating the flesh of someone who died two thousand years ago."

Smile. Thank you.

"He was a good guy, my dad. I miss him."

Yes. I miss him too. I wonder if he told her about the bombed out churches we went to.

***

On the following Tuesday a telegram came from Reuven saying that Uncle Kalner had been released. Two days later, a letter from Reuven gave more details; fortunately, Kalner was a citizen - barely. His naturalization date was only three months prior to his detention. Once he was able to prove his citizenship, he had either to be charged immediately or released. Since they had nothing concrete to charge him with, he was let go.

On the Friday, a letter came from Uncle Kalner describing his whole ordeal, from the time the federal agents broke into the union hall and detained everyone in the building, through the terrible crowded and unsanitary conditions of their confinement, to the interrogations which included threats against his family, and then, finally, his release. He said that his fire for the work he did was intensified by this experience and he "would never be intimidated by a gang of government thugs!" He also wrote that he and Mary were coming for a quick visit on Saturday and Sunday.

"We need to give something to Reuven," my mother said. "Without him who knows what would have happened to Kalner."

"I'll see Reuven tomorrow. I'm going to Boston after work."

"Come home before you leave. I'll have something for you to bring to him."

I convinced Virginia to come with me to see Reuven. I had been to his apartment before going to her house, but he was not there and the place was in even worse condition than it had been the week before, so I assumed he was at work. My mother had given me a small package and a sealed envelope to give to Reuven. I had no idea what was in either.

We entered the office to find no one at the reception desk. "I know where his desk is," I said, and we went down the hallway. The door to Reuven's office was closed but we could hear he was in intense discussion with someone. "We'd better go back and wait."

After about ten minutes, Wendy arrived carrying boxes of food. "Lunch for the boys," she said. "You're here for Mr. Novitz?"

I nodded.

"I'll let him know." As she walked down the hall, Reuven and another man, dressed in faded work clothes and heavy boots, came towards us. Reuven walked with him to the door, shook his hand and said, "Come back on Wednesday. I think we'll know a lot more by then." The man thanked him and left.

"I came by to thank you, Reuven. My mother asked me to bring these to you." I hugged him. "Kalner and Mary are visiting this weekend."

"I had a very warm letter from him. I'd love to see him sometime."

"Can you get away tomorrow?"

"Not a chance."

I put my hand in his shoulder. "I guess we should go. Thank you, Reuven."

"Do you have a few minutes for a cup of coffee?" Virginia asked.

He looked at his watch. "Nope. I have someone coming to see me in fifteen minutes and I'm not prepared. Thanks. I have to get back."

Virginia and I spent the afternoon wandering through the Boston Common. The pathways had been cleared of snow and the sun was shining brightly reflecting off the whiteness. Without really thinking, I said, "Well, since Reuven can't make it tomorrow, why don't you come and meet my uncle and Mary?"

"I'd love to meet them, and I'd love to see your mother again," she replied. "I'll have to ask my parents."

"Of course."

We started walking toward her house and the enormity of what I had just asked hit me. And then I thought that her parents would never let her go. But I was wrong. We made arrangements for her to take specific trains to and from Lawrence and to ensure that she would be accompanied to and from the station at either end of her short journey. I could not imagine how my mother would react to the news of our sudden guest.

I arrived home to find Mama, Mary and Uncle Kalner sitting at the table drinking vodka and talking. I hugged each of them and sat down. Uncle Kalner offered me a glass, but I declined. "Time has run out - it is no longer legal to buy this stuff. So, have a drink, Itzik!"

"I have never enjoyed vodka, Uncle, so now would really be a foolish time to start."

"True. This country is crazy. Pious and paranoid at the same time."

"So, how are you, Uncle?"

"I'm fine. They treated me no worse than they treated everyone else. It was not fun. I told your mother the whole story; she can tell you all about it. There are still a lot of people in danger of being deported. Your friend, Reuven, and his associates are doing important work. Shake his hand for me next time you see him. No - give him a big hug!"

"I will. I tried to convince him to come for a visit tomorrow, but he's too busy. He's been working non-stop for two weeks."

"I knew he was a good one the moment I met him at Ellis Island." Uncle Kalner poured himself another glass of vodka.

"But," I said, and I waited to make eye contact with my mother, "We *are* having a visitor tomorrow. Virginia is coming."

"Coming here?" My mother said. "Tomorrow! How can we make this place ready for her in a few hours? Are you nuts, Itzik!"

Everyone stopped talking and the room grew quiet. They were all looking at me as if I had horns growing out of my head. "It will be fine. She is anxious to see you again, Mama, and also wants to meet Mary and Uncle."

"But look at this place. Compare it to where she comes from."

"Mama, she knows we are not like them; it is a topic that comes up over and over again in our conversations. She doesn't care; if it was important to her she wouldn't be inviting me to her home every week, she wouldn't be in love with me. It will be fine, Mama. Don't worry!"

She drained her glass and leaned back in her chair. "We need to get some sleep," she said, "We have a mountain of work to do in the morning. What time is she arriving?"

"I am meeting her at the station at one-thirty."

She stood, leaned across the table and ruffled my hair. "I'm looking forward to seeing her again. She's a good girl."

It was an uncomfortable night with four adults trying to sleep in our small apartment. I got up early and walked to the bakery about two blocks away to buy fresh bread for breakfast. The sky was changing colors by the minute - from deep blue to deep oranges and reds which faded and gave way to palest blue. I lingered, watching the spectacular sunrise, then I looked around me at my neighborhood - the drab rows of identical buildings, the uneven street, the smoke hanging low over the houses. When I looked closer I saw all the broken windows, the cracked steps, the missing shingles, the piles of refuse covered with dirty snow. This was so far from Virginia's world.

Mama and I were in a better situation than many of our neighbors. We both worked, and I was making a decent wage, and we only had ourselves to worry about. Most families on our block struggled to maintain full-time jobs for both spouses, and there were children in almost every home who needed food, clothing and attention.

When I arrived home the others were up and dressed and were sipping tea at the table. I joined them and sliced the bread. Mama found a jar of peach jam. We ate our breakfast in silence. No one had slept well. Finally, Mama announced she had come up with a plan of action to prepare for Virginia's visit. Everything that did not need to be in the front room was to be moved into her bedroom, then we were to sweep and dust and clean the front room from top to bottom. Also, the bathroom needed to be thoroughly cleaned and organized.

"You didn't plan on this when you came to visit," I said to Uncle Kalner, as we carried baskets of miscellaneous items into the bedroom and set them against the far wall.

He smiled. "I told you long ago I would do anything for you. I am anxious to meet this young woman you hold in your heart."

By the time I left for the station the apartment was shining - at least as much as the well-used old furniture and fittings would allow. It was a bright day and despite the cold, dozens of children were playing in the street. I became aware, even though I had seen them so many times before, of the raggedness of their clothes, the inadequacy of their footwear, the lack of gloves, coats or hats. A few years ago I was one of them.

Virginia stepped down from the train carrying a bouquet of flowers and a box of chocolates. She had come straight from church and was wearing a calf-length dark blue dress under a full length pale blue coat. As usual, she wore little jewelry - a simple beaded necklace with matching ear-rings. "You look amazing," I said, as we embraced.

She smiled and asked me to carry the chocolates. "They're for your mother, but I'm sure she'll let you have some."

"Shall we take a cab?" I asked.

"How far is it?"

"Less than a mile."

"Let's walk. I feel like I've been sitting for hours."

She took my hand and we exited the station and walked across the Duck Bridge. From the bridge one could see the mosaic of mills and factories on both sides of the river. The wind was bitter, and we wrapped our arms around each other as we walked. By the time we turned onto our street, Virginia had seen the industrial core of the city, as well as the teeming neighborhoods that provided the workers for that core.

The street was loud, with dozens of children running around, playing, shouting, squabbling. Two little girls came charging in our direction, trying to escape a boy who was chasing them. One of the girls ran into me and almost knocked me over. "Sorry, sir!" she shouted, and ran on.

"Is it always like this, Isaac?"

"Only when the weather permits." We walked a little further. "It's the next building." I looked up and saw my mother briefly at the window.

"Is your mother panicked?"

"You could say that."

We climbed the narrow stairs to the apartment. My mother was waiting on the landing. "Thank you for coming to see us, Virginia." She opened her arms wide.

Virginia handed me the flowers and they hugged.

I introduced Virginia to Uncle Kalner and Mary while my mother arranged the flowers in a vase and put it in the center of the table. "Thank you, dear, they are beautiful."

"Virginia brought you chocolates, too, Mama."

"Lovely. Sit, all of you. Eat chocolates while I get the tea going."

I took Virginia's coat and set it on the sofa, then we sat at the well-scrubbed table, staring at the flowers not knowing what to say. Finally Virginia broke the silence; "You know, Isaac, you have not said a word to me about the oil paints. Have you been using them?"

"I have experimented a bit, but I find it so different and difficult I'm afraid that anything I do now is just wasting them. I found an instruction book in the library a couple of days ago, but haven't had the time to read it yet. Next week I hope to jump right in."

"I'm dying to see the results." She turned to my mother. "Mrs. Simon, did Isaac show you the pair of pictures he did for me?" I noticed that she did not say, "For Christmas," and smiled to myself.

"Of course he did. I liked them, but I'm not sure why."

"I did a portrait of you, Uncle. Let me show it to you."

"I put all your sketchbooks away, Itzik. You'll have to show it some other time. Let's have our tea."

We hadn't had this many people in our apartment since the strike ended. I don't think anyone sitting around the table at that time noticed the tea cups did not match each other or the saucers and cake plates. The different patterns jumped out at me now as Mama poured and distributed the tea, then sliced the cream cheese cake she had baked.

"Virginia, Isaac tells us you will be taking some college courses soon," my mother said.

"Yes. Mrs. Simon. In fact I started this week with three classes; English literature, American history and something they call domestic science, which is cooking and sewing and so on - skills I really do need to learn. I'm enjoying it. In the fall, I'll start full-time working towards my teaching certificate."

"That's wonderful," said Uncle Kalner, "We can never have too many teachers."

"I think, Kalner, if you were to have chosen a different profession it would have been teaching," Mary said. "You are never without a book, and you love to talk about what you read."

"Very true," I said, "Uncle Kalner taught me things from the day I was born. He would make a great teacher."

"Well, I have other work to do," he responded. I sensed a wistful note in his voice.

The conversation continued easily. Virginia was relaxed, delightful. My nervousness about this visit finally faded and I, too, began to relax. Kalner talked a little about his detention and the mass arrests that were happening across the country, but my mother did not allow things to get too heated. Mostly we talked about everyday things - family, friends, and our plans for the future.

And then it was time for Virginia to leave. "We'd love you to come for another visit, Mrs. Simon," she said as she stood in the doorway, "and sooner rather than later."

"Thank you, I'd like that. I'll write to your mother."

Walking back to the station Virginia seemed to be absorbing everything around her. She kept turning to look at people and buildings, the chimneys billowing smoke, the murky river turned orange from the dyes used in the mills. "This is another world to me, Isaac," she said while we waited for her train. "It gives me so much to think about."

I was not sure what she meant by that, but was afraid to ask.

The train arrived. We kissed. "See you Saturday at two," she said.

***

Wanda is singing softly as she checks my tubes. It is a hymn I do not recognize - not that I have an encyclopedic knowledge of hymns - but I have heard many in my lifetime, and Wanda sings them often. I can't quite catch all of the words, but the refrain is, "Surrender to the love, the love of the Lord," or something like that. It's a lovely, gentle tune. I listen until the song is over, then I let her know I am awake.

"Good morning, Isaac. It's good to see you." She adjusts the pillow. "Everything all right this morning?"

Yes.

"Your neurologist, Doctor Jerzak, is coming to see you today. He is fascinated by you."

Laugh. He doesn't know the half of it. He can attach his wires to my head and watch the signals go up and down, but wouldn't it be something if I he could actually read my stories as those brain impulses create them.

"He should be here in about an hour."

Her singing and her voice are replaced by my cat-machine and its eternal purring and occasional puff-puffs. A poor substitute! Maybe I should try moving my eyeballs around before Doctor Squeak get here. That would make his day. I go through the motions, if one could call them that. Up, down, left, right. I try it six or seven times then give up.

I focus on my breathing and realize that it is very shallow and quite fast. I try to inhale deeply. No real change. I try to force the air out. Nope - pretty much unchanged. I try this several times but have no success. I guess the reason I make no sound, except the occasional snore, is that my lungs are so weak I can't draw enough air into them to get any vocal cord vibrations going.

I hear Doctor Squeak approach my bed. He is not alone. In fact, I hear the sounds of several people. I have a sense that he will start doing whatever he plans to do whether I tell him I am awake or not. The group quiets. There is an expectant pause. Doctor Squeak clears his throat but says nothing. I realize they are waiting for me to initiate the dialog. I kind of like the suspense.

Finally, I blink that I am awake.

"Mr. Simon. Good morning. It is eleven-fifteen on Monday, June third, 2002."

Thank you.

"I am here with five medical residents who have expressed an interest in meeting you. Is that all right with you?"

Yes.

I hear them titter. One of them says, "Look at the chart above the bed."

Do I dare to have fun with them? Why not? I signal "hug."

"Did you say 'hug?'" a female student says.

Yes. Hug.

There is a shuffling of feet, then I feel someone gently touch my upper arms and place her head on my chest for a moment. "Thank you," she says.

Thank you.

"I see you have a few new words since I was here last week," the doctor says. "It looks like you have asked people to read the newspaper."

Yes.

"The chart also has a note to start with the sports news because world news upsets you. Is that true?"

Yes.

"I don't blame you. Things are pretty tumultuous out there."

One of the students asks, "Doctor, Jerzak, if his mind is so active, do we have any idea what he is experiencing inside his head when no one is interacting with him?"

"Doctor Scott, let me first remind you that Mr. Simon is aware of everything that is said in his presence, so do not talk about him as if he is not here."

"Sorry."

"Second, that's a good question and I hope that someday we will know."

How about I tell you. I indicate new word.

"You want to create a new word, Isaac?" Doctor Squeak sounds excited.

Yes. Then I blink the pattern I have come up with. Five letters.

He proceeds to slowly recite the alphabet. It is a tedious process, but we finally create the word.

"Is the word 'story?'"

Yes.

Doctor Squeak sounds confused. "Do you want me to read you a story?"

No.

"Tell you a story?"

No.

"I think it's the answer to Doctor Scott's question," one of the students says.

Yes.

"You tell yourself stories?"

Yes. Smile.

The excitement in the room is contagious. I can almost feel their smiles. "Can I give you another hug?"

Yes.

I receive hugs from two different people. Then Doctor Squeak says. "Have you been doing your eye exercises, Mr. Simon.?"

No. Well, I have made a half-hearted effort, but not really. To be honest, 'no' is the closest answer, given my limited vocabulary.

"Let's give it a try, anyway," he says, and he leans in so close to me that I can feel his breath on my face. I don't like it. "Please look up. Down. Up again. Down again."

I really do try to do what he asks, but don't feel like I am actually doing anything. I'm also getting tired.

Finally he straightens up and says, "Not much going there, I'm afraid."

C'est la guerre. I'm not sure why that expression popped into my head. My son Albert used to say it; he picked it up in France when he was there.

Chapter 39

In early June 1920, Mr. Wilkins called me into his office and told me I should move to Boston and start taking classes at the Boston Architectural Club, of which he was a member. He said he hated to lose me, but he encouraged the move to further my career. He gave me the names of two architects in Boston who he knew were looking to hire good draftsmen.

I was stunned. I had been thinking of moving to Boston for some time. Reuven and I often talked about sharing an apartment, but I was worried about finding a job, and here my own boss was urging me to go and recommending me to his colleagues. "I don't know how to thank you, sir. I have learned so much being here. And now this."

"You're a talented and bright young man, Isaac. You need to be in an environment where you can learn more and do more."

A month later I started working at the architectural firm of William A. Carpenter, who also sponsored my enrollment in courses at the Architectural Club. Mr. Carpenter was fairly young, but he had already made a name for himself as an audacious modernist. His office shelves were crammed with books by and about the innovative architects, artists and designers of the day - Gropius, Le Corbusier, Wright, Behrens, and many others. The walls of his office were hung with abstract and expressionist paintings. I was glad that I had slipped some of my own abstract works into the portfolio I had brought to the interview.

I moved in with Reuven, but after a few weeks we realized that the apartment was too small. I wanted my own room and also a space where I could paint. I was earning enough for me to pay two-thirds of the rent for a larger apartment and still have some money available to help Mama with her rent. We found a bright, three-bedroom place on the top floor of a three story building a little closer to the downtown, and we moved in on the first Saturday of September.

The owners were Italian immigrants who lived on the second floor and ran a bakery on the street level. On our first afternoon in the new apartment, Mrs. DiNapoli came to the door with a basket of fresh-baked bread rolls and pastries. She spoke little English, but certainly enough to make us feel very welcome.

"We're going to get fat in this place, Itzik my friend," Reuven said as he took a bite of a pastry which Mrs. D. called Sfogliatelle, and which took us several painful and comic attempts to learn to pronounce.

"I could use a little meat on these bones," I said.

Virginia and I had arranged to go to dinner and the movies that night. We had been seeing each other almost every weekend for over a year. Her parents now accepted me as a regular visitor and since I was becoming a professional, they appeared less concerned about my presence at social occasions. They even invited me to join them at their church's annual July Fourth picnic held at Franklin Park where I spent some time talking with the Reverend Frothingham about his efforts to put an end to child labor.

Even though Virginia and I had decided within the first two months of our courtship that we were engaged, we had still not told anyone. At the same time, all of our friends and family assumed we were committed to each another and treated us that way.

When I arrived at the Appleton home at around five o'clock that evening, Virginia met me at the door and pulled me aside. "Sorry, we can't go out tonight. My Uncle Peter and his family are here from New Jersey and they insist on meeting you and taking us all to dinner at Locke Ober."

"I will finally get to eat in that place. I'll be on my best behavior."

She laughed. "Uncle Peter has more money than he knows what to do with, and he loves to show it off." She sighed and took my arm. "Well, let me introduce you to everyone."

Peter Appleton and his wife, Alice, were sitting on the couch. Their two daughters were playing the piano rather loudly and erratically in the music room, but came out briefly to shake my hand. Virginia joined her aunt and uncle on the couch and I took the chair near her mother.

"How is the move progressing?" Virginia asked, then followed up, "Isaac and his friend have taken a new apartment and were moving all their belongings today."

"Well, everything is inside, although it still requires a great deal of organization. Boxes everywhere. Our landlady is friendly - she brought up a basket of fresh pastries. They have a bakery on the first floor."

"That's convenient."

"I hope I don't over-indulge."

"My brother tells me you are planning to be an architect." There was something a little unnerving about Peter Appleton's manner; a sense of rigidity, superiority. He was quite a bit younger than Virginia's father and lacked his openness to new and different things.

"I am. I have a position with a firm in Boston and I'm attending classes at the Architectural Club."

"You served in the war?"

"I did. In an engineering company."

"I was a captain in the Service of Supply in Hoboken."

What was I to say? I looked around helplessly, but everyone seemed to be waiting for my response. "I heard that huge amounts of equipment and men shipped out of there," I said, trying to be as non-committal as possible.

"Yes. We received several commendations."

I was able to make eye contact with Virginia. "Aunt Alice," she said, "how are Betty and Diana faring in school?"

Thank you!

"Very well, thank you dear, although Diana's teacher is a bit too free and easy in my opinion."

"There are new ideas about what constitutes a good education. I don't know whether my parents told you that I am studying to be a teacher."

"Does Massachusetts allow married teachers?" Uncle Peter asked.

"Many schools do; but anyway, I'm not married yet."

"How old are your daughters?" I asked, trying to keep the conversation away from the war.

"Diana is almost thirteen, and Betty had her tenth birthday last month." At that moment the two girls started yelling at each other in the adjoining room. Mrs. Alice Appleton excused herself and hurried to calm them down.

There was an awkward silence, which Mr. Peter Appleton seized to ask, "Did you see much combat, Mr. Simon?"

Virginia's father stepped in, "Isaac had more than his fair share, Peter. He was seriously wounded and spent several months in an army hospital in France."

"That's actually how Isaac and I met," Virginia added, then continued with the story of the care package, the drawings, our correspondence and my return home.

"They are at such a difficult age," Virginia's mother said as her sister-in-law returned to the couch.

"They most certainly are. I told them they would miss dinner if they continued to squabble. Which reminds me, what time is our reservation, Peter?"

He glanced at the banjo clock on the wall, then made a show of looking at his impressive gold pocket watch. "Seven-thirty," he announced, "We should leave in half an hour. We can take my car."

"It's such a lovely evening," Virginia said, "I'd like to walk with Isaac. The girls can join us."

"Splendid idea," Virginia's mother said, "The girls need to work off some excess energy before dinner."

"Thank you for this. It is a beautiful evening," Virginia said as we walked through the Gardens. The girls were running ahead, chasing each other, dodging behind tree trunks, circling the flower beds and park benches. Their mother had specifically told them to stay on the path and to avoid getting dirt on their dresses.

"Do we need to rein them in?" I asked.

"Let them be. Their mother is so strict, I don't blame them for going a little wild." She paused, then called to the girls and they ran to us. "I don't mind you two running around like a pair of mares. All I ask is that you don't fall down and get your dresses dirty. Neither you nor I want to have to explain things to your mother."

They nodded enthusiastically and ran off. "They are really quite sweet," I said.

"They are." She took my hand. "I'm so sorry you walked into this. Uncle Peter telegrammed yesterday inviting themselves for the weekend. My mother was rather put out. I rarely hear her raise her voice - except at political rallies, of course - but she went on a bit of a tirade last night. The girls are easy compared to Peter and Alice."

We were approaching the end of the park and found the girls waiting on a bench. "Tired yourselves out, did you?" Virginia said.

Diana was panting. "Just need to catch our breath. We'll be fine."

Virginia looked up at the clock on a nearby church steeple. "We need to hurry - it's almost seven-thirty and you know how your parents hate to be late."

We arrived at the restaurant minutes before the others. It was even more sumptuous than I had expected, with crystal chandeliers, carved mahogany paneling, French and Italian paintings, sculpture and furniture. I think I actually gulped audibly as we entered the dining area; I felt Virginia squeeze my elbow. Virginia's mother took control of the seating arrangements at our table and placed me next to her and as far as possible from her brother-in-law. I whispered a thank you, and she patted my hand, protectively.

The menu was astonishing, both for its variety and the prices. I waited for Virginia to order, then ordered almost exactly the same things. Her uncle and aunt appeared to choose the most expensive item in each course. "It is so strange not to be able to order a bottle of French wine anymore," Mr. Peter Appleton proclaimed. "These Prohibitionists are driving this country to ruin!"

I agreed with him, but said nothing. Virginia's father took up the discussion. The rest of the meal went by slowly but without incident or too much stress. The food was good, but over-priced. The girls were well behaved - I think they had been bribed with the spectacular desserts before we sat down. After dinner, the Appleton brothers ordered cigars and offered me one. I declined. I leaned across to Virginia and asked if it would be too rude to excuse ourselves.

She folded her napkin and placed it front of her. "Isaac and I are going to take a leisurely walk home. Thank you so much for dinner, Uncle Peter. It was delicious." She rose.

I stood and thanked them for the dinner and we left. "Well, we survived that without any scarring," Virginia said, as we stepped out of the restaurant. "I think my mother was ready to run out with us."

"Yes, I noticed a pleading look in her face as we started toward the door."

"Fortunately, we only see them a few times a year, but they do have this habit of coming with almost no warning. It's not right, and poor Bea is really upset because she had to postpone her plans this evening in order to set up beds and rooms and for them."

"Times are changing, Virginia. People are going to have to learn to make their own beds."

"I know. I have actually started doing that for myself. I like it."

***

Danielle is here. She is such a dear, kind person; she is so much like her mother. I let her know I am awake.

"Hi there, old friend," she hugs me gently. "I believe you had a whole flock of visitors earlier today."

Yes. Like.

"Good. I see you have new words, too. You're up to eighteen. Do you have any more in mind for now?"

No.

"So, I asked the nurses whether you could have a CD player. I thought you might like to listen to music and even books or old radio shows that are now available on disc. What do you think?"

What do I think? It would be nice, really nice to be able to hear some music and those old shows Virginia and I used to tune in to before TV came along. But, how do I let people know what I want to listen to, or when I want them to turn the thing off? I'm really not sure how to answer. *Maybe.*

"Well, let's give it a try. I brought the CD player from your apartment and a few discs. Blink once for Louis Armstrong and Ella Fitzgerald, twice for the Beatles, or three times for Harry Belafonte."

Oh, my music. How could I have forgotten about all those albums? I wanted to hear all three, but especially Louis and Ella. I blink once.

The music starts. *Thank you.*

Virginia had bought the album when it first came out in the fifties and we played it often, danced to it often. I can almost feel myself holding her, moving gently together, growing old together. It has been so long since she died, but those memories are right in front of me as clear as can be.

The album comes to an end. I feel Danielle wipe my eyes and cheeks. I must have been crying. "I can just see you and Virginia swaying to 'Nearness of you.' I think that was one of your favorites."

Yes.

"Would you like another? I also brought Simon and Garfunkel and

Peter, Paul and Mary, and a few others."

No. I feel kind of worn out.

I have said that thinking of Danielle makes me think of her father, Reuven. But she also reminds me so much of her mother, Yvette, who lived through hell the first part of her life. As I recounted earlier, during the war Reuven and I were billeted at one time with the Chaisson family in France. Yvette was the only daughter and her first husband and child both died during the war. She had remarried and moved with her new husband to Brest where he worked on the docks loading American troops and equipment onto ships for their journey home.

About a year after we came home, Reuven sent a letter to Monsieur Chaisson asking how things were going now that his sons were there to help on their farm. They exchanged short letters every few months for several years. In November 1923, Reuven received a letter from Yvette; she was back living with her father after her second marriage had fallen apart because of her husband's drinking and womanizing. She was distraught. As he tells it, Reuven replied something like, "If we were not separated by an ocean, I would be beside you to comfort you, as I did five years ago."

The response from Yvette was a simple request to be with him in America. Three months later he met her at the port of Boston, brought her back to his apartment and they were married within a few weeks - March eleventh, 1924. Somehow, I had sensed the love between them in the midst of the war. That love lasted until the end.

Danielle was born three years later, the same year as my Emma. They were best friends for years even though we only saw them occasionally; Reuven's work brought him and Yvette to Detroit not long after they were married. I can still see Emma and Danielle as little girls in grubby overalls, playing with dolls and trucks to the horror of the senior Appletons who happened to be visiting us at the same time as Reuven and family.

Chapter 40

Virginia and I were married on the afternoon of September twenty-fourth, 1922 by the Reverend Paul Revere Frothingham in the Appleton home. That was the compromise - Unitarian minister, but not in the church. It was a small affair, about thirty family members and close friends, because neither Virginia nor I wanted to have anything extravagant. We saw no reason to spend a huge sum of money for just that one day. And besides, we had around us all the people we wanted.

Virginia had insisted on inviting Bea and her husband. Bea thanked us, but replied that she felt their presence would be awkward for all. "Honestly, Virginia, I don't see too many Black people at your parties, except the servants."

"But, Bea, you've been with us for years, since before I was born. You're ..."

Bea cut her off, "But I'm not one of the family, Virginia. That's just the way it is."

And we left it at that. Bea took the day off.

My mother, Uncle Kalner, Mary, Uncle Ben and his wife all arrived together in a car that Mr. Appleton had arranged to pick them up at the station. They were in their best clothes, but appeared out of place between the crystal and porcelain, the paintings and carpets, and the fine jewelry and Paris-inspired couture of the women of the Appleton family. I noticed them huddled together in the parlor, looking at the paintings. Since she had been in this house a couple of times, my mother was acting as guide and diplomat.

I could not leave my post at the door with Virginia and was relieved to see Mrs. Appleton go over to them, hug my mother warmly and begin to engage them all in conversation. Reuven joined the group and introduced his companion for the afternoon, Irma, who was a legal assistant he had met while attending a conference on civil rights and labor law in New York a few weeks earlier. The romance did not last.

Uncle Peter, Aunt Alice and their two girls arrived as the ceremony was about to begin. "You look absolutely beautiful, Virginia my dear," Alice whispered loudly as the Reverend was taking his position. "The perfect bride."

Virginia smiled, thanked her, and turned her attention to the Reverend and me.

The ceremony was brief. The Reverend had allowed us to have some say in the content, so there was no "honor and obey," and not a whole lot of God and Jesus - enough to satisfy the Unitarians, although it did astonish the Presbyterians in the room (Uncle Peter and family). The Jewish folks had been forewarned, and did not seem to care one way or another. I noticed Uncle Kalner approach the Reverend immediately after the ceremony. My uncle told me later he had congratulated the Reverend on his skill at walking a tight-rope.

Mr. Appleton brought out half a dozen bottles of French champagne he had been saving for this occasion. He offered a warm toast in welcoming his guests, then asked Reuven to toast the bride and groom. Close to three years of Prohibition had lowered people's tolerance for alcohol and we were all quite light-headed for most of the party. I remember little of Reuven's remarks except his comment that he'd known me since I was in short pants, and also that the moment he heard me talk of Virginia while we were still in France, he knew she and I would someday be married.

The Reverend did not stay much past the first glass of champagne, but before he left he pulled me into the far corner of the music room, away from most of the hubbub, and asked me to sit and talk with him for a few minutes. "I know you to be a thoughtful young man, Isaac," he said. "You are not a person to make important decisions without a great deal of consideration. I also know you are devoted to Virginia as much as she is to you. It is for these reasons, and out of my high regard for the Appleton family, that I was willing to perform this ceremony here, and not in my church. I wish you every happiness in your future, Isaac, and I want you to know that you are welcome in our church at any time. I know, too, that you would never stand in the way of Virginia's involvement in the church."

"Sir," I replied, "I appreciate your thoughts and good wishes on our marriage. I am truly happy you agreed to officiate. As to your concerns; I would never obstruct Virginia's path to happiness and fulfillment."

"You are both young. You have a long road ahead and I pray you can hold to what you have said."

"I'm sure we can and we will."

He stood and I followed. "Best of luck, Isaac. I hope I will see you and Virginia often." We shook hands. "By the way, Isaac, I finally had the opportunity to meet your mother today. She is a fascinating person. I see where you get your intelligence." And with that, he left.

Virginia and I were both so very young, twenty-two, but we were in love and ready to spread our wings. I was near the end of my formal architectural studies and Mr. Carpenter offered to keep me on as a junior architect. Virginia received her teaching certificate and found a position at an elementary school in Cambridge. She actually started working there a few weeks before the wedding.

As a wedding gift (and, I believe, in gratitude for her not wanting an expensive, elaborate wedding), Virginia's parents bought us a small house about a mile north of Harvard Square and not too far from Virginia's school. We had two bedrooms and a bathroom upstairs, and the living room, dining room, and kitchen on the first floor. There was a sunny patio off the living room in the back, and the lot was big enough for us to add a couple of rooms as they were needed.

For me, it was an unimaginable gift. The idea that I was a homeowner was outside my experience, and that we owned the house outright, with no mortgage, was incomprehensible. When Mr. and Mrs. Appleton told us about a month before the wedding that this was the gift they wished to give us, I was completely at a loss for words. How could I possibly thank them!

We moved in to our new home the weekend after our wedding. We would live together in that house for fifty-seven years and I lived there alone for fifteen more, until I was ninety-four. I hated selling that home.

A different gift also had a profound influence on our lives. My boss and our friend, William Carpenter, had traveled to Munich in the spring of 1922 to study at the Bauhaus under Walter Gropius. One of the instructors at the school was Wassily Kandinsky, who is often credited as being the first abstract artist. William was completely taken by his paintings and brought home several of them, as well as works by another instructor at the Bauhaus, Paul Klee. He hung a few of these in the office.

William arrived at the wedding alone carrying what was obviously a fairly large painting wrapped in colorful paper. He handed it to Virginia and me as we stood at the entry to the parlor greeting our guests, but before he could say anything he was distracted by the Metzinger hanging on the wall behind us. "Marvelous! Absolutely marvelous!" he exclaimed, then refocused his attention on us, "I know you will enjoy this. It's going to the right home."

When we opened William's gift after all the guests had left, Virginia and I were astonished to find a Kandinsky oil. It was vibrant, alive in the sense that it never seemed to be still. The way it was composed, the colors, lines and shapes, forced one's eyes to keep scanning the surface. I spent countless hours studying that painting, and the others in the office and, later, in William's home. Not that I tried to emulate them; it was more an attempt to understand how the artist made the colors and shapes interact in the ways that I saw them.

***

I hear Damon the Good at my bedside. It's been a while since he was last here. I am awake.

"I didn't mean to wake you, Isaac. How are you doing? Everything OK?"

Yes.

"It's quiet up here; early, early morning before sunrise on June fourth." He checks my pulse and blood pressure, fiddles with my plumbing and scribbles some notes. "Another long weekend. It's hard to sit around my apartment with nothing to do, no one to talk with. I listen to a lot of music, drink too much coffee which results in me not being able to sleep, so I watch dumb TV at six in the morning. I'm beginning to think that working this overnight shift is dragging me down; it really prevents me from seeing the few friends I have 'cause I'm sleeping when they're not working. I'm becoming a hermit." He sighs and I hear him fall into the chair.

I wonder how old he is. He said he had been a medic in Operation Desert Storm; that was ten or eleven years ago, which puts him at least in his early thirties. Too old for Ginnie? Although I have detected a little something between them. They both could benefit from having a new friend.

"Enough of my problems. I see you've got a few more words going. Doctor Jerzak noted that you tell yourself stories; that is amazing. I'd love to climb in there and listen."

Laugh. Yes, I suppose in some ways one's life story is wasted on oneself. It would be much more interesting to have an audience and to hear and see their response. Come on in and grab yourself a beer! Get me one, too.

***

Virginia's teaching career got off to a fiery start. When the principal of her school found out she had gotten married barely three weeks after the beginning of the school year, he called her into his office and threatened to fire her. Fortunately, the teachers in that school had recently joined the American Federation of Teachers, and the union shop steward, who was herself about to get married after six years as a teacher, told the principal he would face a strike if he followed through on his threat. He backed down.

However, at the end of the school year, in June 1923, when Virginia's pregnancy was noticeable even to the most unobservant, her contract was not renewed and the specific reason given was her pregnancy. Married teachers in the classroom was one thing - but pregnant ones were deemed completely unacceptable and a threat to the proper and moral education of the children! The union felt it had no power under their existing contract to make a stand. Virginia was incensed and wrote a letter to the school board, and sent a copy to the Cambridge Tribune.

She pointed out that the gentlemen on the board, as well as the ladies, all had mothers who were not virgins, and that all those mothers had been pregnant, and had given birth. If the board members had moral problems with human biology and our reproductive system that was for them to resolve, but they had no right to thrust their misconceptions on the children of the city, many of whom, living in small, over-crowded apartments were well aware of how babies came into the world.

The letter was, not unsurprisingly, never published, nor did she receive a response from the board.

We had not planned on having a child so soon after getting married, but once the reality set in we were overjoyed. The second bedroom, which I had been using as my studio and office, had to be converted to a baby's room. We stripped the old wallpaper and painted the walls a soft yellow. Virginia, thanks to her classes in domestic science, made curtains using bright, colorful fabric.

I designed a two story extension to the house that would give us an extra room upstairs, and my studio and a bathroom downstairs. We started work in late July and were done with the major part of the construction within four weeks. I then spent most evenings and weekends for the next two months painting and varnishing, and building shelving.

Albert was born in the early morning of Wednesday, October tenth, 1923, at the Cambridge Hospital on Mount Auburn Street. It was, thankfully, a relatively short labor and there we no complications or concerns. He was a seven pound, eleven ounce wonder, with all the requisite fingers and toes and mighty lungs which he exercised frequently during the first months of his life.

Mrs. Appleton and I sat anxiously in the waiting room during the birth. She told me the story of Virginia's arrival in the world which was quite dramatic - three weeks early while the young Appleton couple was visiting her mother in Washington D.C. It was a difficult birth which resulted in Mrs. Appleton being advised not to have another child. Why she told me this right then, as we waited for Albert, is impossible for me to understand, but it reminded me of my Uncle Kalner telling me of the loss of my infant sister, Tzipora, while we were in the middle of the Atlantic and my mother was suffering terribly from sea-sickness.

It was not until the Saturday afternoon that my mother could get away from work to come to see her first grandchild. I met her at the Harvard Square subway station, then we took a street car to the hospital. She brought with her a small suitcase of her things - she was to stay with us for four days, her first vacation that I could remember - and a large bag of baby clothes.

Mrs. Appleton had earlier offered to have Bea come to our house to help with the baby, but neither Virginia nor I liked the idea. Then my mother stepped in and invited herself. "Just for a few days, I promise. I will help. I will not take charge, don't worry."

"So, Itzik, how do you like being a father?" she asked, as we hurried up the front steps of the hospital.

"Mostly, I miss Virginia and the baby. I spend as much time as I can here, but the nurses throw me out at eight in the evening and I go back to an empty home. The little one is so sweet. I love to hold him, to look into his eyes."

"When are they coming home?"

"Tomorrow morning - at last."

"So, my boy, you and I have a lot of work to do tonight!"

When we arrived at Virginia's room she was nursing the baby. My mother moved close to them and leaned over slightly, touching Virginia's hair and gazing at her first grandson. The three of them were so beautiful together, I wanted to paint them right there, in that moment.

"He looks a lot like Chaim," she said, "peaceful and beautiful." She kissed Virginia on the top of the head then sat down in the chair beside the bed.

"Thanks for coming," Virginia said.

"I wish I could have been here earlier, but..."

"I know. The important thing is you are here now, and will be around to help for a few days."

The baby began to fuss; he had eaten enough. Virginia lifted and straightened him so that he was upright against her and looking over her right shoulder. She patted him gently on the back until he burped loudly.

"Good boy," Virginia smiled. "Would you like to hold him, Mom?" She held Albert up to his grandmother who took him carefully, cradled him in the bend of her arm and began singing a song in Yiddish that I vaguely recognized. Within minutes the baby was asleep.

"You're pretty good at this," Virginia chuckled.

"It's something you never forget, my dear. It's a mother's heart and it is always there." A distant look came over her face, as if she were remembering something from long ago. Virginia and I sat watching her and smiling.

A nurse came in to take the baby back to the nursery but my mother waved her away. The nurse tried to insist, but my mother simply said she was not ready. The nurse relented, saying she'd be back in a while, and my mother began to sing again, very softly. I noticed Virginia's eyelids closing and her head drooping.

"Sleepy?" I whispered.

"Mmm. Sorry."

"It's OK. We'll wait for the nurse to come for the baby. See you around ten in the morning."

"Mmm." And she rolled onto her side and fell into a deep sleep.

It was dark outside. The clock above Virginia's bed read eight-fifteen. I sat quietly, listening to the gentle breathing of my wife and son as they somehow blended with the lullaby my mother was singing.

***

Ginnie is here. It seems like ages since her last visit. I can tell it's her because I heard her talking to Damon a few minutes ago. I think they were actually talking about the Rolling Stones, who are still touring and were going to be in Boston in September. If Virginia were still alive, she and I could go to that concert to celebrate our eightieth wedding anniversary. That would be something - I can see us dancing to "Honky Tonk Woman," just as we did at Allen's wedding!

Laugh.

"You're awake, Grandpa Isaac. What are you laughing about?"

Story.

"You were telling yourself a story?"

Yes. I wish I could tell it to you.

"Did you hear Damon and me talking?"

Yes.

"Did your story have something to do with that? With the Rolling Stones?"

Yes.

"You're not going to tell me that you knew them?"

Smile. No.

"Did you see them live?"

No.

She sits next to me. I can visualize her narrowing her eyes and clenching her teeth as she tries to come up with the right question. Finally she says. "I'll have to ask my dad. Will he know?"

Yes. It was quite a wedding. The music was really good and I danced like a fool, mainly because I had to stay away from Allen's new in-laws who were driving me crazy.

Ginnie is patting my hand rhythmically. She is thinking. Finally, she exhales loudly and says, "Do you remember when my parents got into a big fight about whether I should have a bat-mitzvah?"

Yes. I remember it well. Allen, Martha and Ginnie came to visit me on the Friday evening before Ginnie's twelfth birthday. The argument had started in the car, but continued into the house. I remember hugging Ginnie and asking her what the fight was about. "My stupid bat-mitzvah! It's a year away and they're already arguing about it," she replied.

"Do you want a bat-mitzvah?"

"I don't know. Almost everyone has one, or a communion, or something. My mother wants me to have one. Dad thinks it's archaic."

"What do you think?"

"I don't know."

She was sitting next to me on the couch in the living room while her parents had, fortunately, taken their disagreement into the kitchen. "You know, Ginnie, when I was growing up there was no such thing as a bat-mitzvah; girls didn't feature in the religion. Now, it seems, the status of girls has changed - and that's a good thing. On the other hand, it appears that the bat-mitzvah has become just like the bar-mitzvah; more about showing off than anything else."

"I know. It's crazy. My friend Leah's parents spent over ten thousand dollars on her sister's bat-mitzvah. I'd rather put the money into a trip to Europe or something."

"Are your parents giving you that choice?"

"Well, my dad has said several times that they should let me decide, but my mother thinks I'm not mature enough to make this decision."

"It's a Catch-22. If you make the decision she wants, then you're mature enough to make a decision, but if you go the other way, then you're immature."

"That about sums it up. So what do I do?"

I took her hand. "You need to decide if any parts of this are important to you - the bat-mitzvah ceremony itself, the party, being with friends and extended family, the gifts, what your parents want, and anything else associated with it - and then tell them what *you* want and why."

"Will that make a difference?"

"Hopefully. You still might end up doing exactly what your mother wants but at least you will have clarified your feelings for yourself and for them."

In the end, Ginnie did the most unexpected and wonderful thing; she went through with the ceremony, asserting her right as a young woman to have a voice, but she refused to have any kind of party or receive any gifts. She would not be drawn into the materialism and extravagance of the event, and in so doing, she set in motion a mini-trend among her friends. I was so proud of her - and she got her trip to Europe the summer after she graduated from high school!

"Are you still with me, Grandpa Isaac?"

Yes. Story.

"You were remembering that argument?"

Yes.

"So, I found myself thinking about it because it was such an important time when you helped me figure out my solution to a problem." She pauses. "I wish I could have a similar conversation with you now. Jake was like that. He reminded me of you because I could talk with him and he would just hint at a direction for me to think about that I hadn't thought of before, and it would help me to sort things out. He gave me different perspectives."

I wonder where she is going with this. It is more than her loss of Jake; she is grappling with a different question.

"It's nine months since Jake was killed. Some days it seems like yesterday, others it's far off like a bad dream that never happened. What I have realized recently is that I can't live in the past. I need to do more than work at Starbucks, read books and watch TV. I need to meet people; the problem with my old friends is that they still see me as 'poor Ginnie' and they either want to console me or create a fake atmosphere of fun.

"I have experienced something that not many others have lived through. In some ways, I feel like I have been to war and I need people near me who have had similar experiences. In some deeply profound ways a feel like I have been forced to become old before my time." She sniffs loudly, then continued. "I have been going to a grief counseling group for about a month. We meet at the Arlington Street Church, strangely enough, but I find the place comforting. There are ten people in the group. I cannot say anything about them because of our confidentiality agreement, but I can say that it is helping me." She falls silent.

Hug.

She does not respond, so I indicate "hug" again.

"Thank you for listening, Grandpa Isaac." I feel her hands gently on my arms and her head on my chest.

Suddenly she straightens up. "Shit, I'm going to be late for work! See you later. Thanks."

Chapter 41

Virginia lost her teaching position because of the baby, but having a baby did not stop her from working once Albert was weaned. She received a letter of introduction from the Reverend Frothingham to the minister at the First Parish in Cambridge, the Reverend Samuel Crothers, who hired her to assist part-time with parish administration and in the religious education program on Sunday mornings.

She also became more actively involved, with both her mother and her mother-in-law, in the fight against child labor. The United States Senate passed a constitutional amendment in June 1924 banning child labor and it was sent to the states for ratification. The Massachusetts house refused to vote on this; instead they made it a ballot question for the November elections, which ended up being a three-way race between the Republican, Coolidge, the Democrat, Davis, and the Progressive, LaFollette.

On the Saturday before the election Virginia, Albert and I went into Boston for a rally to urge people to vote to ratify the amendment. My mother came from Lawrence and Mr. and Mrs. Appleton came, too. The crowd gathered in the same place as the women's suffrage rally we had participated in five years earlier. Virginia was one of the speakers, and she was almost eight months pregnant. I stood to the side of the stage holding Albert who had become an active and squirmy toddler, but when his mother began to speak he calmed down and seemed to be giving her his full attention.

Virginia's style was reminiscent of my mother on the picket line. She talked in short, clear, un-flowery sentences. She described what she had seen in the poor neighborhoods of Lawrence, as well as the Cambridge classroom where she had briefly taught. As she came to the end of her speech, she said, "Let me close with a simple assertion that I heard from my mother-in-law, who works in a mill in Lawrence; 'Children should be in school, not in factories!'"

After the rally we walked to the Appleton home for tea. Virginia seemed withdrawn, but said nothing. Albert loved coming to this house: his grandfather doted on him. The stern, aloof, very proper Mr. Appleton would completely transform into a playful, silly and creative man when in the company of his grandson. The two of them would go off into the music room to play. Every so often we would hear peals of laughter, or uncoordinated pounding on the Steinway, or the soft deep tones of Mr. Appleton's voice as he read a story.

I had not seen my mother in a couple of months and as I sat opposite her in the parlor of the Appleton home she did not look well. Her eyes were deep and ringed and her skin was pale. She was only a year older than Virginia's mother, but she looked like an old woman next to her. They were talking with each other about the rally and also about the presidential election and I noticed that my mother often stopped in mid-sentence to catch her breath.

We were all supporting the Progressive candidate, LaFolette, even though we knew he had little chance of unseating Coolidge who was strongly anti-union and pro-business and the banks. The Democrats, of course, still clung to their antiquated views, not much different from the Republicans, but with the added feature that they could not even adopt a policy to distance the party from the Ku Klux Klan. It was not a good time for working people, immigrants, Blacks, or children.

Veterans did get a scrap tossed in our direction; after a great deal of wrangling, threatened vetoes and lamentations about the budget, the veterans bonus bill was passed in 1924 that would enable us to each collect one thousand dollars from the government - in 1945!

Bea brought in the tea and an apple pie. The conversation stopped while Mrs. Appleton poured and Virginia sliced and distributed the pie. Albert waddled in from the music room, followed by his grandfather. "I thought I heard the tea arriving," Mr. Appleton said, and sat down in his usual chair. Albert pulled on his trouser legs until he was helped up onto his grandfather's knee which immediately began bouncing up and down; Albert shrieked with laughter.

I glanced at the three women; they all were smiling although there was a hint of envy on each face. I wondered if a grandson would have lit a small spark in my own father's heart. We drank our tea, ate our pie and succumbed to the joy of the child.

340

Albert finally tired of the horsey ride and began to cry. Virginia picked him up and began to slowly pace back and forth, patting him on the back. "We need to get going," Virginia said, "I still have to prepare for Sunday school tomorrow."

"I should go, too," my mother said. "It was so good seeing you, Jane. Keep on fighting!" They embraced.

"We will. Keep well, Rivka. Write to me."

We walked together to the subway station. "I never got to tell you what a great speech you gave, Virginia," my mother said, as we stopped inside the station before heading off to our different trains. "You're a brave young woman!"

"Thank you, Mom. It felt good up there."

***

Allen is here. I blink to let them know I'm awake.

He sits beside me. "You doing OK, Grandpa Isaac?" There is a nervous texture to his voice.

Yes.

"The doctor says you had an episode this morning, but that everything is back to normal now. Do you remember?"

No. Episode? What the hell does that mean? I don't remember anything unusual happening to me. Am I losing my short-term memory? Let me think; who was here earlier? Ginnie was here, and Damon. My short-term memory is just fine.

"Are you feeling OK?"

Yes. I'm feeling OK - whatever that means!

My cat-machine seems to be getting a little louder and its noises a little more frequent. I consciously force myself to calm down - a trick I learned back in the trenches - and I listen to the machine returning slowly to its normal pace and volume. I feel pretty good that I can still do this.

"Good," says Allen. "So, the time-stamp. It's four-thirty in the afternoon of Tuesday, June fourth. It's a warm and humid day, around eighty-five degrees, with low clouds and a threat of thunderstorms. The semester is almost over; we are preparing for finals week and then all I'll have to do is correct the exams for three classes and finish grading my senior class essays. Then I'm off for the summer and I can devote my time to my next novel."

Like. Smile.

"I see you're up to eighteen words, and telling stories."

Yes. It runs in the family.

"Do you have any other words in mind?"

Yes. I actually have three words I want to create; good, happy and sad. We zip through these; we're getting pretty good at this. I hear Allen take down the chart and add the new words.

Happy.

"This is great, Grandpa Isaac. I'm so impressed that you can make these up, and remember them."

Good. Smile.

Allen laughs and gives me a hug.

I hear someone entering the room. "Good evening, Mr. Simon. Everything rolling along OK?"

It's Trainwreck. I do have to find another name for her; she was just having a bad day when I came up with that name. I'll have to think about it.

"He's doing fine," Allen says. "He came up with three new words today."

"Wonderful!"

Happy.

***

A Boston newspaper article the day after the rally described Virginia as a "rabble-rousing fireball," a fitting description and one she was most proud of. It also carried a lengthy guest editorial written by a Mr. Chester Kingman, who happened to also be the chairman of the Cambridge school board that had dismissed Virginia because of her pregnancy. In his piece, Mr. Kingman extolled the virtues of work and opposed the ratification of the anti-child labor amendment. He also lamented the financial burden the removal of children from the workforce would impose on business owners, and proclaimed that businesses should be free to hire whoever they wanted, and all people, of all ages, should be free to work.

When Virginia read the editorial after she returned from Sunday school she uttered a string of words that would not have been appropriate for church. She immediately sat down to write a fiery response to Mr.

Kingman. She pointed out that families do not send their children to work as an exercise in freedom but rather as a matter of economic survival. "Freedom implies choice," she wrote, "and since working class families have no choice because of the inadequate pay in the mills, mines and factories, there is no freedom."

Then she launched into his earlier pronouncements as school board chairman concerning the duty he has to protect the "moral and spiritual life of each child," and contrasted it with his inability to see the "physical and spiritual burden imposed on the young minds and bodies of boys and girls working long hours under the harshest conditions." She closed with wondering "whether Mr. Kingman's views are more influenced by his family's interests in the dye houses of Massachusetts and New Hampshire, than by any real concern for the well-being of children."

The next morning, the day before the election, she took Albert and made her way by street car and subway to the offices of the newspaper and demanded to see the editor. I would have loved to have been there. In recounting the story, Virginia laughed about how intimidating she must have appeared, with a belly "out to next week and a feisty one-year-old in tow."

She explained that she was one of the speakers at the rally, then handed him her letter, which he read while she tried to prevent Albert from pulling books from the bookcase. He agreed to insert her letter into the evening edition, and went on to praise her writing ability. A few years later, the editor moved to the weekly Cambridge Banner and hired Virginia to write a regular column on what she called, "social commentary." This was to become a significant platform as the financial markets crashed in 1929 and the depression set in.

Her letter was published, but it did little to help the vote. The amendment was defeated by the voters of Massachusetts; the "No" vote was seventy-four percent. Parents were not convinced that the loss of the income their children brought home would be offset by raises in their own wages. It was a matter of the family's survival. "The bastards have working people in a trap. The only answer is to organize, unionize," Virginia said, then added, "and I won't apologize for my language!"

Mark was born six weeks later, on December twenty-second. I spent Christmas day visiting Virginia and Mark in the hospital. Albert was with my mother at our house; she was staying through the weekend. A few of the parents whose children were in Virginia's Sunday school class came to visit after church, as did the Reverend Crothers. While they were still there, the Reverend Frothingham showed up with Virginia's parents. He was absolutely delighted to bless a "Christmas baby," despite the obvious fact that Mark had been born three days earlier.

It was a rather odd gathering. After they all left, Virginia said, "I do love old Frothy, but he has become such an emotional old man. Mother said next year will be his twentieth at Arlington Street and there were rumors of an announcement of his impending retirement. She said he was 'very teary-eyed' in church today. They'll miss him. So will I. He was always so kind, and so welcoming of you, Isaac, and of our relationship."

"He certainly gave me a different perspective on religion; a much more positive one. Not that you should expect to see me as a regular in church, but I have liked and respected him since that first rather chess-like meeting at your parents' house."

"Who could forget that?"

The nurse brought the baby in for his evening feeding. I waited until he was done and then took my turn holding him and walking with him back and forth across the room. I did not want to leave, but I needed to get back to my mother and Albert, and to prepare for Virginia and Mark's return home the next day.

As loud and active as Albert had been, Mark was quiet and calm. He slept well, fussed little and was happy to entertain himself with the rattles, soft stuffed animals and other toys we gave him. More than anything, he was captivated by his big brother who never tired of performing for him.

Virginia had to give up her job in the church office to look after the boys, but continued with the Sunday school while I took care of them.

My work with William Carpenter and Associates became more interesting and rewarding. In the spring of 1925 I was given major responsibility for the design of a country home for one of his high profile clients. The client not only wanted the building, but asked us to design the living room and dining room furniture and lighting as well. I had never done anything like this, but William urged me to work on it. He was much more than a boss; he was a mentor and a good friend.

The client, a couple in their early thirties with two daughters, drove me to look at the land they had purchased overlooking Lake Sunapee in central New Hampshire. It was a beautiful seven acre lot that sloped gently down to the water, with close to six hundred feet of shoreline. The land was thick with red maples, red oak, white pine and scattered stands of white birch. I made a few quick sketches of the site; rock formations, the natural breaks in the vegetation at the shoreline, the changing contour of the land, and the locations of useable trees. I was able to correlate these with the surveyor's map I had been given.

The Sloans were inspired by the work of Frank Lloyd Wright, and wanted their home to blend in with the landscape, not dominate it. They wanted to remove as few trees as possible, just enough for the house itself, for a small vegetable garden and for a view from the house to the lake. This was to be their summer home; they wanted it relatively small, intimate, but with enough rooms for their family to relax in and to host up to ten overnight guests. I smiled at the idea of small, with room for fourteen people to sleep, relax and play.

The nearby village of Newbury was served by the electric grid, but it was going to be a big investment to bring electricity to the house. That did not bother the Sloans; they had the money to do all they wanted. Mr. Sloan was a banker, and the son of a banker. Mrs. Sloan came from a wealthy insurance family in Connecticut.

When the Sloans dropped me off in Boston after our visit to the site, we set an appointment two weeks off to discuss the design approach I was to develop. It was a dream project and I threw myself into it. William gave me my own office. I moved my desk and drawing board into it, hung some of my own oil paintings on the walls, as well as a few watercolors I had created for presentation of design concepts to clients, and got to work sketching out ideas, and writing notes for the Sloan house.

The design had to incorporate several contradictory objectives like an unobstructed view of the lake without removing too many trees, and a small building, comprising somewhere in the vicinity of eight or nine bedrooms plus living, dining, kitchen, bathrooms and storage.

Two days before the Sloans were due to arrive for their first look at my ideas the design began to coalesce, and I made some preliminary sketches. I had decided on a few things: the building was to consist of two separate sections joined by a fairly large, single level open informal combined living room, games room and dining area for use when there were guests. The main section of the building would be a self-contained two-level living space for the family. It could be closed off from the rest of the building if they wanted to. The second section comprised the guest quarters; six bedrooms and bathrooms on two floors. All the living spaces faced south-west, toward the lake. I planned to make this face of the building almost entirely of glass. The result was a long - about a hundred and twenty feet - and fairly narrow building.

I wanted to use as much wood as possible from the trees we cut down in the construction of the house, as well as in the furniture. The down-side to this, of course, was that the wood needed to cure two to three months before it could be used. We could kiln cure it, but I had read that this took away some of the natural texture and beauty, which was especially problematic when it came to the furniture.

William came to my office to see how the design was developing. I showed him my sketches and went over my ideas. He liked the basic concept, but, ever practical, he asked detailed questions about the location of the septic system, about the driveway from the road and where automobiles would be parked; he was concerned about the view one would have of the building as one approached. I worked late that evening, and the next.

Virginia was not happy; they were long days for her, alone with an inquisitive eighteen-month old and an infant, but she understood. Albert, on the other hand, did not understand why Daddy stayed at work so long. This situation tipped the balance in one respect; we decided it was time to get a telephone.

***

I hear several pairs of shoes scraping on the floor; there is a bunch of people standing around. I think it is Doctor Squeak back with his group of students, although I didn't hear his shoes. I don't feel up to performing for them. I wait for someone to talk, to give me a clue about what is going on. Maybe I can have *them* entertain *me*.

Finally a woman I don't recognize speaks. "Right, everyone," she says, in a smoker's gravelly voice. (In fact, I can detect the sour smell of cigarette smoke clinging to her clothes.) "The patient is Mr. Isaac Simon. He has been with us for six weeks. He came here in a completely non-communicative state, but, as you can see from the chart which Dr. Jerzak briefed us about, Mr. Simon is now able to communicate twenty-one words. He can hear us, and his mind and memory are active, as you saw in the EEG graphs."

I don't like being talked about as if I am not here. Who is this woman, and who is with her? What are they doing here? I think I need to learn how to signal, "Fuck off!" Yes, I'm a hundred and two, but I still know those words! I learned them a long time ago.

Dr. Gravel-pit drones on, having switched now to more technical medical terms that mean nothing to me. I try to tune her out.

Finally, I hear Dr. Squeak say, "Mr. Simon, this is Dr. Jerzak. I am here with my colleague, Dr. Weintraub and four of her students. Are you awake?"

I'd love to ignore them, but I've also hatched a little game. I signal that I am awake.

"Good," he says, "are you doing OK?"

Yes.

"Folks," he says to the group, "you'll need to get closer and pay careful attention to Mr. Simon's blinking. As I mentioned, there are short, medium and long blinks and their sequence denotes a word."

I hear the shuffling of feet again, and some twittering among the students.

"Is there anything you need, Isaac?"

Yes.

"Did anyone get that?"

Silence from the group.

"It is subtle, but discernable. Can you say that again, please, Isaac?"

Yes.

One student says, "Short, short. Yes."

"Correct. What is it you need, Isaac?"

Sing.

"Anyone get that?" Silence. "Could you repeat the word, please?"

Sing.

"Anyone?" Silence.

"Perhaps, Mr. Simon," Dr. Gravel-pit says, "you could demonstrate a short, then a medium, then a long blink. I think that would give us a better chance of reading your signals."

"Does that make sense to you, Isaac?" Dr. Squeak asks.

Yes.

"Go ahead, please."

I give them the demonstration of my three different duration blinks. This is getting to be a pain, but I still want someone to sing!

"OK, then, Isaac; let's try that word one more time."

Sing.

"Anyone?"

A tentative young voice says, "Short, medium, medium. Sing."

Yes. You got it young man!

"You want someone to sing, Isaac?" There is a note of suppressed humor in Dr. Squeak's voice.

Yes. Sing.

More shuffling of feet. I can just imagine the sideways glances and shaking of heads. Dr. Gravel-pit coughs loudly.

Finally, the same tentative young voice says, "I'd be happy to sing to you, Mr. Simon." There is a long pause, then he breaks into a beautiful, haunting rendition of "Danny Boy." Everyone else in the room is frozen in silence. It is wonderful.

When he comes to the end of the song I signal, *Thank you. Hug.* And I feel him lean over me and hug me gently.

"Thank you, too," he says.

Smile. Happy.

"My name is Patrick Dolan," he whispers. "May I visit you again, Mr. Simon?" His voice is no longer tentative.

Yes.

***

By the time the Sloans arrived I had sketched a scaled outline of the house on tracing paper so it could be over-laid on the surveyor's site drawing. I also had a preliminary plan view showing the various rooms, as well as the garage, parking, driveway and patio. And I had produced a sketch showing a view of the house from the lake.

We met in the conference room, and much of the discussion was about room sizes and schedule. They wanted the building to be completed as soon as possible, although they liked the idea of using wood from the existing trees. We compromised; we would kiln dry the wood to be used for the construction and naturally dry the wood for finishing and the furniture.

With regard to the design itself, the Sloans liked the basic concept, but wanted the building to be smaller, and were willing to drop the number of guest bedrooms from six to four and to reduce the size of the connecting common room. We seemed to spend an inordinate amount of time trying to decide where to put the small vegetable garden because we would have to cut down a large number of trees to provide enough sunlight.

Two weeks later the Sloans returned to review the modified design. We were anxious to get the basic footprint approved so that we could start cutting and curing the wood. The details of the design could wait. The meeting was over in under an hour; the only change they wanted was to increase the size of the garage to accommodate two cars rather than one - they would not want their parents to have to park their automobile in the open when they came to visit. And, not unsurprisingly, they had completely forgotten to mention earlier that they would need a servant's room with bathroom. This was to be added alongside the garage.

William and I set off the following Monday to work at the site. We had contracted a logging company to cut and cure the lumber and arranged to meet their representative at the Sloan property. We spent two days trudging through the woods and thick brush marking the trees with paint, using different colors to indicate which needed to be kiln cured, which naturally cured and which should be discarded.

It was mid-May and the migrating ducks and birds were returning for the summer. The lake and the woods echoed with their sounds. As we worked, William would stop from time to time to point out a large, gawky pileated woodpecker or the small pine warblers in the trees, and the wood ducks and mallards on the water. I was reminded of my boyhood excursions into the woods near Linkeve and the drawings I had done of the creatures I had seen.

We spent the overnight at a small inn in Newbury. This was the first time we had been together in a setting other than work, except for my wedding and an office Christmas party, neither of which circumstances gave much time to talk. The conversation over dinner started off a little awkwardly; as we sat down he asked about Virginia and the children and whether they were all right with me being away for a couple of days. I replied that they were fine, but that I should probably try to find some small gifts before we left the area. He said we'd stop at the general store on the way home.

I realized that, while he knew a fair amount about my life - my family, my origins in Lithuania, my time in the war - I knew nothing about him other than the fact that he was not married. I asked where his family originated.

"We're originally from England. We go almost as far back as the Mayflower, at least that is what my father claims. I grew up in Philadelphia. My father is a politician. I left home when I was eighteen to come up to Boston to study art and architecture. My parents did not approve. I arrived here with almost nothing but my portfolio of drawings and a small inheritance from my grandfather. I was lucky to soon find a job as a draftsman. The rest, as they say, is history."

"They must be proud of your success, though," I offered.

He slowly placed his knife and fork on his plate, then responded, "I have not seen my parents or communicated with them since the day I walked out their front door."

I couldn't imagine having no connection with my family.

He folded his napkin, dabbed his mouth and continued, "I design buildings and I paint, much like you, except I have little else to distract me." There was a note of resignation in his voice. "And I like to travel," he added. "How about you, Isaac? Travel much?"

"I've been back and forth across the Atlantic, but it was not exactly a vacation."

"But you did learn things and see things. You figured out what you wanted to do with your life, so it couldn't have been all bad."

I took a bite of my steak, followed by a sip of water while I tried to figure out how to change the course of the conversation. Finally, I said, "I think I would have come to the same conclusion about architecture had I stayed home."

"Perhaps, but you would not have seen those marvelous Gothic cathedrals and small churches. You would not have learned how to build things."

"I guess not, but it cost me more than I can describe."

We sat silently, uncomfortably.

"Were you in the war?" It just came out.

"They didn't want me," he replied. "It's a long story that can keep for another time."

Chapter 42

It is quiet; my cat-machine is the only thing that lets me know I can still hear.

Dr. Gravel-pit said I have been here six weeks. That surprises me. I feel it has been much longer. Where was I before I was brought here? I know it wasn't my house. I had to sell it ages ago and then I moved into an apartment. How long was I there? There were only three rooms - a bedroom, a living room and a kitchen that had a table where I ate. I didn't cook much, even though I had learned to be a pretty good cook during our marriage. People brought me food; usually Allen or Danielle came, but sometimes it was Ginnie and even Martha, and a woman from Meals on Wheels stopped by twice times a week.

She was in her seventies and would natter on about television shows, most of which I had never heard of. She was always in a good mood and she seemed to have made it her mission to cheer me up. Her name was Mrs. Pratt. I nicknamed her the Prattler which she found quite funny. I remember her stepping into the apartment and announcing loudly, "Hello Isaac, the Prattler is here!"

I fell one time and could not get myself off the floor. It was a terrible feeling of loss of independence, of loss of control over my body and my life. I hated feeling so helpless. It was the Prattler who found me after I'd been lying there for three or four hours. She insisted on calling an ambulance even though I told her I was in no more pain than usual. It took a couple of days in the hospital to confirm there were no broken bones.

That's the thing about getting old; every day it seems like more and more of you is being drained away, more and more of your ability to do for yourself is going. For me, it is all those physical things. I used to be strong and good with my hands; I could make things and fix things, and I could draw and paint. It was in that apartment when I realized those things were going.

I had set up my easel and paints in one corner of the living room. It was cramped and the light was not good, but I tried to force myself to paint every day. And then one day I didn't have the energy to stand for more than a short while, so I readjusted the height of the easel and reorganized the area to bring in a chair. That worked for a time, until I realized my arms ached so badly I could no longer hold a brush for more than about ten minutes. So I broke up my painting sessions into short bursts.

But at some point I noticed I couldn't see what I was putting on the canvas, I could differentiate colors, but all lines and shapes blended together. I tried to talk myself into thinking that life was giving me a new way to look at the world, and I even created a handful of paintings in this phase. Once, Danielle visited while I was into one of those paintings and I found myself expounding on my new philosophy of art and sight. I could not see the expression on her face but I could sense from her voice that she was skeptical.

And then one day all the colors had merged to gray. I knew it was all over.

Over the following months I worked almost exclusively on the Sloan house. I had weekly meetings with William to review my progress, and one or both of the Sloans would come by every so often to see how things were developing and to make or approve small adjustments as we went along. We would normally meet in the conference room, but one Wednesday afternoon in early August they arrived unexpectedly and that room was unavailable; they were shown into my small office. "So this is where the magic happens," Mrs. Sloan said as they entered, "Sorry to drop in without an appointment."

"So long as you can tolerate my brand of organization," I said, gesturing to the piles of sketches, reference books, and drafting equipment that cluttered every surface. "Let me find a couple of chairs."

When I returned Mrs. Sloan was looking back and forth at my two paintings hanging on the wall opposite my drawing board. "One of the many things I like about coming here is the artwork that Mr. Carpenter displays in the entry-way, the hallways and the conference room, but I have never seen the works of this artist. They are quite marvelous. Who is it?"

"They're my own work."

"I love them. When we're done with the house, I'll commission you to do a few paintings for it."

"I'd be honored," I stammered.

"And I'll suggest to Mr. Carpenter to display your works in more accessible places around the office. Have you ever had a gallery show, Mr. Simon?"

"No. Between working here and having a young family, I don't have much time for my painting. I'm lucky if I can manage a few hours a week, so I haven't built up a collection to show."

"Just another thing to work on after our house is completed."

That would be nice, I thought. "Well, talking of your house, I'm sure you came here with some questions."

"No questions, really; more a status update."

"As you know, the design is nearly complete. On the property itself all the designated trees have been taken down and are being cured. The electric company had extended its lines so that we had power. The foundations are dug, and the well is operational. The septic tank with its leach field is completed.

"William and I are scheduled to go to the site next week to inspect the reinforcing steel, the electrical conduit and so on before the concrete is poured for the foundation and floor slab. It's a big step, and we need to be sure everything is correct."

"Excellent. Give us a call when you return. How long will it take?"

"Two or three days. I'll keep you posted."

When I told Virginia of this upcoming trip she suggested we turn it into a short family vacation. She would ask her father to let us borrow his automobile; we could drive up to the lake together and she and the boys could play while William and I worked, and then, when the site work was completed, I would join them for an additional couple of days. "You've been working so hard these last few months, Isaac - we all deserve a break," she said.

I was apprehensive about raising this idea with William, but felt it was worth a try. I'd been working for him for five years and the only few days I'd taken off were around my wedding and the birth of my boys. We needed a vacation, and the timing was actually not bad; the design for the house was essentially completed and what remained to be done was the furniture and lighting. It would be a good idea to clear my head of the details of wiring and plumbing before tackling something I had never attempted before. "Telephone your father. If he can lend us the car, I'll talk with William."

I approached William the next morning and, after a short pause he agreed to my request, on condition I visited the site for an hour or so every day. "That way I can tell myself you're working and I can pay you for your vacation time." I telephoned Virginia to let her know William's response.

"Our first family vacation! This is going to be fun! I'll call the inn right now and make the reservations."

***

Damon the Good is humming a gentle lilting tune that I don't recognize. I wait for the end of the song then let him know I'm awake.

"Hi, Isaac. Good morning." His voice is tired. I wonder if his nightmares are keeping him up again. "Telling stories again?"

Yes.

"I wish I could be there. I'm sure you've got a lot to say."

Yes.

"You've led a full life, I know. I can see it in your hands, your face, and in the people who come to see you."

Yes. Smile.

"I think your beard needs a little attention. OK?"

Yes.

I hear him open the drawer next to the bed. Then I feel him sit beside me and he begins to comb my beard. "Golden white," he says. "Beautiful."

Smile.

I listen to my cat-machine purring softly. I could sleep. I could sleep a long time.

"I forgot your time-check," Damon the Good interrupts. "It's past seven on the morning of Thursday, June sixth. It's going to be another hot and humid day. The sunrise this morning was intense; the sun was like a giant red blister ready to burst."

What an image. I wish I could pick up my brushes and paints right now.

I hear someone enter the room. "Hi, Ginnie," Damon says, "You're early."

"I woke up at five and couldn't get back to sleep, so I thought I'd come visit before work. How's he doing?"

"Good. He's awake and as chatty as ever."

Ginnie laughs then sits on my bed. "Your beard looks very grand this morning, Grandpa Isaac."

Smile. Hug.

She leans over me and touches her cheek to mine. "So I asked my dad about you and the Rolling Stones and he told me all about the wedding party; how you and my great-grandmother were dancing up a storm!"

Laugh.

"He says you danced the night away in a gallant effort to avoid having to talk with Mom's parents. Is that true?"

Laugh. Yes.

"I don't blame you - not for one second." She giggled, then paused and her voice dropped. "I wish I'd known her; Virginia, who gave me her name and died a week after I was born."

Yes. Hug. You are so like her. You would have been great together.

***

Early the following Tuesday we packed the car and set off on vacation. Albert, almost two, was excited about everything: the car, the piles of suitcases, the wind in his face as we drove, stopping for gas, even stopping to fix a flat tire. Everything was so new for him. He had not been out of the city before, and the open road making its way through the fields and forests and passing through small villages was an unimaginable adventure. "What's that?" he shouted over and over as we passed things he was seeing for the first time.

But it was the lake that enthralled him. As we came out of a long curve and began to descend to Newbury, the lake came into view and Albert went suddenly silent. "Wow! Is that the lake? Wow!"

"That is Lake Sunapee, Albert," Virginia said, "and pretty soon you and Mark and I will be swimming in it."

"Really?" His voice was somewhat apprehensive.

"Really. It will be a lot of fun. And we can play on the beach."

He did not answer, but he smiled broadly.

By the time we had checked in at the inn, unpacked the car and brought all our things to our room, it was past noon. I asked at the front desk whether William had arrived and they said he had called to say he would not be arriving until around three o'clock, and would meet me at the site. We ate a quick lunch in the dining room, then Virginia and the boys walked down to the beach and I drove the five miles to the site.

The driveway from the road down to where the building was located was awful and I feared I would damage my father-in-law's automobile, so I found the first spot I could to park and I grabbed my roll of drawings and walked the rest of the way. I tried to view this place and what we were doing to it with fresh eyes. It truly was a beautiful spot; the way the lake spread out, the slope of the land, the variety of trees, the sounds of the birds.

It seemed a shame to be changing it at all, but the house was going to blend in and, at the same time, reflect its environment. Using the locally harvested wood along with large expanses of glass and simple lines would accentuate the natural beauty without crowding or dominating it.

I stopped for a moment and listened to the buzzing and pounding of machinery and the voices of men working, then made my way toward the small temporary shack where the construction supervisor had his office. Mr. Ballard must have seen me approaching because he emerged from the shack to greet me. We shook hands and he pointed at the roll of drawings under my arm. "Please tell me you're not here with more changes, Mr. Simon."

"No more changes. Just a clean set of blueprints we can use to mark up as we verify everything before you start pouring concrete."

"That's a relief. Where's Mr. Carpenter?"

"He's running late; I expect he'll be here by mid-afternoon. Is everything all in place for us to start checking?"

"All except the reinforcing for the garage floor. That'll be done by the end of today."

"Good. I'll start at the other end of the building."

"Very well. Take your time, Mr. Simon. No room for errors or oversights."

It was a tedious, exacting process, made worse by the oppressive heat and humidity and the fact that it had rained the night before leaving large puddles and mud and swarms of mosquitoes. By the time William arrived at around three-thirty I was soaked in sweat and itching all over. He took one look at me and suggested I take off my shoes and jump into the lake to cool off.

I followed his advice. As I floated on my back staring up at the few clouds suspended in the sky I remembered a day not long before we left Linkeve when Chaim and I had walked to a pond hidden in the woods. We stripped to our bare skin and jumped into the water. We swam and splashed around until we tired and then lay down on the warm flat rocks to dry. He asked me how I felt about leaving Linkeve and moving to America. I told him I was not sorry to leave the village, but I couldn't imagine leaving without him. I asked him why he would not come with us, why he felt he had to go to Africa.

All he said was, "I need to make my own way," and no matter how hard I tried to get him to explain, he would not tell me any more than that. Instead, he asked me how I felt about our father who had died about three months before. "Do you miss him?" he asked.

"No. He was not good to us or to Mama. I don't miss him at all. In fact, I feel like we are better without him."

"You know, Itzik, he taught me to swim when you were little. We came to this pond and he taught me. It was special - just him and me. I loved it; until the day he brought me here and instead of swimming, he sat on these rocks with his bottle of vodka. And when the bottle was empty he threw it at me because he said I was making too much noise and he wanted to sleep. I ran home, leaving him there to burn in the sun."

Neither of us said a word for some time, then Chaim sat up and leaned over me. "No matter what happens or where we are, I will always be your big brother." He ruffled my hair, playfully. "We should get home to Mama."

William was unusually quiet as we worked. I made a few attempts to engage him, but his responses were short and non-committal. It was clear that something was bothering him and he had no intention of talking about it. When we returned to the inn at around seven-thirty, he went directly to his room, saying he did not feel like dinner.

I went up to our room and found Albert and Mark already asleep and

Virginia sitting on the bed, reading. "How was your day?" I asked, and sat in the arm-chair beside her.

"We had a great time. Both boys really enjoyed playing in the water, as did I."

"I took a plunge at some point, too. It was so hot and sticky. Lots of mosquitoes; I did not enjoy being afternoon tea for a horde of bugs!"

"Did you have dinner?"

"No, and I'm starving. How about you?"

"I fed Mark and Albert, but waited for you. Of course, we can't leave them alone so I asked if the kitchen would send dinner up to the room. They gave me a menu."

"I have to take a bath before I do anything else," I said. "You know what I like. Surprise me."

We enjoyed a quiet dinner and went to bed early. I drifted off to sleep listening to the breathing of my wife and two sons.

The next morning William was waiting for me at the breakfast table. "Sleep well?" he asked. "Virginia and the boys not joining us?"

"I slept like a log, as they say. They'll be down in a couple of minutes." I hesitated, "And you, did you have a good night?"

"I'm fine, even though I was up half the night." He lifted his coffee cup, then set it down again. "There are some personal issues that have been bothering me recently, but I'll get through it. I'm sorry I was so unbearable yesterday, Isaac. I'm in a better frame of mind today."

Virginia and the boys entered the dining room and joined us. "So, Virginia, what are your plans for the day?" William asked.

"Lake!" Albert said.

"Yes, we are going to the beach in the morning. Then, after a midday nap, we'll probably take a little walk and read a book or two in the shade near the water."

"Sounds delightful!"

"It certainly does," I said, "I look forward to being able to join you in those noble endeavors in a day or two."

"Do you drive, Virginia?" William asked.

"I have learned to drive, but need more practice before I'm willing to risk it on my own."

"Pity. There's a beautiful view of the lake from the mountain, and there are lovely picnic spots up there. You could build a fire and have a cook-out."

"Perhaps we could do that on Friday or Saturday; what do you think, Isaac?"

"I like it."

William suddenly stood. "Time to go," he announced.

I kissed Virginia and the boys and we left.

We worked methodically through the day, stopping only briefly to eat a lunch of cheese sandwiches and fruit the inn had prepared for us, and to take a couple of short dips in the lake to cool off. William was focused intently on our tasks, not saying much, always friendly but a little detached. We worked until it was almost too dark to see. Mr. Ballard was not happy to be staying late and even less happy when we presented him with our marked up drawings showing several areas that needed to be corrected.

On the drive back to the inn, William said he was returning to Boston first thing in the morning. "I'll rely on you to complete the few remaining details and verify that Ballard has taken care of the problems we found."

The dining room and kitchen were closed by the time we reached the inn. "I'm sure Virginia made arrangements for us to have something to eat," I said. "Let me go up to the room and check in with her."

"Don't worry about me, Isaac. I'll be fine; I always keep a supply of fruit and snacks when I travel." And with that he went to his room.

"I'm sorry I'm so late," I said to Virginia as I came into the room, quietly, and sat beside her. "William was hoping we'd be done today."

"And are you?"

"We're close enough for him to leave in the morning. I'll go up to the site right after breakfast and will probably be back in time for a midday nap."

"I'd love to see the place."

"They'll be starting to pour the concrete on Friday." I looked over to the corner where both boys were sleeping in their cribs. "There'll be lots of noise and big machines - Albert will love it!"

"Sounds like an exciting day." She paused. "Is William all right? He rushed the two of you off rather suddenly this morning."

"Something is upsetting him, I think, but he said nothing. I offered him dinner, which I assume you ordered for us. He declined and went to his room."

"I'm afraid it must be cold by now."

"It will be fine. I'm starving."

"Good, because I did order for William as well."

"I can handle it."

***

Ginnie and Damon are talking. I must have drifted off because they seem to be ignoring me. I'm OK with that; there's only so much one can get from a blinky-blink talking man.

"He's sleeping now, I think," Ginnie is saying. "I'll see you downstairs in the cafeteria."

"I'm off in about ten minutes. See you there."

I hear her leave. I let Damon know I'm awake.

"You heard that, Isaac?"

Yes.

"We're just having breakfast together. Are you OK with that?"

Yes.

"She's a very kind person."

Smile. Yes. She's also very vulnerable.

He fidgets with my plumbing one more time. "See you later, Isaac. Wanda will be in to see you in a bit."

Chapter 43

We had arranged with Virginia's father to return his automobile on the Sunday afternoon. We were late getting on the road and it was approaching five o'clock by the time we reached our house. We unloaded all our baggage and the boys, who had finally fallen asleep less than thirty minutes before we reached home, and then I continued alone into Boston.

It had been a good break from the day-to-day; we enjoyed being together, playing in the water, taking scenic drives and looking for birds and flowers in the woods. The highlight for Albert was the visit to the construction site with the big trucks and noisy mixing machines. Virginia, too, was quite impressed with the process and all the designing, planning and coordination and physical work that went into it.

"When will it be completed?" she asked.

"We should have the walls and roof up by the beginning of November, then the work on finishing the interior can be done during the winter months. It's amazing how much there is to do, especially since everything here is custom designed and built. I still have to design the furniture and light fittings - something I have never attempted before. And then I have paintings to do for the house; I'm not sure how many or how large they need to be."

"So, when do the Sloans move in?"

"The goal is March first."

"It is exciting!"

I parked the car on the street in front of the Appleton home and was greeted by my father-in-law who was clearly disappointed to see that I was alone. "The boys were exhausted from so much sun and fun," I said.

"Did you just get back? It is rather late."

"We had a late start. The boys, surprisingly, slept late this morning, so our usually reliable little alarm clocks didn't wake us until eight o'clock. And then, of course, it being such a beautifully sunny day, we needed one last swim in the lake. It was difficult dragging ourselves away."

"I can understand that. Well, come in, Isaac. Have a cup of tea or coffee."

"Thank you, but I must rush back, Mr. Appleton. Virginia is waiting. I'll have her telephone you during the week; perhaps we can visit on Saturday. Thank you so much for the use of your automobile, sir."

"You're welcome, son."

As I rode the subway home it occurred to me that I had never before heard him call me "son," and I had never called him anything other than "Mr. Appleton" or "sir." His use of that word seemed to have come so naturally to him, but I wondered if he had rehearsed it many times, as lawyers do. Either way, it caught me off guard; no one had referred to me as "son" for a very long time. I thought, again, of that time at the pond near Linkeve with Chaim and what we had both said about our father.

For the next several months either William or I made frequent trips to the Sloan house to review the progress. Initially, he allowed me to borrow his Packard automobile, but after my third visit up north he called me into his office and told me I had to make other transportation arrangements. An architect needed to be able to get around, and he had to have his car available at all times. He had missed an important meeting with a client. He was not angry; simply practical and to the point.

This was not an expense I wanted to take on, but I had no option. Virginia and I talked it over that evening after Mark and Albert were asleep. We had just enough money in our savings account to buy a Ford Model T. "We have to do this," I said. "It'll be a whole new phase of life."

"I know. I only hope it doesn't put us in the poor house."

"We'll manage."

Virginia was mending the children's clothes while we talked. "You know, Isaac," she said, and she set her sewing on the table beside her and looked directly at me, "You need to sell some of your paintings, and I have a feeling your Mrs. Sloan has some connections."

"I have to find time to focus on creating some new works. So much is old."

"They're still good."

A few days later I arrived home with a brand new Model T. Albert was all over it, pretending to drive and ready to head off for another vacation. Virginia took her place behind the wheel and said, "Well, I'm going to have to learn to drive this thing. But not now; it's almost dark and the boys need their dinner."

It was late October. I had spent a good deal of time working on the designs for the furniture and lighting for the Sloan house and felt ready to show them some drawings and watercolors. After William reviewed and approved them, we invited the Sloans to the office to take a look. I also brought finished samples of the wood we were planning to use.

The designs, like that of the house itself, were simple, refined, unadorned, allowing the natural beauty of the wood to dominate. For the easy chairs and couches in the living rooms, I envisioned curved light oak armrests with dark leather cushions. The dining tables and chairs were all maple. The lampshades would be bell-shaped and turned from sections of maple; the sconces were made from similarly turned maple, then cut in half so that they could be mounted on the wall. In place of a chandelier for the center of the large living area I proposed a cluster of seven maple bells of different sizes suspended at different heights from the ceiling.

The Sloans took several minutes looking at the watercolors as well as the detailed drawings. "Beautiful, I love the chairs and tables," Mrs. Sloan finally said, "And I love the shades, too, but I wonder whether they'll give enough light, and are they robust enough to survive over time? Will they dry out and crack from the heat of the light bulbs?"

"I have had turned maple shades in my own home for six years," William said, "and I've had no problems with them."

"Good. I'll take your word, then, William."

We saw them out and William and I returned to the conference room to gather up my drawings and wood samples. "We are almost there, Isaac," William said, "and you've risen to the challenge. Thank you. A long period of late nights and endless sketches and drawings is almost over and I hope we can return to a more normal pace - at least for a short while."

"I've learned a tremendous amount doing this project. Thank you for your trust in me and your guidance."

"How long have we been working together?"

I was touched that he phrased his question in such a personal way; he did not ask how long I had worked for him, or how long I had worked there. Rather, he asked about us working together. "I arrived here in August 1920."

"Over five years. Amazing. I think ..." he hesitated, then walked toward the door. "I think it's time for you to go home to Virginia and the boys."

The walls and roof were in place by November tenth and work was started on the kitchen and bathrooms and also on the paneling for the entrance hall and living rooms. I spent a great deal of time working alongside our master carpenter going through the wood to select matching grains and organizing the boards so that when installed they would give the right sense of connection to the outside environment as well as warmth and comfort to the people in the house.

December blasted in with a storm that deposited more than a foot of snow in Boston and even more up north, followed by several days of below freezing temperatures. Travel to the site was impossible, so we talked with Mr. Ballard by telephone every week. In every conversation he assured us they were making progress and were on schedule. I was skeptical of his optimism and was anxious to visit.

The arrival of winter along with the slowed pace at work, allowed me to spend time in my studio after the boys went to bed. The first thing I did was to put away all the paintings that were propped up against the walls, as well as a couple I had hung. I wanted to cut myself off from all past works and start anew. I tried to clear my mind of everything I had ever done.

It was both terrifying and liberating to stand in front of a blank four foot by three foot canvas with a blank mind and nothing in my hand. I don't know how long I remained like this, but suddenly I was painting, almost without thinking. I will not say that I was in a trance, because I knew exactly what I was doing and was in full control of the brushes and colors, but I was not planning ahead. Everything happened in the moment; one shape or line or color suggesting the next.

I did not hear Virginia come into the studio to say good-night. I was unaware of time. It was only when I noticed the change in the light that I realized I had worked through the night. I heard a sound in the house so I left my studio and found Virginia in the kitchen sipping a cup of coffee.

"What time is it?" I asked.

"Seven fifteen."

"Are the boys still sleeping?"

"They've been up for a while. They're in our room, which is where you were not?"

"I got carried away; I couldn't stop. It was a strange night. Hard to explain."

"Can I see what you're working on?"

"Sure."

It was an odd feeling standing in front of that painting. I remembered everything I had done to create it, every brush-stroke, every combination of colors, and I remembered being aware of how the painting progressed, but what I did not see until I stood there with Virginia was how the whole painting vibrated back and forth between abstraction and realism. In one moment everything was a blur of merging forms and colors, and in the next one could see a landscape with a lake and forest and a low glass-fronted building.

"It's the Sloan house," Virginia said, "dancing in a cloud of color. It's stunning!"

I did like it. It was actually not much different from some of my more recent works, but it projected a more confident grasp of how my eye, hand and brain work together. For the first time I felt that I really understood not only how to paint, but how to see. I put my arms around Virginia and kissed her. "This is good. I can finally see where I'm going."

Our moment was interrupted by the sounds of a crying child. "I'll go," I said.

I went to the bedroom to find Albert sitting on the floor, wailing and rubbing his forehead. I picked him up and sat him on my lap on the bed. "Bumped my head," he cried and wrapped his arms around me. I saw a small red circle above his left eye and kissed it gently and patted his back rhythmically.

"Did you have breakfast yet, Al?"

"No."

"I didn't either. Let's go together."

He hopped off my lap and ran to the kitchen. I picked up Mark and followed.

Albert and I ate oatmeal while Virginia fed Mark. I looked at the clock on the wall. "I'm late. I need to rush to work."

"You need to sleep, Isaac. I'll telephone William and tell him you'll be in after lunch."

Chanel Number 5. Danielle. I signal that I am awake.

"Hi there, old friend. I'm here for a quick visit - I'm meeting Martha and Allen for dinner at some fancy new joint that Martha has been raving about. She says they serve authentic Middle Eastern food."

Smile.

"So, it's around six on Thursday, June sixth. I don't have a whole lot of news to report. I did chat with Ginnie a short while ago; she says she'll be seeing you early in the morning."

When Damon the Good is working.

"She seemed to be in a good frame of mind. I think she's finally beginning to surface after everything." She paused and took my hand. "And how have you been doing? OK?"

I hate that question because I have no way to answer it. Even if I could talk what the hell would I say; I'm stuck here like a plank with my brain running like a buzz-saw. I have nagging, gnawing pain almost constantly and I'm being fed and I'm shitting through a complicated web of plumbing. On the other hand, I'm alive and, in a strange way, I am enjoying telling my story. It's been an interesting life. It would be nice to share it, though. I wish I had written it down when I was still able to.

So, am I OK? *Smile. Yes.*

"The Red Sox beat Detroit eleven to nothing yesterday. Do you want me to read the newspaper report on the game?"

No. I'm not in the mood for the sports news. I'm actually not in the mood for anything. My old war wound has started aching.

"I brought a book of O'Henry stories. I don't have time to read one now; maybe Ginnie can read a story later." She leans over me and kisses me on both cheeks. "Afraid I have to go, now. See you soon."

***

Mark started walking the day before his first birthday. Virginia called me at work to tell me the news, and also to give me the latest arrangements for the upcoming Christmas holiday. We were to be at her parents' home by six o'clock on Christmas Eve, then we would all go to the evening service at seven, and return to spend the night with the Appletons. In the morning, after presents had been opened, we would drive to Lawrence and spend the rest of the day with my mother.

"We are bringing our two little boys into church? I can't imagine them being able to sit and be quiet through an entire service."

"I know, but my parents insist. I think they want to show them off."

"And they believe church is the place for that?"

"Apparently so, Isaac. Anyway, there'll be dozens of children there; I'm sure our two will fit right in with the general commotion."

"They do love being grandparents," I said. "While we're talking about holiday plans, William has invited everyone in the office and some clients to a New Year's Eve party at his house in Concord. I'd like to ask my mother to spend the night with the boys."

"New Year's? OK, it sounds like fun. I'm dying to see his house. Yes, let's ask your mother when we see her on Christmas."

"I've often wondered what his house looks like. It was one of the first buildings he designed, and he keeps on modifying it."

The Christmas Eve service went better than expected; the boys were fascinated by the crowd, the lights, and especially the singing, although Mark fell asleep in his grandmother's arms about halfway into the service. She beamed. Albert remained uncharacteristically quiet between his grandfather and Virginia and managed to stay in his seat throughout. There was a large number of children in the sanctuary and the Reverend Frothingham took their normal distractions in stride, even smiling broadly when a portion of the crowd burst out laughing near the end of "Silent Night," right after the line, "Sleep in heavenly peace," when a child called out, "I don't want to sleep,"

After the service, the Reverend stood by the door wishing everyone a "Merry Christmas." When Virginia and I approached, he shook my hand warmly. "I saw your parents with the little ones a minute or two ago, Virginia. Those boys are so sweet, and their grandparents couldn't be more delighted. They invited my wife and me for a late supper," he said. "I look forward to seeing you all in a little while."

It was a clear but chilly night and few people were milling around outside. The Appletons, each carrying one grandchild, walked quickly up the path to the house. "Let's take our time," Virginia said, "It's such a lovely night."

I wrapped my arm around her and we walked slowly toward the house. "Do you miss all of this?" I asked, gesturing to the Garden and the surrounding buildings.

"Not often. I do miss this church and old Frothy, and I sometimes miss the ability to just step outside and stroll through these beautiful gardens whenever I want, but I wouldn't trade it for what we have done together in our little house across the river in Cambridge. We've come a long way. My life is so much more real. Before we met, Isaac, I never even thought about college or working. I couldn't even fry an egg or sew a button on a shirt. I talked a lot about women's independence, but I was dependent on everyone from my father to Bea for almost everything in my life."

I squeezed her closer to me. "Yes, we have both come a long way."

The furniture in the parlor had been re-arranged to make room for a floor-to-ceiling pine tree in front of the bay window. The tree was hung with garlands of large colored glass beads, ornaments of spun cotton, and painted glass shaped like bells, stars, shells and orbs. At the top of the tree, almost brushing the ceiling was a figure of an angel in flowing red and silver robes and carrying a golden harp. At the foot of the tree on a rumpled white blanket were several brightly wrapped boxes of various sizes.

No guests had arrived yet and Mrs. Appleton was in the kitchen giving instructions to Bea. Mr. Appleton and the boys were warming themselves in front of the glowing fire that was burning in the fireplace. Virginia and I joined them.

"The boys were so good in church. I was so proud of them," Mr. Appleton said.

"You boys certainly were," Virginia responded as she bent down to give them each a hug. "Did you enjoy the service, Albert?"

"Yes. Mark slept."

"I know. He was tired."

She kissed them both then straightened up. "How many people are you expecting this evening?" Virginia asked her father.

"Your mother has the final tally, but I think it will not be a large gathering. I know the Winslows will be here with their son and his wife; both their daughters have moved away, one to California and the other to

London. Also, the Adamses and the Newcastles and a few others. You'll just have to wait and see who comes - or ask your mother."

I looked forward to seeing Mr. Winslow again. He was the civil rights and labor attorney that Reuven worked for before moving to Detroit. Reuven had a lot of respect for Mr. Winslow senior, although he was not too enthusiastic about the son, who was now a junior partner in the firm.

"I must join Jane to greet our guests," Mr. Appleton said and walked off towards his wife who was speaking with a cluster of new arrivals. I did not recognize any of them. I knelt down next to Mark and Albert. "How are you two doing?"

"Good," Albert replied, while Mark pulled himself upright and opened his arms. I picked him up and went over sit near the tree. Virginia and Albert followed. Bea was circulating with a tray of appetizers - a spicy red bean paste on crackers topped with a marble of sour cream. "Good evening Mr. Simon," she said. "Please try one of these; I got the recipe from a Mexican woman I met in the park many years ago, when Virginia was a little girl. It has taken all these years to convince Mrs. Appleton to serve them."

How could I say no? I took a bite, as did Virginia. It was so different from anything else I had ever eaten, but it was delicious. I took another. "These are really wonderful, Bea."

"Thank you, Mr. Simon. What do you think, Virginia?"

"Very unusual and very good," she said.

"Your boys look so sweet in their holiday outfits," she said. "Well, I must keep moving. I watched her offering her tray around the room. Many people took a small bite and returned the remainder to their plates or surreptitiously folded the remaining portion into their napkins.

Mark had fallen asleep on my lap and Albert was beginning to get fidgety and whiney - sure signs that he was ready for bed. "I'll bring them up to the room," I said.

"OK. I'll be there in a few minutes to kiss them good-night."

As I stood, Mrs. Appleton came over to us with the Winslows close behind. "These are our lovely little boys," she said. "Is Mark asleep?"

"He nodded off about five minutes ago, and Albert is sleepy too, I'm afraid," Virginia replied. "Isaac was about to put them to bed." On cue, Albert grabbed at his mother's dress and wailed.

"Good night everyone," I said. "Al, take my hand and we can go upstairs to bed." He wailed again, so I picked him up and carried the two boys to the room. Virginia had taught me how to change diapers when Albert was little and she was pregnant with Mark. I was completing this task when Virginia entered the room. I could see immediately she was angry about something, but had to restrain herself while we readied the boys for bed.

"I think I'll wait in my father's study - the last door on the right," she whispered. "Please come find me there."

"What happened?"

"Come find me in the study as soon as you can."

I finished reading the book, made sure they were both asleep and tucked in safely, and then went in search of Virginia.

She was seated in a large leather armchair in front of her father's desk. Her teeth were clenched and she clasped her hands together. I knelt down in front of her and placed my hands on hers and waited for her to speak.

"It's the little things that get to me, Isaac," she said at last. "Little things, details that six or seven years ago I was clueless about, oblivious, but now they jump up at me."

"What happened?"

"There's a list. A long list, but the final straw was that wife of Andrew Winslow!" She took a deep breath. "After you went up with the boys, we were chatting about how sweet and well-behaved they are, when Millie Winslow said they looked really splendid in their holiday clothes, and everyone sighed approvingly. I said that I had made the outfits myself, expecting some praise, some positive comment, but Millie sniffed and said, and I quote; 'How odd. I thought that's what maids and seamstresses were for.' I wanted to poke her pretty little eyes out!"

She squeezed my fingers. "But what made it even worse, Isaac, is that she made her stupid remark as Bea was approaching with a tray of her puff pastries. I could see in her eyes that she had overheard Millie's comment and she turned aside with her tray and returned to the kitchen. I excused myself, saying I wanted to check on the boys, and ran up here.

"You remember, Isaac, when we first started seeing each other how you pointed out Bea's shoes to me? How you made me realize that she was a person first, not just a servant."

"I remember," I said, "and I remember saying that our class differences would be harder to overcome that the religious ones."

"That's so true. I don't know how to relate to Bea anymore now that I cook and sew and clean and look after the babies. When I'm here, and Bea is cooking and serving food and baking, and doing all those million other things, I feel uncomfortable. I feel out of place in my parents' home - my childhood home!"

Tears began to well up in her eyes and roll down her cheeks. "One other thing I never told you, that I've tried unsuccessfully to ignore. Do you recall my speech at the rally against child labor?"

"I do. You were brilliant!"

"Remember at the end of that speech I mentioned that my mother-in-law works in a textile mill?"

"Of course I remember. She was happy you quoted her, and I was, too."

"Well, as I returned to my seat on the stage, one of the women exclaimed loud enough for the other speakers to hear, 'Oh my Lord, Miss Appleton has married into the lower classes!' I was so taken aback I could not respond. The lady in question is Mrs. Adams, who is downstairs right now in my mother's parlor!"

I heard the floorboards creak in the hallway outside the door, followed by Mrs. Appleton's low voice, "Virginia, is everything all right dear? Our guests are asking after you."

Virginia opened the door. "We'll be down in a minute, mother. Isaac and I needed to discuss something."

"Very well, dear. Please don't delay." Her mother's footsteps receded.

"Will you help me avoid Mrs. Adams?"

"Point her out to me and I will be your shield."

We looked in on the boys to be sure they were both sleeping. "I wish I could just stay up here with them," Virginia said, as we closed the door to the room.

"Well, they are the best excuse to disengage from your mother's guests."

The parlor was now filled with people. The music room doors were open and several people, including the Reverend and his wife, were gathered around the piano singing Christmas carols. "The lady who has seated herself at the Steinway is Mrs. Adams," Virginia whispered to me, and then she pulled me towards the buffet table that had been set up against the wall below the Metzinger. "I'm starving," she said. We filled our plates with sliced ham sandwiches, roasted root vegetables and Brussels sprouts and found a couple of chairs next to the Christmas tree.

"I thought this was going to be a small gathering," I remarked, "There must be close to fifty people here - more than we had for our wedding."

"I guess my mother and father have developed a different understanding of 'small' since I lived under their roof." She laughed.

Bea snaked her way through the crowd, picking up dirty dishes and glasses. I looked at her shoes; I could swear they were the same ones she had worn when I first came to this house. She approached us for our dishes. "The food was lovely, Bea. Thank you," Virginia said. Bea smiled briefly, and moved on without saying a word.

"I wonder how late she's working tonight."

"I overheard my mother ask her to stay till eleven, and then she'll have tomorrow off - after breakfast."

"It's almost eleven now."

"I told my mother I'd be happy to make breakfast so that Bea could leave earlier, but she wouldn't have it. You'd have thought I volunteered to work in a coal mine."

Mr. Winslow made his way towards us. I stood up to greet him. "Good to see you and your family, Isaac. How are things with you?"

"We're all very well, thank you sir."

"What do you hear from your friend, Reuven, and his French wife? He's a fine young man, and the kind of lawyer this country needs."

"Reuven and Yvette are happy in Detroit. As you probably know, sir, Reuven is always busy. I receive a letter from him perhaps every couple of months. He was able to go to Tennessee for a few days to observe the Scopes trial which he said was both anti-climactic and outrageous."

"Yes, a lot of high-priced lawyers managed to make a circus out of that." Mr. Winslow responded. An uncomfortable silence followed. "Well, do give them my best wishes."

"I will, sir."

The crowd was slowly beginning to thin, although the singing in the adjoining room continued with as much enthusiasm as ever. Virginia went to check on Albert and Mark, leaving me at the mercy of whoever decided to come up and talk to me. I did not know any of the Christmas songs, nor could I sing, so I remained in the parlor trying to be as inconspicuous as possible. The song ended and Mrs. Adams announced she was exhausted and needed a break from playing. She stood up, turned and before I realized it she had marched over to me and seated herself in the chair Virginia had recently vacated.

"We did meet once before, Mr. Simon, after the church service commemorating the first anniversary of the end of the war. I'm Mrs. Adams." She shook my hand. "Virginia looks lovely. And those boys! My, how perfect they looked this evening. I believe Virginia made their costumes herself."

"She did." The fact that I did not acknowledge knowing her did not seem to register with her at all.

"I'm not sure I approve of this young generation and its new sense of independence."

"The world is changing, Mrs. Adams."

"Well, I like the old days!"

"Before women could vote, perhaps?"

"Of course not, Mr. Simon."

I saw Virginia enter the parlor, see who was sitting with me, and exit in a hurry.

The Reverend Frothingham and his wife, tired of singing, came into the parlor and saw me with Mrs. Adams. They walked over to us and I stood to greet them. "Such a wonderful little party," Mrs. Frothingham said. "We so love singing Christmas songs, and Mrs. Adams, you were a splendid accompanist. I did not notice you in the music room, Mr. Simon."

"I'm not much of a singer, Mrs. Frothingham."

"Mr. Simon's talents are in the visual arts, I believe, not the musical," Mrs. Adams chimed in. "Is that not so, Mr. Simon."

"I do paint, but I spend much of my time at that intersection between art and engineering - I am an architect."

"Now, there's a never-ending argument," the Reverend said, "In a building, what is more important, more dominant; the beauty of the building or its structural accomplishments?"

"Come now, Paul, this is a party. It is not the time for a discussion on aesthetics and philosophy." Mrs. Frothingham tugged on her husband's sleeve. "It's getting late, and these good people will be up early with those boys to unwrap presents." They headed for the door, followed by Mrs. Adams.

Virginia waited until the Adamses were in the front hall, thanking Mrs. Appleton for the lovely party, before she reappeared. "The boys are sleeping soundly," she said. "How was your conversation with Mrs. Adams?"

"Uncomfortable, but polite."

Virginia laughed. "You are becoming quite the diplomat."

With the Frothinghams and Adamses gone, the rest of the guests quickly made their exits, leaving Virginia, her parents and I standing in the cluttered chaos that was now the parlor; overflowing ashtrays, dirty dishes, napkins and glasses crowded every horizontal surface. Virginia picked up a few things and brought them to the kitchen, returning with a large tray which she began to load.

"Oh, Virginia, Bea will take care of all of this in the morning," her mother said.

"It's no bother, mother. Bea is off after breakfast for Christmas day with her family. It will be a lot easier and quicker for her if we bring all these dirty dishes to the kitchen."

"If you insist, dear. Your father and I are going to bed."

Virginia started washing the dishes while I gathered up the rest of the mess in the parlor and music room. Then I dried and began putting everything away. "I'm so looking forward to seeing your mother tomorrow, Isaac. She's so genuine and straightforward; she doesn't act like she needs to impress anyone. Not like this crowd with everyone vying for position, trying to be smarter or funnier or wealthier than the next. I love my parents, Isaac, but I am having a difficult time identifying with them. Our lives have become so different."

"When we first met, you often talked about how open-minded they were, and that they encouraged you to think independently. Have they changed?"

"No, I don't think they've changed. I think there was always a disconnect between what they believed and the reality of those beliefs." She stopped washing and turned to me. "It's easy to be open-minded in your head, and even in your heart, but it is a lot more difficult to embody that in your actions and your relationships."

Chapter 44

Damon the Good is checking my plumbing. I wonder why they have to check these tubes so often; it's not like I move around or shake them loose. He's humming. He is always humming or singing. I love it. I remember that Danielle brought in a CD player and some music. I'd like to hear Louis and Ella again. I don't have blinky-blink words for that. The closest I have is "sing," so I give it a try.

"Hey, Isaac. You said something? Sorry, I missed it."

Sing.

"You'd like me to sing?"

Maybe.

"Maybe? Are you fooling with me?"

No. Maybe.

He laughs loudly. "Let me think a minute."

Yes.

"You want music? A CD?"

Yes. He is a smart young man!

"OK, then. I believe your favorite is Louis Armstrong and Ella Fitzgerald; is that the one you want?"

Yes.

"Then let's fire this thing up."

Thank you.

The music starts and a few moments later I hear someone else enter the room. Damon says, "Hi! D'you want to dance?"

Ginnie giggles. "Not exactly my kind of music." She remains near the door and I hear Damon move towards her. "Thanks for listening to me yesterday morning. It was good to have someone a little detached to talk with," she says.

"I appreciate your trust in me, telling me all that."

"Thank you." She hesitated, then says, "How's he doing today?"

"He's good. He requested the music."

"Yeah. I remember he played this often when we visited. I think it reminds him of his wife, Virginia, whom I'm named after. She was quite a woman."

Yes she was!

"Oh - look at the time! I gotta go," Damon says. "Do you want to do breakfast again?"

"Sure. Same time, same place."

"Good. See you in about half an hour."

Ginnie sits down beside me.

"Did you hear all that?" she asks.

Yes.

"No matter. He's a good guy and easy to talk to. But, don't worry, Grandpa, he's too old for me; I could see us being friends, though."

Good.

"Did he give you your date-stamp?"

No.

"Well then; it's around seven-thirty on Friday morning, June seventh. It's drizzling, and it's supposed to continue drizzling all day."

Thank you.

I hear her fidgeting. "So, I think I've decided to take a year off before grad school. I need the time to be sure I'm going in the right direction. My deal with my folks was that they'd pay for my undergrad degree, but I'm on my own after that. There's not a lot of scholarship money out there for post-grad Liberal Arts studies. I need to be damned sure of what I want to do before I put myself fifty-thousand dollars in debt! "

That's a lot of money. Ridiculous. When Virginia went back to school in 1947 to get her Masters of Education it cost a few hundred bucks a year - I imagine that's less than two thousand in today's money.

***

Virginia and I had not made a big deal of the presents waiting for the boys under the Christmas tree; in fact, we had not mentioned them at all, and the boys had shown little interest in the colorfully wrapped boxes. I think they thought the boxes were part of the decoration. We came downstairs to find Bea sweeping the parlor. Virginia went directly to the kitchen to start the coffee while the boys and I waited for Bea to finish her work. "Thank you for doing the dishes," Bea said, "It was a great help."

"You're welcome, Bea. I hope you have a good day with your family."

"I'm looking forward to it." She continued sweeping.

Albert and Mark sat in front of the tree; it looked different in the daytime - less dramatic, although the colors we more pronounced. Virginia came in, "Come to the kitchen, boys, your breakfast is ready."

Bea smiled at her.

"They might as well eat now," Virginia said, "They can't open their gifts until my parents come downstairs, anyway."

The four of us went into the kitchen, leaving Bea to finish in the parlor. "Granny bought Wheaties for you, Albert, and we've got applesauce that Bea made for you, Mark." We helped the boys onto their chairs by the kitchen table. She poured milk for them as I poured coffee for us and then sliced bread for toast.

"When do you think they'll be up?" I asked. "It's after eight o'clock. I'd like to be on the road by ten."

"They'll be down soon. I've never known them to sleep late. Do you want anything else for breakfast?"

"Toast and butter will be enough. I think I'm still full from last night."

The boys finished their meals and we all returned to the parlor. Bea had lit a fire and we drew near to it. "I'm going up to pack our things so we can leave on time," Virginia said. "I'll listen for my parents and come down as soon as I hear them."

Mark, Albert and I sprawled on the rug in front of the fire, playing. We were getting pretty rowdy and did not notice that Virginia and her parents had entered the room until they were all standing over us and laughing. "Well, I think you should crawl over to the Christmas tree because there is something special waiting for you," Mr. Appleton said.

Albert began to crawl and Mark mimicked him, as did I. I remained on the floor with the boys and watched as Mrs. Appleton gave them each a colorful box. "You can open them, boys," she said. Albert ripped the paper off and opened the box inside and pulled out a bright red cast iron automobile.

"Car!" he shouted, and began to push it across the carpet while emitting beeps and roars.

"Just like Daddy's," Mr. Appleton said.

Virginia helped Mark open his box to discover a large soft Teddy bear wearing a blue cap. Mark hugged the bear tightly then flopped forward onto it. A similar bear, but with a red cap, emerged from another box for Albert. Mark also received a set of brightly colored stuffed fabric blocks with pictures of animals.

I'm pretty sure those bears are still around; Albert had his by his bedside when he was dying. Its hair had mostly been worn away, but both eyes were still bright and the red cap still sat happily on its head. Danielle says she has it now next to her bed. Mark's bear stayed with us, of course. Virginia kept it on her dresser, and it remained there until I had to sell the house. It got put into a box; I'm actually not sure where it is. I wish I could ask Allen.

***

Louis and Ella have stopped. I don't remember Ginnie leaving, but I guess I drifted off, thinking of Teddy bears and toys. And everyone who has gone. The thing about still being around at one-hundred and two years old is, of course, that just about everyone you once knew is dead. Not only the people you grew up with, but even the next generation. A person shouldn't outlive his children. It doesn't seem right.

I liked to paint our little ones. I would paint realistic pictures of them sleeping, playing, reading - sometimes alone, sometimes together. Then I would create a completely abstract piece that reflected the realistic one, and we would hang them side by side in our home. I only exhibited and sold the abstract halves until years after Virginia died and a gallery in Boston wanted to do a retrospective of my work. The matched pairs, of which only three remained, caused quite a stir and sold surprisingly well.

I hear movement in the room and blink that I'm awake.

"Morning, Isaac. It's good to see you."

It's Wanda. *Smile.*

"Thank you, Isaac. Dr. Jerzak will be here in a couple of minutes. He's alone this time - no students." She goes through her usual routine. "Everything's looking good. See you later."

I am left with the purring of my cat-machine. I wonder what Dr. Squeak has in mind today. I'm too old for new tests. I wish he'd leave me to my stories. I think I'll ignore him.

I hear his squeaky shoes walk up to the side of the bed. "Good morning, Mr. Simon. Dr. Jerzak here."

I don't respond. I feel him lift each of my eyelids and I think he's shining his bright light into my eyes, moving it from side to side. Then he feels for my pulse. Does he think I'm dead! I'd better let him know I'm here, else they'll be wheeling me down the hall!

I'm awake.

He does not respond.

I'm awake.

Is he messing with my head? My cat-machine begins to pick up the pace. I consciously try to calm down.

I'm awake!

He finally responds, "Good morning, Mr. Simon. Have you been doing the eye exercises?"

No.

"How about your hands - any movement there?" He picks up my right hand and asks me to squeeze his fingers. Then he repeats with the left. I'm pretty sure I did nothing, although I did make a bit of an effort. "I'm going to have the physical therapist make another try at doing something with your hands."

And then he is gone.

Minutes later Megan and Tracey arrive to bathe me. This is a busy day. They chat with each other as they sponge me, ignoring me as if I were a sack of potatoes. They roll me slowly onto my good side, and their chatting stops. "I'll get the nurse," one of them says and hurries out the room.

This is not good. I feel the cool air on my back and am suddenly aware of an itching, searing ache near the base of my spine.

"Mr. Simon, it looks like you've developed a pressure ulcer." It's Dr. Fish. "Fortunately it is still stage one. Nurse Wanda will apply a topical pain killer and a dressing, but the main thing is that we have to keep you off it for as long as possible. The nurse knows what to do. I'll check in on you tomorrow."

He leaves. Wanda tells Megan and Tracey to go, too, then she comes to the side of the bed that I'm facing and touches my cheek gently. "I need that bed sore to get some air; I'm going to prop you up with pillows so you can lean back a little and take the weight off your hip and ribcage. Then we'll dress the wound. Are you OK on your side for a while?"

Yes. Actually, it doesn't feel too bad in this position and it gives me a whole new angle on things.

***

We bundled the boys and ourselves into the Model T and drove to Lawrence to see my mother. Both boys slept most of the way. We arrived shortly before noon. My mother must have been watching out for us because she was downstairs while we were still unloading the car. She hugged and kissed the boys, then Virginia and me. "Come up. I'll put on tea to warm you up from the trip. Your faces are frozen! Lunch will be ready in about an hour."

My mother's small apartment was warm and smelled of roasting chicken and lavender soap. It had been some time since we'd visited and Albert was a little shy. He squeezed himself between Virginia and me on the sofa and clutched his bear. Mark, on the other hand, stretched out his arms to his Nana and she picked him up and walked slowly back and forth across the kitchen singing a tune which I recognized was from the picket line. I smiled; she wasn't going to let that part of our story go away.

"I need to get the vegetables going," my mother said. "Take the little one." She handed Mark to Virginia, and as she did this I noticed her wince.

"Are you all right, Mama?"

"Yes. Yes. Just the normal aches and pains of old age."

"You're not that old, Mama."

"I'm forty seven. When you work where I work, that's ancient." She dropped a pile of potatoes on the table and started to peel them. I moved to help, but she told me to stay on the sofa.

"How much longer do you intend working?" Virginia asked.

"It is not a matter of intention, my dear. It is a matter of necessity. Most likely, I'll work till I drop dead one day at my machine." She chuckled, "Hopefully I won't fall forward - that can get kind of messy."

"Mama! That's not funny."

"I know, but it's the truth."

By now Albert and Mark had both found their way to the floor and were becoming noisier and more active. It was a small room with a hot wood-stove in one corner. I parked myself on a chair near the stove to make sure they couldn't get to it, while Virginia moved to the table to help with the vegetables. It was amazing that families survived in these apartments, with kids running around amongst all the hazards of daily life.

And then I suddenly thought of Roland Ramsay who I hadn't seen since Christmas Day five years before. I wondered if he would return to that spot downtown where we had last met.

"How long before we eat, Mama?"

"Half hour, maybe forty-five minutes."

"I have to take a quick walk." I put on my jacket. "Albert, come with me. There's someone I want you to meet." Virginia squinted at me. "I'll explain when I get back."

I helped Albert into his coat and hat and gloves, picked him up and hurried down the steps into the street and half jogged towards the center of the city. Ten minutes later I turned onto the street where we had met years before, and there he was, standing in front of an easel near the same low wall.

"You see that man, Al? He's an old friend. We used to work together before I even knew Mommy."

I called his name, and Roland turned. He was smiling and raised his deformed right hand in the air. "It's so good to see you, Isaac." We embraced. "And who is this young 'un?"

"This is Albert, my oldest. He's two and he has a one-year old brother, Mark."

"Pleased to meet you, Albert, my name is Roland" He nodded his head toward Albert, who wriggled and smiled.

"He's a little shy."

"Of course. One is always a little nervous about meeting new people," he said, then continued, "I've been coming here every Christmas day. I hoped you would show up, but then I heard through the grapevine that you had moved to Boston. I continued coming, anyway. I like the quiet in the middle of the city."

"I somehow had a hunch you'd be here. My mother is doing a big meal for us; we can only stay a minute or two."

"Well, I'm glad you showed up. What are you doing now, Isaac?"

"I'm an architect. I'm also painting as much as the job allows. We live in Cambridge. How about you?"

"Believe it or not, I am working as an advertising artist for a different paper. We have another child, Adam. He's the same age as your Albert here. We're all good."

Albert was staring at the bright colors of the painting that Roland had been working on. "Paint," he said.

"Yes, my friend Roland is a painter, just like me."

I heard a church bell chime. "We have to rush off, Roland, but I'm so glad we had this brief time. Our best wishes to your family."

"Yours, too, Isaac. Next year?"

"I'll do my best to make it."

My mother was quiet through most of the meal, except for sporadic little coughs. These, coupled with periods of shortness of breath, were not good signs, but she refused to talk about her health. She kept her eyes and the conversation on Albert and Mark. After dinner Virginia helped her clean up while I took the boys for a walk to look at the frozen river.

The sun was low, casting long shadows of trees and skaters on the ice. Albert was fascinated by the people whirling around on the ice. "You need to be a little bit older before you can do that, Al. Maybe next year, when you're three." That did not pacify him one bit. He wanted to be out there and he began crying when I said we had to leave.

As we got the boys situated in the car, my mother kissed them. "Albert, Mark - I'll see you next weekend." She kissed them again, then embraced Virginia and me.

"Thanks, Mama," I said.

"It will be nice. I'm looking forward to it."

***

My ribs are killing me. I don't know how long I've been lying on my side - but it's too long. I listen to hear if anyone is around, but all I hear is my cat-machine. The burning pain of the bed sore continues. What do I do? I'm dependent on their routine, and their adherence to that routine. Someone has to come through here at some appointed time, so long as there are no distractions, emergencies or random omissions. I have no control, no way to call out!

The purrs of my cat-machine speed up. Perhaps I do have some way of getting their attention. Perhaps the calm-down trick that I learned in the trenches can be reversed and I can increase my level of agitation. I begin shouting, "No! No! No! No! Dammit! Dammit!" in my head and the pace of my cat-machine increases to the point where it emits a series of beeps. Wanda arrives moments later.

"What's happening with you, Isaac?"

Pain.

"You hurting?"

Yes. Pain.

"The bed sore?"

Yes.

"I'll apply some more of the local pain-killer." She removes the dressing and rubs the cream around my tail bone. "There. That should help."

Pain.

"Give it a minute, Isaac."

Pain.

"I said ...," she stops. "You have pain somewhere else as well?"

Yes.

"Your leg again? Your old wound?"

No. At least not now.

"Your side?"

Yes.

"Shoulder?

No.

"Ribs?"

Yes.

"You're feeling pain in your ribs because you are lying on your side?"

Yes.

"Hmm, that's something I feared might happen. We have to keep you off that bed sore because if it gets worse it can become infected and then it's really a problem. And, of course, we can't put you on your other side because of your bad shoulder. Let's try adjusting the pillows. I need to get some help."

When I was in the hospital in France and the nurses were setting me up on that traction contraption they would always tell me to focus on something pleasant. I always would think about Mama and her determination and courage, and her powerful singing on the picket line. And so I thought of her again, standing on that box and breathing fire in the faces of the paid goons and militia men.

***

I met my mother at the Harvard Square station on the afternoon of New Year's Eve. She had one small suitcase for the weekend, and a shopping bag from a toy store in Lawrence. "A little something for Albert and Mark," is all she said. "I'll give it to them after you've left for your party."

It had been about six months since she'd visited us and she could not stop commenting on my "strangely beautiful and unexplainable paintings" that shared the walls of our home with the Kandinsky William had given us for a wedding present. She was also intrigued by an early, rejected, sample of one of the dining room chairs I had designed for the Sloan house. "Why did they not like this one, Itzik. I think it's beautiful, and so comfortable for such a simple design."

"They liked it, but they wanted higher backs - Mr. Sloan is quite tall."

"Well, now you have it. Good."

We were sitting in the living room, having a cup of tea and watching the boys playing on the carpet with a pile of colored wooden blocks. "They play well together," my mother said.

"Most of the time," Virginia said, "but they do have their moments."

"Of course; they're people," my mother replied and moved herself to the floor beside the boys. "Can I play too?"

Albert laughed and hugged his grandmother. Mark climbed into her lap. She started teaching them a clapping game and the song that accompanied it. I remembered the song, but I had no recollection of my mother ever being down on the floor with Chaim or me. I had never thought of her as playful. I hurried off to my studio and returned with my sketchpad and pencils.

Virginia sat watching, a huge smile on her face. Finally she stood. "I'll get supper ready for you and the boys, Mom," she said, and she ruffled my hair as she passed me on the way to the kitchen.

I managed to almost complete one quick sketch before the game broke up and their supper was ready. My mother led the boys into the kitchen while Virginia went upstairs to start getting dressed for the party. I remained in the living room finishing up the sketch and listening to my boys chatting and laughing with their grandmother. Then I raced upstairs to change.

Virginia looked beautiful. She wore a round-collared long-sleeved steel blue dress that flowed from her slim shoulders down to below her knees. Over this she wore a matching deep V-necked long jacket with darker blue pockets on the hips and the same dark blue wide bands around the bottom edge of the jacket and the cuffs. A bright red scarf complemented the ensemble.

"You look lovely, my dear," my mother said, "Doesn't she, boys?"

"Lovely," they said in unison.

"Have a nice time with Nana, boys. Be good, OK."

"We'll have a good time. And I'm sure you will, too."

"We'll be home late," I said, "long after midnight."

William had distributed maps and instructions on how to get to his house, situated on a small side street in Concord, overlooking the Sudbury River which curved through the town. We arrived shortly before nine o'clock. There were at least twenty cars parked on the street and along the driveway leading to the house, which featured large areas of glass walls and was lit up in colorful lights. We could hear the jazz band as we walked towards the house. "This is going to be fun," Virginia said, and she reached up to kiss me.

A butler took our coats and led us towards the music. "Drinks are on the table on your left," he said, "You'll find Mr. Carpenter there."

The five piece jazz band was set up on a platform in the far corner and many people were dancing, but I was immediately taken by the house itself.

The house had an open design: there were no walls between the living room, the dining room and the kitchen. This large space was divided only by the flooring material, the furniture, the lighting, and a few free-standing screens displaying abstract paintings. The wall facing the river was all glass. It was a remarkable place - wide open, but at the same time, comfortably intimate. The man was a genius; one could see it and feel it.

"We should say hello to William before we hit the dance floor," I said, and we made our way through the crowd to the drinks table. William was there, playing bartender, and he welcomed us warmly. "So glad you're here, Isaac, Virginia. I'm afraid the zealots will only let me serve you wine which I made myself," he said. "I have actually become quite good at it over the last few years. I recommend the red." He poured us each a glass. "Enjoy!"

I knew many of the people who were there, either as colleagues or clients of the firm. The Sloans were on the dance floor and I pointed them out to Virginia. "I'll introduce you to them when we get a chance." Waiters circulated with trays of finger foods, cheeses and glasses of wine. The music alternated between sedate waltzes and fox-trots and freer more boisterous dances. It seemed like almost everyone had learned the Charleston and Virginia and I soon found ourselves caught up in the revelry. We hadn't let go like this since before the boys were born. It was exhilarating and exhausting.

The band took a break just before eleven-thirty, promising to return to play us into the New Year. I noticed the Sloans standing alone admiring a Kandinsky that was hanging on one of the divider panels. Mrs. Sloan saw us approaching and reached out to hug me. I think she had been enjoying William's wine. "So nice to see you, Isaac! And this must be Virginia who you have talked about so much." She hugged Virginia. "This is my husband, Ernest."

"Pleased to meet you, Mrs. Sloan," Virginia said. I detected a note of embarrassment and caution in her voice.

"Please, call me Lizzie."

"You are building a lovely house," Virginia said, "Isaac has shown me some of the watercolor renderings."

"William and Isaac are wonderful, brilliant and so creative. I cannot wait to move in." She turned to me. "Are we still on schedule for March?"

"I talked with the construction supervisor the day before yesterday; everything is still on track. The furniture and the lamps are in process, too."

"How about those paintings we talked about?"

I was rather surprised by this question. Our "talk" was little more than her saying that she'd like to commission me to do some paintings. There was nothing definite about how many, how big, how much or when, and making those decisions at a party with someone who was not exactly sober did not seem like a good idea. On the other hand, here was an opportunity I could not walk away from.

"My time has been concentrated on the house, but..."

"Lizzie," Virginia interjected, "perhaps you and Ernest would like to come by Isaac's studio one evening next week to look at what Isaac has been working on. I'm sure you'll be impressed."

I was stunned at Virginia's bold but practical suggestion.

"Excellent idea, my dear. We would love to do that, wouldn't we, Ernest?"

"Absolutely. Isaac, I'll telephone you at your office to set it up."

The music resumed with a splash of vibrant sound and the singer broke into "Sweet Georgia Brown." Everyone was up on their feet, swaying and dancing, and singing along. I noticed that William was not dancing; he remained near the drinks table, not drinking, but looking intently at the party swirling around him. As I watched him, the butler approached him and they stood close together without talking. I saw the butler look at his watch and then say something to William.

William made his way toward the band and climbed onto the platform. The music stopped. He stepped behind a microphone. "I want to thank every one of you for coming this evening to welcome in 1926. It is now one minute to midnight by my watch, so we will begin the countdown shortly. Let me also thank this fantastic band - The Fivespot - for their music tonight." The crowd cheered and whistled. William held up his hands. "The music will continue for another hour, so don't run away." More cheers.

He held his pocket watch high. "All right, then. Ten, nine..."

A moment after he called midnight, the band struck up a chorus of "Auld Land Syne," and then immediately broke into a raucous rendition of "Yes, sir, that's my baby." William returned to the drinks table, the butler exchanged a few words with him, and then returned to the entrance hall.

Virginia and I did not get home until almost two o'clock. As we were leaving the party, William pressed a bottle of his red wine into my hand, insisting that the festivities should not end so soon. My mother and the boys were asleep, but Virginia and I were still bubbling with the fun of the evening. We sat together on the couch and I poured us each a glass of wine.

"That was a mighty bold invitation you made to the Sloans. I'm in awe of you!"

"Sometimes you forget that I know rich people, Itzik." We both laughed at her use of my mother's nickname for me. "And the ones who are patrons of the arts like nothing more than to see the artist in his natural surroundings - his studio."

"I should probably sweep and neaten the place up a bit."

"No, no, my dear man - the patron enjoys the raw ambiance of the studio."

"I have so much to learn!" I sipped my wine and leaned into her.

"You do. And the Sloans can be a doorway to others. I really think we should take the opportunity of their visit to see if she can recommend you to a gallery in Boston."

"Really?"

"Really. Isaac, your art is good and deserves to be seen. Like everything else in life, it is all about who you know. You know the Sloans; they expect you to seek their support in the art world."

Chapter 45

Lizzie and Ernest Sloan arrived at our little house in their black and gray Packard Phaeton at eight-thirty on Thursday. The boys were in bed, and Virginia and I had raced around the place picking up toys and straightening up the living room. "How charming," Lizzie exclaimed as Virginia opened the front door. I took their coats.

Lizzie advanced slowly across the small entry hall into the living room, stopping every so often to take in the paintings on the walls. "I do love your work, Isaac. Marvelous!"

"Let me take you through to the studio." They followed me down the short hallway. I had hung a few paintings and had propped a few more against the walls, but, on Virginia's advice, had left several in a stack one behind the other just inside the door. My canvas drop-cloth was on the floor under the work table and easel which held a canvas I was still working on.

The Sloans circled around the room staring at the paintings, then flipped slowly through the pile by the door. They conferred with each other and selected one of the paintings from the pile. "I do so love what you have here, Isaac, and I think we will take this one for the entrance hall, but we need larger works for the big room. So, we would like to commission three paintings, each about four feet by eight feet."

"Thank you."

"We're planning a house-warming party for the first Saturday in April; we would very much like to have the paintings by then. And of course, you two must come to the party," said Lizzie, and she gave Ernest a little nudge.

Ernest cleared his throat. "So, we should deal with the financial matters. First, how much is the work we selected?"

I looked at Virginia; I was never good with the money side of things. "That painting is eighty dollars, Ernest," she said.

He didn't respond, other than to ask if we would accept his check. I was the one a little shaken by the price; eighty dollars was two weeks' pay for me! But Virginia continued; "For the three paintings, each more than twice the size of this one, I think four hundred and eighty would be in order, payable, of course, when the works are delivered."

"That's not unreasonable," Lizzie said. "Let's shake on it!"

"I wish I could offer a drink to seal the deal," I said.

"Oh, we have some Champers in the auto," Lizzie giggled. "Ernest, dear, why don't you take the painting to the auto and bring in the bottle?"

I didn't ask how they managed to have a bottle of champagne five and a half years after the start of Prohibition. I knew that wealthy people operated by their own rules. I walked with Ernest to the Packard, while Virginia and Lizzie went into the living room. He wrapped the painting in a blanket then placed it behind the front seat and retrieved the bottle of Champagne. "I'll write the check as soon as we get inside. I would hate to forget it."

Ernest joined our spouses in the living room while I went in search of four champagne glasses - not an easy undertaking. I knew we had received a set of eight as a wedding gift, but since we never used them I had no idea where they might be. It took a full ten minutes before I located them on the bottom shelf of a storage closet in the pantry. They were pretty dusty, so I had to wash and dry them before bringing them into the living room.

"Isaac, Lizzie says she has a good friend who owns a new gallery on Clarendon Street."

"Yes," Lizzie said, "Marjorie specializes in avant garde artists: she is looking for people to represent. I think she'd snap you up."

"What's the name of her gallery?" I asked.

"Nouvelle Vision. It's in the first block down from Boylston."

"Thank you. I'll try to drop in sometime next week."

"I'll send her a note telling her to expect you."

It's all about connections!

***

Allen is here. He is talking with someone I don't recognize. They are speaking too softly for me to make out anything that is said. It's a weird situation I am now in; for a long time, before they knew I could hear them, the people who came in here acted like I was no more than a lump in the bed that breathed every now and then. They said whatever they wanted to say. When they figured out I could hear them, two things happened - some people began to talk to me almost expecting a conversation, or if not that, at least a sounding board for their problems and uncertainties. Or, they withdraw, having quiet conversations out of earshot from me, which, frankly, I consider rather rude. If you are in my space, you should not be having private conversations, you should not exclude me.

Finally, the stranger leaves the room and I feel Allen rest his hand on mine. I blink to let him know I'm here.

"Good morning, Grandpa Isaac. I see they have you propped up on your side. The nurse was telling me that you have the beginnings of a bed sore."

I am painfully aware of that fact.

"Are you doing OK?"

Yes. What the hell else could I say? Relative to a lot of other situations I've been in, I'm OK.

"It's Saturday morning, June eighth, around ten o'clock. The weather is perfect; mid-seventies, dry, sunny, light breeze."

Thank you. I'd love to go for a walk. I wonder if they can move me to a wheelchair without breaking me. Wheel me outside where I could feel that sun and that breeze.

"I plan to waste the rest of the day on the deck reading a cheap suspense story and drinking beer. Martha is spending the weekend with her sister in New York. If I get a little ambitious, I might even do some preliminary work on the next novel; I have a pretty good idea on the main characters and the general direction and key elements of the plot." He stops abruptly. "Sorry, I don't need to bore you with that."

No.

He laughs. "So, Ginnie has decided to take a year off before grad school. I think that's a good idea; she's had to deal with an awful lot. A break from the stress will do her good. Do you agree?"

Yes. Although, Allen, I wish I did not detect a note of concern in your voice. I wish I could provide a more nuanced response. Yes, I do think she could benefit from a break, but I also fear the interruption could become an ending of college. I fear her grief could take her down a dark path. On the other hand, I've always thought of her as a smart, creative person - even when she was quite little - so I am confident she can re-create herself and move on without Jake. So, Allen, in response to your question about whether I think a break is a good thing for Ginnie, my answer is "Yes, with reservations, but I would never tell her that."

He stood and began pacing, which was a sure sign he had something he wanted to ask me. I wish he'd just spit it out. Surely he knows by now I know what his walking back and forth means; he's been doing it since he was six years old.

He sits, at last. "Grandpa Isaac, do you remember a short while ago I said I had found letters and other papers from you and Chaim from the First World War?"

Yes.

"They are fascinating for both what they say and what they don't say."

The censor had a hand in that.

"My next novel is set in that era, and I would like to somehow incorporate those letters into the story. Are you OK with that?"

I'm not sure how I feel. If you'd been reading my mind for the last few weeks you would have the real story. Wouldn't that be something! How do I feel about my experiences, and Chaim's, being interpreted by Allen? He's a good writer, but how well does he really know me? And, of course, he only knows Chaim through those letters, documents and the stories I've told.

On the other hand, I'll be dead by the time his book is published, so why do I care? If those letters help him create a successful novel, that's great.

"Grandpa Isaac, did you hear my question about the letters?"

Yes. Give me a minute; I'm thinking.

"Can I use them?"

Why not? *Yes.*

"Thank you." He hugs me gently. "This is going to be my best work. You'll be proud!"

Realistically, Allen, I'll be in a hole in the ground. There are limits to poetic license.

***

It was three weeks before I could get an appointment with Marjorie

Ross at Nouvelle Vision. She asked me to come on a Saturday morning and to bring examples of my work. Parking near her gallery was not easy, and I circled the block a few times till I finally settled on a spot a block away. It was a cold, windy day and I had a heck of a time carrying the four oils I'd brought to show her.

She saw me struggling along, and opened the door for me as I approached. "You must be Isaac Simon. I'm Marjorie," she said in a smoky voice. "Lizzie has told me about you. Here, let me help you with that." She took two of the paintings and, without even glancing at them, led me to her desk in the far corner of the room. "Put those against the wall," she said, waving her hand at the paintings I still carried.

"I'll get us some coffee. In the meantime, take a look around."

"Thank you."

The gallery had two display areas: in the front room, the walls were hung with the works of a variety of artists. A wide archway led to the larger rear space containing a solo show of an artist I had not heard of. I stayed in the front room, looking at the works on display; I felt that my paintings would fit well in here.

She returned with the coffee and we sat down at her desk. "Lizzie says you're an architect, working with William Carpenter."

"I've been with him for about five years."

"A lovely man and a most innovative architect."

"Yes. I was most fortunate to find a position with him. He's taught me a great deal."

"He also has a keen eye for what is happening in the art world. Do you know he was one of the first to bring the works of Klee and Kandinsky to America?"

"I know. He gave us a Kandinsky for a wedding gift. He's very generous."

"He certainly is. However," she placed her coffee mug loudly on her desk and stood up, "you did not come here to talk about William. Let's look at your paintings!"

She arranged the four oils side-by-side along the base of the wall and stood back a few feet. Then she walked back and forth looking at them in silence for what seemed like half an hour, but was probably no more than a couple of minutes.

"I like your work, Isaac. I would like to have it in my gallery. So, if you're amenable, let's get the business side of things out of the way, first."

"Sure," I stammered.

I left the four canvases with her, and promised to deliver four more over the next month. She had a show of new artists planned for May and she would include my paintings. As I drove home that cold January morning it suddenly struck me that I was a "professional" artist. I wasn't sure what that meant, but it felt very, very good!

***

Chanel Number 5. Danielle.

I'm awake.

"Hello, old man! It's nice to see you. I bumped into Allen on my way in. He told me about the bed sore. Does is hurt a lot?"

Yes - no.

I've been thinking about taking a wheelchair ride in the sun. I need to create new words. I blink that I have a ten-letter word.

"Ten letters?"

Yes.

It is a tedious process, especially since the first letter, "w," is way down at the end of the alphabet, but when we get to the "c" Danielle says, hesitantly, "Is your word 'wheelchair'?"

Yes.

"Do you want a ride in a wheelchair, Isaac?"

Yes. New word.

"Another word?"

Yes. This one is short - three letters. Soon we have established the signal for 'sun'.

"So, you would like to take a ride on a wheelchair in the sun?"

Yes.

"That would be lovely. It's a gorgeous day out there. Let me find a nurse and we'll see if that's possible." I hear her walk quickly from the room.

This is exciting, I can almost hear birds singing, smell the lilacs. I feel my body drifting, hovering over Virginia's garden behind our house. We had a huge wild blueberry bush that produced thousands of berries year after year. One year I put a net over it to keep the birds from eating all the fruit, but I ended up trapping a pair of cardinals. Virginia saw them struggling to get out and she had a terrible time freeing them. After that we decided to share; the birds got most of it, although one year a red-tailed fox enjoyed the berries, too.

"Isaac. I talked with the nurse and she said she needs a doctor's approval to move you. She's trying to contact someone. I hope it doesn't take the whole damned day!"

Smile.

"What are you smiling about? I'd be pissed if I were you."

Smile. What else can I do? I'm at the mercy of everyone around me. I have no option but to take it as it comes. Not that I like it.

Danielle sighs deeply. "How about some adventures of Pooh Bear?"

Yes. I'm not really in the mood for it, but at least it will get her out of her huff, and it will pass the time.

The story is interrupted by a nurse who says the doctor was afraid that riding in a wheelchair would put too much pressure on my bed sore and he wants to wait at least another couple of days before letting me take a ride.

"Sorry, old man. The doctor's probably right." Danielle kisses me on both cheeks and continues reading.

***

William returned extremely angry from a visit to the Sloan house in late February, just a few weeks before our target completion date. One of the large glass panels in the big room had been blown out during a heavy, windy three-day snow storm. The shattering glass had gouged the wooden floor and snow had swept into the house and ruined the finish on a large section of the floor. On closer examination, he had determined that the glass had been improperly installed. He checked the other panels and found similar concerns; we were lucky only one of the six had given way. It was also fortunate our furniture delivery was late, or we might have lost some of that, too.

"I don't believe you have ever heard me raise my voice, Isaac, but I blasted Ballard and his crew. This is bad and our insurance does not cover poor craftsmanship. I certainly hope Ballard is covered or this could be an unspeakable disaster!"

He was standing in the doorway to my small office.

"We don't need this shit, Isaac!" He flopped down onto a chair. "We've put too much into this to be upended by incompetence!" He buried his face in his hands and sat silently. Finally, he straightened up and said, "Other than this little disaster, the place looks spectacular. It has really come together. I love it, and the Sloans will love it, and all their friends will be jealous!"

"Will we make their grand opening on April third?"

"Yes, unless some other thing blows up in our faces. Lizzie Sloan said they commissioned a few paintings from you. Congratulations!"

"Thank you. But, getting back to our immediate problem, are the floor boards repairable?"

"Those that are gouged will have to be replaced, then we're going to have to re-sand and re-finish the whole damned area to ensure consistency. Fortunately, we do have enough boards available."

"How soon can we get the glass?"

"I telephoned the glass company. They can't deliver until March eighth. I was hoping to hand over the keys to the Sloans on the twelfth, but that's out of the question, now."

"Do you want me to tell them?"

"No. That's my job."

The next week I drove up to the house. Thankfully, I had not been involved in the negotiations with Mr. Ballard and the insurance companies. Judging from William's mood and occasional comments during those few days after his visit, things had been mostly sorted out. The Sloans accepted the postponement of their move-in date to March twentieth. This was their summer home, after all; it was not as if they were waiting on the sidewalk for their new place.

It had been two weeks since my last visit. I found Mr. Ballard in his make-shift office, reviewing drawings and piles of paperwork. I greeted him, but he barely acknowledged me. I decided I would avoid him for the moment.

Despite the obvious sheets of plywood in place of the glass panel in the big room, there had been tremendous progress in the house. The main wing was complete, except for the installation of the kitchen appliances and cabinets. The guest rooms were receiving their final coat of paint. In the big room, the floor had been redone, all the wall and ceiling paneling was installed. Two men were working on the stone surround for the fireplace. None of the lighting fixtures had been installed.

Outside, despite the cold and the coating of snow on the ground, men were working on setting the stone for the patio. I walked all around the house a couple of times then went down to the lake, which was still frozen.

I heard someone crunching through the snow behind me and I turned to find Mr. Ballard. "Sorry I was so short with you back there, Mr. Simon. This glass business has set me on edge. More paperwork than I've ever seen. Damned insurance companies! And lawyers!"

I was surprised by the mention of lawyers, but decided not to pursue the matter. "Assuming the glass arrives by the eighth, Mr. Ballard, when do you think you'll be all done?"

"I plan to pack up my things, pick up my check and be out of here on the seventeenth. So, I'd like to do the final walk-through on the fifteenth."

"I noticed none of the turned wood lighting fixtures are up."

"Ah, those. We have not received them. I meant to tell Mr. Carpenter last week, but, well, you know about that."

"I do. I'll talk with Mr. Carpenter about the lighting first thing tomorrow."

"I have the electrician waiting. He's not happy and he's not cheap; those fixtures were supposed to be here two weeks ago."

"I'll find out what's happened to them."

"Good. Thank you. Anything else, Mr. Simon?"

"No, Mr. Ballard. It's looking good."

"It's the most beautiful home I've ever worked on." He made his way through the snow back to the house, stopping to inspect the work on the patio along the way.

***

Someone is sitting on the chair next to my bed. I can hear the breathing, but I have no idea who it is. I listen intently for clues. Nothing. I'm pretty sure the person is reading a book; I hear pages turning. I blink that I am awake.

"Good evening, sir." That tentative voice, soft. I know him. "It's Patrick Dolan, Mr. Simon. Do you remember me?"

Yes. How could I forget that beautiful voice of the student with Dr. Gravel-pit?

"You said I could visit you. Is that OK?"

Yes. Smile.

"Forgive me; I am slow in learning your language. I caught the 'yes' but missed the second word."

Smile.

"You want me to smile?"

Here's a dilemma. Of course I want him to smile. I want everyone to smile, but that is not what I meant. I signal 'maybe.'

"I'm sorry, Mr. Simon, I didn't get that."

Maybe.

"You said 'maybe'?"

Yes.

He took some time to respond. "So, maybe you want me to smile, maybe not. But that isn't what you were saying. Right?"

Yes.

Again, a long pause. "You said that you are smiling."

Yes. Laugh.

"Now you're messing with me. You're also laughing."

Yes. Hug.

He laughs then squeezes my hand gently. "I'm so happy you said I could visit you." That tentative quality has returned to his voice. "I'm doing my neurology residency here. I'm far from home and I'm missing my family. I don't think about them much - I'm so busy, spending long days in the hospital, studying, conferencing - but, when I have even a little down time, I don't know what to hold on to."

I can understand that; that feeling of being adrift, unconnected in the midst of chaos.

He was still holding my hand and I sensed a slight tremor in his. "I come from a small town in Southern California, a place called Tehachapi. Have you ever heard of it?"

Yes. I'm not sure why I know the name, but I definitely do. It's such a lovely, musical name.

"Really? Have you ever been there?"

I don't think so. I answer "No".

"My grandparents moved there from Delaware in the nineteen-sixties. They thought the clear desert air would be good for his health. He died when I was in my second year of med school in San Francisco. You remind me of him; he had long white hair and a beard to match. He had a great sense of fun and always had a way of making people feel good."

Patrick's voices trailed off and his breathing slowed. I began to think that he had actually fallen asleep; I know medical residents are overworked and are forced to endure long shifts. I waited a while, not that I had anywhere else to go. Tehachapi - where had I seen the name?

"Oops. I almost dozed off," Patrick said. "I also forgot the first requirement for your visitors - the time-stamp. It is almost four o'clock on Saturday afternoon, June eighth. 2002. I actually have a few hours before my next shift so I'm going to run back to my apartment for a nap. Can I swing by here in a day or two?"

Yes. Smile. What an odd little visit.

"I'm smiling, too."

Tehachapi! Mark wrote about the town in a couple of his letters while he was training at Edwards Airforce Base. He talked about going to the movies there.

Mark, as I have said, was a quiet, contented baby. As he grew he reminded me of myself; he loved to play with his big brother, but he also liked to be left alone to explore. We had to watch him carefully, because he was apt to quietly slip away. We often would find him in the back yard playing in the dirt of our small vegetable patch. It was his favorite spot for years, from the time he could walk.

At first, he'd make patterns in the dirt at the edge of the patch, but then he progressed to digging up handfuls of immature carrots and beets which he arranged in patterns on the grass. Virginia was not happy. The next spring, she had him help with preparing the area for planting, and she also set aside a small section just for him. They pushed four sticks into the soil at the corners of "Mark's Acre," as they called it, and strung bright red ribbon from stick to stick to clearly mark his plot. Then they planted rows of carrots, beets and radishes.

The wait until the first sprouts of green emerged was interminable. Finally one afternoon he came running into the house. "Leaf, leaf," he shouted, and grabbed Virginia's hand to lead her outside to see the first sighting of the plants. Within a few days, Mark's Acre was all green. He was ready to taste his produce. Virginia tried to explain that he had to wait for there to be even very small edible vegetables. "Let's pick one of each kind and see how they look," she said.

"OK," he replied, dejected.

"Go ahead, Mark. Can you see that the leaves are different? These are little and curly - they are the carrots. And these are big leaves and they have little red lines in them - they are the beets. And the radishes have leaves that are smaller and not as dark as the beets."

"And no red lines."

"Right. You do look very carefully at things."

"Uh huh." He carefully pulled one of each from the ground. The vegetables were small but discernable and as he examined each one, he announced its name.

"They need to stay in the ground some more, so that they can get bigger," Virginia said.

"How do they get bigger in the ground?"

Virginia was a firm believer in what she called *in situ* education; if a child asks a question that child wants to know the answer and you need to answer it right there and then, and you need to find a way to present the answer in a way that the child will understand it. So, she explained how all things need food and water to grow and that vegetables grow because they are able to take in their food from the soil. She reminded him that he had seen her give the vegetables water. She also talked about how plants need sunlight, and they set up an experiment in which they covered a couple of the young plants with a cup. "We'll see what these plants look like after three days with no sun."

"OK." And then he got a curious look on his face, and he pointed at Virginia's pregnant belly. "Does the baby need water and sun?"

"When it's still inside me, it gets its water and food from me. After it comes out, it will need its own water and food and it will also need some sunlight, just like you."

"OK."

Emma was born on June seventeenth 1927. It was a perfect New England summer day.

Chapter 46

When I reported to William that none of the lighting fixtures had been delivered he asked me to drive to the craftsman's workshop and find out what was going on. Andre Boisvert's home and studio were set far back in the woods about three miles outside Acton, Massachusetts. I had been to the studio twice before; once in November to deliver the drawings for the fixtures, and then about a month later, with William, to see how things were progressing. At that time, Andre had rough-turned all of the pieces and had begun the painstaking process of thinning them down and smoothing them prior to final finishing and polishing. He assured us they would all be done by February first.

I arrived at the workshop to find it locked and unoccupied. I peered through a window and was able to see several of our lampshades on a workbench. I could not tell whether they had been touched since our last visit. I looked at the adjacent house and saw smoke rising from the chimney. "At least someone is home," I thought, so I went to the front door and knocked. It took some time before the door was opened by a tall, gaunt woman.

I introduced myself, and asked if I could talk with Andre.

"My husband is not well," she said. "I will ask him if he can talk with you."

She closed the door and left me standing on the front step. This gave me the opportunity to marvel at the delicate twirling vine carving on the door and its frame, and to contemplate the enormity of the problem I was facing. Those fixtures were essential to the design; as aesthetically important as the furniture, the paneling, and the lines of the house itself. Not to mention that William had already given Andre a significant check for the work.

Finally, the woman returned and showed me into the small, warm parlor where I found Andre on a sofa in front of the fire. "Please sit, Mr. Simon." His voice was weak.

I sat on a chair close to him and stared into the flames. "How are you feeling, Andre?"

"Uh! Not good."

His wife sat beside him. "As you can see, Mr. Simon, Andre is not well. He had a heart attack not long after you were here. He has not been able to work since."

"I'm so sorry. But why didn't you tell us?"

"I kept thinking I'd get better, stronger. And then..." He looked at me helplessly. "I tried to work, but could not hold the tools steady enough, and I tired quickly."

"Were you able to finish any of them?"

"The sconces are complete: all six big ones and the two smaller ones. I've also done the basic shaping of all of the shades, but the fine work and finishing needs to be done."

At least there was something to work with. "That's good. Can you recommend someone who can complete them? The clients are moving into the house in about three weeks"

He sighed. "I don't know. Perhaps Pierre Dupont. He's young but quite good. Maybe I can have him come here and work under my supervision. But three weeks - it can't be done."

Why didn't he call this person weeks ago! "I understand your situation, Andre, I really do, but you need to get this Pierre person here as soon as possible. Is there anything I can do to help?"

"We do not have a telephone. I will give you his number. Call him and ask him to come here."

"I'll find a pay phone in the town center and call him." I stood and shook his hand. "I hope you feel better soon, Andre."

He instructed his wife where to find Mr. Dupont's number, then she accompanied me to the studio and helped me load the completed sconces into my car.

I drove into town and called William to fill him in on the situation. Then I called Pierre Dupont who sounded quite young and was awed by the prospect of working beside Andre Boisvert, who he called "the master." He promised to see Andre that afternoon. I gave him the office phone number and asked him to keep us posted on the status of the work, then I called William again. He was remarkably calm.

"I think you should drive those sconces up to Ballard now," he said. "I'll contact Virginia and let her know you're on a mission and won't be home till late. Call me at home when you get back to town."

It was after ten by the time I walked into our house. Virginia was sitting in the living room, reading, and sipping a glass of red wine. "William dropped it off; he thought you'd need it." She poured a glass for me.

"Thanks. I have to call him before I can relax."

I dialed William's number. It took a while for him to answer the telephone and he sounded somewhat distracted. I told him I was back from the Sloan house.

"Would you say things are under control?" he asked.

"Well, Ballard was happy he had something, but we know nothing about this kid, Pierre, and we know there is no chance they will complete the work by the fifteenth."

"The kid, as you call him, called me before I left the office. He said he had been to see Andre, the master, and that he will start working tomorrow. He is actually moving in to their home until the work is done."

"Did we just dodge a bullet?"

"Well, we haven't seen his work yet," William replied, "but he did say he expected his work to be nearly as good as the master's. He thanked us profusely for giving him this opportunity to learn by the side of Mr. Boisvert."

I sighed deeply. "Thanks for the wine, William."

"Goodnight, Isaac. We should take a trip to Andre's workshop on Monday."

***

I am still on my side. It feels like I've been this way for days. My hip and ribs and shoulder are numb; at least there is little pain. My cat-machine is purring quietly, rhythmically. Most of my time is spent alone with Kate, the name I have just bestowed upon the cat-machine. We have a symbiotic relationship, Kate and I - we are keeping each other alive, although it's obvious which one of us has a better chance of survival.

I'm not sure what it is that Kate does. I think she has something to do with my supply of nutrition, but she also responds when I am stressed. I'm actually not even sure if Kate is one machine or more than one. In my mind, her physical form changes from boxy and clinical, to soft and feline. She doesn't move much.

We only ever had that one cat that Emma named Bunny. I wanted to get one when I moved into my apartment, but the management company wouldn't allow it. It would have been nice to have a companion, to have someone to care for. When Allen would bring me to his house I was able to sit with their cat, named Kitty-bee - a silly name that Ginnie had invented when the cat first came into their home when Ginnie was six or seven. Kitty-bee liked to sit next to me and rest her head on my thigh. She appreciated my quiet, and having her head scratched. I'd love Kitty-bee to visit me. She's calm and even-tempered; she must be around sixteen years old and probably has as many aches and pains as I have, poor thing!

Someone has entered my room. "Are you awake, Grandpa Isaac?" Ginnie says softly.

I'm awake. What perfect timing! I'm going to ask her about Kitty-bee.

"It's late on Saturday night - after ten-thirty. I thought I'd pop in for a few minutes on my way home from work."

Smile. And, perhaps see Damon the Good. I don't know if he's working tonight.

"Everything OK? I see they still have you on your side."

Yes. New word.

Ginnie hesitates. "Sorry, Grandpa Isaac, I missed that. I think you signaled something."

New word.

"You want to create a word?"

Yes.

"I haven't done this before, but I'm willing to give it a try. Danielle wrote instructions on your chart."

Eight letters.

She gets it on the first 't'! "Kitty-bee," she shouts. I can hear the laugh in her voice.

Yes.

"Kitty-bee is doing OK. She rests a lot - but, then again, she always slept a lot. She sometimes has trouble jumping up onto the bed or sofa. Other than that she's good."

Smile.

"But, why are you asking about Kitty-bee? Do you miss her?"

Yes.

She takes my hand. "I wonder if they'll let me bring her in to see you."

Yes. Smile.

"That would be so nice. I'll ask around."

Hug.

I feel her cheek against mine and her hand gently on my shoulder. "Are you still telling those stories in your head?"

Yes.

"I wish we could hook you up to some machine that could write them down."

Smile. Although I'm not sure I'd like my unfiltered mind-ramblings to become public. There are times when my thoughts go into unusual places. A person can't control what pops into his head.

***

A heavy snow had fallen over the weekend and the rough driveway to Andre Boisvert's house and studio was impassable. We parked on the side of the road and walked through the untouched carpet of snow. Smoke was rising from the chimney of the studio and the sound of machinery carried through the trees.

We found Andre in his wheelchair positioned a few feet from Pierre who stood at the lathe. One of the lighting fixtures was spinning at high speed. They both ignored us as we entered. We could not hear the instructions being given by Andre, but the tone was calm and encouraging. Pierre picked up a chisel with a rounded tip and slowly began to remove a thin layer of wood on the inside of the bell-shaped lampshade. Then he stopped the lathe and measured the thickness of the wood.

"Good, Pierre," said Andre, "One more pass and we'll be there." He turned to us. "You have come to check up on me, Mr. Carpenter?"

"We just wanted to be sure that Mr. Dupont measured up to your expectations."

"He's good. Young, but good. He moved in the day after you were here, Mr. Simon, and he hasn't stopped working."

"Do you have any idea when you will be done?"

"We started working on the smaller ones first. He's still learning and it makes sense. It will build his confidence. The bigger you go, the more the danger of catastrophe. So, if there are no catastrophes I think we can deliver on the last day of March."

"We need to focus on the seven pieces for the main chandelier," William said, and he pointed to a watercolor I had created of the chandelier design which Andre had pinned up on the wall. "As you see on the illustration, the bells are of different sizes. You have the detail drawings for each of them. Work from smallest to largest if that makes sense to you, but don't spend time on the other three shades until these are done."

"We can do that."

Pierre flipped the switch on the lathe and kissed the spinning wood with the chisel. A moment later there was a loud crack and bits of wood exploded off the machine. Pierre recoiled in shock, and turned away from us.

"Merde! Our first catastrophe!" Andre exclaimed, then continued softly, "Well, Pierre, this will give me the opportunity to show you how to start one of these from a solid block. Come, roll me to the raw blocks and I'll explain how to select the right wood."

"I think we had better leave," William said.

On the drive back to the office, William asked how my paintings for the Sloan house were progressing. "Two are done. I'm working on the third."

"So here's a question I've wanted to ask a painter of abstract art: you know how I love abstract art, but how do you know when a painting is done? I mean, in an abstract work there is nothing that tells you that the images on the canvas are complete." He waited patiently as I tried to formulate my answer.

"Perhaps art will be reduced to a single dot of color located somewhere on a white canvas. What would vary would be the size of the canvas, and the size, color and location of the dot. Someday, someone will do this, but I'm not there, yet."

William burst out laughing. "I can see that!"

"So, to return to your question; I know a work is done when I have achieved an unstable balance between movement and quiet. I know the words don't really make sense, but in a painting I am somehow aware of that uncertainty, that contradictory state."

He nodded his head slowly. "Well, I'm looking forward to seeing those paintings for the Sloans. When are you delivering them?"

"I'm meeting Lizzie and Ernest at the house on the Sunday before the big party."

We drove on in silence for a while, then William said, "I've started working on another project, quite a bit bigger than the Sloan house. It's for a country club; it consists of a large main building with dining and entertaining facilities, as well as a number of guest cottages. The client has approved the basic layout for the complex."

"Sounds interesting."

"The client is coming in first thing tomorrow. I'd like you to sit in on the meeting.

I wore my best suit for the meeting. Our client, represented by the chairman, treasurer and membership director of the organization arrived promptly at eight o'clock. William made the introductions and then moved directly into discussions on the specific requirements for each structure, followed by matters of schedule and budget.

The trio brought with them a brochure promoting their club and, during a mid-morning break for coffee, they passed one of these to me. I scanned it quickly then excused myself, saying I needed to check on something in my office. It did not take much before I found what I had expected and feared in the brochure; the club catered to an "exclusive membership that valued refinement, decorum and high standards."

I returned to the conference room and sat quietly, not quite sure how I would deal with these people. I was being asked to design buildings that I would not be allowed to enter once they were completed. I wondered whether they had already quarantined me because of my very Jewish name.

"What do you think, Isaac," William said. I had no idea what he was talking about, since I had completely lost track of the discussion. He must have seen the confusion in my face. "What do you think about the suggestion that we try to incorporate motifs from ancient Greece and Rome into some of the structural and decorative elements of the design?"

The first word that sprang into my mind was, "Bizarre," but I pushed that thought aside and said, "I think it is difficult to successfully blend classical forms into a modern design. The structures that the ancients developed were dictated largely by the materials - stone and wood - that they had to work with, and they achieved marvelous things. But we have so much more available in terms of materials, so much more variety. I think it would be limiting to try to incorporate those old elements."

"There needs to be an heroic and lofty sense to the structure," the treasurer persisted.

"Adding Corinthian columns and frescoes of chariot races won't necessarily achieve that," I said.

"Well, it's your job to find the elements that will achieve it."

"We'll give it some thought," William interjected, before I could respond.

The meeting ended shortly after that little exchange, with William agreeing to work on the idea. He and I remained in the conference room. "What the hell was that all about?" he demanded.

I slid the brochure across the table to him. "Read the first paragraph."

Anti-immigrant sentiment was rampant at the time. Laws were passed barring Asians from entering America. The KKK was at the height of its power and influence, spewing their hatred of Blacks, Jews and Catholics and non-English speaking foreigners. Lynching and mob riots plagued the South. In his infrequent letters, my friend Reuven wrote disconsolately about trials gone wrong, of Black men being convicted on non-existing evidence, and labor leaders being arrested on trumped up charges. The world-wide appeals to save the Italian anarchists, Sacco and Vanzetti, were going unheard in the courts.

I had refrained from talking politics with William during our entire association, but these issues of overt and often violent discrimination had become part of daily life, and here they were embodied in this country club project. And so I waited for his response.

He read the brochure, then slowly and methodically crushed it in his fist and threw it into the waste-basket. "Jack-asses! I don't need their bloody money!"

"Thank you!" I reached out to shake his hand.

"They most likely would not allow me into their club, either," he said. He stood and closed the door to the conference room, then sat down in the chair next to mine. "I am going to tell you something I have told only a few people, and you must promise you will not repeat to anyone else, not even

Virginia." He was staring hard into my eyes. "Do you promise, Isaac?"

I thought a moment. "In all honesty, William, I do not keep anything from Virginia, but you can be sure that she would not say anything to anyone."

He placed both hands palm down on the table, and fixed his eyes on them. "Do you remember the person who was my butler at the New Year's party?"

"I do."

"Anthony is not my butler. He is my life-partner. We have been together for years, since high school. He is the reason I have no contact with my parents."

I did not know what to say. Homosexuality was illegal. It was not talked about. Of course I knew it existed, had existed since before recorded history. The fact that there are even a couple of mentions of it in the Bible suggests that it was not uncommon, but I had never had someone openly confess his homosexuality to me. And this was my friend, my mentor, a creative genius who I respected and admired!

"You don't have to say anything, Isaac. I know what I've said comes as a shock to you, but, please think about the fact that I am now still the very same person I was ten minutes ago."

I had this image of William standing alone beside the wine table during his party, visited only occasionally and briefly by Anthony. "That's not quite true, William," I said after a long silence. "You are now a little less burdened than you were, and that can only be a good thing."

"Thank you."

"Honestly, William, I don't understand it, but I don't have to. Thank you for taking me into your confidence."

***

"Allen is elbow deep in grading papers." It is Martha come to cheer me up. Can I pretend that I don't know she's here? That probably wouldn't stop her. I have a feeling she's not unaccustomed to talking to herself. "He says he'll come by tomorrow evening."

I'm awake. I relent; I am awake, anyway.

"It is Sunday afternoon, June ninth. It was nice all day, until about an hour ago when dark clouds started moving in and it looks like it will be

411

pouring any minute."

Thank you.

"I see you're on your side. Is there a reason for this? Actually, I remember Allen saying something about a bed sore. I hear those are extremely painful. Are they giving you something for the pain? My Great Aunt Channah had bed sores; she was stuck in bed for about six months and they didn't take care of her properly and she developed them all over her back and even on her elbows. It was terrible! Does it hurt?"

No. Well, not as much as your continual prattling. I'm pretty sure she has not bothered to learn my blinky-blink signals.

"But wait, I have a surprise for you," she says, and I hear her walk to the door and close it, then I hear the sound of a zipper being opened followed by a long-ago but familiar purr.

"Kitty-bee has come to visit." I feel the cat beside me - her soft fur against the papery skin of my arm. She inches forward and lays her head on my shoulder. I feel the tears come to my eyes.

"I said to Ginnie and Allen that if you want to see Kitty-bee, then I'll bring her. I just walked right in, carrying her in a big old gym bag. No one tried to stop me, so here she is - and she looks so happy to see you!"

Thank you. Thank you. Smile.

"You're welcome, Grandpa Isaac."

I think I fell asleep with Kitty-bee rubbing her head against my upper arm.

***

Early on the last Sunday of March I drove up to the Sloan house to deliver my three paintings. On the way I stopped at Andre Boisvert's studio to pick up the seven lampshades for the big room. Pierre had done excellent work under Mr. Boisvert's gentle supervision. Andre was teary-eyed, explaining over and over how proud and appreciative he was of his protégé. Pierre, for his part, stood behind his mentor and smiled.

I arrived at the house shortly before noon on the clear but chilly day. Ernest came out to greet me and help with my cargo. The painting they had bought from me a few months earlier was hanging in the entry hall opposite the front door; it was a wonderful feeling to see it.

"Lizzie has been up here all week organizing the furniture in the guest rooms and in our sleeping quarters, and also preparing for the house-warming party," Ernest said. "I came up on Friday with the girls. They love it here."

"Lizzie was here alone all week?"

"Well, she did have one of our maids with her."

Of course. I couldn't imagine Lizzie actually moving furniture.

We carried the paintings and lampshades into the big room and set them in the middle of the floor. "I'll get Lizzie. She's busy up in our bedroom."

"Actually, I'd like to hang the paintings first and then invite you in. If you wouldn't mind all waiting in the parlor. It shouldn't be more than a couple of minutes."

"Very well. You want us to have the full effect. I understand that."

He left and I set to work. I knew where I wanted to locate each painting, so it only took a few measurements and three picture hooks nailed carefully to the walls and the paintings were up. I made sure each was straight then placed myself near the center of the room and slowly turned to take in the three works. I really liked it. The room, with the simple furniture and warm paneling, the glass front looking over the lake, and now my paintings, was an inviting and interesting space, a space one could relax in and enjoy. Everything worked so well together, and when the central chandelier was installed, it would feel even better.

I took one last look around, then went to the parlor and invited the Sloans, all four of them, to come in to the big room. Lizzie walked to almost the same spot near the center of the room where I had stood a minute earlier. She turned slowly from side to side, several times. Finally, a smile spread across her face and she placed her hands on her cheeks like a child surprised.

"Beautiful! Absolutely beautiful and so perfect for this room!"

"Yes," said Ernest, "they go perfectly."

The girls were more interested in the lampshades, one of them pretending they were hats. "Those are very delicate, and very expensive, Lydia. Do not touch them!" Lizzie said emphatically. The girls withdrew.

"Mr. Ballard's electrician will be here in the morning to install those," I said.

"Yes, William telephoned us," Ernest replied.

"I'm so happy you like the paintings," I said. "How are you finding the house?"

"We love it, Isaac. It is intimate, but big enough for us to do whatever we want to do in it. I can't wait till the summer. Nor can the girls."

"Well, I must be going. Virginia has something planned for us this evening."

"So soon? Let me have Betty fix you something for the road."

"Thank you, but I brought several snacks. I'll be fine."

"We will see you and Virginia next Saturday?" Lizzie asked.

"Of course."

"I'm sorry that we don't have enough rooms to accommodate everyone, but…"

"You can blame the architect for that," I interjected. "We'll be at the inn in Newbury."

"Along with several other of our guests."

Ernest handed me a check for four hundred and eighty dollars as he accompanied me to my car. It was the equivalent of almost a quarter of a year's pay!

Chapter 47

Someone is poking around with cold fingers near the base of my spine. I'm guessing it's Dr. Fish.

"It's looking much better."

I'm correct. It is Dr. Fish.

"Let's keep him fifty percent on his side, and fifty on his back."

"Yes," Wanda responds.

I hear the doctor leave the room and I blink that I'm awake.

"Good morning Isaac. Did you hear what the doctor said?"

Yes.

"So I'm going to roll you onto your back in a minute. OK?"

Yes. I feel her apply a new dressing over the bed sore. She takes away the pillows that are propping me up, and gently tips me backwards.

"How's that bed sore? Too much pressure on it?"

No.

"Any pain?"

No. Well, nothing I can't deal with.

"Wonderful."

Sun.

"Did you say 'sun'?"

Yes. Sun.

"You want to take a ride in a wheelchair and sit in the sun for a while?"

Yes.

"That would be nice. It's early now - before nine - but it's going to be a warm day. I'll see what I can arrange."

Thank you.

She finishes checking my plumbing. I hear her humming as she moves about.

***

The Sloan house-warming party was a roaring success. We arrived a little late, as planned, and found the party in full swing, with jazz reverberating through the surrounding woods, and the champagne flowing. The thirty or so guests were impressed with the building and all it contained. Lizzie introduced me around as the architect, furniture designer and artist, and Marjorie Ross promoted my participation in her May new artists show.

William was not there. He had called Lizzie that morning to say he had a last-minute emergency.

"He does that quite frequently," Virginia said to me. "I find it so out of character."

"No, I think I understand," I said. "I'll explain later."

We knew few of the Sloans' friends, and frankly, I still felt uncomfortable surrounded by so much finery - the silk dresses and emerald and diamond jewelry. But I recognized from a business point of view it was important for me to circulate, to be charming and even a little eccentric. Although, of course, being a working class Jewish person in this upper-crust environment was exotic enough.

During the course of the evening several people engaged me, asking about my architectural experience and philosophy, or about my paintings. Three people asked for my card, and quite a few said they would be at the Nouvelle Vision opening. I felt like I was being launched into space - terrifying and exciting.

"Let's take a walk to the water," Virginia said. "It's a lovely evening and the smoke is getting a little thick in here."

There were a few couples on the patio in quiet conversation or embrace. We stood looking out at the lake and the sliver of moon hovering low above the mountains. I put my arm around Virginia. "This is a long way from Linkeve," I said. "Although, when I'm in nature, it seems like yesterday I was tramping through those woods near the village, sketching leaves and bugs and frogs."

Virginia sighed.

"And then I turn and look at this building I designed, and all the work that went into making it, and I realize how far away I am from my beginning."

"Yes, Isaac, but you will always have that link back across time. You will always have your art."

She kissed me. "Let's go in and dance!" She grabbed my hand and we hurried back.

We were among the first to leave the party, shortly after midnight. As we drove to the inn, Virginia asked about William.

"Before I say anything, William asked me to promise to keep what he told me in the strictest confidence, even from you. I told him I shared everything with you, but I knew you would honor his request."

"I can keep a secret." There was a note of apprehension in her voice.

And so I told her about William and Anthony. She was quiet for the rest of the short journey, but when we got to our room, she said, "I had thought there was something unusual about their interaction at the party. It makes sense now."

"So, what do you think?"

"I think it's their business. I cannot imagine how difficult it must be for them. It certainly explains his reluctance to come to parties."

"Do we need to be concerned about him being with our children?"

"Gracious, Isaac, you surprise me sometimes. William is a homosexual, he's not a pedophile!"

I took her face between my hands and kissed her. "Thank you for straightening me out. But who else could I feel comfortable with to express my dark, irrational fears?"

"They are irrational fears. I know a few homosexuals, both men and women, and I know they live in fear of discovery and in fear of not being themselves. It's a difficult life. They need people like us to just be accepting of who they are, even if we don't understand it."

"During the strikes before and after the war, when strikers of different nationalities sometimes got into squabbles, my mother would say something like; 'people are people - get used to it.'"

"Your mother is one of the wisest, warmest people I know."

Virginia was lying in the bed, I was sitting in an armchair nearby, "My mother is quite amazing, but I am beginning to be concerned about her health. Did you notice when she was making snacks for the boys before we left that she was having difficulty breathing?"

"I've noticed her shortness of breath a few times."

"She also looks worn down; her skin is yellow, her eyes are sunken, she walks bent forward. But, she refuses to see a doctor; she thinks they're a waste of time and money."

"Maybe she'll listen to a woman. I'll talk with her when we get home tomorrow."

***

The lovely smell of Chanel Number 5 - Danielle. I signal that I'm here.

"Good afternoon, old man. It's a bright sunny day and Wanda and I have a treat for you!"

"I'm here with Marcus," Wanda says. "He's going to move you into a wheelchair. Are you ready?"

Yes. I wish I had a signal for an exclamation point. Am I ready? You bet!

"Mr. Simon, I'm going to pick you up now." His voice is high and lilting. I feel his one arm under my thighs and the other across my shoulder blades. And then I am floating for just a moment before he sets me down on a soft pillow. I seem to be in a cup-shaped chair with most of my weight on my upper back and legs. It is remarkably comfortable.

"The doctor said we can disconnect you from your machines for only a half hour. OK?" Wanda says.

Yes. Sun.

"Marcus is going to wheel you down the hall to the sun-room. It has a glass roof and walls, and we have the windows wide open."

I feel myself moving. I am holding my breath, listening to every sound, imagining where I am going. I remember the hallways at the newspaper where I worked as an illustrator before the war; the wood paneling and the portraits. So long ago.

We slow down, I hear a door open and immediately I feel a light breeze on my face, rustling my beard. We go over a bump and I feel the warmth of the sun pour over me. Maybe this is what the last moment is like - cool breezes and warm sunlight, movement wrapped in comforting light. There is a poem or a prayer of sorts in those thoughts.

"I'll be back when it's time," Marcus says.

I wonder what he means by that.

"What a delightful afternoon, Isaac." Danielle says. She is sitting next to me, resting her hand gently on mine.

Yes.

"Would you like me to tell you what I see?"

No. I would just like to be quiet and enjoy feeling everything I feel and hearing whatever sounds come in from the outside. I wish Kitty-bee were here, sitting in my lap. But you can't have everything.

***

"How was the party?" William asked when I arrived at the office on Monday morning.

"Good. Great music, lots of champagne and food, good weather."

"You know that's not what I'm asking."

"I know. People were exuberant in their praise of the house. It really did look and feel right. I made some contacts - we might even get some work out of it."

"Good. And your paintings?"

"Well received. Marjorie was there and she made sure to let everyone know my work was hanging in her gallery."

"So, how does it feel to be on your way?"

"A little intimidating, but good. Lucky."

"Luck has only a small part in this, Isaac. You're an exceptional artist."

"Thank you." Despite the enthusiastic smile on his face, he appeared somewhat depressed. "People asked after you, William. They missed you."

"I know I've become somewhat of a hermit," he said, lowering his voice, "I don't like to go to parties on my own, and I can't bring Anthony, so..." He turned and began to walk toward his office, then stopped and said. "I gave those country club fools a call on Saturday. I told them we had aesthetic differences. They weren't happy, but I don't really give a damn. We have plenty of other work. In fact, I need to talk with you about a new client who will be coming in this afternoon."

A month later, on the afternoon of Sunday May ninth, Virginia and I were at Nouvelle Vision for the opening of the New Artists Show. We came to town early and left the boys with their grandparents who promised them a romp in the Garden and a trip on the Swan Boats. It was a big day for them, and for me.

The gallery was crowded. For each of the seven artists represented this was our first real show, and we had all invited just about everyone we knew. Virginia sent invitations to old school and college friends, as well as people she knew from both churches she was associated with. William came, as well as most of my colleagues at the firm. My mother arrived at the same time as Roland Ramsay whom she had never met, but apparently had taken the same train with. I hugged them both, then introduced them to each other.

"I couldn't miss this," Roland said. "Do you know there is an article about your show in our old newspaper? The writer waxed eloquent, mentioning that you had once worked there."

"Publicity is good. I'm so pleased to see you. How are things?"

"We're good. Really good, in fact."

Marjorie tapped me on the shoulder. "Sorry to interrupt; the Globe wants to take a photograph of the sensational seven. Would you join the others in the back room?"

"You're a busy man. Stop by next time you're in town."

"I will, Roland. Thanks for coming."

By the end of the afternoon there were red dots pinned to the wall next to three of my six paintings. "You did very well, Isaac," Marjorie said. "In fact, the show has done well - fifteen of the forty-three works were sold today, and we will sell several more before the show closes in six weeks. I need you to bring me at least eight pieces to have in stock. "

"I'll get to work. What a wonderful afternoon, Marjorie. Thank you."

"Get those painting to me as soon as possible." She strode off to consult with another of her flock.

I squeezed Virginia's hand. "This is quite amazing! I have a lot of work to do."

"I wonder who bought your paintings," she said. "It's odd to think that pieces of you are going to be hanging in strangers' homes or offices." She laughed.

***

I feel like the rays of sunlight are lifting my body. I am held in an embrace of light. I feel no pain, no pressure. I am wrapped in gentle warmth.

"We need to go back inside now, Isaac." Danielle's voice cuts through the light. I feel like I've been dropped back into the reality of my life. A sharp pain stabs me in my old wound.

I feel the bump as I am wheeled over the threshold and back into the sterile cool of wherever I am. One of the wheels on my chair squeaks loudly. We stop. I am lifted into my bed, my plumbing and wiring are reconnected. I am back where I was.

"Did that feel good out there, Mr. Simon?" Wanda asks.

Yes. Thank you. In more ways than I could express.

"Would you like to do it again sometime?"

Yes. All the time. Day and night. It would be nice to feel the stars, too.

Chapter 48

On a brutally hot, humid day in August 1928 my mother collapsed at work. I received the urgent phone call in the middle of a conference with a client, excused myself and rushed up to the Lawrence General Hospital. She was suffering from advanced emphysema and was told she could not return to work. A week later, when she was discharged, I brought her to our home. We settled her into my studio which Virginia and I had converted into a bedroom. She felt a little better, but could not take more than a dozen steps without having to pause to regain her breath.

The following Sunday, we left her and the children at home in the care of Virginia's mother and went up to Lawrence to pack up my mother's things and to close the apartment. We had not visited her in over a month and the deterioration in her health was reflected in the state of disarray in her home - she did not have the strength or energy to take care of the place. We packed all we could into boxes and suitcases, trying not to get emotional or side-tracked by the mementoes she had kept; the letters from Chaim and me, my drawings, locks of hair, a silver spoon that I think was her mother's, photographs with names of people I barely remembered.

As we drove home with the car piled high I remarked to Virginia that I had seen nothing of my father among her things - not even a photograph.

"How long has it been since she wore a wedding ring?" she asked.

The question had never occurred to me and I could not remember when last I had seen that thin band of gold on her finger. "I think she must have sold it to help pay for the passage to America, but I'm really not sure."

The boys, now five and four, and Emma, fifteen months, loved having their Nana at home, but did not understand her inability to play with them, or even sing to them as she used to. It was not easy on Virginia, having to be available to help her on a daily basis, while taking care of the children. And my mother hated being dependent on others and not being able to contribute.

She found a role for herself; feeding Emma in the morning. She could do this sitting down and she could speak in short sentences to her granddaughter. The two would be huddled together at the kitchen table, giggling and playing while the rest of us ate our breakfast.

With my mother occupying my studio, I had to construct a new space for me to work. I built a small studio behind the house, adjacent to the garage. I saw it as a temporary solution, so I did not put any more time, money or effort into getting it built than I had to. So long as it kept the weather out and provided enough light, both natural and artificial, it would be fine. There was real pressure in getting it built; I had committed to Marjorie to do my first one man show in March 1929 and she wanted at least thirty paintings.

My mother took a serious turn for the worse three days after Christmas. I sent a telegram to Uncle Kalner who was still in New York and he arrived with Mary on New Year's Day. He sat with her, holding her hand and talking to her in Yiddish, until she died two days later.

It was a small but unusual funeral. She wanted to be cremated, and she wanted no religious "characters," as she called them, saying things about her. She didn't like them, nor did she know any of them, so why should they have the last word?

We held a memorial service in our home, with her ashes in a simple unglazed covered earthen pot placed in front of the fireplace. A few of her co-workers came, as well as some of mine and Virginia's. Her brother Ben told stories about her childhood and Kalner talked about her courage and commitment on the picket line. Virginia's mother recounted their first meeting at the Votes for Women rally in Boston where my mother had unfurled her "Freedom for Women" banner. I found myself talking about how she warned me, while somehow simultaneously encouraging me, in the early days of my relationship with Virginia. And I talked about the loss of Chaim, her first-born, and how she stoically dealt with my own abandonment of her during the war. And then I talked of the last few months with her living in our home, being a part of our family life.

She had only lived with us four or five months, but she left a huge hole. The children were bewildered by her absence and even though we explained to them that Nana was not coming back, they asked for her often, especially Emma. The death of a loved one is finite only in a very narrow sense, since we continue to think about them and remember them. For children who have not yet learned to distinguish between reality and fantasy, it seems like that distinction between being here and not being here is very unclear.

***

I am thinking how my life has changed over the last couple of days. Such small things; the sunlight on my face, the breeze in my beard, the soft purr and gentle touch of an old cat. I lie here and try to re-experience them all. I feel like I am smiling.

I remember one summer morning playing in the back yard with Emma. We were sitting on the grass and rolling a small soft ball back and forth. The cat, Bunny, joined us and started chasing the ball. Every time she caught it she'd grab it in her teeth and bring it to Emma. It was a behavior more common to a dog than a cat, unless one thought of Bunny as the hunter-cat delivering her prey to her favorite person. She did, in fact, drop the occasional dead mouse at the foot of Emma's bed in the middle of the night, an act that annoyed Virginia but didn't seem to upset Emma at all. "It's part of nature, mom," she'd say, repeating the words that Virginia had said to her after the first such incident.

I was, frankly, getting a little bored with the game so I flopped back and closed my eyes, feeling the sun on my face, focusing my vision on the changing colors and patterns playing through my eyelids. Bunny climbed onto my chest and started butting my chin with her head. "Bunny wants you to sit up and play, Daddy," Emma said.

"I'm sleeping!"

"You're not sleeping. You can't sleep and talk at the same time."

"Come lie next to me."

"OK."

I felt her rest her head on my upper arm. "Pretend the warm sunshine is like a pond and we're just floating on the pond."

"Nice. Is Bunny with us?"

"Of course. Bunny loves to be in the sun. What do you see?"

"Hmm. I see blue sky and birds."

"A few small puffy clouds."

"I see sun-trees and sun-flowers."

I smile. "What do you hear?"

"Hmm. Birds and sun-frogs and sun-Bunny splashing in the sun-pool."

"I do too. I also hear Mommy calling us for lunch."

I continue to feel that warmth, to float on the sunlight. It holds so much.

1929 was quite a year, starting with my mother's death and ending with the crash on Wall Street and the immediate collapse of the economy. In between Virginia started writing her weekly column for the Cambridge Banner on topics ranging from the speculation on Wall Street and the fragility of the economy to, believe it or not, contraception. A popular topic of the day was Eugenics, which Virginia called a "phony science designed to promote colonialism and the notion of white superiority." The proponents, many of them her fellow Unitarians, believed the Eugenics approach would over-all improve human life. There were a lot of letters to the editor and even a couple of calls from some quarters for her to be removed from her position as the religious education director at the Cambridge Unitarian Church. She stood her ground.

I had my first one man show at the Nouvelle Vision gallery and sold almost half of my paintings. In parallel with the escalating stock market prices, Marjorie had been raising the prices on my works, so by the time I received my check from her after the show, I had earned what was to me a small fortune; three-thousand, two hundred dollars!

An associate of Marjorie's from New York invited me to show my work at his gallery. I shipped four works to him in July and in September I received a large check from him and a request for more paintings.

William advised not putting the money into the stock market - he viewed that enterprise as little more than legalized gambling and backed up his beliefs with charts and graphs showing the rise and fall of stock values over the last few decades. "There is more speculation than sound investing going on right now. It can't continue," he said. He kept half of his assets in gold which he secured in a safe in his house. The balance of his money he kept in a trusted bank. Virginia was even more skeptical of the state of the economy than William; she bought some gold which we kept hidden in the house, and she spread our remaining money between four different banks. I don't know how she had the foresight, but it served us well.

The architectural firm was extremely busy and William promoted me to senior architect. He hired a junior architect and three more drafters, bringing the firm's number of employees to twelve - any more and we would have to find new office space - but we still had to work long hours to meet our deadlines.

And there were parties, many parties. As I became more acknowledged on the art scene, we were invited to more and more gatherings - fund-raisers, exhibit openings, private events. I never felt comfortable at any of these and we rarely stayed more than an hour or two. Having small children was always a good excuse to make an early exit.

One party, however, stands out. William and I had designed a modest country home for a shy, guarded young woman, heiress to a small manufacturing group that supplied the automobile and aircraft industries with a range of springs and clips. Grace had no interest in the business, and simply wanted to retire to her secluded home with her companion, Celia, and raise chickens and write poetry. She invited us to the house-warming party in early September, and it was the first time I had seen William and Anthony relaxing and having fun together.

During a pause in the music, Grace read a few of her own poems, followed by a selection from her idol, Elsa Gidlow. I remember the ending of one poem in particular;

> I shall never have any fear of love,
> Nor shrink weakly from its touch;
> I have loved too terribly and too much
> Ever to have any fear of love.

As Grace read the poems, couples drew close in silence, holding hands, embracing. There was an air of quiet defiance. I put my arms around Virginia and kissed her. "You and I have it so easy, Isaac," she whispered.

***

Damon the Good is here.

I am awake.

"Good morning Isaac. Everything's looking fine over here. You doing OK?"

Yes.

"I'm told you were in the sun room for a while yesterday. Was it good?"

Yes. More than I am able to express - even if I had translated all the words in the English language into blinky-blink!

"I need to turn you onto your side and take a look at that bed sore. Ready?"

Yes. Not that I can ever feel ready for this, but it has to happen. He tilts me gently and tucks a couple of pillows behind me. I feel him poking around near the base of my spine.

"It's looking a little better. We're going to leave you on your side for a while. Wanda will turn you back later."

Like a slow-cooking potato latke!

"I gotta go. I'm meeting Ginnie in the cafeteria for breakfast. She'll be up to see you after."

Smile. I'm not sure why I signal that word; maybe it's a knowing smile, or an ironic smile, or a smile of encouragement, or is it embarrassment?

"Don't get any ideas, Isaac. Ginnie and I are friends. I was going to say, 'Nothing more,' but that phrase kind of devalues friendship. Anyway, we share a lot and we like talking to one other."

Smile.

"And, in case you hadn't figured it out yet, I'm gay."

Smile. Hug.

Damon laughs, then gently touches my beard and leaves the room.

So, a long time ago I had thought he might be gay and I had dismissed the notion because I felt I was stereotyping men who worked in professions which in my day were generally reserved for women. It still does not mean that stereotyping is correct; all it means is I had no way of knowing then, and, in fact, no way of knowing now until Damon actually told me.

The world is a little easier for him than it was for people I knew when I was his age. The oppression and the fear were real, wrapped up in words like 'pervert,' 'unnatural acts,' 'lascivious depravity,' and more. The broader society just could not understand or accept the nature of love. Things are finally changing. I read a while ago that in the Netherlands, same-sex marriage is now legal; it can't be too long before some of the states here will follow.

"Hi Grandpa Isaac." Ginnie kisses me on the cheek. "On your side again. Are you feeling OK?"

Yes. It's good to see you.

"I had breakfast with Damon. He says he told you he was gay."

Yes.

"I told him you were a warrior from way back - you and Virginia. I told him the story about you testifying to the character of your boss who'd been arrested. Damon was quite amazed."

Who could forget that terrible time? It was the summer of 1934 and business was slow. William had all but closed down the firm; he kept one drafter and had me working for him as needed. He and Anthony took a vacation together in Martha's Vineyard. They booked separate rooms in the same quiet hotel, but some busy-body became suspicious and reported them. The police raided the place at around three in the morning and found William and Anthony fast asleep in the same bed, and bundled them off to jail where they were held for two long days before being released on bail.

The trial started on December third and lasted three days. It was a press circus. William asked me if I would be one of his character witnesses and of course I agreed. The prosecution repeatedly threw around those despicable words, trying to make the two men look like depraved perverts, pedophiles and monsters. Many people rallied around them; former clients and colleagues, friends in the art world, and people from a variety of charitable organizations that had benefitted from William's generosity. There were many who did not show support, either because they disapproved, or because they were afraid.

In the end, the prosecution was unable to prove a crime had been committed; there was no one to testify definitively that they had seen the two men even touching one another, let alone engaging in "lewd acts." They were released to a crowd of supporters who escorted them through the snow to a celebration at the Parker House bar, which had reopened about six months earlier with the repeal of Prohibition.

But the experience was devastating for William and Anthony. They went home after the party and sometime that night over-dosed on a mixture of pills and alcohol. They were found side by side in bed late the next day by an old friend who had stopped by to visit.

Virginia's column that week was an obituary for them, and she asked a simple question; is there a limit to the state's invasion of privacy? She ended her piece with a couple of lines from a poem that Grace had written in response to William's death;

I never thought you were so fragile,
but now I know how mirrors shatter.

"Are you still with me, Grandpa Isaac?"

Yes. You reminded me of a terrible time. I wonder if you were told the rest of that story.

"I'm going to visit Jake's family in Seattle. I'm flying out on Thursday afternoon and will be back on Sunday." She pauses. "After I moved out of our apartment I shipped his things to them, but I kept some of his stuff, too. Some of what I kept really should be with them - a Teddy bear from his third birthday, a photograph album from his childhood, and a few other things. I talked with his mom last night and told her what I wanted to do; she was so kind and thankful."

I hear her blow her nose and sniff. She puts her hand on mine.

"It will be hard, but I need to find a way to say good-bye. My grief counseling group is very supportive, and so is Damon." She sniffs again. "It's a process. A long, winding, back-tracking, crisscrossing, painful process."

I know. *Hug.*

***

I wish Virginia had been able to convince her father of the impending financial collapse that she saw so clearly. He had a portion of his fortune in property, but the bulk of it was in stocks and in bank interest-bearing savings accounts. When the stock market collapsed at the end of October 1929, Mr. George Appleton lost about sixty percent of his wealth. The runs on the banks which followed over the next few years and the subsequent failure of two-fifths of the banks in the country reduced his holdings even more.

By 1932, the man who previously could purchase just about anything he wanted was down to counting pennies to keep his home warm in the winter and provide food for himself and his wife. Still, he was more fortunate than most. Bea was let go. Virginia spent time with her mother teaching her how to cook, clean, do laundry and other household chores. She had to teach her how to shop: how to tell if meat was fresh, fruit was ripe, bread was moldy.

We were visiting them one Saturday in April 1932. We had come into Boston early in the day and had all spent the morning in the Garden. There were many people living there in tents and box-houses. The Victory Gardens which had been planted during the war had been reintroduced to feed the people and to give them something worthwhile to occupy a small portion of their time.

We returned to the house in silence. Even the children had been moved by the sight of so many destitute people. Mrs. Appleton served a roasted chicken with potatoes and carrots, followed by a custard pie and coffee. A somber mood enveloped the meal. When we were done, we sent the children to play in the parlor. Mrs. Appleton poured another round of coffee. "I don't think I ever realized how much Bea did for us," she said, "how much she had to know. It all seemed so mundane. But now that I am forced to do it all myself, I am astonished." She set her cup on its saucer, then leaned forward and pressed her fingertips together, a gesture of thankfulness, even prayer. "I am more than astonished - I am ashamed. We, no I, took so much for granted."

She stood and began piling the dirty dishes on a silver tray. "I found myself looking for her among all those people. I have no idea where Bea is, what became of her."

"I'm sure she's fine," Mr. Appleton offered. No one responded.

Our drive home was difficult; how do you explain to children why so many people are living in the park and are hungry? We had survived the worst of it, at least the initial impact of the depression, due to Virginia's foresight. I was working sporadically and even selling a few paintings, and Virginia continued with her column at the newspaper and her part-time position at the Unitarian church. We were doing well compared to many others, but it was impossible not to be concerned about the future.

I received a letter from my Uncle Kalner shortly after that visit to Virginia's parents. He told me he was involved in organizing the veterans march on Washington in June to demand that the government pay out the bonus now, rather than many years hence. It was a movement that was spreading rapidly and they expected more than fifteen thousand veterans to participate. He asked me to join and to bring any veterans I knew.

"I should do this," I said to Virginia and handed her the letter.

"You should."

"I think I'll visit Roland and see if I can persuade him to come, too. He and I can drive down together."

"What about Reuven?"

"Oh, I'm sure Reuven will be involved, somehow. I'll write him."

It was strange and disquieting visiting the old neighborhood. I hadn't been there since Virginia and I had emptied my mother's apartment before the start of the depression. Many buildings had boarded up windows and doors, some of which had been ripped away allowing squatters to enter. I passed a long line of families waiting for a church to open its doors to serve an evening meal, and I also saw a line of men waiting stoically outside a union hall.

I did not know how Roland was faring. I had written a letter telling him I wanted to come and see him to talk about the march in Washington. He sent a postal card in reply and said simply that it would be good to see me. I found him in the street in front of his apartment building playing catch with his children. It was wonderful that his terribly deformed hands were now flexible enough for him to participate in this game.

I parked the car a short distance away and he came over and climbed into the seat beside me. "I didn't expect to see you on a Tuesday afternoon," he said. "Not working?"

"I work from time to time. The firm is slow. We're down to only one full-time drafter. How about you?"

"I held on till two weeks ago, then they had another round of cutbacks and they got me."

"Sorry to hear that, Roland."

"My wife is still working twenty or so hours a week. We have a little in savings which somehow survived the bank bloodbath. I took it all out and hid it in the apartment - it's not worth risking keeping it in the bank. We'll be OK for a while."

"So, do you want to go on one last march with me in Washington?"

"When is that?"

"Early June."

"How long will we be there?"

"I really don't know. I've heard that many folks are bringing their families and are planning on camping there until Congress acts."

"Well, I can't do that. Are you planning on bringing Virginia and the children?"

"No. Just you and me, Roland. I can't see us staying there more than a week, but I want to show my support. I'm hoping, also, to see a few old friends."

"I'd like to join you, Isaac. Let those bastards have a piece of my mind. Give me a few days to think about it and talk it over with my wife. I'll send a card."

The game of catch petered out and the children came to find their father. "There's an ice-cream stand nearby, isn't there Roland?" I said in a low voice, "I'd bet the kids would like to take a little trip."

He nodded. "Hop in, you three," he called to them. "We're going on an adventure."

Chapter 49

Roland and I set out for Washington early in the morning of Saturday June eleventh, 1932. We spent the night in New York City at my Uncle Kalner's home. He was already in Washington, but Mary was there and she filled us in on all she knew about what was happening with the march.

She had received several letters from Kalner describing a camp that had been set up across the river in Anacostia. People were pouring in. It was well organized with places laid out for folks to erect their shelters. There were kitchens and latrines, places for musical and other performances, ball games and the like. A small city was growing every day.

One of the remarkable things, she said, was the degree of racial integration. While the military units had been completely segregated during the war, the Bonus Army that was forming was quite integrated. Kalner wrote of a concert where a Black jazz-band followed a mountain-music group and the mixed crowd cheered wildly for both and then even more loudly when the two groups came on stage together and figured out a way to blend their music.

We arrived on the outskirts of the capital in the early afternoon. We pulled into a gas station for gas and to use the restroom to freshen up and put on our army shirts and medals. The elderly man pumping gas refused to take my money - instead he gave us each a bottle of milk and a sandwich and wished us well.

The Bonus Army camp was spread out across a wide field. Roads were laid out and a kind of police force had been formed to register new arrivals, provide security and to give us directions on where to set up our campsite. They gave us a list of camp rules and a map of the place, showing where all the facilities were located. Roland and I were assigned a spot between a group of five men from the Twenty-eighth division from Pennsylvania and three men from the Buffalo division - a division made up of Negro soldiers from all over the country.

We put up our tents and organized the few things we had brought with us, then set out to explore. Near the music stage we found a large bulletin board which carried posters and flyers announcing the events for the next couple of days, including meals, concerts, several baseball and basketball games, boxing, and a chess tournament. Most prominent, however, was a call for volunteers to walk the halls of the House and Senate office buildings to lobby members to vote in favor of the bill authorizing immediate payment of the bonus. The House was expected to vote within a few days, and the Senate shortly after. Roland and I went to sign up - and there was my old friend Reuven in the tent as one of the organizers of the lobbying effort.

We hugged and I made the introductions. "So, why am I not surprised to see my old lawyer friend in this very place?" I said. "It's so good to see you."

"When I heard about this campaign I knew I could help. I've been in this city more than once over the last few years. I know those building pretty well. Some senators might say too well." He hugged me again. "Man, it's good to see you! How are Virginia and the kids? How are you faring in this crazy world?"

Reuven signed us up and told us to meet back at the bulletin board at nine the next morning. He was going to be busy for a while, but promised to look for us at the jazz concert that night. Roland and I wandered about the campsite. The larger portion of the site was set aside for families. I was amazed at how many men had brought their wives and children with them. Some had even brought their parents. As we walked, we were both looking for men we had known fourteen, fifteen years before, hoping to find some old comrades, and in some ways, hoping not to.

We approached the baseball field. A game was underway and we stopped to watch. We asked one of the spectators who was playing and were told it was the south against the north-east. As a north-east batter approached the plate Roland let out a shout, "Philip Flipper Ferguson!" The batter turned, then dropped his bat and ran toward Roland who himself was advancing toward the field. While the two men hugged and talked excitedly, everyone watched and waited without a murmur.

"That man dragged me out of the fire," Roland said, when he rejoined me. "He saved my life!" There were tears in his eyes. "He just told me he'd thought for all these years that I didn't make it."

We stayed till the end of the game and then walked with Flipper back to his camp where he introduced us to his wife and two daughters. After a short while I withdrew, saying I was sure they had a lot of catching up to do. I went back to our site, found my sketchpad and a few pencils, and climbed onto the back of my car and began to draw.

One of the neighboring Negro men came up beside me and introduced himself; "Willie Smith," he said, "from Detroit, Michigan." He extended his hand and I shook it.

"Isaac Simon, Boston."

"You an artist during the war?"

"I wish. I was in the Engineers. I dug a lot of holes, but I drew things whenever I could."

"You an artist now?"

"I am."

"Can you draw a picture of me and my buddies?"

"Sure."

He returned to his companions who were sitting on blankets on the ground, chatted with them and then said to me, "So, how should we be?"

"Just sit together and keep doing what you're doing."

"That's it?"

"That's it. Pretend I'm not here."

They resumed their conversation. It had been quite a while since I had drawn realistic portraits, but the technique returned as I got more and more into the drawing. It took about an hour, but I was able to complete a drawing for each of them. I slid off the car and handed the sketches to them.

One of the men said, "Isaac Simon? Should we have heard of you?"

"Probably not. I do mostly abstract stuff and I've only shown it in Boston and at one place in New York."

"These are really good. Thank you."

"You're welcome. It's what I like to do."

I returned to my car and my sketchpad, and they continued their conversation. I was fully absorbed in a detail of a beat-up old Model A parked right across from me when I became aware of someone standing beside me, looking over my shoulder.

"I don't remember your name," he said, "But I know you from the hospital in France." He was a big man with a painfully distorted face. His speaking was slurred as a result of his injuries.

I thought I recognized him, too. "YMCA hut, Rouen?" I asked.

"Yeah, that's it. I still have that picture you did of me. They nicknamed me Gorgeous George."

"I remember. Good to see you made it home," I said.

"Yeah. I made it back to nothing!" He shrugged. "Well, good to see you," he said and walked off.

The next morning about a hundred men gathered and received our lobbying instructions from Reuven and a couple of others experienced in this practice. We were divided into two groups - most were assigned to the House, while about twenty of us were to visit the senators, under Reuven's guidance. We then lined up and proceeded to march in loose formation towards the houses of power. We all wore our uniforms and our medals and service bars. At the foot of the steps of the Russel Building, Reuven divided us into five groups and handed each group a list of approximately twenty senators. He emphasized the importance of spending some time with each senator, rather than rushing through. This was an operation that was going to take most of the week.

I looked down the list in my hand and saw the name of Senator J. Hamilton Lewis from Illinois. A flood of memories engulfed me and a raw, visceral anger rose up inside me. "I'm not sure I can talk to this guy," I said.

"Why not? What's the problem?"

"I saw him at the July Fourth ceremony at the hospital center in France. He was such a pompous, arrogant bastard!"

"All the more reason for you to call on him," Reuven said. "Just don't slug him. Let him know that you saw him in France saying encouraging things to the troops. Use his presence in France as a basis from which to appeal to him, to influence him. Challenge him not to give up on the support he showed for the troops back then - even if you personally sensed his lack of sincerity at the time. It's a hook - use it!"

"I'll try not to kick his ass," I muttered.

Roland and I and another man, Manny DeMarco from the Yankee division decided to start with the two senators from our home state of

Massachusetts, David I. Walsh and Marcus A. Coolidge, both Democrats. We spent about thirty minutes waiting for Walsh to emerge from his inner office, then he deigned to give us five minutes of his valuable time to lecture us on the state of the economy - as if we were not fully aware of how dire things were - and why it would be fiscally irresponsible to pay out the bonus now. Senator Coolidge kept us waiting even longer, but when he finally invited us into his office, he was effusive in thanking us for our service and dedication. He asked about Roland's disfiguring wounds and praised him for his courage to persevere and find work. He remarked on Manny's Bronze Star and my purple heart. Then he shot us down with the same argument about the state of the budget.

"Let's go'n see your old buddy, Senator Lewis," Roland said.

"Why not?"

Senator Lewis had grown an impressive golden brown beard and moustache since I'd seen him in France. He welcomed us warmly into his inner chamber, asked his assistant to bring in sandwiches for us then asked us each to introduce ourselves. I was the last of our trio to speak. "I doubt you remember me, sir, but we did meet briefly."

"We did?"

"Yes, sir. At the hospital center in Rouen on July Fourth 1918. I was in a wheelchair with my leg straight out in front of me. I was seated next to a soldier from your home state who had lost both legs. The two of you had a brief but intense exchange."

He pushed his chair back slightly from his desk, bowed his head and locked his hands together, flexing his fingers several times, then said. "I remember that encounter all too well. I think about that young man often."

"Sir, there are tens of thousands of hungry veterans and their families out there calling on you and your colleagues to act, to do the right thing. We urge you to support us."

"I have not yet made up my mind on this vote. As you are all aware, our economy is in a mess. The government does not have the money to pay out the bonus. We would have to borrow, to go even further into debt. On the other hand, we here in this building are fully aware of the suffering and the need." He stood up. "Thank you for coming to talk with me. I will take your concerns into consideration."

I ignored his outstretched hand. "Senator, what we have expressed are not simply concerns - we are talking about veterans, men who sacrificed more than you can imagine, who are now living in cardboard boxes with their wives and children. This is more than a concern, sir, this is a national disgrace and you folks who pushed us into that war need to take responsibility."

The day was not going well. When we all met for a debriefing at five-thirty it was clear that most of the senators were either against us or wavering; we had found few who would definitely be with us. On the House side things looked more encouraging; the vote had been set for the Wednesday, so our leaders decided to send everyone back the next day - Tuesday - to talk with members of the House.

After we broke up, Reuven and I went to one of the dining areas for dinner. "How was your favorite senator?" he asked while we shuffled down the canteen line.

"Slimier than a slug. Although he did not definitively say no."

"Then we'll send another group to see him on Wednesday or Thursday."

With our trays laden with a large bowl of thick soup, a big chunk of bread and an orange, we found seats at one of the trestle tables. "Have you seen my Uncle Kalner around here?"

"Kalner," Reuven looked at me and smiled. "He's in a camp about half a mile from here. He was identified as a Communist and the organizers decided to exclude them. There are about a hundred and fifty of them down the road. I advise you not to go there - the security folks here might not let you back in."

"Wow. Why are they so scared of the Communists?"

"They don't want the press writing this Bonus Army off as a commie undertaking. Stupid, but not an unrealistic fear."

"I'll track him down on my way out of town."

"How long do you plan to stay, Itzik?"

"At least until the Senate votes."

"Rumor is that will be on Friday, but you never know."

"How about you?"

"Who knows? Till it's over. "

We finished eating in silence and began to walk back to our respective sites. Before we parted Reuven said, "I have a bad feeling about this situation; it's been too easy. They've let us do whatever we've wanted to do, go wherever we wanted to go. A bunch of men even took over some abandoned buildings not too far from the Capitol. The police just let them in." He exhaled loudly. "It's been too damned easy. I don't like it!"

The House voted on Wednesday in favor of the bill. Our leaders called everyone to the ball field and urged us to increase our determination and to "lobby like hell! Don't let those senators forget we are here and that they need to vote for us!"

Thursday morning over three hundred people showed up to make the final push on the Senate. Most of the senators did their best to avoid us, many not even showing up for work. Those who were in the building acted like we were out to lynch them - one even threatened to call security. We returned to our camp walking into a spectacular sunset, with the low scattered clouds burning pink and red and fringed in shimmering gold, but we could not enjoy it; it had been a long and frustrating day.

The next morning the majority of the camp assembled and then marched up to the Capitol building. We spread out over the steps and onto the lawns. We were in our uniforms and the families were dressed in the best clothing they had. Thirty people had been selected to enter the visitors' gallery and observe the proceedings. We all cheered loudly as we watched them go through the huge doors into the building.

Reuven, Roland and I were standing together when about forty members of the Capitol police arrived and stationed themselves in front of the door and along the front of the building. Minutes later our observers returned. One of the men climbed up onto a platform at the head of the steps. "The bastards voted 'No!'" he shouted, and the entire crowd started yelling and booing. Police reinforcements arrived, but most of us were more upset than angry about the vote, and the crowd soon dispersed in small groups.

"Bastards!" Roland exclaimed as we returned to the camp. "Is there any point in staying?"

"I can't see it. Let's leave in the morning."

"Drive safely," Reuven said. "I'll write to you if anything important happens."

***

Danielle is here. Sweet and lovely. Her father was such a champion for the people. How I miss Reuven!

I'm awake.

"Hi there, old friend," she says. "It's Wednesday, June twelfth, two-fifteen in the afternoon. A beautiful bright, warm sunny day!"

Smile. June twelfth? It was seventy years ago today that Roland and I joined the Bonus Army. I was just remembering it all. Strange how past and present merge sometimes.

"Are you up for a trip to the sun room?"

Yes. Anytime.

"I'll find someone to help - don't go anywhere."

Not funny, Danielle.

"Ready for a ride, Mr. Simon?"

Yes. It's Marcus, the same person who had moved me to the wheelchair the last time. He lifts me and I have that same floating sensation. I wish it could last longer, much longer, but he lowers me into the chair and we start rolling. I hear the door open and feel the breeze through my beard. We bump over the threshold into the sun. Miraculous! The warmth penetrates my body, soothing, regenerating. I feel it down to my bones and coursing through my arteries and veins, caressing my muscles.

Thank you. Smile.

After a while, Danielle says, "Ginnie's off to see Jake's parents the day after tomorrow. She's so brave. It's a hard thing she is doing."

Yes. She's trying to navigate those ever-changing seas between yesterday and tomorrow. It's hard to do, especially when you're carrying a heavy load. My mother had this expression - I'm not sure whether it's an old Yiddish saying, or if she made it up: "You can't climb a mountain with rocks in your boots." You can always look at the past whenever you want - you just don't have to drag it around with you. It's not easy.

"I had a letter from my brother, Sam; he had such a good time visiting out here a few weeks ago that he's decided to sell his condo and move back to the Boston area. I was surprised he'd leave San Diego, but he really misses this part of the world. It will be nice to have him around. I'm thinking about suggesting we share a place. Why not? We know each other well and we get along. Why should we both be on our own?"

There is a flicker of apprehension in her voice. But, the reality is that any two people thinking of sharing their living space will have some doubts. I think it's a great idea.

Smile. Good.

"I brought the Globe. Would you like me to read something? The latest Red Sox game?"

Yes. Why not.

"The Sox lost to the Rockies, three to one. Arrojo pitched seven shut-out innings, but the bullpen collapsed."

She reads on, but I soon lose interest. It was too nice a day to get wrapped up in the ups and downs of a baseball team, even the one I had supported since I was a boy. I prefer to let the breeze and the sunlight lift me up and carry me off.

***

I could not find Kalner at the Communists' camp; several people had seen him around, but no one could find him that morning, so we drove off. We were not the only ones to leave the encampment that morning. The roads were jammed with unhappy, hungry, angry people in their worn out automobiles. We noticed many broken down along the way. We stopped several times to help. For some, the problem was simply being out of gas, and we shared what we had from the two spare cans I carried. For others there was real mechanical failure and there was little we could do. Few of the men wore their uniforms.

Compared to so many of the folks we had seen in Washington and on the roads, Virginia and I were living well; our house was paid for, we both worked part time, I was able to sell the occasional painting and our savings had, thus far, survived the initial onslaught of the depression. Only one of the four banks that Virginia had put our money in had failed.

Roland's situation was different. On the ride home he confided in me how desperately close to eviction they were; his wife's earnings did not quite cover the rent, while his pittance from the government for his war wounds allowed them to eat little more than eggs and potatoes. He had planted a vegetable garden and was hoping it would soon supplement their diet. "My kids are going to school hungry and with holes in their shoes. I really need that bonus money. Bastards!"

Somewhere north of New York City we pulled over and set up our tent for the night. Roland got the campfire going. We had picked up a couple of cans of beans, bread and cheese when we'd stopped for gas a few miles back. It was a cloudless night, lit by a full moon that was so bright it obliterated all the stars in a huge arc around it.

"I've never been hunting in my life," Roland said, "but come winter, I think I might have to." He took a bite of bread and cheese. "Thanks for this, Isaac. I appreciate it."

He stood up and I watched him walk slowly into the nearby field. When he returned I could see that his face was streaked with tears. "I've been lucky, that's all," I said.

He sat down opposite me, took another bite of bread. "What happened, Isaac? How the hell did we end up here? Begging for a few crumbs! Dammit, we gave blood for this country, we gave everything, and all we have left is our nightmares!"

Yes, the nightmares. One night in the Bonus Army camp I was unable to sleep, so I got up and started walking around. It was eerie, frightening. Every so often, too often, I heard panicked yells, screams, whimpering. In the section of the camps for families I heard those same awful sounds often followed by the soothing voices of women; "It's OK. It's just a bad dream. I'm here."

I bumped into one of our security men on patrol. "I'm glad I'm on the overnight shift," he said, "I love to come to this part of the camp and hear those comforting words."

We all had our nightmares. When I'd returned to our campsite Roland was awake and sitting in the back seat of the car. I didn't have to ask him why.

Late the next afternoon, Sunday, I dropped him off at his home in Lawrence. "I'm glad I went to D.C. It was good to be with all those people, even though we didn't get what we needed from the bastards on the hill," he said. "It was good to spend time with you. Thanks, Isaac."

"Will you let me loan you money for shoes for your kids, Roland?"

He shook his head.

"Seriously, Roland. I can spare it. I know you'll pay me back when things straighten out." I took a ten dollar bill from my wallet and pressed it into his hand.

"Thanks." He turned and hurried into his apartment building.

It was almost dark by the time I walked into our home. The children had finished their supper and were playing on the floor in the living room. They ran to me and tackled me around the knees; I sank to the carpet and hugged them. Virginia joined us.

"You were away so long, Daddy!" Mark said.

"Where were you?" Emma asked.

"He was far away, in another town," Albert responded.

"I was far away, in Washington. I went with my friend, Roland. We were there with a lot of other people trying to tell the government to do something to help people who are having hard times."

"Why does the government have to be told to help?"

"That is an excellent question, Mark. I really wish I had the answer to that one." Mark always had a way of cutting to the core of a situation.

"Are you hungry, Isaac?" Virginia asked, "There's leftover casserole. It's probably still warm."

"I'm starving. Thanks."

"I'll get this little mob to bed. Come on everyone!" There were groans and grumbles as they climbed the stairs.

"I'll come and tuck you all in in a few minutes," I called after them.

"Don't be long, Daddy."

It was wonderful to be home. I spooned a heaping pile of dinner into a bowl and went to sit on the couch in the living room. Virginia joined me about ten minutes later. She clasped my hand and kissed me. "How was it down there, Isaac?"

"Desperate. Let me go up and say goodnight to the kids, then we can talk."

I went up and read them each a short story. I was exhausted; I could easily have fallen asleep next to any one of them, but I made it downstairs.

"Things are bad. I can't tell you how many men brought their whole families with them - they had nothing left to lose. The final vote was devastating. We had been so optimistic after the House voted for us, and then to be blown out in the Senate…"

I told her about Reuven and Kalner, about the camp and its organization, Roland's reuniting with the man who saved him, and my brief meeting with Gorgeous George. I told her about talking with the senators, especially Lewis, and about the nightmares. And in telling about much of this, I had to tell the back-stories that I had barely mentioned to her in the past; The July Fourth celebration with Senator Lewis and the legless soldier from his home state, the YMCA tent in Rouen and the bizarre nicknames, the horrors of flame throwers used in close combat.

It was past midnight before we went up to bed. Virginia held me tight as I fell asleep, but it seemed like only a few minutes before I felt her stroking my hair and face and whispering calmly into my ear; "It's a bad dream, Isaac. You're home. I'm here. Everything is OK."

Chapter 50

Allen is sighing. I'm not sure how long he's been sitting in my room, but I think it's been a while. He's flipping pages and sighing. Occasionally he'll say something like, "good," or "interesting idea," but he also mutters, "yuck," and "that's lazy." No doubt he's grading papers. This is finals week; he's anxious to be done with his responsibilities at school so he can get to his novel.

I'm awake. He does not respond; he's obviously totally absorbed in his work. I wish I could just say his name. I wait for him to shuffle the papers again, then give my signal.

"Hi there, Grandpa Isaac. You awake?"

Yes. Got him!

"I'm grading final exams. One more on Thursday, then I'm done!"

Good.

"I've had to put my prep work for the novel aside until I get through this week, but I've made progress. I'm feeling really good about the story and the characters."

Good. I'd really love to be around to see how Allen portrays me. How often do you get to look into someone else's head, see through his eyes?

"Oops - time-stamp. It's late Wednesday night, after ten. June twelfth. It was a beautiful day, although I didn't get to enjoy much of it because of school work." He paused. "I know you've heard about Ginnie's trip to Seattle to see Jake's family."

Yes.

"Do you think it's a good idea?"

In one word or less. *Yes.*

"I'm worried it might be too much for her. She's still pretty fragile."

But, she needs to find ways to lessen her load.

"She still chokes up when she talks about him."

Of course! Jake's sudden death was a huge blow. This is all part of coming to terms with an incomprehensible reality. It's hard to accept it;

mostly you just get used to it. Well, not really.

"She won't even let me drive her to Logan; she says she wants to take the subway." I hear Allen stand then start to pace about the room. Finally, he sits and takes my hand. "I've been thinking a lot about Colin lately, wondering how my parents handled the news." He hesitates and his voice drops. "Well, of course I know how my mother handled it, but my dad. He said nothing. I remember him holding on to me so tightly I could barely breathe and I have this image of him sitting on the deck in the dark, in the rain. I could see him from my bedroom window and he just sat there alone without moving a muscle. It was terrifying."

I remember Albert in that time, too. All his experiences during the war came crushing down on him. He went through hell - worse than me.

***

A little over a week after we left the Bonus Army camp in Washington D.C. the uneasy feelings Reuven had expressed became real, exploded. He sent me a detailed account of the police attack on the occupied buildings, and then the army, under Douglas MacArthur, moved in on the camp with tanks, tear gas and fixed bayonets. They burned the shacks and cars, and they threw men, women and children into the street. The conflagration could be seen for miles - thousands of people came to witness what was happening. President Hoover hid in the White House and offered support for his general.

Two men were killed, dozens injured including children, and many more were arrested. Reuven's letter was borne out by reports in newspapers and on the radio and the Movietone News shown in theaters. Virginia and I went to the theater in Cambridge just to see the film of the attack on the Bonus Army. I recognized some of the folks being evicted - Roland's friend Flipper Ferguson and his family were shown staring blankly at their burned old car. Gorgeous George, with his scarred and twisted face was seen yelling, "Stop! Stop!" as a soldier torched a tent. It was horrifying, and Virginia leaned into me and wept. I could not move.

A letter from Kalner a few days later gave even more graphic details. He described an incident in which a thirteen year old boy was hit in the face by the butt of a rifle wielded by one of the soldiers. And the sight of those huge tanks rolling over the campsite, crushing everything in their path. People who had so little - losing it all.

The only good thing to come out of this travesty was that Hoover was booted in the November elections, and FDR was elected. The Bonus March had blown Amelia Earhart's trans-Atlantic flight and related awards, galas and accolades off the front pages of the newspapers for a few days, but she was back soon enough. Politicians and the papers soon forgot about the worst action ever taken by the US Army against its own people. Cries of "Commie extremists" bubbled up for a while, but even they soon dissipated.

Reuven, Yvette and their two children came to visit a few months later. The visit happened to coincide with Armistice Day - November eleventh. Reuven and I were sitting on the patio behind the house, deep in our own thoughts and watching the children playing in the yard. It was a chilly gusty day, threatening rain.

"There's nothing quite like seeing men wearing the uniform you once wore burning down the miserable dwellings of the men you fought alongside." He brushed a tear from his eye. "It was one of the most devastating experiences of my life, Itzik. I felt so hopeless. It was worse, in a strange way, even than that day you were injured - at least then I felt there was something I could do. But in Washington, I could do little more than watch."

"I hate what this day has become. It's that Senator Lewis speech magnified a thousand times. Thank you for your service and sacrifice - now get lost, don't bother me."

"I will never wear that uniform again," he said bitterly. "It has been tarnished beyond recognition."

The sky had darkened and one could hear the faint rumble of thunder. "We'd better round up the kids before the rain gets here," Reuven said. Not unsurprisingly, the children did not want their game interrupted, but a louder roar of thunder and the arrival of a few large raindrops convinced them it was time to go inside. They ran upstairs to continue their game. Reuven and I joined Virginia and Yvette in the living room.

"How are things in Detroit?" Virginia asked.

"Are you asking about my work, or about things in general?"

"Well, Yvette has told me about your family, so, how is the mood of the city?"

"It's depressing. The auto companies are taking advantage of the economy to keep wages low. It seems like there are ten people looking for work for every person actually working. The union is getting organized, slowly and with great difficulty. I think it will take a few years before we reach a tipping point, before we can actually challenge the companies."

"Years?" I said.

"I'm afraid so." He leaned forward. "Here's a story that explains just how low things are, and how far we have to go to turn things around. I met this man, a union organizer, who was trying to get a job at one of the big plants in Flint, and he told me about arriving early one morning, before six, to apply. There were several hundred men in line waiting for the hiring office to open its doors at eight o'clock, as had been advertised. It was pouring rain and quite cold, but the men stood there and waited. At eight the doors did not open. Nine o'clock came, then ten. By eleven some of the men had given up and left, and by twelve, even more men had departed. That's when the company opened the door, figuring that men who had waited half the day in the cold rain would be docile enough, beaten down enough, and desperate enough not to become union men and trouble-makers. That's the kind of situation we're up against."

"Bastards!" Virginia exclaimed. "Can I use that story in my column, Reuven?"

"Sure."

"It's despicable!"

***

Damon the Good checks my plumbing and wiring. I'm on my side. My leg wound aches.

He is singing softly - a James Taylor song, "You've got a Friend." I love this song. David, Allen's Wall Street hot-shot son, believe it or not, used to sing it when we went on road trips together. He used to sing quite well as a teenager; I wonder if he takes the time now.

I focus on the song, listening to Damon's lovely deep voice, enjoying the words and the sound. The song ends and I signal I'm awake.

"Hi there, Mr. Simon. I need to check that bed sore. OK?"

Yes. He gently touches around the base of my spine.

"It's looking really good. I'm going to roll you on to your back. OK?"

Yes. Finally.

He rolls me back gently. "Your beard's gotten all messed up and is looking a little scraggly. Would you like me to trim and comb it?

Yes. I love it - it's like a soft face massage.

I hear him look in the drawer for the scissors and comb, then I feel the slight tugging on my face and hear the snipping of the scissors. "Ginnie told me about your exploits in the thirties. Man, the more I know about you, the more I want to know you. What a life!"

Smile. It would have been nice to have had you visit when I could still get around. I'd like to try to paint your voice - so rich and genuine, down-to-earth.

"And your wife, Virginia, too. Ginnie says she was quite someone; a real fighter."

Yes. That she most certainly was. She was never half-hearted about anything.

"She supported you when you gave testimony on behalf of your boss?"

Yes. Absolutely. She was the person who first made me understand that Love is Love, plain and simple.

"There, that's looking a whole lot better! Your golden white mane is glowing."

Thank you.

"Well, I have to leave you Mr. Simon. My shift is almost over. It's seven-thirty on Thursday morning, June thirteenth."

I am left with my glowing mane and Kate, my cat-machine.

***

I never really came to terms with William's death in December 1934: he had been a mentor to me and had even become like an older brother. We talked so much about our work, and even more about things that had nothing to do with the architecture firm, but he never mentioned that by mid-1934 the firm was essentially without money. Few private opportunities came in. He had entered, and lost, three different contests for public buildings. He was paying the one remaining draftsman and me out of his own funds.

In the hours before he took his life he had written his will in the form of a letter to his friends. It started with the words; "I have had enough, but I do not apologize one moment for my life." He then went on to leave his entire art collection, except one Klee which he left to me, to the Boston Museum of Fine arts. I couldn't help but notice that in the list of paintings attached to the document was one painting that I had given to him. That painting is, perhaps, still buried deep in the basement of the Museum.

What was left of his estate, after the lawyers and other creditors had been paid off, he left to Anthony's daughter, who I did not even know existed, but apparently had visited William and Anthony many times in recent years and had been very supportive of them.

He regretted the closing of the architecture firm and said that Grant, the draftsman, and I should take from the office whatever furniture, materials and supplies we wanted, and sell the balance to benefit one of the many soup kitchens in the city.

I met Grant at the office on the Friday morning before Christmas. We did not discuss William; we just went to our respective work areas and packed up the things we wanted. All the paintings, except my Klee, had already been removed by William's attorney and a representative of the museum, who had left a note taped to the wall beside the Klee asking me to contact him should I ever decide to loan or donate the painting. I went through the telephone directory and found a used furniture dealer who might want to buy what was left in the office, but when I tried to make the call, the phone line had already been shut down. I made a note of the number.

Grant had borrowed a friend's truck and he loaded it up with his drawing board, desk, chairs and filing cabinet, as well as a couple of boxes of equipment and supplies. After he drove away, I locked the office and found a pay telephone and called the furniture dealer who grudgingly agreed to come into town at two o'clock to look at what we had. I had almost three hours to kill. I called Virginia's parents but they were not home, so I set off aimlessly to walk through the Common and the Garden.

A bitterly cold wind whipped across the expanse of the snow-covered gardens. I turned up my collar, pulled my hat down tighter and walked briskly, not really paying much attention to where I was going. About halfway through the park I saw a man with his two small children building a snowman together. Their clothes were threadbare and he had no coat or gloves or scarf, but they laughed and played and cavorted in the snow as if everything in the world was wonderful. As I approached I noticed that his shirt was Army, and I saw the emblem of the Yankee Division on his sleeve.

I approached. "I was in the Yankee Division," I said. "One-hundred and first engineers."

"I was infantry - but that means nothing. At least the shirt is quite warm."

"Can I get you and the kids a square meal?"

He hesitated, looked me up and down, then said, "My wife is in the house," and he pointed in the direction of a cluster of make-shift shacks constructed of wood, cardboard and tar-paper, that huddled against the trunks of a stand of ancient birch trees.

"Let's get her," I said, and he sent his older child running to get her mother.

"My name's Isaac Simon," I said, extending my hand.

"Stan Kowalski."

His daughter returned with his wife. Stan introduced us and we made our way across the park, in the direction from which I had come. I knew that the old restaurant that Virginia and I had eaten at several times so many years ago had miraculously survived and that they still served hearty meals, so we headed there.

We ate together; thick beef soup, bread and butter, meatloaf, potatoes and squash, and apple pie with ice cream washed down with strong coffee. There was not much to talk about; what could one say that wasn't obvious. Every so often I would notice Stan glance at his wife and children, and a sad smile would flash across his face. He had been a machinist in an electrical equipment plant that had shut down eighteen months before, putting over two hundred people out of work.

As I was finishing my meal I remembered I had seen some items hanging in the closet in the office. I ordered another round of pie and ice cream for the kids and coffee for Stan and his wife, paid the bill and asked them to wait for me while I made a quick run to the office. It was almost one-thirty when I returned to the restaurant with a winter coat that William had left. Tucked into the outer pockets was a pair of gloves and a scarf. In an inside pocket, William had left two ten dollar bills.

"I've been clearing out the office. My boss passed away recently. He left this there." I handed the coat to Stan. "I need to get back - I have a furniture dealer coming to pick up some things."

"Thank you, Isaac."

I shook his hand and before I turned to leave, I said: "Don't forget to check the pockets."

The furniture man arrived twenty minutes late and displayed little enthusiasm for what I had to show him. I managed to talk him into paying sixty dollars for the lot. While he and his assistant loaded his truck, I stood in my now almost empty office trying to understand the impact William's death had on my life. It was far more than the end of the firm; it was about the daily bruises he endured - small and large - and how I was no longer oblivious to the pain he, and so many others like him, suffered. I was forever changed by his life and his death.

I arrived home with my car packed with drafting equipment and supplies, which I dumped in the temporary studio I had built while my mother was living with us. Over the following days, I converted the room into my architecture office. No one was hiring; it seemed like the only way I could possibly continue practicing. We hung the Klee in the living room next to the Kandinsky William had given us as a wedding gift.

Our old clients, Grace and Celia, had invited us to a gathering on the Saturday evening. It was not to be a Christmas party - gifts were emphatically not allowed - it was more a gathering to honor and remember William and Anthony. We brought our children to Virginia's parents' home; they were going to spend three nights with Grandpa and Granny, and we were to join them on Christmas morning. This also meant that Virginia and I had a short vacation alone, together.

We arrived at the gathering around nine in the evening. The first thing I noticed when Celia opened the front door was one of the large paintings I had done for the Sloan house hanging in the entry hall. I gripped Virginia's hand and let out an involuntary gasp. Celia put her hand on my arm. "We wondered how you would react. I guess you have not kept track of Lizzie."

"No, but this is not a good sign," Virginia said.

"Come." Celia led us to one of the bedrooms. "It's a terrible situation. Ernest, as you know, was in banking. When Wall Street crashed he lost a lot of money. Six months later his bank collapsed. He went up to the house on the lake, rowed a boat out into the middle of the water, and drowned himself. As you can imagine, Lizzie was devastated. She refused to return to that beautiful house. She called up an auctioneer and sold off everything - the paintings, the carpets, the furniture and the house itself. Grace and I bought your four paintings. I told Lizzie we would keep them for her, that she could have them whenever she wanted them. We only display the one - the others are in storage."

"Where is she now? What is she doing?"

"We've lost touch. She doesn't answer letters and her phone number is dead. I wrote to her mother, but received only the briefest response, saying that Lizzie wanted no part of the past."

"That's terrible," Virginia said, and her voice faltered. "There are too many victims, of all kinds."

The three of us stood in silence for a while, then Celia said she needed to return to their guests. Virginia and I followed. We were acquainted with some of the people from the house-warming party a couple of years earlier. Celia introduced us around and made a point of bringing us over to a young woman, no more than twenty or twenty one years old, sitting alone in a large leather chair facing the glowing fireplace. She stood as we approached, extended her hand to Virginia and said, "I'm Maryanne, Anthony's secret daughter."

"Not so secret anymore," Virginia said and took her hand. "I'm Virginia Simon. This is my husband, Isaac. He worked with William for close to fourteen years. They designed this house together, in fact."

"And you're an artist, too, Mr. Simon. I believe it is your work in the front hall."

"It is."

"Lovely. Are you still with Marjorie Ross, the Nouvelle Vision gallery? Grace told me your work was there."

"Yes, I am, not that there's much movement given the state of things."

"There are always some people with money, Mr. Simon."

"Hopefully they will spread it around where it's needed," I replied, without really thinking about what I was saying.

Grace called everyone to silence. She thanked us all for coming to this evening to recognize the lives of our two departed friends. She lit two tall white tapered candles and then asked us all to close our eyes and to observe a time of silence. She ended the silence by saying, "Anthony and William would not have been welcome in any church, but we know that their lives were sacred, that love is the most potent force in the universe, and so we honor them and all they did."

More silence, then she asked everyone to fill their glasses and to drink a toast. "And now I would ask whoever is so inclined, to talk about William or Anthony or both of them and how they have contributed to our lives."

Maryanne immediately stood. "I need to talk," she said. "I met most of you for the first time this evening. Many of you did not even know that I existed until that letter was read. So I want to tell you the story." She took a sip of wine, then continued; "William and my father fell in love as seniors in high school in Philadelphia. Of course they could not tell their parents, but their parents somehow found out. They fled Philadelphia for Boston and shared an apartment together. To the outside world they were college room-mates."

She paused and took another sip from her glass. "You probably know all that, because that was the story they told the folks in their close circle. But, what they rarely talked about was that when they were both around twenty-five they had a terrible fight and they separated. I never learned what the fight was about, but it was pretty serious and they had no contact with one another for eight years. Anthony moved to Hartford where he worked for an insurance company. A young woman in the typing pool was very taken with him and set about courting him. That was my rather brazen mother, who got him drunk at an office party and dragged him back to her apartment where she seduced him. She fell pregnant and they got married."

She drained her glass and walked to the drinks table to refill it. "They looked great together - I have the photographs - but it was a terrible marriage. Just after my sixth birthday he moved out and, I learned later, came back to Boston to find William. He traveled to Hartford at least once a month to see me. When I turned sixteen a few years ago, I asked if I could come and visit him in Boston. It was then that he told me about William. I remember taking his hand and saying that I'd love to meet this very special man. I remember his smile in response to my words. He gave me money for the train and met me at South Station the following Saturday morning. He brought me back to their home and introduced me to that lovely man, William, who was the love of his life.

"Why, then, was I kept a secret?" She sighed. "I don't really know. After I finished high school I moved to Boston to be near them and to go to the teacher's training program at the University of Massachusetts. Keeping me secret just seemed easier at the time. It made no sense to me, but that's what they wanted. When that horrible episode happened on Martha's Vineyard, I was visiting my mother in Hartford. A phone call from my father begged me to stay away, to avoid being caught up in the craziness and the drama."

Her voice had dropped and I noticed a slight tremble in her hand. She took a sip of wine and continued, "During that dreadful time I talked with either William or my father almost every day, but I respected their request to stay away until the dust settled." She slumped into her chair. "Of course, the dust never settled. I miss them. I miss them so much!" She was sobbing loudly, uncontrollably. Celia squeezed in next to her on the chair and hugged her tightly.

***

"Sorry to wake you, Grandpa Isaac. I thought I'd stop in on my way to the airport." Ginnie is sitting on the bed beside me.

I'm awake. Smile.

"Damon fix your beard? You're looking pretty good."

Yes. I love to hear her talk.

"I'm nervous about this trip, but I need to do it. You know, I only met Jake's parents three times - twice in Boston and once in Seattle. We went there for a few days during spring break; it's when we told them that we were moving in together. It was a difficult conversation, and an uncomfortable visit. They try to be open-minded, but they were not happy about our announcement, and they definitely did not want us sharing a room in their house. I slept in Jake's old bedroom; he slept on the couch, and we didn't dare break the rules." She exhales loudly. "I wonder what they've done with his room. I wonder if they'll have me sleep in it or on the couch. I'm not sure how I'll feel whatever they decide to do with me."

She kisses me on both cheeks, then rests her head gently on my chest. I feel her hair in my beard, hear her breathing.

Finally, she sits up. "Well, it's time for me to go," she says. "I'll see you Monday, Grandpa Isaac."

Hug.

She kisses me on the forehead. Be strong. Be good to yourself.

Wanda is here. She fiddles with my tubes. "I'm afraid it's drizzling out there, Mr. Simon, so no sun room this morning. Supposed to be like this through tomorrow."

Don't like. Sad.

"I don't like it either, Mr. Simon. Although we really need the rain. There have been several brush fires around the area. A good steady rain should help a lot."

***

By the late summer of 1935 our funds were running low. I had not had any architecture work in months and had sold only one painting the whole year. What Virginia earned through her column and her position at the church was barely enough for food and basic household needs; anything extra, like property taxes, auto repairs, maintenance on the house, and my painting supplies had to come out of our savings. I decided to apply to the newly established Federal Arts Project, a section of the Works Project Administration - the WPA.

It was not until November after several interviews and bureaucratic delays, that I was finally accepted, but once on the payroll, I found it to be a remarkable program. I became a muralist under the tutelage of an expert, and I taught art classes two afternoons a week to school-children in Cambridge. Mark was in the class; it was difficult not to favor him. He had real talent. I earned twenty-four dollars a week; enough to survive on.

The down-side of the program was the decided preference for realistic art and the rejection of anything abstract. It was pointless trying to argue. I worked on murals depicting rural and city scenes in three different post offices in Boston, then was sent up to Plymouth, New Hampshire for a month to assist with the work in a school there. It was June 1936 and the weather was perfect. I was housed in a WPA camp on the edge of the White Mountain National Park, where about thirty men were employed clearing trails, building rest rooms and improving pedestrian bridges.

On my way home from this assignment, I took a detour to drive by the Sloan house. The last time I had seen it was shortly after the house-warming party when I'd delivered the last light fittings for the main part of the house. I was so proud of the work we had done.

The road had been upgraded since then, probably with WPA funds, and the driving was easy. The lake stretched out below me as I turned into Newbury. I stopped for a sandwich at a kiosk next to the town beach, then drove on. Every so often I could see the lake sparkling through breaks in the trees.

I finally arrived at the driveway to the Sloan house and turned in but had to stop immediately; the driveway had become totally overgrown with brambles and even a few young pines. I could barely make out the structure through the undergrowth, and what I could see made my hands tremble. I got out of the car and carefully made my way toward the building. As I got closer, what I feared became real. The place had been burned; the walls that still stood were charred, the roof was gone. I rounded the house and found myself in a sea of shattered glass lying beneath layers of dead leaves and burned wood. I entered what was once the big room, looking for something, anything that could conjure up what had been here.

I wandered through the ruin and found nothing. Apparently everything, down to the last knife and fork, had been removed from the house after the auction - and then the structure was torched.

As I began walking up the path back to my car I saw a smooth curved shape protruding from the carpet of dead leaves about fifteen feet into the woods. I knelt down beside it and carefully moved the leaves and twigs aside. Slowly I unearthed one of the smaller turned wood light fittings. Miraculously, it was undamaged, other than the weather staining. I did not try to imagine how this could have happened, how it could have survived. I carried it back to the car, wrapped it in an old towel that I found on the back seat, and placed it next to me. Tears rolled down my face.

Chapter 51

This was a desperate time in the country. By the mid-1930's workers had been so hard-pressed, so pushed down by repeated pay cuts, increasingly oppressive working conditions and management policies designed to divide people, that working men and women began to feel there was nothing left to lose, so they might as well fight back. It was the longshoremen on the west coast first, shutting down the ports and gaining the support of several other unions including the Teamsters. The California National Guard was mobilized and pitched battles were fought. A short state-wide general strike stopped just about everything and a few concessions were gained.

The resistance spread to the industrial cities of Ohio and Minneapolis and then to the textile industry in the east. Towards the end of 1936 the auto industry became a major focus of union activity which coordinated a cascading number of job actions and sit-down strikes. Reuven by this time was on the legal staff of the United Auto Workers. When the workers shut down and occupied the three major General Motors plants in Flint, Michigan in the last days of 1936, Reuven found himself in the middle of a whirlwind. Several other big General Motors plants in four other states were taken over by the workers a few days later. The giant General Motors was stopped.

Vigilantes organized by a consortium of auto industry leaders in Flint threated to attack the workers occupying the buildings. In response, thousands of union men and women from the Midwest poured into Flint and the other striking towns and set up enormous picket lines. They came to reinforce the lines already established by those workers who were not inside the buildings, along with whole families of the strikers. Reuven wrote about looking out over the scene in front of the Chevrolet Four plant and seeing huge numbers of men, women and children marching and singing and facing off against the police and militia.

As the sit-down dragged into its third week, the men inside issued a statement warning against any attempts by the government or the company to evict them by force, stating they would fight till the last man. Reuven later learned that the men had gathered stockpiles of metal objects they could use as projectiles and clubs. Sometime towards the end of January, General Motors officials turned off the heat in the plants, hoping to freeze the men out.

President Roosevelt was trying to get negotiations going. He sent senior officials to Flint to bring the two sides into the same room but essentially nothing happened. The auto companies refused to recognize the union and refused to offer anything meaningful at the meetings. Reuven wrote at length about sitting in an office adjacent to the room where the union officials and the company management were meeting and being aware that not a word was said for hours on end. At one point a union negotiator came in to talk with Reuven and his colleagues and commented; "sitting across the table from a billion dollars was like sitting next to a giant fart - all stink, no substance!"

In the meantime, the press and the business community were calling for action to evict the strikers. Reuven found himself in court arguing against an injunction sought by the owners which could lead to force being used to remove the workers. The judge signed off on the injunction, but it was soon shown that the judge held a large number of General Motors shares, so the injunction was invalidated.

Attempts were made to stop the women from bringing food to the men inside. A fierce battle raged for over two hours outside one of the plants. The police used tear gas and then opened fire on the women and the men who were helping them to deliver the food. Dozens of people were injured and gassed, but the food got through.

The strike stretched into its second month and still the men inside and the men and women on the picket line outside held strong. "The mood among working people on the street is electrifying," Reuven wrote. "Everyone you talk to is energized by the events at the GM plants. Every day those strikers hold on, is a day closer to victory. It is long overdue."

Virginia came home from church one Sunday and said the minister had spoken mildly in support of the strikers. This caused quite a stir in the congregation, the vast majority of whom were not from the working class and had fallen for the popular notion pushed in the newspapers that the strikers were all communists and anarchists and were out to destroy the country. A special meeting was called, but the Reverend, who had served the church for more than twenty years, stood his ground.

In a letter a few days later Reuven wrote: "Every day there are rumors the vigilantes are about to attack and the governor is sending in the National Guard. It is thirty-eight days since they shut the place down. The tension is frightening. I cannot sleep and I'm working non-stop. Yvette and the kids never see me. I just hope the companies realize they have to give up something. This could be a blood-bath."

On the forty-second day of the sit-down strike the strikers sent a telegram to the governor appealing to him to stand against the economically and politically powerful and reiterating their determination to stay where they were. They stated that sending in armed police and the army would result in many people being killed, and "you are the one who will be responsible for our deaths." The telegram appeared in newspapers across the country.

At seven in the morning of the forty-fourth day of the strike, Reuven got a phone call to hurry to the negotiation site and prepare to write actual contract language. GM had agreed to recognize the union and to bargain in good faith. Word spread quickly to all the plants. Huge ecstatic crowds lined the streets as the sit-down strikers marched out of the plants and through the streets of the city. Reuven still had several long weeks ahead of him, but a deal was finally struck setting working hours and conditions and almost doubling the hourly rate for many workers.

After the contract was signed Reuven, Yvette, Sam, and Danielle came out to visit his family who were still living in Rhode Island. They made a day-trip up to see us on the Saturday. Reuven looked exhausted but could not stop smiling. "We beat them, Itzik! We won! I am in awe of the bravery and determination of those men and their families."

It was a clear spring day, still a little chilly, but bright and calm. The children were in the back yard; Reuven, Yvette, Virginia and I were at the kitchen table drinking coffee. "It is impossible to grasp just how big this victory is!" Reuven said. "Men are flocking to the union. The whole auto industry will be under contract to the UAW within a couple of years. Finally, some dignity!"

I thought of my mother on the picket lines in 1912 and again when I returned from the war. I remembered my fear when she was injured and did not come home for days, and then that sense of elation and strength and pride when she brought me with her to march and sing. I remembered, too, the real difference the extra money and the slightly shorter work week made in our lives.

"Do you recall the story I told you about the men waiting for hours in the rain for the hiring office to open?" Reuven asked.

"I do."

"Well, I ran into the man who told me that story. He did eventually get hired and he was inside Chevrolet Four during the sit-down. He told me all about how they organized themselves, how they worked to keep their spirits up. He talked about sticking the firehoses through the windows to fend off the police and to allow the women to get to the building to deliver the food. He talked about how important it was for them inside to know that working men and women everywhere were taking a stand for them."

"You do good things, Reuven, my friend!" I said.

"I'm a paper-pusher."

"Reuven is always too modest," Yvette said. "He might not be marching on the picket line - although he has on occasion - but he writes the words and he does battle in the court."

Reuven refilled his coffee mug. "But I'm afraid there are more battles to come, both in this country and overseas."

"Hitler in Germany?" Virginia said.

"Hitler and Mussolini. The Japanese advances into China. And, of course, the Klan and their political mentors in this country."

"Mentors?"

"If you look closely at all the New Deal legislation that is coming out of Washington you will notice one glaring omission - the rights and benefits given in the new laws are denied to many Negroes and other non-white people, particularly in the South. Agricultural and domestic workers are excluded from the labor laws and from receiving Social Security or unemployment benefits. The discrimination even extends to things from school lunches to small business loans. This is the work of the Southern Democrats in congress. The big battle for equality and civil rights will be coming. In the meantime, lynching continues, phony convictions continue. I hate to admit it, but even within the labor movement anti-Negro and anti-immigrant sentiment is high."

He stood and said; "I think I'll go'n check on the kids - they seem awfully quiet out there." Then he stopped and added: "And I fear that Hitler's anti-Semitism is resonating inside those Klan hoods. Fascism is taking hold in parts of Europe; we'd be foolish to think there are no supporters here."

***

I hear the door to my room close. "Hello Isaac. I brought you a visitor." Martha. I hear the sound of a zipper followed by a purr. Kitty-bee flops down against my arm and rests her head on my shoulder. I feel her tail brushing back and forth across my hand. I try to move my fingers.

Thank you. Smile.

"I snuck her in under cover of dark. It's eight-thirty on Thursday evening, June thirteenth. She looks so happy to be with you."

Smile. As I am happy to be with her!

"Ginnie said she dropped by this morning, before her flight. She called shortly before I came in to see you. She's at Jake's parents' home. I'm so proud of her."

Yes. I am too.

"So, anything new going on with you?"

No. Well, actually quite a bit is going on inside my head, but I've resigned myself to the fact that whatever is happening in there is staying there.

"I'm working on our annual bazaar at the Temple. It takes a lot of planning and endless meetings. I'm chair of the book sale and they'll probably put me in charge of the antiques and art table as well, because the lady who used to run it had a heart attack and they can't find a volunteer to replace her. She had an antique store in the town center for years, but retired last year and promptly had the heart attack! Just doesn't seem right, does it?"

No. I try to tune her out and give my full attention to Kitty-bee who is purring softly and still swishing her tail about.

There is a knock on the door. I feel Kitty-bee jump off the bed.

"I just need to check a few things." It's Trainwreck. Kitty-bee must have been quick enough to avoid being caught. The nurse examines my tubes, takes my wrist to check my pulse and sneezes suddenly. "That's odd," she says. She sneezes again and walks out mumbling something about allergies.

Martha giggles then closes the door and puts Kitty-bee back on the bed. "Smart kitty," she says. "The instant the door opened she was under the bed behind the sheet that's hanging down."

Smile. Laugh.

"Your poor nurse must be pretty sensitive - she wasn't here more than a minute before she sneezed. I couldn't imagine being allergic to cats."

Kitty-bee positions herself exactly where she had been before the interruption, and I focus my attention on her again. I try to move my fingers. I think I might have actually moved one or two! Wasn't Dr. Squeak, the neurologist, supposed to have been here this morning? I'm sure Wanda said he was going to be here, but I don't remember him coming. I don't like this - is my mind failing me, or are people not following through on what they tell me?

"I will have a lot to learn about antiques, but I'm sure I'll manage."

What on earth is she talking about! Kitty-bee adjusts her position and rests her head on my chest. I can still feel her tail waving slowly.

Martha chatters on. Finally, I hear her say; "Well, we have to go home now, I'm afraid. It's late." She kisses me on the forehead and lifts Kitty-bee off the bed. I hear the zipper and a stifled little purr. "We'll be back."

Thank you.

***

1937. Our kids were not little kids anymore; Albert was fourteen, Mark a year younger and Emma would soon be ten - on June seventeenth. Emma wanted a big party for this "most important birthday," but she did not want her brothers around, or her father. "No offense, Dad, but I want this to be an all-girls party, a sleep-over," she declared while we were all together one Saturday morning.

"Can I spend the night at Robbie's?" Albert chimed in. Robbie was a school friend. His family were long-time members of the church where Virginia taught.

"I'll talk with Robbie's mom and dad," Virginia said. "What about you, Mark? Anyone you'd like to stay with?"

Mark said nothing.

"Do you want to go camping with me?" I asked.

"No."

"Well, you can't stay here," Emma said. "You and Dad have to go somewhere."

"It's still a couple of weeks away. Mark and I will come up with something."

The following Tuesday was the afternoon art class I taught at Mark's school as part of my contract with the WPA. After the class, as he and I were walking home I suggested that we go into Boston to visit the Museum of Fine Arts on the day of Emma's party.

"OK," he said, and I noticed a smile on his face and he straightened up just a bit. "Where will we stay?"

"I think we can find a spot at Granny and Grandpa's."

"I think that's a great idea, Dad."

Phone calls were made to Robbie's parents and to Virginia's, and invitations went out to ten girls for the sleep-over.

"Will you survive it?" I said to Virginia, "Eleven ten-year-old girls!"

"We'll have fun. They're a good bunch."

Right after lunch on the Saturday of the birthday party Mark and I took the subway into Park Station. We made a quick stop at the Appleton house to drop off our bags and then headed back across the park towards the subway station. I kept an eye out for Stan Kowalski and his family, hoping not to see them, hoping they had been able to move on from here. The make-shift shacks were still under the birches, but I recognized none of the people who were in the vicinity.

"Remember when we were here in the spring a few years ago, Dad, and there were so many homeless people in the garden."

"Yes, I do. And there still are quite a few."

"Does it have something to do with why you went to Washington?"

"You remember that, Mark? That was five years ago. And yes, the situation here with these people has everything to do with what we were fighting for in Washington."

"Has it always been like this: so many people without work, without real homes?"

"Things have never been easy for poor and working class people, but eight years ago, in 1929, the economy took a sudden nosedive and millions of people lost their jobs within a matter of months. And things have not gotten any better since then. In fact, more and more people still lose their jobs every month. I think the number right now is around one out of every five workers has no work."

"That's a lot of people. It's not right."

"No it isn't."

We arrived at the entrance to the station and descended to the platform. It was too noisy to continue the conversation so we rode the train in silence. When we got off near the museum, Mark said, "Are Granny and Grandpa rich? They have a huge house, almost a mansion, and all those paintings and fancy plates and things."

"The answer is yes and no. They used to be very wealthy. When I met Mom they had a lot of money. They were also pretty skeptical about their daughter going out with a poor foreign working class kid whose mother worked in the textile mills in Lawrence. They traveled a lot, all over the world, and gave fancy parties and wore glimmering jewelry and clothes. Most of their money was inherited family wealth, although your Grandpa has always worked; he is a highly respected lawyer in Boston. When the economy crashed in 1929 a huge chunk of the family fortune disappeared. So now they have to live much more simply. Granny even had to learn how to cook and keep house, because they had to let their servant go."

"They had servants?"

"Just one." I checked my watch. "But we came here to look at art - let's go inside. We can talk more about this later. OK?"

"OK."

We ambled through the large galleries, not saying very much. Mark was unimpressed by the huge dramatic Renaissance works; he was more drawn to the stylized medieval compositions and the works of Cezanne and Pissarro. The Modern Art was in a small side room and half the collection appeared to consist of the paintings that William had donated. There were William's four paintings by Kandinsky, the two by Klee, a Picasso and a Braque. It was unnerving coming face to face with paintings I had seen hanging in our office and my friend's home; paintings now arrayed so formally in this most prestigious museum.

Mark walked directly up to one of the Klee's, stood in front of it for some time, then said, "This looks like the painting we have in our living room."

"You have a good eye, Mark. It's by the same artist, Paul Klee."

"Wow! We have a painting by someone whose work is here!"

"Do you remember my friend, William?"

"The one who died a few years ago?"

"Yes, and when William died, he left the Klee painting to us. He gave most of his paintings to this museum; several of them are hanging right here." I guided him over to a Kandinsky. "Do you recognize this?"

"Like the other painting in our living room?"

"Yes. William gave that one to Mom and me as a wedding present."

"Wow!"

"He was a very generous man."

We spent a good half hour in that gallery and then headed back towards the Appleton home. Mark was quiet, deep in thought throughout the subway ride and the walk across the Common. As we approached the Appleton house, Mark stopped and looked at me. "Those two paintings - do they make us rich?"

"I'd never thought of them in that way, Mark. They are wonderful gifts given to us by someone I admired, respected, even loved." I put my arm around his shoulders. "Fortunately we have enough to get by on. I have a job and Mom works part-time. Every now and then I even sell a painting. We're lucky. I have no idea how much those paintings are worth - probably quite a bit, but they're not for sale."

Virginia's mother opened the door. "I'm almost done preparing supper. Why don't you gentlemen wash up, then join me in the kitchen. I hope macaroni and cheese is still your favorite, Mark," she said.

"It still is, Granny."

"Good. It will be ready in about ten minutes. Grandpa is at his club for dinner. There's some big meeting going on that he could not miss. He'll be home later."

Mark and I went to clean up while she went to check on the dinner. When we joined her a few minutes later in the kitchen, she said, "So, Mark, how did you enjoy the museum?"

"It's so big - I think I could spend a week there and still not see everything."

"Yes," she said, and then added, "Their collection has been growing significantly in the last few years." There was a touch of bitterness in her voice that I did not understand, but did not question.

Mark and his grandmother chatted on about the museum and his favorite paintings. He talked about the Kandinsky and Klee. "They don't have a Metzinger, do they?" she asked.

"I don't think I saw that name," Mark replied. "Is he good?"

"You tell me. When you finish supper you can take a look at it - it's the big abstract in the parlor."

"Oh, I remember that painting. I really like it!"

We finished our dinner. Mrs. Appleton sent us off to the parlor saying she would join us shortly with coffee and dessert. Mark hurried ahead of me and planted himself about ten feet in front of the Metzinger. As I entered the room I immediately noticed that most of the fine porcelain and silverware was gone, and the large glass display cabinets were no longer in the room. The horizontal surfaces were now covered with simple cloths. As I looked around I saw, too, that the banjo clock was no longer there, and two landscapes were missing.

Mrs. Appleton entered with a tray of milk and coffee and cookies. She placed it on the small table in front of her usual chair and sat. "I can't tell you how much work it was to keep up with all those things - the dusting and the polishing," she said, obviously aware that I had seen the changes in the room, "so I decided it was time for them to go."

"Yes." What could I say? I sat on the edge of the couch near her and she handed me my coffee.

"I did put a few of the best pieces into storage - George's family heirloom silver, and some of my grandmother's Wedgewood and Meissen. We donated some pieces to the museum; others we sold. You've no idea how much it costs to keep this old house running."

She fell silent, twisting a silk handkerchief around her fingers. Mark came to sit next to me on the couch. "No, Granny, I don't think there was a Metzinger in the museum. Was there, Dad?"

"I didn't see one."

"More coffee, Isaac?"

"Yes, thank you."

As she was pouring the coffee, the telephone rang. I looked at my watch; eight-twenty.

"It's Virginia for you, Isaac. She sounds a little agitated, but who wouldn't be with all those little girls running around."

I went to the phone. "Albert has hurt himself." Her voice was quavering. "He broke his leg horsing around with Robbie. They brought him to Cambridge hospital. He's OK, but they're keeping him overnight."

"You can't leave those girls. I'll go to the hospital. Mark can take the subway home in the morning."

"OK. Call me when you've seen him. Tell him I love him."

"I will."

I told Virginia's mother and Mark what had happened, grabbed my things and jogged to the subway station. Saturday night; trains were infrequent. It was past nine-thirty when I arrived at the hospital, long after visiting hours, and was told I could not see Albert. No matter how much I tried to argue, the receptionist would not bend the rules.

"Will you at least give him a note?" I pleaded.

"If he's awake."

I scribbled a quick note telling him we loved him and we'd see him as soon as the hospital would let us in the next morning. I made a quick sketch of two boys jumping around like fools and handed the note and my pencil to the receptionist. "Tell him to write something, please." She disappeared into a back room.

I called Virginia to fill her in on the situation. She uttered a rare curse and asked me to call again after I had Albert's response and had talked to the doctor.

About fifteen minutes later a nurse emerged and handed me the note. "I'm OK. Don't worry. Tired. See you tomorrow."

"Short and sweet," the nurse said. "Don't worry, he'll be just fine. Dr. Andrews will be out to talk with you in a couple of minutes."

The couple of minutes became close to half an hour. When the doctor finally arrived he explained that Albert had broken his right tibia; it was a clean fracture and did not require the bone to be re-set. "He's in some pain and we have him on medication for that. He will have to be in a cast for about eight weeks."

I called Virginia again, then had to walk home because I'd just missed the bus and I had no idea when, or whether, the next one would be along. It was close to midnight by the time I reached home. Virginia met me at the door with a hug. "The girls are finally asleep - they're spread out on the floor in both kids' bedrooms. I wish you could have seen Albert. "

"Me too. Visiting hours are at ten tomorrow."

"Did they say when he could come home?"

"No. And somehow I forgot to ask."

"We'll know tomorrow. Tea?"

"Thanks." I sat at the kitchen table while she made a pot of tea. "We had a really good day, Mark and I. He enjoyed the museum. Many of William's paintings are up. It was strange seeing them. Mark recognized Klee and Kandinsky; he asked if we were rich."

Virginia laughed. "I'm glad you had a good time. What did my mother feed you?"

"Mark's favorite - macaroni and cheese, and a big salad."

She poured the tea. "I saved you a slice of birthday cake."

"Thanks. Did you know that your parents have been selling off things?"

"No. What things?" She sat opposite me and clasped her hands.

I told her about the cleared shelves and missing display cabinets, the paintings and clock. "She said that it was too much work to clean it all."

"I thought they were doing OK. I never realized it had come to this."

"She did say she saved your father's heirloom silver and her grandmother's Wedgewood."

"That stuff goes back four or five generations. It's probably worth more than this house. Is the piano still there?"

"I didn't go into the music room."

"The Metzinger?"

"It's still there. Mark loves it - he stood and studied it for quite a while."

Virginia cleared the dishes and began washing them. I stood beside her with a dish towel.

"Isaac, how much *do* you think those two paintings are worth - the Klee and Kandinsky?"

"I have no idea. Why do you ask?"

"I'm trying to figure out how we're going to pay for Albert's doctor and hospital bills. This little mishap was not in our budget."

I had not thought about that. "We'll figure something out," I said. "I'm too tired to worry about it now."

Albert came home after a second night in the hospital. He had a cast from six inches above his knee to his toes. Well, at least he didn't have to be in traction. Within a couple of days he became a speed demon on his crutches, refusing to let his temporary disability get in the way of his school or social life.

That same week, Virginia was told that the church could no longer afford to pay her for her services. They asked her to continue as a volunteer, and promised that when the economy improved her pay would be reinstated. She agreed. The timing of these two events - her loss of the job and Albert's broken leg - came when we had depleted all of our savings and were entirely dependent on what each of us brought in week to week. It came down to needing to sell something, and the most obvious was either the Klee or the Kandinsky, since my own works were not selling at all.

Virginia broached the question first; she was, after all, the one in our family who kept track of our finances. "It's a tough decision, Isaac, but we need to part with one of these. We'll be able to pay the doctors and the hospital and we'll have enough left over, I hope, to get by for some time."

"I have no idea how to go about selling either one of them."

"I know - Freeman's Auctions. They're in downtown Boston and our families have been acquainted for ages. I'll give them a call in the morning. If anyone knows the market, they will."

A few days later, Virginia and I were in the Freeman office with the Kandinsky and consigned it to their next auction of paintings, two months off. I wondered whether the missing pieces from the Appleton house were somewhere in this expansive, over-decorated space. They estimated the painting would realize around two thousand dollars. Why did we decide on the Kandinsky over the Klee? Virginia and I could not make the decision, so we put it to Albert, Mark and Emma. The only one who had any strong opinion on the issue was Mark; he begged us to keep the Klee.

We fended off our creditors with small payments for several months until we received a check from Freeman's for slightly under fifteen hundred dollars. And just in time, too; the funding for the WPA arts program that kept me going for a few years had been reduced and I, along with many others, was cut. The only income we now had was the few dollars a week Virginia was getting for her column in the Banner.

Chapter 52

Danielle. Her soft scent close to me.

I'm awake.

"Good morning, Isaac." I hear her place something on the table next to me. Lilacs; their aroma complementing hers. We had a few bushes beside the house. Virginia tended them and kept them from getting too woody, but after she died, I let them go - and they got to be tall and unkempt. And they never flowered as brilliantly and plentifully as when Virginia had watched over them. I could see them through my studio window; in the early summer, that light purplish pink encroached into my paintings.

New word.

"You have a new word?"

Yes.

"OK, I'm ready."

We quickly create the blinky-blink signal for "flowers." I hear Danielle writing it on the chart.

Like. Flowers. Thank you. Almost a complete sentence!

"You're welcome, Isaac. The lilacs are from my new neighbor's garden; she saw me leaving to come to see you this morning and asked if I'd like to bring some in for you. She's a sweet young thing. She and her husband and baby girl moved in about three weeks ago and I brought them a welcome apple pie. We've been very chatty ever since."

Smile. That is so like Danielle - to be warm and friendly to the newcomers.

"It's around eleven on Friday morning, June fourteenth, 2002. It's a lovely, warm, sunny day. Before I came into your room I asked the nurse if you could go to the sun room. Someone will be here soon to get you into the wheelchair."

Thank you. You are so like you father, Danielle; always thinking of others, always trying to find ways to make people's lives just a little easier. Reuven was always the smartest person in the room, and also the kindest and most self-deprecating. He gave credit for his accomplishments and achievements to all those around him, yet he took personal responsibility if things went wrong. If they made saints out of Jews turned atheist, they'd be begging him to join the club. I'm sure he would decline the offer.

"Marcus is here, Isaac. Are you ready to roll?"

Yes.

My plumbing and wiring are disconnected from the cat-machine. "Thirty minutes," Wanda says.

"I'll watch the clock," Marcus replies in his lilting voice. Those strong arms lift me carefully. Again that wonderful sensation of floating. I feel my body relax, sense my breathing slow and deepen. Then he lowers me into the wheelchair and off we go!

Just before we bump over the threshold I feel the breeze on my face and I hear wind-chimes jingling. These are new. I am immediately reminded of the set of hand-made bells mounted on the wall of the bombed out church in France; the church where Reuven, Benny and I had stopped for a while, not long before the shell exploded in the road, killing Benny and smashing my leg and throwing me to the ground. I see the flash of the blast, hear the deafening roar. I feel my pulse quicken, my blood pressure rise as fear grips my throat. Someone touches my arm and it burns.

This is not good. I am not connected to Kate, my cat-machine. Nothing is monitoring me. If I slide into panic no one will know. I fight to push the sounds and images from my mind, to focus on the warm sun on my face. I hear myself saying, "I'm OK. That was long ago. Be calm. Be calm." I cannot get the noises out of my head. My leg is throbbing, the old wound is on fire.

It is out of control. I blink my eyes furiously. I hear Danielle's voice; "Something's wrong! Help!" I feel the wheelchair bump over the threshold - the vibration sends out ripples through my body that seem to converge on my rib cage.

I feel a cold stethoscope on my chest. I hear someone say, "DNR," and I tell myself I'm not ready to check out - I still have a long way to go in my story! I focus all my senses on the cold spot of the stethoscope. At some point I feel the pain in my ribs begin to recede. The pounding in my ears slowly decreases. My leg is numb.

The door to the sun room must have been left open; I can hear the wind-chimes, faintly, and I know what they are and I am no longer afraid. Our children bought an elaborate set of glass and metal chimes for Virginia's fortieth birthday. I had a similar reaction then, and we had to take them down. It was the first time I told them anything about my experiences in the war.

The stethoscope moves around. I follow it. "He seems to have stabilized." It's Dr. Fish. "Let me know if his vitals change."

"Yes, doctor." Wanda is patting my forehead with a cool cloth. "I don't know what happened out there in the sun room, Mr. Simon, but you scared the heck out of us."

New word.

"You want to create a new word? Now?" Danielle asks.

Yes.

"OK, let's do it."

I create the blinky-blink signal for "chimes." It takes some time for her to get it - I guess we are both a little on edge.

"Chimes?" Wanda asks. "What does he mean by that?"

"I'm not sure. Are you saying, Isaac, that the chimes had something to do with you having that episode?"

Yes.

Danielle and Wanda are silent. I can almost hear them scratching their heads. It is really important for them to know that my reaction was not to the sun room itself; I'd be devastated if they blamed this situation on the sun room and stopped bringing me out there.

"Does he still have nightmares?" Danielle and Wanda have moved away from the bed, but I can still hear them talking.

"On a few occasions we've thought he was having bad dreams," Wanda replies.

I hear Danielle approach the bed. She puts her hand on my cheek. "Do the chimes have something to do with the war, Isaac?"

Yes. Smart woman! I've said before how you remind me of your father.

"I don't understand the connection, but before we go out next time, I think the chimes should be taken down."

"I'll note that in his chart," Wanda says.

Thank you.

They called it "Kristallnacht." The night in November 1938 when Nazi goons rampaged through Germany vandalizing synagogues, Jewish homes, cemeteries and businesses, and beating up Jews. It was the night the Nazi movement's anti-Semitism added an even more sinister dimension to its operation; it expanded from bureaucratic and controlling to openly vicious and violent. Some English language newspapers called it "The Night of Broken Glass." But more than glass was broken; Western civilization itself had gone off a cliff.

Hitler had been on the move for over a year, annexing Austria in March, and grabbing the Sudetenland from Czechoslovakia in October. Twenty years after the end of the Great War - the "war to end all wars"- the world was on the brink of another catastrophe, but, unlike my war, there actually was a good reason to fight this one.

Relegated to Section C of the *Sunday Boston Globe* on November thirteenth was the headline: "Nazis wipe out Jews' Business." The article described the new measures taken by the Nazis to essentially destroy the Jewish community in Germany. From prohibiting Jews from owning or managing large business enterprises, to barring them from owning retail businesses, to blocking them from concerts, movie houses, theaters and other public places. It even included cancelation of insurance policies so that repairs to the property and homes damaged during Kristallnacht were the responsibility of the owners. The article also described the arrest of thousands of Jews across Germany.

I was reading the paper alone at the breakfast table. Virginia was at church with Emma, and the boys were upstairs doing their homework. It was impossible to grasp what was going on in Germany. It seemed insane, but all too real. I had vague recollections of armed men on horseback rampaging through Linkeve, burning houses and slashing at people. I remember running into the forest with my mother and father and Chaim and waiting until the noise went away before we returned to find several homes and the synagogue burned to the ground along with the store where my Uncle Kalner worked. No one was killed that day, but many were hurt. It was awful, scary. But what was going on in Germany was on a scale unimagined before.

Albert came downstairs to get a snack and saw the headline in the paper. "We're kind of Jewish, aren't we, Dad?"

"Kind of," I said. "I was born Jewish, but was brought up without any strong religious connections. Mom, of course, grew up Unitarian. My mother never went to the synagogue, nor did my Uncle Kalner who lived with us for a few years. If you remember your Nana's memorial service, there was no rabbi or any religious symbols. That was per her strict instructions to me."

He sat down opposite me at the table and took a big bite out of an apple. "If we were in Germany today we'd be considered Jewish."

He'd been reading the newspapers, too. "Probably. But, then what is going on in Germany is insane."

"Insane, but terrible and inhuman."

"Yes, it is."

"What's going to happen? I mean, will the rest of the world just stand by and let the situation get even worse?"

I looked into the eyes of my fifteen-year-old son. Do I tell him what I hope will happen, or what I think and fear will happen? I opted for the latter, at least some of it. "I think the world will protest, send letters, and threaten diplomatic action, but will essentially do nothing. They did nothing when one of the first things Hitler did - back in 1933, soon after he came to power - was to take control of the trade unions, shut down all leftist and communist publications and arrest union leaders and left-leaning activists. That was Hitler's first move against democracy and civil rights and he got away with it. Hell, the world even participated in the Olympic Games in Berlin two years ago."

I tossed the newspaper on the floor. "These latest outrages are not his first move against the Jews, nor will they be the last. And Hitler has territorial ambitions as well - he's already grabbed Austria and part of Czechoslovakia, and he won't stop there. Right now, Hitler and Mussolini are actively supporting the Fascist forces in Spain. We, the American government that is, have adopted a policy of wait and see. The rest of Europe, too, is just standing by and watching. Europe will not move against Hitler until they feel directly threatened. America? Who knows when we'll get involved, but it will happen."

"War?" It was a question weighted with fear and innocence.

"Probably." What else could I say? All I could hope for was that it would be over before he and Mark were old enough to get caught up in it.

He tossed his apple core in the trash. "I still have a paper on Macbeth to write. See you later."

I made myself another cup of tea, then picked up the Globe again. Buried on page forty-three was a short article about the Boston police providing protection to the German consulate - apparently the consul had received death threats against himself and his family. Similar threats were made against German representatives in other parts of the country. Some people were paying attention.

I drained my tea and went into my studio. I replaced the half-finished work on my easel with a blank canvas, squeezed large mounds of scarlet and black paint onto my pallet, picked up a wide brush and set to work. I envisioned this rigid, mechanized Nazi cloud descending over the world, crushing down, destroying everything but a few sparks of color. My mind was churning, absorbing and translating these abstract images of life fighting back against the pressure of dull, deadly uniformity.

I worked on four canvases simultaneously and I did not stop until sometime late at night. I slept in the easy chair in the studio and woke up to the sound of the blue jays at the feeder, and I continued painting. Virginia came in every so often with tea or sandwiches; she said nothing. The children went to school and came home; I kept painting. I had never worked in such a sustained, focused way before. It was not trance-like; I knew what I wanted to paint, what I envisioned, and I was intensely aware of how the paint on the canvas was illuminating that vision.

Finally, long after midnight, the paintings were done. I put my brushes down and stepped back. These were different. Certainly, they carried my style and built on everything I had done in the past, but they were bolder, more assertive. There was nothing passive about these four canvases; they demanded a response. I sat down in the chair and soon fell asleep.

Virginia was standing with her back to me looking at the paintings. She had brought in a tray with tea and toast, and was still holding it. I moved my feet and she turned. "My God, they're powerful, Isaac!" She placed the tray on the small table next to me and turned to look at the paintings again. "I'm sorry, the toast is cold - I've been here for about ten minutes, unable to move."

"No matter. I'm so hungry right now I could eat cardboard." I devoured the toast and gulped down the tea, then stood behind her and wrapped my arms around her. "What an amazing couple of days it has been. I gained a whole new understanding of my art. Thank you for allowing me to just go."

She twisted her body and kissed me.

***

Allen is talking to Dr. Fish. It is hard to hear what is being said. The word "episode" has come up more than a couple of times. Also, "more tests" and "very old." As if we all don't know that I am very old. And I don't want any more tests: as you say, I'm very old - there's not much left to test. No more needles, no more electrodes! I've had enough of all of that. As far as I can tell, nothing has changed since my "episode." I can still blink. I can remember and, apparently, I can still have pretty good arguments in my head!

I hear Allen approach the bed and sit in the chair.

I'm awake.

"Hi, Grandpa Isaac."

Smile. Flowers. I can still smell the lilacs that Danielle brought in.

"Sorry. I missed the second word," he says, then adds, "Oh, I see you've got a couple of new words on the chart."

Flowers.

"Flowers? The lilacs - they're in full bloom. Danielle was here this morning. Did she bring them?

Yes.

He pauses and touches my shoulder. "Dr. Watson says you had an episode when they took you out to the sun room this morning."

He waits for my response, but I remain still.

"He's not sure what caused it. He wants to run some tests."

No. No.

"You've had enough tests?"

Yes. More than enough.

"That's what I told him. But, do you know what happened?"

Yes. Chimes.

"I wondered why that word was on your chart. Your episode had something to do with chimes?"

Yes. Talk to Danielle - she gets it.

"I'll tell the doctor I do not authorize further testing on this episode - whatever the hell they mean by 'episode!' I really hate that word."

Me too. *Thank you.*

"So, to other things. It's just before four on Friday, June fourteenth. It has been, as you know, a warm and sunny day, and I'm done with school for a couple of months. I submitted the last grades this morning, then Martha and I went out for a leisurely lunch, came home and we did a bit of weeding in the garden, and here I am."

Smile.

"Tomorrow morning, around six, I start chapter one. My brain is buzzing - I have written a hundred variations of the first line in my head, and I'm still not sure what I will actually put on the paper. It's both terrifying and invigorating; there's nothing quite like it."

This is the third time I've heard variations of this speech. The previous two times I could at least respond with some degree of shared excitement at the commencement of a new novel. This time, all I can do is use blinky-blink to say; *Like. Story. Smile.*

"Thanks, Grandpa Isaac. I'll read you the first chapter when it's written."

Smile.

"Sorry to interrupt." It's Wanda. "I just need to go through the usual." I feel her fiddle with the tubes.

"Excuse me, nurse, were you here this morning?" Allen asks her.

"I was. Isaac had what I would describe as a panic attack. He was able to communicate why it happened. Those wind-chimes triggered some traumatic memory from the war. It's all in his chart."

"Dr. Watson said nothing about that. He was talking of running more tests."

"Dr. Watson, between you, me and Isaac, is not the most imaginative doctor. He also doesn't always find it necessary to read the chart. I'll talk with him."

"Thank you."

Thank you. Wanda is wonderful.

Quite unexpectedly I received a call from our old client, Celia. She and Grace wanted me to design an extra room and a large covered deck for their home. I had not done much architecture work over the past few years so I jumped at the opportunity. She invited Virginia and me to visit the following Saturday afternoon for tea and to discuss their ideas. It was so good to hear from them.

It was a cold January day with a light snow falling on and off all morning. But by the time we arrived at their house the sun had come out and the world sparkled. Everything stood out in brilliant relief against the white backdrop. I stopped on the path to the front door to watch a crimson cardinal sitting on a branch of a bare young maple and calling to his mate, who arrived moments later.

When we entered the house I saw immediately that my painting they had acquired from Lizzie Sloan was no longer in the hallway. Celia noticed my reaction. "Lizzie is finally back on her feet," she said. "She's remarried and they moved to Virginia. We sent the paintings to her once she had settled in to her new home."

"I'm glad to hear that," I said. "Are you still in touch with Anthony's daughter?"

"Not much. She finished her studies and is teaching in Bedford, I think," Grace said. "She lives alone in that lovely home in Concord. I heard she's written a novel she's trying to get published. I reached out to her a few months ago: we invited her to dinner, but she declined."

We sat in the parlor, looking out over the snow-covered back yard. Celia showed me a rough sketch of the changes they wanted to make to the house, and we talked about specifics of location, access, size and what these spaces would be used for. I set about drawing a quick plan view of the house with proposed additions. Then I stepped out into the snow to take the needed measurements.

When I came back inside, Virginia and Grace were seated on the couch in deep conversation. Virginia was holding a magazine written in German and Grace was explaining what it was all about. "It is an underground publication put out by a small group of homosexual men in Germany. I'm sure you've read about the trade unions being crushed, and the Nazi's attacks on Jews, but no one talks about the arrest and imprisonment of thousands of homosexuals, many of whom have been tortured or executed, or both." She was on the verge of tears. "This magazine exposes what is going on. I've tried to get the Globe to write about it, but they've refused."

"There's this prevailing idea that these men are not worth fighting for or even talking about, that they deserve to die," Celia added.

"Let me take some notes," Virginia said. "I still have my weekly column in a small Cambridge paper." She took out a note pad and pen.

"There's also a short article about Hitler's special police rounding up thousands of physically and mentally handicapped people," Grace said. "No one is quite sure what has happened to them. There are rumors that these people are being used for medical experiments."

"Horrifying," Virginia exclaimed, and kept on writing.

We all sat silently. There was nothing that could be said.

After some time, Grace asked, "How is your painting going, Isaac?"

"I really like my most recent work - it's somewhat darker than my previous paintings."

"A reflection of the times, perhaps?" Grace replied.

"Very much so."

"We'd love to see it; we need to replace Lizzie's painting."

"I'll bring a few paintings when I come back to show you some ideas for the modifications to the house." We made an appointment for three weeks away - the first Saturday in February.

As we drove home, Virginia was quiet. When I tried to engage her in conversation, she reached across and lightly touched my shoulder. "I'm thinking," is all she said, and we drove on in silence. Back at the house she went directly to our bedroom, and asked not to be disturbed. It was close to supper time so I decided to cook one of the few things I knew how to make - macaroni and cheese.

The kids were on the floor in the living room, playing *Anagrams,* a board game they had received for Christmas from their grandparents. They had apparently fixed themselves a snack sometime during the afternoon and left a sticky mess in the kitchen. My first impulse was to make them come and clean up the place, but they were doing so well together and were having so much fun, that I let it go. It only took me a few minutes to straighten it out, anyway.

Once the casserole was in the oven, I went to sit in the parlor with the day's newspaper, to which I paid little attention, preferring to listen in on the conversation that was taking place between the three young people on the carpet.

"Are we really Jewish?" Emma asked.

"Dad said we're kind of Jewish. I asked him," Albert responded.

Mark, said, "We can't be Jewish. Mom's a Christian and under Jewish law a person is Jewish only if their mother is Jewish."

"But, in Germany, the Nazis go back three or four generations on both sides to figure out if a person is Jewish."

"That doesn't make sense," Emma said. "To be a Jew you have to believe in the Jewish religion. If you have no religion, you can't be Jewish!"

"Not according to the Nazis," Albert replied.

"Well, the Nazis aren't here and I don't care what they say. I'm not a Jew. Not even according to Jewish law."

There was a brief pause, then Albert said, "That still doesn't make what Hitler is doing right!" He paused again. "Dad thinks there will be another war."

"Do you, Dad?" Emma asked, and she came to sit next to me on the sofa.

I took her hand. "Unfortunately, Emma, I don't think Hitler's going to suddenly reverse direction. At some point the world will decide they have to stop him from taking over other countries, and from hurting groups of people he doesn't like."

The kitchen timer sounded. "Supper's ready. Go'n wash up, everyone."

We sat around the kitchen table and I served the macaroni and cheese. "Where's Mom?" Emma asked.

"She's working on her column for the paper. She told me not to disturb her."

"You'd better put aside supper for her before those monsters devour it all," Emma said, pointing at her brothers who, surprisingly, did not respond.

"Good idea."

Chapter 53

It was a short article under the headline; "Hitler's strategy to numb us into complacency." Virginia described a consciously planned sequence of actions that the Nazis had executed against different groups of people, starting with the ones most Westerners either did not think about, or despised or feared. The Communists, Socialists and Anarchists were attacked first, followed almost immediately by the trade unionists because the elites of the industrialized countries would themselves have been happy to see these people removed from their own political and economic landscapes. These attacks were reported, but no one urged any action.

Then they went after the homosexuals, because the whole world had little understanding or sympathy for them and was unmoved by their plight. The arrests, torture and murder of homosexual men was barely reported in our newspapers. We chose to ignore it because, while we didn't like torture and murder, we also didn't condone homosexuality. We even had laws against it.

And then the Nazis escalated their attacks on the Jews. While anti-Semitism had been fundamental to the Nazi movement, the large-scale arrests and totalitarian regulations, followed by organized violence, were not implemented until the other "undesirables" were out of the way, and the world was lulled into accepting Hitler's repressive actions. And even regarding the Jews, Hitler relied on a significant underbelly of anti-Semitism in Europe and America.

In his quest to craft a master race, Hitler was weeding out everyone that did not fit his vision. While the major round-ups of Jews were gaining most of the headlines in the newspapers of the world, a less publicized campaign was waged against smaller religious groups, gypsies and also the mentally and physically disabled.

"The world has been lulled into inaction," Virginia wrote. "My fear is that nothing will be done until Hitler marches again. My fear is that we are on the brink of another war, one made more inevitable tomorrow because of our inaction yesterday and today."

Virginia concluded the article; "As I write this, my husband is in the parlor talking about the prospects of war with our children, aged eleven to fifteen. This is not what any father wants to be doing. It is not the future he fought and bled for in the mud of France twenty-one years ago."

She finished the article around ten-thirty in the evening. I heard the bedroom door open, then I heard her go into the kids' bedrooms and kiss them and whisper something to each of them. When she came down to the parlor she had tears in her eyes. She handed me the article and walked into the kitchen. "You saved me supper. Thanks."

She ate her cold macaroni and cheese in the kitchen while I read the article. She had captured so much in the three-hundred-and-fifty words she was allowed. She had a remarkable ability to see the relationship between events, how they intersect and influence one another.

She entered the parlor and sat beside me.

"Your article is really powerful, Virginia: very perceptive and thought-provoking."

"You paint it, I write it."

"Hmm."

"Seriously, Isaac, I found myself flashing on your paintings as I wrote the first draft. That dark, sinister, calculating undertow; it's how they operate. The Nazis have figured out what they can get away with. They push and push with arrogance and impunity. And, in the meantime, they are stockpiling weapons and aircraft and God knows what else..."

There was a heavy silence between us. "Can I change the subject?" I said.

"Sure. I'm exhausted thinking about war and Hitler."

"How are our finances?"

She grunted. "Not good. This work for Celia and Grace has come at the right time. Another couple of months, and we'd have been thinking about selling something else. And, hopefully, they'll buy a painting or two. Why do you ask?"

"I'm running out of paints and canvases. I have no problem painting over old pieces I'm no longer happy with - the process might even elicit some unexpected results - but I can't do anything without paints. Also, I need to replace some brushes; they're plain worn out. I'm probably going to need to spend around twenty dollars."

"Can you wait until you get paid by Celia and Grace?"

"We're that tight?"

"We are."

"I had no idea. I suppose I could ask for partial payment on the design work up front. It's often done."

"I think it's worth giving Marjorie Ross a call, too. Perhaps she can showcase your new works."

"I'm amazed she's been able to hold on to Nouvelle Vision this long."

"Rich people still have money; maybe not as much, but enough to add a little color to their lives every now and then."

"I'll call her Monday morning."

I looked up at the space where our Kandinsky used to be. "How long can the economy continue like this, Virginia? You seem to have some insight into the way the world works."

Virginia looked at me with a faint smile, which suddenly changed into a grimace of fear. She took both my hands in hers. "There are several economists and politicians saying that what we need is a 'good war.' It looks like we're going to get it. It might be good for the economy, but not much else." Her eyes glanced upwards to where our children slept.

***

Damon the Good is here; he is humming softly.

I'm here.

"Hi Isaac, why are you awake at this crazy hour? It's four-fifteen Saturday morning. The whole world is sleeping except you and me."

Smile.

"Yeah. I love the way you smile. Would you like me to comb that golden white beard?"

Yes. Like.

He sits on the bed and gently massages my face, then begins to brush my beard.

"A long time ago, I told you about splitting up with my wife soon after I got back from the desert. That was only partly true, of course. There was no wife." He sighed loudly. "Adam and I had been together a couple of years before I signed up. He was really mad at me for joining the army.

He was right - at least he was right when he said it would not be what I expected, and that it would drive us apart. But I hadn't worked in ages, I'd run out of unemployment and I figured I'd learn something in the army - which I did. I'd taken a few pre-med classes before I ran out of money and dropped out of college so they sent me off to be a medic, and here I am."

Damon stopped brushing and rested one of his hands on mine. "Adam and I got back together after I came back from Iraq, but it didn't work out. I saw him at a party last night. I almost never go to parties, working this crazy shift, but someone convinced me to go. He was alone, like me. We talked; it was awkward, but we made plans to have lunch tomorrow."

Smile.

"I'm really nervous. It's been so long since we've seen each other, since I've even been on a date." He started brushing again. "We have a lot of history - good and bad."

How do I encourage and support him? *Hug.*

"Thanks, Isaac," he says, and hugs me gently. "I have to stop in with Mrs. K. next door. See you later."

***

Nobody wanted another war and Hitler knew it and exploited that reluctance. The news from Germany grew worse every day, and thousands were trying to get out as the repression increased. But the flood of refugees was not welcomed. Refugee ships arriving in Cuba were sent back to Europe. America seemed open to accepting wealthier, educated Jews, but there was resistance to the destitute. And as the tide swelled, the voices of isolationism and hate swelled, too. Laws were passed limiting immigration. Thousands were turned away.

My Uncle Kalner, still with the Ladies' Garment Workers Union in New York, became actively involved in a campaign to open the doors to the refugees. Members of his union worked extra hours to send money to help people escape. He traveled the East Coast building support for the campaign and came to Boston for a few days in June 1939. I met him at South Station in the late afternoon. The last time we had seen each other was when he visited the area briefly on union business six years before, but he was unchanged - at sixty-four he still had a full head of dark hair and he carried himself with that same air of confidence and energy. His bear hug was the same, too.

"I have a busy schedule of meetings," he said, as we waited for the subway. "Tonight is my only time off - after that, morning noon and night I'm talking to unions, Jewish groups, other religious groups, including Virginia's Unitarians, and several student groups." He put his hands on my shoulder, like I was a little boy. "So, Itzik, if you don't mind, I would prefer not to talk about Hitler or refugees or politics tonight."

"OK."

"How are you and Virginia doing? Are you working, painting? I know that the WPA funding for artists was cut."

"We're getting by, probably better than most. I finished a small architecture project a couple of weeks ago and have even sold a painting or two. I spend most of my time in my studio."

"And Virginia?"

"She continues to write her column for a small local newspaper. She's been negotiating with a few other papers in surrounding towns, trying to get them to carry it, too. She is, as you know, very outspoken and she gets people thinking and talking about important issues. She generates flurries of letters to the editor, which is also good for business. But, we said we weren't going to talk about politics. How is Mary?"

"She's been with me on most of these trips, but she's worn out. She came down with a bad cold, so she had to take a break. She was really looking forward to seeing you, but just did not have the energy."

We arrived back at the house to find Virginia and all three of our children in the kitchen preparing dinner together. "We're having a triple celebration feast tonight," Emma yelled as we entered. "First is to welcome Uncle Kalner, who we haven't seen in forever. Second is because Mom just heard from the church and they are going to start paying her again, and number three is that Marjorie called to say that she sold two of your paintings this morning!"

"Wow! A feast indeed - and well deserved," Uncle Kalner said as he embraced Virginia and each of our children.

"I bought beer," Virginia said. "Help yourselves and go'n sit in the parlor. I'm sure you have a lot of catching up to do. We'll join you in a little while."

Kalner told me he planned to retire from the union the following year and devote all his time to the refugee situation. He also talked about word leaking out of Germany describing ongoing and escalating mass evictions, confiscation of property and arrests. And he talked about the concentration camps where tens of thousands were being held. I showed him the article Virginia had written and he confirmed the treatment of non-Jewish religious minorities and homosexuals. He also said that he had compelling information about the mentally and physically handicapped being used for medical experimentation, confirming the reports in that underground magazine that Grace and Celia had shared.

"Hitler's not going to stop anytime soon." He stood up and placed himself in front of the Klee. "Do you know that this artist, and many other modernists are regarded as degenerate? Their work has been removed from galleries, museums, and even private homes and has been burnt in the streets, or stolen by SS officers." He sat down heavily. "The world is in for another war - it's a matter of when, not if."

He stood again and began pacing. Finally he stopped in front of me. "But I said I didn't want to talk about all of this! I'm sorry. Tell me about the boys and Emma."

Dinner was spectacular; fresh salad, followed by roast beef with potatoes, broccoli and summer squash. For dessert we had apple pie with vanilla ice cream. Uncle Kalner told stories of picket lines and union battles. He also went into great detail recounting the story of our arrival in America and how I met my good friend Reuven at the immigration center on Ellis Island. Virginia, Albert, Mark and Emma were entranced, as was I; I was fascinated to hear that story told from his perspective.

The next morning he was out of the house by nine and we didn't see him till ten in the evening. He had a quick cup of tea, then went straight to bed, exhausted. The next day was the same. On the third morning, the last of his visit, I accompanied him to the subway station. He was on his way to talk with a group of local church leaders in Boston. He had his suitcase with him. He looked worn out.

"It was so good to see you, Kalner. I just wish we could have spent a little more time together."

"Yes, it was wonderful to be with you all. You have great children, and Virginia is a remarkable person; you two are so good together." He hugged me, then stepped back and said, "But time - there is none. The world is out of time."

How does one respond to that? So I said, "Give our love to Mary. I hope she's better soon."

As it turned out, Mary's cold was far more serious. Uncle Kalner never talked about it, but she grew steadily worse, losing a lot of weight, until she finally died in February the next year. The weekend of the service the East Coast experienced a monumental snow storm that shut down trains and roads for days. We were unable to be there. I tried to make plans to go in March, but Kalner was already off to Washington to meet with senators and congressmen about the refugees.

War had broken out in Europe; Germany had advanced into Poland and set up Nazi rule. Hitler's police were rounding up Jews and herding them into ghettos.

Nine years after the end of the war we were visiting Kalner in his tiny apartment in New York City. He was not at all well; his heart was failing as was his eyesight, as a result of the diabetes which had gone undiagnosed for years. He rarely went out, and seemed to spend much of his time listening to and swearing at the radio. "They're trying to rewrite history, those bastards. Right after the war, when the camps were opened up, those mindless, heartless bastards in Washington started saying they didn't know. Bullshit! They knew. I told them many times about what Hitler was doing. Many people told them. We brought them documentation and letters, even photographs that had been smuggled out, but they did nothing. Worse than nothing - they turned people away, sent the overloaded ships back to Europe. Now they're trying to say they never knew. Lying anti-Semitic bastards - the lot of them! They knew. They just were too cowardly to do anything. I don't believe in hell, Itzik, but for them I am willing to make an exception!"

As war exploded through Europe, the economy here began to improve, just as Virginia had surmised. By the end of 1940, Hitler controlled most of Eastern and Western Europe. The first British attempts to defend France had led to chaos and the evacuation at Dunkirk. The American unemployment rate dropped three-and-a-half percent. The next year it would drop another five percent to just over nine-and-a-half. And then came Pearl Harbor and our entry into the war; unemployment plummeted to almost zero.

Albert graduated from high school in June 1941. He had been a good student - not great, but good enough to be accepted at Massachusetts State College in Amherst to study history and economics. During the summer between high school and college I was able to get him a job on a construction crew building a small office complex in Cambridge I had designed. No one but the construction foreman knew he was my son, although I'm sure many of his co-workers saw the physical resemblance and the fact that we shared a last name. They knew he was a short-term worker, and nick-named him "Harvard." He responded jokingly to the ribbing and applied himself with determination to the job.

I had to visit the site fairly frequently and I did my best to ignore him, which he appreciated. I could not help but watch him from afar, though, and feel pride in his ability to learn the job and do it well. He handed a quarter of each pay packet to Virginia and put most of the rest into his savings for college.

In late August we saw him off at South Station. He returned home for Thanksgiving and the next time we saw him was on our doorstep on December twelfth. A couple of days after the attack on Pearl Harbor, Albert and almost all the men in his class had dropped out of college and signed up. He was home for a few days before having to report for his physical. He was assigned to the 1st Division, nicknamed "The Big Red One," and spent Christmas at Camp Devens, which, judging from the postcards he sent still looked much like it did when I returned from France. By the end of February he was in a training camp in Florida, and then to Camp Benning in Georgia.

I don't know how he found the time or the energy, but he managed to write home two or three times a week throughout his whole time in the Army, except, of course, when other things prevented him - those long, stress-filled, inevitable periods when we heard nothing. We kept all his letters and cards. His letters, like those of millions of other soldiers over the years, talked about trivialities and tried to reassure the folks back home that everything was fine, the food wasn't terrible, and he was with a good bunch of guys. Occasionally he'd let us know how tired or bored he was. Or he would ask after people he knew, went to school with, played ball with. Sometimes he'd actually write about some humorous incident in the camp, or about someone from home he'd run into. I knew these letters; I'd written them myself.

Towards the end of August, a letter arrived with a new, rather obscure return address, saying that he had been moved again and could not say where they were because their mail was now being censored. He also said we might not hear from him for a while. That night at our dinner table Virginia started the meal by asking us all to hold hands and be quiet for a minute. Then she said, simply, "Let Albert be safe. Let them all be safe." This became our family practice every dinner. The war had become personal. We added Mark's name after he enlisted in the Army Air Forces after his eighteenth birthday in December 1942.

Albert's next letter arrived almost a month later. It was dated September twenty-fourth, 1942. There was no mention of where he was, but he referred to spending days on a ship in cramped quarters, being seasick, and being glad to be on "terra firma" again. He was clearly no longer on American soil. His new address, one he would have for some time, was Company B, 26th Inf., APO 1. Two days later, a letter came from "Somewhere in England." My nightmares returned with greater frequency. I remember waking up many times to Virginia's soothing voice and cool hands on my brow.

The newspapers, understandably, were vague about the details of the war. They would write articles, and show maps, but would say little or nothing about which units were involved. It wasn't until late November that the Globe reported on American troops being involved in the battles for Tunisia. Albert had been there a month; his letters simply said, "Somewhere in Africa," but he wrote of desert sandstorms and miles of nothing.

There are enough books out there on the history of the First Division in World War Two; some even tell things from the perspective of the poor bastards on the ground. Albert was with the Big Red One through Tunisia, Sicily and Omaha Beach. He was injured a few days after the landing, was sent to recover in England and then returned to another unit in Belgium just in time for the so-called "Battle of the Bulge." From there they went into Germany, bringing supplies and medical relief to a recently liberated small concentration camp along the way. He came home in time for Thanksgiving 1945. These are the bare bones of what he went through.

He came home having been through hell, to a home where his brother and sister were gone, both casualties of the war. While the rest of the country was dancing in the streets, having parades and celebrations, we were in mourning. I remember that afternoon when he appeared at the front door. He had telephoned a couple of days before to say his unit was being dismissed from Fort Benning, Georgia and he had a train ticket home. He was not sure when he'd be getting to town. He did not want us to meet him at the station.

So there he appeared on the doorstep, in uniform, with a big duffle bag over his shoulder. He had done his best to look good; he had pressed his shirt and shaved, but he had lost a lot of weight, and his eyes were dark and sunken as if he had not slept in months. As Virginia reached out to embrace him, he dropped the duffel bag and clung to her. I watched them with tears rolling down my face. "You're home, Albert! You're home!" She said it over and over again. I wrapped my arms around them both.

When he entered the house, he went straight upstairs to the room he and Mark had shared from infancy. "I'll be down in a minute," he said.

"I prepared macaroni and cheese," Virginia said. "I'll put it in the oven."

We could hear him pacing back and forth in his room, then going into Emma's room which had been left virtually unchanged since her death. We heard him sit heavily on her bed.

He came down after about half an hour wearing a pair of dark blue slacks and a flannel shirt. We all sat at the kitchen table. He kept shaking his head from side to side. "They're really gone," he said. "You get a letter with news like that, and you're in a crazy, unreal situation yourself - you just file it away. You can't deal with it. You can't do anything about it, so you just push it aside." Tears were flowing down his cheeks, dripping from his chin onto the table. "And here I am, home, safe, and the first thing I do is to go up to check on my little brother and sister, and they're not there. I've seen a lot of people die, but those empty beds upstairs…"

We stayed up well after midnight talking about Emma and Mark. Not a word was spoken about Albert's experiences on the other side of the ocean.

Chapter 54

I still ran my architecture practice out of the house, and when I had no architecture to work on I had the studio. I was home most of the time. Virginia had taken on extra duties at the church, so she was out of the house in the mornings.

Albert spent most of his first two weeks back home sleeping. He would get up around noon, have a meal, lie on the sofa until supper-time, eat, and then go back up to bed. Virginia and I took our cues from him. We had no idea what he had seen and done; we knew he needed time and distance to recover, and besides, he was exhausted.

Thanksgiving was difficult. He did not want to leave the house to go to Virginia's parents who had invited "a few family members to welcome him home." We promised we would stay only a couple of hours and he reluctantly conceded. The "few family members" turned out to be almost a dozen of the Appleton clan, one of whom arrived in his lieutenant uniform, and he made a bee-line for Albert telling of his exploits in an intelligence unit posted to Iceland for the duration of the war.

Albert looked at me helplessly. I flashed on my own experience meeting the officer sons of rich people who had served far away from the war zones. I remember feeling they talked so much because they had nothing to talk about. I took Albert's arm. "I don't think you've said hello to your grandfather yet," I said and steered him away in the direction of the drinks table. He poured himself a large whisky. Virginia joined us.

"Mom, can you ask Gran not to seat me near that man," Albert said, gritting his teeth.

"I'll talk to her," Virginia said, and strode off toward her mother who was circulating through the room with a tray of appetizers. Virginia virtually pushed her out of the parlor and then returned moments later with the appetizers in hand - apparently her mother had gone to the dining room to rearrange the seating cards.

But, the revised seating arrangements still had Uncle Peter sitting across the table from Virginia, Albert and I, and Peter asked Albert the same question he had asked me the first time I was introduced to him; "Did you see much combat?"

"More than I'd care to remember," Albert said. He stood and excused himself. I followed and found him in the parlor pouring another large whiskey. "I'll be back in a minute, Dad. Don't worry. Do you think I'd bypass a big turkey dinner?" he laughed. "Go back; I'll join you in a minute." He took a big gulp of his drink and waited for me to leave.

"Don't be too long, Albert."

"Don't worry."

He did, in fact, return to the dining table soon after me. He sat quietly and ate his dinner. He answered, politely, but briefly when conversation was directed at him. I could feel his discomfort; he was not ready for this. When the meal was over and Mrs. Appleton announced that she would bring the coffee to the parlor, I whispered to Virginia that we should leave. She agreed. We said our good-byes to her parents who had stayed behind in the dining room.

Albert hugged his grandparents warmly. "I'm sorry about ..."

"There's nothing to apologize for, Albert my dear young man," Virginia's mother said. "I understand." We slipped out without talking with any of the rest of the clan.

On December seventh, the anniversary of the attack on Pearl Harbor, I woke early and went into my studio and started painting. At some point Virginia came down and she brought in a tray of coffee and toast. She sat in the chair for a while and watched me work. "I'm worried about him," she said.

"So am I."

"It's been weeks and he can barely get out of bed. He needs to begin to look for something to do."

"I'll see if I can get him to help with some chores around the house."

"That would be a good start." She stood and kissed me. "I have to go. See you around lunch time."

Minutes after she left I heard Albert moving about upstairs. When he descended, I set down my paints and brushes and hurried to the kitchen. He was dressed, shaved and appeared ready to go out. "There's only so much lying about a person can do," he said. "I need to get off my butt."

I hugged him. "Coffee?"

"Yes, thanks. I'm going to write to the college and find out when I can resume my studies. Then I need to buy some clothes - everything hangs off me like a refugee." He gasped as the words slipped from his mouth. "What an insensitive thing to say," he muttered.

"One does get desensitized," I said. "I've been there, Albert. Whenever you want to talk about it, I'm here. OK?"

"OK. I'm going to fry some eggs; d'you want a couple?"

"Sure." Clearly he was not ready to talk.

We ate our breakfast together, talking about Virginia's work at the church and my on-again, off-again architecture practice. He washed the dishes, then said he needed to write some letters. I returned to my studio. At around eleven he popped his head in to say he was going to mail his letters and buy some clothes. I asked if he'd like me to go with him, but he said he wanted to do it alone.

He returned late in the afternoon with several shopping bags in his hands and the smell of whiskey on his breath. "Mission accomplished," he said. His words were a little slurred. He struggled going up the stairs to his room.

Virginia and I looked at one another. "We have to say something, Virginia, before this gets out of control."

"Yes," she said, moving her head slowly from side to side. "I wonder how long he's been doing this."

"From the ease with which he gulps it down, it's been way too long."

"On the other hand, he did get up and out of the house for the first time since Thanksgiving. He also wrote to the college about resuming his classes." She stood and began walking to the kitchen. "I need to start on dinner."

"I'll try to find a way to talk with him in the morning."

***

I hear the door close and then the sound of a zipper being opened. *I'm awake.*

"Hi Grandpa Isaac." It's Allen. "I snuck Kitty-bee in to see you. Martha told me her tricks."

I feel the cat move beside me, squeezing between my body and my arm, resting her head on my shoulder. *Happy. Thank you.*

"Two days of writing and I'm into chapter two. It's going well. I put in six hours yesterday then went for a long walk in the Arboretum. Seven hours today. I'm really excited about this story!"

Smile. Amazing how he can change gears like that! One day he's teaching English literature to a bunch of high school kids, the next day he's inside his head in a novel. Kitty-bee is purring loudly. I hope she doesn't attract any attention.

"It's almost eight o'clock on Saturday night, June fifteenth. I talked with Ginnie just before I came here. She called. She's OK. She says it's been a difficult but important few days for her, and for Jake's mom and dad. She'll be home around this time tomorrow. I'm picking her up at Logan."

Yes. I so look forward to seeing her. She keeps a lot to herself, and then she lets it all out in torrents; reminds me of Albert, her grandfather.

"It's kind of like she is trying to rearrange her life, to reorganize everything that was turned over and thrown into chaos nine months ago, to figure out what stays and what must go." He sighed. "It must be so hard. I wish there was something I could do to help her! I'm her dad. I should know, but I feel helpless."

All you can do, Allen, is be there. How do I say that in blinky-blink? *Hug.* He does not respond to my little word. I repeat, *Hug.*

I feel him hug me. The cat squirms then settles down. "Kitty-bee and I need to go - before she's discovered." He picks up the cat and zips her into the bag.

***

About ten days after Albert's shopping day, Virginia and I were having breakfast before she went off to work. Albert came down, poured himself a mug of coffee and announced that he had heard from the college and was going to resume his studies after the Christmas break. He had applied for benefits under the GI bill and he expected the government would pay his tuition and give him money to live on while in school. He still intended to study history and economics, but was also going to take education courses.

We both breathed sighs of relief; he was getting himself focused on the future, setting goals and making plans. "He's going to be OK," I said to Virginia as she left for work.

That night Albert had his first nightmare since returning home. We were woken by loud howls followed by shouts of, "No! No! No!" and then intermittent whimpering.

"I'll go," Virginia said, squeezing my shoulder, "I have dealt with this before."

I listened to her open his bedroom door and gently call his name. I could hear him thrashing around in the bed. Something crashed to the floor. "It's OK, Albert. I'm here. You're home. You're safe." She repeated these words several times until he finally quieted down. She stayed in his room for an hour or more.

"He's calm now," she said when she came back to bed, "although he never woke up."

The next morning he made no mention of his nightmare. He seemed well rested, at ease. He went out soon after lunch and did not return until almost ten; a taxi deposited him on the front step. He was too drunk to stand. I paid the driver and guided Albert to the couch where he collapsed. "I'll stay with him tonight," I said to Virginia. "You should get some sleep."

I removed Albert's shoes then fixed myself a pot of coffee and settled down in one of the comfortable chairs opposite the couch where Albert lay. All I could think about was my father and the way he treated my mother, Chaim and me when he was drunk - which in my mind seemed to be a constant state. I remembered him shouting and stumbling around. I remembered being afraid and hiding outside with Chaim. I remembered the relief in my mother's face when she heard that he was dead.

And here was my son, my only surviving child, lying drunk in front of me, snoring like an animal. I wanted to shake him awake, slap his face and yell at him. Yesterday it seemed like he was taking control of his life - now this! The longer I sat staring at him, the angrier I became. I could feel my teeth clenching and my nails digging into my palms.

Finally, I stood and strode into the kitchen and made another pot of coffee and a peanut butter sandwich. I looked at the clock on the wall - almost three. I took my coffee and sandwich into my studio and began to paint. After some time I realized I didn't know what I was doing; I seemed to have no control over my brushes, so I abandoned the effort and returned to the living room.

The sky was just beginning to lighten. Virginia came downstairs and I joined her in the kitchen for another coffee. "How's he?" she asked.

"He hasn't moved."

"Did you get any sleep?"

"No. I was too angry."

She reached across the table and patted my cheek. "You need to talk to him, Isaac. Today."

"I will."

Albert woke up some time after Virginia had left for work. I was dozing in the living room when I heard him stir. I opened my eyes; he was sitting up and looking intently at me. "I need to tell you about Red," he said.

I nodded.

"Red was one of my best buddies, even though he was about five years older than me. He was from Orange, Mass. We were partners on a B.A.R. team. We went through training camp, Tunisia and Sicily together. And we landed at Omaha Beach together. We called him Red because of his red hair. He was a big guy - six-three or more - and strong as an ox. He was the star on our regiment's baseball team. He was also funny as hell." Albert lifted himself off the couch. "I have to pee. I'll continue about Red in a minute."

He was gone for quite a while, but when he came back downstairs he had showered, shaved and dressed. "I'm putting on a pot of coffee. Do you want some?"

"No thanks. I've been drinking coffee all night."

When he returned he sat on the couch opposite me. "As I was saying, Red and I were together through everything, until Omaha Beach - well, till a couple of days after we landed. We somehow made it through the chaos on the beach and began climbing up the ridge, lugging that big gun and the ammo. The paratroopers had landed on top of the ridge and were in fierce battle with the Germans who were firing on the guys coming off the landing craft. It was horrific. Our lieutenant was killed before he even reached dry land. I saw him floating by, blood pouring from his face. His second in command was useless. We didn't know where we were, where we were supposed to be and what we were supposed to be doing, other than climbing up and shooting at Germans, wherever the hell they were.

"Somehow we made it to the top by the second day. Our company was able to regroup - at least the hundred or so men that had survived. Red and I set up our gun on this flat area overlooking the valley, facing away from the beach. We thought we could see everything, but the underbrush and hedgerows were deceptively thick. That night a German patrol found us. I was on the ground in position to fire. Red was ready to feed the ammo. All of a sudden Red sees these Germans at the edge of the brush to our right, silhouetted against the bright night sky. I swing the gun and start firing and three of them go down. The fourth hurls a grenade which lands a few feet behind me. Pain blasts through both my feet and lower legs.

"The next thing I remember is Red lowering me into a ditch, and then he yells and falls over. I wake up the next day in an aid station. My feet and legs are bandaged and are killing me. They tell me I'm lucky to have survived and that I'm being sent to England for surgery. I ask about Red and no one knows where he is. After almost two months in an army hospital in England a letter from that useless second lieutenant, who is now number one, finally finds me. He asks after my health. He also writes that Red is dead."

Albert's hands start trembling, and tears are dripping down his face. "My last memory of Red is that he saved me, then I remember him shouting and falling down like he was hit. He saved me, and he died for his trouble. He had a wife and a three-year-old daughter. He carried their pictures with him wherever he went. He showed them to me dozens of times. He showed me the scribbles and pictures his little girl had drawn for him. And he was killed carrying me to safety." He shook his head slowly. "How do I carry that, Dad?"

I moved to sit beside him, wrapped my arms around him and let him sob into my shoulder. There was nothing I could say.

***

Danielle is here. I hear her breathing evenly in the chair next to the bed. I hear her turning the pages of a book.

I'm awake. She does not respond. I guess she's been here a while. I wait until she turns another page and I signal again. She closes the book.

"Hi there, old man. Good to see you."

Smile.

"It's almost six-thirty, Sunday evening, June sixteenth. Allen and Martha have gone to the airport to pick up Ginnie. I brought a bunch of roses - dark red. Can you smell them?"

I try breathing in deeply. *No.*

"Let me hold them closer."

I feel the soft petals brush my cheek and nose. I inhale. Lovely. *Thank you. Happy.*

"Any new words?"

No. I think I've reached a point where I have enough; at least, I have accepted the fact that the twenty-five or so words I have created will have to suffice. It's hard enough remembering all of them. I actually only use about half of them most of the time, anyway.

"Would you like me to read the Globe?"

Yes.

"Red Sox?"

No. I think I need to know a little about what is going on in the world besides sports.

"Arts?"

No.

"News?"

Yes.

"OK." She rummages through the paper. Here's one we're all going to have to deal with. The headline is; 'Backlash felt far from Ground Zero, anti-Muslim sentiment will be focus of forum.' Interested?"

Yes. Those nine-eleven terrorists were Muslim fanatics, but why do people blame all Muslims? We didn't blame all Christians for Oklahoma City. The common thread is not religion, it's fanaticism, and underlying that is disconnection from humanity. Why is it we are so quick to judge who our enemy is, who hates us, but we have such a hard time recognizing who loves us and cares about us? But, enough of my preaching! I do find it encouraging that this forum is to take place in a Christian church.

She comes to the end of the article. "Shall I read something else?"

No. Thank you. I've had enough.

***

Albert and I sat together on the couch a long time without talking. Finally, I said, "Albert, I don't know how you carry that burden, but I do know that drinking will not make it go away."

He shook his head angrily and moved to stand up. I grabbed his arm and pulled him back down. "You need to listen to me, Albert. I haven't finished." He slumped back. "There is one thing I think you should consider doing."

"What?"

"I think you should visit Red's family. I know it will be hard, but they will want to know about your friendship with him and about what he did for you. I believe that if the situation were reversed, if that grenade had hit him, you would have dragged him back to a safe place. Mom and I would have liked to meet him. War is horrible, and horrible things happen. It is also random." I paused and put my arm around him. "If you want, Albert, I'll go with you to Orange to see them."

"I'll think about going to see them," he said. "Can I leave now?"

"No. We need to talk about booze."

"I'm not in the mood."

"Do you remember your Grandmother Rivka, my mother?" I said, ignoring his protest.

"Of course; she lived with us."

"You were only five or six when she died, so you probably don't remember too much."

"I don't. What does she have to do with the subject?"

"You were too young to realize she never talked about my father, her husband. There were no pictures of him in her apartment in Lawrence, and none in her room here. He died when I was ten. I remember him well, too well. He was a nasty drunk; he yelled at us and smashed things. My mother, brother and I lived in fear of him. She intimated to me a few years after we came to America, that he had raped her. When he died of exposure, having fallen drunk into a ditch on his way home from the tavern, my mother finally breathed freely, she came to life."

I paused, waiting for him to look at me. "Albert, when I sat here last night listening to you snoring drunk on that couch, all I could think about was my father. It scared the hell out of me, and it made me incredibly angry. I had to get up and walk away so I wouldn't hit you." I placed my hand on his. "This is very personal to me, Albert. The hurt runs very deep. You need to stop."

He did not answer, but he held my eyes for some time. Finally he stood and went up to his bedroom.

When Virginia came home from work I told her about Red and about what I had suggested, and also what I had told him about my father and his drinking. "That poor boy," she said. "I cannot imagine the pain, the guilt. My poor Albert!" She fell against me and wept.

Albert came downstairs. "I'm going to mail a letter. To Orange. I won't be long, I promise." He returned within ten minutes.

***

"Hi Grandpa Isaac. Are you awake?" Ginnie's back!

I'm awake. Hug.

I feel her head gently on my chest, her hair tangling a little in my beard. I wish I could look into her eyes - so much like her namesake, my Virginia.

"I came home last night. My flight was delayed because of thunderstorms in Chicago. I didn't get in till almost ten. My folks picked me up; they were not in the best mood when I finally arrived. Nor was I. Anyhow, it's back to work today. It's nine-thirty Monday morning. I have to be in at eleven. It looks like that Chicago weather will be arriving here any minute - dark, heavy clouds and that strange yellow light you get before a big storm."

She takes my hand and strokes my fingers. "It was a good trip. I'm glad I went. Jake's parents were so nice to me. We talked a lot, and cried a lot. On the Saturday afternoon I went out in a rowboat on a nearby pond with Jake's sister, Dana. She told me about growing up with him - he was a year older than her - and some of the things they did together as kids. They used to swim in the pond we were on, and look for frogs and birds and salamanders. She also talked about watching the television as the towers came down, and then getting the phone call from me a few hours later telling them that Jake had gone there for a job interview. Thinking about making that call still makes me tremble." She sniffed. "But, it was a good day on the pond. Dana and I probably would have been sisters-in-law, and now that isn't going to happen. We said we'd email." She grew quiet.

"I couldn't tell them I had turned down his marriage proposal, that I had said I wanted to wait." She sniffed again, loudly.

Sad. Love. Hug. It took her a few moments to de-code my signals, then she put her head on my chest again and lay there for a while.

***

I drove Albert to Orange; it was an easy two hour drive on a bright, cold morning, on the second last day of the year. Albert had received a reply to his letter less than a week after mailing it; Red's wife invited him to visit, and asked if he would also like to meet Red's parents. He said yes. We drove in silence, each of us exploring our own thoughts.

It was a small Cape Cod style house with an American flag out front and a back yard that sloped down to Millers River, which ran through the heart of the town. I parked the car on the road, and before I could open my door, Albert touched my arm. "I think I want to do this alone. OK, Dad?"

"If that's what you want, Albert. I'll find a place to get a cup of coffee."

"Thanks. Come back in an hour."

I watched him walk slowly up the short straight path to the front door. He carried a plain box containing a doll he had brought home from France for Red's daughter. He had shown it to Virginia and me that morning. He knocked and almost immediately a man of about my age opened the door, shook Albert's hand and stepped aside for Albert to enter. They both looked briefly in my direction and then the door was closed. I stayed there a few moments, then checked my watch and drove off in search of somewhere to spend an hour.

I found a place not too far away to pull over near a bend in the river. I took my sketchpad and colored pencils and walked through about eight inches of snow towards the water. The river moved quickly and had not yet frozen over although fingers of ice had formed along the water's edge, and the rocks and logs that projected above the water were glazed in ice. The sun flashed and sparkled off the different static and moving surfaces. I cleared the snow off a large rock just above the water and sat down and sketched whatever I saw. I realized how rarely I took myself out of the studio, and how much I loved drawing out in nature. I could never walk

503

away entirely from realism.

I made it back to Red's family's house about an hour after I had left Albert there. I sat in the car for another fifteen minutes or so, waiting. Finally, the man who had opened the door for Albert came out onto the front step and motioned to me to come in. He waited for me, then introduced himself as George Lambrakis, and led me into the living room. Albert was sitting on the couch between Red's wife, Marie, and Red's mother. A little girl was playing with the doll on the carpet at her mother's feet. I sat on a chair facing them. Red's mother offered me a cup of coffee and a shortbread cookie.

Marie had a photograph album on her knees; she was showing Albert family pictures. Every so often Albert would say, "He showed me that one," or "I remember this." He stopped and looked at one particular picture a long time, then said, "He kept that one of Anna in his shirt pocket - I saw it many times."

We did not leave until nightfall. They thanked Albert for coming to see them. They hugged him and kissed him and gave us a bag of cookies for the drive home. The first thing Albert said as we drove away was, "Thanks for suggesting this. The truth is that Red and I had promised each other we would visit each other's family if either of us did not make it home. The promise had been made half in jest, half in fear while we were waiting on board the landing craft before Omaha Beach. I even got that doll while on furlough in Paris, assuming that I would somehow get it to Anna. I'm so glad I came. They are really nice people."

I reached across the seat and patted his shoulder. "I'm proud of you, Albert. Really proud."

"Thank you."

We drove on in silence for a while. "On a lighter note, I think," I said. "How did a guy from Greece end up with red hair?"

"Actually, during a lull in the conversation I asked Red's father that very question. He said it was rare, but he had an uncle who had the same color hair. Red used to joke about being the Big Red Greek in the division that was nicknamed The Big Red One."

Chapter 55

Three weeks later Albert moved to Amherst and was taking classes. He had found a room in an apartment with two other ex-soldiers. We visited on the first weekend in February and he said he was settling into the flow of his school-work, and got on well with his room-mates. Virginia and I returned to our home optimistic that Albert was on the right track.

During this same period, Marjorie Ross called and asked me to stop in at her gallery for "a chat." I had no idea what she meant, but I arranged to see her on the Monday morning after our visit to Albert. It had been some time since I'd visited Nouvelle Vision; in fact, the last visit was over a year before, when I went to pick up a couple of old paintings that had never sold and which no longer matched my more recent work. I half expected this visit was to ask me to remove all my remaining works. I was not looking forward to it.

I entered the gallery and immediately noticed it was brighter, with a new highly polished gray and white marble floor. Bright red, stylish chairs and sofas were sparingly placed in both the front and back rooms. Marjorie's new desk and office furniture matched the chairs. She looked up as I entered, then came around the desk and embraced me. "So good to see you, Isaac. How are things?"

"We're doing OK. I see things here have been rejuvenated. I like it."

"Thank you. We just felt that after the war we needed to inject some color, some vitality into the place."

"We?"

"Ah, yes. That is what I wanted to talk about. Sit. I'll get coffee."

I sat and waited, like a school-boy outside the office. I tried not to fidget.

Marjorie returned with a tray of coffee and a couple of Danish pastries. "You remember Karl Lodge from New York; he sold some of your works before the war."

"Sure, I remember him."

"Well, Karl and I are now business partners. I will bring some of his artists up here, and he will show some of mine in New York."

"That sounds like an excellent arrangement."

"It is. It means that you, and my other artists, will have permanent representation in New York City, which is, as you know, *the* market for art in the country."

"If you don't mind me asking, Marjorie; I see the benefit to you and your stable, but how does it benefit Karl?"

"Without getting into any details, let me just say that Nouvelle Vision did not make it through the depression simply on the sale of art - there is a large supply of Ross family assets that kept the gallery afloat, and kept Karl Lodge's gallery in business, too."

I smiled to myself. "OK. I will not ask any more about that. It's none of my business. If you feel confident this arrangement will benefit us up-country artists, I can work with it."

"Good. Which brings me to my next idea; I want to mount a one-man show of your work here for the month of March 1947. We'll then replenish it and send it to New York for a May showing. I will need about fifty pieces for both shows, and I don't want anything older than 1943. Can you do it?"

"I can do it," I replied. "Thank you, Marjorie, this is really exciting."

"Your work is beginning to do quite well - slowly gaining attention over the last couple of years. We need to give it a real boost. You deserve it." She opened the top drawer of her desk. "I have a check for you - we sold two paintings last month."

As I left Nouvelle Vision the enormity of the commitment I had just made hit me; I had no idea how many of the paintings I currently had stored in my studio would be suitable. Not many, for sure. These shows could make or break me.

When I arrived home I went directly to my studio and started sorting through everything; I counted a total of sixty-three paintings, of which I felt only seven would work for the one-man show. Not that I thought the remaining pieces were bad, but many were just too old. I could save these for some future retrospective exhibit if I ever achieved that level of recognition! I laughed out loud at that idea.

Wanda is quietly singing one of her hymns; one I don't recognize. She has a beautiful voice so I wait for her to finish.

I'm awake.

"Good morning Mr. Simon. Everything OK today?"

Yes.

"Good. Everything's looking fine. Dr. Watson will be here shortly to follow up on that episode you had a couple of days ago." She grunts in disapproval.

Not like. Dr. Fish. He really is an arrogant ass! We explained it all. That 'episode' was a minor panic attack.

Wanda leaves and minutes later Dr. Fish arrives with a pod of students in his wake. I can hear them squeezing into position beside the bed. I wonder if Dr. Fish is going to present me as a filleted side of salmon on a slab, or as a still-living wild fish swimming upstream.

"Mr. Simon is a one-hundred-and-two year old male..." He lost me right there - not even a "Good morning." I guess I'm the fillet. I tune him out, focusing my attention on the non-verbal sounds; my cat-machine, the occasional shuffle and scrape of a student's feet, the infernal bell of the elevator, a sudden boom of thunder followed by raindrops slapping against the window. It's quite a symphony!

"Dr. Watson, what's that big chart on the wall about?" Her voice is unusual - high-pitched and nervous, just strong and different enough to break through my enjoyment of the random music.

"Hold that question until our meeting after rounds."

They all go, leaving me to listen to the storm.

***

Albert, like me, rarely talked about the war. He continued a distant friendship with Red's family, exchanging the occasional letters and sending Anna a gift on her birthday in July and at Christmas. When Marie remarried in May 1947 she did not invite Albert to the wedding. He took that as a hint; it was time for him to stop the letters and gifts.

When he told us about not receiving a wedding invitation, Albert added, "You know, I almost married someone in England." Virginia and I had sensed that possibility, in fact; we received a couple of letters from a young woman Albert had met in Swanage while he was on the south coast of England training for the Normandy invasion. She had written to introduce herself to us. She thanked us for producing such a kind and caring young man. After Albert was injured and returned to England, she visited him a couple of times in the hospital, but the spark was gone. In her last letter she said he had broken things off.

"There were too many war widows - I didn't want to risk Dottie becoming another one, and since I couldn't get away from the war, I had to drop any idea of a relationship."

And then, quite unexpectedly, he began to talk about Belgium. "When I was released from the hospital they didn't send me back to my old unit; they sent me to the twenty-ninth Infantry Regiment where they gave me a jeep with a heavy machine gun and a couple of guys and we became a kind of reconnaissance unit. We were in the forest of Belgium, gathering for a final push into Germany. No one expected the Germans to put up much resistance and our generals were taking their time building up a huge force.

"Our job was to drive all over the place, delivering packets of information, ferrying officers to meetings and generally to keep our eyes open for anything going on. It was pretty easy and laid back. As I said, no one expected the Germans. Then, one morning about two weeks before Christmas, we were sent off to check in on an army hospital. We were barreling down this icy dirt road when all of a sudden we see a column of about thirty soldiers crossing a couple of hundred yards ahead of us. I couldn't believe my eyes - they were Germans! They saw us at about the same moment we saw them and they started firing. Fortunately they were carrying light weapons and we had that big fifty-caliber machine gun. We hit a few of them and the rest ran off into the woods. We high-tailed it back to base and reported what had happened. Our CO thought we were making it up, but the couple of rounds embedded in the jeep's front bumper and the bullet holes in the windshield convinced him. Turns out this was one of the first engagements in what came to be called the 'Battle of the Bulge.'" He paused and lowered his head into his hands.

We - Virginia, Albert and I - were sitting on the patio of our house enjoying fresh-made lemonade and cheese and crackers. It was a warm day in mid-June and Albert was home for a brief visit before returning to Amherst for summer classes.

He took a sip of his drink, then slowly placed the glass on the table. "But that was not the worst of it, by far," His voice was shaking, hesitant, but he continued, "Shortly after this incident, on December eighteenth, we were sent off early in the morning to investigate a rumor that some Americans had been ambushed near the town of Malmedy. We were driving along, approaching our destination, when we saw this American soldier walking zombie-like down the middle of the road towards us. It was a freezing cold day, but he had no gloves or jacket. His uniform was soaked in blood. We pulled over and helped him into the jeep. We found a blanket and wrapped it around him. His teeth were chattering, his eyes were blank and he did not say a word. He just pointed back in the direction he had come from. We drove ahead slowly for about a thousand yards. As we rounded a bend we saw them - dozens of bodies in the middle of a snow-covered field. You could see the tracks of heavy vehicles - tanks and half-tracks - that had churned up the mud and snow, forming a large circle around those dead men. They had been massacred, over eighty men lying there, their blood frozen in the snow.

"My sergeant said, 'We have to see if any of them are still alive.'

"'They're not,' our passenger said, 'I checked.' He was the only survivor. His whole unit had been captured, disarmed and wiped out." Albert voice dropped to barely more than a whisper.

"We climbed out of the jeep to check. It was so real that it was unreal. I felt detached, like I was watching a movie. I remember thinking that you, Dad, might have found the patterns of men and blood and snow and broken branches, interesting. I had this momentary vision of you sitting on the hood of the jeep with your sketchpad in hand.

"We found no one alive. We drove back to HQ, got our traumatized passenger to the aid station and delivered our report. Then I went into the woods and puked my guts out."

His hands were trembling. He tried to lift his glass to his lips but could not do it without spilling. Virginia stood and went behind his chair and began to massage his neck and back. After several minutes Albert stood. "I need to take a walk," he said. "Don't worry, I'm not going for a drink."

Two days later he left for Amherst and on the train met Charlotte who was also returning to school. She, too, was planning to be a teacher.

On his next visit home Albert told us about Charlotte. She was from Winchester and was in her final year studying to be a math and science teacher. She was smart, funny and loved to walk in the woods and along riverbanks and lakesides. She was an avid bird-watcher, and was urging Albert to take up the past-time, too. "But, most importantly," he said, "we just click. I can't explain it, but we just seem to understand each other."

"That's the most important ingredient in any relationship," Virginia said, taking his hands. "Everything else comes from that feeling of belonging together. I'm so happy for you, Albert, so very happy."

They were married in Amherst on the last Friday in September - a small civil ceremony with only us, Charlotte's mother, and a few college friends in attendance. They stayed in Amherst another two years. Charlotte took a job in the high school while Albert completed his degree.

***

I hear soft footsteps approach the bed then stop. *I'm awake.*

"Good evening, Mr. Simon. Do you remember me?"

Yes. It is my Irish tenor, Patrick Dolan. *Smile.*

"Patrick Dolan, the neurology intern."

Good. As I said, I remember you. I also think to myself that I have to practice some of the words I don't use too often.

"It's six-thirty on Monday evening, June seventeenth. We had quite a storm today. Did you hear it?"

Yes. And I enjoyed listening to it.

"I just finished an eighteen hour shift. I thought I'd stop in to say hello for a few minutes before I go back to my apartment."

Thank you.

He tried to suppress a yawn. "I used to sing in the church choir back home. I miss it."

Sad. Actually, Patrick, don't be sad - do something about it. I'm sure you can find a church around here that would love to have you, even if your attendance is inconsistent. I need a new word, dammit! I signal *New word.*

He hesitates. "Did you just indicate that you want to create a new word, Mr. Simon?"

Yes.

"I'll give it a try."

It takes quite some effort, with several detours, but we finally get the blinky-blink word for 'Church.'

"You want to go to church?"

No. Foolish boy - how can you be so lacking in self-awareness!

"You want a minister?"

No. I wish I had a way of indicating an exclamation point or three.

"You think I should go to church?

Yes. Finally. *Sing.*

"I should go to church to sing? Yes, Mr. Simon, I should probably do that." I feel him lightly touch my hand. "Would you like me to sing something before I head off?"

Yes. Happy.

And before I have finished my word he starts an old Bob Dylan song, one of Allen's favorites, "Girl from the north country." I wonder how one so young knows this old song. As he is singing I hear someone else enter the room. Ginnie kisses me on the cheek and waits for the song to come to an end. She holds my hand gently.

"That is one of our family's historic songs," Ginnie says. "You sing it so beautifully. Thank you. I'm Ginnie, Isaac's great-granddaughter."

"Patrick Dolan, neurology intern."

"And wonderful singer."

"Thanks." He hesitates, then says, "I'm afraid I need to go home and get some sleep - I've been here since I don't remember. Nice to meet you."

"He's cute," Ginnie says after Patrick leaves.

Smile.

***

1947 was quite a year for us. In addition to Albert's wedding, Virginia started work on her Master's in Education degree, and I had my first one man shows in Boston and then in New York. Virginia and I went to New York for the opening there on July twelfth. The show had been pushed back a couple of months so that I could produce a few more pieces because we had sold more than expected in Boston. I was flying high. We arrived in the city soon after lunchtime. Albert had called about a week before and said he'd like to join us in New York. We arranged to meet at my Uncle

Kalner's apartment for a visit with him in the afternoon.

When we arrived at Kalner's, Albert was already there and they were talking about the work Kalner had done during the war to try to get the government to allow more Jewish refugees into the country. I could see Albert's fists clenching. "I didn't know you'd been involved in all that, Uncle Kalner. I'd always thought you were a union man."

"I was and still am all union, but during the war the refugee crisis is what I devoted myself to."

Albert exhaled loudly. "However bad you imagined the situation, it was a thousand times worse," Albert said. "I carry a million images of the war around with me, but the ones that haunt me most are from a place called Zwodau in Germany, near the Czech border. It was a small camp, a sub-camp of Flossenburg, and was set up to produce equipment for the German air force. All the inmates were women." His voice dropped. "It was liberated in April 1945 by some of my old buddies in the First Division. The Germans had abandoned the place a few days before the First arrived - and they'd taken every last scrap of food with them, chained the gates and ran. My unit just happened to be nearby at the time, as we advanced into Germany, so we were called upon to bring in whatever food and clothing and medical supplies we could find. We essentially looted nearby German towns and headed to the camp."

His bottom lip was trembling. "I think we smelled the place before we actually saw it. Almost a thousand women, all just skin-covered skeletons, with sunken eyes, and balding heads. You couldn't even tell they were women. They stood or sat in small silent groups, too weak to approach our trucks as we entered the camps. We had three medics with us, and I followed one of them around, distributing cleaning supplies and cotton cloths. We had a water truck, and were able to set up showers, but not many of the women were strong enough to use them. I do remember this one woman advancing slowly behind the curtain we had strung up in front of the showers. I couldn't tell if she was twenty or a hundred and twenty. Moments later I swear I heard her laugh, just a short burst. When she emerged she was smiling. She caught my eye for a moment, then she turned and went to a friend and helped her to the shower.

"Our mess guys started a couple of fires and began cooking whatever we had gathered. Many of the women were unable to even eat - their teeth had rotted, or they had some awful disease that did not allow them to keep anything down. We were woefully ill-equipped to deal with the situation, but we did what we could until a Red Cross team of about thirty doctors, nurses, and other support people arrived the next afternoon, and we moved on. I felt less guilty about killing German soldiers after Zwodau. I still have nightmares in which I see that woman with her wet straggly hair and her toothless smile."

Albert pressed the tips of his fingers together, a gesture reminiscent of my mother, then he continued; "I couldn't sleep that night - none of us could. I was sitting in my jeep with one of the guys in my crew. We weren't really talking, just uttering words of disbelief at what we had seen that day. I remember it was a clear cold night with no moon - the sky was carpeted with stars. In another place, another time, it would have been breathtakingly beautiful, but the smell of this place hung in the air, and all you could hear was the drone of a power generator which lit up the medical tent we'd set up earlier. A long line of women waited patiently and quietly in the dark for one of the medics to call them in, one at a time. I decided I should see if there was anything I could do to help. I spent until after dawn washing wounds that had gone untreated and were now infected. I held the hands of women while the medics drained pus from swollen limbs then applied ointments and bandages. Of course, we couldn't understand one another, but I just talked about whatever pleasant things I could think of - home, family, school, art. Mostly I talked to try to take my mind off what was going on. I was not the only regular soldier working with the medics that night, each of us trying to find a way to cope with the horror of this place.

"I learned later that almost all of the women were political prisoners from various parts of Europe; a few were Jews. You know how Nana Rivka would throw out a Yiddish word every now and then? I swear I heard some of those words during that long night."

Kalner, Mary, Virginia and I sat and stared at Albert as he talked. We could not keep our eyes off him. There was nothing we could say. Everything seemed frozen in time; no one moved. Finally, Albert stood up and came over to me and hugged me. "I really didn't mean to go off on this, but once I started I just couldn't stop. We're here for Dad's New York show; I expect it will be a wonderful evening."

I looked at my watch - six-fifteen; we needed to be at the downtown gallery before seven. We grabbed our jackets and rushed to the subway station. On the train, Virginia sat next to Albert and patted his knee over and over again. At some point he placed his hand on hers. He leaned toward her and said, "I'll be OK, Mom. Don't worry."

The Karl Lodge gallery looked similar to Nouvelle Vision in Boston - the same polished gray and white floor and the same red furniture. It was smaller than Nouvelle Vision - with the main gallery in the front section and two smaller rooms in the rear. We meandered through the space, looking at my work and searching for Karl Lodge. The lighting was wonderful, arranged to enhance each painting. The gallery was full, but not over-crowded. Waiters circulated with glasses of wine and wedges of toast topped with soft cheeses. Over on one side a pianist sat at a baby grand playing mellow jazzy tunes. It was a sparkling evening in New York.

We eventually found Karl in the far corner of the main gallery in deep conversation with a fashionably dressed young couple. "Ah! The man of the hour," he said as he saw me.

"I'm sorry we're a little late."

"You're the artist. No one expected you to be early!"

I introduced Virginia and Albert and commented on how beautifully the show was set up.

"Thank you - but it is your work that people are here for, not the lighting. In about twenty minutes I'll give a little speech presenting you to the gathering, then I'll call on you to say a few words. You don't need to say anything more than to thank people for being here. OK?"

"I can manage that. Thanks, Karl."

If someone had asked me to come up with a theme for the show it would have been: "War and the End of War." I stumbled upon this idea during that frantic couple of months between the close of the Boston show and the opening in New York. Everything I painted during that period had this dual atmosphere, captured in rigid versus free-form shapes, and dark tones splashed with bright color. In many of these paintings I introduced a small, realistic vignette of a flower, bird or animal. This was a new departure for me; I liked that juxtaposition of abstraction and realism. Apparently the attendees at the opening were of opposite opinion; while little red dots indicating "Sold" appeared next to six of the paintings that evening, not one graced the description cards next to my most recent works.

But, six paintings sold was a great success. After the gallery closed that evening, Karl and his wife took us out to dinner at a nearby restaurant. He was happy and optimistic. "There were art critics from the *Times* and the *New Yorker*. I talked with both of them - they were both impressed. The *Times* man was surprised that none of those paintings with the realistic vignettes sold; he thought they were the outstanding pieces of the show."

***

Ginnie is still here, still resting her hand on mine. "Patrick has a beautiful voice, doesn't he?"

Yes. Smile.

She pats my hand again, and breathes in deeply. "Do you remember me telling you about going out on a pond with Dana, Jake's sister?"

Yes.

"While we were out there Dana said she was seriously thinking of joining the army."

No. Now I really wish I had the signal for exclamation point. I need a few dozen of them! I don't trust President George W and I don't believe a quarter of what he says. And even if his claims were true, I don't believe sending American soldiers into the Middle East will do anything positive.

"You disapprove?" Ginnie asks. "You don't think we should go after the terrorists and those who give them shelter?"

My lack of language is now painfully clear to me. I can't continue. *Stop.*

"Well, I think she's pretty brave."

And stupid. *Stop. Please. Sad.*

"OK, I won't say any more about this. Is there anything I can do for you?"

I need a diversion. *Sing.*

"You want music? How about Ella and Louis?"

Yes. Thank you. I much prefer *Dancin' cheek to cheek* to talking about the state of the world and the increasing drumbeat for war. I hope I cash in my chips before things get out of control again. I only hope Ginnie doesn't get the same terrible idea as her almost sister-in-law, Dana.

Chapter 56

Reuven and his family came to visit over the Thanksgiving holiday, 1947. They had left Detroit and moved to Washington towards the end of the war without any explanation. I had assumed it had something to do with the inner workings of the United Auto Workers, but I was wrong; well, kind of wrong.

We were sitting around the kitchen table on Thanksgiving morning after breakfast. It was a cool, gloomy, lazy day. We were expecting Albert and Charlotte and her mother, Gladys, to be arriving soon. I asked Reuven why they had moved.

Reuven, not one for chit-chat, explained, "There were a lot of labor actions during the war, fighting for better wages and working conditions, and I was involved in many of those negotiations. I really enjoyed it and felt I was doing good work. But, one of the results of the ramping up of war production was an influx of people coming up from the South looking for work in the more industrialized northern cities. And as more and more Negro workers moved into previously all white jobs, that old divide-and-conquer strategy insinuated itself into the equation. Open racism and violence coupled with strikes and other work stoppages sprang up all over the place, with white workers demanding the exclusion of Negroes. The unions held frantic meetings trying to figure out how to deal with the situation. I had many angry and frustrating discussions, but unfortunately, too many of the union leaders gave in to the push towards whites-only union membership. I decided it was time to leave."

He stood, walked over to the stove and poured himself another mug of coffee. "I had been reading about cases of lynching and phony trials where Negro defendants were being convicted and sentenced to death by all white juries and without adequate legal help, so I contacted some of my old friends in the NAACP and asked for a job. They said 'yes,' if I'd move to DC - so that's how we ended up there. Lots of work to do."

"And Danielle, what have you been up to?" Virginia asked.

"I'm following in my father's footsteps - I'm taking undergrad courses to prepare myself for law school. I know there are not many women in law, but change is coming and I'm happy to help push it along."

"Very much like your dad!" I said.

"During the war, with all those men away," Danielle continued, "so many jobs previously closed to women suddenly became available, and we showed that we could do them, and do them well. Now, the men are home and we're told to stay in our kitchens. The genie is out of the bottle! You can't shove it back."

My thoughts drifted to our Emma who held one of those jobs, briefly.

"The same holds true for Negroes entering the workforce." Reuven added. "They're here to stay - white folks better get used to it, and more importantly, to see all working people as allies in the fight for better lives." Reuven could get a little preachy. "The rise of the Klan over the first half of this century presents the most dangerous threat to American democracy since the Civil War. For some folks the Civil War never ended and there has been violence against Black people unceasingly almost since the day the Emancipation Proclamation was issued. Those racists just cannot accept that the world has changed."

"So, Reuven, what kind of cases are you involved with?" I asked.

"D'you want me to talk all day, Itzik?"

"Well..."

"Give them the shorter version, Reuven," Yvette said.

"OK, I'll try. There was a Supreme Court decision last year called the Irene Morgan Decision, and it basically says that segregation cannot be enforced on interstate buses. I was involved in preparing the legal arguments and written briefs - it was my first assignment after moving to Washington. Anyhow, since this decision, an organization called CORE - the Committee on Racial Equality - has been staging a series of protests in which white and Negro activists ride the buses trying to ensure the implementation of the High Court ruling. They call these protests, 'The Journey of Reconciliation.' The problem, of course, is that in some of the Southern states the riders are being arrested. A large part of my work is working on the defense team for them."

"We've seen nothing about this in the local papers, not even the *Boston Globe*," Virginia said.

"Not surprising! What is happening to Black people is not reported much anywhere. Black people don't seem to matter, until we need them to fight our wars or clean up our mess. Well, there are now a whole lot of Negroes who came back from the war who have been trained to fight. They weren't fighting and dying in Europe and the Pacific so they could come home to be discriminated against, abused and treated like farm animals. The next wave of the Civil War is about to begin, and it's going to be a battle of Negroes and their progressive allies, against the die-hards who are still yearning for the Confederacy. It will not be pretty!"

"It's that bad?" Virginia asked.

"The way I see it, there'll be blood in the streets within ten years."

Unfortunately, he wasn't far wrong. Fourteen years later, during the Freedom Rides, Danielle went down to Jackson, Mississippi, as a legal observer, and Yvette, at sixty-one years old, insisted she go with her daughter to show support. They were in of a group of around two hundred people who met the bus when it arrived on May twenty-fourth. The situation was tense; there were scuffles with police and racist thugs. Many of the riders and their supporters were arrested. Yvette was knocked down but said she was not badly hurt; "Just a little pain in my side," she wrote to Reuven. She and Danielle went to the hearing of the men and women who had been arrested and charged with trespassing for using restrooms designated for people of a different race. In a letter to Reuven, Yvette described how the judge sat with his back to the defendants, refusing even to look at them, let alone hear them. They were sentenced to thirty days in jail. These sentences were fought all the way to the Supreme Court where they were eventually overturned.

About half-way through the bus ride back from Mississippi, Yvette suddenly began to experience increased pain in her side. She soon felt disoriented and faint. By the time they reached Washington, Yvette was short of breath and coughing painfully. Danielle took her directly to a hospital, then called Reuven. Yvette had sustained three broken ribs, which had shifted during the bumpy bus ride and punctured a lung. She died the next morning.

***

I have been lying awake for hours. Ginnie's defense of Jake's sister,

Dana, joining the army has me angry and upset. I'm consciously fighting to keep my pulse under control - the last thing I need is for the doctors and nurses to think I'm having another "episode!" I wish Kitty-bee would just show up - she knows how to calm me down.

I hear someone enter the room. *I'm awake.*

"Hello Mr. Simon."

It's Damon the Good.

"Everything OK?"

No. I'm not OK. I'm worried about Ginnie.

"Are you in pain?' The bed sore?"

No.

"Something else bothering you?"

Yes. But I don't really want to talk about it. I don't know how to say what I need to say.

"Can I help?"

I wish I knew how. *No. Thank you.*

"OK." He checks my plumbing, takes my pulse. "I'll be back before the end of my shift to check in," he says and is gone.

The minute he walks out I realize he is just the person I need to talk with Ginnie; he's her friend, a war veteran, and most importantly he's good and kind. Dammit! Why did I let him leave? I have to talk with him when he comes back.

Do I sleep now and run the risk of missing him when he returns later, or do I try to stay awake and run the risk of falling asleep before he arrives? He'll probably be gone about six hours. How long is that? How could I measure it?

I try to visualize a clock face and suddenly the beautiful old banjo clock which hung on the wall near Virginia's mother's favorite chair in the parlor appears before me. I have seen it so many times but not for about seventy years, yet the shape and the details stand out so clearly; the rear-painted marine scene on the glass panel of the base, the delicately shaped brass rails on the tapered neck, the simple white face with Roman numerals, and the brass eagle with outstretched wings at the top. I can almost hear it ticking. The Appletons sold the clock during the Depression - I wonder what became of it.

Albert and Charlotte arrived much later than expected that Thanksgiving day; they apologized, saying they had car trouble, but Virginia sensed something else was going on. They had only been married a few months and neither of them looked comfortable. Virginia asked me to help with something in the kitchen. I followed her.

"Charlotte looks like she's going to burst into tears any second," Virginia said.

"And Albert looks ashen, depressed. He's barely said a word since they arrived."

Virginia placed both her hands on my shoulders and looked into my eyes. "Please don't let him be drinking again. That would be unbearable." She leaned up against me. "I think I'll find a way to talk with Charlotte. We need to help."

"We can't meddle in their lives."

"They need help. If he's drinking then we need to know and we have to have another talk with him. They're just starting out, Isaac - new jobs, school - they can't risk all of that!"

"OK. You talk with Charlotte. If she says Albert's drinking, I'll talk with him."

The Thanksgiving meal went without incident; the food was good and we managed to keep the conversation light. When the main course was over, Virginia suggested we all go to the living room and take a break before coffee and dessert. Charlotte, by now a little less withdrawn, talked about her first day in the classroom with thirty ninth-graders - which was both funny and somewhat frightening.

After about twenty minutes Virginia asked Charlotte to give her a hand with the coffee and pies. I watched them enter the kitchen. It was only a minute or two before we could hear Charlotte sobbing uncontrollably. I looked at Albert. He said nothing, but stood and raced into the kitchen. I did not know what to say to Reuven, Yvette, Sam, and Danielle who each had a look of concern and confusion. Yvette finally offered, "I did think that Charlotte looked a little tense."

"So did Virginia and I. We have no idea what it's all about. Virginia said she'd try to talk with her."

The sobbing stopped and we heard kitchen chairs scraping. "I suspect coffee will be a while," I said.

It was a long uncomfortable silence. I was with my oldest, closest friend and I did not know what to say. The low voices coming from the kitchen were present but undecipherable. Reuven looked around the living room, searching for something to talk about. "The Kandinsky is gone," he said, finally.

"A victim of the Depression, unfortunately. It was sell the Kandinsky or don't eat. We did manage to hold on to the Klee." I paused. "Has it been that long since you were in this room?"

"We've been here a few times," Reuven said, "but I never noticed that the Kandinsky was missing." Of course they had been here, not that long ago. Reuven had come to see us after we had word of Mark's death, and they had all come for Emma's service.

Virginia emerged from the kitchen carrying two pies. "The coffee will be out in a couple of minutes." She placed the pies on the low table in the middle of the room then brushed my shoulder as she began to make her way back to the kitchen. She stopped. "Everything is all right. We'll explain it all shortly."

She returned with a tray carrying the cups and plates. Albert and Charlotte followed with the coffee pot, milk and sugar. Charlotte had a weak smile on her face. She sat down next to Virginia on the couch and the two held hands. "I'm sorry about my crying," Charlotte said.

"I had my first nightmare since our wedding," Albert said. "I had warned Charlotte about them, but I guess the real thing is a lot scarier than the warning."

"It really frightened me. I didn't know what to do. He was shouting and thrashing about. At one point he was pounding his pillow. I was afraid he'd hurt me."

Virginia put her arm around Charlotte's shoulders and hugged her.

"Reuven was like that, too," Yvette said. "He would sometimes even get out of bed in his sleep and move around the house like he was looking for someone. The only thing you can do, Charlotte, is make sure you're safe and then talk to him calmly and lovingly and let him know you are there with him, that he is safe and there is nothing to fear. Massage his brow if he will let you."

"Do they go away in time?"

"Reuven will sometimes shout something in the middle of the night, but the worst episodes went away after a while. Some people say it is good to talk about those terrible events, other experts say the exact opposite. What I did with Reuven was just let him know that if he wanted to tell me what happened, I was there to listen. He has told me some things, many things, but I suspect there is more inside."

Reuven and I both nodded our heads, but said nothing.

**

Wanda is humming one of her hymns. Dammit! I missed Damon. She goes through her usual routine. I pretend to be asleep - I'm not in any mood to deal with anyone. I can't believe I slept through Damon's return visit. I have to get him to talk some sense into Ginnie.

It's raining again. I can hear the drops bouncing off the window, and the sporadic booms of thunder. I remember during that summer between the end of the Second World War in Europe and Albert's return home, Virginia and I had taken a two-room cottage for a few days on the shores of Lake Winnipesaukee in New Hampshire. We wanted to get away from our empty house. It rained every afternoon. We did little more than sit on the front porch of the cottage watching the rain rolling across the water. At night, we'd listen to the thunder and rain and watch the lightning bouncing through the sky. We cried a lot, too. For Mark and Emma. When we returned home, the house was still empty.

**

Colin, our first grandchild, was born on Saturday, July seventeenth, 1948. Virginia and I drove out to Amherst the next morning to see him and his happy parents. We arrived at the hospital during feeding time and they would not allow us into Charlotte's room. Stupid rules! Albert was in a waiting area nearby. We hugged and he chatted about the events of the last twenty-four hours.

Finally they let us in to see Charlotte; she was tired but beaming. "He's so sweet," she said. "They've taken him back to the nursery - you should go'n see him." The three of us filed out, went down the hall and stood in front of the glass panels that closed the world off from the newborns. A nurse approached and we pointed to the crib in which Colin lay. She picked him up and brought him to the glass for us to get a better look. He was wide awake and stared back at us as we waved, made cooing noises and laughed at ourselves. Colin seemed amused.

"I got to hold him earlier. He's so little, but has a pretty good grip - he grabbed my finger and didn't want to let it go."

"I'd love to hold that little bundle," Virginia said.

"I know, Mom. You'll get your chance."

We stood by the window for some time, until the nurse grew tired and returned Colin to his crib. When we finally returned to Charlotte's room, she was asleep. "She needs it," Virginia said. "Why don't the three of us go out for breakfast? I'd bet you haven't eaten in a while, Albert."

"I had a coffee and part of a stale bun in the cafeteria downstairs."

We found a diner not too far from the hospital. "Is the baby's room all set up? Do you need help with anything?" I asked once we were seated.

"It's painted and carpeted and everything is waiting. It's been a busy time since graduation - the move to a new house, the new job, and now Colin."

"I've been working on a large painting for Colin's room," I said. "It's mostly soft colors, with pictures of children and toys and stuffed animals."

"It's very cute," Virginia said.

"Kind of outside your usual work."

"Far outside my usual work, Albert, but I like to do realistic things every now and then. Anyway - I'd think that a picture of a chicken or a truck looks pretty much like an abstraction to an infant."

"Probably so. Thank you."

"I can bring it over one evening this week, after you come home from visiting Charlotte and the baby."

Our breakfast arrived. "Charlotte's mother is coming to stay with us for a few weeks after the baby and Charlotte come home. I tried to convince them both that it wasn't necessary, but I was over-ruled."

"I think it's nice for a new mom to have her mother around for a short while. Do you get on OK with her?" Virginia asked.

"She's fine, most of the time. She tends to be a little more of an organizer that we are. She couldn't resist commenting when she discovered our towels are not arranged by color in the closet." He laughed. "But we get along OK."

"Are you sleeping OK?" Virginia asked, tentatively.

"Don't worry, Mom. I do still have those dreams occasionally, but Charlotte's able to bring me back. The talk we all had last Thanksgiving really helped both of us."

***

Allen is here. I hear him talking with nurse Trainwreck. (I do have to come up with a nicer name for her!) I wonder whether Ginnie has said anything to him about Dana's foolish idea. Ginnie is taking a year off before starting grad school - this is a vulnerable time. She hasn't talked about her plans in a while; that scares me.

I hear Allen say, "Thank you," to the nurse, then he sits beside me.

I'm awake.

"Hi Grandpa Isaac. It's almost seven o'clock in the evening on Tuesday, June eighteenth. I popped over for a quick visit after writing almost all day. I also needed to escape: Martha is working on this big fund-raising event and about a dozen people are coming over to the house this evening for a meeting. I volunteered to leave for a while. Ginnie's covering a shift for a co-worker tonight; I think I'll stop in there and have a cup of coffee and read a bit."

Well, at least he mentioned Ginnie's name, but they apparently haven't talked about Dana and the army!

Martha is the one in the family with the money. Allen's a teacher and the son of teachers. His first two novels were moderately successful; he never told me any details, but they seem to supplement his income nicely. On the other hand, he's still teaching, so they couldn't have brought in that much. At one time there was hope for a movie of his second book, but that fell through.

Allen and Martha met at the Hebrew University in Jerusalem in 1972. They were both there doing their junior year. Allen was doing a double major - ancient history and English, and what better place to study ancient history than Israel? He spent most of his spare time wandering through the Old City of Jerusalem and its surroundings, photographing ancient structures. He came home with thousands of pictures he had taken - from the Al Aqsa Mosque and the Shrine of the Rock, to the Church of the Holy Sepulchre, and many less well-known archaeological sites, mosaics, beautifully carved doorways, and the stone walls and market places of the city. It was a time of relative stability in the area and he was able to go just about anywhere. He confided in me that he had moved out of the student dorms and lived in a residential hotel inside the Old City for his last two months in Israel.

Allen likes to tell the story about how he and Martha met. It was Christmas Eve and he and a couple of friends decided to go to Bethlehem to see what was going on. When they arrived there by bus in the early evening, the town was packed. They made their way toward the Church of the Nativity, which stood at the far end of a huge open space aptly named "Manger Square." The church itself was closed to all but a select few. As the evening wore on, it began to look like every hippie within a fifty mile radius had descended on Manger Square.

It was a chilly night, so people tended to gather around the fires of the many vendors selling fresh roasted chestnuts and peanuts. There were also dozens of other street vendors, selling various trinkets and souvenirs as well as long white tapered candles. And there was also the unmistakable sweet smell of hashish in the air. The post office was open, so Allen decided it would be a nice idea to send a few postcards postmarked in Bethlehem on Christmas Eve. While waiting in line for stamps he met Martha, who was with a small group of students from Brandeis. They chatted and ended up spending the rest of the evening together and traveling back to Jerusalem early in the morning on the same bus. Allen would always end this story with the comment, "Like it or not, it was the baby Jesus that brought us together." To which Martha would always respond, "Actually, I think it had much more to do with the hash."

"Are you still with me, Grandpa Isaac?" Allen's voice displays a touch of nervousness.

I guess I did go off on one of my little diversions. *Yes.* I wonder what time it is. I have to be sure to be awake for Damon.

"Martha's meeting is supposed to end at nine, but will probably go until after ten. They don't know how to stop talking. I can't stand being around them - they fawn all over me and insist on questioning me about my writing."

Smile. I thought you liked talking about your writing? You do it when you come to see me. I guess, the plus side of talking to me about it is that I don't ask any questions.

I hear him stretch and yawn. "Nurse Melinda says that your bed sore is healing well. Is it still painful?"

No. Who's Nurse Melinda?

"Good." He stands. "Well, I have to be off. I'll tell Ginnie you said 'hi.' One of us will be back tomorrow evening. We'll bring Kitty-bee."

Thank you.

Chapter 57

In the early summer of 1948 Mr. Appleton retired from his law practice and sold his car. Virginia's parents were still living in that large house overlooking the Boston Public Garden. They were both in their seventies and the arthritis in Mr. Appleton's knees kept him from climbing stairs, so they sold the Steinway and converted the music room into a bedroom. They closed all the doors to the upstairs rooms and essentially lived only on the first floor. The large sofa and heavy chairs in the parlor were replaced by a much smaller set, and the room was divided by a low bookcase to provide an office area for Mr. Appleton. The Metzinger still occupied its place of prominence.

When Virginia telephoned them with the news of the birth of their first great-grandson they were thrilled. On the Saturday after Charlotte and Colin went home, Virginia and I drove in to Boston early to pick up her parents and bring them to see the baby. George Appleton sat up front with me. Despite the nagging pain in his knees and hands, he was more relaxed than I ever remembered. Retirement seemed to be good for him.

"I received a letter from your friend Reuven a while ago congratulating me on my retirement. That was most thoughtful of him. Are you still in touch?"

"Yes. In fact, he was up here for a visit with his wife and children last Thanksgiving. Reuven thinks very highly of you, and he's forever grateful to you for helping him get his foot in the door."

"What's he up to?"

"He's working with the NAACP legal group based out of Washington, DC."

"Good for him! I had a good sense about that young man. Please give him my regards the next time you talk with him."

"I'll be happy to," I replied. "Are you finding enough to do in your retirement?"

"More than enough. I'm still involved with the law; I act as a review attorney for briefs and contracts - another pair of eyes to look things over before signatures are attached. I only do things I'm interested in and I do them on my own time. It's great. I'm also working with someone in my old firm to establish a mediation approach to disputes, rather than adversarial. It's quite a new field, but has promise and is long overdue. After all, the best resolutions are when all parties involved feel like they have come away with something."

"Seeking agreement rather than conquest."

"Indeed. And, of course, I've become more active in the church. I've been elected to the board of trustees, a position I held thirty or more years ago." He paused. "The only thing limiting me is my difficulty in getting about; my damned knees hurt much of the time. But I refuse to let it bother me; in fact, I've been forcing myself to walk a mile every day and it does help, but there are days…"

We arrived at Albert and Charlotte's home in Amherst and were met at the front door by Charlotte's mother, Gladys, who signaled with her finger on her lips that we should be quiet. "Charlotte is putting baby to sleep," she whispered as she guided us into the living room. We sat, uncomfortably, as she tiptoed into the kitchen. Albert came into the room and hugged each of us, in turn, then sat on the couch beside his grandmother.

"I'm afraid your timing was lousy," Albert said, clearly ignoring his mother-in-law's admonition for quiet. "Colin decided he was hungry about thirty minutes ago, so Charlotte nursed him and he promptly fell asleep."

George and Jane Appleton suppressed their disappointment. "I'm sure he'll be calling for us before too long," Jane said. "So, how are you both adjusting to having a baby in the house?"

"It's lovely. Sure, we don't sleep enough or eat regular meals, but I just love to hold him and look into his eyes, and feel his little fingers holding me tight. He loves to lie in his crib and look at that painting, Dad. It's almost like he knows it was done just for him."

Gladys arrived with a tray of tea and cookies. Moments later Charlotte entered and plopped herself down beside Albert. "He does tire me out," Charlotte said. "We're so happy you're all here." Gladys poured the tea and distributed it, along with the cookies.

It wasn't long before the baby started wailing. Gladys started to rise from her chair.

"I'll get him," Albert said.

We all listened, following Albert's footsteps up the stairs. Then the baby stopped crying, and we heard the footsteps descending. Albert placed Colin in Jane's arms. She smiled and cooed and held out her finger for him to grasp, which he did. "It has been so long since I held a baby," she said, "I can't even remember." I could - it was Emma.

After some time she reluctantly handed the baby to George, who cradled him in his arms and began to hum a tune. He held Colin so close to his face that the baby was able to pat his cheeks, which elicited a giggle from the old man. I looked at Charlotte; her eyes were sparkling, delighted.

After Virginia and I each had out turns with Colin, Albert asked me to go out back with him to take a look at a problem he was having with the fence. "Gladys is driving me crazy, Dad," he said, the moment we were out of the house. "I know she means well, but she's living in the nineteen-twenties. Hell, Charlotte and I are both educators; we've learned something about child development. And she's so damned adamant!"

"Have you and Charlotte talked about it?"

"Of course. She just tries to ignore it, but we both know that's not possible."

I looked around the small, well-groomed back yard, with its rows of tomato bushes and cucumber vines along the side fence. "Are you asking for my advice, or are you just blowing off steam?"

"Both," He paused. "Seriously, Dad, what do you think?"

"I think that tension in a home is not good for the baby or for your relationship with your wife. You and Charlotte need to find a gentle way to tell Gladys you appreciate her help, but now that you've been home with the baby for a while, you feel you are able to handle the challenges of being parents on your own. Promise her to visit often."

"She'll be hurt."

"She'll get over it. Look, she has always known her stay in your home would be limited. If she's driving you crazy after a week, what do you think a month would look like?"

"You're right. I'll talk it over with Charlotte." He hugged me. "Thanks, Dad."

Damon is finally here.

I'm awake.

"Hello, Mr. Simon. Is everything OK with you?"

No. I need a new word. I give him the signal.

"New word. We can do that." He sits in the chair next to the bed. We create the signal for "Ginnie." I hear him write it on the chart, then he sits again. "Something about Ginnie, your great-granddaughter is upsetting you?"

Yes.

Damon sits silently for some time. "You want me to talk with her?"

Yes. Please.

He is quiet again. Finally he says, "What do you want me to talk to her about?"

I need another new word. I signal.

"OK, another word. I'm ready."

It takes longer than one would think to create the signal for a four letter word beginning with an 'A', but we eventually create the signal for "Army." He adds it to the chart.

"You want me to talk with Ginnie about the army?"

Yes. Then I continued, trying to emphasize my feelings. *Stop. Ginnie. Army.*

"Are you saying that Ginnie is thinking about joining the army and you want me to dissuade her?"

Yes. Yes. Yes.

He was silent, again, for quite some time. "We're not really supposed to get involved with patients' family issues," he said, at last, "but since you can't really talk, and since Ginnie and I are friends, I can at least try to find out what's going on."

Thank you. Hug.

"I'll be back near the end of my shift - hopefully she'll come to see you around then as she often does."

Thank you.

"FYI - it's two a.m. Wednesday morning. See you later, Mr. Simon."

***

We visited Albert and family the following weekend. Gladys had moved back to her house and the level of stress in Albert's home was noticeably lower. We sat on the back covered patio lazily sipping iced coffee on a warm July afternoon. Colin was sleeping in a large basket at Charlotte's feet.

I remember that beautiful feeling of tranquility.

***

It seems like I've been lying here forever, waiting for Damon to return and for Ginnie to visit. I need him to talk to her, but what can I realistically expect. Three generations of our family experienced the horrors and consequences of war and we all shied away from telling those who were not there about the experience. We wanted to spare them our pain and despair and guilt. I fear that by our silence we might be perpetuating the madness; we might have spared them nothing and instead, condemned them to repeat what we have done. We told some of it to our wives and parents, never to our children.

There is this poem, *Lies,* by the Russian poet, Yevgeny Yevtushenko. Allen lent me the book. It was written in the early sixties. The poem starts with the stark and simple statement; "Telling lies to the young is wrong," and ends with the even more ominous observation; "and afterwards our pupils will not forgive in us what we forgave." I think about this poem a lot; too much. It seems to raise a warning finger for every half-truth, evasion, omission. I think about those stories I made up - the ones about Charlie the mouse. They were fine for Ginnie and David when they were little, but maybe I should have reframed them when they got older. Made them much closer to reality. Maybe I should have talked about myself as well as my brother Chaim who they only knew of as a character in a child's story, a fiction.

I hear someone walking towards my bed.

I'm awake.

"Hello, Mr. Simon." It's Damon the Good. "I've been keeping a lookout for Ginnie, but I haven't seen her this morning. Was she here? Did I miss her?"

No. Dammit. She didn't come in this morning.

"I'm afraid it's time for me to take off. I hope I'll get to see her tomorrow."

And he's gone. Damn!

***

You want to know about guilt. I talked about Albert's experience after the landing on Omaha Beach, when he was wounded and his friend, Red, was killed while bringing him to safety. Three years after he came home, on June ninth, the anniversary of that day, Albert submitted a few lines to the Personals column in his local newspaper; "In memory of a friend who carried me to safety, and then he fell. How do I carry him?" He repeated this year after year and, it turns out, every time he submitted these lines, Albert went off and drank himself into oblivion. He even scheduled that day as a vacation day from work every year.

The first year he got drunk, he promised Charlotte it would never happen again. The next year he said he needed that one day of self-destruction. But the sad truth is that within a few years he was finding more and more days in the year to justify his self-destructive behavior. He was not mean or loud or abusive during these bouts; he just disappeared for a day or two. Their two boys were now old enough to recognize things were not right. Charlotte made excuses for him to the kids, to his school, to us, but eventually she broke down and a day before that fateful anniversary in 1957 she came to our home and told us what was going on. Albert's job was in jeopardy, and their marriage was beginning to unravel. She had begged him to seek help, but he insisted there was nothing to seek help for, he was fine.

I went to see him. It was the evening of June eighth. Charlotte had dropped the boys off at her mother's home before coming to us. I searched all over the house, but could not find him. I was about to leave when I glanced out the kitchen window and noticed the light was on in the garden shed. I ran there and found Albert lying between empty whisky bottles on the concrete floor. His skin was pale blue and he was barely breathing. I ran into the house and called for an ambulance, then I raced back to the shed and tried to revive him. He began to vomit, so I turned him on his side. The ambulance arrived within a few minutes and they rushed him to the hospital. I rode with him, trying to get him to respond to my voice, but he did not.

He was brought into the emergency room and I was told to wait. I called Virginia. She and Charlotte hurried to the hospital. It was almost dawn before Charlotte was allowed to go in to see him. Virginia and I sat, holding hands, saying nothing. Finally, Charlotte returned; she had a slight smile of relief on her face. "The doctor says he'll be fine. They're going to keep him for a few days." Then she started crying. "He almost died. He was this close to killing himself. If you hadn't found him, he'd be dead!" We hugged and let her cry.

Albert was finally moved from the emergency room to a ward; he looked weak but managed a small smile. "I'm sorry I put you all through this," he said. "I will stop."

"Thank you, Albert." Charlotte kissed him on the cheek. "We need you back."

And Albert kept his word. When he was discharged from the hospital, he immediately joined Alcoholics Anonymous.

But the story doesn't end there.

Twenty-three years later, in September 1980, two years before Albert died, a letter arrived at our house addressed to Albert. It was from Anna Lambrakis Cousins of Brattleboro, Vermont. She had written, "Please Forward," on the envelope. I called Albert and he asked me to open the letter and read it to him. It was short and to the point.

"Dear Mr. Simon, I'm not sure if you remember me; I am the daughter of George 'Red' Lambrakis who you served with in the army. I hope this letter finds you and that you are well. We met one time when I was a child, and you sent me gifts for a few years. I have been looking into my father's war records and related papers. I also found photographs of you and my dad in an old album. My mother told me the details of your visit to us many years ago. She still has letters from you from around that time, which is how I got an address. I have information I'm sure you would want to know. Please contact me; if you are still in New England I would be happy to visit and talk." She added a phone number.

Albert was silent a long time after I finished reading. He, at this time, was married to Danielle, his second wife. He had continued to place that small notice in the Personals every year, and he continued to maintain his sobriety. "I wonder what she means," he said. "Do I really want to rake all of that up again?"

"Talk with Danielle about it. Whatever you decide to do, you'll need her by your side. I'll be there, too."

"Would you read the address and phone number again, Dad? I need to write them down."

He called Anna Cousins the next day, and she and her husband made the trip to visit on the Sunday of the following week. I was with Albert and Danielle when they arrived; Anna was carrying a large manila envelope which she placed on the coffee table in front of her as she sat down next to Albert on the couch.

"You haven't changed much since I saw you last," Albert quipped, and laughed nervously.

"Nor have you. I still have that doll you brought me when you visited us thirty-something years ago," she said. "She's still very special. She is one of the few connections I have to my dad. In fact, in a way, she was responsible for me seeking my father's military records." She tapped the envelope in front of her.

Danielle stood. "I'll get the coffee," she said, and went to the kitchen.

"Is it OK if I just jump right into what I found out?" Anna asked. "It's been boiling inside me for months."

"Go ahead." Albert leaned forward as she opened the envelope and extracted a small pile of aged documents.

"I spoke to my mom after I received this information and asked her to tell me again what you had told her. She said that my dad, Red, had carried you to safety after you had been badly wounded on June ninth, a few days after the landing at Omaha Beach, and that my dad had been killed while saving you."

"That's correct." Albert's voice was hoarse.

She looked into Albert's eyes, then tuned her face towards the papers in her hands. "His records don't mention the incident at all; they document his participation in the invasion at Omaha Beach, but they say he was killed on June fifteenth when he stepped on a land mine."

The blood drained from Albert's face. "Impossible. I heard him shout." He looked up. His eyes were wide. "The bastard! That bastard lieutenant wrote that Red was killed. He never said how and when. I just assumed..."

He stood and began pacing back and forth. We all waited quietly, unable to speak. Finally he sat down and reached for the documents. Danielle handed him his reading glasses, and he read the official record of Red's death. "I don't know what to say." He dropped the papers onto the coffee table. "I need to take a walk."

"I'll go with you," I said.

We left the house and began to walk briskly up the street, in the direction of the river. It was hard for me to keep up, but Albert did not slow his pace or say a word until we were at the water's edge. He turned to me and tears were rolling down his face. "Is it possible to feel guilt for one's guilt? What I put you all through, Charlotte, the boys! What I did to myself!"

He knelt down, picked up a small flat stone and skipped it across the surface of the river. He repeated this several times then said, "Let's go back. Thanks for walking with me."

Albert and I did not talk about that day until shortly before he died. The cancer that had started in his pancreas had spread rapidly, and he was heavily sedated for the pain. I was visiting, an unwilling observer to the death of my last surviving child. In a rare moment of lucidity he said, "I'm so glad you walked with me that day. When I stood up to leave the house I had it in my head that I was going straight to the bar at the Legion Post. Thank you. The Mystic River was so much nicer."

***

Danielle is here. I've just been thinking about her. *I'm awake.*

"Hi there old man. It's good to see you on this bright sunny Wednesday afternoon." She kisses me on both cheeks.

Smile.

"There's big family news. David called from New York to tell us that he is engaged! Who'd have thought it; he's so engaged with his career I didn't imagine he had time for fun, let alone maintaining a relationship. But, that's just my opinion. I'm happy for him, and I hope his young lady knows what she's getting into."

Smile. David has been so wrapped up in making money and in himself. I think this could be a really good thing for him. I hope it all works out.

"The two of them are coming up for the weekend so we can meet

Kari, and she can meet us. He wants to take the family out to a fancy restaurant on Saturday evening. I wish you could join us."

Yes. Me too. It would be quite something. But let's do something that's a little more realistic. *Sun.*

"You want a trip to the sun room. I'll see if I can order you a cab." I hear her walk off in search of a nurse. Kari - that's an interesting name. I hope she comes to visit me.

Danielle returns with Wanda, Marcus and a wheelchair. "I made sure the wind-chimes are not dangling in the breeze," Danielle says. "We don't need another little episode."

Thank you. Wanda disconnects me from my cat-machine and Marcus lifts me then floats me down into the wheelchair. He wheels me down the hallway and into the sun room. *Thank you.*

"You're welcome, Mr. Simon," he says. I notice for the first time that he has an island accent, possibly Jamaica. I will never know.

"I picked up the newspaper on my way in. Interested?"

Yes.

"One blink for sports, two for news."

I think I want to know what's going on in the world - particularly the Middle East. *News.*

"News it is. Let's see what's on page one." I hear the paper crackle. "The main headline is; 'US says bombing won't halt Bush initiative.' There was another terrible suicide bombing in Jerusalem. Nineteen people were killed." She paused, "Do you want me to read the article?"

Not really. They're all crazy. Both sides. *No.*

I hear her turn a few pages. "How about an editorial? 'Aiming at Saddam.'"

Do I want to hear about this? *Yes*, with reservations.

"OK. 'Administration officials have been talking up a new Bush doctrine that is said to transcend Cold War models of containment and deterrence, replacing them with a strategy of preemptive action that can be applied as readily to Al Qaeda as to Saddam Hussein.' Shall I continue?"

No. I've heard enough. That idiot Bush is going to lead us off a cliff into a preemptive war! What the hell is that! Another 'War to end all Wars!' We've been there before! Stupid!

I feel Danielle's hand on my arm. She must have sensed that I was getting all worked up. I try to control my breathing, my heart-beat. She knows me as well as her father did. Maybe better. *Smile.*

She pats my arm several times. "This shit really gets you fired up, doesn't it?"

Yes. It sure does. I need to stop Ginnie.

Chapter 58

Albert and Charlotte moved to Medford, not too far from us, after he graduated in 1949. He found a teaching position in the local middle school. Allen was born two years later. Virginia and I drove in to Boston to pick up her parents to see their second great-grandchild. They invited us in for a light lunch before going to Albert's.

George and Jane Appleton were enjoying life; they had sold most of their unused antique furniture and miscellaneous other treasures that had survived the Depression, and they spent their time and money on the theater, opera and travel. They had recently returned from a four week eastern Mediterranean cruise during which they had visited Egypt, Israel, Turkey, Greece and the Islands, and Italy. George vowed he would not let his arthritis slow him down, and judging from the photographs of him in all these various ancient sites, he certainly was able to climb to some remarkable places.

"Of course, I'm paying for it now," he said, "But it was worth it. It was the trip of a lifetime."

"He amazed me," Jane said. "Every time we docked he'd be one the first in line to go ashore. By the end of the third week, coming into Salonika, half the people on board were too worn out to take the day trip, but George was there, dragging me along."

"America is so young. When you see these structures built thousands of years ago, you get a sense of how much of a baby we are. I could have spent six months in Egypt alone."

"And it was not just the places we visited. George was definitely the most adventurous when it came to the local food. There were few things he wouldn't try."

"Indeed, when everyone was heading back to the ship for an 'American' meal, Jane and I were sampling the delights of the Mediterranean - tabbouleh, hummus, baba-ganoush, souvlaki, and a dozen other names I don't remember. And the flaky honey-drenched Greek desserts - wonderful!"

Jane began to clear away the lunch dishes. "We should go. I can't wait to see the new baby."

"Before we leave," George said, "we brought you a little something from Egypt." He produced a wooden box about the size of a shoe-box and handed it to Virginia. Inside was a black stone sculpture of the Egyptian cat goddess, Bastet, wearing a broad beaten gold necklace. "To be honest, I have no idea whether it's real or fake, but I think it's beautiful. We bought it from an antiquities dealer in the market in Alexandria who claimed that it was from an ancient tomb on the Upper Nile."

"We know you like cats," Jane said.

"It's lovely, Dad, Mom. Thank you."

Colin was not taking well to the arrival of his baby brother. He had enjoyed being the center of attention and now this squalling little thing came along and stole the limelight from him. When Charlotte placed Allen in Jane's arms, three year old Colin started crying and screaming and stomping his feet on the floor. Albert took Colin's hand. "Let's go outside, Colin," he said gently, but firmly. Colin protested, but Albert simply dragged him until they were both on the patio in the back. I joined them.

It took only a few minutes before Colin calmed down. "You know, Colin," Albert said, "instead of getting upset that Allen is sitting with Granny Jane, you could sit with Grandpa George. And then, when Allen is tired of sitting with Granny, you can sit with her."

Colin thought for a moment, then hurried back inside and climbed up onto George's knee. "You're getting pretty good at this, Albert," I said as we followed the little fellow into the house.

***

Allen is here. I recognize his footsteps. He closes the door and walks up to my bed and places something on it. I hear the faint meow of Kitty-bee. He unzips the bag and Kitty-bee's jumps out and I feel her prowling around my feet, then up beside my body until she finds her spot between my arm and my ribs. She settles down with her head on my shoulder. She is purring, putting my cat-machine to shame.

Thank you.

"Kitty-bee positioned herself next to the front door when she saw me getting ready to leave as if she knew where I was going and wanted to come along. She seems to like being here. She looks very contented lying there with you."

Yes. Smile.

"Well, it's almost eight o'clock on the evening of June nineteenth. Danielle said you were out in the sun room today. It was gorgeous out. Did you enjoy it?"

Yes. Feeling the sun and the breeze on my skin is wonderful. I'm like a plant - I need those things.

Allen was quiet for a short while, then he said, "I see you have two new words - 'Ginnie' and 'army.' What's that all about?"

Stop. Ginnie. Army. I wonder whether she has said anything about this to her father. Something tells me she has not. I think she knows Allen would not be happy.

"Are you saying that Ginnie is joining the army?"

Maybe.

"She has not mentioned it. She did say that Jake's sister, Dana, was thinking about it, but I didn't get the impression Ginnie was, too."

What can I say? Ginnie didn't tell me directly she was thinking about it, but there was something in her voice that got me concerned. And that, on top of her putting off graduate school for a year, could set her down a terrible road. I didn't want to take any chances. *Stop. Ginnie. Army. Please.*

"I'll talk with her."

Thank you.

Allen falls silent again. I try as hard as I can to move my fingers to rub Kitty-bee's stomach - something she used to love.

The door opens. Nurse Trainwreck squeaks. Kitty-bee does not move - she is far too happy to be disturbed by the arrival of a nurse. "Has the cat been here before?" Trainwreck asks.

"A few times. I hope it's OK. Isaac loves to have Kitty-bee come to visit."

"So long as she doesn't escape there's no harm." Nurse Trainwreck sneezes. "Of, course, I'm terribly allergic, but I'll be all right." She checks my pulse, fiddles with my tubes and wires. "The cat really looks like she belongs right where she is." She sneezes again and leaves.

"Well," Allen says, "I guess we don't have to worry about Kitty-bee being expelled from here."

Smile. Happy. But, you have to talk to Ginnie. *Ginnie.*

"Don't worry, Grandpa Isaac. I'll talk with her."

I try to move my fingers again. Kitty-bee readjusts her position. Did she feel my fingers move?

***

The June before Allen was born Virginia completed her Masters of Education degree and started a new job working on curriculum development in the school superintendent's office. I was painting almost full-time, with the occasional architecture project thrown in every so often. I liked the mix.

Marjorie Ross in Boston, and Karl Lodge in New York, continued to represent my art. I was scheduled to do another group show with two other artists - a sculptor and a potter - in both galleries in October and November. Marjorie had thought the mix of media and our own individual styles would work well together, so about a year before the show she invited the three of us to a "working dinner" at a restaurant near the gallery to discuss our art and to see if we could arrive at a common theme for the show.

I was late because of delays on the subway. When I entered the restaurant I was shown to a small secluded table in the rear. Marjorie was seated with a man of about my age and a younger woman. I was introduced to Vincent Dellano, the sculptor, and Vanessa Ramsay, the potter. "Vanessa is taking pottery to another realm, Isaac," Marjorie said. "You just have to visit the gallery and see her work."

"I'd love to."

Vanessa gave me an inquisitive look. "Mr. Simon, I believe we've met; a long time ago, when I was a little girl."

"You're not Roland Ramsay's daughter, are you?"

She smiled. "I am." Then she looked away and when she turned back her eyes glistened. "My father died a few years ago."

"I'm sorry to hear that. He was a good man."

"Yes, he was. He talked about you often; he said he came to your first group show at Marjorie's gallery." She sighed deeply, sipped her wine. "Let's talk about our show."

"Yes, let's get right to it. I decided to group the three of you because I sense a common theme running through your work. Each of you has an unusual way of combining strong, rigid almost structural elements with amorphous, organic elements. I see in this something dynamic and exciting. So, this sense I have about your work, coupled with a look at the world today as it emerges from the war, suggests to me a theme of Rebirth." She looked slowly at each of us. "What do you think?"

Vanessa was the first to respond. "The idea of Rebirth implies something that is shedding its past; something reborn is not exactly new, but it denies its own history. I, personally, do not think we can, or should, escape the past. I think the world is not in a period of rebirth, but in a phase of recovery. I would suggest *that* - Recovery - as our theme."

"I like it," Marjorie said after a long pause. "Gentlemen?"

"OK." Vincent Dellano was not a man of many words.

"I like it. The idea of Recovery extends from the individual journey to social change, as well as the physical reconstruction on the ashes of structures that were destroyed. It gives us a wide area in which to work."

"Recovery it is. Well that was a lot easier than I'd anticipated." Marjorie raised her glass. "To Recovery."

The rest of the evening was a little uncomfortable. Marjorie tried to keep the conversation going, but with not much success. Mostly what was said was about the food and the weather. Vincent was the first to leave, before dessert, making the excuse that he had to feed his dogs.

Marjorie went to the restroom, leaving Vanessa Ramsay and me alone at the table, eating delicious bread pudding with vanilla ice cream and sipping our coffee. "I know you'd like to ask me about my father," Vanessa said, "but I really don't have much to say."

"Some other time, perhaps," I said.

"No. I'll tell you the bare bones of it. In the last few years of his life my father barely worked and was more often drunk than not. My mother gave him chance after chance but eventually she threw him out and told him not to come back. I saw him only a few times - he came by when he knew my mother wouldn't be there. I fed him and let him bathe; he helped me with my drawing." She folded her napkin slowly and placed it on the table in front of her. "He jumped off a bridge into the Merrimack River in December, 1946, a week before Christmas."

"I'm so sorry, Vanessa."

Marjorie returned to the table.

"It's getting late," Vanessa said as she stood. "I'll be in touch, Marjorie. Thank you." She left Marjorie and me sitting there.

"She looked upset. What happened?"

"She told me about her father."

"Oh. A very sad story."

"The man went through hell. Did you ever meet him?"

"No."

"I worked with him doing advertising illustrations for a newspaper before the First War, and then I met up with him after I came home. He'd been badly burned in the war - his hands were like claws. He joked that Vanessa used to call him lobster man. He taught himself to draw and paint again with those terribly deformed fingers and even found a job, until the depression descended. We saw each other in 1932 - we went together to Washington for the Bonus March. We kept in touch for a while, but then our lives went in different directions, I guess. I thought he was getting along OK. When I knew him he was absolutely devoted to his family."

"Drink can do that."

"It's war that drowns some men in the bottle."

"Women, too." She offered no explanation, but on the subway ride home I found myself thinking about Charlotte and how war and Albert's drinking had damaged her life.

On July Fourth 1970, still grieving for Colin who had been killed in Vietnam, Charlotte went down to the river after Albert was asleep, to the same spot, almost, where Albert led me many years later, and swallowed a mixture of pills washed down with Bourbon. Her body was found early in the morning by a fisherman. In her pocket-book she carried Colin's senior prom photograph, many of his letters from the war and a lock of hair from his first haircut.

While Colin could have been buried at Arlington Cemetery in Washington, Albert and Charlotte had wanted him close by, in the Mount Pleasant Cemetery in their home town. She was buried next to him. There were no more than fifteen people at her funeral. Virginia and I stood on either side of Albert and Allen at the graveside on that sticky, gloomy afternoon; it was one of the saddest days of my life. Most funerals are followed by a reception with food and low-key chatter. Albert wanted none of that. The four of us went back to his home and sat in the living room, and looked at albums of family photographs. "I knew this was coming," Albert said. "I just could not stop it."

***

Damon the Good is back. I wonder what time it is. *I'm awake.*

He does not respond. He adjusts my plumbing, checks my pulse. There is a stiffness, a tenseness in his movements. *I'm awake.*

"Hi Mr. Simon." His voice is clipped, holding back a deeper feeling. He touches my beard. "Would you like me to give it a brush?"

Yes. I always find it so relaxing when he brushes or combs my beard.

He stands beside the bed, passes a brush through my beard a couple of times, then stops and sits down. "This will be the last time I do this, Mr. Simon. I've been laid off. This is my last shift."

No. No. Sad. This can't be! He's so good. He is so good at what he does.

"They're cutting ten percent of the staff and a couple of management positions. Since I'm one of the newest, I'm one of the first to go."

What do I say? How do I say it? I feel tears in my eyes. *Sad. Hug.*

He dabs at my tears with a tissue. "I have to go now, Isaac. I'll be OK. Good luck." He pats my shoulder and is gone. The tears return to my eyes. It's not right. He's been through more than his share in life - he doesn't deserve this. No one does.

I lie awake thinking about Damon. I always worked for myself. I come from the working class but I was lucky - I fell in love with a woman from a wealthy family and she fell in love with me. In addition to the love and true companionship Virginia and I shared, I received more advantages from that marriage than I could have imagined: not only the house and the financial safety net, but also the connections and introductions to people who helped my career immeasurably. Sure I had talent and I worked hard - many people do - but I was given the opportunity to grow that talent and turn it into my life's work as well as a reasonable income. When things got tough during the depression, we were able to sell one painting - the Kandinsky - and survive for the next few years until the economy improved. How many others had that!

I think of Roland Ramsay who tried so hard and couldn't make it through. I wonder how many of those thousands of men and women we saw on the Bonus March in Washington were able to make it through. I wonder if Damon and the many others from this place who are now without jobs will make it through. The economy is down - not nearly as bad as the 1930's - but to the family without an income, history and statistics are meaningless. My mother was a union activist; so was my uncle. They're needed now more than ever! Life should not be so hard.

I feel the blood pounding in my ears. My blood pressure is rising along with my pulse. Pretty soon my cat-machine, Kate, is going to start buzzing. I wonder how long it will take for someone to get here, now that they've cut the staff. Part of me wants to see what happens, while the more rational side of my brain is telling me to calm down, breathe deeply and slowly, focus on relaxing. My rational brain wins. I feel the pulsing in my ears begin to subside.

I try to sleep but my mind keeps going back to Damon the Good and I suddenly remember how much I was counting on him to talk to Ginnie about the army. That conversation won't happen. It's a conversation that could possibly change the entire arc of Ginnie's life, and it won't happen! The random machinations of a downturned economy and how they play out in one medical facility in Boston have set in motion a chain reaction that could result in monumental misunderstandings and bad decisions in the life of someone dear to me. It's the opposite of the so-called "butterfly effect." I think I'll call it the "volcano effect" - where huge events are seen and understood in the specific impact they have on specific individuals. I wish I could write this all down.

Chapter 59

Wanda is not singing. I know she's here because I know her movements and I recognize her touch when she takes my pulse. *I'm awake.*

"Good morning, Mr. Simon. Sorry, I can't stay to chat; with the layoffs, guess who has more work and less time?"

Sad. She doesn't respond.

I hear her move toward the door. "Dr. Jerzak is scheduled to see you this morning," she says. "I'll be back later." I hear her footsteps depart.

In an instant, the feeling of this place has flipped from warm and caring to cold and efficient. I don't like it.

My father was like that - switching from kind to nasty. On Saturdays, instead of going to the synagogue, he would sometimes take Chaim and me for early morning walks in the woods. When we started out he was upbeat and enthusiastic; he would point out the birds and plants, teaching us about the things we saw. But, he always brought his bottle, and after a while he'd tire of us and give his attention to his drink. He'd become dark and uncommunicative and he would bark at us and tell us to leave him alone, not to bother him. More than once we left him and found our own way home. Every time we started out on these "explorations," as he called them, I would feel excited and optimistic, hoping that on this walk the day would not end the same way previous ones had ended. It never happened. By the time I was seven he had given up all pretenses at being a father; the "explorations" stopped, and his anger and meanness grew.

"Are you awake, Grandpa Isaac?" Ginnie says.

Yes. I'm thankful for her interruption. Those memories of my father always end up in a bad place.

"I just got off work. It's four-thirty in the afternoon. Thursday, June twentieth. Are you doing OK?"

No. How do I tell her about the changes in this place? If it's four-thirty then I missed both Dr. Jerzak and Wanda's second check-in. Was I asleep or did they just not come to see me? I don't like this!

"I see you have two new words on your chart - my name and 'army.' Is what I said about Dana worrying you?"

Yes. And that you might follow her.

"It's her life, Grandpa Isaac. You don't even know her."

I know that! I also know that joining the army will not bring Jake back, and that revenge is the worst and the stupidest of all human emotions. I know because I tried it and I continue to pay the price to this day; the flashbacks and nightmares are as vivid as the experiences themselves.

"Dad said Kitty-bee was discovered last evening, and the nurse was OK with her being here. That's a relief."

Yes. Smile. But don't change the subject young lady. *No. Army. Please.*

"I hear you, Grandpa Isaac. I am not really considering the army. Don't worry."

Good. Hug.

She hugs me gently. "I had hoped to come in before my shift today to see Damon, but I overslept."

She hasn't heard about the layoffs. *New word.*

We create the pattern for 'Damon'.

No. Damon.

She hesitates. "What do you mean - 'no Damon'? I thought you liked him. Did he do something to you?"

No. Damn. How do I tell her?

"What happened? Did he leave?"

Yes.

"He just left! That's messed up! How could he just do that!"

This is too frustrating. I think I need a change of scenery. *Sun.*

"What? I missed that."

Sun.

You want to go to the sun room?"

Yes.

"It's kind of gloomy out there today. You sure you want to go?"

Yes.

"OK. I'll see if I can find someone to help."

I hear her leave the room. I review our conversation; what did she mean when she said that she is "not really considering" the army? It does not sound like she has completely shut the door on that idea. I need to make sure both Allen and Danielle talk with her.

Ginnie seems to have been gone a long time. When she finally returns she says she had a hard time tracking down a nurse who said she'd try to get to you but she wasn't sure she could organize a wheelchair and an orderly to move you. "They seem particularly under-staffed today."

Yes.

"You know they are under-staffed?"

Yes.

"And Damon's departure has something to do with this. He didn't walk out, he was laid off!"

Yes.

"That's terrible. Mom might know what's going on; she knows everyone, I'd bet she has a friend or two on the board. I'll call her."

It's all about who you know.

***

The October 1951 three-person show in Boston at the Nouvelle Vision Gallery was well-received. The place was packed for the opening and the critics generally thought the grouping of the painting, sculpture and pottery was "bold, innovative and provocative." Marjorie was ecstatic. Sales were modest at the opening, but picked up somewhat over the month.

Virginia and I planned to be in New York for the November eighth opening reception there, but her father had a heart attack at the end of October. He was released from the hospital after a week, and Virginia went in to Boston to be with her mother. I offered to skip New York, but she insisted I go.

It was strange traveling alone after all the years we had been together. The train ride was long and uneventful. As usual, I had a sketchbook with me and a bunch of pencils, so I set about drawing everything I saw in the train car, in the minutest detail. It was a fascinating exercise. I arrived at my hotel in the late afternoon and telephoned Virginia to find out how they were all doing and to let her know I had arrived in New York. Then I showered, dressed, and left for the Karl Lodge Gallery. It was a walk of only a few blocks. On the way I ran into Vanessa Ramsay. We continued the walk together, chatting about New York and its various modes and moods.

As I opened the door to the gallery, Vanessa said, "I hope they have food - I was so anxious to get here I forgot to eat."

Vincent Dellano was already there, standing alone in a corner pretending to look at his own sculpture. Karl Lodge was circulating, but noticed Vanessa and me the moment we entered, and he headed directly toward us. "It's so good to have you in my gallery again, Isaac. I believe the show in Boston did quite well. Congratulations." He turned to Vanessa with a slightly confused look. "I don't believe we have met," he said.

"I'm Vanessa Ramsay," she said, "the potter."

His expression changed immediately and he beamed, "Of course. I did not recognize you from the photograph Marjorie sent, but I see it now. I'm so pleased you are here, Miss Ramsay. People are fascinated with your work."

"Thank you."

"Well, I must circulate. I'll introduce the three of you in about a half hour."

Vanessa laughed. "He thought you and I were together."

"I don't think so. He just didn't recognize you."

She laughed again. "Well, I think I shall circulate, too - in the direction of the food and wine."

The evening dragged on. I was hungry, and tired of smiling and being polite to complete strangers on whom I was, in a very real sense, dependent. By nine-thirty the crowd had thinned. I found Karl, thanked him and told him I was going back to the hotel. "You might want to assist Miss Ramsay," he said, "she appears to have had a little too much wine; she's not at all steady on her feet. I believe you're both at the same hotel."

He went to the back of the gallery to his private office and returned a little while later leading a rather wobbly Vanessa Ramsay. "I had her drink a black coffee. She's a little better, now."

We left the gallery, Vanessa leaning heavily on my arm. I hailed a cab. The driver was not too happy to have a drunken lady in the car, nor was he thrilled about a fare that went only a few blocks. I tipped him well and he helped me get her out of the car in front of the hotel.

"Thanks, Isaac. You're a good guy."

"Let's just get you inside, Vanessa."

"I'm still hungry as hell. Those little cheesy things couldn't fill a fucking thimble."

"You can eat in the morning."

"No! I'm starving." She looked around and amazingly was able to identify a restaurant across the street. "Let's go there!" She straightened up. "I'm OK." She grabbed my arm. "I bet you're hungry, too."

"I'm fine," I said.

She leaned in towards my face. "Bullshit," she whispered harshly. "You're as hungry as I am." There was a tone to her voice I found most uncomfortable.

I took her elbow. "I think you need to sleep it off." I managed to steer her into the hotel lobby and up to the front desk. "Miss Ramsay seems to be in need of assistance. Could you please help her to her room?"

"Certainly, sir." The receptionist had a hard time suppressing a smirk, but I thanked her and hurried off.

The next morning Vanessa found me in the hotel's breakfast room. She asked if she could join me, and sat before I answered. "Thank you for getting me back last night. To be honest, I don't remember much more than you getting me out of a cab and into the hotel. I apologize for my behavior - I hope I was not too difficult or inappropriate."

"Nothing I couldn't handle, Vanessa." I wanted to lecture her, to plead with her to never drink again. Surely she had seen what it had done to her father, her family. She was such a talented artist - this would rob her of that talent!

She placed her hand on mine. "I know what you're thinking, Mr. Simon. Please don't say anything; I am fully aware of the guilt and the shame."

"But are you aware of the danger?"

She took a bite of her toast and a sip of coffee. "I am. I really am."

***

I am awake. It's quiet - just my cat-machine and me. With Damon laid off, I wonder what level of coverage this place will have for the overnight shift. I'm guessing this is the overnight shift. I don't like not knowing.

***

When Mark was around fourteen he tried out for his high school baseball team. He was a little guy, but very athletic and agile and he wanted to be a short-stop. I went with him and Albert to the try-outs. They put the kids - about sixty of them - through a whole series of exercises and Mark looked like he was doing better than the average, particularly in base running and fielding. As we sat in the bleachers waiting for the coaches to tally up their evaluations, Mark said, "Not knowing is much worse than knowing, even if what you know is bad - at least you can deal with it."

He did not make the team that year. He tried again the next year and was selected. It was his determination, his agility and his hand-eye coordination that got him there. It was those qualities, together with his small physical size, that got him into the tail gunner's bubble on the B-24, Liberator.

Emma used to call him "li'l brother," even though he was two-and-a-half years older than her. They argued a lot as kids but by the time she became a teenager she had stopped teasing and they grew close. Her diaries talked of long conversations they had, well into the night. She had confided in him that she "didn't like boys." He had replied that he didn't like them either and had told her not to worry. I wish we had told her the whole story about William Carpenter and about our friends, Grace and Celia. (That Russian poet lifts his admonishing finger again; "Telling lies to the young is wrong.")

She also wrote about her fear that her brothers had gone to war. She missed them, particularly Mark. When we received the news that he had been killed, Emma went into the room he had shared with Albert, lay face-down on his bed, and wept. She stayed in his room for hours, inconsolable. How could she be consoled! When she finally emerged and came downstairs to join Virginia and me, she was dressed in Mark's baseball uniform.

***

George Appleton, Virginia's father, died on December third, 1951. The Reverend Dana McLean Greeley of the Arlington Street Church, the church the Appletons had attended for generations, conducted the memorial service the following Sunday afternoon. It was a cold, bright day, with the colors of the Tiffany windows filling the space. George had been an active and popular member of the community; the church was crowded. Virginia and I sat with her mother in the front row, straining our necks to look up to the Reverend as he stood in the pulpit high above the gathered crowd and spoke of his friendship with George.

The eulogy from the minister was unusual. He said little about God and heaven and other religious matters; he talked about the man and what he had done in his life - for his church, his profession, his community, and the world. I learned for the first time that my father-in-law was an early member of the American Civil Liberties Union and that he was a generous supporter of the NAACP and various anti-colonialist movements including the African National Congress in South Africa and Gandhi's Congress Party in India.

When the service ended, as we filed down the aisle I was aware that this was the first truly integrated gathering I had ever attended. George, apparently, was known in the immigrant and African-American communities, and people from these communities came to say good-bye to him. Many of those people walked from the church to the Appleton home for the reception. Virginia and I were in the midst of the crowd when an elderly Black lady approached and stopped right in front of Virginia. "Do you remember me, Virginia?" she said, staring directly into her eyes.

"Bea?" Virginia reached out and hugged her. "Thank you for coming today, Bea."

"Your father was a good man. It was an honor to be here today." She took Virginia's arm and we walked slowly toward the house.

"Does my mother know you are here?"

"I have not seen her yet." She stopped and took both of Virginia's hands in hers. "Did you know that about three months after I was let go, your father found my address and sent me some money? He did that almost every month for years, till I found a job."

"We thought you'd disappeared. He never mentioned he knew where you were."

"I asked him not to, and he kept my secret. During the war, when his grandsons and mine were away, we exchange letters of support every now and then. I almost came to your Mark's service but I couldn't. Too much history. I wrote you a letter, but didn't mail it. Emma, too. I wish I had mailed them."

"Me too, Bea." Virginia squeezed her hand. "So how are you?"

"I'm a seventy-six year-old Black woman - strong as an ox, and feel like I'm ready to die." She laughed. "I'm fine. Let's walk on."

We joined the line of people waiting to enter the house. Jane Appleton was standing in the doorway, greeting people as they arrived. When she saw Bea she gasped and fell forward into her arms. "I always said you were part of the family, Bea! And here you are. Thank you for being here today." Jane left her post at the door and guided Bea into the parlor. They sat on the couch together and talked for about twenty minutes. No one attempted to interrupt them. Virginia assumed the role of greeter and Charlotte took charge of the food and drink.

By around five o'clock everyone had left except for Virginia and me. "I have two important things to say," Jane said as we helped straighten up the house. "Let's sit a while; there's plenty of time for me to finish clearing up in here. I'll make a pot of tea."

We sat at the kitchen table. "First, your father's will. I have not seen the actual document, but he and I talked about it recently. He has quite a bit of money as well as an office building downtown. And this house, of course. Except for a few specific things, everything is left to me. My will, naturally, will leave everything to you. He set aside four thousand dollars each for the education of Colin and Allen. He left another six thousand to the church. His lawyer will be here tomorrow evening for a formal review if you'd like to be here."

"No, Mom, these are your personal financial matters. You really don't have to tell us anything," Virginia said, and then asked, "But, what will you do with the house and that office building?"

"I have no interest in the office block. I will sell it and give most of the money to George's causes. As for the house - that brings me to the second important thing I wanted to tell you. Bea is moving in next month. She is alone and I am alone, so we decided to give being housemates a try. I'll stay in the music room and she'll have the master bedroom upstairs. We'll split the cost of food, utilities and so on. I tried to convince her that George left more than enough to cover all these expenses, but she insisted she would not move in if she did not pay her own way. So, that's it. I'm quite looking forward to it. We're going to share recipes. We have a lot of catching up to do."

Jane and Bea became good friends. They entertained frequently and worked together to raise money for the civil rights campaigns of the 1950's. They participated in marches in support of the Brown vs Board of Education decision and of the Montgomery bus boycott. They attended arts functions and were a fixture at various charity events. There were rumors about their relationship; even our old friend Grace enquired. Jane and Bea intimated nothing, so we assumed there was nothing to talk about. They lived together until the 1957 Asian flu pandemic claimed both of their lives within days of one another.

***

Someone is holding my wrist, checking my pulse. I do not know who this is. *I'm awake.*

No response. The person drops my wrist and walks over to my cat-machine, then returns to the left side of the bed. I hear the Velcro on one of those blood pressure straps being separated. This person is going to lift my left arm and strap that thing on me. Didn't they read my chart - my left shoulder hurts!

Stop. No.

No response. My arm is jostled as the strap is slid under my upper arm. *Stop. Pain.* I hear the Velcro being reattached, hear the air pump, and feel the pressure building on my arm. My shoulder is throbbing. *Stop. Pain.* This person has no idea that I am trying to communicate! This is bad. Finally the air pressure is released. More pain as the device is removed. I don't bother to signal anything - suffer in silence, Isaac! I've been there.

I hear the footsteps leave my room. I have no idea who that person was; they didn't even have the courtesy to say their name. I'm guessing this person is now covering some of Damon's shift. I think I will assign the name 'The Nameless One' to him or her; it has an ominous sound to it which captures how I feel about him/her!

The place is quiet again. I remember being awake in this quiet before - I don't know whether it was an hour or two ago, or a whole day, or more. I have become unmoored.

***

The reference points have vanished; blocked out by the smoke. Stumbling over the churned up mud which yesterday was where we buried our dead in no-man's land where they had fallen the day before. One day blurred into the next, we are running, screaming, jumping over the uneven ground which we can barely see, not knowing where we're going. Following the whistle and the shouted commands, headlong into the flashes of gunfire dead ahead. I know Reuven is on my left; I hear him and whenever there is a slight clearing in the smoke I glimpse his ghost running beside me. This is insane; I just want to stop, to sit down in the mud, to let the noise and turmoil charge ahead and away from me. But I gallop on like a panicked horse. I yell Reuven's name, and he yells mine. The whistle is sounding piercing bursts at ever-shortening intervals. I have no idea what this means. I call Reuven's name again.

Wanda's voice breaks through the chaos. "Isaac, can you hear me? Mr. Simon, can you hear my voice?"

I struggle to emerge from that horrific place. The whistle begins to slow. I recognize my cat-machine's beeps. I feel Wanda's hand on mine.

Someone in the room says, "Does he have a DNR?"

"Yes," someone else responds.

I'm not ready to go yet.

Wanda, again; "Can you hear me, Isaac?"

Yes. I'm awake.

"Good. Good." The beeping has stopped. "Did you have another bad trip down memory lane, Isaac?" Wanda asks.

Yes. Army.

"I thought so." She squeezes my hand gently. "Mr. Simon had another flashback. He'll be OK," she says to the still hovering group in my room. I hear them shuffle off. "I got into work as your monitor started beeping. I haven't even had time to take my coat off. Give me a minute and I'll be back to check all your tubes and wires," she says.

A short while later I feel her fussing about me. "I told you before I'm not going to let you check out on my watch, Mr. Simon." She laughs. "You're everyone's favorite around here."

Smile. Thank you.

"You're very welcome, Mr. Simon. I do have to go now, though."

She lightly touches my beard, then leaves.

***

My Uncle Kalner died in New York in April 1954. He was seventy-nine years old. His old union comrades arranged a memorial service for him at an International Ladies' Garment Workers hall in the garment district. Kalner had spent many years of his life as an organizer for this union; it was a fitting place for his service, which was attended by over a hundred union members and leaders. I was asked to give a short talk. The four other speakers all talked about his role in the union, in the important strikes in the twenties and thirties. I decided I would focus on the man I knew back in Linkeve, our shtetl in Lithuania.

I talked about him spending all his money on his collection of books, and sharing them with me, teaching me to read and to acquire a broader view of the world. I told them the story of an argument I overheard one day when I came to the village store where he worked. The rabbi, a rigid self-important man only a few years older than Kalner, had come to the store to buy some lumber and nails to repair the roof of his house - one of many homes damaged by a violent windstorm.

"Thank God no one was hurt," the rabbi said.

"I don't understand, rabbi. What's to be thankful for? Did not God cause this wind, why not be angry at him for causing so much damage?"

"It's not for us to question God's actions," the rabbi responded.

"If *we* don't, then who will?"

"It is not our place."

"Rabbi, I want to understand how the weather works. I cannot simply allocate that power to God. If we can understand the weather, then perhaps we can predict it and even prepare for it."

I concluded my eulogy by saying that Kalner had not, as we all knew, become a weather-man, but his underlying need to understand how things worked drove him in everything he did. He learned to understand the machinations of industry and power, and the role that unions needed to play in confronting that power.

Chapter 60

Danielle is here. I smell her Chanel Number 5.

I'm awake.

"Good morning, old friend. It's good to see you."

Smile. I like that she calls me "old friend" even though she is much younger than me - she was born the same year as my Emma, and married my son, Albert. Albert and Danielle had known each other since childhood.

Danielle married someone named Danny three years after she finished law school. I only met him the one time - at their wedding, and I did not get the best impression of him. He reminded me of my old boss, Mr. Hardwicke, who always got what he wanted, and when he didn't became mean and moody. I said nothing, but was not surprised to learn that they were divorced a few years later.

After Charlotte's death in 1970, it seemed almost inevitable that Albert and Danielle would meet up again and be together. I think she had a crush on him from the time they were young teenagers. She found a job with a law firm in Boston. They were married in September 1972 and spent ten good years together.

Danielle helped me take care of Virginia in her last years, while she also spent many weekends on Cape Cod with Reuven who died just a year after Virginia. And then, of course, Albert died a couple of years after her father. She has done a lot of sitting by the side of dying loved ones, and she has become more loving as time has passed.

There are too many dead people in my life, too - an obvious consequence of living so long.

"I talked with Ginnie last night," Danielle says, pulling me out of my reflections. "She told me about Damon being laid off. That's not good. Are you OK."

Sad.

"Martha is on the hospital board; she's going to look into what's going on."

Good.

She pats my hand. "Ginnie also said something about you worrying she might join the army."

Yes.

"She and I talked about it. Don't worry, Isaac, she assured me she has no intention of signing up."

Good. Ginnie. No. Army. I wanted to underline it ten times, a thousand times!

Danielle gently takes my hand between hers. "She says she won't, Isaac. You have to take her at her word. And don't worry, I'll be watching her."

Good. Thank you.

"Now, how about a little Winnie the Pooh? We haven't heard from him in ages."

Yes. A nice little distraction.

"But first - a time check. It is ten-forty in the morning on Friday, June twenty-first, 2002. It's a hot, humid day out there; a day when you are thankful if you have air conditioning. I don't have it in my place, so I might be spending most of the day here."

Good. I'd like to go to the sun room, but it probably is not air conditioned. Worth a try. *Sun.*

"You'd like to read in the sun room? I'll see what I can do."

She leaves and returns less than a minute later. "There's a notice on the door saying the sun room is closed until further notice. I'd bet it has something to do with the layoffs!"

No. Why is it that when money is tight, the first things to go are the things that bring us joy and enrich our spirits - arts in the schools, libraries, school orchestras, the sun room in this place? Are these any less essential than the cops, the guards, the guns, the administrators, the book-keepers? I think if we had more music, art and literature teachers in the schools we'd need fewer cops on the beat and fewer cells in the prisons. Allen and I talked about this not long ago, when he was concerned the city's budget problems would impact his job. Fortunately, he survived, but several younger colleagues in his department were let go.

"This infuriates me!" She drops into the chair. "Well, at least we have the stories about that little bear and his friends."

I was no longer too interested in the bear, but let Danielle read, anyway. It was a harmless distraction.

***

Allen loved to visit Virginia and me when he was little. His favorite thing was to squeeze as tightly as he could between us as we sat on the couch. He would wriggle his way in, back-side first, then ask us to read to him. He liked to play his own made-up word games, rearranging the sequence of words to make them sound funny. He would take a sentence like, "The old black cat sat on the mat," and mix the words up to something like, "Sat cat the black old mat." "The House at Pooh Corner," one of his favorite books, became "Pooh house at the corner." I could never figure out what the joy in this game was, but he would squeal with laughter every time he came up with a new revised sentence. He wrote poetry in middle school, much of it characterized by the same kind of juggling with words. These word games propelled him in the direction he took after college - English teacher and novelist.

Allen was lucky. His military draft number was around three-hundred and thirty; there was no chance he'd be called up. We all breathed a huge sigh of relief when the numbers were pulled, live on television. What a crazy way to form an army. Charlotte had killed herself months before Allen's lottery; I think the prospect of that day weighed on her, along with everything else. After our Mark was killed, the dread of every knock on the door was magnified, knowing that Albert was still somewhere in Belgium, then somewhere in Germany, then somewhere else … who knew where the hell!

When Allen and I marched against the war in October 1969, it was only a few months after Colin was killed. I wore that wild shirt I'd painted, and I pinned my ribbons and medals on it. Allen wore jeans and a flannel shirt, and he carried Colin's Purple Heart in his breast pocket. "His heart close to mine," he said.

When he told me this, I began to cry. I remember marching down Boylston Street in the midst of that huge throng of mostly young people, with tears rolling down my face. I could not stop. A man about my age came over to me and put his arm around my shoulders. "I know," is all he said. I saw the sunlight glinting off the medals on his chest. We marched together and he stayed with me till the end of the rally.

I never learned his name or anything about him, but I think about him often. Sometimes I'm not even sure he was actually there, although I do remember him saying before he left, "I love your shirt, and I particularly love your banner." I had momentarily forgotten what I had painted on the banner. I looked up to read it. "A Soldier's Dream - Death by Natural Causes. Stop War Now!" When I turned back, he had disappeared into the crowd.

I guess I am approaching that dream.

Those were intense times; people who had been put down, marginalized, and oppressed began to organize, fight back, and demand their humanity be acknowledged, protected and respected. It had started with the civil rights movement, then the anti-war movement, and then the women's rights movement exploded across the country. Along with these came the fight to protect and organize farm workers, while Native Americans fought to reclaim their history and heritage and to expose the truth about what had been done to them.

A month after Colin was killed in Vietnam, another turning point; in New York the police raided a gay bar, the Stonewall Inn. This was in no way the first raid on this bar, but this time the people in the bar had reached their limit - they fought back in what became known as the Stonewall Riot. Hundreds of gay men, drag queens and lesbians fought it out with the cops over a period of about five days. Reuven left his retirement home on Cape Cod and went to join Danielle who was living in New York at the time, to help in the legal defense of those arrested.

Our old clients, Grace and Celia - still living in the house that William and I had designed - invited Virginia and me to a Sunday afternoon party to celebrate Stonewall. The house had changed little since we'd last visited several years before, except that the flower gardens surrounding the building were even more extensive and colorful. It was mid-July and so much was in bloom. "A few years ago we ripped up just about everything and started again with native plants only," Celia said. She was sitting on the covered deck with about a dozen of their guests. "It's remarkable how they thrive when given a chance! And the butterflies and birds that come by. It was worth every drop of sweat we put into it. Grace and I spend most of the day out here."

Grace came out of the house with a few more guests. I looked around; we were a group of twenty or so folks, none younger than sixty, and Virginia and I were a distinct minority - there was only one other straight couple. I thought of William and what he had endured, what he had, in the end, been unable to endure, and I wondered what all of these people had gone through, experienced, every single day of their lives. I thought of our Emma and her brief love, who we saw only for a moment, but never met. Virginia clasped my hand; I believe she was having similar thoughts and memories.

"To the young fighters of Stonewall!" Grace proclaimed, as she raised her wine glass. "This is just the beginning."

***

Martha has brought Kitty-bee who is lying in her favorite place, between my arm and my body, with her head resting on my shoulder. She is purring softly. I try to scratch her tummy, but who knows if my fingers actually move. Allen is here, too. I don't remember Danielle leaving.

"I called a couple of board members," Martha says. "None of them was aware of the layoffs. The board chair said that hiring and firing was not a board responsibility; it was entirely up to Annabelle Duke, the chief executive officer."

Kitty-bee shifts her body so that she is leaning more heavily on my arm. Maybe she senses I'm trying to move my fingers.

"I requested a special meeting of the board with Mrs. Duke; the chair said he would poll other members and let me know. That's about all I can do for now, although I imagine word will get back to Mrs. Duke that at least some board members are not happy and want an explanation."

I wonder if she is aware of the sun room being closed. *Sun.*

"Sorry, Grandpa Isaac, I missed that," Allen says.

Sun.

"Sun? I'm afraid it's after seven in the evening, the sun is pretty much gone by now."

Sun.

"You want to go there, anyway. I'll see what I can do."

I hear him leave the room. Martha has stopped talking. I appreciate her attempts to find out what's going on.

Thank you.

"I'm afraid I wasn't paying attention."

Thank you.

She hesitates, then says, "You're welcome, Isaac."

Thank you. Kitty-bee.

She pats my hand. Allen returns and announces what I already know; "The sun room is closed until further notice."

"I will report that to the chair. He has to call a meeting: if quality of service is impacted, Annabelle Duke has to explain."

Martha could be formidable. She was not one to let things go too easily.

A sneeze. Nurse Trainwreck is here.

"Good evening Mr. Simon," she says, and sneezes again. "The cat really likes to be with you, but I must ask your son to hold him while I check on you. OK?"

Yes. Poor Trainwreck sneezes again. Allen picks up Kitty-bee and I hear him walk away from the bed. I can't imagine this could help the allergy too much, but it's worth a try, I suppose.

I feel her checking my tubes and wires. "I'm going to roll you onto your side to see how that bed sore is doing. OK?"

Yes.

She gently tips me on my side. Her fingers touch the area. It hurts a little. "We'll leave you like this for a while to take the pressure off and get some air to it." She props a few pillows behind me. "I need to roll on."

Laugh. It's almost like she knows my nickname for her, telling me she has to "roll on."

Allen returns to my bedside and places Kitty-bee up against my stomach then lowers my hand onto her. Lovely. I try to flex my fingers. I believe Kitty-bee senses my effort although I'm pretty sure nothing moved. She purrs softly. *Smile.*

Chapter 61

We held Virginia's memorial service at our home on the Saturday afternoon after she died in late October 1979. It really was a celebration of her life, a retrospective. Danielle and Albert had created several displays of photographs. Scrap books containing her weekly columns were put out on a table with the photographs. People came from all phases of her life; many of whom I had never met. Parents who had been children in her religious education classes, women she had marched with for the right to vote and against child labor, old friends from college and her work in the education department, artists and collectors we had met through my work; all sorts of people of all ages.

Reuven was too sick to be there, but he sent a letter expressing his joy at having known her and his sorrow for my great loss. He enclosed the two drawings I had given him hours before we entered the line in France; the drawings I had done of the desolation of the war-scarred French country-side and my vision of what it had been like before the war. Reuven wrote; "I have held these for so many years, my good friend, and they have always brought me hope. Thank you."

Albert was the first to speak about Virginia, his mother. "My Mom was warm, compassionate and had complete faith in the limitless power of love," he said. He recalled her response to his announcement that he had signed up after Pearl Harbor. "My Dad hugged me, then went off to his studio to process what I had said, but my Mom took my hand as if I were a child and led me to the couch where we sat silently for some time. She looked deep into my eyes, seemingly searching for the words she needed to say. Finally, she placed her hands on my shoulders. 'If you are doing this out of hatred, Albert, nothing good will come of it,' she said. 'But I believe you are doing this because it is the right thing to do.' She kissed me, then went to join my Dad who was not having an easy time with my decision."

After Albert's remembrance, Brian Fleming, editor of the Cambridge Banner for which Virginia wrote the weekly column until she was too weak to write stood and introduced himself. He talked of her fire, her insight, her unflinching way of looking at the world, and her ability to put her understanding in very human, personal terms. "The last time I saw her was about two months before she died," he said. "She didn't want to talk about her illness. She wanted to discuss her column on nuclear disarmament in light of the tests both the US and Russia had carried out early in the month. She was as passionate and articulate as she was the day I first met her in 1924, when she was almost eight months pregnant, and with one-year-old Albert in tow, and she had come to see me about the fight against child labor."

There was lots of food and drink and lots of singing and talking - just as Virginia would have wanted.

By the time everyone left and Albert and Danielle were helping to clean up I was in awe at how many lives she had touched, and how deeply. I sat on the patio and surveyed the bare trees, the lawn covered in fallen leaves, the empty space.

How could I have known that I'd still be around more than twenty-two years later?

I am racing across the ocean, flying low. The closer I get to land the faster the fear circulates through by body. It has invaded my bloodstream. As my heart pounds more rapidly the panic spreads. France again, but I don't recognize this place. I hover for a moment above the smoke. The pounding of the guns is deafening. I see fountains of mud spray up through the fog of smoke where the shells land followed by the sickening cries of men. There is a break in the smoke and I see Chaim, by brother, standing on a mound of dirt, his one fist raised above his head, his other clutching at his gaping chest. I drop heavily to the dirt beside him and immediately the choking gas burns my nose and throat. I struggle to fit my gas mask, and as I fight with it I see Chaim collapse just a few feet away. I scream into the mask.

And suddenly I see myself sprawled in the mud. My eyes are wide and white peering through the glass of the mask. I try to crawl to where my brother lies. I am shouting his name over and over. My throat is raw. By the time I reach him, he is gone; his eyes are staring blankly at me. I cradle his head in my arms and curse. And then I begin to sob. "He is dead. I am broken." The words repeat in my brain, getting louder and louder. I cannot breathe. I cannot breathe. The noise and chaos of this place close in on me. I hear sirens.

***

"It was worse than usual. His pulse elevated rapidly as in previous episodes, but this was the first I've seen where he was having trouble breathing. He was gasping for air. It took a long time for him to stabilize." It is Wanda.

"Thank you for calling me," Allen replies.

They are both quiet for a few moments, then Wanda says. "I think his time is coming soon. I'll leave you, now."

Allen touches my shoulder and sits on the bed beside me. "Are you awake, Grandpa Isaac?"

I try to answer, but I cannot remember the signal for "Yes," so I just blink my eyes a few times.

"Hi, there," he says, "the nurse says you've had a rough day. I hope you feel better."

I flutter my eyelids again. He touches my cheek, strokes my beard. "It's two o'clock on Saturday, June twenty-second, 2002."

All the twos! Life is random. I've said that several times already. So is death. It seems like mine is about to happen on this day in June. I said at the beginning of this story that I'm ready for it, and I still am.

Watching Virginia slowly dying was the hardest thing in my life. In the last weeks she slept most of the time, the drugs for the pain taking her mind even before her shrinking body had a chance to go. I would sit by her bed for hours, listening to her shallow breathing, her occasional sighs, hoping for a few moments of lucidity which did surface unexpectedly and briefly like a brilliant flare above the battlefield, glowing brightly then giving way to the gloom.

During the evening before she died she suddenly said my name, quite loudly and clearly.

"I'm right here, dear."

"Do you still have the colored pencils I sent you?"

"Of course I do," I said, "I use them every day."

"They drew us together," she said, and smiled weakly at the pun she had made.

I laughed. She died that night while I slept in the chair next to her bed.

We had known each other for over sixty years, and every day was new and important. We loved to be in each other's presence. We loved to share each other's experiences. And we honored each other's need for solitude. We came from such different worlds, but we knew that our love could transcend history. And we tried together to be good and kind and supportive. We had a belief that the world could be a better place, and we fought for that.

So, I sound a little preachy - but, who's listening? This is all inside my head. I know.

And, anyway, it's time to go.

Notes and Acknowledgements

A few notes about the intersection of fiction and non-fiction.

With the few exceptions noted below, all the characters in this book are fictional, and any resemblance to actual people is incidental and unintended.

First exceptions - actual historical figures, like presidents, attorneys general, senators, and so on.

Second exceptions - This book is dedicated to, "Uncle Max and Uncle Frank." The war experience of Isaac's brother, Chaim, is based on the military records of my grandmother's brother, Max Simon, who went with my grandmother from Latvia to South Africa in 1912. I want to thank my sister, Thelma Buchanan, for sharing her family research with me.

The character of Isaac's son, Albert, is based on the life of my wife's uncle, Frank Rogan, a man I knew quite well. In the last years of his life he shared many of his stories with me, as well as all his letters home from the war and the scrap book he created.

Third exception - The Reverend Paul Revere Frothingham of the Arlington Street (Unitarian) Church. I had not intended to use a real person in this role, but when I researched the history of the church, I found that a gentleman named Paul Revere Frothingham had, in fact, been minister in this church for the first quarter of the twentieth century, from 1906 to 1926. I could not resist the name! What could be more upper crust Boston? I read several of his speeches and sermons as well as a biography written shortly after his death (*The Life of Paul Revere Frothingham* by Howard Chandler Robbins, published by Houghton Mifflin, 1935). He was an interesting man in the more progressive, humanist wing of the church. While, obviously, his interactions with fictional characters like Isaac and the Appleton family are made up, I believe that his character as presented in this narrative is quite true to who the Reverend was.

There are many people to thank. My wife, Laurie, who encouraged me, read the manuscript several times and made suggestions that helped to improve it. Some early readers, particularly Tanya Prather, Mark King, Ellen McCormick and Jodie Holway, who all spent more time than I could have hoped, reviewed early drafts, marked them up and made insightful and careful recommendations that helped sharpen the story. I am so grateful.

Roy Goodman
Nashua, NH
December 2019

About the Author:

Roy Goodman grew up in South Africa during the era of Apartheid. He studied Architecture in Pretoria, then Art History and African Studies at the Hebrew University in Jerusalem, at the start of the settler movement in the West Bank. He moved to New England in 1972. His first job was on the factory floor where he helped to organize a union. He has been involved in social justice issues all his life.

His novel, *Angel Play,* was published in 2013.

His poetry has been published in anthologies, including *The Anthology of New England Writers 2001* and *The Other Side of Sorrow.*

www.roygoodmanwrites.wordpress.com

Made in the USA
Monee, IL
04 February 2020